Cynthia Harrod-Eagles studied English and History at the Universities of Edinburgh and London. Her novel THE WAITING GAME won the Young Writers' Award in 1972.

Cynthia Harrod-Eagles, who lives in London, will be taking the story of the Morland Family to the present day.

Also in the *Dynasty* Series from Futura:

DYNASTY

11

The Emperor

Cynthia Harrod-Eagles

Futura

A Futura Book

First published in Great Britain in 1988
by Macdonald & Co (Publishers) Ltd
London & Sydney

This edition published by Futura in 1988

ISBN 0 7088 3925 8

Reproduced, printed and bound in Great Britain by
Hazell Watson & Viney Limited
Member of BPCC plc
Aylesbury Bucks

Futura Publications
A Division of
Macdonald & Co (Publishers) Ltd
Greater London House
Hampstead Road
London NW1 7QX
A member of Maxwell Pergamon Publishing Corporation plc

SELECT BIBLIOGRAPHY

W.J. Ashley   *The Economic Organisation of England*
Jacques Bainville   *Napoleon*
H.L. Beales   *The Industrial Revolution*
Geoffrey Bennett   *Nelson the Commander*
Asa Briggs   *The Age of Improvement*
John Fielden   *The Curse of the Factory System*
Pauline Gregg   *A Social and Economic History of Britain*
Christopher Hibbert   *George IV Prince of Wales*
William Howitt   *The Rural Life of England*
William James   *Naval History of Great Britain*
William Jesse   *Beau Brummell*
Michael Lewis   *England's Sea Officers*
Michael Lewis   *A Social History of the Royal Navy*
R.S. Liddell   *Memoirs of the Tenth Royal Hussars*
H.C. Maxwell-Lyte   *History of Eton*
George Rude   *Revolutionary Europe 1783-1815*
J.M. Thompson   *Napoleon Bonaparte, His Rise and Fall*
Oliver Warner   *A Portrait of Lord Nelson*
J.S. Watson   *Reign of George III*
R.K. Webb   *Modern England*
E.L. Woodward   *The Age of Reform*

The Morland Family

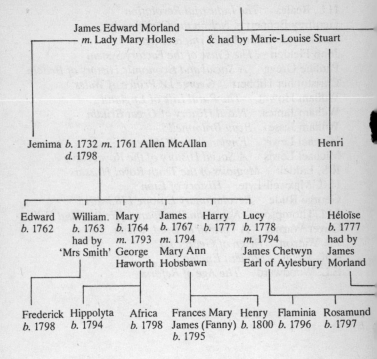

James Edward Morland
m. Lady Mary Holles   & had by Marie-Louise Stuart

Jemima *b.* 1732 *m.* 1761 Allen McAllan   Henri
d. 1798

Edward	William.	Mary	James	Harry	Lucy	Héloïse
b. 1762	*b.* 1763	*b.* 1764	*b.* 1767	*b.* 1777	*b.* 1778	*b.* 1777
	had by	*m.* 1793	*m.* 1794		*m.* 1794	had by
	'Mrs Smith'	George	Mary Ann		James Chetwyn	James
		Haworth	Hobsbawn		Earl of Aylesbury	Morland

Frederick	Hippolyta	Africa	Frances Mary	Henry	Flaminia	Rosamund
b. 1798	*b.* 1794	*b.* 1798	James (Fanny)	*b.* 1800	*b.* 1796	*b.* 1797
			b. 1795			

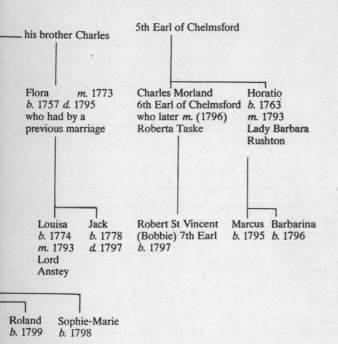

his brother Charles

5th Earl of Chelmsford

Flora   *m.* 1773
b. 1757 *d.* 1795
who had by a
previous marriage

Charles Morland
6th Earl of Chelmsford
who later *m.* (1796)
Roberta Taske

Horatio
b. 1763
m. 1793
Lady Barbara
Rushton

Louisa
b. 1774
m. 1793
Lord
Anstey

Jack
b. 1778
d. 1797

Robert St Vincent
(Bobbie) 7th Earl
b. 1797

Marcus
b. 1795

Barbarina
b. 1796

Roland
b. 1799

Sophie-Marie
b. 1798

To my mother

BOOK ONE

Eagle Chained

I loved a love once, fairest among women:
Closed are her doors on me, I must not see her.

Charles Lamb: *The Old Familiar Faces*

Chapter One

One day in March 1795, Hawkins, the butler at Chelmsford House in Pall Mall, paused on his way through the great hall to speak to Bunn, the porter.

'The Countess of Aylesbury is expected today, Mr Bunn,' he said – ceremoniously, because Bunn's boy was at his elbow, his mouth open in wonder.

'Was hany time o' day mentioned, Mr 'awkins?' Bunn replied in kind.

'His lordship did not specify, Mr Bunn. Her ladyship is coming from Wolvercote today, was all I was told.'

'I'll set the boy to keep a lookout for Lord Aylesbury's travelling chariot, then, Mr 'awkins,' said Bunn. The boy, who was new and had, in Bunn's opinion, a deal too much of what the cat cleaned her paws with, spoke up shamelessly in the presence of his betters.

''Ow will I know the kerridge then, Mr Bunn? Pall Mall is full o' gentlemen's kerridges.'

'Not of travelling chariots, it ain't,' said Bunn quellingly. 'Four 'orses – her ladyship wouldn't travel with two. Matched, most like. With postilions an' prob'ly a couple of outriders, all in the Aylesbury livery. You get out there on them steps, and when you see that lot a-coming, you sing out.'

'What colour livery is that, then, Mr Bunn?' demanded the unquellable boy.

'Sky blue, o'course. Don't you know *nothing*? Get along now. Boys!' he exclaimed to his superior as the child scuttled off. 'Don't know nothing, don't want to know nothing. I don't know what the world's coming to, straight I don't, Mr 'awkins. It wasn't like this when I was a boy.'

'It's the war, Mr Bunn,' said Mr Hawkins condescendingly. 'Stands to reason. War changes everything.'

It was hardly the boy's fault, however, that Lady Aylesbury took the household by surprise, for instead of

13

arriving in the travelling chariot, she confounded everybody by bowling up Pall Mall at a clipping pace, driving herself in a smart curricle drawn by four enormous York chestnuts, with her maid beside her and her groom up behind.

'You was right about the four 'orses, anyway, Mr Bunn,' the boy piped up, and this time Bunn thought it right to see how far a clip on the ear would go towards teaching the boy a more respectful demeanour towards his betters.

'Good morning, Bunn!' Lady Aylesbury called cheerfully as she entered the black-and-white tiled vestibule, stripping off her long gloves. 'How is your leg now? Did that salve do any good?'

'Yes, your ladyship. Thank your ladyship,' Bunn replied, blushing with pleasure. Only last year the Countess had been plain Miss Lucy Morland, and her appearance had hardly changed since then. Her sweet, pleasant face was speckled with mud from the journey, which mingled with her own natural freckles; her hay-coloured hair, which she wore in a short crop, was a tangle of wind-blown curls; and her movements were brisk and boyish. She was only sixteen, after all – yet there was a kind of authority in her bearing which made it perfectly natural for Bunn to bow low to her and call her 'your ladyship'. He noticed, too, that Mr Hawkins received her with genuine respectfulness, and Hawkins was capable of a very withering irony towards mushrooms and nabobs and others he considered not quite of the first consequence.

'I trust your ladyship had a good journey?' Hawkins asked.

'Very pleasant. The road is very good from Oxford – I'm told we are never cut off now, even in the winter. Ah, Charles!'

Her cousin, the Earl of Chelmsford, had come down into the hall to receive her. He kissed her, and then glanced out into the street, where Lucy's groom, Parslow, was leading the horses away, and grinned.

'Don't tell me you drove yourself in that thing! Yes, I can see from the mud on your face that you did. You really are a shocking girl, Lucy! And laying out your horses as if you were at Newmarket, I dare say. Is this your maid? She looks

14

scared half to death.'

'This is Docwra – she's new since Christmas,' said Lucy, turning to smile at the maid, who came into the hall, pushing back the hood of her cloak to reveal a face snub-nosed, rather grim, and very pale. She began to regain some natural colour now that she was on terra firma.

'To be sure, me lord, her ladyship's a very fine driver. Indeed she is. I'll soon get used to it,' she said with more determination than conviction, and a broad Irish accent.

'I told her she could come with the luggage if she liked, but she wouldn't have it,' Lucy said.

''t'wouldn't do for you to be travelling alone, my lady,' Docwra pronounced firmly.

'She fears for my reputation,' Lucy said with amusement as they started up the stairs. 'I told her that since I dressed up as a boy and ran away to sea when I was fourteen I had no reputation to lose, but she wouldn't believe it.'

'You delight in being shocking,' Charles said, looking her over with amusement. 'Are you never going to grow your hair again?'

'It's comfortable like this,' she replied. 'Besides, Mother says that now it is growing out curly, it suits me better. You can't imagine what a comfort it is to be able to ride fast without shedding pins everywhere.'

'I like long hair in women,' Charles said mildly, and Lucy snorted.

'You men have no notion of discomfort. Besides, it's very modish to crop. They call it *à la guillotine*, but I think that's rather horrible.'

'And you have another new maid. That must be the fourth in a year. What happened to the one you had at Christmas?'

'Oh, you mean Penney? She gave me notice. I never liked her. She disapproved of me, you know, Charles. Those expensive lady's maids always do. She told Flora's maid, Mrs Phillips, that I was more in need of a keeper than an abigail. She said I behaved like something out of Bedlam.'

'So you do,' Charles agreed. 'How do you know what she said to Phillips, anyway ?'

'Parslow told me. It went all round the servants' hall. But

15

I think Docwra will stay. She's of a very different breed. The poor thing almost starved to death in Ireland before she got passage to England. She came from a poor family – eleven brothers and sisters – and worked her way up from kitchen skivvy to abigail.'

'In that case, she must be tough enough to endure life with you, even if you do make her travel in an open carriage! But why didn't you come in the chariot? Would it not have been more comfortable?'

Lucy shrugged. 'I was perfectly comfortable, thank you. Besides, Chetwyn has the chariot. He has gone up to Morland Place again, to visit Ned.'

'And you did not wish to go with him? After all, we saw you at Christmas, and we ought not to be selfish, if you wanted to go home for a visit.'

'Oh Charles!' Lucy laughed. 'Calling it home, when I have been married more than a year! Wolvercote is my home now, and Chetwyn my husband – though I confess he seems much more like my brother,' she added, perhaps a little unguardedly.

Charles said curiously, 'Don't you mind that Chetwyn spends more time with your brother than with you? You could have gone to Morland Place with him, or he could have come to London with you.'

'Don't be so Gothic, Charles. I know you and Flora like to spend all your time together, but you will never succeed in making it fashionable. Chetwyn couldn't live another minute without seeing Ned and Mother and Morland Place, but I had a lot of shopping to do, that's all. I'm bound to go up to Yorkshire in the summer, so they won't miss me. Where is Flora, by the way?'

'She's in her room,' Charles said. 'I don't know how it is, but she has not been just quite well since Christmas. I have persuaded her once or twice not to get up in the mornings. The rest seems to do her good.'

'What is the matter with her?' Lucy asked with quick concern. All her life she had been interested in medical matters, and it was when she had discovered that women could not be doctors that she had determined to dress as a boy and run away to sea, to be a ship's surgeon.

16

'I don't know, except that she seems unable to digest her meat properly,' Charles said. 'She has bile and sickness, and sometimes cramps in the stomach. Dr Abse has been dosing her, but it seems not to have helped very much.'

Lucy looked grim. 'I told you before not to have Dr Abse in. He is the most abominable quack that ever lived. Don't you remember what he put in that remedy he gave Horace last autumn? Powdered mummy!'

'His reputation is very high,' Charles said feebly in self defence. 'All the people of fashion swear by him.'

'All the people of fashion die by him, and the more fool them! If I had my way, I'd tie him to a bed and dose him with his own filth until he choked on it. The harm such people do is not to be believed! Spirits of lead and powdered dung and ground woodlice; blistering and fomentations and bleeding; all the old witches' brews and hocus pocus! Oh, why didn't God make me a man?'

It was her old cry, and Charles could only pat her arm and say, 'I really can't imagine.'

'You must promise me you won't have Abse in again, Charles. I'll do what I can for Flora. If Abse has not poisoned her, Docwra and I will make up something for her, and we'll have her on her feet in no time. Docwra is the greatest help to me, you know. She had the doctoring of all her brothers and sisters in Ireland, and brought her mother through the childbed fever. And when I had to pull a tooth last week – one of the housemaids at Wolvercote, and, Lord! you would think I was going to murder her, the noise she made – Docwra held her down for me. It is a knack, you know, Charles – not everyone can do it.'

'I begin to see her attraction,' Charles smiled. 'Penney was right about your not needing an abigail.'

They arrived at the door of Flora's room. Charles scratched upon it, and they went in to find Flora lying on the day-bed by the window. Lucy was shocked at the change that had occurred in her in the two months since she had last seen her; but Flora's face lit up at the sight of Lucy, and she began at once to get up.

'Dear Lucy, I knew you would come. Now I shall be comfortable again!'

17

A few days later Lucy's elder sister, Mary Haworth, arrived at Chelmsford House, on her way back to Morland Place from Portsmouth. She had just had three days' blissful reunion with her adored husband, George Haworth, who was a sea officer, commanding His Majesty's ship *Cressy*. The *Cressy* had put in for some necessary refitting after eighteen months at sea, and had now gone back to resume her task of bottling up the French ships in their harbours.

Mary and Flora were old friends, for Flora had been brought up with the Morland children before Lucy was born. When Flora married Charles in 1782, Mary had gone on their honeymoon tour with them as bridal companion, and thereafter had made her home permanently with them, until her own marriage two years ago.

Mary presented a very different picture from her younger sister, for where Lucy was only quite pretty, Mary was truly beautiful. Introduced by Flora into society, she had become a leader of the *ton*, and had had scores of suitors of the greatest eligibility. Barons and earls had been dying for love of her, but she had led them all a dance and remained provokingly heart-whole, so that Flora began to fear that she would end as an old maid. Then when she was almost thirty, and more beautiful and sought-after than ever, Mary had fallen in love almost at first sight with a very unremarkable sea-captain, a friend of Flora's far more dashing naval friend, Hannibal Harvey.

Marriage and motherhood had not diminished Mary's beauty nor affected her style. She arrived at Chelmsford House with all the dignities of a post-chaise, a maid and a man, and a suitable quantity of luggage; wearing moreover an extremely modish pelisse of *bleu céleste* velvet and carrying an enormous muff of black sable. Her gloves were of French kid, and her glossy dark curls fell from beneath a perfectly distracting Russian hat of the same fur, decorated with a red-and-white hackle.

'I hope you can stay for a good, long time,' Flora said. 'Apart from my party to celebrate the Prince of Wales's marriage, which I must have you for, you know that Louisa is in Town, with John, to shop for her confinement, and I know she would value your opinion on what to buy.'

'She had far better ask yours, ma'am,' Mary smiled. 'After all, you are her mother; and besides, your budget is closer to hers than mine is. I am only a poor sea-captain's wife: I can't afford to patronise the shops you and Louisa go to.'

'How can you say that, when you arrive in the most delicious hat I have seen all winter?' Flora said. 'Where did you get it?'

'I designed it myself, and Farleigh made it up. She is wonderfully clever with her fingers.'

'You and Lucy have maids perfectly suited to your needs,' Charles remarked. 'Farleigh dresses hair and makes hats, and Docwra dresses wounds and holds down patients.'

'Hush, Charles! You will stay, won't you, Mary? Louisa's John will beg off my party with some excuse about being needed at the House, unless I tell him you are to be there.'

'I'll stay with pleasure, if you think I won't spoil your numbers,' Mary replied, wisely ignoring the last part.

'Oh no, as to that, I shall invite Lord Tonbridge for you. He has not courted any woman since you refused his offer, you know. Everyone says he stays single for love of you.'

'Everyone?' Mary queried with a wry smile.

'His mother,' Charles elucidated. 'It will be most cruel of you to invite him to have his heart broke all over again, my love, for Mary is prettier than ever. And it will do nothing for your numbers, because you will have to invite his mother too. She certainly won't let him come without her.'

'Never mind,' Flora said peaceably. 'I shall ask Horace to bring along some single men. There are some quite respectable officers in his regiment.'

'I should think there may be!' Charles exclaimed, amused at this slight upon the Prince of Wales's own regiment.

'And Hannibal shall bring one of his fellow admirals. I'm sure there must be plenty of them in London, for one cannot walk down Bond Street without bumping into half a dozen. It makes me wonder who there can be at sea.'

'It's a good system, which allows for keeping the bad sailors on shore while the good sailors command at sea,'

Mary said from the depths of her two-year acquaintance with matters nautical. 'But you must be so pleased that your friend is raised to flag rank at last.'

'Indeed I am,' Flora said. 'Now he will be able to pay his account at Fladong's. I never knew anyone build up debts so fast! If he did not eat here three days of the week, I am sure he would starve to death. It is a very good thing, you know, Mary, that you did not accept him, because I am sure you would not have been happy, though I thought otherwise at the time.'

Mary looked mystified. 'At what time, ma'am? How could I accept Captain Harvey when he never offered for me?'

'Oh, as to that, I expect he meant to,' Flora said, and Mary, catching Charles's eye, could not prevent herself from laughing.

Later that day, Mary found Lucy alone in the library, searching for a medical book to read.

'Nothing but novels,' she said with a sigh as she looked over her shoulder to see who had entered.

'Oh, don't!' Mary begged. 'You sound just like James's wife. There is nothing wrong in reading novels.'

'Of course not,' Lucy replied, 'if that is what you like. It's just that I never have time for them. Does Mrs James say they are bad, then?'

'Oh no. If she would only say so, one could argue with her. But whenever she sees me reading, she is bound to ask me what book I have, and when it turns out to be something jolly like *The Recluse of the Lake* or *The Mysteries of Udolpho*, she turns up her nose and says 'Oh, a novel!' as though I had done something vulgar; and then she takes up a piece of sewing from the poor-basket, or a book of sermons. She only asks me to make a point of her own superiority. There's no bearing it.'

'Poor Mary. And poor Mrs James, too,' Lucy added thoughtfully.

'I notice you haven't gone home with Chetwyn, for all your sympathy,' Mary said caustically.

'As to that, I think Chetwyn prefers it when I don't go with him. And there's nothing much for me to do there, with you out visiting your friends, and Ned and Chetwyn and Mama out around the estate all day, and James – God knows where! Probably in the Maccabbees Club; and that leaves me all alone with Mrs James, and I've nothing in common with her. All the same, I can't help feeling sorry for her. You know and I know, Polly, that James only married her out of duty, and he is not the sort of person to make the best of things.'

'You mean he only married her out of spite, because he couldn't have Héloïse,' Mary amended, 'and he's not the sort of person to forgive her for not being the woman he loves.'

Flora and Charles had no children of their marriage, though Flora had two of her first marriage, her daughter Louisa, now married and expecting her first child, and a younger son, Jack, who was serving in the navy aboard her brother William's ship. The heir to Charles's title and estate was therefore his half-brother, Horatio, who was a Captain in the 10th Light Dragoons, a very smart and fashionable regiment, permanently safe from actually having to go abroad and fight, because the King refused to allow the Prince of Wales to risk himself in active service.

Horatio had married Lady Barbara Rushton, the daughter of the Duke of Watford, and now that she had presented him with a son, Marcus, the line seemed to be secured. Horatio had removed from Chelmsford House after his marriage, and set up his household in Park Lane. It had been something of a relief to Flora, who could never quite convince herself that Horatio was not simply waiting and hoping for Charles to die; though she acknowledged to herself that the feeling was probably unreasonable, and that her dislike of Horace's pale, protruberant eyes and white eyelashes had prejudiced her.

He was certainly an ideal guest for her dinner party, for he was a personal friend of the Prince himself, and had been present at the wedding ceremony, and so could furnish all the details that everyone would be eager to hear. He brought with him on her request two other Dragoons officers: a Mr Danby Wiske, an extremely fashionable younger son of a Yorkshire family, and a Mr George Brummell, whose father had been a Treasury official and much valued by the King.

The small dining parlour, with its sea-green draperies and peacock-blue upholstery, and the handsome mahogany table which just held fourteen to a nicety, was as comfortable as it was elegant. Dinner advanced with the afternoon, and the candles and the dessert were brought in together, the curtains drawn to cut out the grey twilight, and the atmosphere set for a little cosy scandal.

'Is it true that the Princess never washes? And that Lord Melbourne had to tell her to change her linen when they were on the boat coming across?' Lucy wanted to know.

'Who could have told you that?' Charles asked, amused.

'Chetwyn, of course. And he said that the Princess's father, the Duke of Brunswick, told Melbourne that she was mad and ought to be locked up.'

'I don't suppose any of those things is true,' Flora said hastily, seeing Lady Tonbridge looking disapproving.

'At all events, it seems that the Prince does not mean to give up Lady Jersey,' said Lucy.

'He never did,' Charles said. 'Princess Caroline was told from the beginning that Lady Jersey was to be a Lady of the Bedchamber. What is more surprising is that Lady Jersey should ever have ousted Mrs Fitzherbert. I for one always thought that she was permanent.'

'There's plenty of precedent for it, after all,' Mary said unconcernedly. 'Kings have always made their mistresses serve in their wives' households, and the wives have simply had to put up with it. We learned that in history.'

'I have always thought,' Lady Tonbridge said, addressing the air with massive disapproval, 'that education of *that* sort ought to be confined to boys. It was never considered in my dear father's household that education contributed to that delicacy of mind which one looks for in females. My sisters and I were taught to be accomplished, not learned, and we all made extremely good matches. *That* was my dear father's plan for his daughters.'

A brief silence followed this unanswerable remark, while Lord Tonbridge looked unhappy and embarrassed at his mother's suggestion that the Morland girls lacked delicacy. Lady Tonbridge had been infuriated at what she considered Mary's presumption in making her son fall in love with her, and had been triumphant when she married an obscure man of neither fortune nor family; and not all the evidence to the contrary would convince her that it was Lord Tonbridge who had pursued Mary, or that she had chosen Captain Haworth of her own free will.

Flora rescued the conversation. 'You were in the escort which was sent to meet the Princess at Greenwich, were not you, Mr Brummell?' Mr Brummell bowed assent. 'I believe the coach was much delayed – was that Lady Jersey's doing?'

'No, your ladyship,' said Mr Brummell, 'though I believe Lady Jersey would be glad to take the credit. When the coach did arrive, she demanded to be allowed to sit beside the Princess, instead of taking the backward seat.'

'Claimed it made her sick, riding backwards,' put in Mr Wiske.

'Dear me! What did the Princess say to that?' asked Flora.

'Oh, she was not obliged to notice it,' Brummell said. 'Malmesbury told Lady Jersey that if riding backwards really made her sick, she should have refused the position of Lady of the Bedchamber, since taking the backward seat was one of its duties. After that, her ladyship could not argue further. She vented her spleen by criticizing the Princess's clothes and appearance in a very audible voice.'

'The poor Princess,' said Louisa. 'I feel so sorry for her. I should hate to travel hundreds of miles from a foreign land, all to be insulted by Lady Jersey.'

'Indeed, ma'am,' Mr Brummell said with a droll look, 'you need not put yourself at so much trouble. You might go tomorrow only to Carlton House and be insulted by her there.'

'It's Mrs Fitzherbert I feel sorry for,' Lucy said. 'To be put aside like that, after ten years' service, is very hard.'

'Mrs Fitz will be all right,' Horatio said. 'She has moved into a very nice house in Tilney Street, just round the corner from us, and there she sits, all right and tight, out of the way, but not too far to be called back.'

'Thought she'd turn up at the wedding,' Mr Wiske remarked. 'Lady Jersey did.'

'I believe the Prince was drunk?' said Flora.

'We all were – as wheelbarrows,' said Mr Wiske. 'Can't think why royal weddings are always put on so late in the day. At Carlton House we are always three parts foxed by that hour.'

'Lord Melbourne said that the Prince looked like Macheath going to his execution,' murmured Mr Brummell. 'A man doing a thing in desperation.'

'He'd had several glasses of brandy, according to Bedford,' Horatio admitted, 'but, damnit, a man must get his courage up for a thing like that. I could have done with a glass or two myself, just to get through that tedious long ceremony.'

'And the Archbishop did nothing to shorten it,' Mr Brummell said innocently, 'lingering as he did over the passages which refer to lawful impediments to marriage. I wonder what he could have been thinking of?'

'Mr Brummell, I do believe you are very wicked,' Flora said approvingly.

'Dashed good fellow, George,' Mr Wiske remarked to Lucy, who was his neighbour, in what he evidently thought was an undertone, 'only, too particular about his waistcoats and neckties and such. As good a fellow as ever lived. True as turnips.'

And Lucy, liking him both for his loyalty to his friend, and for the unexpectedly rustic simile, bestowed on Mr Wiske a smile that made him first blink, then blush.

In the drawing-room, Lady Tonbridge was soon wanting whist, and Horatio and Lady Barbara hastened to oblige her, for she was a notoriously bad player who nevertheless liked to play high, and Horatio was not so plump in the pocket as to be able to resist such easy prey.

John Anstey and Charles retired to a table where the newspapers were spread, and discussed politics. Flora and Hannibal Harvey took possession of one sofa, and soon had their heads together in the old manner, while Mary good-naturedly took Louisa to another and let her talk about babies and confinements. This left Lucy to entertain the three unmarried gentlemen, and the division seemed natural enough, despite her being a married woman. She had been brought up with her brothers, and her weeks in the ward-room of the *Diamond* had taught her how to converse with men on equal terms. Their group was the liveliest in the drawing room.

They had been talking of hunting, and Lucy had noticed that Mr Brummell's face was fixed in an expression of ironic disapproval.

'Do you not hunt, Mr Brummell?' she asked.

'I fear I am obliged to, your ladyship,' he sighed. 'When society is so misguided as to go out of Town in the middle of winter, one is obliged to follow, whatever the inconvenience.'

'Do you mean you don't like the country? Why ever not?' Lucy asked in astonishment.

He gave a delicate shudder. 'It is cold, Lady Aylesbury, and wet, and muddy. I am a hothouse creature, I cannot bear discomfort; and yet in a country house I am obliged to creep from one inadequate fire to another, across the seas of icy draught, and to spend a great part of each day in severe discomfort slaughtering birds and beasts to whom, really, I wish no harm at all. How could civilization have gone so far astray?'

'What would you consider a civilized occupation?' Lucy asked.

'To spend my time in well-heated, well-lit rooms,' he said promptly, 'with elegant surroundings, beautiful women, and witty conversation.'

Lucy glanced at Danby Wiske. 'He is so different from you, sir. How came you to be acquainted?'

Mr Wiske entirely missed the implied insult, which made Mr Brummell smile, and replied, 'We were at Eton together, ma'am. George and his brother William and I all entered in

25

'86, and lodged together at Dame Yonge's.'

'Such lodgings!' Mr Brummell exclaimed. 'Forty boys with beds for twenty, food for fifteen, and coals for ten. Eton was such a perfectly *barbarous* place that I do not think I shall ever be able to forget it.'

'Really, sir?' Lucy laughed.

'Really,' Mr Brummell affirmed. 'Not only were we starved, but we were beaten – flogged, my dear Lady Aylesbury, like dogs, upon the most frivolous of pretexts, positively in *batches*! I remember on one occasion, the headmaster gave ten strokes a-piece to seventy boys, after which he was confined to bed for upwards of a week, with such pains in his arm and shoulder he could scarcely sit upright.'

'I wonder you survived it,' Lucy said, her eyes alight.

'It don't do to take him too seriously, ma'am,' said Mr Wiske. 'Beatings were as common as blackberries at Eton, but I don't recall that George was flogged once the whole time we were there. He was such a favourite, you know, and though he was always playing tricks, he was never punished. The praepostor would come down upon him, arm raised, and George would just smile, and it would all be forgotten.'

'I was fortunate in my smile,' Mr Brummell admitted. 'But it was only what was fair. God gave me my charming Irish smile to make up for my unfortunate Irish nose.'

'I think Mr Brummell is making game of us,' Lucy said to Danby Wiske.

'He don't take anyone seriously,' said Mr Wiske.

'Indeed, you wrong me,' Mr Brummell said gravely. 'My Irish ancestors have always been my affliction. One can discourage history in one's family, but one cannot entirely escape its geography.'

'Talking of geography,' Lord Tonbridge interposed at this point, 'don't I hear that the Dragoons are going down to Brighton Camp this summer?'

'Yes, and the Prince and Princess will be there too. Brighton will be the place to be this year.'

'Brighton will be well enough, when all the rebuilding is finished,' said Mr Brummell. 'At the moment, the dust is intolerable.'

'But we have famous dinners, Lady Aylesbury, and the theatre is very pretty. I wonder you do not come to Brighton,' said Mr Wiske a little wistfully.

'Perhaps I may,' Lucy said carelessly. 'I have recommended Lady Chelmsford to try the sea-air for her health. Perhaps I may join her there for a little while.'

'Of course, you will drive yourself to Brighton,' Mr Brummell said mischievously. 'In your curricle and four, you may even beat the Prince of Wales's time. You know that he drove down from London in '84 in less than five hours, and it has never been bettered.'

Lord Tonbridge was looking alarmed, but Lucy's interest was already caught, as Danby Wiske said, 'It was four hours and fifty minutes, George, in a three-horse phaeton. A devilish difficult rig to choose, I always thought.'

'Four hours and fifty minutes does not seem so very fast,' Lucy said thoughtfully. 'It cannot be more than sixty miles, I suppose? And perhaps the road may be better now.'

'Very true – and four horses, you know, must be faster than three, if the driver is as good,' said Mr Brummell seriously.

'He is teasing you,' Lord Tonbridge told Lucy anxiously. 'Do not rise to his bait. You cannot possibly drive yourself to Brighton in a curricle and four. Think of the scandal!'

Lucy's smile was calm and determined. 'Of course I can, Tonbridge – and as for the scandal, I don't regard it. And I'll beat the Prince's time, you see if I don't. Only it must be made worth my while. What do you all say to a wager? I am sure enough of the result to put a hundred guineas on my own performance.'

Lord Tonbridge looked more than ever distressed. 'This grows worse – to make a wager on it, too! I beg you, consider.'

'Don't be so gothic, Tonbridge – what is there in that? Ladies make wagers all the time. Look at your mother, playing whist, and what is that but a wager on her skill with cards?'

'It is not the same thing at all. What would your husband say?'

'It seems exactly the same to me,' Lucy rejoined stoutly,

'and as for Chetwyn, don't trouble yourself about him. He will think it very good sport. He has always said that I am the best driver of my family, and I will be very surprised indeed if he doesn't put something on me too, when he hears.' She smiled round at the three men. 'It is just what I was wanting – something to amuse me. I was just beginning to feel bored with life. I am very grateful to you for suggesting it, Mr Brummell.'

Mr Brummell smiled and bowed, and murmured, 'And I am grateful to you, dear Lady Aylesbury, for exactly the same reason.'

He and Lucy looked as though they understood each other perfectly, and Danby Wiske was regarding her with an expression little short of adoration. Only Lord Tonbridge looked unhappy, and he was made even more so when Lucy told him that she hoped he would lend her his greys for the race.

'I shall need three changes, you see. My chestnuts for the last, and I'll send for Chetwyn's bays, which are eating their heads off at Wolvercote, and I'm sure Charles will let me use his team. But I must have one more, and yours would do. They are a neatish team, and fast, though their knees are weak. But there's nothing much to the first stage, except for the hill at Brixton, and I'll nurse them up that like babies, you may be sure, and send them back to you no worse than I took them.'

'There now, Lord Tonbridge,' said Mr Brummell with a seraphic smile, 'how can you possibly refuse to lend them to her ladyship after that?'

'And when she has spoke of them so handsome, too!' Mr Wiske added, and could only look on in bewilderment when Lucy and Mr Brummell burst simultaneously into laughter.

Chapter Two

The news of Lucy's race to Brighton was, on the whole, well received in a Season whose scandals were otherwise of the bad-tempered sort. One or two high-sticklers – what Mr Wiske called 'mossy-backs' – thought it shocking, not so much that Lucy should drive herself in an open carriage down a busy road accompanied only by her groom, for indeed she was a Countess, and what was the world coming to if a peeress could not travel according to her fancy; but because she had made herself the subject of a wager, and won a great deal of money by backing her own performance.

'Envy,' said Mr Wiske tersely. 'Wish they'd thought of it themselves. Wonder if we don't see dowagers organizin' wheelchair races and madeira-drinkin' contests, hoping to win enough to pay off their mortgages.'

Danby Wiske had constituted himself Lucy's faithful attendant, admirer, and unofficial protector. That he admired her to distraction was obvious from the way he gazed at her with his mouth open and hung on her every word as though it were Holy Writ. He had attended her during the race, riding behind the curricle on horseback, despite the serious disadvantage of the dust and mud thrown up at him.

'See fair play,' he offered as an explanation, when Charles at the starting line looked surprised; and then added with a blush, 'Take care of her la'ship – see no harm comes to her.'

When the race was done, and Lucy had beaten the Prince of Wales's time by a full fifteen minutes, Mr Wiske's admiration was secured for ever. His continual appearance thereafter by her side, or rather half a pace to the rear, might have created a real scandal, had his devotion not been so evidently dog-like and innocent. As it was, Lady Aylesbury was in general considered a dashing and enter-

29

prising young woman; her health was drunk at Carlton House twice in one week, and in the officers' mess of the 10th Light Dragoons every night for a fortnight; and Mr Wiske's devotion was thought no more than her due.

At Morland Place, her brother James laughed and called her 'a trump', and her brother Edward wanted to know where she had changed horses. Her mother sighed and shook her head and said that there was no taming Lucy; and her husband, though laughing with James and Edward and agreeing that it was a capital stunt, and a great joke against His Highness, grew very thoughtful afterwards, and cut his visit short. Her escapade had served to remind him that he had married her in the first place to provide him with an heir, and that if she broke her neck with one of her hoydenish pranks before she had done so, he would have to go through it all again with another woman. The idea turned him cold, and he hurried home to remind her of her duty and, if possible, to make her pregnant.

The one person at Morland Place who remained unmoved by the event was James's wife, Mary Ann. She listened without either admiration or disapproval, indeed with no other emotion than a faint surprise that any female should wish to expose herself to so much dirt and discomfort. Her life so far had not contained such desires. As Miss Hobsbawn, her father's adored only child, she had lived a well-regulated and peaceful life in their large modern house in Manchester. Her mother had died when she was very young, and she had been brought up by a nurse, now her maid, Dakers. At the age of nine she had been sent to a convent school for three years, where she had learned to read and write and sew and speak French; thereafter she had had a fashionable governess for four years to teach her the accomplishments, and at sixteen had entered into society as her father's companion and housekeeper.

Her days had been an uneventful round of ordering the household, receiving and paying morning visits, taking her walk in the garden, dining, and spending the evenings reading, working, or playing for her father upon the pianoforte. Her upbringing and religion had taught her obedience, and she had always known that Papa would arrange her marriage at the right moment. Trusting him, she had been content to leave such things to him. She had never wished to choose for herself. She did not read novels; she had no romantic notions.

Her experience of the male sex was limited. There were her father's friends and colleagues, most of whom had known her since her infancy, and treated her accordingly. Occasionally a clerk or foreman would come up to the house from one of the mills, but these, like priests and male servants, did not really count as men at all; and the young men she encountered were usually husbands of the women her father considered respectable enough for her to visit. Young unmarried men did not come in her way.

So her interest was keenly aroused by the news that she was to meet her future husband. Would he be tall, short, fat, thin? Would he be gruff or cheerful, bad-tempered or kindly? Everyone, she knew, had good qualities, and since it was her duty before God to love her husband, it would be her business to find them out, and respect him for them. Her first sight of James Morland was reassuring. He was not tall, but he was graceful and strong, and definitely handsome, with his fair skin, fine features, reddish-brown hair and dark blue eyes. He played upon the pianoforte at her father's request, and did it well; he spoke little, but sensibly; and the only words she had privately with him, gave her to think well of his character, for he told her that he did not wish her to marry him against her will, which seemed a kindness. He would be considerate to her, she thought.

But Morland Place had proved more strange than she could have imagined. To be living in the country instead of in a busy town, and in an old castle with a moat, instead of a neat modern house with all the conveniences, was strange enough, but she was no longer mistress of the household. She now had to get used to the ways of servants who took their orders from her mother-in-law and resented any suggestion that they should change their methods. There was a continuous flow of people through the house, bringing noise and movement, unexpected guests and even more unexpected absences, so that it was hard from moment to moment to know where anyone was. There were dogs and

31

bits of saddlery everywhere, strange smells, and an incomprehensible accent to unravel.

And marriage was not what she had expected, either. The physical side of it, which her religion had prepared her to endure, was not intolerable; but after the first two weeks at Morland Place, her husband had removed himself without explanation to another bedroom, leaving her to sleep alone in the great bedchamber.

She saw little of him. He was out all day, either in the city or helping his brother to run the estate. Often he did not return to dinner, and sometimes not at all before she went to bed; and from time to time he would go away for several days to Harrogate or Scarborough, for what purpose no-one seemed to know or ask. When she did encounter him in the house, he would greet her politely, or make some enigmatical remark she did not understand.

She was fascinated by him: he seemed so unlike other people. He not only played well, but also sketched and painted, and there were many examples of his talent about the house. He was strange and moody, too silent upon some occasions, and on others laughing inexplicably at the wrong things. She saw that he often drank too much, and had reason to suppose that his absences were not always upon respectable business; and yet he never missed mass, and often sat alone in the chapel for an hour together at other times.

After the Christmas season, when all the guests had gone, and a certain flatness seemed to prevail in the house, he had suddenly reappeared in her bedchamber, and for a few nights had resumed physical relations with her. He left off again as suddenly as he had begun, but it had been enough: she proved to be with child. She had waited for an evening when he was present in the drawing room before announcing the news, and though she addressed herself to her mother-in-law, she had covertly watched her husband's face. His first reaction, she was sure, had been one of pleasure; but afterwards he had looked bewildered, and then unhappy, and had very soon made an excuse to leave the room.

Since then she had seen as little of him as before, but her

32

own life had settled into a sort of pattern which, as far as she could manage it, recreated her life in Hobsbawn House. Dakers came to wake her and dress her at eight, and she spent an hour in private prayer and reflection before going down to the chapel for mass, and then to breakfast. At eleven she took her exercise, always in the gardens, for Morland Place was designed for riders, and the estate had no walks suitable for ladies. For the rest of the day until dinner she read, worked, wrote letters, and practised her music, though there was no pianoforte, and she found the old harpsichord a severe trial, not suited to the sort of music she was accustomed to play. After dinner she conversed with such of the family as gathered in the drawing-room, and after tea and evening prayers retired early to her bed.

That the Morlands found her as strange as she found them rarely occurred to her and never worried her. She did not doubt that her place amcngst them was understood and secure, for her father had arranged it all, and what her father decided upon always came to pass. She missed him sometimes, missed his affection and praise, and was occasionally puzzled by her husband, but she was not unhappy. Her life assumed a placid and untroubled course, as she sewed baby-shirts and prepared for the birth of her child. Her son would inherit Morland Place and the whole of her father's estate, and the mother of that child could never be less than respected.

'Every autumn, God sends one perfect day, when the colours of the trees are so beautiful they would break your heart,' said Jemima, as she and Mary rode past the beech hanger which sheltered Knapton village on the north-east. The beech leaves seemed to burn against the autumn-blue sky, gold and copper and orichalcum and flame, tiger-brindled with their black branches. The air was as mild as summer, but the horses' hooves struck out no smell of earth or bruised grass, sure sign that the world was cooling into winter.

Jemima, though over sixty and white-haired now, rode easily and very erect with all the skill of a lifetime in the

33

saddle. Her workaday habit of black worsted was cut for comfort rather than elegance, and her hat was an old-fashioned tricorne which had happened to come to hand as she prepared to go out. Mary's habit on the other hand, was of fine cloth cut tight at the waist and long-skirted, and her fashionably mannish tall hat was secured with a veil which covered her whole face in a way that was particularly becoming; but after what was for her a long ride, she was struggling to keep her back straight, and had long ceased to attempt to direct her horse, content to allow him to pick his own way home while she held onto the pommel for support.

As they passed through Ten Thorn gap, a partridge rattled out from under the hedge right under their horses' hooves. Mary's mount, a steady old schoolmaster, acknowledged the event only by a flicker of his ears: nothing would distract him from taking the quickest way home to his box and hayrack. Jemima's chestnut was a young horse she was schooling to carry sidesaddle, and he snorted with alarm, jumped sideways, and tried to get away up the lane. Jemima sat him unperturbed, soothing him with hand and voice, and in a moment he consented to follow old Badger through the gap.

'He's very good, isn't he?' Mary remarked when they were side by side again. 'Your dear old Poppy would have stood up at half the provocation, and you'd have been two counties away by now.'

'Yes, he's very sensible for a youngster,' Jemima said. 'I think he'll be just right for Louisa Anstey by the time she's out of childbed. But then, you know, I've often thought that geldings are more suitable for ladies than mares. They're usually better-tempered and more reliable, in my experience.'

'You've always ridden mares yourself,' Mary pointed out.

'But then I like the challenge,' Jemima smiled. 'Louisa has never been adventurous, but she likes to go out on horseback, so this fellow will be just right for her in another month. It was well thought of by John Anstey. He is a most attentive husband.'

'And you benefit by the commission. Clever John! And clever Louisa, to get a boy first time. What are they going to call him?'

'John, of course.'

'Yes, of course. I imagine Lucy must be hoping very hard for a boy next March, so that she won't have it to do again.'

'Why should you think she is not pleased to be pregnant?' Jemima asked in surprise.

'Oh, perhaps she may be,' Mary said, 'but it will restrict her other activities so much I dare say she will not wish to be often increasing. No curricle racing for her – no hunting this winter, nor skating on the great lake at Wolvercote – no travelling at all, if Chetwyn has any sense. Poor thing, she will be so bored.'

'Do you think it is boredom, then, that makes her do such – unexpected things?'

'Oh yes,' Mary said simply. 'You gave us both too much education to fit us for the usual female life of sewing and sitting and smiling. Lucy was more restless than me, because she was cleverer, but she was better off really, because my interests were never fixed on horses. I didn't know what I wanted, until Flora and Charles took me to Italy and then set me up in London.'

'Is that what you wanted,' Jemima smiled, 'to be a leader of the *ton*? Yes, I remember, you always said you intended to marry an earl. Poor Captain Haworth!' Mary laughed in acknowledgement of the jibe, and they rode on in silence for a while, each occupied with her thoughts.

Jemima said eventually, 'It's strange how one's children turn out so differently from the way one imagines them. William, for example: he was so small and frail as a child – do you remember, Mary? – and we often thought we should never rear him at all. And now he's the captain of a seventy-four, a tall, strong man, and a great martinet! You remember that last letter from Harry, where he said that William is such a strict disciplinarian that the men call him "Bloody Bill"? And then there's James.'

'Ah yes, James,' Mary said thoughtfully.

'I often wonder why James has turned out the way he has. He was such a quiet, good child. Perhaps he was too much alone. You and Edward and the twins had each other to play with, but Jamie was too young to join in, and by the time Harry and Lucy came along, he was too old for them.

And your Papa was abroad a good deal while he was growing up, and I was always busy. Yet he was very fond of Father Ramsay. I can never understand what made him do that dreadful thing with Mary Skelwith. That's when he began to go wrong.'

'I think he was in love with her before she married, when she was still Mary Loveday.'

'Do you? But she married Skelwith of her own free will. Why would she have done that if she meant to –' She frowned. 'All that apart, when the scandal broke, what could we do?'

'Only what you had to.'

'But from that moment, he has seemed so lost. If only he could have married Héloïse.'

'Do you really think that would have made any difference? In a few months he would have grown tired of her, and been just the same. He is discontented by nature. I think he has loved her far more since he lost her than ever he did when she was there.'

'Oh, no, Mary,' Jemima said, quite shocked. 'You didn't see them together as I did. He adored her, and she would have fixed him for ever. She was so strong and energetic, and she would have guided him into proper habits of thought and behaviour; so that even if he did fall out of love with her later, the lessons would have been learned.'

Mary shrugged. 'Well, it makes no difference now, anyway. He is married to Mary Ann, and about to become a father, and we'll all have to make the best of it. At least he doesn't get drunk quite so often – not falling-down drunk, at all events.'

'Mary!'

'And he does help Ned, in a half-hearted sort of way. But you notice he still visits Scarborough.'

Jemima grew a little pale. 'You surely can't mean – '

'I mean that I think it would have taken a love-match to make him give up those trips, even temporarily.'

'But who – no, don't tell me, even if you can guess. I had much rather not know. I hope you are mistaken.'

'I hope so, too,' Mary said. She was growing bored with talk of Jamie. 'Lord, my back does ache! How you can stay

36

in the saddle all day long I can't think.'

'It's because I do, that my back doesn't ache,' Jemima said, deflected. 'You should be more regular in your exercise, my love. As soon as Hippolyta is old enough, I hope you will encourage her to be out of doors a good deal. Your Papa was very firm about the value of fresh air, especially for growing children, and regular outdoor exercise is the best way to guard your health. I don't like to see young women sitting indoors all day.'

'Yes, Mama,' Mary said meekly.

It was in the early hours of the following morning that Mary Ann went into labour. Jemima and Mary remained in the house all day suffering vicarious pains, and Edward found things to occupy him within earshot of the house; but James, without even waiting for breakfast, went out at ten in the morning, and did not return until five o' clock, the usual dining hour. To judge by his eyes and his breath, he had consumed a great deal of brandy, but on learning that his wife was still in labour and dinner was not ready, he rang for more, and sat himself in the farthest corner of the drawing room, hunched over his glass.

It was not until six o' clock that day, the third of October, that the ringing of the house-bell proclaimed to the village that the heir to Morland Place was born. Those gathered in the drawing-room heard a baby's wail from the great bed-chamber above, and after what seemed like an endless delay, the sound of quick footsteps crossing the hall outside. Then the door opened, and Farleigh appeared, followed by the nursery-maid, Jenny, carrying a white bundle.

'A girl, ma'am,' Farleigh announced to Jemima, and Jenny, her face wreathed with smiles, gave her the child, saying, 'A lovely little girl, my lady, a companion for dear Miss Hippolyta. And the mother's doing very well, the midwife said to say.'

Jemima heard her son's quick sigh at the first words, and glanced at him, wondering if it were a sigh of disappointment, but his face was inscrutable. She held out her hand for him to come to her, and turned back the edge of the wrapper to look at her second grandchild. James crossed the room reluctantly, and as Jemima said, 'Look, Jamie,' she thought the expression in his eyes was one of apprehension.

James looked. Within the white folds he saw a tiny head, fragile as a robin's egg, despite its covering of draggled black hair, and below, the small face, still a stranger's, composed in a sleep of the most unutterable innocence. Her half-hour's acquaintance with the world, he thought, had not yet been able to tarnish that. Around him he heard people talking and exclaiming, but their voices were distant and muffled, as if they were beyond a curtain, and he seemed alone with his strange fear as he reached out his hands in dread to take hold of his daughter.

She was so small, so light! He looked down at her and knew he had been right to be afraid, because the first touch of her pierced him with a terrible love from which he knew he would never be able to escape. His lips trembled but he could not speak; he could only stare at her, and allow the pain to absorb him. She lay in his arms in her utter helplessness, an innocence beyond trust. One tiny hand rested against her cheek, half-curled like a new leaf, so that he could see the miracle of her nacreous fingernails; her sleeping face quivered, her lips and eyebrows moved, as though with the force of new life flowing through her, strong and invisible, like light flowing through crystal.

That part of James which was an artist was in love with perfection, and had always sought it in vain; and now here it was, in this new, unused, and perfect child. He wanted to cry out with love and pity, for now she was born, and now everything that would happen to her was inevitable, life and love and pain and death. The world would harden around her still-damp tenderness like a shell; and time would drive her second by second further from this moment of absolute innocence, down into the darkness of self-knowledge where he lived.

Amongst the voices around him he heard that of Farleigh saying, 'Madam expressed the wish that, as tomorrow is St Francis's day, the child should be named Frances.'

Other voices followed, commenting and discussing, but he shut them out, retreating from them into the silence

38

which contained only him and his daughter. Frances! Yes, already the name seemed right, as if it had come with her. Through the pain of his new love, he smiled at her, and her eyes moved under her closed eyelids as if she saw him, and her lips moved as if in response. Her vulnerability made him vulnerable: now would begin the struggle to protect her from the things against which there was no protection; but her love would make him strong. She was his fate; she would be his salvation.

He brought his face near so that she alone would hear him. 'I love you, Fanny,' he whispered.

Mr Hobsbawn came of a generation which regarded journeys as momentous events which required careful preparation, if they were to be survived; and so though the express bearing the news of his grandchild's birth reached him on the following day, it was another week before he appeared at Morland Place.

He travelled in his ancient and ponderous berlin, with his own horses, four massive, hairy-hoofed beasts whose merits lay not in speed or beauty, but in endurance. Inside there was ample room for himself, his manservant, and his lawyer, Mr Yardley, and all the apparatus of travel, the furs and rugs, hot-water bottles, cushions, and a hamper of food and drink, against emergencies. Hobsbawn had a special travelling-cap of fur, with long lappets to protect the ears, and travelling-slippers, which had to be changed for boots at every stop, before he could descend.

He travelled slowly, going only as far as Leeds the first day, with two other stops, besides a long bait at Huddersfield at midday. His own coachman and groom sat up on the box, protected against the elements by box-coats so heavy and stiff that the servants could have slipped out of them and left them sitting up there; and against possible highwaymen by a loaded shotgun of primitive design. They reached Morland Place by dinner-time on the second day, having taken something over six hours to cover the twenty-five miles from Leeds.

All this he explained at great length to the family as they

39

sat down to dinner together, supposing in his innocence that his audience was enthralled by his tale of hills scaled and ditches narrowly avoided, of cold and damp endured, and cozening inn-keepers bested. Everyone was of course far too polite to do other than listen in silence, but as they left the dining-room for the drawing-room. James took the opportunity to mutter to Mary as they passed through the door together, 'What a piece of work to make of it! You would think he had rounded Cape Horn in a hurricane!'

Dinner had taken so long that tea was brought in almost at once, and afterwards Jemima was just about to propose whist for the entertainment of their guest when Mary Ann rose to retire, and Hobsbawn said, 'Yes, you're right, my ... it's time we were all a-bed. Do you say prayers, Lady Morland.

Jemima rose too, seeing out of the corner of her eye the looks of amazement from James and Mary, for it was not yet nine o'clock, and forestalling them by saying, 'Yes, indeed. Shall we go to the chapel? Father Thomas, will you lead the way?'

James seized her arm in the hallway to protest. 'Really, Mother, are we to go to bed at this hour every night, just because *he* says so? I won't stand for it!'

'Don't make such a fuss, Jamie. Remember, his habits are probably very different from ours, from having to supervise his factories at all sorts of strange hours. Besides, once he has gone up, there is no reason why you should not sit up, if you want to.'

James muttered something inaudible, but probably uncomplimentary, and Jemima spoke to him sharply, in a low voice.

'Jamie, he is a good, kind man,, and adores his daughter, and is prepared to be very generous about settlements. I insist that you treat him with respect. I won't have you being impolite to any guest in this house, least of all to –'

'Our saviour?' James interrupted sourly. 'The man whose money is to build you your new stables?' He regretted the words instantly, and his mother's look made him feel ashamed. 'I'm sorry,' he said, before she could reply.

Jemima looked at him with a mixture of anger and pain.

40

'Jamie, what is the matter with you?'

'You know the answer to that,' he muttered.

'I don't know. You chose this marriage yourself. No-one forced it on you – it was your own suggestion. And you seemed so pleased with the baby – '

James made a restless movement of his head. 'Leave me alone, Mother, please.' And he walked away before her into the chapel, leaving Jemima to stare after him in dissatisfaction.

Edward and Jemima were always up at dawn, and usually took a first breakfast of bread and chocolate together, before going off to their early morning tasks. Edward was a restful companion, not inclined to be talkative, and the world was quiet, except for the sounds of waking nature, and Jemima valued this peaceful time, when the world seemed hers, and there was space to breathe deeply and compose oneself.

It took self-control, therefore, to greet Mr Hobsbawn warmly when he appeared in the hall just as she was about to go out. He, too, was an early riser, and since politeness could not admit of leaving him to his own devices, there was nothing to be done but to propose shewing him round the pleasure-grounds.

They made a circuit of the moat, followed hopefully by the swans, who had not yet been fed, and Mr Hobsbawn was shewn the rose garden, the Italian garden, the Long Walk, the orchards, and the American garden, before returning by the barbican and the courtyard in time for morning mass. This was followed by breakfast proper, to which everyone had come down. Mr Hobsbawn approved the number of dishes spread, and ate heartily of smoked cod, mutton chops, sausages, and fat pork fried with onions, which he helped down with a quart of small beer. He was evidently curious about his son-in-law, and tried several times to engage him in conversation, but James was more than equal to frustrating his design. Mr Hobsbawn was obliged at last to leave off, without having formed any more certain opinion of James than that he ate too slight a breakfast – buttered eggs and toast, only enough for a woman – and that he was like to ruin his nerves and digestion by washing it down with coffee.

They were still sitting amongst the bones and eggshells when Oxhey came in to say that Pobgee, the lawyer, had arrived, and was waiting in the steward's room.

'Well sir,' said Edward, getting to his feet, 'shall we begin? Mother? Mr Yardley?' There was a general rising from the table, but it was only when they were out in the hallway that Hobsbawn realised James was heading in the other direction, and asked him in surprise, 'Why, sir, do you not come with us?'

James smiled and said lightly, 'The steward's room will not hold more than five comfortably.' Then, seeing his mother frown in disapproval, and Hobsbawn about to make further enquiries, he added firmly, 'My mother and brother attend to the business, sir. I know I may trust them to take care of my little Fanny's interests.' This went down well, but he spoiled the effect by adding cynically, 'I can have nothing to contribute to the discussion. I own nothing but my horse and my clothes.' With that he bowed deeply and made his escape to the stables.

He spent the day at the Maccabbees Club in Stonegate, sitting over the fire with a bottle of brandy. When he arrived back at Morland Place, he found his servant, Durban, waiting for him in the yard. Durban came up quickly to take Nez Carré's head, and shot his master a look of mingled enquiry and warning.

'Where is everyone?' James asked. 'Have I been missed? Are search parties abroad for me?'

'I believe your absence was noted, sir,' Durban said. 'The dressing bell has gone, and everyone is upstairs. The coast is clear for the moment, sir.'

James dismounted, and patted Durban's arm in acknowledgement of the sympathy. The house was before him, waiting, but today his childhood home looked forbidding in the fading light. It contained his unloved wife and her sharp-eyed father, his anxious mother and cynically amused sister. It threatened him. Everyone wanted something from him, he thought, clenching his fists in frustration. Why would

'Jamie, what is the matter with you?'

'You know the answer to that,' he muttered.

'I don't know. You chose this marriage yourself. No-one forced it on you – it was your own suggestion. And you seemed so pleased with the baby – '

James made a restless movement of his head. 'Leave me alone, Mother, please.' And he walked away before her into the chapel, leaving Jemima to stare after him in dissatisfaction.

Edward and Jemima were always up at dawn, and usually took a first breakfast of bread and chocolate together, before going off to their early morning tasks. Edward was a restful companion, not inclined to be talkative, and the world was quiet, except for the sounds of waking nature, and Jemima valued this peaceful time, when the world seemed hers, and there was space to breathe deeply and compose oneself.

It took self-control, therefore, to greet Mr Hobsbawn warmly when he appeared in the hall just as she was about to go out. He, too, was an early riser, and since politeness could not admit of leaving him to his own devices, there was nothing to be done but to propose shewing him round the pleasure-grounds.

They made a circuit of the moat, followed hopefully by the swans, who had not yet been fed, and Mr Hobsbawn was shewn the rose garden, the Italian garden, the Long Walk, the orchards, and the American garden, before returning by the barbican and the courtyard in time for morning mass. This was followed by breakfast proper, to which everyone had come down. Mr Hobsbawn approved the number of dishes spread, and ate heartily of smoked cod, mutton chops, sausages, and fat pork fried with onions, which he helped down with a quart of small beer. He was evidently curious about his son-in-law, and tried several times to engage him in conversation, but James was more than equal to frustrating his design. Mr Hobsbawn was obliged at last to leave off, without having formed any more certain opinion of James than that he ate too slight a breakfast – buttered

41

bits of saddlery everywhere, strange smells, and an incomprehensible accent to unravel.

And marriage was not what she had expected, either. The physical side of it, which her religion had prepared her to endure, was not intolerable; but after the first two weeks at Morland Place, her husband had removed himself without explanation to another bedroom, leaving her to sleep alone in the great bedchamber.

She saw little of him. He was out all day, either in the city or helping his brother to run the estate. Often he did not return to dinner, and sometimes not at all before she went to bed; and from time to time he would go away for several days to Harrogate or Scarborough, for what purpose no-one seemed to know or ask. When she did encounter him in the house, he would greet her politely, or make some enigmatical remark she did not understand.

She was fascinated by him: he seemed so unlike other people. He not only played well, but also sketched and painted, and there were many examples of his talent about the house. He was strange and moody, too silent upon some occasions, and on others laughing inexplicably at the wrong things. She saw that he often drank too much, and had reason to suppose that his absences were not always upon respectable business; and yet he never missed mass, and often sat alone in the chapel for an hour together at other times.

After the Christmas season, when all the guests had gone, and a certain flatness seemed to prevail in the house, he had suddenly reappeared in her bedchamber, and for a few nights had resumed physical relations with her. He left off again as suddenly as he had begun, but it had been enough: she proved to be with child. She had waited for an evening when he was present in the drawing room before announcing the news, and though she addressed herself to her mother-in-law, she had covertly watched her husband's face. His first reaction, she was sure, had been one of pleasure; but afterwards he had looked bewildered, and then unhappy, and had very soon made an excuse to leave the room.

Since then she had seen as little of him as before, but her

And your Papa was abroad a good deal while he was growing up, and I was always busy. Yet he was very fond of Father Ramsay. I can never understand what made him do that dreadful thing with Mary Skelwith. That's when he began to go wrong.'

'I think he was in love with her before she married, when she was still Mary Loveday.'

'Do you? But she married Skelwith of her own free will. Why would she have done that if she meant to –' She frowned. 'All that apart, when the scandal broke, what could we do?'

'Only what you had to.'

'But from that moment, he has seemed so lost. If only he could have married Héloïse.'

'Do you really think that would have made any difference? In a few months he would have grown tired of her, and been just the same. He is discontented by nature. I think he has loved her far more since he lost her than ever he did when she was there.'

'Oh, no, Mary,' Jemima said, quite shocked. 'You didn't see them together as I did. He adored her, and she would have fixed him for ever. She was so strong and energetic, and she would have guided him into proper habits of thought and behaviour; so that even if he did fall out of love with her later, the lessons would have been learned.'

Mary shrugged. 'Well, it makes no difference now, anyway. He is married to Mary Ann, and about to become a father, and we'll all have to make the best of it. At least he doesn't get drunk quite so often – not falling-down drunk, at all events.'

'Mary!'

'And he does help Ned, in a half-hearted sort of way. But you notice he still visits Scarborough.'

Jemima grew a little pale. 'You surely can't mean – '

'I mean that I think it would have taken a love-match to make him give up those trips, even temporarily.'

'But who – no, don't tell me, even if you can guess. I had much rather not know. I hope you are mistaken.'

'I hope so, too,' Mary said. She was growing bored with talk of Jamie. 'Lord, my back does ache! How you can stay

36

they not just leave him alone?

'I think I'll walk in the gardens first,' he told Durban. 'It may clear my head a little.'

'Very good, sir,' said Durban, but the non-committal words held a clear note of warning.

In the Italian garden, there was privacy. It had been laid out more than a century ago, and was too dark and formal for modern taste, with high, carefully clipped yew hedges, narrow gravelled paths, and gloomy alcoves containing marble benches and statues brought back from Italy by some long-dead Morland from his Grand Tour. Its coolness was sometimes sought on hot summer days, but the servants shunned it, especially after dusk. There was one place where the grass grew differently, and the story was that Lord Ballincrea fell there, run through by his step-brother in a duel: his blood soaking into the ground was said to make the grass come up discoloured, and his ghost was thought to haunt that spot.

James was not afraid of the Ballincrea ghost, and the effect of drinking brandy all day while eating nothing was to produce a mood of such gloom and depression that the atmosphere of the Italian garden could hardly deepen it. He sat down on a bench, sank his chin in his hands, and gave himself up to reflection.

His life seemed to him to have gone wrong from the very beginning. He had been isolated as a child between the two extremes of the family, with no companion but the chaplain-tutor, Father Ramsay, a man of strange humour and a saturnine turn of mind, who had influenced James intellectually, without being able to give him the warmth and affection the boy's nature craved. James had grown up thoughtful, reserved, inward-looking, too lonely to be happy, too sensitive to be able to ask for love where there was any chance of rejection.

His passion for Mary Loveday, some years his senior, and her subsequently arranged marriage to John Skelwith, had confirmed him in his view of the world. When she bore his child, she refused to leave her husband and run away with him, and his share of the shame and scandal had been unrelieved by any share in her love or that of their son.

43

Chapter Three

Mary Ann was woken abruptly by the crash and rattle of someone knocking down the poker into the hearth. A soft human sound of distress, followed by muted noises of reparation told her that it was a housemaid making up the fire, something that was usually done silently without her knowledge before she woke.

She opened her eyes. Above her and around her were the red sarsenet tester and curtains of the enormous Butts bed. They were old, and a little faded, and really ought to have been replaced for her marriage to James. Someone had failed in their duty there. She pondered for a moment on colours and materials. The heavy carving which covered the ancient oak of the frame demanded the splendid rather than the dainty; something brocaded with gold, perhaps?

She knew from the light coming through the curtains that it was still early, but she was wide awake. Yesterday her father had gone back to Manchester: once the business of wills and settlements had been concluded, he had begun to be anxious about his mills. She had clung to him, wanting foolishly to beg him to take her with him, back to Hobsbawn House where she belonged, where she had been mistress for so long, where everyone loved and admired her. Pride sustained her, and she swallowed her tears and waved him goodbye with a watery smile. She was married to James, and nothing but her death or his could change that: she had no choice but to stay here and make the best of it she could.

Morning brought new counsel. She looked at the faded curtains some other mistress of Morland Place had ordered, and thought, this is my home for the rest of my life. I must make something of my situation, carve contentment out of the materials to hand: that is the Christian way. It was a philosophy which owed as much to her father as to the nuns who had educated her, a restless energy which despised weakness and could not be content merely to endure. I will which warned her that there was more to come.

'Secondly,' he said, lifting his head a little, 'you must remember that you are no longer Miss Hobsbawn of Hobsbawn House. Your father is no longer your guardian – that authority has passed to me, and under the law I have complete control over you. You must know that it is in my power to compel you to obey me.'

Now she was too angry to speak. She glared at him, as he continued, 'I am not an unreasonable man, madam. I do not wish to ill-treat you. I have left you pretty much alone, to do as you please. Anything you want, within reason, you shall have. But you will obey my orders. You will not touch the phaeton.'

'Why not?' she demanded defiantly.

'Never mind,' he said, and taking her arm gently, turned her towards the house. She shook herself free, but walked with him. 'If you want a park carriage, I will have one made for you. You need only ask.'

'I should like,' she said in a low voice, 'to kill you.'

'I dare say,' he said wearily. 'But the feeling will pass. Everything passes, good and ill. Come, madam,' he added, seeing her white, set face, and feeling a little sorry for her, 'we are wed, and we must make the best of things. I have no wish to make you unhappy.'

They went into the house, and James swept her past the hovering, anxious Oxhey, and brought her to the foot of the stairs. 'You had better go to your room,' he said. 'I'll send Dakers to you.'

He sent up not only her woman, but a good supply of hot water and a bottle of arnica, and with Dakers' tight-lipped help, she undressed and bathed. The hot water soothed her and allowed her time to think. Fury and tears alike must be held back in front of her waiting woman, but behind her calm face, her thoughts seethed. He was right, of course. It was no accident that up here in the north, the people used the word 'master' instead of 'husband'. The law permitted him to do what he liked with her, short of actually killing her – beat her, starve her, lock her up, deprive her of every-thing, even of her children.

She belonged to him; and even if she ran home to her

father, it would avail her little. She could not be divorced from James, and however strongly her father sympathized with her, she would for ever afterwards be disgraced. Society would not receive her, and she would not be able to marry anyone else, but would remain a prisoner in her father's house for the rest of her life. And when her father died, what then?

No, she must stay here, and behave submissively to James. That galled her pride abominably, and part of her wanted to go home to Papa, just to shew him that he could not govern her. But that would not be sensible, nor consonant with duty. It would be much more sensible to let James think he had won, and by behaving meekly towards him, to enjoy what freedoms she had.

She remembered with an inward blush her recent folly in thinking that they might come to love each other. That was obviously impossible: he had married her, as he said, simply to get an heir for Morland Place, and now that he had one, he wanted nothing more from her than her quiescence. But she was sure now that there was some other underlying reason for his moodiness she had not found out; something in his past, which the family and servants must know about.

By the time she went downstairs in answer to the summons of the dinner bell, she was completely calm. The bruises on her wrist were covered by the long sleeves of her sage-green silk dinner gown, and no-one could have known by looking at her that anything untoward had happened. When she entered the drawing-room, the first thing she noticed was that the pianoforte had gone, and the harpsichord was back in its place, but she was so well under control that she merely raised an enquiring eyebrow towards Edward.

'James seemed to think it would be better upstairs in the long saloon,' Edward said apologetically. 'It will be the very thing when we have dances up there, and indeed, it was very large for this room. Too large, perhaps.'

'You are quite in the right,' Mary Ann said calmly, not glancing at James. She sat down in her usual chair and took her sewing from the little table beside her. 'It was too large. The harpsichord suits this room a great deal better.'

watched as a successful union was achieved between the two. His wife recalled his attention, saying, 'Chetwyn, why have we no house in Town?'

'Well, we have, of course. Aylesbury House, in Piccadilly. You must have passed it a hundred times. Why did you think we hadn't?'

'Because ever since I've known you, you've always stayed with Flora and Charles when you've been in Town. Why did we never stay in Aylesbury House?'

'It's let out on lease, to the Staplers' Club. It's a horrid great barn of a place, quite suitable for a gentlemen's club, but there was no living in it. Grandfather let it after Grandmother died, and Papa used to rent a house for the Season, if Mama wanted to go up to Town. When he went up on business, he always stayed in an hotel. Why do you ask, anyway?'

'I've been thinking that after the baby is born, I should like to spend some time in Town. I shall have had enough of rustication for a while, but with poor Flora gone, it would be rather awkward to be staying at Chelmsford House.'

'Especially if Charles don't invite us,' Chetwyn agreed cheerfully.

'And we haven't heard a word from him since Christmas. Do you think he's all right?'

'I imagine so. I expect he's just getting things sorted out. Well, Luce, there's no problem here. We can perfectly well rent a house for the Season, if that's what you want; and if you should happen to see a place that strikes your fancy, we might take it on a long lease.'

'Really? Oh Chetwyn, you are a trump card!'

Chetwyn grinned. 'We'll have to find a house near to the Park, so that you can drive out every day in your curricle-and-four and shock the dowagers. We ought to have a place of our own: it's time we gave our own dinners and balls.'

'Think of me, a hostess!' Lucy marvelled.

'Oh, you'll be first-rate. And I'll give you any odds, that our parties are the most talked-about of the Season.'

At the end of February Mrs Haworth came down from

65

Morland Place to Wolvercote to be with Lucy during her lying-in. She found her sister larger than ever, but still cheerful and practical, despite her discomfort.

'I shouldn't be surprised, from the size of me, if it weren't twins,' she said. 'Wouldn't that be a splendid thing, Polly? Two for the price of one – or rather, for the pains of one.'

'As long as they were boys.'

'Yes, that's the worst of it. I don't mind for myself, but Chetwyn must have his heir. But tell me all the news of home. How do you all go on?'

'As well as can be expected, in the circumstances,' Mary sighed.

'Oh dear, that does sound gloomy. What's the matter?'

'Mrs James, as usual. It makes such a bad atmosphere in the house, her and James not being upon terms. One can never feel comfortable.'

'Poor thing! It must be hard to be forced to leave home and marry a stranger, just to give him an heir.'

'Like you, in fact,' Mary said.

'Not at all like me,' Lucy said, surprised. 'I wasn't forced – and Chetwyn wasn't a stranger. He and I are the best of friends, always have been. Do you think I would have married him if it weren't so?'

'But you weren't in love with him,' Mary said.

'Oh, love!' Lucy made a face. 'I know nothing of this *love* of yours! You females are always talking about it, but I think you invent it, to make yourselves mysterious.'

'You're a female yourself,' Mary pointed out, and Lucy frowned, and then placed a hand over her belly and smiled ruefully.

'Just now, I am forced to agree with you. Well, what has Mrs James done now, to make you so cross, Poll? I'm sure she's a very good creature: why can't you get on with her?'

'Her upbringing has been so different from ours; and she has been mistress of her own house so long, she can't seem to understand that she is not mistress any more. You heard about the affair of the pianoforte? Her father's breach of delicacy was beyond anything, in sending such a gift, accompanied by a letter saying that as we would not provide her with the things she needed, he must do it for us –'

eggs and toast, only enough for a woman – and that he was like to ruin his nerves and digestion by washing it down with coffee.

They were still sitting amongst the bones and eggshells when Oxhey came in to say that Pobgee, the lawyer, had arrived, and was waiting in the steward's room.

'Well sir,' said Edward, getting to his feet, 'shall we begin? Mother? Mr Yardley?' There was a general rising from the table, but it was only when they were out in the hallway that Hobsbawn realised James was heading in the other direction, and asked him in surprise, 'Why, sir, do you not come with us?'

James smiled and said lightly, 'The steward's room will not hold more than five comfortably.' Then, seeing his mother frown in disapproval, and Hobsbawn about to make further enquiries, he added firmly, 'My mother and brother attend to the business, sir. I know I may trust them to take care of my little Fanny's interests.' This went down well, but he spoiled the effect by adding cynically, 'I can have nothing to contribute to the discussion. I own nothing but my horse and my clothes.' With that he bowed deeply and made his escape to the stables.

He spent the day at the Maccabbees Club in Stonegate, sitting over the fire with a bottle of brandy. When he arrived back at Morland Place, he found his servant, Durban, waiting for him in the yard. Durban came up quickly to take Nez Carré's head, and shot his master a look of mingled enquiry and warning.

'Where is everyone?' James asked. 'Have I been missed? Are search parties abroad for me?'

'I believe your absence was noted, sir,' Durban said. 'The dressing bell has gone, and everyone is upstairs. The coast is clear for the moment, sir.'

James dismounted, and patted Durban's arm in acknowledgement of the sympathy. The house was before him, waiting, but today his childhood home looked forbidding in the fading light. It contained his unloved wife and her sharp-eyed father, his anxious mother and cynically amused sister. It threatened him. Everyone wanted something from him, he thought, clenching his fists in frustration. Why would

42

they not just leave him alone?

'I think I'll walk in the gardens first,' he told Durban. 'It may clear my head a little.'

'Very good, sir,' said Durban, but the non-committal words held a clear note of warning.

In the Italian garden, there was privacy. It had been laid out more than a century ago, and was too dark and formal for modern taste, with high, carefully clipped yew hedges, narrow gravelled paths, and gloomy alcoves containing marble benches and statues brought back from Italy by some long-dead Morland from his Grand Tour. Its coolness was sometimes sought on hot summer days, but the servants shunned it, especially after dusk. There was one place where the grass grew differently, and the story was that Lord Ballincrea fell there, run through by his step-brother in a duel: his blood soaking into the ground was said to make the grass come up discoloured, and his ghost was thought to haunt that spot.

James was not afraid of the Ballincrea ghost, and the effect of drinking brandy all day while eating nothing was to produce a mood of such gloom and depression that the atmosphere of the Italian garden could hardly deepen it. He sat down on a bench, sank his chin in his hands, and gave himself up to reflection.

His life seemed to him to have gone wrong from the very beginning. He had been isolated as a child between the two extremes of the family, with no companion but the chaplain-tutor, Father Ramsay, a man of strange humour and a saturnine turn of mind, who had influenced James intellectually, without being able to give him the warmth and affection the boy's nature craved. James had grown up thoughtful, reserved, inward-looking, too lonely to be happy, too sensitive to be able to ask for love where there was any chance of rejection.

His passion for Mary Loveday, some years his senior, and her subsequently arranged marriage to John Skelwith, had confirmed him in his view of the world. When she bore his child, she refused to leave her husband and run away with him, and his share of the shame and scandal had been unrelieved by any share in her love or that of their son.

43

And then he had met Héloïse. He lifted his head and stared sightlessly round the dark garden. Here – she had been here, in this very place. These hedges had heard her laughter; he had walked with her along these paths, holding her hand. His memory retained the exact impression of her hand, its size and shape, the warm grip of her child-small fingers, though he found it hard now to bring her face to mind.

She had come here as if to a home which had long awaited her, come to be queen of a kingdom which was glad to be hers. She had loved everything, from the least kitchen boy riddling the grate to the swans on the moat. From the moment of her arrival, the servants had seemed to accept her, without its ever being discussed, as Jemima's natural successor; and she had opened her guileless heart to him and chosen him king.

The loss of her was like endless darkness. With no further chance of happiness, he had turned to duty. Morland Place needed an heir, and neither of his elder brothers seemed likely to provide one, so in a fit of noble self-sacrifice he had proposed the match between himself and Mary Ann Hobsbawn. The difficulty was that the momentary spasm of self-sacrifice involved a lifetime of living with the reality, and commonplace, day-to-day disappointments were harder to bear than great tragedy and noble grief. He found it hard to think about Mary Ann as a person, or even as his wife: she simply loomed in the background, an inescapable fact; his gaoler.

He sighed deeply, and then started violently, as he came back to reality to find the inescapable fact standing not ten yards away, watching him. She was a tall woman, well-formed, handsome, with a statuesque calm of bearing which made her easy, for him, to dismiss. She had evidently changed for the evening, for she was wearing a gown of twilled lilac silk, with a heavy, expensive Persian shawl over her shoulders. James did not recognize it – probably a new gift from her father, he thought. Her hair was up, and bound by a fillet of purple velvet ribbon. It was fine, light-brown hair, thin and silky like a child's, difficult to manage, and already it was slipping the battery of pins Dakers had used to confine it, and escaping in wisps about her brows. She ought to have it cropped, he thought: it would suit her, with her long, graceful neck; but he did not speak the thought aloud.

'Had you not better change?' she said at last. 'It is almost dinner-time.' Her voice was light and cool and careful, with no hint of her father's accent, or of any emotion of her own.

'What are you doing here?' James asked. It sounded accusing: he might as well have asked why she was spying on him.

'I wished for some air,' she said unemphatically. 'I was just going in.' She did not move, however, and at length James felt obliged to rise and walk with her back towards the house.

'You should not walk out at dusk,' he said after a moment, since some speech seemed necessary. 'You will catch cold.'

'My shawl is very thick,' she replied.

'Have they all done, in there? Is it all signed and sealed and witnessed?' he said next. She assented with a silent nod. 'And so now Fanny is an important heiress.'

'She will inherit your mother's and my father's estates, to be held in trust until her majority, provisionally, of course – '

'Provisionally?' James leapt upon the word so sharply that Mary Ann almost flinched. 'What do you mean, provisionally? Fanny is to have everything. That was the bargain.'

'Indeed, she will – unless the next child is a boy. Naturally a boy would take precedence. If we have a son, he will inherit the estates, and Fanny will have a very handsome dowry, enough to see that she marries as – '

'No!' said James furiously, and he turned to face her and backed off a step, like an animal at bay. 'That was not the bargain! I do not consent!' They were trying to cheat him: he had done his part, and now they were trying to cheat him of the reward.

Mary Ann regarded her extraordinary husband with puzzlement. 'Your consent was not required,' she said. 'Your mother and my father may dispose of their wealth as they please, and you surely – '

'They were to leave everything to our child!'

45

' – and you surely must realize that my father, at least, needs a male heir for his spinning mills. A daughter could not follow him *there*, whatever your mother – '

'I'll have *you* realize one thing, madam,' James said fiercely. 'I married you for the sake of producing an heir for Morland Place, and that is what I have done. Fanny *shall* have everything. Do you think I will stand by and see her cheated? Do you think I would have anything to do with breeding a boy to steal what is rightfully hers? As to your father, he may keep his promises, or go back on them; he may leave everything to Fanny, or give it all to the next beggar he meets on the street. But there will be no more children of this marriage, of that you may assure yourself.'

The ordinary sounds of the garden at dusk fed themselves back into the space where his voice had been: a movement of leaves, a last sparrow chipping away at the grey half-light, the dabbling of some water-bird on the moat, and farther off the sounds of the house and yard, a dog rattling its chain, a cockerel, the clank of a bucket, a man's voice calling.

For a long time they stood still, looking at each other. She seemed farther from him than a star, yet he was aware of every breath she took, almost of every heartbeat, as though he were feeling with her nerve-endings. He had said something that could not be unsaid, and now for the first time he wondered what she was feeling, what she had ever felt, about being married to him. It would have been appropriate if she had stretched out her hand and blasted him with retributive lightning, like an enraged Juno, and in that long moment he felt her powerful enough to do it. He waited for oblivion, aware that he would have welcomed it, done nothing to evade it.

Then she turned and left him without a word, walking lightly and gracefully, her thin slippers hardly disturbing the gravel of the path. James, unpunished, watched her go. Always in his life, less happened than he expected, or hoped for: that was his tragedy. When she was out of sight, he turned the other way, and went in through the barbican. The night beacon had been lit in the window above the archway, and its yellow light made the dusk seem suddenly greyer.

46

Chapter Three

Mary Ann was woken abruptly by the crash and rattle of someone knocking down the poker into the hearth. A soft human sound of distress, followed by muted noises of reparation told her that it was a housemaid making up the fire, something that was usually done silently without her knowledge before she woke.

She opened her eyes. Above her and around her were the red sarsenet tester and curtains of the enormous Butts bed. They were old, and a little faded, and really ought to have been replaced for her marriage to James. Someone had failed in their duty there. She pondered for a moment on colours and materials. The heavy carving which covered the ancient oak of the frame demanded the splendid rather than the dainty; something brocaded with gold, perhaps?

She knew from the light coming through the curtains that it was still early, but she was wide awake. Yesterday her father had gone back to Manchester: once the business of wills and settlements had been concluded, he had begun to be anxious about his mills. She had clung to him, wanting foolishly to beg him to take her with him, back to Hobsbawn House where she belonged, where she had been mistress for so long, where everyone loved and admired her. Pride sustained her, and she swallowed her tears and waved him goodbye with a watery smile. She was married to James, and nothing but her death or his could change that: she had no choice but to stay here and make the best of it she could.

Morning brought new counsel. She looked at the faded curtains some other mistress of Morland Place had ordered, and thought, this is my home for the rest of my life. I must make something of my situation, carve contentment out of the materials to hand: that is the Christian way. It was a philosophy which owed as much to her father as to the nuns who had educated her, a restless energy which despised weakness and could not be content merely to endure. I will

47

make myself useful to Lady Morland, and take some of the burdens from her shoulders; I will learn to be mistress of this great estate, and then teach my daughter all I have learnt. With these resolutions, she pushed back the bedclothes and slipped out of bed between the curtains.

A shriek and a more prolonged clattering greeted her, and she gained her feet to find herself facing a diminutive housemaid whose clothing had evidently been designed for someone better-nourished, and who had just dropped the box in which she carried around her rags and brushes. Her eyes were wide, and her hands were clasped where her bosom would be in a few years' time.

'Oh, you startled me!' the child exclaimed, and then, remembering herself, curtseyed and said, 'I beg your pardon, m'lady. I'm very sorry, m'lady.'

'Not my lady,' Mary Ann said automatically. 'You address me as ma'am.'

The child reddened and curtseyed again. 'Beg pardon, ma'am,' she mumbled, but seemed too paralysed with embarrassment to move. Mary Ann looked her over with the interest a mistress always accords to new servants, to find what they are good for.

'I haven't seen you before, have I? What's your name?'

'Betsey, ma'am.'

'Are you happy here, Betsey?'

'Oh, *yes*, ma'am!' she cried fervently; then, 'Only there's such a lot to remember all at once, and all them different stairs an' corridors. I'm sorry I woke you, ma'am.'

She looked subdued now, and Mary Ann reflected that most mistresses would complain to Mrs Mappin about being woken by a clumsy housemaid. She felt an unexpected sympathy with this skinny child, and to her own surprise heard herself saying, 'It doesn't matter. I was awake anyway.' Betsey curtseyed again and knelt down to pick up her spilled brushes, and Mary Ann, watching her curiously, said, 'Where do you come from, Betsey? You are new, aren't you?'

She looked up with a glowing face. 'Yes, ma'am, I came up on Monday from St Edward's.'

'St Edward's? Oh, you mean the orphan asylum.'

'Yes, ma'am. Me an' my brother Timmy, we're orphans, ma'am. We've lived there all our lives, until Mrs Mappin brought me up to the house to train for a housemaid, on account of the master's plan, and your father's, ma'am, begging your pardon. Such kind gentlemen, ma'am, as ever could be, and I'm that grateful, you can't imagine.'

'My father? What plan?'

'The plan they have, ma'am, the master and your father, to send the boys from St Edward's to Manchester, to be 'prenticed to your father's mill. The master came hisself to explain it all, so they shouldn't be afraid, and he told how they should be made 'prentices and learn a trade so that they could keep themselves respectable-like all their lives, and never come to be beggars. My Timmy was to be one of them, and we didn't like above half to be parted, ma'am, until master said I was to come up to the house. And Mrs Mappin told as how her ladyship once went to visit a spinning-mill, and how it were a lovely green place, and how the 'prentices lived in a lovely house, all white and clean, and so I were pretty well pleased, ma'am, to think of Timmy so well provided for. And one day Timmy might come back, when he's learned to be a weaver, and we might set up house together, for weavers earn a deal o' money, ma'am, and then I might keep house for him, just as I've learned here.'

The rapid and breathless stream ceased, and the child beamed up at Mary Ann in artless delight and gratitude, so that she could not find it in herself to rebuke the freedom her question had provoked. She was pleased with what she had heard about her father and Edward. This was behaving as a Christian should, placing the poor and dependent in the way of keeping themselves respectably. She had never seen her father's mills, and knew nothing of his business, except what she had gleaned in conversation; but she did know that weaving was done by hand, not by machine, and that weavers were therefore the elite of the cloth-trade and might well, as Betsey said, earn a 'deal o' money'.

'I hope it may happen as you wish,' she said graciously. 'You must shew your gratitude by being a good girl. Work hard and say your prayers, and then your bother may be proud of you, as you are of him.'

'Oh yes, ma'am, thank you, ma'am,' Betsey beamed, bobbing like a cork on water as she backed out of the room. Mary Ann looked at the clock on the chimney-piece, and saw that it was still before her usual time of rising. She might ring for Dakers, of course; but in the end she decided to dress herself for once, and to go and visit her baby. The nursery, surely, would be astir early, babies requiring to be fed regardless of the hour.

She put on her clothes, and being unable to dress her hair herself, merely brushed it and concealed it under a cap, and went out. At the end of the corridor a housemaid came out of the red room and stopped, startled, at the sight of her; but being older than Betsey, she did not drop anything, only curtseyed and gave her a puzzled look. Mary Ann turned the corner by the backstairs and walked along the corridor to the nursery. She passed several bedroom doors: this was the bachelor's wing, and behind one of these doors her husband was sleeping, but she did not know which. She reached the end of the wing and opened the door to the night nursery, and paused on the threshhold.

Her husband was there before her. His back was to her; he had drawn up a stool beside Fanny's crib, and was leaning over, talking to the baby in a soft voice. Mary Ann could not hear what he was saying, but she could see that Fanny was awake, and that her eyes were fixed on her father's face, while one hand was clenched firmly round his right forefinger. Mary Ann took a silent step forward, and James's next words became audible to her.

'Then when you're older, I'll teach you to ride, and you shall have a pony of your own, and we'll go riding together, over the moors, everywhere. I'll shew you everything, your whole kingdom.'

Fanny smiled as though she understood, and James made a sound that could have been a chuckle. Mary Ann withdrew from the room and closed the door after her. In the corridor she considered what she had witnessed, and it pleased her. Men, she knew, did not usually notice their children until they reached a rational age, and that James should care enough for Fanny to rise early and sit in the

50

nursery talking to her, seemed another point in his favour. He *had* good qualities, and a heart capable of affection, and if she took more pains to get to know him, she thought that they might still learn to be contented together.

That same day an express from London disturbed the newly restored routine of the house, bringing the news that Flora, who had been a little ailing all year, had taken a sudden turn for the worse, and was not expected to recover. Within hours Jemima, Mary and James had left for Chelmsford House in the hope of being in time to say goodbye. Edward wished to go, but could not leave the estate at such a time; but though he remained at Morland Place, he was hardly company for Mary Ann, being absent all day in body, and even more absent in mind on the occasions that she saw him.

A few days later, the pianoforte arrived. It came on an enormous carrier's cart, well packed and muffled with cloths and sacks, and put Oxhey into a great taking, for he had not been told to expect it, and felt at a disadvantage before the carrier's men.

A letter came with it, addressed to Mary Ann.

'My darling girl, I beg you to accept this gift from your old Papa, and hope that it will give you many hours of pleasure. I thought of it when I heard you playing on the harpsichord at Morland Place. Such superior performance as yours deserves a better instrument! You were used to have a pianoforte at home, and it was never my intention that you should be less comfortable as a married woman than you were as a maid. So play upon it to your heart's content, my love, and think sometimes of one who thinks of you constantly, and loves you best in the world.'

Oxhey was hovering, looking unhappy, and Mary Ann folded the letter with a smile and said, 'It is from my father, a present for me.'

'Yes, Madam. I understand,' he replied, looking gloomy. 'What would you have me do with it?'

'Why, have it brought in, of course,' she said in surprise.

'Yes, of course, Madam, but where would you have it put?'

51

'In the drawing-room, Oxhey,' Mary Ann said patiently. 'Where else does one keep a pianoforte? It can stand in the corner, in the place of the old harpsichord. It will look very well there,' she added in satisfaction. 'Now what is the matter?'

'But madam!' Oxhey actually waved his hands in his anxiety to convey to her the problems inherent in the command; but Mary Ann thought that he was concerned only with the physical problems of the removal, and grew impatient.

'Really, Oxhey, it is perfectly simple! The carrier's men will know how best the thing is to be moved, and if you have two of our men help them, I am sure it can be done with no trouble at all.'

'And the harpsichord, Madam?'

'You will move that first, of course. I dare say the legs will remove, and it can be wrapped in the cloths that came with the pianoforte, and stored somewhere until we decide what to do with it.'

'It belongs to Miss Mary – Mrs Haworth, I mean – madam, and she is accustomed to play upon it,' Oxhey said, making one last effort, and Mary Ann frowned.

'Mrs Haworth is a married woman, and this is no longer her home. That she lives at Morland Place while her husband is at sea is beside the point. While Lady Morland is away, I am mistress of the house, and you will obey my orders. Now let us hear no more argument, Oxhey.'

By dinner time the pianoforte was installed in the corner of the drawing-room, where it glowed handsomely, rose-wood casing, satinwood inlay, gilded candle-holders, all complete; while the harpsichord, carefully wrapped, had been put into one of the storerooms. The tuner had been sent for from York, and Mary Ann was sorting through the piles of music to choose such as were suited to the more modern instrument.

If Oxhey had hoped for Edward's intervention on his behalf, he was disappointed. The master was so busy about the estate at this time, especially with Jemima away, that it was two days before he even entered the drawing-room; and when Mary Ann brought the new instrument to his notice, he only said vaguely, 'Oh yes, ma'am, very handsome. I congratulate you,' before excusing himself to return to his reports in the steward's room.

The pianoforte did add to her comfort and pleasure, but an unusually fine burst of weather made her discontented with her solitary indoor pursuits, and one day she put down her sewing and wandered, on impulse, out into the court-yard. It was a time of day when everyone was about their business elsewhere, and the yard was deserted, except for the dog chained in its kennel, three brindled cats sleeping in a strip of sunshine along the wall, and a large number of pigeons roosting on the roof-slopes. The doors to the stable building stood open, and the shadows within looked very black by contrast with the sunshine.

She felt confined and for once longed to go outside the walls and view the grounds. There were, of course, plenty of horses at Morland Place, but she had never cared to ride, and though her father had given her a very pretty vis-à-vis for her wedding, it was not the sort of carriage in which to go driving about the rough estate tracks. The silence of the yard was growing unnerving to one accustomed to the noise of a town and to being surrounded by servants, and she began to feel absurdly as though something disagreeable might pop out of one of those dark doorways; or at the very least, that someone might come and rebuke her for being here.

A thud and a shriek close behind her made her jump almost out of her skin, and she had cried out in alarm before she realized that it was only one of the peacocks flying down and landing clumsily. She felt foolish; but her cry had had the effect of bringing a young groom out of the nearest stable door, a brush in his hand and his eyebrows almost in his hair, and though it would be hard to tell which of them was blushing the more violently, it was necessary for her to command the situation.

'Is Mr Humby about?' she asked. She did not know any of the grooms, but she had heard Humby's name mentioned in connection with the horses.

'Oh, no, ma'am, he doesn't come up to th'ouse. He's at Twelvetrees,' said the boy in surprise.

53

'Then who is in charge of the stables here?'

'Mr Hoskins, ma'am, but he's out at the moment. He's over at Twelvetrees as well. There's only me here.'

Mary Ann considered him. He looked reasonably intelligent. 'Then you will have to do. What is your name?'

'Birkin, ma'am.'

'Very well, Birkin. I want a small open carriage, in which to take a drive about the estate. Is there such a thing in the coach house?'

The boy thought deeply. 'Master's took his curricle – not that that would be suitable for a lady, ma'am. There's the gig, and the cocking-cart – but they're not very smart. Wait, though – there is something, ma'am, all shrouded up right at the back. It's never used, but from its size and shape, it might be some sort of light phaeton. Shall I have a look, ma'am?'

In a moment he was in the back of the coach-house, dragging the covers off the vehicle, while Mary Ann stood at the door watching, mindful of her dress. 'I was right, ma'am, it is a phaeton,' he cried, growing less shy as he grew more excited. 'Look – it's a beauty, too, and quite new, I should say – not a scratch on it. I wonder why it's all shrouded up? It seems a shame not to use it.'

'It is suitable?' Mary Ann asked, not able to see much of it from her vantage point.

'I'd say it were made for the job, ma'am,' Birkin said enthusiastically. 'It's right pretty, small, and light as a spider-web. It's a lady's park-phaeton all right. I wonder –'

Mary Ann was not interested in his wonderings. 'Is there a horse to draw it? A quiet horse, that I could manage?'

'There's old Strawberry – he's quiet as a ewe-lamb.' He examined the phaeton more closely. 'This is rigged for a pair – ponies, I should say – but I can soon change that. If I take the shafts off the gig –'

'Very well, Birkin, do so, if you please. Can you drive?'

'Yes, ma'am.'

'Then you shall teach me. Can you have the phaeton ready and the horse put to in half an hour?'

'Well, yes, ma'am – but –'

'Very well. Have it waiting at the door for me.'

54

When Mary Ann came down into the hall again, dressed in her habit, and pulling on a pair of York tan gloves, she saw the phaeton waiting for her at the foot of the steps, and looking very smart. Birkin was holding the head of the horse between the shafts, and Mary Ann was pleased to see that the animal looked very quiet, and, being a pink roan, nicely matched the coral-coloured upholstery of the phaeton.

She was not pleased when Oxhey came hurrying forward, looking anxious, and tried to prevent her from taking the drive she was so much looking forward to, especially as she could make nothing of his incoherent reasons.

'Really, Oxhey, I cannot understand you. I gave Birkin instructions to make the phaeton ready for me, as I wish to drive in the park. What can you have to object to in that?'

'Oh, Madam, I only meant – that phaeton you see, Madam, is Mr James's own –'

'Well, and I am Mr James's wife. What of that?'

'I am persuaded he would not like it used, Madam. He gave instructions it was not to be used.'

'Why? Is it unsafe?' Oxhey didn't answer. 'What reason did he give?' Oxhey only looked miserable, unable to tell her the reason, and not quick-witted enough to invent anything, and after a moment Mary Ann shrugged. 'I will not be delayed by any more of this foolishness,' she said, and swept past him down the steps.

Mary Ann enjoyed her drive, and she liked Birkin, who, revelling in his meteoric promotion, was firmly established as her champion, praised her progress, and enlivened the drive for her by telling her the names of every tree and flower they passed. His manner was respectful, but his intelligence was too lively to allow him to remain silent until spoken to, and Mary Ann had been lonely for so long that she found his company refreshing.

She liked Strawberry, too, for his steadiness, though Birkin said with affectionate contempt that he had only two paces, slow and slower. She was not a natural horsewoman, and was slow to learn the handling of the reins; but the phaeton was a perfect thing of its kind, and Strawberry knew his business well enough to pick his own path. She returned from her drive exhilarated and determined to go out again every day while the weather held.

When they drove back into the yard, she saw a sweating horse tied up to the ring by the door, which Birkin told her knowledgeably was a post-horse, and she was not surprised, therefore, on entering the great hall, to find an express there. His business she could guess. She hurried to the drawing-room, but it was empty; then she tried the steward's room, and there found Oxhey standing before his master, and Edward, the letter in his hand, and his face very grave.

'Is it news from London?' she asked.

Edward nodded, tried to speak, and had to clear his throat before any sound would come. 'Flora is dead,' he said. 'She died very quietly in her sleep. Charles was with her, and my mother.' He swallowed again. 'They will remain there until after the funeral. Charles is – bewildered with grief, my sister says.'

'I am so very sorry,' Mary Ann said. She could see how upset he was. 'Shall I send Father Thomas to you? A special mass should be said –'

'Thank you,' Edward said, and Mary Ann inclined her head, and left him alone.

James came home after the funeral, leaving Jemima and Mary to keep Charles company a while longer. He came on the night mail, setting down at the Hare and Heather a little the worse for wear, and was easily persuaded to take a leisurely breakfast in the inn parlour while Durban walked up to the house to fetch the horses. A good fire and the fragrance of fresh coffee raised his spirits, and the smell of bacon frying in oatmeal was so tempting that he made a much heartier breakfast than was his habit.

The potboy stuck his head round the door while James was addressing a second toasted bun, to say that Durban was back. James was so comfortable that he found himself in no hurry to go home, and he poured himself another cup of coffee, buttered another bun, put his feet up on the fender, and slipped into a half-dream. A pleasant digestive sadness came over him. Life could have been so different, he thought, and the barrier between what was and what might have been was so thin and transparent that it was hard to believe that events were irreversible. One small, apparently unimportant event could change everything; the essence of human tragedy was its inconsequence.

Pondering the mysteries of life was, of course, a good way to delay going home to a house which held the wrong wife; but then he recollected that it also held a dear, good brother, probably eager for news, and a darling daughter who was at the age when every day brought its changes, so he dragged himself out of his chair and went out into the yard, yelling for Durban.

They had just come in sight of the house, and the horses were beginning to pull and jog, when a one-horse phaeton came out from under the barbican and turned onto the track, heading away from them.

'Visitors?' James said aloud. 'It's a little early. I suppose –' The nagging sense of familiarity resolved itself as he spoke. He broke off, his face whitening, his lips compressing themselves grimly. Durban opened his mouth to speak, but James had kicked Nez Carré sharply enough to make that well-bred animal snort with indignation and leap straight from a walk into a canter, and by the time Durban had controlled his own excited mount, his master was well ahead of him.

Mary Ann heard the bellowing and the sound of hooves, looked over her shoulder, and after a moment's apprehension that she was about to be attacked by highwaymen, recognized her husband and pulled up.

'Ma'am –' began Birkin in sudden fear, his sharper eyes noticing the expression on James's face, but there was no time for more. James, carried past by the speed of his approach, wrenched Nez Carré round on his hocks, and swirled round them, his horse trampling and snorting and spattering the unfortunate Strawberry with foam from his tossing head.

'Get down!' James bellowed, beside himself with fury, trying to drive Nez Carré near enough to grab the reins of the phaeton. 'Get down this instant! How dare you take out

57

my phaeton? Get down, I say!'

Birkin, supposing the command for him, turned as pale as his master, scrambled over the side of the phaeton and ran to Strawberry's head.

'What ever is the matter, Mr Morland?' Mary Ann said composedly. 'Why are you so excited?'

'How dare you take out this carriage?' James shouted furiously. 'I gave orders it was not to be used. No-one is to touch it, no-one, do you hear? You will get down from there at once. How dare you disobey me? By God, if this were my regiment, I would see you flogged for this!'

Mary Ann could only assume that the last sentence was meant for Birkin, though from his expression he might have meant either of them, or both. She faced him firmly and said, 'Birkin was obeying my orders, sir. And indeed, why should I not use this carriage? It was there in the coach house, unused, and it perfectly suits my requirements. You cannot suppose I am harming it by driving in it a little, about the estate?'

'No-one is allowed to use it,' James said. He was no longer shouting, but his voice was no less angry. 'Everyone understood that order. Why were you not informed?'

'To be sure,' Mary Ann said, blithely throwing away her exculpation, 'Oxhey did try to dissuade me, but I thought he was talking nonsense. He would give me no reason except that the phaeton belonged to you, and I said to him, that as I am your wife, there could be no objection.'

James jumped down from his horse and flung the reins to Durban, who had caught up with them, took one step to the phaeton and dragged Mary Ann by the arm out of the driving seat. She staggered as she landed, and he shook her upright, his fingers like shackles round her wrist.

'My wife, yes, you are my wife!' He shook her back and forth, and she resisted him, trying to pry his hand loose, but though she was tall and strong, he was wiry, and made stronger by his anger. 'By God, there is no chance I will forget that! Well, as *my wife* you will learn to obey my orders and to keep your place! You *will not* touch anything of mine without my permission, do you understand?'

Mary Ann, angry herself now, though frightened, began

58

to protest, but James only shouted again, 'Do you understand?' and pushing her back from him violently, at the
same time released her arm, so that she staggered, and fell,
or rather sat down, on the bare earth of the track.

The stillness and silence that followed was one of shock.
It was James who recovered first, though he was still so pale
that even his lips were white, and his eyes looked dark, like
bruises, in comparison. He could hardly believe what he had
done, but the sight of Mary Ann sitting on the ground, her
hat fallen off, her hair coming down, her eyes fixed on him
more in astonishment than fear, horrified and sobered him.
He spoke tersely to the two grooms.

'Durban, take the horses in. You, Birkin, take that
phaeton and put it back exactly as you found it. I'll speak to
you both later. Now go!'

They left him reluctantly. James went to Mary Ann and
helped her to her feet, and she was too surprised to resist
him, but once upright she recovered enough to thrust him
from her angrily. She straightened her clothes and dusted
herself down; James fetched her hat and gave it to her, and
they faced each other, she with growing indignation, he with
a sort of doomed calm.

'You are not hurt, beyond a bruise or two?' he said at
last.

'Not hurt? I am shaken to pieces! How dare you use me
so? And to speak to me so, in front of the servants!'

'Oh, yes, the servants,' James said wryly, looking away
from her.

'I have never been so used in all my life! If my father
were here, he would – he would *strike* you! Who is it you
think you have married? Do you think you can –'

'Be quiet,' James said, so intensely that Mary Ann
stopped, realizing that she was now alone with him, and
unsure how far he would go. 'Listen to me – two things.
Firstly, I am truly sorry that I hurt you. It was wrong of me,
but I was too angry to know what I was doing. It is not my
way to use violence. I am shocked and ashamed, and I beg
you to forgive me.'

She was silent, watching him cautiously. She thought his
apology was sincere, but there was no humility in his voice,

which warned her that there was more to come.

'Secondly,' he said, lifting his head a little, 'you must remember that you are no longer Miss Hobsbawn of Hobsbawn House. Your father is no longer your guardian – that authority has passed to me, and under the law I have complete control over you. You must know that it is in my power to compel you to obey me.'

Now she was too angry to speak. She glared at him, as he continued, 'I am not an unreasonable man, madam. I do not wish to ill-treat you. I have left you pretty much alone, to do as you please. Anything you want, within reason, you shall have. But you will obey my orders. You will not touch the phaeton.'

'Why not?' she demanded defiantly.

'Never mind,' he said, and taking her arm gently, turned her towards the house. She shook herself free, but walked with him. 'If you want a park carriage, I will have one made for you. You need only ask.'

'I should like,' she said in a low voice, 'to kill you.'

'I dare say,' he said wearily. 'But the feeling will pass. Everything passes, good and ill. Come, madam,' he added, seeing her white, set face, and feeling a little sorry for her, 'we are wed, and we must make the best of things. I have no wish to make you unhappy.'

They went into the house, and James swept her past the hovering, anxious Oxhey, and brought her to the foot of the stairs. 'You had better go to your room,' he said. 'I'll send Dakers to you.'

He sent up not only her woman, but a good supply of hot water and a bottle of arnica, and with Dakers' tight-lipped help, she undressed and bathed. The hot water soothed her and allowed her time to think. Fury and tears alike must be held back in front of her waiting woman, but behind her calm face, her thoughts seethed. He was right, of course. It was no accident that up here in the north, the people used the word 'master' instead of 'husband'. The law permitted him to do what he liked with her, short of actually killing her – beat her, starve her, lock her up, deprive her of everything, even of her children.

She belonged to him; and even if she ran home to her

father, it would avail her little. She could not be divorced from James, and however strongly her father sympathized with her, she would for ever afterwards be disgraced. Society would not receive her, and she would not be able to marry anyone else, but would remain a prisoner in her father's house for the rest of her life. And when her father died, what then?

No, she must stay here, and behave submissively to James. That galled her pride abominably, and part of her wanted to go home to Papa, just to shew him that he could not govern her. But that would not be sensible, nor consonant with duty. It would be much more sensible to let James think he had won, and by behaving meekly towards him, to enjoy what freedoms she had.

She remembered with an inward blush her recent folly in thinking that they might come to love each other. That was obviously impossible: he had married her, as he said, simply to get an heir for Morland Place, and now that he had one, he wanted nothing more from her than her quiescence. But she was sure now that there was some other underlying reason for his moodiness she had not found out; something in his past, which the family and servants must know about.

By the time she went downstairs in answer to the summons of the dinner bell, she was completely calm. The bruises on her wrist were covered by the long sleeves of her sage-green silk dinner gown, and no-one could have known by looking at her that anything untoward had happened. When she entered the drawing-room, the first thing she noticed was that the pianoforte had gone, and the harpsichord was back in its place, but she was so well under control that she merely raised an enquiring eyebrow towards Edward.

'James seemed to think it would be better upstairs in the long saloon,' Edward said apologetically. 'It will be the very thing when we have dances up there, and indeed, it was very large for this room. Too large, perhaps.'

'You are quite in the right,' Mary Ann said calmly, not glancing at James. She sat down in her usual chair and took her sewing from the little table beside her. 'It was too large. The harpsichord suits this room a great deal better.'

'I'm glad you think so,' Ned said gratefully, 'because, now I come to think of it, Mary would have been very upset to come home from London and find it gone. And you can always go up to the saloon when you want to play.'

'Yes,' she said serenely, taking the first tiny stitch of a long, long hem, 'I can always do that.'

Chapter Four

By February 1796 Lucy had grown so large that moving around was difficult, and she began to stay in bed until late in the morning. It was a habit Chetwyn thoroughly approved, saying that for the first time in their married life, he could be sure where to find her. It became his pleasant custom to visit her in her chamber, timing his arrival to coincide with her breakfast tray.

Following the servant in one morning he paused on the threshhold to look at her with affection. Their marriage had been a contented one. After their wedding, they had consummated the marriage for the first few nights with some solemnity and a great deal of shyness, but as nothing had immediately come of it, they had left off, both having many more interesting things to do. Time had passed more quickly than they realized, as he had reminded her after the curricle race. They had slept together for a fortnight in a spirit of sober endeavour, and at the end of that time Lucy had been able to inform him in a brisk, matter-of-fact way, that their efforts had been rewarded. Since then they had resumed the relationship which seemed so much more natural to them both, that of brother and sister, of childhood friends.

She looked up now and saw him, and gave him a welcoming smile which was more like an urchin's grin. Her short-cropped hair was sleep-ruffled into a crest, and the shawl she had pulled on was slipping from her shoulders. Her bed was a comfortable nest of letters and parcels and books and cats and handkerchiefs, and a hound puppy peaceably chewing one of her shoes; and for a moment Chetwyn was quite tempted to get in with her, for the sheer cosiness of it.

Since she had been rendered immobile, the household had shifted its focus to her bedchamber. The cats had been the first, with their instinct for comfort, to colonize her bed, but gradually everyone gravitated towards it. The servants brought her news or a splinter to be removed, or asked wistfully if there was anything they could do for her; gardeners came to bring her flowers and fruit, stablemen to ask her advice, villagers to have their disputes settled and their problems solved.

The servant with the tray managed to find room to place it across her knees, and the compression of the bedclothes revealed the huge bulge in front of her. Chetwyn grinned.

'You look exactly like a little girl dressed up with a pillow, not in the least like a pregnant woman,' he said.

'I feel *exactly* like a pregnant woman, thank you,' Lucy said sternly. 'And let me tell you, Chetwyn, I wouldn't do this for anyone else.'

'I sincerely hope not!' he laughed. 'Let me pour your chocolate for you. Did you sleep well?'

'No,' she said simply. 'Do you know what I most look forward to, after this baby is born?'

'Going riding,' he said certainly.

'More even than that – to being able to lie on my front again. As soon as I'm out of bed, I'm going to go and find myself a good patch of grass, and lie down flat on my face for hours and hours and hours.'

'It won't be so very long now,' Chetwyn comforted her.

'I think it must be an elephant child I'm carrying,' she grumbled, but not unhappily. 'None of those little shirts and dresses Docwra has been labouring over is going to fit. We'll have to wrap it in tablecloths and push it around on a cart.'

'Fool!' said Chetwyn, examining her breakfast tray critically, and choosing a dried fig to nibble. 'What on earth is that extraordinary-looking mess in that bowl?'

'Mrs Gordon makes it for me. She calls it brose. It's oatmeal and honey and cream and some other things, I can't remember. It's supposed to ensure the baby will be sweet-tempered. Will you eat some of it for me? I don't like to hurt her feelings by sending it back untouched, but I can't relish anything so sweet first thing in the morning.'

'Not me!' Chetwyn said hastily. 'Give it to the cats.'

'They'd be sick. Try the puppy.'

Chetwyn obediently put the bowl on the floor, detached the puppy from the shoe and placed it beside it, and

64

watched as a successful union was achieved between the two. His wife recalled his attention, saying, 'Chetwyn, why have we no house in Town?'

'Well, we have, of course. Aylesbury House, in Piccadilly. You must have passed it a hundred times. Why did you think we hadn't?'

'Because ever since I've known you, you've always stayed with Flora and Charles when you've been in Town. Why did we never stay in Aylesbury House?'

'It's let out on lease, to the Staplers' Club. It's a horrid great barn of a place, quite suitable for a gentlemen's club, but there was no living in it. Grandfather let it after Grandmother died, and Papa used to rent a house for the Season, if Mama wanted to go up to Town. When he went up on business, he always stayed in an hotel. Why do you ask, anyway?'

'I've been thinking that after the baby is born, I should like to spend some time in Town. I shall have had enough of rustication for a while, but with poor Flora gone, it would be rather awkward to be staying at Chelmsford House.'

'Especially if Charles don't invite us,' Chetwyn agreed cheerfully.

'And we haven't heard a word from him since Christmas. Do you think he's all right?'

'I imagine so. I expect he's just getting things sorted out. Well, Luce, there's no problem here. We can perfectly well rent a house for the Season, if that's what you want; and if you should happen to see a place that strikes your fancy, we might take it on a long lease.'

'Really? Oh Chetwyn, you are a trump card!'

Chetwyn grinned. 'We'll have to find a house near to the Park, so that you can drive out every day in your curricle-and-four and shock the dowagers. We ought to have a place of our own: it's time we gave our own dinners and balls.'

'Think of me, a hostess!' Lucy marvelled.

'Oh, you'll be first-rate. And I'll give you any odds, that our parties are the most talked-about of the Season.'

At the end of February Mrs Haworth came down from

65

Morland Place to Wolvercote to be with Lucy during her lying-in. She found her sister larger than ever, but still cheerful and practical, despite her discomfort.

'I shouldn't be surprised, from the size of me, if it weren't twins,' she said. 'Wouldn't that be a splendid thing, Polly? Two for the price of one – or rather, for the pains of one.'

'As long as they were boys.'

'Yes, that's the worst of it. I don't mind for myself, but Chetwyn must have his heir. But tell me all the news of home. How do you all go on?'

'As well as can be expected, in the circumstances,' Mary sighed.

'Oh dear, that does sound gloomy. What's the matter?'

'Mrs James, as usual. It makes such a bad atmosphere in the house, her and James not being upon terms. One can never feel comfortable.'

'Poor thing! It must be hard to be forced to leave home and marry a stranger, just to give him an heir.'

'Like you, in fact,' Mary said.

'Not at all like me,' Lucy said, surprised. 'I wasn't forced – and Chetwyn wasn't a stranger. He and I are the best of friends, always have been. Do you think I would have married him if it weren't so?'

'But you weren't in love with him,' Mary said.

'Oh, love!' Lucy made a face. 'I know nothing of this *love* of yours! You females are always talking about it, but I think you invent it, to make yourselves mysterious.'

'You're a female yourself,' Mary pointed out, and Lucy frowned, and then placed a hand over her belly and smiled ruefully.

'Just now, I am forced to agree with you. Well, what has Mrs James done now, to make you so cross, Poll? I'm sure she's a very good creature: why can't you get on with her?'

'Her upbringing has been so different from ours; and she has been mistress of her own house so long, she can't seem to understand that she is not mistress any more. You heard about the affair of the pianoforte? Her father's breach of delicacy was beyond anything, in sending such a gift, accompanied by a letter saying that as we would not provide her with the things she needed, he must do it for us –'

'I'm sure he said no such thing.'

'Those were not his words, but that was certainly the sense of it. But her father's indelicacy was more than matched by hers, in accepting such a gift, and having it put in the drawing-room in place of the harpsichord, without asking Mama's permission, or thinking for a moment of anyone's convenience but her own. And that was not the only thing. He is constantly sending her things, not just personal gifts, but horrible great pieces of furniture, all covered with gilding and scroll-work, and statues and ornaments, which she places about the rooms in common use, so that you would hardly recognize the place now.'

'Can't Mama speak to her?'

'Oh, you know Mama – she's hardly ever at home anyway, and she hates to hurt anyone's feelings. Though I think even she thought Mrs James had gone far enough when she changed rooms with her while Mama was out.'

'Not really!'

'Oh yes: she said that it was more suitable for Mama to have the great bedchamber, and that Mappin had told her that Mama never liked the red room, which you know is not true, because it always used to be Great Uncle George's room, and Mama was very fond of him. Mama was most put out, but she didn't like to make a fuss when Mrs James had done it for a kindness, which was how it appeared, so she said only that she wished Mrs James had asked her about it beforehand, so that she could have saved the servants all the trouble of changing back. But Farleigh told me afterwards that Dakers told her that Mrs James's real reason for wanting to move was that she had taken a dislike to the great bedchamber.'

'Why?'

'It seems that one of the housemaids – a new one, that Ned took in from the asylum – told Mrs James a story about somebody hanging themselves from the chandelier hook, and Mrs James couldn't sleep for thinking about it.'

'Oh yes, I've heard that story. It's perfectly true. It was our great-grandmother. She was discovered having an affair with the domestic chaplain, and hanged herself out of remorse: one of the maids told me when I was quite little.

67

But that's no reason to take an aversion to the room, or the chandelier hook. After all, think of all the people who have slept in that room and *not* hanged themselves.'

Mary burst out laughing. 'Oh Lucy, you are like a breath of fresh air! I wish you were still living at home. You would restore everyone's sense of proportion.'

'Well it certainly seems you've lost yours, Polly. I've never known you get so far into the dismals over nothing at all.'

Mary sighed. 'The truth of it is, I miss George so terribly, and there's nothing at Morland Place to distract me. Mrs James is so dull and pious, and Jamie so irritating with his sulks and his martyred airs; and Mama is never home, and Ned is growing more bucolic by the day! How I long for the sort of company I was used to when I lived with Flora and Charles.'

'It's obvious you are wasted in Yorkshire. Why don't you come and live with Chetwyn and me? We are going to get a house in Town for the Season, and even when we are here at Wolvercote, you know, it is so close to London, that all sorts of people come and visit us. If they knew you were here, all your old beaux would come flocking! We should never be dull. Oh, do say you will, Polly! Chetwyn would like it of all things, I know, and I think it would be *prime*!'

'Such language, child! I think you need me to keep you in hand. I should like it very much,' Mary said, 'but I should be loath to leave Hippolyta at Morland Place, to be influenced by Mrs James.'

'Don't leave her, then – bring her with you. She'll be company for my child. They can be brought up together: what could be better? Anyway, you know you promised I could have her, if I should start up my school.'

'I only said I'd think about it. But how could I leave Morland Place, without looking as if I had been driven away by Mrs James? I should hate to do anything that seemed particular.'

'Say you want to be nearer London, in case Captain Haworth should put in somewhere for a day or two. That makes perfect sense.'

Mary smiled, and laid her hand over Lucy's for a

moment. 'You're a good, kind girl, Lucy, and I do thank you very much. I will come, if you think Chetwyn will not mind it.'

'We'll shake down together, never fear. You and I never quarrelled when we lived together in Bath, did we? And don't worry about Chetwyn – he is the sweetest-tempered man in the world.'

Lucy went into labour on the eighth of March, earlier than she had expected. Chetwyn surprised her by exhibiting a great nervousness, and begging her to send for London's most eminent surgeon. Lucy only patted his hand comfortingly and retired to her room with the faithful Docwra, who turned back at the last moment to say to her master, 'No don't you be fretting, me lord. Haven't I helped me po mother through six confinements, and her no more hea than a breath o' wind on a hot day? Sure, and her ladyshi s as strong as the bog-heather: we'll bring it off between s, never fear.'

The baby was large. and Lucy was small, and despit all her determination and her medical knowledge, despite her veterinary skills and Docwra's experience, it went hard with her. She would not cry out, and remained in control throughout, but when at last the baby was born, she had a moment of weakness when she could only clutch Docwra's hand in relief and croak, 'Animals do it all so much more easily.'

'Sure, and animals never give birth to young the size o' this one,' Docwra said cheerfully, wiping the sweat from her mistress's face. 'I vow and swear, me lady, there was never a bigger babby in the whole o' history.'

'Boy or girl?' Lucy whispered.

'A girl, and as stout as can be!' Docwra replied. Lucy closed her eyes in weak dismay.

'Are you sure? Docwra, is there only one?'

'One's enough to be going on with,' Docwra said firmly. 'You thank God it's whole and healthy, and leave the planning and worrying to Him. There, now, me lady, drink this, and then I'll clean you up and make you comfortable.'

'I don't think I'll ever be comfortable again,' Lucy groaned. 'Mary, are you there? Will you go and break the news to Chetwyn for me?'

The cordial Docwra administered, and the effect of hot water and clean linen, restored Lucy to something like her normal spirits, and enabled her very soon to receive her husband's visit. They faced each other down the length of the bed, smiling shyly.

'Well, then,' said Chetwyn at last, at a loss for words.

'You've seen the child?' Lucy asked anxiously.

'Yes. She seems very healthy; and she's certainly large. You were right,' he added, trying to make a joke, 'about carrying an elephant child.'

'I'm sorry it's a girl,' Lucy said. 'That must be a blow to you. It is to me. Now we shall have it all to do again.'

'But not immediately,' Chetwyn said hastily. 'Sure you will want a good, long rest before you begin again!' A silence followed. 'I was wondering, Luce, what we shall call her? What do you say to Jane? That was my Mama's name.'

Lucy frowned. 'It's very well; but the thing is, that she will be growing up with Mary's child, and if she has a plain name, it will sound ridiculous next to Hippolyta.'

'Hippolyta and Jane – well, perhaps.'

'I think we ought to give her a name something the same.'

'Hmm.' Chetwyn mused, and then his brow lightened. 'What about Flaminia?'

Lucy tried it, and smiled. 'Oh yes, I like that. That's very well. What made you think of it?'

'I don't know. It must be something I picked up from m'tutor, at Balliol. It's Latin, you know.'

'Well, I know that, you dunderhead,' Lucy exclaimed indignantly. He met her eyes, and his expression softened.

'I'm glad you're all right, Lucy,' he said gruffly. 'Worried about you!'

Lucy fed the baby herself for the first couple of weeks,

expounding to Mary the theory that it was good for both mother and baby. 'The next time you have one, you must try it,' she said, and Mary shuddered delicately. At the end of March, Lucy tried to transfer the baby to a wet-nurse, but she did not take to it, and there was a distressing period when she cried constantly with colic. Every time she cried, Lucy's breasts oozed milk in sympathy, ruining her clothes, and embarrassing Lucy and Chetwyn almost equally.

'You'll have her on your hands for ever,' Mary warned, and Lucy was obliged to fall back on Morland Place lore, dismiss the wet-nurse and send out for a milch-ewe. Flaminia took to ewe's milk, and throve, and grew into a placid and quite pretty baby. Lucy's milk dried up, and Chetwyn found a pleasant small house in Upper Grosvenor Street, and at the end of April the household moved up to Town.

The news that Lord and Lady Aylesbury had arrived, and that Mrs Haworth was with them, acted like a charm on Society, and from the day the door-knocker was hung, it was never still. Amongst the very first of callers was Mr Danby Wiske, who came to pay his respects, and to gaze at her ladyship with six months' accumulation of unexpressed adoration. As prompt in his *devoirs* and far more articulate was Mr Brummell, who bowed over Lucy's hand and congratulated her on producing a daughter.

'Since the Princess of Wales had a girl, and an *immense* one at that, it would not do to produce a child of any other sex, or requiring any other epithet. Dear Lady Aylesbury, you have such exquisite taste!'

'It's very good to hear you talking nonsense again,' Lucy said. 'And haven't you to be congratulated, too? I think you are promoted to Captain, are you not?'

Brummell bowed. 'Though the pleasure is not unalloyed,' he sighed. 'One must spend even more hours before one's glass before one is fit to parade before one's troop. Thank God I do not have to groom my horse myself, or we should never have done.'

Danby Wiske gave a positive bark of laughter. 'Idea of *you* groomin' a horse, George!'

'Nothing, I assure you, surprises me more about the

army,' Brummell replied solemnly, 'than finding myself in it.'

'Tell her la'ship what happened the other day,' Mr Wiske urged him. 'About old Blue-nose.'

Mr Brummell bowed. 'I had a scheme, you see, for recognizing my own troop, for in general soldiers all look so much alike, and it is horribly embarrassing to be forced to ask where they are when going on parade. But one of my men had a nose quite blue in all weathers, so I gave instructions that he should always be placed in the front row.'

'Ingenious,' Lucy remarked.

'So I thought,' Captain Brummell went on. 'But the other day I was sitting on my horse in front of my men, when the Colonel came galloping up to me shouting, "Captain Brummell, what the devil are you doing there? You are with the wrong troop, sir!" I was greatly taken aback; but then I looked over my shoulder, and there was blue-nose, right in the middle of the front line. I was not to be so taken in! I smiled engagingly at the Colonel, and said, "No, sir, no, I know better than that! A pretty thing, indeed, if I did not know my own troop!" The Colonel's face turned quite purple, poor thing, which clashed horribly with the scarlet of his regimentals, and proceeded to bawl at me in a most unrestrained way. It was only afterwards I learned that my troop had received some new recruits, and my dear old Blue-nose had been moved on to another.'

'I'm not entirely sure I believe you,' Lucy laughed, 'but pray don't stop! Tell us all the latest scandal. Mary and I pine for the news.'

'What can I tell you? You will have heard about your cousin, the Earl of Chelmsford, of course?'

'About Charles? No, what has he done? He left his card as soon as we came up, but we were out at the time, and we haven't had a moment yet to visit him. Have you seen him?'

'Everyone in the 10th has seen him forever,' Danby Wiske said. 'What makes it so gallin' for Captain Morland!'

'For Horatio?' Lucy enquired, puzzled. 'What can you mean?'

'The *on-dit* is, your ladyship, that the Earl has fallen a

victim to the little blind god,' Captain Brummell said with a smile.

Lucy and Mary exchanged an astonished look, and Lucy said, 'Charles in love? It can't be true. You can't mean it?'

'It is sad to see it happening to a man of sense and years,' Brummell agreed solemnly, 'but indeed it is so. The lady in question is the daughter of one of our company commanders, Colonel Taske.'

'But it's barely six months since Flora died – and he was inconsolable!' Lucy said unguardedly, and Mary, sitting beside her, pinched her hand warningly. These were not things to be said to mere acquaintances, however shocked one was.

Mr Brummell bowed. 'Colonel Taske is a widower himself,' he went on, 'and his daughter is his sole comfort, and much beloved, so he is not best pleased by Lord ..¹msford's attentions. On the other hand, it would be a brilliant ...atch for Miss Taske, for though she is perfectly amiable, and rather pretty than not, she has no portion at all – as, I believe, Captain Morland has been at pains to point out to his brother.'

'Oh dear, has Horace been making a spectacle of himself?' asked the incorrigible Lucy, who could never learn to have any reserve with people she liked.

'Lucy!' Mary reproved.

'Pray don't concern yourself, Mrs Haworth,' Brummell said gently. 'Wiske and I are entirely to be trusted. And nothing could be more suitable than the attentiveness Captain Morland and Lady Barbara have been shewing his lordship. Indeed, more than once Lord Chelmsford has begged them not to put themselves at such pains, and not to be afraid to leave him sometimes on his own! It was in the course of a mild indisposition of Lady Barbara's – she is increasing again, you understand – that Lord Chelmsford formed his acquaintance with Colonel Taske and his daughter; and by the time Captain Morland was able to resume his custodial duties, the damage was done.'

It appeared that Charles had gone out of Town for a few

days, but Lucy and Mary had not long to wait before meeting the other protagonists in this family drama. Miss Taske they came across while calling on Lady Tewkesbury, a sharp-nosed, garrulous woman who prided herself on being always the first with the gossip. It was plain that she had invited Miss Taske for the purpose of pumping her, and equally plain that Miss Taske was either too innocent or too wise to be pumped.

She seemed very young, too young, almost, to be 'out'. From her appearance she might be no more than sixteen, and Mr Brummell had done her less than justice in saying she was 'rather pretty than not', for in fact she was very pretty indeed, with golden curls, a pink-and-white complexion, and violet-blue eyes. Her dress was very plain, which might be attributable either to poverty or modesty; but though she was quiet, even reserved, there was no shyness or awkwardness about her, and her air and manner made her seem older than her years.

All Lady Tewkesbury's remarks about 'beaux' and 'future plans' and 'happy news' eliciting no response from Miss Taske, she turned with evident relief to the Morland females, whom she might legitimately ask if they had yet met with their cousin Chelmsford; but as they had not, and as the mention of his name drew no blush to Miss Taske's rose-and-ivory cheek, the dowager found herself baffled at every turn, and was obliged to allow the conversation to turn to fashions.

'Well, she seems a very pretty girl, at least,' Lucy said to Mary when they were in the carriage again. 'One can see why Charles fancies her.'

'One can't,' Mary said crossly. 'When he was so devoted to Flora, how can he so soon be in love with nothing but a pretty face?'

'She might be very intelligent,' Lucy said fairly. 'It's hard to tell, when she says so little, and who would not keep silent with that disagreeable old hag needling and probing away like a glutton at a snail?'

That made Mary laugh. 'It was to her credit, I suppose,

74

that she did give so little away. But how can a girl of her age be so composed? She *ought* to have blushed. It's unnatural.'

'There's no pleasing you, Polly,' Lucy said. 'But at least, having met her at Lady T's, we can invite her to our ball next week without comment. Now all we have to do is to find a way of meeting her father.'

It proved easy enough, for since all of Society was longing to know how much of the scandal might be believed, and what Chelmsford's family thought about it, it wanted nothing better than to throw Morlands and Taskes together at every possible opportunity; and at a dinner the following day given by a fashionable hostess, Mary, Lucy and Chetwyn found amongst their fellow-guests not only Colonel Taske, but Captain the Honourable Horatio Morland as well.

Colonel Taske was a gaunt man in his fifties, with the upright carriage of a cavalryman, and though his wig and coat were rather old-fashioned, his eye spoke a lively intelligence. During dinner the conversation turned to the conditions in France, where the Directory was proving as corrupt and inefficient as the government it had replaced, and where mismanagement had led to internal bankruptcy. Colonel Taske proved himself an intelligent commentator.

'The only hope of financial relief for the French must be the conquest of Italy. This young General Buonaparte's army seems to be sweeping right across the country.'

'How does that help finances, sir?' Chetwyn asked.

'Plunder, my lord, plunder, sent home to France by the shipload! And of course, as long as the army is on foreign soil, it feeds itself on the produce of that country,' the Colonel replied. 'France, you see, is in the position of one who has grasped a tiger by the tail. She dare not let go. If she makes peace, that army of half a million Frenchmen will come home, and it will want to be fed, and it will want to be paid; and there is not gold and corn enough in France to satisfy one of them, far less half a million.'

'So what will happen?' Chetwyn asked.

'The Frogs will go on fighting. They must. They will press on outwards, extending their frontiers until the conquered territory is so unwieldy it becomes unmanageable. Then it will collapse under its own weight, and the other nations will drive the French back into France again. Then we shall have peace.'

'How long will all this take?' Chetwyn asked.

'Who can tell? Five years – ten – twenty? Perhaps I may not live to see the end of it. But it will happen. You may read it all in your classics: it is the way all empires grow, and die.'

There were several dinner-guests who looked as though they did not agree, and one of them, an elderly politician, broke in at this point to say cheerfully, 'Stuff and nonsense! All this talk of empires, Colonel – there ain't a man in France fit to be emperor! Look at this Directory of theirs – thieves, rogues and vagabonds! Not a gentleman among 'em! No, no, we'll lick the Frogs in no time, and have 'em back under hatches within the year, you'll see.' As this was evidently the popular view, it had the last word, and the conversation turned to other topics.

After dinner, in the drawing-room, Horatio took the opportunity of the general mobility caused by the advent of the tea-table to come to Mary's side, and address her in an urgent undertone.

'Thank heaven you are here! Now Mary, I beg you, you must talk to Charles and make him leave off. You always had more influence with him than anyone, perhaps you can talk some sense into him.'

'Make him leave off what?' Mary said discouragingly.

Horatio was not to be deterred. 'You know very well. And what the devil was Aylesbury doing, encouraging old Taske like that? Everyone will draw their conclusions. It is making us all ridiculous. A man of Charles's age, dangling after a chit of a girl like Roberta Taske!'

'Oh come, Horace, the girl is respectable enough, isn't she? Why should he not be polite to her?'

'She's respectable, I suppose,' Horatio said unwillingly. 'As respectable as anyone can be, who has neither rank, family nor fortune. But you don't understand: he is not just being polite to her. His attentions are become so particular that everyone is saying he means to marry her!'

'Well, if he wants to, surely that is his business?'

Horatio stared, reddening. 'How can you say that, you of

76

all people? Good God, it's not six months since Flora died! It is in the worst possible taste for him to be running after a girl young enough to be his daughter, and his wife not cold in her grave! Of course,' he went on bitterly, 'it would be a fine match for her. Taske is penniless, with nothing but his army pay to live on. You can see what they have been about, on the catch for Charles, casting out lures for him. If you don't do something, he will have *offered* for her, and then we shall all be done up!'

'Now do stop exaggerating, Horace,' Mary said calmly. 'You've just been complaining that Charles is dangling after her, and now you're saying it is *she* who is on the catch for *him*. I agree it is a little soon to be paying such attentions to a woman as to be talked about, but Charles knows what he is about, and I am perfectly sure he would not make her an offer within the period of mourning. What he does after that is his business.'

'Don't you see, he is making us all ridiculous!' Horatio cried, exasperated.

'If anyone makes us ridiculous, it is more likely to be you,' Mary said quietly. 'If you go on making your hostility so obvious, people will say that you wish to stop the affair because you are afraid of losing the title.'

Horatio turned extremely red. 'What do you mean?' he spluttered. 'How dare you?'

'Oh, I know it isn't true, of course,' Mary said sweetly, 'but there are always those who will put the worst construction on things; and it is common gossip that you have often borrowed money on the expectation of becoming the seventh earl.' This was a guess on her part, but she saw by his expression that it had found the mark.

'That's a damned lie,' he muttered feebly.

'Indeed? Well if I were you, Horace, I should be very careful not to give people any idea you are jealous, because that would tend to confirm the notion that you had been banking on the reversion.'

The Aylesburys' first ball was a great success, with at least twice as many people present as had been invited, and almost twice as many as the rooms would comfortably hold. With everyone so eager to be invited, there was no need for Chetwyn to provide anything more than the best of food, wine, and musicians; though Lucy felt her reputation for being outrageous was at stake, and wore a gown in the latest fashion, of spotted Indian gauze with a deep embroidered hem, so fine it appeared to be transparent, an effect which her flesh-coloured under-garment did nothing to diminish.

She enormously enjoyed her own ball, which was not at all the fashionable thing to do. Danby Wiske would have danced every dance with her had she permitted it. He was her constant companion, and she liked to have him at her elbow, for he was reliable and undemanding. He left her free to observe with amusement the growing crowd around Mary begging her to dance, though she continued to protest that she was too old a married woman to take the floor.

She also watched Charles dancing with Roberta Taske, looking down at her with an expression of such tenderness that for an extraordinary moment Lucy felt almost jealous, almost sad that no man had ever looked at her like that. They were a silent couple. It was evident to the most casual observer that they danced in a world of their own, and that gazing at each other left them in no need of words.

She was standing, just for that instant alone, as Danby Wiske had walked off for a moment, when a voice close behind her said quietly,

'Well well, if I don't mistake me, it's Mr Proom of the *Diamond.* I am glad to meet you, sir.'

Lucy started violently, and swung round, to find herself looking up into the laughing brown eyes of a tall, handsome, elegant young man, who took advantage of her speechlessness to take her hand and bow over it gracefully, saying, 'You must allow me to say that you are the most versatile ship's surgeon I ever encountered. I never saw another who looked as much at home in a ballroom as on the orlop deck of a seventy-four.'

'Lieutenant Weston!' she cried, and in her excitement, retained his hand in hers and smiled at him more welcomingly than was perhaps quite proper.

'Your servant, ma'am,' he said, shewing his admirable

white teeth as he returned her smile. 'And, let me add, I never saw a ship's surgeon who looked more ravishing in a gauze ball-gown.'

'Oh, hush!' she cried, reddening. 'That is all forgotten – or at least, it is supposed to be. I am very respectable now, you know.'

'Indeed, I do know. The Countess of Aylesbury, no less,' he said, and there was a pleasant mockery in his smile. She gave a puzzled frown.

'But how do you come to be here? I did not invite you. Indeed, I would have, with pleasure, had I known you were on shore,' she added hastily, realizing what a social predicament she was initiating.

Weston laughed, and said, 'I am glad to find you are still more Mr Proom than Lady Aylesbury! And now you may have me thrown forcibly into the street, for I must confess that I have no very good right to be here, having been invited only at second hand. Lord Chelmsford – your cousin, I believe? – met me in Fladong's where he was dining with Admiral Harvey, and knowing of me from what you told him of your time aboard the *Diamond*, he took the liberty of inviting me to your ball, and I took the even greater liberty of accepting.'

'Oh, but I am *so* glad that you did!' Lucy exclaimed fervently. 'Oh those happy days on the good old *Diamond*! Why will such things pass away? I should like to talk with you about it for ever!'

'But not, I hope, on the dance-floor, or everyone will be in a stir,' Weston smiled. 'I have been watching you dance this half-hour, your ladyship, and I am glad to find you dance admirably, with all the grace and spirit of a senior warrant officer in His Majesty's navy! But I am curious about your last partner: surely that was not your husband?'

'Oh, no, that was only Mr Wiske, a friend. Here is my husband now – I must introduce you! Chetwyn, may I present Lieutenant Weston? Mr Weston, my husband, the Earl of Aylesbury.'

The two men bowed, and eyed each other consideringly as they straightened up. 'Servant, sir,' said Chetwyn. 'I've heard a lot about you.'

79

'Then you have me at a disadvantage, my lord,' Weston replied. 'But you arrive most opportunely: I was just about to solicit the honour of leading Lady Aylesbury to the set.'

'Do, if she wishes. Do you want to dance, Luce?' Chetwyn said languidly.

Lucy's smile was all the answer he needed. Weston led her to the set, and as they took their places, he asked, 'Why do you call him Chetwyn? Is that his given name?'

'Oh no, it's his family name. When he was at school with my brother, we all knew him as Chetwyn, and I got so used to calling him that, I have never left off,' Lucy replied. 'He doesn't mind me dancing with other people, you know,' she added carefully. 'He doesn't care to dance himself.'

Weston looked across to where Chetwyn was standing at the edge of the dance floor, chatting to some other young men of fashion, and a thoughtful expression crossed his face for a moment. 'Yes, I understand,' he said.

Lucy found Mr Weston a graceful dancer, and a most satisfactory partner, able to talk amusingly on a great many subjects, and she was sorry when their two dances were over, and he led her back to her husband. One subject in particular she longed to discuss with him, but it was the one he had already banned from the dance-floor. That it was on his mind, too, was evident from his saying, just before they reached the group where Chetwyn was standing, 'You can't imagine, Lady Aylesbury, how very dull the wardroom seemed after you had left it.'

'And you can't imagine how dull my life seemed, after I had left you – and the other officers. To be expected always to talk about sewing and such ladylike subjects! '

He paused and took her hand again, and looked down at her with a quizzical expression. 'Then, may I hope to be allowed to give you the opportunity to talk once more of professional matters? Dear Lady Aylesbury, may I do myself the honour of calling on you? Will you be at home tomorrow morning?'

'Oh *yes*,' said Lucy, comprehensively, her eyes shining with pleasure, and Weston, as he bowed formally over her hand, allowed his lips to brush it before releasing it, and yielding her up to her husband.

80

Chapter Five

Héloïse stepped out of the house into Yeman's Row, and closed the door behind her, shutting herself into the darkness of a frosty night lit only by stars and the dim gleams of light filtering through the shutters of the houses. She shivered as she adjusted to the cold. There seemed to have been so little summer that year. Late spring frosts had spoiled the young wheat, and now winter had come early, and there had been no relief from the high prices. The price of bread had more than doubled since last year – because of the war, they said. A quartern loaf cost a shilling now; meat, even the cheapest, most indigestible cuts, fivepence a pound; coals sky-high at five pounds a chaldron.

Coals were her greatest problem. She glanced involuntarily over her shoulder at the tiny, sluttish cottage she had just quitted. The doctor said that Vendenoir must be kept warm at all costs, and though the cottage was only one room below and one above, it was hard to keep it warm when it had only an earth floor and the roof leaked like a sieve.

Two small rooms; a stair, so narrow and precipitous that she had to descend it sideways for safety; a tiny, beetle-infested scullery: of this she was mistress. Behind was a common yard which gave access to the common water-pump and the common privvy. She gave a quirky smile as she thought of the house in Paris she had once owned. Even in England, she had known glory: King George had once kissed her cheek, and acknowledged her title of Countess of Strathord. Now she and her faithful Marie ate lentil porrage and rice pudding so that Vendenoir could have the little bit of stewed mutton they could afford.

The contrast was ridiculous, and made her laugh more often than repine. She was of a cheerful, trusting nature, and believed that God had not lost sight of her, and her sense of humour saved her when things seemed darkest. There were things that tried her severely. It was not the loss of those luxuries she had been used to, nor even the hard work and poor food. She had learned to be an inventive cook, and to make surprisingly tasty dishes out of very little. Marie brought the provisions, trudging all the way to the market at World's End to find the best bargains; and Héloïse, troubled with guilt over the hardships her former maid endured, would sometimes joke that though Marie had promised to follow her to the ends of the earth, it was rather too much to ask her to go to World's End twice a week.

She didn't mind having to work for her living, either, for she had been brought up to be useful and active, and teaching French and music and Court etiquette to the daughters of the bourgeoisie was not exacting work, and was occasionally even enjoyable, when a pupil shewed aptitude, or succeeded at last in understanding something that had been eluding her.

What did trouble her was the cold and the dirt. She had not been brought up to clean houses or wash clothes, wash dishes, lay fires, pump water. Marie did these jobs as far as she could, to save her mistress, but Héloïse would not let her entirely shoulder the disagreeable burden. It was very hard to get things clean, when the water itself was far from pure, or to dry them, once washed, on any but a hot, sunny day. The smell of poverty was something that Héloïse had found very difficult to bear; now she worried even more that she had stopped noticing it.

She set off briskly down the lane towards the main road, picking her way carefully over the ruts. One good thing about the frost, she thought with an inward smile, was that the mud and other filth that accumulated in the lane were frozen hard, and much more pleasant to walk over. Pride prevented her from wearing pattens, the same pride which had made her only moments ago refuse Marie's offer of a shawl. Her pelisse, though not very warm, was still smart enough if you didn't look too closely, but Héloïse refused to go out with a shawl over her head and shoulders like a peasant. When I come to that, she had told Marie with a smile, you will know I am beaten.

Yeman's Row fed itself into the main Brompton road, which linked the village of Brompton in one direction with

Kensington, and in the other with Piccadilly and Park Lane. Nicely placed, as Héloïse put it, between the homes of the gentle and the homes of the genteel, Brompton housed a large population of French *émigrés* who, displaced from a variety of social stations in France, now made a living by teaching their accomplishments to the rich, by making their gowns and shoes and hats, or by dressing their hair or their meat. Héloïse was walking to Sydney Street, and it was safer to stay upon the main road. In hard times there were always footpads about, and though a footpad was likely to have but poor pickings off her, she could hardly expect one to take her word for that and go away without trying.

It was Sunday, the day of the week she really looked forward to, though she had had to struggle long and hard for the right to do what she was doing. Even now, Vendenoir did not like it, and had he been stronger, he would have prevented her; but his condition had worsened steadily over the past year, and now he was bedridden, leaving it only on his better days to drag himself as far as the sofa. She had worn him down on the subject of her Sunday evenings to the point where, though he complained bitterly that she was deserting him for a parcel of traitors and decadent royalists, his tirades were more habitual than passionate, and soon petered out into self-pity.

'You wish me dead – don't you think I know it? And by God I'd as soon oblige you as lie here day after day suffering as I do. Nobody knows what I suffer!' he said as she put on her pelisse.

'You need not blame yourself for that,' Héloïse replied, 'for I'm sure you tell us often enough.'

Vendenoir glowered. 'Yes, and precious little sympathy I get, too!'

'You have so much for yourself, you cannot need more for Marie and me,' she said cheerfully. 'Come, why not resign yourself? You know that I *will* go; and perhaps I may be able to bring you back a newspaper.'

'Yes, a newspaper a week old,' Vendenoir said bitterly. 'You starve me of news as of everything else. I know your tricks, madam. I know why you moved me here to this cold, damp place: you thought it would finish me off.'

Héloïse looked at him with some compassion. He looked like an old man, though he was only a few years older than she; his face was skull-like, his skin pallid and unhealthy, his thinning hair already going grey. If her life was hard, his had been harder, and was made harder still by a bitter, resentful spirit which doubled all his burdens, while her resilience lightened hers. She knew he felt the cold more than any of them. The fire over which he crouched, taking all its warmth, was the best she could afford, and the coals were eked out with kindling gathered at a great expense of labour by her and Marie from such woods as were within walking distance; but there was no sense in expecting him to be grateful, and in her better moments she knew that his inability to feel anything but resentment was something for which he should be pitied.

'Now, Olivier, you know we moved because we could not afford the other place. And you always said you hated it.'

'At least it was dry, and the air was not so foul. We afforded it before.'

'Yes, when Marie was working. Now she is obliged to stay home and care for you, we have only half the money, and everything costs twice as much as before. But you know these things – you are only trying to delay me. I must go or I shall be late.'

She gave his forehead a dutiful kiss, and Marie's cheek a loving one, and hurried away to Vendenoir's parting plaint: 'That's right, go and spend an evening in luxury, while Marie and I huddle over this miserable fire.' His voice rose to follow her as she closed the door. 'I'll wager they even have *candles*!'

The house in Sydney Street was old, but in good repair, and large enough to seem luxurious to most of the *émigrés* who hurried there every Sunday evening. A torch flared by the entrance door, but no light escaped the windows, tribute to the good fit of its shutters. Héloïse was alone in the street as she lifted the knocker – everyone must be already here, she thought.

In this house lived one Madame Chouflon, who had been

84

a mantuamaker of some renown in Paris, and who, fleeing to England at the beginning of the Revolution, brought with her all her skill and some of her reputation. Consequently, she lived well in a London hungry for fashion, earned enough to be comfortable, and was successful enough to ignore the new style of gown she designed for her customers, and to dress herself as she always had, in the fashion of thirty years back, when Madame de Pompadour led society.

She opened the door to Héloïse herself, and the lights from within revealed her in a gown of black satin, the bodice stretched tight over whalebone stays, the skirt full and deeply flounced, the whole tinkling and flashing with a multitude of jet beads and spars. Madame's white forearms emerged from the stiff triple ruffles of her sleeves, her neck was encircled with a little starched gauze ruff, and her soot-black hair was elaborately piled and curled and embellished with ebony combs and black feathers. In all, she presented to Héloïse's affectionate amusement the appearance of a rich French widow of the 1760's, though as far as she knew there had never been a Monsieur Chouflon.

'My dear child, come in, come in! I knew it must be you – you are the last. How cold it is – you must be starved in that poor little pelisse! I wonder that women should ever have given up cloaks, especially in this cold, damp country. A cloak is such a comfort, and holds in the warmth, you know. Depend upon it, these pelisses are the cause of a great deal of ill health.'

Héloïse was enfolded briefly but affectionately in a stiff and nubbly embrace, and led into the drawing-room, where the rest of the party was assembled.

'There is such a good fire, I think you may take off your pelisse at once, don't you? But, love, have you no shawl? And those poor little shoes! You must have the seat by the chimney. Thiviers, come, give up your seat to the poor Countess; you have had it long enough. Now, if we are all ready, I think we may begin. Father?'

Here was true comfort, Héloïse thought blissfully, easing her way through the familiar group towards the great roaring fire, exchanging smiles and nods with old friends, and settling herself like the others, facing towards the far end of the drawing-room where Father Jerome, the Jesuit priest, was preparing to say Mass. It was the invariable beginning to their Sunday gatherings, and a great comfort, though she never mentioned it to her husband, who, like many young revolutionaries, had abandoned the Catholic Church along with privilege and monarchy.

After the Blessing, there was a moment of thoughtful silence, and then everyone began talking at once, and the noise and movement was like a flock of starlings suddenly descending on a tree. In a moment the double doors to the dining-parlour would be thrown back, and the *émigrés* would rush as fast as their various states of ill-health and decrepitude would allow to the buffet table, which was spread with a supper which to many of them was a feast.

Many a dull old eye took on a youthful shine at the sight of the cold meats and pies, cheeses and brawns, bread, cakes, sometimes even fruit on display. There was beer to wash it down with, sometimes wine, though the war had made French wines hard to come by. Madame Chouflon provided the bulk of it, but others brought what they could to add to the board. Héloïse, still warming herself at the fire, watched her countrymen pass her, their faces alight with pleasure; shabby, most of them, thin many, some still attempting to maintain a former elegance, all speaking the French tongue, words tumbling over one another in their eagerness to express seven days' worth of ideas in one evening. This, she could see, for them as for her, was as strong a reason for coming here every week as the food and the fire.

There was old Merlot, telling anyone who would still listen how he used to have two-and-forty indoor servants; and Madame Chard, whose once-mighty flesh hung sadly about her like borrowed clothes, describing dish by dish in loving detail a banquet she had attended long ago at Cheverny. There was the Comte de Thiviers discussing wines and vintages with Romorantin, who, having no teeth left, was rendered speechless and thus a good listener while he laboriously mumbled his food about with his bare gums. There was the Vicomtesse Limoux looking about her for someone to whom she could explain once again how she had had to leave her carriage horses behind when she took ship at Nantes, and what she supposed the revolutionaries would have done with them.

Héloïse filled her plate and stepped back from the buffet table, and was trying not to eat like a starving peasant when Madame Chouflon came up and dropped a shawl about her shoulders.

'There, child, that's better. Charivey lends it for the evening – don't forget to return it before you leave. My dear Héloïse, I can't bear to see you looking so pale and thin. I am sure you do not get enough to eat.'

'Dear Flon, I assure you I am quite well,' Héloïse smiled. 'I am too much confined within doors, that's all. I was used to take a great deal of exercise in the old days, riding and walking –' She stopped herself abruptly. In her eagerness to divert Madame's attention, she had fallen into a trap, and now she laughed. 'Ah, no! I promised myself I would not talk about the old days, like our poor friends. I am not yet come to that.'

'You could never be like them, my love. You are too brave and merry. Oh, yes, don't turn away your face like that, just because a poor old woman gives you a compliment! I may be silly – I am sure I am – and nothing but a mantuamaker; and who my father was, only the dear Lord knows; but I know that there is something very fine about you, my love. You are better than the rest of us, and it hurts me sadly to see you go hungry, and support your worthless husband by the toil of your hands. It should be he who works to keep you!'

'You should not say such things,' Héloïse said, reddening. 'Vendenoir is too ill to go out to work, indeed he is.'

Madame sniffed. 'I suppose that is what *he* tells you!'

'The doctor tells me so,' Héloïse countered. 'He says Vendenoir may never recover his strength.'

'Ah, but is he a good doctor?' Flon asked suspiciously.

Héloïse smiled. 'Doctor Cranton is a *very* good doctor. He never presses for payment of his bills.'

Madame snorted. 'Always the jokes! But I know that you starve yourself while this Vendenoir eats meat – aye, and a pint of wine a week, which I suppose you will say this *doctor* tells you he must have. And what has he done to deserve all this care? We all know what he was in Paris, who he served, and who perished by his connivance.'

'Oh, Flon, please don't!' Héloïse cried. She tried not to think too often of those she had left behind, who had died while Vendenoir lived. Papa, her dear Papa! She missed him still, so much. 'Vendenoir is my husband, and it is my duty to take care of him.'

'Duty!' said Madame with robust contempt. Héloïse bit her lip.

'It sustains me,' she said. 'And, don't you see, if I loved him, I might sometimes eat meat with him. But I hate him so much, that only by taking the very best care of him, can I atone for the sin.'

Madame Chouflon looked with puzzled admiration at this child of eighteen who spoke like a nun of eighty, and then offered her her own comfort. 'Well, he cannot last for ever, and then you will be free. And the war cannot last for ever, either. One day the revolutionaries will be beaten, and the King will return, and we can all go home and be happy.'

It was what they all said, with varying degrees of belief, but Héloïse would not allow herself to cling to that particular illusion. She hoped that she might return one day, but it was without any assurance. And if they did go back, France would be very different, of that she was sure. There could be no return to the old way of life, whatever happened; but she was young, and she understood that the older *émigrés* could not adjust to the new world, and needed to believe that Paradise could be regained. To live one day at a time was her way of coping with harsh reality; to think neither about the past nor the future. Hope and regret equally would disarm her.

'Yes, perhaps,' she said, and changed the subject. 'How are your hands, Flon? Are they any better? Perhaps you should see a doctor.'

'Perhaps I should see yours,' Flon retorted, 'and have him tell me I am too ill to work any longer. Yes, and perhaps he might also tell me where to find a young man to keep me!'

The evening went on in its usual way, the food and warmth acting on the *émigrés'* spirits like an excess of wine, so that they became first cheerful, then merry, and a suggestion of cards was brushed aside in favour of a boisterous game of charades. Héloïse was holding her sides, almost crying with laughter at the spectacle of the toothless Romorantin, as the goddess Diana, in a borrowed pelisse and with a silver fruit-bowl on his head for a helmet and the poker for a sword, tackling a lion, nobly portrayed by Madame Chard in a moth-eaten, fur-lined cloak worn inside out; when the party was disturbed by a violent knocking at the street-door.

There was a silence, and apprehension in every face: they had all had cause to fear the unexpected summons in the night. A few minutes resolved the apprehension for all but one. The visitor was a skinny urchin sent by Marie to summon Héloïse home: Vendenoir had suffered a seizure.

Even the meanest of funerals was beyond Héloïse's reach, but she was reluctant to have Vendenoir consigned to a pauper's grave. Madame Chouflon solved the problem by putting up some money herself, and dunning the better-off *émigrés* for the rest, though when she presented the purse to Héloïse she told her very sourly that the money would be better spent on new clothes for her and Marie. Héloïse was deeply touched by the generosity of the *émigrés*, for they could hardly hope to see the loan repaid. It was the final irony of Vendenoir's life, and in keeping with the rest, that he should be buried by the kindness of those he had so much despised.

Only Héloïse and Marie were at the graveside; Madame Chouflon had wanted to attend, for love of Héloïse, but she was suffering from an attack of rheumatism which, spreading from her hands to other parts of her body, confined her to her bed.

It was a cold day, and the sky was a blurred pinkish-grey. The mist condensed on the bare trees in the graveyard and dripped dismally on the women's bent heads, as the priest hurried through the service, longing to get back to his fire.

His imperfect and hasty rendering of the words was punctuated by sniffs, and accompanied by the sound of dripping water and the cawing of rooks.

When it was over, and he had departed, Héloïse remained for a while, head bent, thinking about Vendenoir's life, and praying for forgiveness, for herself as well as for him. Forgive me if I am too joyful, dear Father. I have tried to do what is right, truly I have. I think he did too, most of the time. Let him be at peace now – and those he injured. Let this be the end of all the bitterness.

She raised her head, and saw Marie trying not to shiver, her nose red and her eyes damp. 'Home,' she commanded, taking her arm. 'And when we get there we'll put every last bit of coal we have on the fire, and sit so close to it we scorch!'

When the fire was blazing, Héloïse made Marie sit down in what had been Vendenoir's place, while she found the remains of his last bottle of wine, added some water to it, a little cinnamon, and the whole remaining lump of their sugar, and heated it over the fire. When it was steaming, she poured out a cup for each of them, and said, 'There, now, drink that! It will warm you through.'

'Madame, that was all of our sugar. It was very extravagant of you,' Marie demurred. Héloïse smiled.

'Never mind. I am feeling extravagant. Dear friend, I give you a toast: to the end of hardship, and to the good times to come! Marie, we are going to be merry from now on, and all your kindness to me will be rewarded, I promise you. Oh, don't look so shocked! Do you think I should be sad and sober because Vendenoir is dead?'

'Why – no, Madame –' Marie was evidently bewildered, at a loss to know what she should think. 'I suppose,' she said tentatively, 'there must be the usual period of mourning, now that you are a widow?'

Héloïse laughed, and shook her head. 'No, no mourning! Oh, Marie, Marie, would you have me play the hypocrite? Yes, I see you would – well, you must comfort yourself with the thought that Vendenoir has already had his due. I mourned him for a whole year the first time I was told he was dead, and I may be a wicked, heartless sinner, but I simply *will not* do it all again! One year was more than he deserved, and nothing in this world or the next will make me give him two!' She stood up and stretched out her arms and danced, while Marie tried very hard not to look disapproving. She had a conventional soul, which was warring with her usual propensity to think her mistress an angel who could do no wrong.

'Madame, what *are* we going to do? We'll have more money now that the master is gone, I suppose. Will we be able to move away from this house?'

'Oh yes, we will leave this place,' Héloïse said, pausing in her dance. 'We will pack our bags tonight – no, by St Anthony, we won't pack our bags, for what is there in this dismal house we could possibly want to take with us? I have a little money I kept back from the funeral – I shall pay them back, by the by, every penny, and more, too! – and that should be enough for our fare, if we go on the stage coach. And if it is not enough, well, we shall go as far as it takes us, and walk the rest!'

'But where, Madame? Where shall we go?' Marie asked anxiously, wondering if Héloïse was perhaps unbalanced by the shock of the last few days. Héloïse whirled again, and flung herself on her knees beside Marie and clasped her hand. Her upturned face, alight with joy and excitement, was like that of an impish child.

'Home, Marie! We are going home, to Morland Place in the County of Yorkshire, to my dear, dearest aunt Jemima, and my cousins, and Oxney and Mrs Mappin and the dear swans on the moat! Oh, I am so happy, I can hardly breathe, sweet Mother Mary forgive me! Tomorrow morning, Marie, and not an instant later, we are going to go home!'

The money was enough, but only just enough. The two women had to take outside seats on the stage, and the journey was long and bitterly cold. They had worn their warmest clothes, and packed all their other belongings in a cloak-bag (Marie having won her point, that it would be foolish to start out on a journey of two hundred miles with nothing), and at the first long bait, they had taken the opportunity to put on as many additional pieces of clothing as would fit under or over what they were wearing.

It would not be quite true to say that Héloïse was too happy to regard the cold, but her sufferings were greatly mitigated by the joy with which she looked forward to seeing Morland Place again. She dreamed and dozed and gazed forward eagerly for some landmark she might recognize, and long before they came within sight of the Hare and Heather, she expected every other traveller on the road to be a Morland.

When they finally drew up in front of the inn, where the coachman had agreed to put them down, she had no idea how cold her feet and legs were, and when she was jumped down, she staggered into the arms of the innkeeper's man, unable to feel her feet at all.

'Tha'd best coom into t' parlour and have a warm, miss,' the man suggested, eyeing them keenly, evidently not quite sure of their status, for while Héloïse's bearing was that of a lady, and Marie appeared to be her maid, there was no great distinction between their clothing, and they had undoubtedly travelled a long way on outside seats.

Héloïse, after stamping a few times, had discovered where her feet were in relation to the ground, and was eager to put them to use. 'No, I thank you. You are most kind, but we must be off at once. Come, Marie. Let me take the bag.'

'Oh no, Madame, I will carry it. It is not heavy. Have we far to walk?'

'I think not. As I remember, it is this way.'

They walked off, and the man watched them go, scratching his head with some perplexity. He had a nagging sense that he ought to have recognized them, and yet they had spoken to each other in Dutch or some such, and he was sure he did not know any foreigners. Oh, well, he supposed it would come to him some time, later in the day, when he was thinking about something quite different. That was the way it usually happened. He turned round to bellow at the boy, who like him had been staring at the foreigners, but with his mouth open. 'Hastow nothing better to do than gawp, tha great gowk? Tek 'old o' that box an' shift it round t'back, if tha wants any wages this week!' And he gave the boy a cuff on the side of the head to encourage virtue and industry, and felt the better for doing his duty by him.

It was a longer walk than Marie had bargained for, and her boots were not stout, but Héloïse walked as though her feet were not touching the ground. She did not remember the way in any detail, but she was sure she could walk straight to Morland Place if she were blindfold and put down a hundred miles off. They were on Morland land now, her heart sang. This was Morland grass and those were Morland trees, and –

Two horsemen had come into sight round the bend in the track. The second was a groom on a workmanlike hack, but the leading rider was mounted on a large and handsome long-eared bay, whose distinctive head had a rather curiously square muzzle.

'*Le nez carré,*' Héloïse whispered.

'Madame?' said Marie anxiously. Héloïse stopped and put down the bag which she had been taking a turn in carrying, but she seemed to do these things involuntarily. Her face was as white as paper, and her wide eyes were fixed on the riders who came cantering down on them, evidently expecting them to move out of the way. Then the bay horse was reined in so suddenly that he was forced onto his hocks in a half rear, and shook his head angrily and snorted as the chestnut almost ran into him. There was a moment of equine confusion, and then stillness. The rider on the bay horse took off his hat with a sleepwalker's movement, his face below the ruffled fox-dark hair as white as that of Héloïse.

'Is it you?' he said. 'Is it really you?'

'Yes, James. I have come home.'

He stared a moment longer, and then flung himself from the saddle, and ran to her, pulling the unwilling Nez Carré behind him, and she was enfolded in his arms, her small, thin body – oh so thin! – pressed against him. He cradled her against his chest and rested his cheek on her head, and closed his eyes, feeling tears of weak relief rising behind his closed lids.

93

'Oh my darling, my darling.'

Nez Carré pricked his ears and knuckered softly, and poked his long nose over James's shoulder to see what was happening. The tip of Héloïse's ear, pink in a black forest of hair, was the only part of her that was visible, and he nibbled it experimentally. Durban jumped down and took the reins from James, and looked on with a troubled frown.

At last Héloïse was released just sufficiently to look up at James. Her face was luminous with joy. She reached up and touched his cheek, and he caught her hand and put it to his lips, and then turned it over and kissed the palm. He had remembered it as it had been, a lady's hand; but he loved it now, bone-thin, calloused and work-stained, even more.

'Where have you been?' he managed to say. 'You are so thin and pale – oh, Héloïse, I thought I would never see you again! Why did you run away? Oh, my darling –'

'James, James,' she said exultantly. 'Oh, I can't believe I am here again, that it is really you! I have thought of you so often. When things were hard – ah, but there is no need to talk of that now. It is all over. I have come home, and now nothing can ever take me away again! Vendenoir is dead! He can never come between us again, and there is no-one else, nothing else –'

She stopped short as the joy in James's eyes was replaced by one of dawning horror, and the blood drained from her face in fear. 'James, what is it?'

His lips moved, but no sound passed them. He touched her face and hair distractedly, and then closed his eyes, and turned his face away in pain and helplessness.

'James, what is wrong?' she asked again. For answer he folded her again in his arms, pressed her so closely to him that she could hardly breathe, and then put her from him. His arms dropped to his sides in a gesture of finality.

'I'm married.'

She stared at him, unable to understand the words, her frightened brain pushing them away. His voice rose. 'Don't you hear me? I am a married man. I have a wife.' He made a violent gesture back along the path which made both horses jerk back their heads. 'Back there in Morland Place there is

94

a Mrs James Morland, my lawful wedded wife.'

Héloïse stared at him. 'It can't be true. It can't be.'

'It's true all right. God, God, the irony of it!' He clenched his fists and turned his face upwards to the grey sky. 'All my life! Oh God, what have I done?' He looked down at her, small and thin as a child, staring at him with those great, dark, sad-monkey eyes, and loved her so consumingly he thought he might just be used up there and then, burn to ash and be blown away on the wind. His brief anger of frustration passed, and left him with a hopeless sadness that was harder to bear, and harder for her to witness. 'My Héloïse, my Marmoset! Oh, why did you go away? That was cruel! I would never have tried to force you to do what was wrong. I could have helped you. You should not have suffered like this. Your poor hands! I would have kept you safe, and cared for you, and then, when he – when you were free –'

'I never thought,' she said in a voice so small he could hardly hear it, 'that you would marry anyone else. How foolish of me. I am so sorry, James. I – I wish you well.' She began to turn away, and he caught her wrist in panic.

'Where are you going?'

'Away. I must go away,' she said.

'No!' he shouted. She did not flinch, but looked up at him with an expression that tore him to pieces.

'There is no place for me here. You are married to some-one else –'

'I don't love her. I love you! You are my only love, you are my soul! Héloïse, you *must not* go away, please, *please*!'

She said nothing, but there was no slackening of resist-ance, and after a moment he loosened his fingers deliber-ately and let her go. When he spoke again, it was quietly, with a control that evidently cost him dearly.

'Please, Héloïse, don't go away. I cannot bear it again. I must know where you are, that you are all right, I must see you sometimes. Come with me to the house. I swear to you that nothing will be said or done to offend you. My wife –' he saw her move her head in pain at the words – 'my wife shall know nothing of our history. There will be no impro-priety.'

'By what right can I come with you?' she said in a low voice.

'Morland Place is your home,' he said desperately. 'You have no other. My mother is your aunt. You cannot disappoint Mama. Think how she would grieve if you went away again without seeing her. Please, Marmoset, come home. We will find some way to arrange things. Everything will be all right, I swear it, if only you don't go away again.'

She gave a little trembling sigh, and the resistance went out of her. She nodded, and his relief was visible. He reached out for her hand, to lead her, but she drew it back with a grave look, and an expression of bitterness crossed his face.

'Ah, yes, I understand,' he said. 'You refuse to touch me, now that I am a married man.'

'What else can I do?' she said. The dream was ended. She felt then that she had lived just five minutes too long.

96

Chapter Six

Jemima received Héloïse into her arms like a mother, kissed and hugged her, rejoiced that she was home, lamented over the evidence in her appearance of the hardship she had undergone, and only then became suddenly aware of the full implications of the situation. Her reactions were repeated over and over again as each member of the household, family and servants alike, first delighted in her presence, then recollected Mrs James, and finally determined that nothing in their behaviour would lead to her being forced to go away again.

Héloïse felt as though she were in a dream: everything seemed remote to her, seen and heard through a veil, slightly distorted. Morland Place was so familiar, but now suddenly was not home; James was not James; and here was a stranger, a tall, fair, composed, cool, very English young woman, who was James's wife. And how could that be? How could something so intimately a part of James, her James, be unknown to her? She tried to make sense of it, and shook her head like a dog shaking water from its ears. The anomaly was too great for her, weary as she was. She took the profferred hand dazedly, and spoke a few dis-jointed words.

Mary Ann received the introduction calmly. She saw a very small, very dark Frenchwoman, who was obviously suffering from the effects of a long journey; and, by the state of her clothes and skin and hair, and by the smell of her, from a longer exposure to poverty and want. The white, pinched face was gaunt and looked older than its years, but Mary Ann allowed that food and rest might improve her appearance, though she would never be better than plain, with that long nose and wide mouth.

Héloïse was introduced to her as the Lady Henrietta Louisa Stuart, Countess of Strathord, a distant cousin who had escaped the Revolution, and lost her father to the guillotine, and had now come, homeless and destitute, to Morland Place for refuge. The explanation was perfectly comprehensible and aroused her sympathies, but troubled her in no other way. If she noticed any tension in the air, it was only what was consistent with the excitement of the unexpected event.

When the first flurry of arrival was over, Jemima thought it prudent to remove Héloïse from the scene, and took her upstairs to her own bed chamber, the red room, giving orders for hot water and food to be sent; and there she undressed Héloïse like a child, and bathed her, and dressed her in one of her own bedgowns, and put her into her own bed. The food arrived, hot soup and bread and meat, and Jemima fed her tenderly as though she were an invalid, and insisted that she drank two glasses of claret, and then bid her lie down and sleep.

'I know it's early, but you are very tired, more tired than you know, perhaps,' she said. Héloïse looked up at her gratefully.

'Is not this your bed? Where will you sleep?'

'Over there,' Jemima said, indicating the small bed in the corner, 'where Louisa slept, when she and Mary shared this chamber. I shall be near if you wake in the night.'

Héloïse caught hold of her hand. 'Give me your blessing, *ma tante*,' she said.

'You used to call me your *nouvelle Maman*,' Jemima said, smiling, and then was sorry when she saw the stricken look in Héloïse's eyes.

'Oh, Maman, what shall I do? What will become of me?' Héloïse whispered. Jemima lifted her hand to her lips and kissed it.

'I don't know. Oh, child, I am so sorry things have happened this way. I would give anything in the world to make it all right for you, and for James.' She sighed, and then gave Héloïse back her hand, and smiled, and brushed the hair from her forehead. 'Sleep now, and try not to worry. Whatever happens, you aren't alone any more. We are your family, and you belong to us, and we'll work things out together, one way or another. But you must promise me you won't run away again. You can't think how I have

98

worried about you.'

'I'm sorry, Maman. I promise.' Her eyes were beginning to close, as her tired spirit longed for escape. 'Please – will you see that Marie is taken care of?' she murmured.

'Of course I will. Goodnight, my love. God bless you.'

There was so much to be learnt; so many things had changed. Madame de Chelmsford, that sweet kind lady, was dead; milord, who had been so devoted to her, had married again, and his new wife, who was younger than Héloïse, was already pregnant. There were more babies: Mary's Hippolyta had been expected when Héloïse had run away, but now Lucy was a mother too, hard though it was to imagine. Horatio and his wife Lady Barbara had two, Marcus and the new baby Barbarina, born in September; and James had a daughter.

That was hard to bear, harder still the pride in his voice when he spoke of her. So many new young lives to come between her and the world she had quitted, and hoped so hard to rejoin! Sometimes she felt like the hundred-year sleeper; at others as though she need only blink to restore things to the way they had been two and a half years ago.

She spent the first days in a kind of convalescence, sleeping long, doing little; eating a variety of delicate and nourishing dishes prepared with loving skill by Monsieur Barnard, who had clung to her hand weeping with joy when she went to the kitchen to be welcomed back; taking a little light exercise in the gardens, and resting long hours on the sofa, while various members of the family talked to her, asking questions and relating the news.

Marie was now quite herself again, and with Farleigh's help was happily making new dresses for Héloïse, having seen with grim satisfaction the contents of the cloak-bag removed and burnt. She sat near her mistress when she could, watching her anxiously, and keeping a cautious eye on Mrs James and her far more dangerous servant, the sharp-eyed Dakers. It was from that quarter she expected trouble, though quite what trouble she would have been hard put to it to define.

James and Héloïse spoke little to each other, each painfully aware of the dangers of the situation. He absented himself from the house frequently, though he could never stay away long. He wanted mostly to be near her, and often sat silently across the room from her, pretending to be absorbed in a book or a piece of work, but in reality simply looking at her covertly. When they did speak to each other, it was with a painful formality, for it would have been fatally easy to fall back into their old, easy familiarity. To give licence to his staring at her, he got out his sketching book and took her likeness, turning the page and beginning again as soon as he had finished a drawing; drawing her again and again with a kind of unappeasable hunger.

As her strength returned to her, Héloïse wanted to be more out of doors. She walked further afield with Jemima, soon leaving Mrs James behind, who was sedentary by nature; and it was the latter who finally suggested to James that he should take Lady Henrietta out riding, so that she could see what had changed about the estate.

'I would be glad to accompany you, except that I am no horsewoman,' she said to Héloïse, 'but as you do not leave Morland land, I am sure there can be no objection to your having no female companion. Mr James Morland is, after all, your cousin.'

Héloïse experienced a moment of panic: though she longed inexpressibly to be alone with James, she was afraid of the outcome. 'You are most kind, Madame, but I have no riding habit,' she said weakly, her accent growing stronger as her self-possession left her.

'Never mind,' Jemima said, 'I am sure we can do something for you with one of mine. Or I might find one of the girls' habits put away, from when they were children. I think you are about the same size that Lucy was when she was twelve.'

Upstairs, Héloïse protested anxiously, 'Maman, I do not think – I had better not – surely it is not wise for me to go alone with James?' Jemima patted her hand.

'My love, do you think I would encourage you to do what is wrong, or what would harm you? I think that you and James need a little time alone together to talk, where no-one can overhear you. I have watched you both these last few days, and I am very sure that unless you have that chance, you will both feel all your lives that there is unfinished business between you. There can be no harm in it, this once. Take your time, and say what has to be said.'

An hour later they left Morland Place, James on Nez Carré, and Héloïse on Goldfinch, the pony she was used to ride before. As soon as they were clear of the house, James put Nez Carré into a canter, and they rode fast and in silence for some time, until Goldfinch began to blow. They slowed to a walk and rode on, still without speaking, neither of them with any idea where they were going, until James found that they were at the edge of Marston Moor. Then he led the way up onto Cromwell's Plump, stopped, and jumped down.

'This will do as well as anywhere, don't you think?' he said, coming to Goldfinch's side to help Héloïse down. She looked at him, frowning a little, wondering whether he had forgotten that it was in this place years ago that they had first spoken of marriage. But then he gave her a rather crooked smile, and said, 'The horses just seemed to find their way here, didn't they?'

He helped her down, and pulled off Nez Carré's saddle blanket for her to sit on, as the grass was damp. She settled herself upon it, and he sat down beside her, close, but not touching.

It was a strange day, cool and still, the colourless sky a high pale blanket of cloud, stretching featureless from horizon to horizon. They were facing north, towards Wilstrop Wood, whose bare trees were pink-brown and wintry, their upper branches blurring into the sky, and even from this distance loud with rooks. Nearer to hand, a shepherd was folding a ewe-flock in the Moor Lane close; it was so still that his cries to his dogs rose small and clear, along with the tinkling of the bells, to where they sat. They watched as one of his brindled hounds frisked up to him and butted his hand with its muzzle, and was rebuked and sent away with an outflung hand, and a 'Gerraway back, you, Dog!': a tiny, faraway drama that seemed both ant-sized and important.

Nez Carré gave a long, groaning sigh, and shifted his weight from one side to the other, and took a negligent sideways snap at Goldfinch before settling to doze; and Héloïse said, 'She seems very nice, your wife. Very English and proper.'

'Very *comme il faut*?' James said mockingly. It had been a phrase she often used. 'I don't particularly want you to approve her, Marmoset. I care nothing about her.'

'Nice – that is a very English and proper word, too. Yes, she is nice, I think. How did you come to meet her?'

'Chetwyn was thinking of marrying her: she is an heiress, you see. But he married Lucy instead, and so she was – available.'

She turned her head to look at him, and he met her gaze without fear: the exchange so far had been so matter-of-fact that they might have been discussing the characters in a book they had both read. Now that she had gained a little more flesh and colour, she looked much more like her old self that he remembered; but the similarity was only skindeep. She was older and sadder, patient in a way he did not like to see – *patiens*, the Latin word, with its dual sense of suffering and bearing. But he did not feel separate from her, now that they were alone together. They were one person again; there was nothing he could not say to her; he could make no room in his mind for any thought of being apart from her.

She saw that curious happiness in him, and understood it, wordlessly, because just then she felt it too. This was a moment out of time, something that they would not be called to account for, something separate from the stream of real life with its actions and consequences, guilt and responsibility.

'Why did you marry her, James?' she asked.

'Why did you run away?' he countered. She shook her head.

'No, I am not meaning to speak of blame; only *why*? Why marry a woman that you cared nothing about? Why marry at all?'

'I thought you were gone for ever. I thought I would never see you again.'

102

'That is still not a reason,' she said.

'Morland Place needed an heir,' he said next. She continued to look at him steadily, and at last he shrugged. 'To spite you. To punish you. Yes, I think I did it to punish you. You went away with your husband; you did not love me enough.'

'What else could I have done? He *was* my husband.'

'That creature? What duty could you owe him?'

'The same I would have owed you, if we had been married. Right is right for all, James, one cannot choose.'

'And what of love?'

'Ah, love,' she said. Her dark eyes were sad. 'The law we live by takes no account of love.'

He smiled painfully. 'I love the way you pronounce "law". Oh my darling, I do love you so much! It isn't fair – it isn't fair!'

'Oh, as to that,' she shrugged, 'no-one ever promised it would be.' She thought a moment, and then said, 'Me, I do not think you married this nice girl to punish me. I think you did it to punish yourself.'

He sighed, and took her hand, and she did not prevent him. The narrow, small-fingered hand rested in his and grew warm, and they were silent a while, their thoughts not touching, but close.

'I am nineteen years old,' she said after a while, 'and I have been twice an orphan and twice a widow, I have been rich and I have been poor, I have been a governess and a countess. This is a great deal for so few years, is it not? *Tiens*, think what I may do if I live to be eighty! And almost I have been married twice – in my heart, my James, *quite* twice, because, Our Lord forgive me, I loved you like my husband all the time I was with Vendenoir. Perhaps that is why I am being punished,' she added musingly.

'I don't believe that. I don't believe –' He didn't finish.

'All our lives – that's what Maman said, that we must say everything to each other now, or all our lives we would feel we had been cheated. But that frightens me so much James – those words! To be apart from you all the rest of my life –' She shook her head in dread, and he looked at her with alarm.

103

'What do you mean to do? I know you – you are plotting something bad! What is it?'

'I must go away,' she said simply. 'I cannot live here at Morland Place with you and your wife and child – *ça se voit*. It is impossible.'

'But where do you think you can go?' he asked her desperately.

'Oh, as to that, I am a rich woman, you know. Cousin Charles has my money safe for me in the Funds, Maman told me, and a great deal of furniture that Papa sent from France before he – before they –' She stopped and started again. 'I am very interested to see what there is. I hope some things from my own house in Paris. But at all events, I am sure there must be enough for me to live on, and so I shall find a little house, and Marie and I will live there quietly and be very –' She stopped again, and had to bite her treacherous lip to stop it quivering, and went on in a small voice, 'I am quite determined I shall not cry. There is not the least need.'

'Have you finished?' James asked. She nodded. 'Good, because you are talking the greatest nonsense! Go away – find a little house – nonsense!'

'What else can you suggest?' she asked quietly. He looked at her despairingly, holding her hand in both of his.

'I don't know. Damn it, I don't know.'

'There is nothing else to do, James, you know it. I must go away. But we shall each know that the other is safe and well, and perhaps, perhaps sometimes we might see each other, at some party or public gathering where it is safe. It is all we can do, *mon âme*. It is all there is.'

James felt himself crying, and one part of his mind was astonished, that it was so easy, and that it eased nothing. 'I know,' he said. 'That's what's so unfair.'

Héloïse's return to London was very different from her quitting of it. A letter from Jemima to Charles recounting her arrival at Morland Place elicited a reply which spoke of his great joy and relief at the news, assured her that her financial affairs had been well looked after by him, and invited her to come as soon as she liked to Chelmsford House. He and Roberta were staying in London all winter.

Spain, alarmed at the conquest of Italy by the French general Buonaparte, had joined the war on France's side, and with Austria beaten to her knees, England was left without an ally. The Mediterranean was virtually a French lake; Ireland was in ferment, and it was feared that the French were planning an invasion of England by way of her convenient shores. With matters standing thus, Charles said, it was impossible for him to leave the capital, even had Roberta's delicate condition not made it wiser for them not to travel.

Héloïse travelled up to London post in great comfort, and was received not only deferentially but almost tearfully by the magnificent Hawkins in the great hall of Chelmsford House. She had barely had time to look about her, when cousin Charles arrived, took both her hands, muttered something incoherent, and embraced her warmly.

'Thank God you are safe! Thank God you are come home!' was all he could say for quite a while. Later she sat in the blue saloon, looking round with satisfaction at the furnishings and pictures she remembered so well, and which had not been changed by the new mistress, telling her story to Charles while the new mistress listened in absorbed silence.

Though Héloïse had been as amazed as everyone else at the news that Charles, who had loved Flora wholeheartedly, had married again so soon, she liked the new Lady Chelmsford immediately. Madame, she saw, was almost frivolously pretty on the outside, but very plain and sensible on the inside, the sort of young woman who would make a good housewife if forced to live on a restricted income, who would find ways to dress herself prettily out of whatever came to hand, and who would cope without fuss with any emergency which arose. She was also, evidently, very much in love with Monsieur le Comte, which pleased Héloïse, for though it was perfectly respectable and praiseworthy for a young woman to make the best match she could in worldly terms, Héloïse had suffered enough misery in her own marriage to wish everyone to marry for love if they could.

It was harder to gauge Charles's feelings. He seemed to Héloïse to have aged ten years since she last saw him. His face was heavily lined, and his bearing and movements were no longer those of a young man. When he spoke to or looked at his young wife, his expression softened with affection; but he seemed more often absent in mind, and then his features settled into lines of sadness.

When her tale was told, it was Roberta who spoke.

'What will you do now?' she asked. 'I don't mean immediately – I hope you will consider Chelmsford House as your home for the present, and stay as long as you need to. But for the future?'

'I thought that I should like to get myself a small house – something comfortable, and just big enough for Marie and me, and to have room for a friend or two to come and stay,' Héloïse said. 'Have I enough money for that, cousin Charles?'

Charles smiled. 'I think you will find your income enough to live on comfortably for the rest of your life, provided you are sensible. A great deal of money came through from your father by various routes, and I have it all safely invested in the Funds for you; quite apart from the furniture. You will want a house in London, I suppose?'

'No, cousin, I think not. London has unhappy memories for me, and though I shall always think of you with gratitude and affection, I think I should wish to be near my aunt Jemima. I should like a house in Yorkshire.'

Roberta looked at Charles. 'My lord, Shawes is without a tenant at the moment. Would you not consider letting Shawes to Lady Strathord? It is always better for a house to be inhabited.'

Héloïse did not wait for Charles to answer. 'Oh, but Shawes is a great deal too big for one person, Madame, and also, I think too close to Morland Place. I should wish to be near, but not too near.'

Roberta nodded. 'Yes, I understand. Well, until you are settled, I hope you will stay here, and be comfortable. You must have a great deal of shopping to do.'

'Yes, do stay,' Charles said, 'and I will have my agent look about for something suitable for you in Yorkshire. And now, my dear cousin, I am sure you would like to see the furniture I have been keeping for you. My dear,' to his wife, 'there is no occasion for you to stir. We shall rejoin you shortly.'

It was all stored in one of the rarely-used bedrooms at the far end of the house, and when Charles unlocked the door, Héloïse could only stare in silence.

'I hope you will find it has not suffered too much from its long journey and longer confinement,' Charles said. 'It came under licence from the French Ministry of the Interior, and by a very roundabout route. I suppose your father had contacts within the ministry?'

'He was employed by it, to auction the royal treasures,' Héloïse said. 'Some of these things must be from the auctions – those chairs, for instance, I do not recognize them. Oh, but there is my bed, my own bed from my house in Paris! And the chaise-longue from my boudoir – how sadly the brocade is stained! And, oh, cousin Charles, my *bonheur-du-jour*, with the Sèvres medallions!'

'Oh yes, the writing-desk,' Charles said with interest. 'It is a very handsome piece.'

'It also was in my private room. Papa bought it from one of the dukes he helped to escape. It was made for the Queen, when she was expected to visit, but she never came. Oh, how many times have I sat there to write a letter, or my journal!' She ran a loving hand over its surface.

Charles snapped his fingers and exclaimed, 'Good God, what a terrible thing! I had quite forgot – my dear, there is a letter which came with the furniture, I suppose from your father. I put it in the drawer of the desk for safety. Wait, let me get it for you. You must forgive me for not remembering it sooner.'

He placed the letter in her hand. Héloïse looked down at it, her face very pale. It was Papa's handwriting, though the direction was hastily scrawled, and the outer wrapping, sealed several times, was much stained from its long and tortuous journey. With unsteady fingers she opened it, and read his last words to her. He had died on the guillotine almost four years ago.

'My dearest little girl, my Marmoset,' it said, 'they are

coming to arrest me – I expect them every moment. Forgive me, child, but I am grown too tired to run any longer. I don't doubt that when they take me, it will be the end, but I find at the last that I am a Frenchman, and I cannot face the thought of being uprooted. You are young enough to begin again in another country, though it may be hard, for I know how tenacious your heart is, and how you will mourn France. I hope this letter may reach you; if it is taken, I hope those who intercept it will have pity, and not prevent a father from taking his last farewell of his child. God bless you, Marmoset, my only treasure. I wish you happiness always. Remember me.'

She looked up, her vision blurred by tears, and in that moment her father seemed very close to her, and she remembered his face and his voice as clearly as if she had parted from him only yesterday. Cousin Charles was speaking to her, but she could not distinguish his words, and at last he had to put his arm around her shoulders and lead her away.

A visit to Upper Grosvenor Street was paid on the following day, and Héloïse received more embraces, told her story again, and was invited by the open-hearted Lucy to make her home permanently with the Aylesburys.

'We already have Mary and her baby, and one more won't be any trouble. Do, if you would like it! It would be very good fun.'

Héloïse explained again her intention to take a small house in Yorkshire. Mrs Haworth only looked her concern, but Lucy voiced it.

'Is that wise? I mean – forgive me, cousin – but, would it not be better for both of you if you were out of temptation's way?'

'Dear Lucy, ever tactful,' Charles murmured, and Lucy looked rebellious.

'We are all family – and Héloïse knows I'm only concerned for her.'

'Of course,' Héloïse agreed. 'But I wish to be near enough to my aunt Jemima for her to visit me – I do not think it would be wise for me to visit often at Morland Place. She is like a mother to me now, you see,' she explained anxiously.

'But you will be very lonely, living all alone in Yorkshire,' Lucy went on. 'For I don't suppose Mother will be able to visit you every week, with all she has to do on the estate. How will you occupy your time? You will be bored, too, with nothing to do, when you have been used to working.'

'I have considered that,' Héloïse said, 'and I thought I might occupy myself with writing a history of the revolution in Paris. I was at the centre of things, you know, and Papa explained things to me that perhaps are not generally known. I think it might interest people to know what really happened.'

'Excellent idea,' Mary said enthusiastically. 'There are several memoirs about at the moment, but most of them seem to have been written by people who left before the most important events, or who had only the vaguest idea of why they were happening. I should very much like to read what you write, cousin.'

Héloïse smiled. 'And perhaps I may ask you to correct my English when it is done, for I do not yet speak it perfectly, I think.'

'Well, if you are determined to go to Yorkshire, I suppose we must make the best of it,' Lucy said. 'But there is no need for you to hurry away. You must have enough things to do in London to keep you until the Season begins, and then you won't want to go away. There is no need to go to Yorkshire until the summer, I'm sure.'

'If you do not go until the summer,' Roberta said in her soft voice, 'perhaps my lord and I might go to Shawes, and then you might stay with us until you find the house you like.'

Shortly after Héloïse's arrival, the Chelmsford household received another addition, when Flora's son Jack arrived in London. His stepfather greeted him affectionately.

'But to what do we owe this visit, my boy? Not that we

aren't delighted to see you, of course, but I wonder the navy can spare you at a moment like this.'

'I hope it won't have to spare me for long, sir. I came in the dispatch boat from Cadiz on Admiral Harvey's recommendation. I'm pleased to be able to tell you that I have passed my lieutenant's exam, and I have a letter from him to Their Lordships which I hope will see me made, as soon as there is a vacancy.'

'Well, that is excellent news indeed!' Charles said. 'But I confess myself a little puzzled. I'm not an expert on naval matters, but I could not be married to your mother for so long without knowing one or two things. Am I not correct in thinking that one needs service of six years to become a lieutenant?'

'That's right, sir – six years at sea, of which two must be as midshipman,' Jack said cheerfully.

'And you went to sea in – '93, was it?'

'Right again, sir, but my mother had the foresight to acquire me some book-time: I was on Admiral Harvey's books long before I went to sea – I was rated A.B. in 1790. I have all my certificates here, all in order.'

Charles smiled drily. 'And I presume you will have thought of a way round the other requirement?'

'Oh yes, sir – as to that, there is not the least difficulty in acquiring a false birth certificate,' said Jack. 'Half a crown to the porter at the Admiralty will do it. Their Lordships know all about it, of course, but they never enquire too closely, for they all have sons and nephews doing the same thing. Why, I've heard of lads of twelve who have gone up with certificates saying they are twenty! At least I'm only two years short.'

Charles lifted his hands. 'My dear boy, I was not implying a criticism. Your ambition does you credit, and I'm sure the navy will not be the loser by your promotion. But is not Harry with you? I always thought you two were inseparable.'

Jack's face clouded. 'That's the one drawback, sir. Harry and I have always done things together, and I hoped we always would – at least until we were both made post. And Harry is every bit as good a seaman as I am – better at mathematics perhaps. But he hasn't got the service. Mama did not have him put on the books, of course, and Bloody Bill – the Cap'n, I mean, sir, I beg your pardon – is too strait-laced to bend the rules, even for his own brother. He – the Cap'n I mean – did it all by the book when he was a mid, and he don't mean to help anyone else do it any other way.'

'That's a great pity for Harry,' Charles said. 'It will put him two years or more behind you.'

'Yes, sir. He won't have his six years until February '99,' said Jack, frowning. 'The worst of it is, it caused bad feeling between us. We didn't exactly quarrel, but we parted coldly, and I'd almost sooner not be made than have a falling-out with Harry.'

'Almost, but not quite,' Charles observed. Jack smiled unwillingly.

'That's the size of it, sir. Harry thought I ought to hold back on his account, so that we could stay together, but – well, sir, who knows what might happen? If I refused Admiral Harvey's help now, he might not offer it again, or he might be killed, or – or *anything*! I couldn't turn down the chance of being made, not even for Harry. But I wish with all my heart he had not taken it so hard.'

'You did the right thing, I'm sure,' Charles comforted him. 'Harry will come to see that, too, when he has got over his disappointment. I dare say he's already wishing he had parted with you more kindly.'

'I hope you're right, sir,' said Jack. 'He's like a brother to me.'

He had plenty to say about conditions in the navy, which interested everyone, but Charles in particular.

'Discipline's fallen off badly, ever since the Quota Act,' he told them over dinner. 'Of course, I know that with the blockade war the press wasn't raising enough men, but the quota-men are of the worst sort. The magistrates use the Quota to get rid of poachers and vagrants and petty-thieves, and even they, if they can find a man worse off than them-selves, can put in a substitute.'

'You can hardly expect seamen from a conscription policy,' Charles pointed out.

111

'No, of course not – but these are the dregs of society, good for nothing but to make trouble. The older jacks don't like the service being filled up with gallows-fodder, sir – they think it an insult. And then there's the bounty: quota-men are getting bounties of seventy pounds a head, though they're only landmen, and many of them are only volunteering to avoid going to gaol; whereas seasoned seamen who volunteered in '93 only got five pounds a head.'

'That does seem hard.'

'I'm afraid there may be trouble over it,' Jack said. 'These quota-men may be worthless, but your true jack's a good man, and he's not being treated fairly, in my view. Conditions on the lower deck are bad enough – well, there may not be much we can do about that, and they're tough enough to stand it – but they don't like to be cheated of their rations, which they often are, or their pay. Did you know the last time the men's pay was raised was during the Commonwealth? That's a hundred and forty years ago!'

'These are rather republican ideas you're espousing, aren't they?' Charles said, and Jack blushed with vexation.

'Good God, no, sir! It's just that I don't like to see gaol-rats treated better than decent, honest seamen.'

'Well, your ideas are very interesting, at all events,' Charles said, 'and I shall see if we can't make the opportunity for you to repeat them to one or two influential people. Though perhaps,' he added with a smile, 'as you have a letter from Admiral Harvey, you may be in the way to meet more influential people than I can introduce you to.'

Admiral Harvey's letter of recommendation was not ignored, and before the end of December Jack was given his commission into the *Excellent*, 74, commanded by Harvey's old friend Cuthbert Collingwood. The first thing Jack did was to write to Harry, a letter speaking such natural joy at his good fortune and such frank and affectionate regret at Harry's lack of it, that Charles, asked to read it over before franking it, thought it must surely heal the breach.

Jack was naturally anxious to take up his commission at the earliest possible moment, but when he received his orders for the *Harrier*, a 16-gun brig which would be taking dispatches to the fleet early in January, he felt secure enough of his future to enjoy the Christmas season festivities to the utmost. Town was unusually full, for a number of people, like the Chelmsfords, had stayed up that year, so there was plenty for him to enjoy. He was young, handsome, and in great good spirits, and popular both with the hostesses and with their unmarried female guests, which caused Charles to remark to his wife that it was perhaps a good thing that Jack was going back to sea so soon. On the day before Epiphany he packed his sea-chest, bid everyone an affectionate goodbye, and strode off to catch the Portsmouth mail, his eyes bright with anticipation of the glorious career he had no doubt was ahead of him.

Chapter Seven

Lady Chelmsford was safely delivered on the fifteenth of February of a son, who was given the name of Robert. It was a terrible blow to Horatio, who felt that as Charles had been so wantonly selfish as to marry again and breed, his wife might at least have had the courtesy to produce a daughter and die in childbirth. The couple however seemed lost to all decency, and made a tasteless parade of their happiness and pride when he called to inspect the infant. It was, without doubt, a boy, a pretty baby, and apparently healthy. Horatio brought home nothing on which to pin hope but a report of the child's smallness.

'But you know, my dear, even healthy children can be carried off,' he reminded Lady Barbara, 'and it is but one life between our little Marcus and what is rightfully his.'

Lady Barbara was not comforted. ' That would be well enough, if we could be sure it would *remain* one life. But now they have begun, who is to say when they will leave off? There will be a string of little ones before we can look around, and then what shall we do? We can barely make ends meet as it is, and as Marcus grows, the expense of launching him in the world will be phenomenal, to say nothing of Barbarina's dowry.'

'It is an awkward business all around,' Horatio agreed with a sigh, and wondered what a gentleman of taste and indolence could do to acquire large sums of money. In former times, of course, a Court sinecure would have filled the gap nicely between reality and expectation; but the King lived as frugally as a German baker, and the Prince of Wales was so far in debt that most of his servants had not been paid for several years. Trade or business of any kind was of course out of the question; gambling was too uncertain, and he had in any case no taste for it; and he had already married as many rich heiresses as the law allowed.

Promotion to colonel would help a great deal – there were a number of ways in which a colonel could make money out of his company – but promotion within a regiment which saw no active service was problematical.

'If I transferred into another regiment,' he mused hesitantly, and his wife raised her eyebrows in surprise. 'I know it is an extreme remedy, but if I were in a regiment on active service, there would be far more chance of promotion, and then, you know, if I acquitted myself so as to win great glory, I might receive a peerage, not to say a pension, and we might bite our thumbs at the Chelmsford title.'

Lady Barbara had never in her life done anything so vulgar as biting her thumb, but she thought there was something in the idea all the same. 'We might hold it in reserve,' she said, 'in case the infant survives.'

While Lady Chelmsford was still confined to her bed, news came in of a great naval battle which had been fought at Cape St Vincent on the very day of little Robert's birth. The French fleet had attempted invasion via Ireland's Bantry Bay late in December, but contrary winds had prevented the landing and driven the ships back to Brest. In January they had been ordered to join with the Spanish and Dutch fleets to make a combined force powerful enough to hold the Channel against the English while a French army was taken across.

The English fleet under Admiral 'Johnny' Jervis, numbering only fifteen of the line, intercepted the Spanish fleet of twenty-seven on its way to the *rendezvous*, at Cape St Vincent. The Spaniards were so spread out and straggling that Jervis was able to order his ships to pass through the enemy line and engage the main section of eighteen ships without interference from the rest.

The action was distinguished by the ingenuity of the young captain Nelson of the *Captain*, 74, who, ignoring precedent, left his station to attack the Spanish flagship, the monstrous 140-gun *Santisma Trinidad.* He was joined by Captain Collingwood and the *Excellent*, and their action

115

slowed down the Spanish fleet and gave the rest of the English ships time to rejoin the battle.

It was a notable victory for Jervis. Four Spanish ships were captured, ten badly damaged, and the survivors forced to flee to Cadiz, where Jervis was able to blockade them in, preventing them from joining up with the Brest fleet and thus ending the threat of invasion. All of London was talking about it, and it was soon known that Jervis was to receive an earldom and Nelson a knighthood; and Horatio thought gloomily that he ought to have joined the navy instead of the army.

He was reading the full account of the battle in the newspaper at his club, The Cocoa-Tree, when his eye was caught by a familiar name in the column at the far right. He read, and his face grew grave. He thought for a long time, and then came to a decision, folded up the paper, called for his hat, and set out to walk the short distance to Chelmsford House.

Charles received him in his business-room, and noticed that Horatio's manner was unusually subdued and hesitant. 'To what do I owe this pleasure?' he asked cheerfully. 'I did not know you were in the habit of paying morning calls, my dear brother.'

'I wondered if you had seen the paper,' Horatio replied. 'The full report of the naval battle is here –'

'Ah yes, our notable victory,' Charles smiled. 'Roberta is determined that when we christen our son and heir, we should give him the second name of St Vincent. What do you think of that, Horace? It has a fine, patriotic ring, has it not?'

It was obvious to Horatio from this that Charles had not read the full report. He offered him the folded paper, and indicated the last paragraph in silence. It was the customary list of officers and men killed and wounded, listed by ship. Under the name *Excellent* was written:

'Lieutenant J. Morland, Midshipman P. Perkins, and Able Seaman J. Oliver killed. No officers and ten seamen wounded, none seriously.'

'I'm so sorry,' Horatio said at length, 'I know how highly you thought of him.'

116

Charles could only nod, seeing in his mind's eye the cheerful boy who had set off so hopefully only six week ago.

Cuthbert Collingwood wrote a letter of condolence to Charles.

'Lieutenant Morland was at his station on the lower gun deck at the height of the engagement with the *Santisma Trinidad*, when an enemy shot entered through a gun-port, killing him instantly, along with the midshipman of his division who was standing beside him, and the seaman gun-layer.

'Although Mr Morland had been with us only a few weeks, he had already proved his worth as an active and efficient officer. He was trusted and respected by the men, and his open and cheerful temper made him a favourite in the wardroom. He is a great loss to the Service.'

Charles read the letter out loud to Héloïse and Roberta, and then stared at it in silence for a long time, before looking up to encounter their grave eyes.

'I shall have to write to Harry,' he said.

They nodded, imagining the difficulty of the task, and what Harry would feel on receipt of such a letter.

Charles tried, unsuccessfully, to smile for them. 'Since time began, young men have been dying in battle. It is a universal, perennial tragedy.'

'One knows that,' Héloïse said, 'but it does not seem to make any difference. Each death is the only one.'

He nodded gratefully, and looked down at the paper again. 'A letter of condolence: not much to shew for the whole of his life.' And it seemed just then that Flora was a little more lost to him.

'The Countess of Aylesbury, my lady,' Hawkins announced, stepping aside as the whirlwind that was Lucy dashed past him into the blue saloon where Héloïse and Roberta were sitting working one bright spring morning. Lucy was wearing a cream-coloured box-coat of felted wool, with four shoulder capes, just like a man's, and carrying large driving-gauntlets and a whip.

'From which I conclude that you are driving yourself this morning,' Roberta observed.

'Yes, in my curricle; and I must ask your indulgence, Lady Chelmsford, and steal cousin Héloïse from you, to come shopping with me to Bond Street. I have to go and interview my mantuamaker, that odious woman, and she always bullies me if I go alone. I would have taken Mary, but she will not step outside the house.'

'She is not ill?' Roberta asked in alarm. Lucy grinned impishly .

'Not the least bit – unless you count being love-sick! The truth of it is she is expecting every moment to hear from Captain Haworth that he is come in to Portsmouth, and she does not want to leave the house in case the message comes when she is out. Lord! I never thought to see my sister acting so foolish, and all over her husband, too!'

'The *Cressy*'s commission is ended, I collect?' Roberta enquired.

'Some months ago, I believe, but it was not possible for her to leave her station until now,' Lucy replied. 'Polly will be hoping Captain Haworth does not get another ship for months, and he will be hoping quite the opposite! It's a foolish thing indeed to fall in love with a sailor! But will you come, Héloïse? I know how fierce you are with drapers and silk-merchants, and I absolutely must have your protection against Madame Genoux. If you will only speak to her in French she will melt away and be as nice as sugar-plums, but if I go alone she will make me buy something hideous. And you shall have a turn in the park afterwards, by way of a reward.'

'Of course I will come,' said Héloïse, jumping up at once. 'If you will wait while I put on my hat.'

'I would never have thought to see you so meek,' Roberta laughed. 'I was always told how strong-minded and care-for-nothing you were.'

Lucy made a face. 'Not where Madame Genoux is concerned. And I shall have to tell her about my expectations, and that will make her completely overpowering, unless I have Héloïse there to distract her.'

'Your expectations?' Roberta asked at once, with

118

interest, Lucy raised her eyebrows.

'Oh, did you not know? I made sure Chetwyn would have told Charles. Yes, it is quite certain now – I expect to be confined in October.'

'You take it so calmly,' Roberta said. 'Are you not pleased?'

Lucy shrugged. 'Oh, there is nothing to it. If I get a boy this time I shall be pleased, that's all.'

Roberta shook her head wonderingly. 'You are so strange,' she said. Lucy laughed.

'I think the same about you, cousin. Ah, here she is! Now we can go. Can I do anything for you in Bond Street?'

'How well you drive,' Héloïse remarked as Lucy swung the curricle round the end of St James's Square, sliding it between a parked removers' dray and an oncoming hackney.

Lucy grinned. 'Do you think so? I'm glad. Mary says my driving makes her sick, and Docwra says it's improper while I'm in a delicate condition. By which I suppose she means it's dangerous. I can never bring anyone to understand that there isn't the least likelihood of my overturning my rig – anyone but Parslow, that is. He trusts me implicitly, which ought to be recommendation enough for anyone,' she added, throwing a glance over her shoulder at her wooden-faced groom, who was perched on his little seat between the rear wheels as impassively as Hawkins standing in the great hall of Chelmsford House.

'Indeed, I feel perfectly safe,' Héloïse declared. 'I suppose you had a good teacher at Morland Place – I mean, your Mama?'

'Oh, everyone had a hand in teaching me,' Lucy said lightly. 'Ned and Mother taught me the basic skills, and Jamie taught me the refinements; but I have outstripped them all. By the by,' she added, quite unconscious of any effect she might be having, 'I still have your ponies, you know.'

'My ponies?' Héloïse repeated, genuinely puzzled.

'Your cream ponies, that Jamie gave you, to go with the phaeton. *He* has that, at Morland Place, put away some-where I believe; but he was going to turn the ponies out, and I said it would be a shocking thing to waste them, when we had put so much work into their schooling. So he gave them

119

to me; but of course they are yours, really, and as soon as you are settled, I will have them sent back to you.'

Héloïse was distressed, and could not speak; but after a moment she regained control of herself, and said, 'I thank you, cousin; but I do not think my establishment will run to the setting up of a stable. I shall have to live quite simply, you know. It will be better for you to keep them.'

'Oh, you will change your mind,' Lucy said, frowning with concentration as she edged her pair past a coster-monger's cart and a barrel-organ. 'Sure you must have some means of getting about, and it don't cost much to keep a pair of ponies.'

Héloïse said no more, though she was perfectly sure that Lucy knew far less about the cost of keeping horses even than she did.

While Parslow held the chestnuts outside the shop in Bond Street, and Lucy conducted her business inside, Héloïse performed her task of deflecting the attention of Madame Genoux with conversation in her native language, and remembered the way she had similarly served her friend Lotti by occupying the nurse while Lotti played with her baby Mathilde. Lucy reminded her a little of Lotti, in her high spirits and rejection of convention; though Lucy was much cleverer than Lotti had ever been, and had also a vein of seriousness that had been lacking in the girl from Leipzig.

Héloïse wondered again, as she had wondered many times, what had become of Lotti's children, Mathilde and Karellie, and whether she would ever see them again. She had promised Lotti she would take care of them if anything happened to her: how poorly she had kept that promise! When the war was over, she must ask Charles's help to travel to Germany and find the children, and make sure they were all right.

They emerged again into Bond Street, and before they had time to exchange a word, a gentleman just that moment passing stopped at the sight of them, lifted his hat, and bowed. Héloïse did not know him, and looked at Lucy, to discover to her surprise that Lucy's cheeks had taken on a warm glow, and her eyes an unusual brightness.

'Why, Weston, what a pleasant surprise. What do you here?'

'What does anyone do in Bond Street, but waste their time in an agreeable manner?' the gentleman replied with a charming smile, and a graceful gesture towards the other loungers who filled the street. 'I might ask your ladyship the same question.'

'Indeed, I have been properly employed ordering gowns, and not enjoying myself at all,' Lucy said. 'But I must make you known to my cousin. Héloïse, let me present Lieutenant Weston – Weston, my cousin Lady Henrietta Stuart.'

Héloïse made her curtsey, scanned Weston's face rapidly, and came to a number of rather puzzling conclusions.

'But where do you go now, ladies? May I have the honour of escorting you somewhere?' Weston asked as he straightened up.

'I was just going to take Héloïse for a drive in the park, to make up for having to talk to my mantuamaker for almost an hour,' Lucy said, her voice rich with a regret she was quite unconscious of revealing.

Héloïse touched her arm. 'But I was just about to say, when Mr Weston spoke to you, that my conversation with your Madame Genoux reminds me I have not yet visited my old friend, Madame Chouflon. It is a visit I ought to pay at once, without delay, and I was on the point of asking you to excuse me from accompanying you to the park, so that I may drive out to Chelsea before dinner.'

'Oh, then I must drive you home again,' Lucy said at once, and Héloïse, carefully not looking at Weston said, 'But no, that is not at all necessary: I can so easily take a chair to Chelmsford House. I am sure you wish to exercise your horses, and it is not worth changing your plan only for that.'

'If you're sure,' Lucy said doubtfully, but her eyes went irresistibly to Weston's. 'It would be a shame not to take them round a time or two, on such a fine day.'

The arrival of a smart town chariot with the Chelmsford arms on its side panels caused a considerable stir in Sydney

Street when it drew up in front of the house of Madame Chouflon, and those wise in the ways of the rich expressed surprise that a lady should visit her mantuamaker rather than send for her. When the footman let down the steps and a daintily-shod foot appeared, two urchins struggled briefly for the right to lay a meagre body over the wheel to protect her skirts from its muddy contamination, and Héloïse felt all the pleasure of being able to bestow a coin where it was sure of doing good.

Madame Chouflon's upper servant opened the door with a promptness that suggested she had been lurking behind it, but the sight of a lady in a hat decorated with wax cherries and a smart cherry-coloured pelisse, rendered her speechless. Héloïse smiled and urged her gently backwards so as to gain admittance into the hall.

'Come now, Elise, close your mouth and find your wits. Don't you know me?' she said in French. Elise gaped a moment longer, and then her face cleared and she dropped a series of rapid curtsies and exclaimed, 'Oh, Madame Vendenoir, I beg your pardon. I did not recognize you; and seeing the coach, I thought you must be the doctor'

'That is worse than foolish,' Héloïse said. 'Don't you see it isn't a doctor's coach? But do you expect him? Is someone ill?'

'No, Madame, not precisely – it is Madame's old trouble, only come on worse these last weeks.'

'Is she in her room?'

'Yes, Madame. Will you go up?'

Héloïse ran up the stairs, knocked, and entered Flon's room, to find her old friend in bed, with a heavy shawl about her shoulders. A meagre fire burned in the grate, and the room felt cheerless and a little damp. Héloïse crossed the room and took Flon's hands, and kissed her cheek, noticing the unnatural moistness of the skin and the parched look of her lips.

'My dear, dearest Flon, what is this? But you are ill! You have the fever. And what a wretched fire!'

'Héloïse, my dear!' Flon cried. 'How glad I am to see you – and looking so well and so prosperous! A new hat and pelisse – my dear, you have come into money. Oh, I am so

122

glad for you. Tell me everything. Has all gone well with you since we last met?'

'First,' Héloïse said sternly, 'you shall tell me why I find you here ill in bed with such a poor fire. Why have you not called Elise to have it made up? Why is the scuttle empty?'

Flon managed a shrug. 'The old trouble in my hands, my dear, has meant I have not been able to complete my orders. My customers have gone elsewhere.'

'You mean you have no money?'

'Oh, it is a temporary state, I assure you, little one. Don't look so troubled. Old Flon has survived many a worse setback. When the fever is gone and the hands loosened up, I shall soon be back to work.'

Héloïse sat down and gazed at her remorsefully. 'I blame myself very much for not visiting you sooner. My dear friend, how have I repaid your kindness? I should have come weeks ago. And owing you money as I do!'

'There is no debt between friends,' Madame Chouflon said. 'The money was given to you, not lent. None of us expected a return – don't forget, it was not I alone who gave.'

'I know who gave the greater part,' Héloïse countered, and rang the bell for the servant.

'Elise, are there more coals in the house?'

'No, Madame,' Elise said, throwing a scared glance at her mistress. 'I used the last this morning, and there was no money to –'

'That will do, Elise,' Flon said hastily. Héloïse drew out her purse and gave some coins to the servant, who gawped at them.

'Take this, and give it to my footman, and tell him to go at once to the nearest coal-merchant, and bring back whatever quantity is convenient to carry, and place an order to be delivered as soon as possible. When he returns, bring the coals up and make up the fire.'

'Yes, Madame.'

When Elise had gone, Héloïse slipped the purse under Flon's pillows. 'That's for now,' she said, 'and there will be more for as long as you need it.' Madame tried to protest, but Héloïse stopped her. 'Is it permissible for me to be helped, and you not? Am I to let my friend starve of cold and hunger after all her kindness to me? For shame, Madame.'

Madame argued no more, only pressed Héloïse's hand gratefully with her stiff and painful one. 'Now, my dear,' she said at last, 'tell me everything that has happened to you, and how you come back to me looking as I have always wanted to see you. Though,' she added with a critical frown, 'the seams on that pelisse are not all that they ought to be.'

Héloïse told her news, the good and the bad, about going home, and James, and her fortune, and her furniture. 'So I shall have enough to live upon comfortably now,' she concluded.

'What will you do?' Flon asked, when she had digested all this.

'I think of taking a house somewhere up in Yorkshire. It is lovely country, Flon – you can have no idea!'

'It is very far away,' Madame said sadly, and Héloïse's face lit up.

'But I have had the most marvellous thought: you shall come and live with me! The air of Yorkshire will make you well again, and you shall taste how good food can be: London bread and milk are so vile! We shall be company for each other, and when your hands are better, you can make gowns for the Yorkshire ladies. Oh, don't turn up your nose like that!' she laughed. 'I promise you there are many fine ladies in York, with every bit as keen an eye as your London belles.'

'It sounds so attractive,' Madame said slowly. 'But I would not be a burden to you. If I can pay my way – may I consider it? You do not go at once?'

'No, I shall stay in London with Lady Chelmsford, probably until Easter. Lady Aylesbury wants me to go to her parties.'

'Lady this and Lady that – you are moving in fine circles now, Madame Vendenoir,' Flon teased.

'Oh, but that is nothing to me, now I am a Lady too!' Héloïse said airily. 'I am the Countess of Strathord, you know, in my own right, which is a very fine thing. In future you shall remember always to call me Lady Henrietta Stuart. Any name must be better than Vendenoir to me.'

Shocking news came in of a mutiny amongst the ships lying at Spithead.

'Jack warned that there would be trouble,' Charles said, reading the *Gazette* over breakfast. 'But I hardly thought it would come to this – a full-scale mutiny!'

'Are all the ships involved?' Roberta asked, putting down the piece of toast she had just buttered. She was a soldier's daughter, and the word 'mutiny' had been known to her from her childhood as the worst thing to be feared. Soldiers, like sailors, were recruited from amongst the lowest classes – soldiers perhaps lower even than sailors – and the harshest discipline was needed to control them. If they were ever to join their strength together and escape the leash ...

'It says the ships of the Channel Fleet – Lord Bridport's ships,' Charles said, looking up from the paper. 'That's the worst of having a whole fleet in harbour at once – communication is too easy between the ships, and the men are idle. If they had been at sea, it could not have happened.'

'They must put in sometimes, I suppose,' Roberta said. 'Pray read on, my lord. Is anyone hurt? What do the mutineers demand?'

'This is only a preliminary report,' Charles said. 'We must wait longer to hear more. A gun was fired, it seems, as a signal, and the men rushed up the masts and manned the yards, shouting and waving their hats. They have refused to put to sea, or do any work about the ship until their demands are met.' He put down the paper and pushed his coffee-cup away, and got up restlessly. 'By God, if this should spread! At such a time, when we are fighting a war without allies! My dear, you must excuse me. I must walk out and see what I can find out.'

The following morning found him at Upper Grosvenor Street, where Mary was worried about the safety of her husband. *Cressy* had been due to come in to Spithead at about the time the mutiny broke out, and though there had been no report of violence, she was convinced that some

125

mutineering sailor, mad with drink, would shoot Captain Haworth dead on his own quarterdeck.

Charles was joining his efforts to Lucy's in reassuring her, when the footman announced a visitor, and Lieutenant Weston walked in.

'I come straight from the Admiralty, Lady Aylesbury,' he said, when greetings had been exchanged. 'I thought you and Mrs Haworth would be glad of the most recent news from Portsmouth.'

'Indeed, Weston, if you can convince Polly that no harm is likely to come to Captain Haworth if he should come in to Spithead, you will have done us all a service,' Lucy said.

Weston smiled his charming smile, and bowed towards Mrs Haworth. 'I can do better than that, Ma'am,' he said. 'I bring you the assurance that the *Cressy* is come in safe and sound, and that Captain Haworth is at this moment on his way to London. I was in the Secretary's office this morning, and was privileged to look over the early dispatches.'

Mary sat down rather suddenly, and was unable to say anything, but the look she gave the young lieutenant was thanks enough.

'Capital!' Lucy said. 'And now my sister is satisfied, you may tell the rest of us about the mutiny. Charles has been reminding us that my cousin Jack foretold trouble before Christmas.'

'Did he, indeed?' Weston said, looking at Charles.

'He thought that the older seamen felt they were being worse treated than the quota-men, and were unhappy about it,' Charles said.

'Ah, but it isn't the older seamen who have stirred up the trouble,' Weston said. 'No, it is the new intake. With the quota, you see, there is a new sort of man coming into the service – spoilt clerks, bankrupts, embezzlers – the sort of men with a little education who, either through vice or weakness or ill fortune, have been forced to take the shilling rather than go to gaol.'

'Yes, a little education, to my mind, is far worse than none at all,' said Charles. 'It gives a voice to discontent.'

'It does worse,' Weston nodded. 'It creates the discontent. The older jacks would never think of rebelling. They

126

are used to the conditions, and they know they would fare worse on land. They haven't the imagination to think that things might be any different. No, it's my belief that if any of the older seamen are involved, it's unwillingly. And I believe it is their influence which has added the caveat to the refusal to put to sea: unless an enemy appears, they say.'

'Well, it's good to know they are not lost to all decency,' Charles remarked. 'What are their demands?'

'Equality of pay with the soldiery; abolition of the more savage punishments; rations at sixteen ounces to the pound,' Weston said. 'Those are the basic demands.'

'Reasonable enough, surely,' Lucy said. Weston bowed.

'Reasonable, yes – but if the Admiralty grants them, does it not encourage mutiny by seeming to condone it?'

'But Mr Weston,' Mary said restlessly, returning to the matter which interested her, 'was the *Cressy* involved at all? When did she come in?'

Weston gave her a sympathetic smile. 'She came in on the night before the mutiny broke out – but her crew was not involved. Whether they were even canvassed by the mutineers is doubtful, but at any rate, they held true. Captain Haworth is greatly loved by his men, you know,' he added, and Mary blushed a little with gratification. Lucy looked at her friend with surprise and doubt, but had the tact not to ask there and then whether he knew that for a fact, or was making it up for Mary's sake.

'Tell us, Weston,' she said, 'what were you doing at the Admiralty this morning? Was it the usual? Have they found you a ship yet, or are you to remain permanently unemployed? Mary says that the system allows for keeping the bad officers on the beach –'

'Lucy!' Mary said, shocked, but Weston only grinned.

'I think that must be what they are doing, ma'am. I have other news, but was keeping it back – the best for last, you see. I have my new appointment!'

Lucy jumped up and clapped her hands. 'Oh Weston, I am so glad for you! What ship is it? When do you sail?'

'You are pretty eager to be rid of me, my lady,' Weston said teasingly. 'I am sorry to have to disappoint you, but I am not going to sea – I have a shore appointment, in the

Admiralty, under the sea-lord; so I shall not only be in England, but in London, and barely ten minutes away.'

'Oh, that doesn't signify,' Lucy said airily. 'Don't flatter yourself that I shall take any pains to avoid you, sir. But seriously, Weston, are you pleased? Had you not rather go to sea?'

'There are advantages either way. At sea there is prize money, and the chance of distinguishing oneself; but my new position will enable me to make myself known to the top men in the service, and to influence naval policy, even if only in a small way. It's an opportunity many men would give an arm for, and you may be sure I shan't waste it.'

'I'm very glad for you,' Lucy said, her expression softening. 'And glad for us, too. We should have missed your company, Mr Weston.' There was a perilous moment when the room seemed to hold its breath, and Mary wondered what impropriety her sister was about to commit; and then she added with her usual cheerful frankness. 'And with two brothers and a brother-in-law in the navy, I shall be glad of a contact within the Admiralty. We shall make good use of him, shan't we, Mary?'

Mary had been worried in recent weeks about Lucy's growing intimacy with Lieutenant Weston, which seemed to her of a different order from her friendship with Wiske or with Brummell; not so much in its external application, for in public Lucy treated him no differently from any other of her cicisbeos, but in what she feared it might come to mean to Lucy herself.

Chetwyn didn't seem to mind what Lucy did, or with whom she did it, living his own life with his own friends and occupations, and treating her, when they were together, with exactly the same older-brother friendliness as always, so Mary had no reason to fear that a scandal was imminent. But she was fond of Lucy, and knowing that her younger sister's affections had never been deeply engaged, was only afraid of their being aroused now, disastrously, by the wrong person at the wrong time.

But that evening all her fears were banished, not by any change in Lucy's circumstances, but by the arrival at Upper

128

Grosvenor Street of her husband, which left her no capacity for any feeling but joy. Captain Haworth looked very tired, and pale under his tan.

'And I'm sure you are thinner. You have not been taking proper care of yourself,' Mary said. They were in the morning-room, locked in each others' arms, and enjoying the first precious moments in privacy, thanks to Chetwyn's exertions in the drawing-room, in keeping Lucy from bursting in on them.

'I'm perfectly well, my darling,' Haworth said, kissing her eyes and brow and nose in rapid succession. 'A little short of sleep, that's all. On blockade, in those waters and at this time of year, one is up and down every few hours for some change of course or modification of the wind; and we have had a hard haul of it up the Channel, too. Oh, my darling, I have missed you so much!'

'Not a fraction as much as I have missed you,' Mary said, revelling in the feeling of his arms around her, the smoothness of his cheek, and the warm smell of his skin which she had almost forgotten. 'At least you have been kept busy. And you had no fears about my safety. I am used to worrying about shoals and rocks and hurricanes, but having to worry about mutinies is something new.'

'I wasn't in the least danger from that,' he smiled down at her. 'In fact, the whole thing was conducted almost in a gentlemanly manner.'

'Gentlemanly! A strange adjective to choose,' Mary smiled. 'What do you think will happen now?'

'I think, if Their Lordships have any sense at all, that they will acceed at least to some of their demands. Most of what the mutineers are asking is reasonable, and we can't afford disaffection in the navy at a time like this. Give them something, the basic things, and they'll go quietly back to work. The steadier men, the older jacks, will see to that.'

'Your ship was not involved, so Lucy's friend tells us.'

'No, my love, so there was nothing for you to fear. My crew are seasoned, and they've been too long on blockade to feel anything but pleasure at being back in port. Besides, we hadn't been long enough in harbour for the mutineers to contact us.'

129

'And how long do you stay this time?' Mary asked in a small voice.

He sighed. 'Only as long as it takes me to find a new ship. Not long, I hope.'

'You hope!'

'I know, I know – it's very hard, hard for both of us. I want to be with you, dearest; but the navy is my career, and we are at war. I must get back to sea as soon as possible; and yet, it breaks my heart to think of parting from you.'

'Oh George,' Mary said, closing her eyes against the pricking of tears, and lifting her mouth to his. A long and tender embrace later, he released her and turned her towards the door, his arm round her shoulder.

'I ought to pay my respects to my hosts,' he said. 'By the by, my love, I saw your brother when I was in the port-admiral's – your brother William. Did you know that the *Pelican* was in Portsmouth? Fortunately she moved there from Spithead before the mutiny broke out, to take a turn at the sheer-hulk – a damaged foremast, I believe – so she was not involved either. He was looking very well, but he tells me your brother Harry is a little under the weather. He took Jack's death very hard, of course. Extraordinary man, your brother William,' he added thoughtfully as he opened the door for his wife. 'He reminds me of a granite statue, so huge, and hard, and unemotional; and yet, you know, my servant on the *Cressy* tells me that he has a mistress of whom he is very fond, and who goes everywhere with him, for all that no-one else can see any virtue in her, for she is not pretty, nor even particularly young.'

'William, a mistress!' Mary exclaimed in amazement

'Why, yes. She's called Mrs Smith, though whether that's her real name anyone may guess. She's a Creole, I believe – certainly he picked her up in the West Indies. I hope you are not shocked, Mary? She is some years older than him, I believe, and gives all the appearance of a staid and respectable married woman, so Dipton tells me. Do not be imagining a painted lightskirt! Dipton calls her "plain and sensible", and says she's a better sailor than most of the *Pelican*'s officers.'

Mary looked up into her husband's smiling eyes, and

thrust aside all this to come to the important part of the revelation. 'But you said she goes everywhere with him. What can you mean by that? You mean she sails with him, in the ship?'

'Yes, my love – she shares his cabin. Of course, it is against regulations, when a vessel is operational, but it is often done, and everyone turns a blind eye to it. The Captain may do pretty well as he likes in his own ship, you know, and many of them take a mistress or a wife with them. It's surprising, I grant you, that William does – he's known as a high-stickler of the most rigid sort – but every man has his weakness.'

Mary actually caught his lapel and shook it in her anxiety to have his attention. 'Do you mean to stand there and tell me, Captain Haworth, that your brother captains take their wives with them when they go to sea, and you have never so much as hinted of it before? That I could have been with you these last three years, instead of pining and fretting on shore?'

Haworth looked at her in surprise. 'It never occurred to me to mention it, dearest. It is very uncomfortable on board a seventy-four. The accommodation is poor, the food worse, and we are not cruising in the West Indies, you know, where one may have fine weather and calm seas. We are blockading the French coast – foul weather, rough seas, and a great deal of danger.'

'As if I should care about that, you fool,' Mary said. 'If you endure hardships, I want to share them with you. If you face danger, I want to be near you.'

'My love, you can have no idea –'

'I have a very good idea, George – remember I have two brothers in the navy. If there is any way in which I can be with you, I am willing to take it. What is my life to me without you? Don't you think I would sooner be with you in whatever conditions of hardship, than apart from you in the greatest luxury in the world? Every moment we spend apart is time wasted to me, however I spend it.'

'Well, if you really feel like that,' he began, and she interrupted him, taking both his hands and pressing them in her anxiety to convince him.

131

'I do, I do! Oh George, let me come with you, when you go to sea again! I don't mind how cramped the cabin or how poor the food, if we can be together. I won't be a nuisance – indeed, I will be a help to you, mend your clothes and cook your food and so on.'

He lifted one of her white hands, and then turned it over, laughing, and kissed the soft palm and unblemished finger-tips. Those hands had never done anything in their lives more damaging than arranging flowers. 'I have servants to do those things, my own love, and I assure you that Dipton would not welcome any interference in his dispositions. If you come with me, it must be solely to bear me company, and receive my love, and dine with me, and talk to me, and sleep with me.'

She lifted her shining eyes to him, and pressed his hand against her cheek. 'Yes,' she said. 'Oh yes, please!'

132

Chapter Eight

Harry's indisposition turned out to be chickenpox, which necessitated his removal to the shore hospital to avoid his infecting the whole ship. While he was in the hospital, the *Pelican* completed her refitting and sailed, and at the end of a fortnight, Harry was sent home to recuperate until passage could be arranged for him to rejoin his ship.

Jemima was delighted to receive her youngest son back into the bosom of the family, and was disappointed only that Harry refused to be coddled or nursed, despite his looking very pale and fagged. His indisposition had not been severe, and he bore only the faint marks of his spots when he arrived home, but he was suffering under the debilitation of the illness, and a lassitude of spirit, which made him by turns mopeish and irritable.

A week of rest and good food did a great deal to restore him to health and spirits, and it was not long before Jemima had the pleasure of having him request permission to accompany her on her morning ride.

'If you have anything that's up to my weight,' he added with a smile. Jemima looked him over critically.

'Yes, I must say it puzzles me where you have this giant's blood from. Your father was a small man,' she said.

At twenty he had grown almost as tall as William, and was shewing something of William's heavy build, together with a roundness of face and fullness of jaw which was all his own. In looks he was unremarkable. His hair was straight and mouse-brown, his eyes blue-grey, and under his tan there was a high colour in his cheeks. He had a pleasant face, and when he was in spirits, an engaging smile, but even Jemima's partiality could not call him better than a personable young man.

'Don't worry,' Jemima reassured him. 'We've plenty of good, plain hacks, and if none of them is big enough, I can find you a plough horse or an ox that will do.'

Now Harry positively grinned. 'Thank you, Mama! Or a circus elephant, perhaps?'

As Harry, like William, was an indifferent rider Jemima put him up on old Badger, the schoolmaster, who could be trusted to look after a tyro; and, mounted on her own new horse, a pretty dark-chestnut mare called Hazel, led the way out of the yard.

'Is it true that Lucy rides cross-saddle at Wolvercote?' Harry asked her as they turned on to the track.

'I'm afraid so,' Jemima smiled. 'Ever since Héloïse told her that Queen Marie Antoinette, poor creature, used to ride cross-saddle on her own estates, dressed in breeches and a man's coat. That girl is for ever doing something shocking. I suppose we should be glad that she confines it to Wolvercote, and does not ride cross-saddle in Hyde Park – though that may yet come.'

'Perhaps it's more comfortable,' Harry suggested.

Jemima considered. 'I cannot think it would be. Women are not made the same as men.'

'I know,' said Harry with a private grin which made Jemima look sideways at him.

'Do you? Now what do you mean by that?'

'Mother, I'm twenty years old,' Harry said, giving her an affectionate look. 'I'm not a child any longer. And the women on the *Pelican* are not nuns, you know. I've seen things below deck you simply couldn't imagine.'

'I hope not,' Jemima said with a raised eyebrow. 'But have you met any respectable women?'

'You mean is there a prospect of my getting married? Dear Mama, always singing the same tune! No, I don't think I shall be getting married for a good, long time yet. Besides, how would you have me support a wife? Though I am twenty, I'm only a midshipman, you know.'

'Are you happy in the navy?' Jemima asked. 'Would you prefer to try some other career?'

He opened his eyes wide. 'Good God, no, ma'am! I could not think of anything but the sea, now. Don't be thinking I am unhappy. I only wish I could get on faster, that's all. It is tedious to be waiting for nothing but length of service, to become a lieutenant. Once I have my commission, I shall be as happy as a porpoise.'

'And then will you marry?'

He gave her a sly look, 'With the left hand, perhaps, like the Cap'n. That will do to be going on with, I dare say.'

'What can you mean?' Jemima asked, and Harry, evidently with great amusement, told her about the mysterious Mrs Smith, who shared the Captain's quarters aboard the *Pelican*, while Jemima listened in growing astonishment.

'What beats all,' Harry concluded, 'is that she ain't at all like a light o'love to look at – at least, not to *my* idea of the thing. She's as plain as a horse – pleasant, mind, but no beauty – and dresses herself as sober as a Methody. She bustles about like a country housewife, doing Bloody Bill's washing and mending, and looking down her nose if anyone should happen to cuss in her hearing, and sitting at the foot of the table when he dines as prim as a pineapple. But she's sea-legs like an old tar, never gets sick, however hard it blows, and turns to in an emergency with the best of 'em. And yet, you know, Mama, the Cap'n worships her, as if she was a goddess, and I've never known him so much as glance at any of the portside beauties. Caps the globe for me, that does!'

After a brief silence, Jemima said, 'But Harry, if he loves her so much, why doesn't he marry her?'

'Oh! He couldn't do that, you know,' Harry said, looking a little nonplussed. He looked sideways at his mother, as though he didn't much want to answer the question, and finally said, 'Not Mrs Smith. She isn't quite – quite right.'

'What on earth can you mean?'

'Well, you see, Mother,' Harry said reluctantly, 'she's a mulatto.'

Jemima had nothing to say. What sons she had, she thought, for falling in love with the wrong person! She had not expected much of William, but she had hoped that when he was older and more settled, when he had won enough prize money to set up his house, he might take a wife. Now it seemed any grandchildren he provided her with would be not only illegitimate, but black, too.

Harry watched her face for a moment, and then tried to comfort her. 'Never mind, Mother, at least Jamie's married, and they may get a boy next time. I think the Cap'n's right not to get married while this war lasts. It would be unfair on a wife, to be leaving her behind all the time. Look how Mary frets for her Captain Haworth. No, depend upon it, a sailor shouldn't marry, not until he's an Admiral, anyway. When I get my flag, Mama, I'll choose a nice, handsome, good-humoured girl, and settle down with her as snug as a hammock. If only I had my certificates! I wish you could have put me onto someone's books, like Jack.' His eyes clouded for a moment as he thought of Jack.

'You must miss him very much,' Jemima said.

'If only he hadn't got himself made without me!' Harry burst out. 'If he had waited for me, everything would have been all right. He was always getting into scrapes, you remember, Mama, but I was always there to get him out of them. Then he needs must go off on his own, and this is what happens!'

Jemima wondered privately what effect Harry thought he could have had on a flying cannon-ball, but she said nothing. Harry's understanding had never been as sharp as Jack's, but they had been very close, depending on each other for different things. Then Harry took an unexpected leap into her thoughts by saying, 'Jack was always the clever one, I know. It was only in mathematics I came near to him. But he was such a fidgety creature, Mama, always seeing difficulties, getting upset over things that weren't worth fretting about, and that's when he needed me, to talk sense into him. He called me his rock. He used to say that between us we made up one very good sort of a man.'

They came in sight of Twelvetrees, and Harry made one of the miraculous recoveries of youth. His face brightened, and he said in a perfectly normal voice, 'What, haven't you begun the rebuilding *yet*? I made sure I would see a vast improvement in the old place, but here it is, as tumbledown as ever! I wonder if you will ever get round to it, at this rate.'

'I wonder myself,' Jemima said with a private smile.

At the end of May, the Chelmsfords came down to Shawes

for the summer, bringing Héloïse with them.

'I rather thought Lucy and Chetwyn might have come too,' Jemima complained mildly when she paid her first morning visit. Harry had gone back to sea, and a slight fall had resulted in her being banned from the saddle for a week, so she was feeling bored.

'Chetwyn had to see to matters at Wolvercote,' Charles explained, 'and Lucy is staying in London, ostensibly to keep the house open for Mary and Haworth until he joins his ship. Have you heard that he's been given command of a new eighty-gun two-decker, the *Africa*?'

'Yes, Mary wrote to me about that. When will she be completed?'

'Very soon, I believe. Haworth's delighted with her, of course. It's a great compliment to have been given one of the few new ships.'

'But Charles, what did you mean by *ostensibly*?' Jemima reverted.

'And I thought you had not noticed,' Charles smiled. 'I think the real reason is that Lucy is trying to fit in as much pleasure as she can, before she has to retire on account of her condition. She and Chetwyn will certainly come in August for the races, but after that I think she cannot expect to go out into society much more before her confinement, so she is making the most of things now.'

'But what does she find to do in London? She was always such a country girl.'

'My dear ma'am, she leads the *ton*!' Charles exclaimed, wide-eyed, and Jemima laughed.

'That I cannot believe! Not my harum-scarum Lucy.'

'Oh, she is every bit the countess now! She wears new fashions before they *are* new fashions, goes to all the best parties, rides and drives in the Park, and is everywhere followed by a jostling crowd of gallants, who tread on each other in their anxiety to be the one to pick up her handker-chief or hand her her gloves.'

Jemima shook her head. 'Mary I could believe it of, but not Lucy.'

'Oh it is quite true, I assure you. Mary is a mature matron now, and in any case has eyes for no-one but her husband.

137

You have heard she means to go to sea with him when he gets his ship?' Jemima nodded. 'That, of course, gives Lucy another excuse to stay in London. She spends long hours telling Mary in minute detail all about the inside of a two-decker, and helps her draw up lists of what to take with her as cabin-baggage. She says no-one else can advise Mrs Haworth so well – and she is probably right.'

Jemima was happier even than she had expected to see Héloïse again. It seemed that she had taken a daughter's place in her affections, and that she had been missing her without realizing it. Charles and Roberta had a great many things to do about the house that first day, so Jemima took the opportunity to suggest that Héloïse take a walk with her.

'We could go down through the formal gardens to the lake,' she suggested. 'One circuit of the lake makes a pleasant round for a morning walk.'

It was a beautiful, early-June day, with a freshness in the air and a glittering clarity to the sunshine which made it seem as though everything had been freshly scrubbed and polished. The sky was a flawless blue, and the chestnut buds were opening juicily. All around everything seemed to be growing so vigorously one could almost hear it; implicit everywhere was the sound of beasts tearing avidly at the lush, rich grass.

'The grass looks so good at this time of year,' Jemima said, 'I feel I could eat it myself.'

Héloïse smiled. 'Yes, and the rose buds: they look so fat and delicious. What do you suppose they would taste like? The pale yellow ones of caramel, perhaps?'

'And those pink ones strawberry cream. And the leaves, of course, would be angelica.'

They walked along the terrace, and Jemima stopped and turned to look at the house. Héloïse looked too, and said, 'It is very beautiful – quite different from the great French houses. It is very – spare. Nothing is in excess, and nothing is wasted.'

'Yes,' said Jemima. 'They say Vanbrugh thought Shawes the best thing he had ever done, for all that it's so small – compared with Blenheim and Castle Howard, I mean. I think it is the most beautiful house I know. I can hardly believe sometimes that it was once mine.'

They turned from the house, and leaned against the terrace wall to look down over the pleasure-gardens. 'When Henry Wise laid these out,' Jemima said, 'the Countess Annunciata requested a mixture of mature trees and saplings – mature trees for her own enjoyment, and saplings for the generations to come. Now, eighty, ninety years later, it's impossible to tell which are which. What would our lives be, if we could not plan for the future, create beautiful things for our children and grandchildren to enjoy?'

Héloïse had no answer. It was not a question for her, who had no children, and no expectation of ever having any; for a moment, all the losses of her life ranged themselves around her for her contemplation. She gazed out over the sunlit gardens in silence, and the penetrating, aromatic smell of box came up to her from the formal garden with its geometrical flower beds divided by gravelled walks. That smell was to her the essence of France in summer, and it was like a gentle hand laid over her aching heart.

'Did you know the Countess?' she asked as they walked on. 'She was a very great lady, I think?'

'I only met her once, when I was a little girl. She was an old lady by then, but she had great presence. I was a little afraid of her. She made much of me, which was odd, because I was of no importance at the time. I had two brothers, you see.'

Héloïse nodded. 'And she had a daughter, no?'

'Her daughter – your great-grandmother – was gone by then, to the convent in France, but her granddaughter lived with her.' Jemima frowned, remembering. 'She could not have known what was to happen; and yet, when she spoke to me, I had the strangest feeling that *I* was her true heir, not her granddaughter. I believed she thought so, too.'

They reached the centre of the terrace and began to walk down the steps. At their foot the lavender bushes were so thronged with bees that they shook and vibrated, and descending step by step was like sinking into a pool of humming, ankle deep, waist deep. The trapped heat rose about them, too, spicy with box and thyme, rosemary and lavender.

139

'When she died, she left me her most precious keep-sakes,' Jemima went on, 'and the diamond collar that King Charles the second had given her.'

'King Charles,' Héloïse said, smiling. 'That is something out of a history lesson. Did she know him well?'

'She was his cousin, and very close to him. She knew all the Stuart family. You, of course, carry on the name.'

'Yes. Papa sometimes used to call me the last Stuart princess,' Héloïse said.

They turned into one of the narrow, box-edged paths, and the gravel felt hot through the thin soles of their shoes.

'One can never be sure how things will turn out' Jemima said. 'Eventually I did become her heir, not only mistress of Shawes, but of Morland Place and the whole Morland fortune, as she had once been. I used to wonder how she knew, but now I think she just hoped. It is a great responsibility, you know, to be guardian of an old name, and an old estate, and I understand better now why Annunciata gave those things into my hands rather than to her own grand-daughter, whom she did not trust.'

She paused at a junction of paths, and looked down at Héloïse. 'The main estate has never been entailed, you know.'

'What is that, please?' Héloïse asked.

'It means I may leave it as I please, and do not have to leave it to the eldest son.'

'Ah yes, I remember James told me so once,' Héloïse said. The sound of James's name on the air surprised her a little, and seemed to hang there, significant, as if it were a key that would unlock further confidences.

'My dear,' said Jemima, 'I was so happy when you and James fell in love; not only for James, though I rejoiced that he had found someone good and true to depend upon, but for myself, because when I first saw you I felt as I believe Annunciata must have felt about me. I wanted to leave Morland Place to you, because I knew that you would not only take care of it during your lifetime, but that you would understand the necessity of choosing your heir as carefully. I wanted *you* to have my kingdom. And now – and now – '

She broke off and resumed walking, a little more rapidly than before. Héloïse caught up with her and said tentatively, 'Maman, though the marriage of James and –' She found it impossible to say, and made a small gesture of dismissal and apology with her hand. 'Though it is not all you must have hoped for, surely the child, surely James's daughter must make everything all right for you?'

Jemima smiled at her painfully. 'Oh, child, not everything.'

They walked on in silence for a while, and then Jemima said in a different voice, 'Fanny promises well, and James does love her, so perhaps he won't neglect her. Things may turn out well. I have to hope so, anyway. One must assume that God knows what He is doing.'

They followed the path round the lake, watching the waterfowl busy in the reeds with their new families. June is a hard month to bear, when everything in nature seems to be pairing and breeding. In every field dams suckled their young; every hedgerow shook and clamoured with birds feeding their nestlings.

Everyone has a mate but me, Héloïse thought; even James, though he does not love his wife, has a child to care for. They paused under a willow tree growing at the water's edge, and Héloïse watched a moorhen paddle past, followed by six impossibly small dabs of young, piping shrilly in her wake. Then she roused herself to a better frame of mind with a shake of her head, and Jemima glanced at her and asked, 'What is it, my love?'

Héloïse smiled. 'I was being self-pitying, which is a great nonsense; especially as my cousin Charles says that his agent thinks he might have found a house for me.'

Jemima tried not to feel dismayed. 'So soon! But you must be pleased. Where is it? What is it like?'

'Charles has not had time yet to talk to him about it, so I know nothing except that it is about fifteen miles away, and in very pretty country. Fifteen miles seems a very good sort of distance, is it not, Maman? Not too far away for you to visit me?'

'If it were twice so far, I should come,' Jemima said. 'But let me see, two hours and a half in the carriage, or three if

141

the roads are bad, would do it. Did Charles mention no name?'

'No. He says he will speak to Athersuch today, and tell me everything this evening. When I go to see the house, will you come with me? I think I shall need advice.'

'Of course I will. If it is a fine day, we might take a picnic with us, you know, and make an outing of it.'

The fine weather continued, and they went to see Héloïse's new house in the open barouche Charles had had built for Flora. Charles and Roberta, Jemima and Héloïse took the seats, and Marie sat on the box beside the coachman, for Héloïse insisted that her maid should have the opportunity of seeing the house before any decision was made. There was an ample basket of provisions stowed behind, and Charles said that if they had time enough, it would be a shame not to go on to Sutton Bank, which was quite near to their destination.

'It's a notable beauty spot, and the view from the top is breathtaking.'

'But what is our destination?' Jemima asked.

'The village of Coxwold – a very pretty village indeed. The house we are going to see is on the outskirts, but there is a good road which passes the door, so it is not isolated. I believe it may suit you very well, Héloïse, but if you have the slightest doubt, Athersuch shall look again. You must not be thinking there is the least hurry in the world. I would not have you leave us until you are quite satisfied with your choice.'

The village was indeed pretty, with a wide main street lined with respectable-looking houses, and a little church set up on a knoll above the road. The countryside was lush and burgeoning, with tidy fields and gently swelling hills, which rose gradually to the high ground of the North York Moors, of which Sutton Bank was a scarp. It was sheep country by long tradition. There were several ruined monasteries nearby: the monks of old had been great sheep-masters, and had grown rich by it, and the legacy of their wealth was seen all around in the continued prosperity of the area.

142

Héloïse loved the house at first sight. They rounded a corner to find it sitting there at an angle to the road, a neat, symmetrical building of rosy red bricks with stone lintels; two stories high, with white-painted dormer windows in the steeply-pitched, lichen-gilded roof. A fence of white pickets enclosed the tiny front lawn, and a pale rose grew up the side of the house and threw nodding sprays of blooms over one of the upstairs windows. All houses have a 'face', and this one was friendly, gentle and retiring.

'I believe there is a more extensive garden at the back,' Charles said as the coachman drew up. 'Ah, the owner's agent is here before us – there's his horse. He said he would meet us here and shew us round.'

The agent opened the door as they walked up the short front path, and after an exchange of ceremonies, ushered them in. A stone-flagged passage led from the front door to the back, and to either side was a good-sized parlour. Behind the principal rooms were, on one side, the kitchen, and on the other a small but very pretty parlour with French windows giving onto the garden. This room, judging by the shelves which lined the walls, had been used as a book-room by some previous tenant.

Upstairs were four bedrooms, with two servants' bedrooms under the roof. The stairs were rather narrow and precipitous, but the rooms were all pleasantly shaped and had good-sized windows.

When they had seen the house, they walked out into the garden, and everyone exclaimed with delight, for though small, it was cunningly laid out so as to disguise its true size and shape with walks which wound in and out of flowering shrubs and screens of climbing plants. It lay humming under the sunshine with a multitude of bees and butterflies, attracted by the sweetly scented flowers and old-fashioned herbs.

The garden was walled all around with the same red brick as the house, and beyond it on the side away from the road there was a small kitchen garden. There were some useful espaliered fruit trees – apples, damsons, apricots, a peach – and a gnarled old mulberry tree grew over the wall from the flower garden. Birds darted and chirped amongst the leaves and swung daringly from the espaliered branches.

As she went round the house, Héloïse had said little, her mind already fully occupied with visualizing her favourite pieces of furniture disposed about the rooms. From the moment she entered it, she had no doubt that this was her house: it seemed to fold loving arms about her, and a great feeling of peace emanated from the sun-warmed bricks. The little parlour with the French windows, she decided, would be her study, where she would sit to write her History of the Revolution. She would put her Sèvres *bonheur-du-jour* just *here*, she thought, so that when she lifted her head she could look out into the garden, for inspiration and comfort.

'Well, my dear,' Charles asked at length, 'what do you think? Do you like it?'

'I love it!' Héloïse cried. 'It is exactly right for me. How clever of your Mr Athersuch to find it, cousin Charles!'

Charles smiled at her enthusiasm. 'You do not have to make up your mind at once, you know,' he began, but she interrupted, 'Oh, but I am quite decided! I wish to live here, and nowhere else. I shall have that little room to work in, and I will plant some white jasmine in a pot outside the window, just like I had at the convent. I shall have a little dog, too, like Bluette, to play with in the garden. I hope the stairs won't be too steep for Madame Chouflon, however. She is not always strong in the legs.'

'The stairs are very bad,' Charles said gravely. 'Not but what they mightn't be improved, if you found you had enough money in hand; but the rooms are good. Four bedrooms will be sufficient, I suppose? And servants – you will want another maid and a man, I imagine. Yes, two attics will suffice for now.'

'Yellow curtains, for my work-room,' Héloïse mused, almost as if she had not heard him, 'and then if I recover the *chaise longue* in yellow silk it will look as though the sunshine is always pouring in to the room. Oh, Maman, don't you think it the loveliest little house in the world?'

'It is very pretty indeed, my dear,' Jemima agreed, 'only there is no stable.'

Héloïse laughed, because it was so like her. 'But I cannot afford horses, so what does it matter? There is a spare bedroom for you for when you come and visit me, and another one besides – *quelle richesse*! What could anyone want more?'

Charles had gone into a huddle with the agent over terms, and Roberta, who had been examining the plants, came towards them and said, 'I like your house exceedingly, Héloïse! But did you know, the agent says it is called Scroggins, because that was the name of the original tenant. Isn't that dreadful?'

'I shall change it,' Héloïse said firmly, looking around her with the sun in her eyes. 'I shall call it *Plaisir*, because this is where I shall find it at last.'

It was late when the carriage, having left the others at Shawes, took Jemima home to Morland Place, pleasantly tired from a long day in the air and sunshine, her head reeling with new impressions, and plans for wallpaper, paint and curtains. Mary Ann had gone to bed, and Father Thomas was in his room, but Jemima found Edward and James in the drawing room, the former reading, the latter with his sketching-book on his knee.

She asked Oxhey to bring her a little supper on a tray, and sat down in the chair opposite Edward, who looked up from his book and smiled questioningly, 'Well?'

'Very well,' she answered. 'Charles's agent has made a good choice. It is a very pretty little house.' She felt James's eyes on her, and turned to look at him.

'But does she like it?' James asked abruptly. 'What does she think of it?'

'She likes it very well indeed. It is all agreed upon.'

'And when does she move in?' he asked, and his voice sounded harsh to Jemima's ears.

'Very soon, I should think. There is a little to be done in the way of painting and papering, which a fortnight should see completed. I imagine she will not delay.'

'A fortnight!' James exclaimed, putting his book aside and getting up to walk restlessly about the room. Edward looked at his mother and shrugged; and Jemima wondered whether James thought a fortnight too long or too short.

'The village is Coxwold,' Jemima went on, addressing herself to Edward. 'It seems a respectable sort of place, and not too far for me to visit, though I suppose I shall have to leave my horses at the inn. The house is too small to have stables. She is going to call it *Plaisir* – charming, don't you think?'

'Will she –' Edward began, but was interrupted by a crash as James knocked something from a side table. It was a tall Chinese vase, a present from Mr Hobsbawn which Jemima privately thought very hideous. Fortunately it fell onto the carpet, and did not break. They watched it roll on its side for a moment, and then looked at James, not knowing whether he had bumped into it accidentally or on purpose. His fists were clenched at his sides, and his face was taut.

He stared at the vase for a moment, and then resumed his restless pacing, catching it with the side of his shoe in passing. It rang, high and sweetly: it was good quality china, at least, Jemima found herself thinking.

'Jamie, please sit down,' she said, quite gently. He looked haggard, as though he had not slept properly for a long time. 'There is no use in this sort of thing. It only wears you out.'

'It wears us all out,' Edward said with scant sympathy. 'I don't know what's got into you these last couple of years, James, but it's time you stopped. Think about someone other than yourself for once.'

'I do,' he said bitterly. 'All the time.'

'It's useless to go on like this,' Edward went on reasonably. 'You made your own choices, you know, and there's no –'

'Shut up!' James shouted, goaded and turning on his brother. 'For God's sake, don't keep on preaching! What do you know of it, you smug, self-satisfied prig? What do you know of love? You've never cared for anyone in your life, and to have you prating and giving advice – it's unendurable!'

With that he crashed out of the door, passing the startled Oxhey, who was ushering in a footman with Jemima's supper tray. When they were alone again, Ned exclaimed

146

angrily, 'It is intolerable. Do you know what he has been doing? I couldn't think why he kept going out on foot – you know he's never been a walker – and today I discovered that he's been walking across the fields to Shawes, and lurking about the grounds hoping to catch a sight of Héloïse.'

'Oh Ned, are you sure?' Jemima asked, dismayed.

'Quite sure. What the devil does he think he's doing? If anyone sees him, they'll think he's gone mad, or worse, they'll put two and two together. You'll have to talk to him, Mama. The next thing he'll be making assignations with her. Mrs James is bound to start wondering sooner or later why he grinds his teeth every time Héloïse is mentioned. I'm not deeply attached to Mrs James, but she is his wife, and she deserves to be treated properly.'

'Even if she does fill the house with Chinese vases,' Jemima said wryly. Ned put his book down and went to pick up the vase and restore it to its table, also a gift from Mary Ann's father, a thing of elaborately carved and gilded legs, with a marble top which made it unstable.

'There's no harm in her,' Ned said, frowning down at the top-heavy combination of vase and table, 'and even if there were, well, it's not *right*, Mother, is it?'

'No, it's not right. But I don't think James will listen to anything I have to say to him. He knows as well as you do how he ought to behave.' She thought for a moment. 'He's like a child who can't stop being naughty, even though he wants to. He has gone beyond his own governance.'

Edward gave her an exasperated look. 'Mother, he's thirty years old! He's a married man, with a child of his own. This kind of conduct in a man of his age is not just wrong, it's – it's unseemly.'

Jemima put down the chicken leg she had been toying with, and looked sadly at her eldest son. 'Oh Ned, how old you sound sometimes.' He stared at her, and his cheeks reddened, and he picked up his book in silence and went back to reading it. Jemima watched him for a moment, and then said quietly, 'I'm sorry, Ned. I didn't mean to hurt you. I know how much of the burden falls on you. But in a way, I think Jamie's right about you. Not that you haven't loved, because I know you do love many people, deeply; but

147

you've never known a conflict of love or loyalty. In a way, you've never been tested –'

She stopped as he stood up abruptly, his cheeks burning and his eyes unusually bright. He pressed his lips together, as a child will to stop them quivering, and laid his book down very precisely. 'After all these years, how little you know me,' he said, and left her.

Jemima knew where to find James. He was sitting in the Lady-chapel, his hands folded in his lap, staring at the pale golden flowers of the candle flames; since Mary Ann had come to the house, the Lady-altar was always illuminated. Jemima sat down beside him without speaking, and after a while put her arm across his shoulder. For a moment he resisted, and then let his head rest on her shoulder and his face in her neck, as he had used to very occasionally in childhood, when he had been unwell and she had had time to notice it.

'I've upset Edward,' she said eventually. 'We take him too much for granted, you know.'

'I know,' James said, his voice muffled. 'Oh Mother, I'm sorry. I don't know what to do with myself. I don't know how to get through the days. They seem so long, and they lead nowhere – only to another day as empty and as pointless. I don't know what to live for.'

'There's Fanny,' she said, but she already knew the answer to that.

'Yes. I love her dearly, but –'

'I know. I love my children, but they can't take the place of Allen,' she said. James sat up, and took her hand into his lap and chafed it.

'You understand,' he said. 'That's what I meant about Edward – he's never lost the one he loves.'

'My darling, God sends each of us our own challenge and our own pain. We can't judge what it is to be someone else. Edward has his own suffering to endure.'

James shook that away as irrelevant. 'But Mother, what am I to *do*?' he asked hopelessly.

'What I do,' she said abruptly. 'Wait, and trust. The pattern will become clear one day.'

'I wish I could believe that.'

'You must. What else can make sense of life? Talk to

Father Thomas about it.'

He gave her back her hand and turned his head away. 'Leave me alone Mother, will you, please? I just want to think.'

Jemima left him, knowing there was nothing more she could say that he would listen to. At the door to the chapel she looked back, and saw him put his dark head into his hands. Thinking was what everyone wanted him to do, she thought. If only they could be sure he would come to the right conclusions.

Chapter Nine

In July Lucy and Chetwyn arrived at Morland Place, with Hippolyta and Flaminia and such a retinue of nursery-maids that Lucy said the children had better stay at Shawes. 'For we don't want to eat you out of house and home, Mother.'

'Nonsense,' said Jemima. 'Do you think I am penurious?'

'I must own, Lady Aylesbury, that the number of nurses does seem excessive. Fanny's may very well look after your two girls as well, you know,' Mrs James said smoothly. 'We have excellent nursery staff at Morland Place.'

Lucy noted her mother's quickly-concealed frown of annoyance at Mrs James's assumption of her role, and, tact not being her longest suit, she said, 'Well, so have they at Shawes, for the matter of that. It matters not a bit to me where they stay, so long as someone stops them swallowing beads or putting their fingers into the fire.'

'Then do let us take care of them,' Mrs James said graciously. 'It will be so good for Fanny to have company.'

Jemima, seeing that Lucy was about to retort, intervened with a change of subject which was bound to deflect her. 'So Mary and Captain Haworth have sailed at last?'

'Yes, and *Africa*'s to join the squadron blockading Brest. She's a capital ship, Mother, the completest thing you ever saw.'

'Did you see them off?'

'Oh yes, I wouldn't have missed it for the world. Even Chetwyn said he was sorry not to have gone, but he was wanted at Wolvercote, and couldn't get out of it. I went down to Portsmouth with them, and Haworth shewed me over every inch of her before they sailed. I dare say Haworth was hoping for a cruise to the West Indies, but he might have known better. Weston says the threat of invasion isn't over, and that the Directory is assembling an army in northern France for an attempt next spring. Of course, they cannot succeed while we hold the seas, but it means every ship available must be kept on the blockade. Poor Haworth looked as though he didn't like it above half! Blockade is so tedious; but Weston says he may still hope for a single-ship action to make his fortune.'

'I dare say Captain Haworth did not want Mary to be exposed to the autumn gales and the navigational hazards,' Jemima suggested, and Lucy shrugged.

'Well, it's her choice, and I couldn't be more surprised at it. I never thought Polly had such spirit. But have you heard that Admiral Nelson's in a scrape? Weston says the First Sea-Lord's in a rare taking about it. He gave him his flag after Cape St Vincent because he was banking on him to do something to keep the newspapers happy and draw the Opposition's teeth. Only Nelson made a mess of things at Tenerife, and half his men got killed and he had to surrender, and lost his arm into the bargain.'

'Good heavens! The poor man!'

'Well, he hasn't died of it. Weston says he's being sent home to recuperate, but it's a great disappointment to Their Lordships.'

'I remember Flora's first husband, my cousin Thomas, talking about Nelson when he was quite a young captain,' Jemima said. 'As I remember, Thomas didn't think much of him – thought him ambitious and rash, even a little mad.'

'Lots of people don't like him,' Lucy said. 'Ask Charles. Hannibal Harvey says he's a little, vain, posturing, effeminate man, and as conceited as a turkey; but Weston says he's a fine sailor, and the men love him, and that his rashness often brings off good results.'

Jemima was noticing that there was an awful lot of 'Weston says' in Lucy's conversation; but Mary Ann was looking frankly bored with all this naval chatter, and as Lucy paused for breath, she said as if it were still the subject under discussion, 'So your ladyship will have the children here with you? I think we should put you and your husband in the great bedchamber.'

'He wouldn't stay there if you did,' Lucy said abruptly. 'Chetwyn always sleeps in the bachelor wing when he comes here. Mrs Mappin will have had his old room prepared, I dare say. Must I have that great barn of a room, though,

Mother? I told Chetwyn when he wanted me to come up early, that it would save trouble if he came on his own; then I could have taken the children straight to Shawes.'

'It's no trouble, my love,' Jemima said hastily, thinking that if Lucy was going to snub Mrs James quite so blatantly, she would have done better to stay at Shawes. 'You can have Louisa's bed in my room; or Ned could move into the bachelor wing, and you could have the north bedroom. Yes, perhaps that would be best. My dear,' she turned to her daughter-in-law with a tactful smile, 'perhaps you would see to that for me?'

When Mary Ann had left the room, Jemima turned to her daughter. 'Really, Lucy, you must try not to be so rude.'

'Was I rude?' Lucy said in surprise. 'I thought *she* was rude, talking in front of you as though she was already mistress, and you dead and buried. Why do you stand for it, Mother?'

'Mainly because she has so much to put up with already, from James,' said Jemima. 'He ignores her almost completely, as though she did not exist.'

'That doesn't sound so hard to bear,' Lucy said. 'I don't see very much of Chetwyn, but I'm not unhappy. Look at the way he dashed off with Ned the moment he arrived – hardly even stopped to make his bow to you. It doesn't trouble me. I have my own life, and she should have hers. Where is James, by the way?'

'He is gone into York, for a sitting with Lord Ashley's new wife – he is painting her portrait. It is good to know for once that he's safely occupied, and not getting into trouble.'

'Does he still see Mary Skelwith?' Lucy asked. Jemima looked startled.

'Why do you ask that?'

'Oh, something Chetwyn said, about something John Anstey had let drop. I just assumed – but I dare say there's nothing in it after all,' Lucy said hastily, and changed the subject. 'So Héloïse is gone to her new house? Have you seen it?'

'Not since she moved in,' Jemima said. 'I mean to go up after race week – I cannot possibly spare the time while that's in the offing. You shall come with me, Lucy dear, and see it for yourself. It is an easy carriage-ride, and the roads are very good,' she added, with a glance towards Lucy's swelling shape. 'Charles and Roberta made her such a generous gift for her moving-in, you know: a full set of china and household linen, very handsome indeed, so Mappin says. Mrs Beech told her, for of course I did not see it myself. And he removed all her furniture for her from London at his own expense. She will hardly need to buy anything, except the furniture for the servants' rooms.'

Then Mrs Mappin came in with an anxious look on her face over some domestic problem, which put an end to conversation for some time.

Lucy was forced to send some of the plethora of nursery-maids over to Shawes during the course of the day, with a note to Roberta asking her to accommodate them for her temporarily in the more extensive servants' quarters there. Even so, it took the nursery all day to settle, and requests kept coming down for arbitration, while Lucy, little as she cared to involve herself with the governance of children of such tender age, was driven to deal with personally, rather than allow Mrs James to make the dispositions.

She was still up in the nursery when James arrived home in time to dress for dinner and, as his custom usually was, went straight up to the nursery to see Fanny.

He arrived in the doorway in his top-boots and breeches, bringing with him a pleasant smell of out of doors and horses, to find Lucy, looking the epitome of fashion in her high-waisted muslin gown and cropped head, trying to soothe Hippolyta, who had discovered that Fanny now slept in the bed which used to be her own when she lived at Morland Place. Fanny, who was clinging to her mattress with both hands, as if she thought it might be snatched from her, and looking mulish, saw her father instantly, and flung herself out of bed to run to him crying, 'Papa's home! Papa's home!'

Lucy turned, and stared, for she had not seen her brother for many months, and was shocked at how worn and haggard he looked, despite the smile he bestowed on his small daughter as she leaped like a monkey into his arms.

'And looking every bit properly dressed for the nursery, in all his dirt and sweat,' she said lightly, to cover her feelings.

James gave her an ironic smile. 'Believe me, ma'am, I look every bit as suited to my environment as you do.' He came across the room, with Fanny on his hip, to kiss his sister. 'Well, Lucy!'

'Well, Jamie,' Lucy replied in kind, returning the kiss.

He looked around him at the confusion of boxes and uniformed maids. 'So you have brought Small Polly and Flaminia to visit my little princess, have you?'

'Papa, that girl wants to sleep in my bed, but she sha'n't, shall she?' Fanny asked, pointing at Hippolyta with a mixture of anxiety and disdain.

'Why, no, my star, why should she?' James said. 'But don't you remember your cousin who used to live here with you?' Fanny shook her head, and then buried her face in her father's neck in an access of shyness.

'It's my bed,' Hippolyta repeated for the tenth time. 'I was here first.'

'True, Little Polly, but possession is nine-tenths of the law, don't you know that?' James said.

'Of course she doesn't,' Lucy said briskly. 'Don't talk such nonsense, Jamie, and don't interfere, please. I had but just got them settled. Hippolyta, you are to sleep over there. Get into bed at once. And you, Fanny, say goodnight to Papa quickly. It's time he was dressing for dinner.'

Fanny looked at her aunt's unsmiling face, and, feeling the safe citadel of her father's arms around her, allowed her lower lip to jut. 'Don't want to,' she said, with the assurance of one used to having Caesar's ear. 'Papa have dinner with me.'

'Nonsense. Kiss Papa goodnight and get down at once,' Lucy said, but Fanny only turned her face away from her to lavish an accomplished smile on her father.

'Me loves Papa,' she cooed, and was not disappointed of the result.

'Who's Papa's little sweetheart?' James inquired rhetorically.

'Me!' said Fanny triumphantly, and turned her head briefly to give Lucy a look which challenged her quite plainly to do something about *that* if she could.

Lucy sighed. 'Really, James, it's quite sickening to see how you go on. Do put that child down and say goodnight. The dressing bell went ten minutes ago, and I want to talk to you.'

But Fanny did not like to be dismissed so peremptorily, and it was another ten minutes before brother and sister stepped outside into the passage, only to find Durban hovering, with hot water and evening clothes in his eye.

'You'd better be quick, Luce,' James said, amused. 'My time is not my own, you see.'

'Oh, never mind,' said Lucy crossly. 'I only wanted to tell you that I am having Héloïse's ponies brought up from Wolvercote. Well, don't look so stony about it – you gave them to her, you know, and I see no reason why she shouldn't have them now she is settled in her own house. She will need some form of transport.'

'As you say,' James said expressionlessly. 'But what is it to do with me?'

'You have her phaeton, of course. I want to know if you will let her have it back, for I can have Parslow drive it up for her when the ponies arrive. He can lead a horse behind and ride back, and I thought –'

'Thank you,' James said smoothly. 'If there are any arrangements to be made, I will make them. When the ponies arrive, you may have them sent to me here.'

Lucy looked exasperated. 'There's no need to sound as though I were trying to steal them! Have a little sense, James. If the ponies come here, it is bound to cause a stir. Questions will be asked. If you have the phaeton sent quietly over to Shawes, it can all be done there without anyone knowing of it.'

'By anyone, you mean my wife, of course,' James said bitterly.

'Oh, for goodness sake!' Lucy exclaimed. They stared at each other for a moment, and then Lucy turned away. 'Do just as you please. I have to dress.'

*

Race week was always a time of great activity and excitement at Morland Place. Apart from all the festivities associated with it, there was a great deal of hard work involved, for Jemima and Ned were producing half a dozen horses for the races, and even with Chetwyn's willing assistance, there was so much to do that James was drawn in to help. Lucy longed to take his place, and bewailed her condition, but Jemima forbade her to come anywhere near the horses, and for once Lucy saw the sense in the ban.

'I'm hoping so much that this is a boy, and then, you know, I shall have it all behind me. It would be foolish to risk it at this stage.'

Jemima's preoccupation at the stable gave Mary Ann an opportunity to be active about the house, and though the older servants still shewed an annoying tendency to want to confirm her orders with 'the mistress', the younger ones accepted her easily enough. There was to be a special dinner on the first day of the races, on which Mary Ann was concentrating her efforts. Though only a family affair, it was to be quite grand: Lord and Lady Chelmsford were to be there, Horatio and Lady Barbara, Mr and Mrs John Anstey, and Charles's cousins, Maurice Viscount Ballincrea and his sister the Honourable Helena McNeill, who were coming down from their Northumberland estate to stay the week at Shawes.

Mary Ann felt that if she organized the dinner, and it went well, it would establish her credit in the household, and perhaps persuade Lady Morland to allow her to take over the running of the house. Organizing the dinner was harder than she had expected, however, for Jemima had long ago stopped trying to interfere with her cook, Monsieur Barnard, and he had become alarmingly autocratic. He refused to admit he spoke any English, but when Mary Ann, who had been taught French by the nuns in the convent where she had her education, went to the kitchen to interview him, he pretended, most maliciously she thought, not to understand her French either.

It was a long and painful interview for both of them. Half way through, Barnard picked up his sharpest butcher's knife from the table nearby, and brandished it as he spoke, a gesture he had often found effective in discouraging interference from his employers; but Mary Ann was made of sterner stuff. She had been mistress of her own household since an early age, was a Roman Catholic, and a daughter of the new class of manufacturing rich into the bargain. She ignored the knife entirely, drew Barnard over to the Household Book on the side table by the sheer force of her steely gaze, and began to turn the pages and suggest menus, overcoming the problem of his non-comprehension simply by ignoring it.

When Mary Ann suggested that the first course remove should be onion soup, in the making of which Barnard was such an artist that his assistants spoke of it with hushed reverence, he looked about him in desperation for a weapon, and picked up the basting-ladle, which was so heavy it needed two hands to manipulate; but when she took up the slate and pencil and began to write her suggestions down, he began to weep in sheer frustration. Half an hour later she left the kitchen glowing with more than the heat of the fires, leaving the Frenchman twitching with outrage; and at the door turned back to deliver what, unknown to her, was the *coup de grace*.

'By the by,' she said with a charming smile, 'I have long thought the kitchen badly in need of modernization. You should not have to cook over open fires: I must see about having a Rumford installed. If you manage so well now, just think what you may do with the right equipment!'

The cream ponies arrived at Shawes, and though Lucy was still cross with James, she decided to give him another chance, and took him to one side after breakfast and asked him to let Parslow come and fetch the phaeton.

'I promise you he will do it very discreetly. If you just have a quiet word with Hoskins they can manage it between them.'

'Thank you,' said James, giving her a boiled look, 'but I shall make my own arrangements. You need not trouble yourself any further.'

Lucy shrugged and said no more, thinking there was time

for him to think things over and come to a better conclusion. She did not think he would act immediately: but only an hour later she was coming down the great staircase and happened to glance out of the window on the landing, and saw Durban leading the cream ponies into the yard.

'Damn Jamie,' she muttered to herself. Why must he be so difficult? she thought. Oh well, I wash my hands of it: I've done all I can. At least he had had the sense to send Durban, who was no talking fool, rather than one of the grooms.

She remained at her post by the window, and watched as Hoskins came out from the stables and conferred with Durban. Then James emerged from the house, and the ponies were tied up while the three men disappeared into the coach-house. Lucy could guess their errand. James was intent on having the ponies harnessed to the phaeton at once so that he could try them out, perhaps to see whether they needed any schooling or exercise before he had them sent up to Héloïse.

They were still in the coach-house when from the corner of her eye Lucy saw Mrs James appear below her in the staircase hall, emerging from the chapel passage, with the little housemaid Betsey trotting at her heels: judging from the basket carried by the former and the watering-can by the latter, they had been arranging the altar flowers. To her own annoyance, Lucy felt herself give a guilty start. Mrs James looked up. She rarely smiled, and did not do so now, only gave Lucy a long and slightly enquiring look, and Lucy came briskly down the stairs, smiled as she passed, and said brightly, 'What a lovely day it is. Let's hope it keeps fine for the week.'

Dinner during race week tended to be an evening affair, for the family spent all day at the racecourse, and even when the races were over, it took time to prise Jemima and Ned away from the stables, where they would spend hours making much of the horses and holding long post-mortems into the conduct of each race.

Mary Ann felt quite at home with a late dinner-hour, for

at Hobsbawn House she had been accustomed to wait until her father had finished his day's business before dining. She went to the racecourse the first day in her own vis-à-vis with James sitting opposite her, while Chetwyn, Lucy, Ned and Jemima rode in Jemima's elderly barouche. The parties united in the grandstand, where the Morlands had their own private box, and there they were joined by the six guests from Shawes.

Mary Ann enjoyed the day very much. The weather was fine, the company agreeable and more than elegant; and if she understood little about horses, she could enjoy the races simply as a spectacle, and with Viscount Ballincrea's kind help, she even made a few wagers. He appointed himself her gallant for the day. She liked his pleasant humour and elegant manners, and it was obvious that he admired her, which was balm to her bruised spirit, suffering under months of neglect and lack of appreciation. He was handsome, rich, and titled, just about her own age, and she felt all the compliment of his attentions to her.

In the middle of the day a large hamper made its appearance, and cold meats, pastries, fruit and cake were brought out, complete with chilled champagne, and ices provided from the Shawes ice-house. Elegant china, glasses and silverware made the meal a little more than a picnic, and Lord Ballincrea stationed himself at Mary Ann's side, supplied her plate, and refilled her glass with such good-humoured punctiliousness that Mary Ann was glad to find James's eyes on them. It was good, she thought, through a haze of sun, excitement and wine, that he should see that other men found her worth talking to. She hoped he might come over to them; but after a moment he turned his gaze away and entered into conversation over the barrier with a lady outside their box whose large hat prevented Mary Ann from recognizing her face.

When the races were finished for the day, however, she had to give up her attendant for the time being, for Lord Ballincrea had to return with the Shawes party to dress. While he was saying goodbye to her, James strolled over. Ballincrea still had hold of her hand, and James gave them both a look of lazy amusement and said in a tone of complete indifference, 'Well, madam, have you had an agreeable day?'

'Most agreeable, thank you,' she said firmly.

'I am come to tell you I do not return with you in your carriage. I am going with my mother and the others to Twelvetrees,' he said. Mary Ann smarted at the uncivility, and even Lord Ballincrea stared a little as with no more ceremony than a slight bow to divide between them, James turned and went away.

Ballincrea's manners were too polished to embarrass her by noticing the incident any further, but he demonstrated his feelings by bowing over her hand and saying with the greatest kindness, 'Allow me to do myself the honour of escorting you to your carriage, Mrs Morland; and pray let me hand you your wrap. It is easy to take a chill when the shadows lengthen after a hot day.'

Oxhey received her in the hallway of Morland Place, with Dakers and Durban hovering in the background; but Durban had the tact to melt away as soon as he saw Mary Ann was not accompanied.

'Mr James has gone with the others to Twelvetrees,' Mary Ann said in her most controlled voice. 'I shall take the opportunity to check the arrangements for dinner, Oxhey. There is plenty of time – I dare say her ladyship will not be back for at least an hour.'

'You're looking fagged, madam,' Dakers said sternly. 'The heat has been too much for you. I am sure you have the headache. It would be much better for you to go straight upstairs and lie down for a while.'

This was one time when Mary Ann did not want sympathy. She wanted to be magnificent, not pathetic. 'I'm perfectly all right, Dakers,' she said crossly. 'Please don't fuss. Oxhey, come with me to the dining parlour, will you? I want to go over the placings with you. Has the table been decorated as I instructed?'

'Let me order some tea for you, at least, madam,' Dakers said, undeterred. 'I dare say you were drinking champagne, and to my mind that is never a good idea in the heat of the day.'

It was necessary to give Dakers something to do, and the

idea of tea was in any case appealing. 'Very well, have some tea sent in to me in the dining parlour. Come Oxhey,' said Mary Ann.

By the time the party from Twelvetrees arrived, Mary Ann was upstairs taking her bath, with Dakers at hand laying out her gown, and the maid Betsey, whom Mary Ann had taken more and more to herself, pouring the water and standing by with the towels.

The marble clock chimed massively from the open door of the drawing-room as Jemima led her party in, and she exclaimed, 'Good heavens, is that the time? I must have my bath. Oxhey, is everything ready for tonight? I haven't time to check anything.' She spoke unconcernedly, long accustomed to trusting her servants.

'Mrs James Morland has done so already, my lady,' Oxhey said gloomily, 'and has seen to the table herself.'

'Well, that was kind of her,' Jemima said, not pausing on her way to the stairs. 'Is Rachel in my room? I will meet you all before dinner, children.'

Mary Ann dressed with great care for that evening, in a gown no-one had seen yet. It was of mazarine blue silk with a three-quarter length slashed gauze over-tunic, and a long train. Her headdress was a chaperon of silver tissue and blue velvet ribbons, and her hair was taken up and wound in and out of it, and finished off with white feathers. The neck of the gown was deeply décolleté, so that the whiteness of her bare neck and bosom were a fit setting for the magnificent sapphire and diamond necklace and earrings her father had given her a wedding-gift. Dakers so far forgot herself as to clasp her hands and cry, 'Oh you look so lovely, Miss!' as she turned from the mirror, and she responded as surprisingly by kissing Daker's cheek before taking her fan and reticule from Betsey and walking downstairs.

She had no competition in the drawing-room from Lucy, whose advanced pregnancy required soberness of dress, or from Lady Morland, who was wearing black silk the better to shew off her diamond collar; and though when the Shawes party arrived, the women were very elegantly dressed, and the Hon. Helena was perfectly beautiful, she had the pleasure of seeing Viscount Ballincrea's admiring look, and of having him come to her side as soon as he had paid his respects to his hostess.

When Oxhey announced dinner, she had to step aside and enter the dining saloon last on John Anstey's arm, for all the other women ranked above her, but it gave her the opportunity to observe people's expressions when they saw how she had decorated the dining table. The centrepiece was the enormous silver epergne which her father had sent after Fanny had been born, and which depicted St Francis surrounded by animals and feeding birds from his hands; it appeared to be rising out of a sea of pink and white roses, which were massed about its base.

At intervals down the table were placed four five-branch candelabra, which bore white candles and were wreathed with ivy, which mingled with long ropes of roses trailing down the centre of the table and branching at intervals to hang over the edge of the cloth between the guests. The wall sconces were similarly wreathed with ivy, and the fireplaces were decorated with ropes of flowers looped in festoons along the chimney-piece.

Most of the family's portraits of horses had been relegated over the years to the walls of the dining saloon. Each was decorated with a garland of laurel, and Mary Ann had had the side tables rearranged so that candles could be set up on them to illuminate the pictures. All the family silver had been got out and polished to a dazzling brilliance; and as a final touch, the fingerbowl before each guest was decorated with a raised relief of galloping horses. These Mary Ann had ordered for the occasion from the silversmith in Stonegate.

She breathed a sigh of satisfaction at the sight of it all, knowing that at last she had done something to be noticed. It was impossible for the guests not to comment. Jemima had been startled into exchanging one unguarded glance with James, but recovered herself almost instantly to reply handsomely to the compliments being offered her by the Ansteys and Ballincreas, saying, 'The credit goes not to me but to my daughter-in-law, Mrs James Morland. It was her

162

own thought entirely. My dear,' to Mary Ann, 'how clever you have been. You have quite transformed this room.'

Mary Ann took her seat happily, replying with a smile and a bow to all the compliments which were being pressed on her. As dinner began, however, she was astonished to find that the dishes on the table were not the ones she had ordered in her long and painful conference with M. Barnard. Only the onion soup was there of her first course, and even that was supported by a chilled pink turnip soup she had not even seen in the receipt book. The dishes were magnificent: a whole salmon dressed with egg-sauce, a glazed smoked saddle of mutton, a ragoo of veal kidneys, a dish of venison steaks in a plum and madeira sauce, another of green peas and spring onions, wine jellies, an orange pond-pudding – these were immediately to her view as she sat down, and there were other dishes further up she could not see – but they were not what she had chosen.

The second course was no better. Instead of the goose she had particularly ordered there were four ducklings in blackcurrant sauce; the oysters she expected appeared under the guise of crayfish, and the piglet seethed in milk was represented by a quarter of lamb stuffed with apricots. Only the cheesecakes, Lucy's particular favourite, remained unchanged, and the Yorkshire curd tarts for which Barnard was famed equally with his onion soup.

She had been mocked, she thought. Looking up the table towards her mother-in-law, she acquitted her of having changed the menu: it was the cook's doing entirely, and since, on reflection, she knew there was nothing she could do about it while Jemima was mistress, she was prepared to forget it and enjoy herself. It was at that moment, unfortunately, that she caught her husband's gaze upon her and, meeting his eyes, received from him a faint and mocking smile.

Did he know? Had he guessed? Surely that was impossible? If he saw her looking about her at the dishes, there was no reason for him to assume anything from that. She was sure he could not know – unless one of the servants had told him? Under his eyes she reddened slowly and turned from his gaze, her pleasure in the evening spoilt. All around

163

her the talk rose like bubbles, a froth of pleasurable comment on the day and speculation about tomorrow, and she listened inattentively, her mind turning resentfully to old wounds.

Suddenly her attention was caught. Helena McNeill had asked James which horse he thought would win the big race the following day.

'I cannot advise you,' he replied cheerfully. 'Whichever horse wins, it will have to do it without my support, for I shall not be there.'

Mary Ann looked at him, and though he did not betray by so much as a flicker that he was aware of it, she knew he was.

'But how can you bear to miss it?' Miss McNeill said, laughing. Mary Ann saw she did not believe it. 'Do not, pray, be telling me you are giving up pleasure for work. I should be so disappointed in you!'

'No, not for work, but for another, greater pleasure,' James said. 'Tomorrow I shall do myself the honour of restoring a piece of property to its rightful owner.'

'What can you mean? What property? To whom?'

'Something precious which has been in my keeping for a long time, until the owner could claim it. There were times when I thought I would never be able to give it back, but I have kept it safe all the while, untouched and unblemished. She shall have it tomorrow. I would not keep it from her a moment longer.'

Miss McNeill did not, of course, know what he was talking about, and teased him obligingly about there being a lady in the case, and he talked some nonsense to her to keep her amused. Mary Ann knew that it had been said not for Miss McNeill's sake, but for hers. There seemed to be a dull ringing in her head, as if someone had boxed her ears, and the talk around the table was drowned by it, as she stared ahead of her at nothing and put together piece after piece of evidence to come to a conclusion.

So many things became clear all of a sudden: James's behaviour towards her since they first married, his violence when she had used the phaeton, his moroseness, his drinking, the extraordinary tension in the house the day

164

Héloïse had appeared; the strange fact that while she had been staying at Shawes she had never once set foot inside Morland Place; the fact that she had not come to stay for race week; and finally James's long day exercising the cream ponies in the phaeton she had been forbidden to touch.

Bitterly Mary Ann considered her own stupidity: that she knew the truth even now she owed not to her own wit, but to James's desire to hurt her, because she was not the woman he loved.

Lord Ballincrea spoke to her; she was aware that it was the second time he had spoken, and she forced herself to answer, to smile, to appear normal. However badly James behaved, he would not goad her into betraying her position and her upbringing. Somehow she must get through the evening; and somehow she did, and stood at last alone at the door of her bedchamber, more weary than she had ever felt before.

Dakers undressed her and prepared her for bed, chattering at first about the evening, and falling silent when she saw her mistress was not responding. 'You get into bed, madam, and have a good night's sleep. You're over-tired, I know. You'll feel a different person in the morning.'

Would to God I could be a different person, Mary Ann thought. Dakers was talking about hot milk, and Mary Ann dismissed her abruptly.

'Let me see you in bed first,' Dakers said cunningly, but Mary Ann only turned away from her with a vague look, and reluctantly the servant withdrew. Mary Ann sat by the window for a long time, until the house settled, and then taking her candle she left her room and walked quietly along to the bachelor's wing. She knew which rooms Ned and Chetwyn had been put into, so James must be in one of the others; but as she entered the corridor, she saw Durban coming out of one of the rooms, so she had no need of guessing.

She passed him without a glance, aware of his puzzled glance at her, and tapped upon James's door, opening it before he could reply. He was in his bed, leaning towards his candle as though he had been on the point of blowing it out. A look of consternation crossed his face at the sight of her, quickly replaced by his blankest look. He sat up straight in bed and said, 'To what do I owe the honour of this visit?'

She stood in the centre of the room, contemplating him. Now she was here, she hardly knew how to begin. In the candlelight he looked very young in his nightcap, with his ruddy hair and his cheeks flushed with wine. He was very handsome; would have been more so if his expression had been pleasant and happy.

'I know where you are going tomorrow,' she said, and was slightly surprised by the words, not having been quite sure what she was going to say until she said it. James raised an eyebrow.

'Indeed. How clever of you,' he drawled.

There were shadows swooping around the room, and Mary Ann became aware that her hand which held the candle was shaking. She felt sick inside with fear and anger, and the horror of facing and articulating what they had both always kept unspoken.

'How dare you?' she said quietly. 'How dare you treat me so?'

'How do I treat you?' he mocked.

'With such – such insolence!' she cried passionately. 'I am your wife, your wife!'

'Do you think I can ever forget it?' he said bitterly.

'In God's name, why did you marry me?' she cried, and then waved the question away with her hand, making the candle flame dip wildly. 'No matter why. That makes no difference. You married me, and that was your choice, and you have *no right* to treat me like – like – '

She could find no simile. James stared at her, not in the least inclined to laugh at her confusion. Her face was taut with fury, she looked magnificent with her fine hair flying loose about her shoulders and her eyes glittering like burning coals in the candlelight. This was an aspect of his wife he had never seen. Her monumental calm, her passivity, her statuesque coolness – he had thought these not the surface but the real Mary Ann. He felt a dawning of some new feeling towards her – respect, was it?

But for the moment he had his own end to keep up. 'You accuse me of treating you badly?' he inquired ironically.

166

'But after all, you married me of *your* own choice. Or was it love?' he sneered.

Her nostrils flared at the tone of his voice. She felt her cheeks burning, and her voice shook as she answered him. 'Yes, I chose to marry you, and God knows I did not expect you to be in love with me, any more than I was with you. I am not a romantic fool. My father chose you as a good match for me, and I accepted you on those terms. I have put up with your breaking of your marriage vows; I have put up with your neglect, with your slights; I have turned a blind eye to your drinking and your – and the other things you do during your trips to the city.' James's eyes shifted at that, and she paused for a moment, her breath coming light and fast.

'But I *will not* have you publicly humiliate me!' she concluded in a rush. 'I am your wife, and I insist that you treat me with respect. Today at the races, you spoke so insolently to me in front of Lord Ballincrea that I saw he was shocked – '

'Oh, yes, Lord Ballincrea! Quite your *cher ami*, isn't he? I wonder if he isn't what's behind this little outburst.'

'You dare to cast your insinuations at me! And if he were more, if he were my lover, what right would you have to reproach me? But you know he isn't. And tomorrow – tomorrow – '

'What I do tomorrow is not your business,' James said sullenly.

'If you drive that carriage and those horses to Coxwold along the public highway, everyone will know where you have gone, and why, and that is very much my business,' she said burningly. 'You must not, you shall not! I will not be humiliated so!'

She stopped, and for a moment they stared at each other, she trembling with outrage, he frozen with shock and then his eyes dropped, and she saw his mouth tremble, and for a moment he looked agonizingly like Fanny trying not to cry.

'Go to bed,' he said in such a muffled tone of voice she could not tell whether he spoke in anger, shame or defiance. 'Go to bed.'

She looked a moment longer, and then knew she must go

167

before her legs gave way under her, before the tears burning behind her eyes forced their way out. She turned and went out, leaving him to the solitude of his own unwelcome thoughts.

Chapter Ten

James greeted the first tentative cock-crow of dawn with the relief and gratitude only known to those who have lain awake all night. He got out of bed and opened his curtains to look out, placing his hands against the window panes with the unconscious gesture of a prisoner. The sky was greenish-yellow, streaked low down with thin purple bars of cloud. Away to his right there was a glow on the horizon where the sun was waiting like an actor in the wings for the cue to enter; then suddenly the edges of the clouds caught fire, deepening their purple almost to black by contrast, and the first gilded fingernail of the sun's rim appeared, broadening to a pool of molten gold as it lifted clear of the earth.

James watched, his mind curiously blank. The hours of darkness had resolved nothing for him. The only action he felt capable of performing was taking the phaeton to Héloïse: that was something which required no thought, a discrete decision, leading nowhere. Beyond it he did not dare to look, as a man balanced on a knife-edge will not look down into the chasm to either side of him.

He dressed himself, and left his room. It was early, and the house was still sleeping, though from up the backstairs came sounds to indicate that the servants were astir; and when he stepped out into the yard, he was observed by M. Barnard, who was taking his morning breath of air at the buttery door. The Frenchman regarded him shrewdly as he walked towards the stables, and then went back into the kitchen, seized the nearest kitchen-boy, and with a surprising access of English, despatched him up to the servants' quarters, to warn Durban that his master was abroad.

James found no-one in the stables but the two boys whose turn it was to do the early watering, but the horses knew what time it was, and their soft whickerings and stampings would soon wake the rest of the stable staff. He set the two boys to groom the cream Arabs while he went to mix them a feed, and when he emerged from the fodder-room, he was met by Durban, neatly clothed, his face expressionless, like a caricature of the perfect servant.

'What are you doing up at this hour?' James asked, knowing nothing of the alarm system he had set off.

'Better let me take those, sir,' Durban said evenly, removing the two buckets from his grasp. 'We'll be needing two more feeds for Nez Carré and Forest. Would you mix them, sir, and I'll start the grooming.'

Durban could guess something of his master's state of mind, and by asking nothing and assuming everything, he hoped to induce James to believe that he had meant all along to take him with him. By the time the rest of the stable staff were tumbling sleepily into the yard to tackle their first tasks, James was driving out through the barbican, with Durban behind riding Forest and leading Nez Carré.

It was clear it was going to be another hot day. The clouds lost their dramatic imperial colouring as the sun rose higher, and the sky grew pale with heat. There was no breath of wind to stir the air or disperse the flies, which hung above them in black clouds as they walked along the narrow lanes between high hedgerows. Durban picked two long sprays of fern as he passed, and tucked the ends under his horses' browbands to protect their eyes. The tormented horses swished their tails continuously, and shook their heads violently with a musical ringing of bit-rings, but there was no relief until James, in desperation, shook the reins and sent the cream ponies into a trot.

There were not many people about yet, but those they passed turned to look at them curiously, for the pale golden phaeton with the coral-coloured cushions was a conspicuous enough rig, even without the addition of two dazzlingly beautiful cream Arabs, trotting exactly in step with their flashy, high knee-action. A woman with a covered basket; three ragged children and a crone gleaning; a farm labourer riding sideways on a cart-mare while he filled his pipe; a respectable-looking farmer on a heavyweight bay; a simpleton in a smock herding geese: all stopped and stared as they went by. In the fields to either side even the brown dairy cattle and the recently-shorn sheep seemed to lift their heads in amazement; in one meadow three horses which had been turned out to graze kinked up their tails and galloped beside them, snorting excitedly, and stopped with three bounces and a dry-grass skid as they ran out of field.

Durban fixed his eyes on the back of his master's head and closed his mind to speculation as he posted along, leading Nez Carré on a short rein, and keeping a respectful eye on the big horse's teeth, with which he tended to express his resentment of cavalier treatment, such as being made to trot beside an inferior horse, rather than in front of it. The long-suffering Forest rolled an eye in mute protest as Nez Carré's teeth clashed like cymbals a fraction of an inch from his neck, and then lowered his ears to their most inoffensive angle, semaphoring self-effacement to his unwilling companion.

The horses began to sweat, and James slowed to a walk, and the flies descended again. The lanes were sickly with the scent of fool's parsley and sweet-nettle. It was a dull time of year for flowers: in the hedgerow only willowherb and white campion and mouse-ear, and along the edges of the harvested fields, fumitory and shepherd's purse and a fringe of scarlet poppies. Now the land was rising a little, and they were in pasture country, and the dry, prickly smell of sheep was everywhere; before them, distant but growing nearer, the high ground of the blue-brown moors was like a line ruled across the sky.

They came at last to the village of Coxwold. James stopped outside the inn and beckoned Durban alongside.

'You'd better take the horses in and stable them, and find out where the house is. I don't know what name they'll know the house by, but they must know the Countess of Strathord. I imagine it caused a stir when she moved into the neighbourhood. I'll wait here.'

Durban nodded and led the two horses in under the arch to the coach-yard. James got down from the phaeton and led the Arabs to the horse-trough at the road's edge. They lowered their heads and blew at the surface of the water, and then dipped their slender muzzles and drank noisily. Bubbles of air hung like silver beads on their whiskers, and the ripples fanned out from their lips, fluttering the reflection of the white sky, and the creeper growing over the inn's face, already beginning to turn to scarlet. A beef-faced young man drove past in a gig with yellow wheels, and turned back to stare with his mouth open.

At last Durban came back.

'To the end of the street, sir, and turn left. It's about half a mile further on, on the left, a red-brick house with a white picket,' he said. He cocked an enquiring eye at his master, squinting a little against the burnished sun. 'They asked if we wanted rooms for tonight, sir. I wondered what your plans were?'

James smiled at him faintly. 'I don't think I have any plans.' Despite his summer tan, he looked pale; there was a white line around his mouth. 'You'd better get up. I shall need you to hold the horses when we get there.'

Durban got up beside his master, and they drove on down the village street. 'This must be it, sir,' he said a few moments later.

James saw a white picket, a red-brick house, a male servant in a dark-blue apron cleaning the front windows, who turned his head at the sound of the horses. A female servant appeared at the open front door with a mat to beat, stared, and ran back inside calling. The ponies stopped at the gate and Durban jumped down and went to their heads, and James got down from the phaeton, seeing his own feet tiny and far away, as if viewed through a perspective-glass. The thunderous noise in his ears, blocking out all other sound, must be his own heartbeat, he thought with distant surprise.

There was a movement in the darkness of the doorway, and Héloïse was there, and suddenly everything came sharply back into focus, sight and sound, colour and detail. She was wearing a plain brown cambric dress, and a big blue apron like the manservant's; her long dark curls were caught back carelessly with a piece of blue ribbon, and a loose strand of hair had fallen across her brow. There was a smudge of dirt high up on her cheek, and she was holding a polishing-rag in her hand.

He loved her so much in that moment that it was like an intense physical pain in his chest and throat, preventing

172

speech or movement. She looked to him more beautiful than he had ever seen her. Her eyes widened as she saw him, and the hand with the rag came forward involuntarily, found itself occupied, and dropped again to her side.

'James,' she said. 'But what are you doing here?'

He opened the gate and stepped through, and then paused, suddenly unsure of his welcome: she looked apprehensive, almost frightened.

'As you see,' he said, gesturing behind him. He heard one of the ponies sneeze, and the characteristic jingling of bit-rings as a muzzle was rubbed against a knee. 'I've brought you back your phaeton.' She said nothing, waiting as though his answer had been incomplete. 'I wanted to see your house,' he added. 'Everyone has seen it except me.'

Then she laughed. 'How absurd you are,' she said gladly, as though his absurdity had released her. 'And surely you must know I have no stable here. Where can I possibly keep it?'

'Oh, miss – m'lady – I know!' cried the female servant, who was hovering behind Héloïse in the passage, trying to see over her shoulder. 'You could keep them at me father's farm, miss. There's a good, big barn where t' carriage could go, and there's plenty of room in t' stables for them two 'osses, miss – m'lady – along'th the plough 'osses.'

Héloïse looked a little doubtful. 'Do you think so, Peg?'

'Certain sure, m'lady. Me father'd be right glad to 'elp, you givin' me such a good place an' all.'

Durban intervened smoothly. 'If the place is near to hand, my lady, perhaps I could take the rig there now and enquire.'

'It is further on along this road, in the direction you are facing – Charlock's farm,' Héloïse said, still undecided. Then she met James's eye for a moment, and seemed to come to a conclusion. 'Peg, why don't you go along with Mr Durban, and shew him the way, and then you can settle it with your father for me. Stephen, you can go too, and help with the horses.'

'Very good, m'lady. Coom on, Stephen, take off your apron,' Peg said excitedly. She dashed past her mistress, dropped a hurried curtsey in James's direction, and was out

173

in the lane in a moment, making a fuss of the Arabs, and asking Durban their names. The manservant followed her, and a few moments later James and Héloïse were alone.

'I think they will be gone a long time,' Héloïse said. 'Peg will want to tell her mother that I have a visitor, and Peg's mother, a good woman, will give them all cakes and ale; and I much mistake my Durban,' she added, with laughter in her eyes, 'if he hurries about putting the horses away. Oh, James, dear James, are you really here? I can't believe it!'

'You aren't angry with me, then, for coming? I thought you were, just at first. I thought you were going to send me away.'

'No, I was not angry, only worried. You should not have come – oh, but I am glad to see you! I should send you away at once, but I am weak, I must have you to myself for a little while, to see you and talk to you, my James. How long do you stay? A few hours, at least, I hope, so I can shew you my house. Do you like it? Is it not the prettiest house in the world?'

'It is very pretty,' he replied, his eyes on her face.

'You are not looking!'

He laughed. 'Very well, I shall look at everything, and admire it all exceedingly. But what were you doing when I arrived? Why do I find you dressed in this absurd apron, which is twice too big for you?'

'The painters only finished in my study yesterday, so Peg and I were arranging the furniture. Oh, do come and look!' And she seized his hand like an excited child and drew him into the house. In the passage he stopped and caught her back, and turned her hands over, examining them.

'This will not do,' he said sternly. 'See here – and here! You have blisters, Marmoset, and positively callouses! This is not a lady's hand, my child.'

'Perhaps I am not a lady,' she said mischievously.

'I fear that may be only too true,' he said with a mock sigh. 'At all events, you evidently haven't enough servants. Are they the only two?'

'Those two, and Marie of course. And that is quite enough, James, for you know I am not a grand lady now. We manage very well. Peg works very hard and she learns

174

quickly, and so does Stephen. He is a sort of cousin of hers, but then, everyone in Coxwold seems to be related to the Charlocks. Even the gardener is Peg's great-uncle, and the woman who comes in to do the heavy work is her sister-in-law.'

'And you sit all day with your hands in your lap?'

'When we are quite settled in, I shall,' Héloïse smiled. 'Or at least, I shall sit at my desk and do my writing, and have nothing harder to do than pick flowers and help Marie with the cooking.'

'Ah, yes, the faithful Marie! Where is she?' James asked.

'She has her day off. She has gone in the carrier's cart to the market at Thirsk: since we do not have to count every penny, she has grown quite passionate about markets. But I think she must be growing rather fond of the carrier, too, James, because every time she has a day off she goes somewhere on his cart.'

'And when does she return?'

'She usually stays all day on market day. I expect she will take her dinner there, so if you will stay for dinner, I shall cook for you. Shall you like that?'

'I shall like it exceedingly,' James said gravely. Héloïse met his eyes for a moment, and gave him a nervous smile; and then pulled him to the door of her study, and said, 'There! Is it not a delightful room?'

It was very pretty indeed, James thought, with the long French windows open onto the sunny garden. The rug Peg had been about to beat was lying in a heap on the floor, and the furniture had been pushed back to take it up, and on the top of the *bonheur du jour* was a pot of beeswax polish to account for the rag in Héloïse's hand. Apart from the desk, there was a *chaise longue* covered in straw-coloured satin underneath the freshly painted white bookshelves, two oval-backed Louis-Quinze chairs with tapestry panels to either side of the fireplace, an exquisite little inlaid low-boy in one of the chimney alcoves and, opposite the window, a massive marble-topped, carved and gilded side table, with a huge gilt-framed mirror on the wall above it.

The bookshelves, however, were empty of books, and the walls of pictures, and James commented on it.

'Oh, I shall begin to be a collector of books now,' she said. 'There is a shop in Thirsk which sells them at second hand; and as to pictures – '

'As to pictures, I shall do something to supply the deficiency, until you can get better,' James said smiling. 'I should like to paint your house, and you in it, and your garden. This is a charming room,' he added, looking around him. 'I shall like to think of you sitting here and working at your book! So this is your writing desk – what is it you call it?'

'*Bonheur-du-jour*,' she told him. 'It was made for Queen Marie Antoinette, but she never used it; see, here is her device. Papa bought it for me when I was first married, from a lord who was fleeing to England.' She gave him a mischievous smile. 'I must hope he never comes here to visit me, or he might want to have it back!'

'Is all this furniture from your house?' James asked.

'No, only the desk and the *chaise longue*. Those chairs I think came from Versailles: they have the royal cipher on them. And this side-table – look, here, James, amongst the carving, a salamander, the symbol of King Francis! I think this table and the mirror may have come from Chambord or Blois. Papa emptied both of them for the revolutionary government.'

She ran her fingers over it appreciatively, and he longed so badly to touch her that it took all his will to remain still. He heard himself say, 'It must be pleasant for you to have a little of your home-land with you.'

She looked up. 'Yes,' she said. 'It is better than nothing, but it makes me very lonely sometimes.' In the silence which followed, they could both hear some children out in the lane, playing a counting-game; shrill and tunelessly they chanted the rhyme:

Queen Anne, Queen Anne, she sits in the sun,
As fair as a lily, as white as a swan;
I send you five letters, I hope you read one.
One, two, three ...

'I wish I had a child to bring up,' she said. Her eyes were wide, undefended, her sadness brimming to the surface, coming too close to him, hurting. He could not shield

176

himself against her, or against the unwelcome knowledge that he added to her unhappiness, that he had done so by coming here today. Then he saw her take up the burden, and smile a little, and she said inconsequentially, 'Or a little dog. I should like to have a little dog, I think, to play with in the garden. I had a dog in France, you know – did I tell you?'

'Yes,' he said automatically. 'You told me.' He pulled himself together. 'Well, since you have sent your servants away, I must try to fill their place. What needs to be done here? You shall command me, as if I were Stephen. Wait, where is his apron? I must look the part!'

He clowned for her, acting the part of a very inept servant to make her laugh, though the ineptitude was not all acting. By the time the real servants returned, they had set the study to rights, and Héloïse was shewing him round the garden. 'I wish I had my sketching-book with me,' James was saying. 'Let this be a lesson to me, never to go anywhere without it.'

It was a pleasant day. Peg and Durban between them prepared a cold nuncheon which James and Héloïse took on the little white bench which stood with its back to the sun-warmed bricks of the garden wall. The branches of the old wistaria arched above their heads, past their blooming now, but full of acrobatic birds. Marigolds burned fearlessly in the sun, and goldenrod and dropwort, and the multicoloured snapdragons; but as the sun passed its zenith, they seemed to cool and fade, and the blue flowers took on vividness, flax and sea-lavender, and tall spikes of delphiniums in their second blooming.

James and Héloïse sat and talked, looked over the house and talked, walked about the garden and talked, endlessly, as if they could never tire. They talked of their separate childhoods, of Héloïse's life in France, the convent, Lotti, her marriage, the house in the Rue St Anne; they talked of London, of the years of her poverty; of Lucy and Chetwyn, of Charles and Roberta. They talked of food, and music, and painting; of horses and racing and hunting; of the changing seasons, of flowers and birds, of gardening of Easter and Christmas. What they didn't speak about was

Mary Ann, the present, and the immediate future.

The sun sank lower, and the conversation faltered; the air hung very still in the garden, and the birds were all silent, as if worn out by their day's activity. Héloïse stood up and turned towards the kitchen, and said, 'I think perhaps I had better start preparing dinner. Don't look so worried, James, I am a very good cook. I learned to be when I was living in Brompton.'

'You cannot do it all alone,' he protested.

'But I will not,' she said. 'Peg and Stephen will do the dull parts, like cleaning vegetables and stirring things. I suppose Durban will help, too.'

'And I am expected to sit in the parlour and do nothing while all this activity is going on?' James queried. She looked wicked.

'But you are a gentleman, James. That is all you are fit for.'

'Very well, my lady,' he said grimly, 'you have issued the challenge, and I shall take it up.' They went in through the kitchen door. 'Tell me what needs doing, and I shall do it, whatever it is.'

Héloïse caught Durban's eye, and could not resist the temptation. 'If we are to eat elegantly today,' she said demurely, 'the silver must be cleaned.'

Durban's lip quivered, and he turned his face away to hide it.

'I shall clean it,' James declared superbly.

'Do you know how?' Héloïse provoked.

'I cannot believe it is a difficult thing to do,' he retorted. Durban took pity on him.

'Better let me do it, sir.'

Héloïse's face was too serious as she said, 'Yes, James, perhaps that would be better. I think you would really do it very ill,' and James rose to the bait. Provided with an apron, he sat down at one end of the kitchen table with the silver, the cleaning-powder, and a rag, and proceeded, partly through ignorance, and partly for fun, to make such a mess that Peg was overcome with laughter and had to sit down and put her apron over her head; and even the solemn Stephen let out a guffaw as James held up a knife he

178

claimed was 'Done – to perfection!'

When the preparations were well advanced, Durban took over with a firm hand, and sent his master and her ladyship away to wash and change for dinner and to sit in comfort and take a glass of something while he supervised the kitchen. James could do no more than wash, and tidy his hair, which was soon done, and he repaired then to the parlour, where he found that his excellent man had laid a fire ready for lighting, lit the candles on the chimney-piece, and put out a tray of sherry and glasses.

Since James was in morning-clothes, Héloïse did not put on an evening-gown, but chose instead a simple but pretty dress of yellow muslin, over which she flung a long-fringed shawl of embroidered Norwich silk. She brushed out her long curls, pulled the side hair up into a knot and left the rest tumbling over her shoulders, and then paused to look at herself in the mirror. In the fading, fluky light, it was as if she were looking at a stranger; she noted the bright eyes, the high colour in the cheeks, the parted lips and the eager expression, and she thought, this is a young and pretty girl, on her way to meet her lover. Then the eyes grew sad, and the lips sighed: she pulled the shawl around her and ran downstairs.

The meal was most successful, and James had to acknowledge that Héloïse was a good cook. 'Though I wish there had never been any necessity for you to become one,' he added. Durban waited at the table with Stephen's assistance, quietly correcting the latter's mistakes and doing more to train him in one hour than Héloïse had achieved in a month; for while Stephen naturally respected her ladyship, he had never seen before, and was much more in awe of, a genuine, magnificent, gentleman's valet.

Durban organized everything. When dinner was over, he ushered his charges into the parlour, trimmed the candles and lit the fire, as it was growing a little chilly; intercepted Marie when she arrived home full of the day's happenings, sent her into the kitchen, and himself took in the tea-things, so that his master and her ladyship should not be disturbed

179

by a new face or clumsy service.

Later, when the kitchen was tidy, he dismissed the lower servants for the evening, made up the kitchen fire and sat over it with Marie. It was a clear night, and though there was no more than a quarter moon, there would be light enough to ride home, if need be; but he had taken the precaution of despatching a boy from Charlock's farm to the inn to bespeak beds for the night, just in case. Thus, having covered all eventualities, he had nothing to do but await developments, and his master's pleasure.

In the parlour, conversation slowed and faltered as the fire burned low. Héloïse had no clock, and nothing was further from James's mind than to look at the watch in his fob, but they both knew it was growing late, and that time was not their friend. Héloïse stood up and walked about the room a little, touching things absently, and James's eyes followed her, unwilling to leave her even for an instant. The fire sputtered and fell in and, glad of something to do, Héloïse walked over to mend it, her fingers reaching the handle of the poker at the same moment as James's.

Her eyes widened, she tried to withdraw, but James closed his fingers over hers, and she became very still, like a threatened animal. Slowly, so as not to startle her, he shifted his grip to her wrist and with his other hand removed the poker from her grasp. Her wide eyes looked down into his, grave, apprehensive, but without resistance. He slid forward off his chair onto his knees on the hearthrug, and drew her gently down before him, facing him in the firelight. Their faces were on a level now, only a few inches apart.

He asked nothing, said nothing, watching her eyes, watching the thoughts and feelings pass through them like fish just under the surface of dark water. She feared, she questioned, she doubted, she wanted; need and longing, regret and bitterness were all there, but not, for once, not resignation. That was his answer, answer enough. He moved his hands up to her shoulders, and placed his lips lightly against hers.

She shuddered at the touch, resisted for the merest part of a second, and then yielded, her lips parting, her hands reaching for him. If time passed then, they did not know it.

Later she pushed him gently away, sat back on her heels, and her burning eyes regarded him in the firelight from the frame of her dishevelled hair. She did not speak, but looked the question that was as clear to him as if she had shouted it: *What do you want? What are we going to do?*

He reached out a hand for her, and she flinched away. 'My love,' he said. 'My darling.' He reached again, and she let him touch her, tilting her head a little, watching him, questioningly. 'I don't want to go away,' he said. 'When I came here today, I had no thought of how it would end. I couldn't think about it. But now, it seems madness to go. Everything I value is here.'

'It would be wrong,' she said painfully.

'Would it?'

'You know it would.'

'Do I? I don't know. I can't know about that. I only know that I love you, only you, absolutely, and that without you my life is meaningless. I can't find any reason to go away from you. If you tell me to, I'll go – but, oh, I won't understand it.'

A long time she stared, doubting, and then closing her eyes, turned her face upwards and cried for help. '*Je ne peux pas! Je ne peux pas décider!*'

He grew strong as she weakened. 'My love,' he said, and gathered her in, kissing her brow and eyelids, her ear, her stretched throat; pushing his hands into her hair to turn her head this way and that for kissing, murmuring her name, feeling the pain and struggle leave her. 'It's all right,' he said. 'Everything will be all right. Only love me, love me!'

'I do,' she cried. 'God forgive me, I do.'

He took her hands, lifted her to her feet, drew her to the door of the stairway. The stairs were unlit, and she had to lead him as they went up into blackness. James was glad of the dark: it seemed to offer safety. He followed her without stumbling, her small, narrow hand warm in his. She opened the door to her bedchamber, and left him for a moment to draw back the window-curtains, to let in what light there was. After the utter darkness, it was enough: everything was limned in a faint greyish glow.

They helped each other undress. There was no embarrassment between them; it was almost as if they were comrades-in-arms, and had done this before, in a thousand camps and bivouacs. When she was naked but for her hair, her slender white body small as a child's, she shivered a little and he stepped close and felt their flesh start into warmth at each other's touch. He kissed the warm place behind her ear where the true scent of her was, and ran his hands down her back and caught her by the hollow of her waist.

'James,' she whispered hesitantly, 'I – I don't – '

'What is it, my darling? Don't be afraid.'

'I am not afraid, not with you,' she said truthfully. 'But I do not know very much. My husband – I am not very experienced, you see.'

He kissed her lips to silence, and turned towards the bed. 'Nor am I, Marmoset, not in love. We'll find our way together.'

He spoke truer than he knew. These were new lands, dark, mysterious, uncharted, wonderful. Time seemed suspended; the night held its breath. Tenderly he touched and kissed her, led her step by step through a country unknown to him; until, dazzled with sensation, he was as helpless as she, and they clung together, lost, drowning. He cried out with his unendurable love, and she answered him in a dark and animal tongue; the stars turned slowly and they went spinning together resistlessly outward through the void to some airless, timeless place where there was no thought or sensation, only a perfect knowledge, a completed, unbreakable circle.

Later, much later, he lay with his head on her breast, her arms folded about him, and she kissed his brow in wordless content.

'I did not understand before,' she said softly into the darkness. 'I did not know. How can this be wrong?'

'It can't be,' he said. 'I love you Marmoset. I will never, never leave you again.'

He felt her arms tighten in reply, heard the smile in her voice as she said drowsily, 'I love you, too, *mon âme*. I am so happy.'

Her breast rose and fell beneath his cheek with her peaceful breathing. I am happy too, he said, but he had already drifted too far into sleep to say the words aloud.

BOOK TWO

Swan Displayed

She walks in beauty, like the night,
Of cloudless climes and starry skies;
And all that's best of dark and bright
Meet in her aspect and her eyes:
Thus mellow'd to that tender light
Which heaven to gaudy day denies.

Lord Byron: She Walks in Beauty

Chapter Eleven

They woke before dawn, that first waking together of lovers which no apprehension can diminish, and nothing ever afterwards can equal. They woke, and looked at each other, and smiled, remembering every moment of shared bliss, knowing it was all to come again. She crept closer into his arms, and placed her lips against his, and they lay breathing in each other's scent, drifting and drowsing while the day broadened and strengthened outside, filling in its faintly-sketched outlines with stronger sounds and colours.

They heard the servants get up.

'They won't disturb us,' James whispered. He kissed her lips and the tip of her nose, and ran his hands luxuriously over her body. To be with her, unfettered, undisturbed, licensed to touch, kiss, speak as he pleased, was wealth beyond counting. Shyly she touched him, tried the effect of stroking his smooth shoulder, ran her fingertips along the line of his jaw.

'You are very beautiful,' she murmured. 'I was never able to tell you that before, my James, but you are beautiful like – like a star!'

He laughed exultantly, rolling over onto his elbows to hang above her, looking down into her dark and serious, glad and laughing, beautiful sad-monkey Stuart face. 'And you, my Marmoset, you are – '

'Not beautiful,' she interposed anxiously. 'You cannot say that.'

'Better than that – you are unparalleled, inimitable, unique!' He punctuated the sentence with kisses, and the last extended itself luxuriously until he was thoroughly roused and wanting her again. 'Shall I?' he stopped kissing her long enough to ask.

'Oh yes,' she said, with a childlike emphasis which made him laugh 'I want *everything*!'

Afterwards, when they were curled contentedly in each

187

others' arms again, he said, 'I remember once before you promised me that when we were married, we should have *everything*. I had no idea, then, how much it would be.'

'It seems to me a very agreeable arrangement of God's,' she said, at her most French, 'that when one loves another, there should be so much one can do about it.' She remembered with momentary wonder her married life: how could something which had seemed to her then so dreadful have become a source of such joy?

'You think it is from God, then?' he asked, and was immediately sorry, fearing it would break her mood. But she only said, 'Oh yes, surely it must be?'

Some time later there was a scratching at the door, and Durban came in with a tray. James, appreciating the tact with which he had elected to make the first approach himself, rather than risk Marie's sensibilities, sat up in bed and grinned at his old friend. Durban was impassive, managing to place the tray on his master's knees without by so much as a glance betraying awareness of the presence of Héloïse, who, in confusion and nakedness, had retreated so far under the sheets that only the tangled crown of her head was visible.

'What's this? Tea?' James cried. 'Durban, my friend, you are a genius, and deserve to be knighted. I'm thirsty as the d – as a man can be, I should say. And hungry, too!'

'There will be breakfast, sir, whenever you care to descend. Stephen has been up to the farm, and the young woman has made bread.'

'Nothing else would tempt me out of bed, I must say,' James grinned, 'but the thought of new bread and – ' Another thought crossed his mind, and he frowned. 'I haven't so much as a clean shirt, to say nothing of a razor.' He ran his hand over his bristly jaw, and then cast a curious look at his servant. 'I notice that you are looking damnably smooth about the chin, Durban. How do you manage it?'

Durban gave a faint smile. 'Stephen's razor, sir. I have cleaned it and resharpened it for your use. I'm afraid there's nothing I can do just yet about a shirt, but I will bring up hot water in five minutes, if that will suit you, sir?'

When the door had closed noiselessly behind his servant,

James pulled the sheet back from Héloïse's face, and found that she had curled up tightly and closed her eyes as an extra precaution. 'Tea, my darling?' he inquired genially. 'You can come out now – it's quite safe.'

She opened a cautious eye, and then sat up, rather red in the face, to take the cup he had poured for her. 'Did he say anything?' she asked, sipping.

James was amused. 'He was discretion itself, my mouse-like creature, but you must know that he knows all about us. You will have to get used to that.'

'I know, I am very silly,' she said apologetically. 'It was just that I was not expecting it. I shall be all right now, very correct.'

'Hot water in five minutes,' James informed her cheerfully, 'and breakfast as soon as we go downstairs. What would you like to do today, my dearest? Should you like to go driving in your phaeton?'

'Will you not have to go back?' she asked in a small voice.

'Back?'

'To Morland Place. To explain. They will not even know where you are.'

'They'll know where I went yesterday. And I don't think, since I did not return last night, that there will be any need of explanation,' James said with grim humour.

'To collect some clean clothes, then,' she said, even more hesitantly. He met her eyes.

'I don't want to go back there, ever. I don't want to leave you for an instant; and also, I'm afraid.'

'Afraid that if you go there, they will make you stay?'

'Exactly so. I shall not take the risk: Durban shall go on horseback, bring back a valise with some essentials, and have everything else packed and sent by carrier. Everything, you see – I shall not be going back.' She was not yet smiling. 'What is it, my heart?'

'Must Durban explain for us? Is it not cowardly to make him face the trouble for us?'

'Not cowardly, just wise. He will not mind it, I promise you. There can be no blame attached to him, and he will simply give them his blankest face, and their words will fall off him like water rolling off a duck's feathers. I shall write him a letter to take to my mother, to explain and apologize,' he added at last, and she nodded, and gave a tremulous smile.

'Oh, James,' she said, and he leaned across to kiss her.

'Don't worry, everything will be all right.'

'They will be angry.'

'For a while, but they'll get over it. I have not been of very much use to any of my family over the past few years, and they will be glad, in the end, that I have gone.'

By the time they went downstairs, James had such an appetite as he did not remember since his childhood. Durban and Marie – the latter looking by far more apprehensive than disapproving – laid the table with new bread, jam and honey, and the good things Charlock's farm had provided, fresh butter, eggs, bacon, pork chops, kidneys, smoked trout, and fat burnished sausages; and James and Héloïse ate with as healthy appetites as if they had been out in the fresh air since dawn.

'It just shews you,' James said, spreading butter lavishly on a warm crust, 'what hard work love is!'

At length Durban came in with the refilled coffee-pot, and said, 'If I could persuade you to write the letter, sir, I could be off. The day is already somewhat advanced – '

'Yes, damnit, very well. I'll do it now. My love, have you any letter-paper, and a pen?'

'In my desk,' Héloïse said, looking grave, and getting to her feet, but James laid his hand on hers and said, 'There's no occasion for you to stir. I shall be back in a moment.'

He called Durban with a glance, and they went together into Héloïse's study. There Durban stood impassively by James's side as he wrote the letter to his mother, hurriedly, before he lost his nerve. He sanded and folded it, sealed it with a wafer, and handed it to Durban saying, 'There. I don't know that it is particularly coherent, but it is the best I can manage.'

'Yes, sir.'

James gave him a curious look. 'Do you think I'm mad,

Durban? Or a villain?'

'It isn't for me to say, sir.'

'Come, my friend – for if you aren't my friend, I haven't one – give me your true opinion, just once. Am I mad?'

'I don't think there was anything else you could have done, sir,' Durban said at length, and, meeting his eyes, James realized that the answer was not unequivocal, was all he deserved, in fact.

'I'm sorry,' he said, 'I really am sorry for everything, and sorry that you should have this disagreeable task. But as you say, there isn't anything else I can do.'

Durban inclined his head in as much consent as he could give, and turned for the door.

'Pack everything,' James called after him. Not that there was much, he thought. He had never been a collector. 'You know what to bring for the immediate necessities? And for God's sake, bring my painting things with you; those I must have. And tell Mother – tell Mother I'm sorry.'

It was well past noon when Durban arrived at Morland Place, to find the yard suspiciously full of loitering servants and grooms. Hoskins came in person to take Forest's head, and murmured to Durban as he dismounted, 'What in the name o' pity's goin' on, Mr Durban? Is thy master run mad, or what?'

'Has the family gone to the racecourse?' Durban asked, relinquishing the reins.

'The master and Lord and Lady Aylesbury has. The mistress stopped 'ome in case your master should come, and the young madam's in her room – hasn't come down at all today. Mad as fire she were,' he added in a burst of confidentiality. 'Miss Lucy's maid told Mr Thorn that Mrs Mappin said she heard madam talking to the mistress as they crossed the 'all last night goin' up to bed: takin' on something marvellous, she were. An' Mr Oxhey says as that Dakers sent word this morning that madam was stoppin' in her room with a fit of the vapours – prostrated, she said – but Miss Lucy's maid says there's no vapours in t' case, and that it's nowt but temper, pure an' simple.'

Durban shook himself free of the elderly groom, reflecting that Mrs James had never succeeded in making herself beloved of the servants. As soon as he entered the hall Oxhey accosted him. Durban knew that he must take the initiative, but as Oxhey had all a butler's traditional dignity to slow him down, it was easy for Durban, with a suitably deferential look, to get his word in first.

'Oh, Mr Oxhey, I have a letter here for her ladyship. I wonder, if she is at leisure, whether it would be best for you to take it to her?'

'Her ladyship is in the steward's room. In the circumstances, I am sure she will wish to see you at once. That is – I assume –' he coughed delicately, 'I assume your master does not accompany you.'

Durban shook his head. 'I'll wait here then, Mr Oxhey, until her ladyship has read the letter,' he said, making it sound as if it had been Oxhey's suggestion, and Oxhey bowed assent, took the letter from his hand, and moved majestically off towards the steward's room.

Durban moved quickly. As soon as Oxhey had gone down the chapel passage, he ran across the hall and up the stairs to James's room, and with a few swift movements flung shirts, stockings, cravats, shaving tackle, and anything else that was easily accessible into a large, soft valise with leather handles which could be tied to the saddle dees. He added the master's latest sketching-book, and the long flat box in which he kept his pencils, paints and brushes, and, on impulse, the book which lay on the bedside table. Then he ran back downstairs and bestowed the valise in a dark corner, under one of the little, hard hall chairs. It was not precisely that anyone could stop him leaving, but there might be difficulty about his packing James's belongings; and at the very least, it would be tactless to ask, or to be seen, to do so.

He was waiting, apparently without having moved from the spot, when Oxhey came back.

'Her ladyship will see you now,' he said. The words were formal, unemotional, but his look was confused and troubled.

Jemima was standing looking out of the window when

Durban was ushered in.

'Thank you, Oxhey. You may leave us. I will call you if I need you,' she said without turning round.

'Very good, my lady,' Oxhey said doubtfully, and backed out, closing the door quietly behind him. When they were alone, Jemima turned, and Durban saw why Oxhey had been troubled: she had been crying. She held James's letter in her hand, and gestured with it as she looked at Durban.

'Do you know what this says?'

'In essence, my lady. I have not read it,' he replied gently. She swallowed, and turned her head away. Durban saw traces of her tears glistening in the light from the window, saw her draw a deep breath and command herself, and turn to him again with the grave and benign look of a great lady, and his heart went out to her. 'My lady,' he said, 'I have served Mr James since he took his first commission, in uniform and out of it and I love him like a son. I beg your pardon for speaking of it, my lady, but – '

Jemima nodded. 'Yes, I understand. It's all right, Durban: I lay no blame on you. You and I, perhaps, are the ones who will feel this most deeply.'

He could say nothing. Just for that instant he felt attached to her across the room by tenuous threads of affection and sympathy, a momentary and oddly intimate sensation of shared parenthood.

'He will not come back?' she said at length.

'I believe not, my lady.'

'Oh God, that it should come to this!' she said from the heart. 'And Héloïse – what of her? Durban, did she not try to persuade him to come back? I cannot believe that she would consent to what she knows is wrong.' Durban was necessarily silent, and Jemima said after a moment, 'I'm sorry, that was not a fair question to ask. You truly believe that he intends to stay with Lady Henrietta – permanently?'

'Yes, my lady.' She was still looking at him, as though unable to accept that this was all, and he added, hesitantly, 'I think they both understand what is entailed, my lady, but they are – happy together. They were not happy before.'

'No,' she said bleakly. She looked down at the letter in her hand. 'Such an irony: it was everything I wished for them, if only it had happened at a different time. But like this – !' She was silent a while longer, and then looked up, meeting his eyes. 'You return to your master, I suppose?'

'He wishes me to take his belongings back with me, my lady,' Durban said unwillingly.

'Yes, I suppose he would. But you will not go immediately. I cannot think all at once what to do. I must have time to consider. You will wait, Durban?'

It was half a question, half a command, as befitted their relationship. He was not her servant; but his master had lived at her expense, and it was she, ultimately, who had paid his wages.

'As you wish, my lady,' he said neutrally, and bowed himself out.

After all the expressions of shock, surprise, and outrage, the family's reactions were very different. Lucy spoke up very promptly for a washing of hands.

'We're all better off without him, Mother – even Mrs James. He's been behaving abominably ever since – well, I can't remember when.'

'But Lucy, dear, consider – we can't just let him do this terrible thing,' Jemima protested.

'Why not? Lord, Mother, lots of married people live separate lives. There's nothing in that. In London nobody thinks anything of it, if someone takes a lover, provided it's done discreetly.'

Chetwyn looked amused at his wife's avowed sophistication, and hastened to reassure his mother-in-law.

'Pay no attention, ma'am – she don't know it from first hand, I assure you!' he said. 'But there's a deal in what she says, all the same. From what I understand, it's all very well to talk about not letting James do as he pleases, but it seems to me it's a matter of what *can* be done. I can't see how anyone is to make him come back if he don't want to. Much better, in that case, to leave well alone. It's not true that people turn a blind eye to that sort of thing – no, Luce, I promise you, a discreet love-affair is one thing, but runnin' off from one's wife and livin' with one's mistress won't do!

194

But if we can't make him come back – and I don't see how we can – it seems to me that it would be better to ignore the whole thing. If we stir up a fuss trying to force him, it will only draw attention to it, and the scandal will be so much the worse.'

Jemima looked bewildered. 'But we can't do nothing! That would be to lend approval to his actions.'

'Do nothing? I should think not!' Edward growled. 'Damn James! Why the devil can't he behave like a normal human being? He's been trying your patience, Mama, since he was in short coats, but this is beyond everything! I can't believe you're advocating letting him get away with it, Chetwyn.'

Chetwyn gave his lazy smile. 'My dear Ned, I'm all for forcin' a man to do his duty, particularly if it's distasteful to him; but I don't care about looking ridiculous, as we certainly should, my dear, if we went up there full of righteous indignation and came back with our tails between our legs.'

'If I go up there, it's James who will be looking ridiculous, I promise you,' Edward said furiously. 'The insolence of it, sending his man to collect his things! All it needs, Mama, is for Chetwyn and me – well, I'll go alone if you don't like it, Chet, and be damned to you – '

'Fire-eater!' Chetwyn murmured, amused.

'– to go up there with a couple of servants,' Edward continued determinedly, 'and bring him back, by force if necessary.'

'And Héloïse?' Jemima said quietly. 'What of her?'

There was a silence. Ned had forgotten her for a moment, and as he remembered, the impossibility of dragging James forcibly from her arms, attractive though the picture was, came home to him. He looked bewildered.

'Well, at least,' he said at last, 'you won't let Durban take his things to him, will you, Mama?'

'Oh Ned, I don't know,' Jemima sighed. 'What good would it do to forbid him? Will a lack of shirts make James come back?'

Lucy glanced at the clock on the chimney-piece. 'At any rate, Mama, we have to decide what to do this evening.

195

There's the dinner and ball at Shawes, and if we are to go, we had better go and get dressed; or if we aren't, we had better send to tell them.'

'Don't be stupid, Lucy, how can we go?' Ned exclaimed. Lucy gave him a withering look.

'Stupid yourself! If we don't go, we might as well write it all up on a board and post it outside the door, for everyone will know.'

'Everyone will know soon enough,' Ned said gloomily, and Chetwyn put an arm round his shoulder.

'We might as well buy time while we can, old fellow. No sense in givin' the scandal-mongers their broth on a plate.' He looked with sympathy at Jemima and said, 'What do you say, ma'am, to Lucy and me going, at least? We can make up some story. And Ned, you'll lend us countenance, won't you?'

Edward laid his hand over his friend's. 'I can't,' he said. 'I should only pull you down. I'll stay with Mother.'

'You had better say that I am unwell,' Jemima said, 'and let it be thought that Ned and James are staying with me on that account. I would not have you tell untruths, but I do feel quite unfit for company.'

'And Mrs James – is she unwell too?' Chetwyn asked wryly. Jemima looked aghast.

'Good God, I had forgotten her! Poor young woman – how she must feel it! I must go up to her and see if there is anything I can do.'

She hurried away, and Lucy and Chetwyn repaired to their rooms to dress. 'I'm afraid she's all to easy to forget,' Chetwyn murmured to his wife. 'James will have no trouble at all.'

Later that evening, Edward went to look for his mother, and found her at last, as she had found James, in the Lady-chapel, just sitting, her eyes upon the golden face, worn gentle with age, of the Lady. He sat down beside her, and after a while she said, 'I was just thinking about your father, and how much I miss him. If only he had been here, he would have known what to do.'

196

'Papa couldn't stop James doing wrong before,' Ned reminded her. 'What about Mary Skelwith, for instance?'

'Oh, but James did heed him, Ned. He restrained himself a great deal on that account; and though what he did with Mary Skelwith was wrong, it was not as serious as this. This is just – the worst thing.' She brooded. 'And yet, I have been wondering, if I had been married to someone else, and loving your father as I did – '

'No, Mama,' Ned said with affectionate amusement, 'you wouldn't have done anything of the sort, and you know it.'

She looked at him. 'The worse my failure then, that my children should be so different from me! For even you, Ned, my dear son, though you are a great comfort to me, even you don't feel James's crime as I do. You are angry with him, because you feel he has wronged us, and made us all appear ridiculous. You are afraid of the scandal, but you don't abhor the sin because it is a sin.'

'Oh, Mother – '

'No, my darling, I don't reproach you. Only I have failed all of you, your father especially; and my father, who left the fortune of the Morlands in my hands. I haven't proved such a good guardian, have I?'

He didn't answer. Jemima brooded, thinking of her childhood; of the Morland history and the sense of family which Allen had instilled into her during their long rides together; how he, unwittingly, had been preparing her for this responsibility at a time when there was no likelihood it would ever be hers. She remembered the Countess Annunciata, who, more than any other, she thought of as her predecessor, and of all the troubles against which she had had to defend the family.

'We have survived so much, we Morlands,' she said at last. 'War and famine and rebellion, poverty, dissension, religious persecution: we came through them all, and they made us stronger. Only now I wonder if we can survive through peace and prosperity. Something has gone out of us, some virtue, and I don't know what it is, or how to get it back.'

She glanced at her son, and saw him listening, but not understanding, and she felt old, and so alone. Allen had

197

been her dear companion through most of her life, her husband and lover for thirty years of it, and five years of widowhood were not enough to blunt the pain of missing him. She had not made a friend of her children when they were young, and perhaps she should not be surprised now that they did not understand each other. In some ways, James had been the child of hers to whom she had felt closest; and yet it was he who had inflicted the deepest wound.

Héloïse would have understood, she thought painfully. She would have been a daughter to me, more truly than the children of my body. It was the bitterest of ironies.

'He'll come back of his own accord eventually,' Edward said. 'I'm sure of it. After a while, when the novelty wears off, he'll get bored and want to come home. It's not to be supposed that there'll be much to do up there, in a little village miles from anywhere, and Jamie's used to his comforts. Héloïse isn't rich, and it's quite a small house, isn't it, Mother?'

'Quite small,' Jemima agreed absently.

'And then, I think he will miss Fanny. He's very fond of her. If we leave him be for a while, it will probably all blow over.'

She turned to look at him; saw his pleasant, gentle, untested face; his hopefulness that he had offered her comfort, and, even more, that the violent winds of life would not come howling down on his quiet haven, and she smiled painfully. 'Oh Ned,' she said.

'I tell you what, though, Mama,' he added urgently, 'I have just thought of it: if we are to keep this business quiet, we must make sure Mrs James does not write to her father, for if he once takes a hand in it, it will be bellows to mend with all of us!'

The thought of Mr Hobsbawn was one jest of fate too many. She buried her face in her hands, and from the noises she made, Ned did not know whether she was laughing or crying, and could only put his arm around her and pat her kindly, hoping that the gesture would be appropriate to either case.

*

When Jemima came up to her room, Mary Ann fended her off, made a cold response to her offers of sympathy, refused all comfort, and finally, triumphantly, drove her away. But left in possession of her solitude, she wondered why she had done it, and gradually with the cooling of her ardour she began to see that she had been at fault. Pride and anger had been her sins that day: anger at the affront to her pride of her husband's actions; hurt pride which led her to reject human sympathy; anger that she had been made to appear ridiculous; pride in standing alone in her martyrdom.

Contemplation led to self-reproach and tears. When she could cry no more, she washed her face, and went to seek out Father Thomas in his room, and he heard her confession, shrove her, and gave her the sacrament. She left his room spiritually comforted, but lonely for human contact. Now was the time to go to her mother-in-law, she thought, to apologize for her coldness, and perhaps, at last, make friends with her. It was a golden opportunity, for not only was Lady Morland in the house and without occupation, but she was also unhappy and troubled, and perhaps needing a companion and confidante as much as Mary Ann.

She looked for her mother-in-law in all the usual places, and finally, as she came out of the steward's room, noticed that the door to the chapel was not properly closed. She pushed it open and saw Jemima and Ned in the Lady-chapel, sitting silently side by side, his arm around her shoulder. A bitterness touched her for a moment: of course Lady Morland did not need her! She had her sons and daughters, and no doubt at this moment was wishing Mary Ann had never been born, so that her precious James could have married the Frenchwoman and stayed at home. Then everyone would have been happy, for it was a plain fact that no-one at Morland Place had ever welcomed Mary Ann, or shewn her the least affection. If it were a choice between her and James, everyone without hesitation would choose James and wish her at the devil.

She caught her thoughts up sharply: she was newly shriven, and in a state of grace. She offered a brief inward prayer of apology and retreated from the chapel as silently as she had come.

She didn't know what to do with herself. She wandered into the drawing-room, sat down and picked up a book, and turned a few pages without the least idea of what she was reading, and was glad of the diversion when Edward's dog Leaky came wandering in from the hall, presumably looking for his master.

'Leaky! Come here, good fellow,' Mary Ann said, holding out her hand. He came out of politeness and nudged her hand, and swung his iron cable of a tail a few times. Normally that would have been all he allowed her, for he was an exclusive dog, and did not care for the caresses of anyone but Edward. But at the moment he was missing Brach, who was in retirement in the kennels where she had just whelped, and he was lonely. When Mary Ann spoke nonsense to him, and began rubbing the place behind the ears as she had seen Ned do, his soul stirred, and he leaned against her, smiling.

A little more of the same, and he forgot his dignity so far as to place one huge paw on her knee, and made the strange whistling noise that Edward called 'talking'. Mary Ann cupped his face, and pulled his ears.

'Yes, you miss her, don't you, old fellow? You're lonely too. Poor Leaky, I understand.'

Leaky yawned and whistled simultaneously, which made him sneeze, and then he put his other paw on her knee for good measure, and tried to climb onto her lap. She hugged him, and he licked her face, and then went on licking, because it was agreeably salty. Mary Ann cried, not the hot tears of passion this time, but the gentler and infinitely more painful tears of the heart, given to the dog because no-one else wanted them; cried because, like Leaky, she had lost her mate, whom she loved, and how ever little he cared for her, she missed him.

Chapter Twelve

James met Durban alone at the door on his return, and led him immediately upstairs.

'You managed to pack the valise, then,' he observed. 'Let's see what you brought. Ah, my painting-box, thank God! And what's this book?'

'It was beside your bed, sir. I had very little time – I had to take what was to hand.'

'Lord, yes, I remember, it was *Tom Jones*. Well, if I am to start a new life with only one book to my name, I suppose that is as good as any. Shirts, cravats – my blue coat, good! Was there any difficulty about bringing my things? What disposition have you made about the rest of them?'

'I left instructions with Mr Oxhey for everything to be packed up and sent on, but I do not know if they will be carried out. There was some resistance to the idea.'

'Well, it doesn't matter, anyway,' James said. 'Here is enough to be going on with, and I don't know what I will need more. We shall be living very quietly, her ladyship and I, quite a country life. I shall not need Court-dress in Coxwold!'

It was intended as a joke, but James's attempt at laughter faltered and failed as he met the terrible sympathy in Durban's eye. A silence fell, in which he could hear the light murmur of women's voices downstairs.

'I'm afraid they won't leave you alone, sir,' Durban said at last, very gently. James tried to smile.

'Well, after all, they can't bring me back by force, and what else – ' He stopped. 'Was my mother – was she very upset?'

It was on the tip of Durban's tongue to tell his master that she had cried, but he thought better of it. All too soon the world would come surging back like a tide, but it was not his business to hasten it.

'She sent you this letter, sir,' he said, drawing it from his breast. James looked as though it would bite him, and then took it reluctantly, as if in spite of himself. The voices downstairs rose and fell, and there was a sudden burst of laughter. He thought of his mother and his wife and his sisters, and in a moment of irritation felt beleaguered by women; and then thought of Héloïse, and shook the idea away.

'I'll read it later,' he said firmly, and folded it inside the book for safety.

He dismissed Morland Place from his thoughts, and was happy. There followed a time of great and extraordinary peace, as if something restless and searching in him, something beaked and taloned, had put its head under its wing and gone to sleep. The anxious, craving feelings which had never let him rest were gone, and in their place was a simple joy which greeted him like the sun when he woke in the morning, filled his days with ease, and sealed his dreamless sleep at night.

Everything in the world seemed somehow closer, more vivid, more immediate; colours were brighter and clearer, sounds and smells sharp and delightful; food tasted extraordinarily good, and he sat down to his simple meals with a clean-edged and healthy hunger.

Every day was full of delight, and every moment was spent with Héloïse, doing perfectly ordinary things, which he would never before have considered as sources of pleasure. He picked fruit, and helped with the jam-making; he worked in the garden, pruning shrubs and planting out next year's wallflowers; he mended things about the house, and with Stephen's help, began to learn carpentry and started to make a cabinet. He caught from Héloïse her interest in cooking, and the hours before dinner were spent in the kitchen with a great deal of noise and occasional hilarity, all six of them chopping and mixing and stirring, arguing pleasantly, experimenting, and getting in each other's way.

He and Héloïse went for long walks, and he taught her the names of the English plants and creatures, which he had hardly known he knew until he discovered the pleasure of

202

instructing her. They drove out in the phaeton, and went to see the nearby places of interest, the ruins of Byland Abbey, and the great white cliff at Sutton Bank. They went fishing together, and never caught anything. Sometimes they would simply find a field with a view, and sit all day, conversing while he drew. In the evening he worked on what he hoped would be the definitive portrait of her, while she talked or read to him.

'I never have time to work on my memoirs,' she complained happily one evening. 'Before you came, I wondered sometimes how I would fill my days. I thought I ought to get a little dog, for company. I even considered adopting a child. Now, the days fly past, and every minute is filled with treasure.'

On the day they drove to Sutton Bank and stood on the top of the scarp, looking out over the great plain of York, with its patchwork fields and little silver rivers, he said, 'It's only when we are silent for a moment, as now, that I realize how much we talk to each other.' She glanced at him enquiringly. 'I mean, in the time since I have been with you, we have hardly stopped talking for a moment, and we never run out of things to say, and yet when I think about it, I can't remember anything we have said.'

Héloïse laughed. 'Oh, but that is the very best kind of talk, my James.'

Never had he shared such intimacy with a woman – or with any human being. He knew every part of her, every expression of her face, every gesture she made. He knew the smell of her, so that if he had been shut in a pitch-dark room with a hundred women, he could have found her by scent alone. In the blind darkness of night his fingertips knew every plain and hollow of her pliant body; he knew her mind, the grace of it which touched him, and the shape of her thoughts.

What he knew, he loved. He loved her laughter, the turn of her head, her quick light movements, the way she wrinkled her nose when in deep thought; he loved her common sense, and the passion with which she would argue over the flavouring of a sauce. And every night in her little boat-bed with the white muslin drapes, he would hold her

203

precious, small body close to him, and wonder at so much love.

'We must never quarrel, James,' she said to him one night on the edge of sleep. 'The bed is much too small.'

He learnt the difference between making love, and what he had done before with other women: this was progression, development, as different as a symphony from a four-bar tune; a shared journey of discovery. When her flux came, and they had to sleep apart for a week, he realized how it would be, how this small monthly disappointment would become a regular and expected thing. It seemed a warm and kindly thing to share. They missed each other, and came together at the end of week with new tenderness.

It was not to be expected that they would be left entirely alone. James had read his mother's letter, and it had made him unhappy. He did not answer it, for no answer was possible. The next approach came two weeks later, when Edward arrived alone on horseback one morning. Durban saw him from the window, and went to fetch James from the garden, where he and Héloïse had been discussing the desirability of digging a pond.

Héloïse looked frightened when she understood who was at the gate, and James, though paling a little, sought to reassure her. He pressed her hand and said firmly. 'Let me see him alone, my love. It is better that way. Don't worry, he can't hurt us.'

He met his brother in the parlour. Edward looked unexpectedly taller to him. His usually cheerful face was set in grim lines, but otherwise he was the same old Ned, and the familiarity roused all James's old affection. The soft brown hair was caught back in a queue with a black ribbon, as always – he did not crop like James, not because he despised the fashion, as some men did, thinking it effeminate or even 'foreign', but simply because he never thought about his appearance. His brown coat and breeches were cut for comfort rather than elegance, and his boots had the soft, dull shine of very old, well-kept leather; his waistcoat was yellow and green striped, a piece of cheerful nonsense which

204

James was willing to wager had been a present from Chetwyn, and his stock was plain white and simply tied.

He looked like a respectable but unlettered country squire, a man who knew everything there was to know about cattle and pigs and crop rotation, tithes and rents and repairing leases, and nothing about fashionable life; he looked also, to James's newly opened eye, like a man who knew nothing about passion and grief. Edward was thirty-five, five years James's senior, but his face, despite the tiredness around his eyes, was indelibly youthful. He is Chetwyn's boy still, James thought; while he is that, he will never be anyone's man.

'It's good to see you,' James said.

'Is it? I doubt you'll be so welcoming when you hear what I have to say.'

'It seems strange to see you looking so grim, not at all like my dear old Ned, my kind brother. Have you been long on the road? Can I get you some refreshment? We live very simply here – ale or buttermilk is about all I can offer you.'

'Oh stop it, Jamie, do,' Edward said irritably.

'Stop what?' James said, with raised eyebrows.

'This play-acting. What the devil do you think you're doing? You must know perfectly well what I have come for, and you go babbling on about buttermilk as though this were a social visit. It isn't a matter for laughter, you know.'

'Ah, but that's where you're wrong,' James said gently. 'My life has become, for the first time, very much a laughing matter. I'm happy, Ned, do you understand that? Do you know what it is to be happy, all day long?'

'How can you be happy? Have you no shame? Don't you know you're breaking Mother's heart? You've plunged us all into the middle of the most terrible scandal. Everything's at sixes and sevens, the house in uproar, and you stand there and talk about being happy!'

James bit his lip. 'I'm sorry – '

'Sorry!' Ned interrupted explosively.

'Sorry to have made anyone unhappy. I didn't want to cause an uproar, and if there were anything I could do, short of leaving here, to make things better, I would do it. But you may as well know straight away that I am not coming back, whatever you say. I love Héloïse, and I'm happy here, more happy than I knew a man could be. Try to understand that, and forgive me.'

Ned listened with growing indignation, tapping his boot with his riding crop. 'I understand one thing, that you are as selfish as the day is long, and haven't the least care in the world for anyone but yourself. Aye, and you've always been like that, from a child upwards. What you wanted, you took, and devil take the rest of us. That's your attitude, isn't it? What about your wife? What about your daughter? Don't you know Fanny looks for you every day? She keeps asking why you don't come to see her any more.'

'Oh,' said James softly, turning his face away. 'That was below the belt.'

There was a short silence, and then Edward spoke more gently. 'Come back, Jamie. Things are bad, but it isn't too late. We've managed to keep it fairly quiet so far. People are wondering, but they don't know anything for sure. Mother will forgive you if you come with me now, and I don't think your wife will say anything. She misses you too, you know.' James looked up, disbelief in his eyes. 'Oh yes, she doesn't say much, but she misses you. She's really quite fond of you.'

'Quite fond,' James said in wonder, and then laughed. The cloud-shadow had passed over. 'Quite fond! My dear brother, it just shews you know nothing of love, if you think I could be summoned by a woman who was "quite fond" of me! What do you know of the rich inner landscape, of the bliss of a shared life and two minds thinking as one?'

'Stuff! Don't try to gammon me with that romantic pish-posh! This is dereliction of duty, plain and simple. You are evading your responsibilities, in the most cowardly way.'

'Cowardly?' James said, hurt.

'Yes,' said Ned, his lip curling with contempt, 'I said cowardly. You're hiding from duty behind a woman's skirts.'

There was a silence, and then James turned away. 'I think you had better go. You can have nothing more to say to me now.'

'You will not come with me?'

'No.'

'And what am I to tell Mother?'

James frowned. 'Tell her I'm sorry, if you please. I can't come back. It will be better if you all forget me, as though I had never existed.'

Edward drew a breath, as though there might still be something to say. He looked at his brother with regret, and remembered their ties of blood, their shared childhood, and the kindness there had been between them in other days; and then he shrugged, clamped his shapeless hat back onto his head, and went out to where Stephen was holding his horse at the gate.

'He won't come back,' said Edward.

'Even now?' Jemima asked.

'Even now,' he said looking down with anxious pity at his mother. It was strange and disturbing to see her so still, sitting in the house all day instead of being out on horseback. 'But don't despair, Mama,' he begged, going down on his knees before her, and pressing her hands. 'Give it time. He is still living in the clouds, full of romantic nonsense. He will come down to earth at last, and then he'll come home and beg your forgiveness.'

Jemima looked up. 'But then he'll be unhappy again,' she said. 'Part of me wishes he might stay in his cloud. The cure will be almost as bad as the illness.'

September came, the best of Septembers, warm, sunny, windless, golden. Edward and Chetwyn spent long hours out of doors shooting rabbits and pigeons, getting in practice for the pheasant season to come; while Lucy grew short of breath and irritable, and longed for her confinement to be over, so that she could get back to London for the Little Season.

Stretched out on a sofa by the window, with her mother and Mary Ann nearby, sewing or reading, she would count and calculate: 'If it is born in the first week of October, I could be in London for most of November. But if it doesn't

207

come until the end of the month, I shan't get to Town until after Christmas.'

'What is so very attractive about London, child?' Jemima asked, puzzled. 'You always liked walking and riding and being in the country.'

'I can walk and ride in London,' Lucy said, 'and there is so much more to do, and more people. I have a large acquaintance in London, Mother. You have no idea.'

'Yes, my dear, I have some idea,' Jemima said with a faint smile. 'I lived in London once.'

Mary Ann looked up and said, 'I'm afraid I have not: I've never been to London at all.'

Lucy looked at her with one of her sudden bursts of pity. She didn't much like Mrs James, but felt that she had had a very poor deal. 'Well, you must come up and stay with Chetwyn and me. There's enough room, now Mary's away. I'll take you around and shew you everything, and introduce you –' She stopped abruptly, as all three women realized simultaneously that it would be impossible to introduce Mary Ann anywhere without some inquiry being made as to the whereabouts of her husband. Damn James, Lucy thought, and was about to express the thought aloud, when Jemima intervened with more tact.

'I'm so looking forward to next year, when *Pelican*'s commission will be ending. We may hope to have William and Harry home again in the spring. I can't wait to see them. I miss my sons when they are from home.'

Mary Ann, stitching away at a vest for Lucy's baby, compressed her lips tightly at the words. But when it came to it, Jemima thought with an inward sigh, there were few topics of conversation that were safe in Mary Ann's presence.

The first part of Lucy's wish, to have her confinement over and done with, looked like being fulfilled. One day in the third week of September she walked over to Shawes to see Charles and Roberta and to demand their commiseration over the fact that they would be back in London before her. It was a very hot day, and she went through the fields, where the walking was rough and the lion-grass long and hampering. When she arrived she was feeling fagged and out of sorts, and Roberta made her sit down and sent for a glass of cold lemonade. At the first sip Lucy opened her eyes wide and gasped. Roberta thought the drink had been too cold for her in her heated condition, and was taking it from her and apologizing, when Lucy cried out and doubled up, and they realized simultaneously that her pains had started.

The pains were immediately severe, and Roberta would not hear of her trying to go back to Morland Place.

'Second babies often come very quickly, and it would not do for you to be having it in the carriage,' she said sensibly. 'Let me get you up to bed, and I'll send for the doctor straight away. There's no reason why you shouldn't be comfortable here, is there?'

Lucy was growing more preoccupied by the minute, and had no further argument to offer. Roberta got her to bed, and sent, on her request, for her mother and Docwra, and on Charles's insistence, for the best surgeon in York.

It was a long and hard labour. It seemed that Lucy did not give birth easily, and the child, like her first, was large. The surgeon emitted such an air of gloom and foreboding that eventually Docwra lost her temper with him, and begged Jemima to send him away. Jemima, despite her own anxiety, exerted herself to be tactful and kept the doctor on hand, just in case, while she and Docwra remained at the bedside.

The child was born at last the following morning, and the first words uttered in its hearing by its mother were hardly welcoming. 'Oh dear, what use is that?' Lucy croaked despondently; the child, another girl, began to yell.

Flaminia had been a pretty baby, and despite her being of the wrong sex, both her parents had been sufficiently interested in her, as a novelty, to carry her over the difficult period until custom made her beloved. But the new baby was misshapen and ugly, and though Docwra and Jemima both swore that the condition was purely temporary, they could rouse no favourable response in Lucy.

'Ah, sure, we'll let her be,' Docwra said at length. 'It was a long labour with her, me lady, and sometimes it hardens

209

the heart to have suffered so. I remember me mother had a bad time with our Joseph, the way she couldn't bring herself to touch him the first few days. She'll come around to it in time.'

'I certainly hope so,' Jemima said, nursing the red-and-blue mottled monster in her arms with love and pity. 'Poor little creature!' She had loved all her own babies from the beginning; but then, she reflected doubtfully, she had dearly loved their father. Perhaps it was different, to have a child by a man you were no more than fond of? She dismissed the idea briskly. Dreadful notion! At that rate, what was to become of marriage and parenthood? What would the world come to?

It was almost as difficult to arouse Chetwyn's interest, although, being in his normal state of health and spirits, he made a polite effort. He was disappointed that the child was not a boy, though not quite as disappointed as Lucy, since his children made their appearance with very little effort or inconvenience on his part, and the thought of having to go through it all again was not nearly so dismaying as it was to his wife; but he could find nothing good to say about the baby.

'Ugly little thing, ain't it?' he said dispassionately when Jemima brought her to him.

'She's not an it,' Jemima said firmly, 'and she's only a little crumpled from the birth. She'll straighten out and get her colour in a few days – like a rose-petal.'

'Rose-petal!' Chetwyn exploded with laughter, and even Edward said, 'Really, Mother, there's not much of the rose about that little brute!'

Jemima found herself growing quite cross in defence of the child. 'You're as bad as each other,' she said. 'I don't suppose you made a very elegant appearance when you were her age, Chetwyn, and I know Ned didn't.'

'I can't help it, ma'am,' Chetwyn said, a little remorsefully. 'I'm only speaking the truth – she is ugly.'

'She's strong and healthy, and she's your daughter,' Jemima said. 'And since Lucy is not feeling herself at the moment, I think you had better give her a name.'

'Oh, Lord, another name? No, ma'am, I beg you will

excuse me, but I shot my bolt last time, with Flaminia. It ain't reasonable to expect me to be brilliant twice in my life, now is it? Ned, I appeal to you – am I the sort of man to ask for a name?'

Edward only laughed, and Jemima glowered at them. 'You are a pair of silly babies,' she said. 'Very well, I shall name the child, and you will have to abide by my choice.'

'Agreed!' Chetwyn said. 'You'll do it very well, ma'am, I'm sure of it. Come, Ned, I want to shew you my Purdeys. They arrived this morning, in good time for the third!'

They went out, laughing, and Jemima turned to Docwra, holding the baby in a fiercely protective grasp .

'Don't pay any heed to them, me lady. They was only trying to provoke you,' Docwra said soothingly. 'The babby's healthy, and that's everything.'

'I know. Well, I shall have to give her a lovely name to make up for it, poor mite. What's the most beautiful name in the world, I wonder?'

'One of the blessed saints' names, me lady, like Miss Fanny – not a heathenish mouthful like Flaminia or t'other one, begging your pardon.'

Jemima, deep in thought, did not hear her. Her brow cleared. 'I have it: the very thing. She shall be Rosamund – the rose of the world! I called her a rose petal, and they laughed, but she'll grow up as lovely as her name, and put the shame on them.'

'Amen to that,' Docwra said fervently, and then flinched as the rose of the world woke up and began to yell with a stridency which betokened at least an extremely healthy pair of lungs.

'What is that you are making, my love?' Héloïse asked, intrigued. James had for several evenings abandoned work on the almost-finished portrait of her in favour of a thick oblong of wood, about one foot by two in size, onto which he had painted a map of the world. It was a very fine affair, the background sea a bright, unlikely blue, sporting ships in full sail and colourful sea-monsters with bulging eyes; the land very detailed, with each country painted a different

211

colour, and decorated with trees and animals and plants appropriate to its climate.

But now, having expended a great deal of time and skill on the painting, he seemed, by his actions, to be proposing to cut it to bits with a saw.

James looked up from his work with a sheepish grin. 'Can't you guess?' he asked.

'Not at all. Will you destroy your own work?'

'No, my love, I am making a dissected puzzle,' he laughed.

'But what is that?'

'Don't you have them in France? It's a child's plaything. You see, you cut out around each country, and divide up the seas, so that it all comes to pieces. Then you give the pieces, muddled up, to the child, and by learning to put the puzzle together again, they can learn their geography without tears.'

'*Tiens*, that is very clever,' Héloïse smiled. 'And who is it for?'

He looked even more sheepish. 'Well – I thought – you see, it is Fanny's birthday on the third of October, and I thought I would make something for her, and send it by post. They would surely not keep it from her, do you think?'

'Oh,' Héloïse said thoughtfully, and returned her gaze to her sewing. 'No, I don't suppose they would do that.' She was silent a while, and then asked, without looking up, 'Do you miss her very much, James?'

'Yes, I do,' he said frankly. He put down the saw, and reached out to take her hand, halting it in mid-stitch. She looked up. 'I love her very much, but not enough to make me want to leave you,' he said. 'I wish I could have you both, but the love of a child can't replace love like ours. There's no question of a choice.'

'I see,' she said. She looked at him gravely for a moment, and he thought she was going to say something more.

'Yes, my darling?' he prompted.

She smiled and shook her head. 'No, nothing. *Rien du tout, mon âme*. Do you think I should make something for Fanny's birthday too? You see, I embroider very prettily, as the nuns taught me. But no, your wife would know convent

212

work if she saw it, and most certainly prevent Fanny from having it.'

He had never heard her speak like that before. He put his work aside and went to her anxiously. 'Don't,' he said. 'You sound like an ordinary, jealous woman.'

'But I am ordinary, and I am jealous. Does that surprise you?'

He kissed her brow. 'You are a Stuart princess – that's not ordinary. And there is no need to be jealous. I love you, only you. I have never loved my wife: you know that.'

'I know,' she said, her eyes downcast. 'All the same, she is your wife, which I can never be; and she has borne you a child.'

'Marmoset, I will never, never leave you. I will love you, waking and sleeping, with every breath I draw, until I die. No-one else has ever had what is yours, nor ever will.'

'Oh, James,' she said, stricken. She folded her arms round him, and he rested his head on her shoulder, and she rocked him, pressing her lips to his hair. 'Oh James, I know, I know. I am so foolish. I love you too, so much, that sometimes I am afraid. I feel the shadows gather round us like wolves, watching us, just waiting for the fire to die down.'

He lifted his head and smiled. 'Now that is foolish! Our fire will never die down. We shall cock a snook at the wolves, and they'll grow bored and go away.'

She pretended gravity. 'Cock a snook? What is this expression?'

'*Faire un pied de nez*,' he translated, grinning. She shook her head disapprovingly at him.

'But this is very *vulgaire*, James, I am quite shocked! And also it is most unfair to do this thing to the poor wolves, who have no fingers, and so cannot make the reply – ah no! James! Do not tickle me! I shall lose my needle! James, no!'

The noise brought Marie from the kitchen, and she smiled to see her mistress romping like a merry child. Holy Mother, Marie prayed, let her go on being happy. But only that morning she had gone down to the village to buy some meat, and had come back with her basket empty, because the village butcher had refused to serve her.

'We will not speak of this to Monsieur, Marie,' Héloïse had said. 'It is not important. We can get our meat from Thirsk, from the market. Your friend the carrier will help us, I am sure.'

'*Oui, Madame.* We can get everything from Thirsk,' Marie had said cheerfully, and Héloïse had smiled too, each pretending for the other's sake; but they both knew that the clouds were gathering.

Chapter Thirteen

Mr Hobsbawn was so outraged that when he made his visit, he abandoned the habits of a lifetime and travelled post, the sooner to confront Lady Morland and bellow at her. Edward took exception to this proceeding, and tried to intervene, but Jemima silenced him with a look and a gesture. Better that Mr Hobsbawn should get his shouting done, so that they could then discuss the matter quietly. Damming up his wrath was only likely to lead to an explosion.

Eventually he ran down for sheer lack of opposition, and stood, red-faced and panting, staring at Jemima and Ned and looking, she thought, as puzzled as a bull which had just charged a shadow.

'Will you sit down, Mr Hobsbawn,' she invited quietly, 'and let me send for some refreshments for you?'

He sat, rather suddenly, and said, 'God damn it, Lady Morland, you're amazing calm about all this! I half wonder if you know what's going on in your own house!'

'Oh yes, I know,' she said, checking Edward again.

'Then why the devil didn't you tell me? I heard about this infamous business from a fellow mill-owner, and deuced embarrassing it was too. "I say, Hobsbawn," says he, "your daughter's married a wrong 'un, seemingly." What was I to say to that? Had no notion what he was talking about. Everyone else in Manchester knew, however. My son-in-law, run off with this French woman, calls herself a countess, but God knows what she really is! More likely a –'

'Sir!' Edward intervened in the nick of time. 'I must ask you to moderate your language in front of my mother.'

'It's all right, Edward,' Jemima said softly. 'Mr Hobsbawn is naturally upset.'

'Upset?' he roared. 'I'll say I am!' He caught himself up, and went on in a slightly moderated voice. 'Don't mean to cuss at you, ma'am,' he said, slightly shamefaced, but then his injuries occurred to him again, and his voice began to rise. 'But why the devil did no-one tell me? Must I hear news of my own family from the gossip-mongers?'

'We intended no slight, I assure you,' Jemima said soothingly. 'There seemed no point in telling you –'

'No point!'

'No point in telling you when we hoped the unhappy situation would resolve itself. And really, as there was nothing anyone could do, we did not wish you to be made unhappy to no avail. Your daughter was with us in deciding not to tell you yet.'

Hobsbawn drew out a violet silk handkerchief and mopped his brow. He looked a little stunned, more than a little bewildered. 'But – but – for God's sake tell me the truth, at least. What has happened? Where is the boy?'

'I'm afraid the melancholy truth is that James has left home and is living with Lady Henrietta Stuart, and so far has refused to come back.'

Hobsbawn stared, his face tragic. 'Dear God!' He seemed unable to take it in. 'Left, ye say? What, just walked away? But why? Why, damnit? Is he mad? Left his wife – my daughter? He must be all about in his head to do such a thing!'

'Perhaps he is,' Edward muttered. Jemima threw him a quelling look.

'The young woman, Mr Hobsbawn, my niece, was engaged to be married to James some years ago. It was a love-match. She had fled Paris during the Terror, and believed her husband to be dead. But shortly before her proposed marriage to James, her husband arrived in London, which, as you can imagine, was a great shock to everyone. She and James naturally parted –'

'Naturally,' Hobsbawn echoed, bewildered.

'And James married your daughter instead. But now my niece is a widow and –' It was impossible to go on. Hobsbawn, who had hardly followed the intricate tale, grasped only this much.

'And your son has run off with her, slighted my daughter, insulted me! By God, Lady Morland, that boy should be thrashed, he should be horse-whipped, he –' He spluttered

216

in his rage. 'What has been done? Why have you not made him come back?'

Jemima looked at her hands in her lap, and said with difficulty, 'I have written to him, and my son Edward has been to see him, but these approaches have failed.'

'But you must *force* him!' Hobsbawn repeated in outrage. 'To the devil with asking him!'

'I'm afraid there is no pressure that can be put to bear on him,' Jemima said, her volume diminishing as Hobsbawn's increased.

'Cut off his allowance!'

'He has received no money from Morland Place since he left, naturally. But Lady Henrietta has private means, and they live very simply. It is to be hoped that – '

'By God, he'll not touch a penny of my money,' Hobsbawn growled. 'I'll cut him off, sharp, like that!' He made a chopping movement of his hand.

'But if you remember, sir, he has never received any money from you,' Jemima said gently. 'Your daughter's dowry was paid to the estate, not to her husband.'

Hobsbawn's eyes bulged dangerously. 'I'll change my will,' he cried hoarsely. 'He won't see a farthing from my estate. I'll leave it all to – '

'Fanny,' Edward finished for him. 'Your will, sir, leaves everything to your granddaughter.' He let that sink in, and then added. 'You see, there is nothing we can do to force James to come back, but – '

'You could go up there, sir, you could go up there and thrash him!' Hobsbawn cried, his voice cracking more with anguish than rage. 'You could drag him back by the hair of his head.'

Edward didn't pursue this line. He waited for Hobsbawn to stop, and then said, 'We are not without hope that he will come back of his own accord. I think he is suffering from a kind of madness, and I am sure it will pass, and he will realize the enormity of what he has done, and come home again of his own will. It's the only way, you know, sir – forcing him would do no good. You must see that.'

'It would do me good to see it,' Hobsbawn said more quietly. He thought a moment. 'What does Mary say?

217

Where is she, by the by? Is she all right?'

'She is in her chamber. You shall see her in a little while, but she wished me to interview you first. The situation is very embarrassing and upsetting for her, as you can understand,' Jemima said.

Hobsbawn's face twisted with sorrow for his child. 'I'll take her home with me,' he said. 'She shall come back to her Papa, aye, her and the child, too! I'll look after them. We'll divorce that worthless, heartless, slack-twisted – '

He broke off at that moment as the door opened, and Mary Ann appeared on the threshold, neatly clad as always, her face pale and composed, her hands folded nun-like before her.

'Mary – my little girl!' Hobsbawn cried, getting to his feet. Mary Ann crossed the room to him, and disappeared in his bear-like embrace. 'Pack thy bags, love – tha s'lt come home with me right away, and our little Fanny, too. We'll shake the dust of this place from our feet. They shan't have a penny of my money, child, I'll see to that. We'll get a divorce for you, and – '

'No, Papa,' Mary Ann said calmly, withdrawing herself from his arms. He looked stricken.

'No? Why not, my lamb? You don't want to stay here, do you?'

'It's my home now, Papa,' she said, meeting his eyes steadily. 'And more than that, it's Fanny's home. She is to inherit Morland Place one day, and I can't take her away from that. As to a divorce – ' she shrugged. 'Even if you could get one, what good would it do me? What good would it do Fanny? Better to try to keep this business quiet, live it down for her sake.'

'But what about your husband?'

Her gaze wavered and moved away. 'If he comes back, I'll forgive him. For Fanny's sake.'

Hobsbawn was lost for words. He stared at his daughter, and then cast around the room, as if looking for words of fire on the walls. 'I don't understand any of this!' he cried suddenly.

Jemima felt it was time for her to intervene. 'Mr Hobsbawn, it has been a great shock for you, as it was for us

218

when we first knew about it; but we have had time to consider and, like your daughter, we feel that Fanny is the important one now. Morland Place goes to her when I die: that has not changed. Now you may change your will, and in the circumstances I don't think anyone would blame you; and if you feel strongly about it, the estate will repay Mary Ann's dowry to you, since she has been wronged by her husband. We do not try to defend James, you see; but there is very little anyone can do in this situation.'

Hobsbawn sat down again, and resumed mopping his face. 'By God, it beats all, does this. You're all so calm, I can't get over it. But – what you say makes sense, all right.'

Jemima drew an inward sigh of relief that the worst seemed to be over. 'Let me send for some refreshments for you,' she said gently. 'The journey must have been most disagreeable.'

Golden September faded into October, and though the sun still shone, the strength seemed to have gone out of it. The mornings were sometimes quite sharp, and James and Héloïse were glad to draw the covers around them; the evenings were often misty, and there was that haunting smell of woodsmoke and blackberries in the mist, which told that autumn was coming.

In the middle of the day it was still warm enough to sit out of doors with pleasure. James had finished his portrait of Héloïse, and had taken to making quick sketches of her in the garden, drawing and re-drawing hungrily as he had done in those few weeks she had spent at Morland Place. She did not prevent him, but it made her nervous.

As the days shortened, their need to talk lessened, and their need to be near each other grew. They were often silent, doing nothing more than sitting together, hands intertwined, watching the cloud shadows drift across the garden. They did not go far from home any more, needing nothing outside their kingdom. The last autumn fruits were ripening against the warmth of the crumbling old wall, and the leaves were beginning to take on tints of gold and red and bronze. A sadness was with them, called up by they knew not what, making them lean closer together, loving each other the more, appreciating what they had more keenly.

They had been left alone since Edward's visit, except for the letters – an angry one from Mary Ann's father, a sad one from Jemima, harder to bear – but the world had other ways of shewing its disapproval. The tradesmen would not call; and there had been the distressing day when Peg had come to them, weeping, to say that she must give her notice.

'My Pa says I'm not to work for you any more, m'lady. He says I'm to go home at once. Oh m'lady, and he says he wants you to take your horses away, too!'

Héloïse had comforted her as well as she could, and over the weeping girl's shoulder had met James's stricken eyes. The Charlocks were a respected local family, and strong church members. Durban had fetched the ponies and the phaeton and had taken them to be stabled at the inn, where they could afford more liberal views. Peg's sister-in-law did not come in any more, either; but Stephen ignored local opinion and stayed on.

'What do we care what they think of us?' James had said robustly, and Héloïse had smiled and agreed; but it had hurt them. Before there had been only sunshine; now there was light and shade.

Héloïse began work on her memoirs, and James would sit in the room with her while she worked, drawing her, or just watching. He could never get enough of looking at her. Her face seemed to change every moment, like the sky, thoughts and feelings passing across it like clouds and light.

'I wish I had my journal,' she said one day. 'I kept it day by day all through the bad years, and it would be so valuable to me now. Papa gave it to me when I went with him to Chenonceau. I went to my very first ball there.' She smiled at the memory.

He came over to stand behind her, and kissed the nape of her neck, where her hair grew in little feathery curls which he found extremely distracting. 'One day, when the war is over, shall we go back there, for a visit? To France, I mean.'

'I should love to see it again,' she said, and then she sighed. 'Ah, but it would not be the same. I should be afraid that they had changed it so much it would not be my France any more. One hears such things about the destruction and the burning and the poverty. War is a terrible thing, James.'

'So I always understood,' he said, gently teasing. She glanced up at him.

'You were a soldier once.'

'Only so long as there was no danger of having to go and fight. As soon as the war began, I sold out.'

'Then why be a soldier at all?'

'Because, my precious angel,' he said, kissing her neck again, 'I looked so very handsome in a red coat!'

'Oh, you are never serious,' she exclaimed as he laughed.

'I'm sorry, darling,' he said resting his cheek against hers and putting his arms around her shoulders. 'I know how much you lost. You still miss him, don't you – your father!'

'Poor Papa,' she said, and automatically reached for his last letter, which was growing worn with frequent handling. 'He used to say he had no drop of French blood in his veins, and yet when it came to it, he could not leave France. This letter – when I think that he wrote it in the last moments before they arrested him –'

'Tell me again what it says,' James said. 'I can't read French handwriting.'

'The writing is bad,' she agreed, 'but he was writing in a hurry, and having to think what he could say that would not make the authorities tear it up, if they found it. That's why it sounds a little strange, I think.' She read it to him again.

'What are those words underlined, at the end – *bonheur toujours* is it?'

'Yes – "I wish you happiness always" he says.'

'But why did he underline just those two words?'

'I don't know. Perhaps he –' Héloïse stopped. After a moment of silence, James removed his cheek from hers to look at her, and was alarmed for she was staring fixedly ahead of her in the most extraordinary way.

'What is it, Marmoset? What's the matter? Are you ill?'

'*Bonheur toujours* – how can I have been so stupid?' she said.

'Darling, what is it? What do you mean?'

'He had to write in code, of course, in case the letter fell into the wrong hands,' she said, as though to herself. 'But he

221

had told me very clearly what he would do, only I was so stupid I forgot it. Listen, James,' she turned to him suddenly. 'On the day I was married to Vendenoir, we went back to the house Papa had bought for me in the Rue St Anne, and while the guests were assembling, he took me to the room he had fitted out as my boudoir. He shewed me the furniture he had bought for me, including this writing desk, and he told me that there was a secret compartment in it. He made a point of shewing it to me, and said there might come a time when I would be glad of it.'

'A secret compartment?'

'Yes, love. I thought it strange that he should make such a point of it on my wedding day, but now I see – '

James was there. '*Bonheur-du-jour*! Of course, the code! He was telling you – but what do you think he has hidden there? Where is it? Open it quickly, Marmoset! I must see!'

Héloïse was pale. 'I am afraid – ' she began.

'Oh, darling, don't be foolish. How can it hurt you? Whatever it is, he meant you to find it, didn't he? Do you remember the trick of it?'

'Yes, of course,' she said. Reluctantly she slid her hand into the drawer to operate the hidden lever. For a moment nothing happened. It was stiff with disuse, and she thought it would not work again. Then there was a loud click which made them both jump, and the false back unlocked. Héloïse opened it, and they both stared in silence.

'You do it, James,' she said. 'I cannot.'

The compartment was filled with soft cloth bags. James drew them out and opened them, one by one.

'Good God,' he exclaimed softly. 'There is a fortune here.'

Héloïse could not speak at all. Just for an instant she remembered Papa so clearly, his face coming to her for once vividly, as though she had only parted from him an hour ago. He had tried to ensure an easy life for her in England, but because of Vendenoir, it had all gone wrong. She thought of her years of poverty and struggle, and imagined the difference even a part of this treasure would have made.

James was still unwrapping things, and spreading them out before her on the desk-top. A bag of golden *louis d'or* –

'God knows what they're worth, especially now the Bank of England has started issuing paper money. No wonder the desk is heavy!' There was a magnificent diamond parure: 'Fleurs de lys here, and here – does that mean they are royal jewels?'

'Perhaps,' Héloïse said, and roused herself to say, 'I think I have seen them before – I think they belonged to the Duchesse de Provence. Papa helped her to escape. And oh, James, look, my rubies! Papa had them reset for me. They belonged to the Queen. And the Queen's cachou box!' More diamonds, unset, loose in a bag. 'Taken out of their setting, I imagine. Look, there are traces of cement, here, and here. I wonder what they were – a tiara, perhaps?'

Héloïse pounced, and held up something that made James wrinkle his nose.

'My love, what can that be? That isn't valuable at all – pink shells and coral?'

Héloïse pressed it to her breast, and smiled rather damply at him. 'It is valuable to me,' she said. 'Papa gave it to me, at Chenonceau, to wear at my first ball.'

'Oh yes, I remember you telling me. So that's it! Hideous, isn't it?'

'I swore to treasure it always, only when I fled, I had to leave everything behind. He must have found it in the house, and put it in – '

'For a joke?'

'No,' Héloïse retorted indignantly, 'for love!'

From the last bag of all came her journal.

'Look, James, it is a miracle! Now I shall be able to write properly, and tell everything! It is all here, from the Bastille, and before, right up to when I left! *La vérité, enfin!* This is most important.'

He pulled her away from her journal and took her in his arms and kissed her on the nose to gain her attention. 'My foolish little one, forget that old diary – don't you realize you are now a rich woman? These jewels are worth a fortune! You can sell them, and live in great comfort for the rest of your life.'

'Not my rubies,' she said firmly, and he laughed.

'You can even afford to keep your rubies! You will be

able to build a stable of your own, now, and cock a snook at the censorious old tabbies of Yorkshire.'

'No more cocking of snooks,' she decreed. 'It is vulgar.'

'I wouldn't be surprised,' he said thoughtfully, 'if this didn't make quite a difference to the way we are treated. There's nothing like a great deal of money for soothing people's sensibilities.'

The shine went out of her face, and he was sorry to have brought her back down to earth. She pressed against him for comfort, and he folded his arms tightly around her.

'I don't care for money, not even a great deal of it. I only care for you,' she said.

'Well, I'm here, Marmoset, so don't be sad.'

'But I am sad, my James. I feel as if the world is pressing in so hard, there will be no room left for us.'

'That's just autumn,' he said, more cheerfully than he felt. 'One always feels melancholy in autumn. But spring will come again. It always does.'

The last week in October marked the completion of the six weeks Docwra considered the minimum safe recovery period for a woman who had given birth.

'Though seein' as your ladyship had such a hard time of it, you ought to take more care this time,' she said.

'Nonsense,' Lucy said. 'I'm as strong as a horse.' The fine weather had helped, cheering her spirits, and allowing her to sit out of doors and get the benefit of "God's good air" as Docwra called it.

'If you are,' Docwra said now, 'it's nothing more nor less than determination, I know that. You're in a fret to get back to London, and fill your lungs with smoke and soot.'

Lucy frowned. 'I don't see that that's any of your business.'

'Haven't you any pity for that poor little babby o' yours, me lady? Will you take her from the sweet fresh country into the dirty town?'

'Oh, there's no need for the children to come up to Town,' Lucy said triumphantly. There had been no nonsense this time about breast-feeding: she had put

Rosamund straight out to a wet-nurse, and her own breasts were now dry. In fact, she was all ready for the Little Season, and anxious to be off. 'The children can stay here, or go to Wolvercote, it doesn't matter which.'

'Doesn't matter?' Docwra queried.

'It depends on whether his lordship is going up or not,' Lucy explained kindly. 'With the shooting so late starting, he may want to stay on here for a few more weeks.'

'And you'd go up without him? You wouldn't, now, sure?' Docwra said coaxingly. Lucy looked at her coolly.

'Of course I shall go up alone, if necessary. Why not? I am a married woman and a countess, not a green girl. Besides, the Chelmsfords are there, and Lady Chelmsford can keep me company, if you think I still need a chaperone, at my age.'

Docwra tilted her head. 'Oh me lady, you're not yet twenty! Our sweet Lord bless you, but you're a green girl all the same, for all you've two babbies, and you're as transparent as a mountain stream, so you are. Only, I beg you, me lady, take care!'

'I don't know what you mean,' Lucy retorted crossly.

'Ah, but you do. It's that young lieutenant you're so anxious to see,' Docwra said, lowering her voice, 'and God knows he's a nice boy enough, but I'm afraid you're going to get yourself into trouble.'

For a moment, Lucy looked frightened; and then a veil came across her expression, and she put on her most lofty air, and said, 'You had better mind your tongue, Docwra. I haven't time to stand here listening to your nonsense, anyway. You can start the packing. I am going to speak to his lordship.'

She found Chetwyn in the steward's room, which he and Edward sometimes used as a gun-room, cleaning his Purdeys, which at the moment occupied all of the affection which he could spare from Ned.

'Hullo,' he greated her cordially. 'How are you feeling? I must say, you are looking better by the minute, quite back to normal, in fact. Childbirth seems to agree with you.'

'Oh, don't talk such nonsense,' Lucy said. 'You know I had a horrible time of it, and all for nothing.'

225

'It is a disappointment,' he conceded, 'but I dare say she will grow up to be pretty enough. And we're bound to have a boy next time.'

'Well, I'm not going to go through all that again, not for a long time,' Lucy said quickly. 'It made me feel very ill. You have no idea.'

'I suppose I haven't,' Chetwyn said fairly, 'but the point is, I must have a son. If it weren't so, I shouldn't dream of troubling you again, but there it is.'

'Oh, I know all about that,' Lucy said impatiently. 'All I'm saying is, not yet. I want a rest.' He said nothing, so she tried to look pathetic. 'I need time to get my strength back.'

He gave her a shrewd look. 'Of course, ma'am, it must be when *you* decide,' he said courteously. 'I have no wish to impair your health.'

Deciding she had won, Lucy gave him a dazzling smile. 'Good,' she said. 'And now, what I wanted to ask you was, what are your immediate plans? Are you ready to go up to Town, or do you mean to stay here longer?'

'A few weeks more, at least,' he said. 'With the weather the way it is, we've hardly got down to the shooting yet, and there's no necessity for me to go to Wolvercote just yet.'

'Very well, then, the children can stay with you,' Lucy said gaily, 'and the maids can take them to Wolvercote when you come up. I plan to go up to Town tomorrow.'

Chetwyn looked taken aback. 'You mean to go up alone?'

'I shall take Docwra, of course, and Parslow. I shall be quite safe on the road,' Lucy said, deliberately misunderstanding him.

'May I ask why you want to go?'

'Well I'd sooner you come too, of course, but I'm bored with Yorkshire, and I want to be in Town for the Little Season, and if you are set on staying – '

'Apart from the shooting, I don't want to leave Ned and Lady Morland while this business about James is still not settled,' Chetwyn said quietly.

'Oh, James! I don't know why everyone keeps fussing about him. But you stay if you like. I'll go up tomorrow, and you can follow when you're ready. Charles and Roberta are at Chelmsford House, you know, so I shan't be all alone.'

'No,' said Chetwyn, 'I'm sure you won't be alone.'

There had been a frost in the night; not a severe one, and it had all melted away as soon as the sun rose, but it made the world smell different. The leaves on the garden path, which yesterday had been crisp and brown, scuttling like mice in the fitful wind, now lay still, wet and black. Héloïse took a shawl with her when she and James went out into the garden, though when they were sitting on their bench under the wistaria, it was sheltered enough for her to let it drop.

'There will certainly be enough money for everything you want to do to the house,' James said. With his sketching book on his knee, he was drawing the house the way it was and the way it should be. 'And it deserves it, Marmoset! It's a lovely house, and it could be perfect, with a little work.'

'I'm glad you like it,' she said. She was looking a little pale, he thought, a little 'all eyes'. He hoped she was not sickening for a cold: autumn colds could be troublesome. His pencil flew, and his ideas limned before them on the paper. 'The thing is, you can't build onto the back of the house without spoiling the garden, which would be a pity, so what I thought was, you could extend it this way, by building a new wing down here.'

Héloïse leaned her shoulder against him, watching.

'Now, you see, the present passageway could be knocked into the parlour to make it bigger, and that could be your breakfast-parlour. The dining room stays as it is, and you take out the stairs, and build a new entrance on the corner, here, with a proper wide staircase. Then the new wing will be your drawing-room – a good, big one, for entertaining – and it will have a pleasant view over the garden this way, and the fields that way. And on the upper floor you'd have room for two more bedrooms.'

'Yes, I see.'

'And the stables – they needn't be very big, say four boxes, a tack-room and a coach-house – can go here, on this piece of waste ground. What do you think?'

'You are very clever, James,' she said. 'It all looks very nice.'

But her voice was listless, and her eyes kept straying from the page and wandering across the garden. The marigolds still blazed, but there were green and curling seed-heads interspersed with the flowers. She shivered a little, though the wind was still just then, and James put aside his sketching book and captured her hand, and stroked its fingers thoughtfully.

'What is it, my darling?' he asked, but his voice was dull with foreknowledge.

'I had a visitor yesterday,' she said neutrally.

'I didn't know – why didn't you call me?'

'It was while you were working on your cabinet with Stephen. I didn't want to disturb you,' she said. 'He didn't stay long. It was – it was the priest, James – or, no, I think you do not call them priests, do you? It was the rector of the parish, from the little church in the village.'

James looked at her in dismay. 'Oh, my darling, I'm so sorry. What did he say to upset you? I've a mind to go and see him, and – '

'Oh, no, James, he did not say anything I did not know for myself.'

There was a long silence. James was still, like a threatened animal, and her hand rested in his like a small flame, vibrantly alive, hard to hold. A late butterfly, slow-moving as they were at that time of year, fluttered down like a scrap of coloured silk blown by the wind, and rested gratefully on the warm gravel of the path, spreading its wings and closing them with a flick. Its white bands were vivid against iridescent purple.

'It is an emperor,' Héloïse said. 'You see how well you have taught me, James? I remember everything that you have told me.'

'You have taught me so much more,' James began, and then stopped.

'Their lives are so short,' she said, watching the silken wings. 'Short and frail, but beautiful. They are fortunate, to dance in the sunlight, and not know that they will die tomorrow.'

James lifted her hand and kissed it, unable to speak. There was a terrible pain in his throat, for he knew what she was going to say.

'We have been very happy, haven't we, my James? And though we did wrong, I can't regret it, not one instant of it.' He shook his head, holding her hand tightly. She turned to look at him, but it was too much for both of them, and she turned her head away again. 'What we have had, no-one can take from us; but you must go back.'

A little wind lifted the fine hair at the nape of her neck, and the butterfly, disturbed, fluttered up and away into the trees.

'We can't be together any more. We should not have done what we did, but perhaps God has let us have these few weeks in the sunshine to make us strong, so that – '

Now she faltered, and James found his voice.

'I can't leave you. Don't tell me to. Why should you let some meddling fool of a priest upset you? He isn't even of your church.'

'Oh, my love, it isn't that. Though everyone is against us, if I knew within me that I was right, I would face the whole world, and care nothing. But no happiness can come from doing wrong, my James – I learnt that long ago. I can't go on shutting myself out from God, and that is what I must do, to be with you.'

'It isn't fair!' he cried.

'No, perhaps not. I don't know. I only know God sees us, and only He knows all of the pattern. We have to believe He knows best. Oh, my darling, if only I thought you understood that, I could bear to part from you.'

She turned to him, and he put his arms round her, and she rested her head on his shoulder, and he stroked her hair: soft, black, lustrous hair, full of life. She was the life of him; without her he was nothing, a dry and hollow shell, to be crushed, to be blown away as dust on a little wind.

'I love you,' he said, which was all he could find in him. 'What will you do, if I go?'

'I don't know, *mon âme*. Just – go on. All we can do is try to obey God's law, and trust that if we do, He will be merciful.'

'I don't have your faith,' he said bitterly; and then he remembered saying the same thing to his mother, after his father had died. She had spoken with this same strength and, under the sorrow, serenity. They were alike, his mother and Héloïse, made of the same strong, shining stuff: was that why he had loved her? Father Ramsay had once said to him, in his childhood, that all love is ultimately love of God. Deep in him, a closed door opened a crack.

Héloïse felt the change in him. 'What is it?' she asked. She lifted her head and looked at him, a long, clear look. She loved him; she called him *mon âme*: how could she live without her soul?

'A little, I begin to understand,' he said. 'I don't accept it. My heart will break, and yours too, but I think –'

She nodded, and rested her hot forehead against him, struggling against the tears. Oh God, she prayed inwardly, give me the strength to do what is right. 'I love you, my James. Nothing can ever change that, and if we are apart in body, we shall not be apart in our souls, so long as we do what we know is right.'

But that is no comfort, James thought. The shadows lengthened across the garden, reaching to their feet, but still they sat, leaning together, their arms around each other; until with the sun's westering the little breeze returned, cool and night-scented, ruffling their hair, and making Héloïse shiver. James kissed the crown of her head, and coaxed her to her feet like an invalid; where she grew weak, he must find strength for both of them.

'It's late,' he said. 'We must go in.'

Chapter Fourteen

James left the road to skirt York, and came back to Morland Place through the fields. It was a pleasant day, cool, sunny, autumnal; but the two men rode in silence, and when Durban glanced from time to time at his master's face he found it set and grim.

They came at last to the top of the home paddock, where Jemima's mare kinked her tail and wrinkled her muzzle, and squealed warning at the two ridden horses. Finding herself ignored, she turned with bared teeth on the two carriage geldings turned out with her and drove them down the field to relieve her feelings, and then came flying back to the fence to goggle and snort.

She was very fresh, Durban thought: the mistress couldn't have been out much lately. He was about to hazard a remark to James, but thought better of it when he saw the preoccupied look on James's brow. Nez Carré also had better things to think about than excitable mares: he had just caught the smell of home. He cocked his long ears forward and knuckered deep down, putting in an extra dancing step or two. Forest joined in as they came to the bend of the track, and James drew rein and looked down towards his home.

He had so often looked on it as a prison, and his wife a gaoler, and had never paused to consider the impropriety of allowing such thoughts. The way one felt, he had assumed, was beyond one's control. But it was not true, of course – it had never been true. The whole of life was a lesson in self-government, in which one grew more and more proficient, unless one was a criminal or a lunatic. He had been a little of both in his time; but he saw now how his crimes and his lunacies had been wilful, how it had always been possible to do right, and how he had always known that. His long hours of conversation spent with Father Ramsay as a child had not left him untouched; but he had chosen wickedness, quite

231

deliberately, because good had not seemed to him suffic-iently challenging.

'Fool!' he apostrophized himself aloud, and Nez Carré grunted in reply. It was the greatest challenge of all, the more so because the rewards were so often intangible. But he thought of his life to come, and for a moment faltered, lost heart for the struggle. I can't, he thought despairingly; it was too great an effort.

Nez Carré, bored with waiting, pretended he had an itch and needed to get his head down to his knee to rub it, so as to loosen the reins, and then used the freedom of his head to edge forward a step or two. It was an old trick of his, trans-parent as air, and James suddenly found himself smiling. Horses were so simple, he thought, like children: simple desires, simple loves, and a transparent wickedness, innocent as milk. Love bubbled up in him, for horses, for children, for home and for his child. Fanny! He had missed her, and the flattering way her face lit up when he came into the nursery. Life could be worth living: at least, he would make it so.

He glanced sideways at his patient servant, and felt love for him, too. I'm so lucky, he thought in surprise. It had never occurred to him before. Durban turned to look at him, and was amazed to see his master smiling, and stared for a moment in astonishment before he was able to govern himself.

'Sir?' he inquired politely.

'I was just thinking it's good to be home,' James said, and Nez Carré took this for permission, and started forward, whickering eagerly.

Their appearance on the track alerted the gatekeeper, who raised the alarm in the house, so that when the two horses came in under the barbican, Hoskins was waiting by the block with two lads, and Oxhey was at the great door with Jemima beside him. James's eyes went straight to his mother, and he thought in sudden shock, *why, she's old.* She seemed to have shrunk since he went away, and though her carriage was as upright as ever, she seemed to be hunching her thin shoulders like a bird against the cold.

Her eyes met and held his, and there was no smile in them, only weariness. He remembered with sudden, sharp regret how she had been in his childhood, energetic, sensible, happy, always smiling, so much in love with his father that the house had seemed to hum with it, as if it were the engine that drove the household. He wanted to cry out to her, don't you realize, Mother, it was you who did this to me, to all of us! You gave us an impossible standard to meet, and knowing we could only fall short took the heart out of us.

He dismounted and went up the steps and stood before her. She looked at him searchingly, but did not speak or move, and he realized that she did not know what his coming portended.

'Forgive me,' he said.

After a moment she nodded, but there was still no smile or embrace for him. There was no change in her expression as she stepped back to admit him. 'Come with me,' she said. 'Oxhey, see we're not disturbed.'

To the steward's room he followed her rigid back, and there she turned to him, looking both fragile and defensive. 'Well, Mother,' he said.

'Jamie,' she said, 'why have you come?'

He looked surprised. 'Good God, Mother, isn't that what everyone's been telling me to do? I've seen the error of my ways, and returned to the fold. Aren't you glad?' She went on looking at him searchingly, and he said more gently, 'I am truly sorry to have caused you pain. I have come to try to make amends.'

'Oh, my dear,' Jemima said, some of the brittleness leaving her. 'Of course I'm glad you've come back. I knew – I hoped – that you'd do the right thing in the end. It's just that – '

'Yes, Mama?' he prompted her.

'The thing is, Jamie, that it isn't just what you do that matters; it's the spirit in which you do it. If you have come back with the intention of behaving in exactly the same way as before, if you mean to make us all suffer because you have been forced to give up Héloïse, well, if that were so, it would almost be better for you to go away again.'

'Almost,' he said wryly.

'Yes,' she said frankly, 'because there is some virtue in doing the right thing, even without a meek heart.'

'You needn't worry,' James said. 'My heart is as meek as you could wish. I know how I have been at fault, and I mean to do better from now on, and to make you happy, if I can.'

'Your wife, too,' Jemima said anxiously.

'My wife most of all,' he said sadly. The last of her resistance left her, and she held out her arms to him.

'Oh, my dear,' she said. 'I have missed you – dearest of my children! I shouldn't say that, but I can't help it. Oh Jamie, I so wanted you to be happy. I wish things could have been different.'

'Now, Mother, no repining. That's all over. I have come to the right way of thinking. Just at the moment it seems obvious, but I know there will be times when I shall have doubts. Then I shall need help.'

'God will help you, my dear. But – ' she stood back from him to look into his face – 'what of Héloïse? I must ask just this once. How does she feel about it?'

So he sat down with her and told her everything, and it poured out of him in a flood like tears, like blood from a new wound, washing everything away, leaving him feeling empty and weak. He knew that if he was to survive, he must not think of her or talk of her again. This was the last time, which must pay for all. Jemima listened, her hand crushed in his, and when it was over, they were both silent, and he gave a little shuddering sigh.

'So now you know everything,' he said. 'And now, I suppose I had better go and face my wife. Will she forgive me, do you suppose?'

'Yes, I think she will. She is a Catholic, and her principles are firm.'

James made a wry face. 'I am to be forgiven because it's the Christian thing to do, am I?'

'What more can you expect?'

'No more, of course. It wasn't expectation, it was hope. And pride – but I can't afford pride now, can I? Well, then, let's get it over. Where is she?'

234

Jemima stood up. 'I think it will be better if you see her here, first, where you can be sure of privacy. I will send her to you.'

The wait seemed very long, and James had time to pass through a number of states of apprehension from nervousness to deep foreboding before the door opened and Mary Ann stood on the threshold.

Tall and pale and serene she was, in a plain dress of leaf-brown sarsenet, her fine hair taken up with tortoiseshell combs. He reflected that when he had first seen her, in her father's house, she had worn clothes too elaborate, in colours too rich, which had done nothing for her looks. Being at Morland Place had taught her to dress, at least.

But then he looked into her eyes, and saw along with resolution and hurt pride, an apprehension as great as his own. Behind that cool, controlled façade, what sort of a woman was she? He had never troubled to discover; but he remembered unexpectedly how on their wedding night, he had cried, and she had comforted him. Shy, she had been that night, and despite her own nervousness, she had offered him understanding. And he knew suddenly, without knowing how he knew, that she had worn those rich elaborate clothes in her father's house, not because she had no taste, but because they had been of her father's choosing, and she was too kind to tell him that they didn't suit her.

As she stood hesitating on the threshold, Edward's dog Leaky pattered up behind her and pushed his nose under her hand, grinning at James but making no movement to leave her side to greet him. James raised an eyebrow, and she said gravely, 'I have been adopted, you see.'

'Yes, I see,' said James. Her light, careful voice gave no indication of her feelings: it was going to be hard for either of them to bridge the chasm between them. James took his courage in both hands. 'I wish, very much, to apologize to you.' She made a nervous gesture of negation, and he gave a grim sort of smile and went on, 'Please, let me say it. It won't be easy, and if I stop, I shall lose my nerve. I have treated you abominably from the very beginning. I was unhappy, through no fault of yours, and I made you suffer for it – you most of all. I am truly sorry.'

There was a silence. She did not answer, and her expression did not change, and James felt a ridiculous disappointment. Then he cursed himself for a fool. What had he expected? That because he apologized she would fall on his neck and become a different person? That she would change miraculously into someone he could love, someone as like Héloïse as made no difference, and they would live happily ever afterwards? That sort of thing only happened in novels, he told himself with contempt. This was real life, and in real life nothing was ever easy.

The tautness of expectation went out of him, and he began to turn away. What must be done, must be done, the hard way, if not the easy way. 'Well, perhaps I should not expect you to forgive me just like that,' he said. 'But in time, I hope – '

'I forgive you,' she said, and her voice was like a breeze moving in the upper branches of a tall tree, faint and light, hardly disturbing the coarse air near the earth, which he breathed. 'I forgave you long ago, before you ever thought to ask.'

He turned back to her, puzzled. 'Then – what?'

'You came here expecting something of me. You came to take, not to give. You were so sure I would forgive you that when I didn't say anything, you were surprised. It was all in your face. You are quite transparent, you know.'

He felt angry. 'I should not have thought *that* was something to blame me for. If everyone was like you, it would be very hard.' He stopped abruptly, hearing himself, and was shocked. 'I'm sorry,' he said.

'Yes, I think you are, but it doesn't go very deep, does it?' she said. He held himself in check this time.

'Perhaps not. It is new to me.' He gave her a rueful smile. 'But in time – with practice – '

She looked down at her hands. She was very young, and alone, and had learned to tread carefully. 'What do you mean to do?' she asked.

'Live here – make amends. Work hard. Be kind to you, if you will let me.' She waited. 'I don't know, Mary,' he said, suddenly disarmed. 'Just – go on, I suppose. Try to do the right thing. I'm a sinner, I don't know much about duty.'

'Duty,' she repeated, rather bleakly.

'I need your help,' he said gently. She looked up at last, and met his gaze, and he saw, wonder of wonders, a blush spread across her perfect alabaster cheek and a very womanly confusion in her light-brown eyes. I have been such a fool, he thought contritely, and something of it must have been in his face, for she smiled suddenly, a short, nervous smile, but a smile none the less.

'I suppose I had better go and meet the rest of the household,' he said. 'Will you come with me?' He offered her his crooked arm, and with only a slight hesitation she laid her hand on it. It pressed no harder than a fallen leaf. 'I was thinking, ma'am, that you ought to crop your hair,' he said as they passed out into the hallway together. 'Oh no, don't look alarmed, I didn't mean it for a criticism. It's just that I have thought for a long time that it would suit you so, and be less troublesome to keep.'

'I didn't think you had ever noticed my hair.'

'Yes, I have noticed. It is very pretty, fine hair, and not all the pins in the world will keep it up for long. But if you cropped, it would shew off your handsome neck, and you need never feel like Saint Sebastian again, stuck full of pins.'

She did not smile, but the hand on his arm rested just a little more firmly. It was a start, James thought, the first small step on the way to wooing his wife. It was not much to put into the emptiness inside him, but it was something.

In the day-nursery there was a breathless hush as the three little girls, round-eyed, watched the completing stages of the wooden horse James had been making. Since his brief introduction by Stephen, he had taken to woodwork kindly, and found it a useful and soothing way to pass the hours which still often seemed long to him. The wooden horse was a splendid animal, solidly made from a piece of beech, handsomely carved and fixed on a wheeled base so that a small person, sitting astride it, could propel herself along by striking her feet against the floor.

The small person concerned was sitting with her enraptured nose perilously close to the glue-pot as she watched her father gluing the real horsehair mane and tail into place. Hippolyta sat a little further back, holding Flaminia, who was still young enough to have to be prevented from eating wood shavings or nails or anything else that came to hand. Flaminia was a placid baby, which was fortunate, as Hippolyta, in her zeal to be a second mother to her little cousin, often lugged her about with her by the arms. The seat of Flaminia's clothing was always grimed with the frequent and forceful contact of her rump with mother earth, but she never cried when she was bumped, and held out her arms and smiled fatly whenever Hippolyta came into sight. Further back still the nurse sat sewing and keeping a discreet eye on things.

'There,' said James, sitting back to admire his work. 'Now when the glue is dry, that should hold firmly enough for you to be able to brush them out like a real mane and tail.'

'He's lovely, Papa,' Fanny breathed. She herself had chosen the horse's unusual colouring: piebald, boldly marked, with blue eyes and a white mane and tail. 'When can I have him?'

'Not until Christmas, my love,' James said, and when Fanny protested, he said, 'You know it was always meant for a Christmas present. And besides, I have to make his saddle and bridle. You don't want to ride him bareback, do you?'

'Yes,' said Fanny promptly. 'I don't care. I want him now.'

'You can't have him now, chick,' James said, and watched the stormclouds gathering over his daughter's face. Since his absence, she had grown not only very possessive of him, but very demanding, as if needing to have it made up to her, that he had defected for three months. He sought for something to distract her, and at that moment Hippolyta said, 'Sir, Uncle James, could we go and see Brach's puppies?'

'Yes, of course,' James said with relief, and looked curiously at Hippolyta – Little Polly as she was often called, to distinguish her from her mother – wondering if it was coincidence or an abnormally precocious tact 'We'll all go, shall we? I'll just put the horse up here, so that it's safely out of the way. Now then – '

Fanny demanded a pick-a-back, and rode downstairs on his shoulders, and the nurse followed with Hippolyta, carrying Flaminia to save her from the thirty-six separate bumps of the great staircase. Brach's puppies were hardly puppies any more, and their mother had long since abandoned them to return to Edward's heel, but they were being kept in a separate pen until Edward decided what to do with them. They were fine big pups, four dogs and a bitch, handsomely marked, with their mother's brindles and their father's dark ears. While the children were playing with them, the doorway darkened, and James looked up to see Mary Ann standing there.

'The servants said you were here,' she said. She did not smile – she still rarely did – but her expression softened a little in greeting. In the six weeks he had been back, James had worked very hard to breach the wall they had erected between them. He sat and talked to her, went walking and driving with her, shewed her the progress of his woodwork, listened to her piano-playing. If he could have slept with her, it might have hastened the reconciliation, but he could not bring himself to do that. He slept apart in the bachelor's wing as before, and if he wept at night in his narrow bed there, she was not to know.

The two things which helped them were their religious observances, in which he was now as regular as she, and love of Fanny. It was unfortunate, perhaps, that Fanny so loudly and insistently preferred her father to her mother, but Mary Ann shewed no sign of resenting it.

'I'm afraid you've lost Leaky's devotion since Brach left the pen,' James said with a smile.

'He still comes to speak to me in the evening sometimes, when I'm sitting by the fire,' Mary Ann said.

'Aye, when you're sitting in the same room as Ned, and Brach is hogging his lap,' James pointed out. 'He's a fickle, ungrateful hound. You should have one of your own.'

He said it casually, but he saw the idea take. Mary Ann's expression brightened. 'Do you think so? Do you think Edward would let me have one? I know he means to sell them.'

'Does he? He didn't tell me that. Well, if he wants a profit from them, I'll pay him a fair price, if you'd like one.'

She looked pleased with his generosity. 'Yes – yes I think I would. It would be interesting to train a dog of one's own.'

'Which would you choose?' he asked idly, watching Fanny tugging the tail of the bitch-pup and getting cussed for it.

'I don't know – they're all so pretty,' Mary Ann said. 'Perhaps the one with the white mark on its face – it has such a comical look sometimes.'

James reached over and picked it up, and it paddled its legs as if it hadn't noticed the ground had gone away, and licked out indiscriminately at any parts of James that were within reach. 'Yes, it's a nice little brute,' he said. 'Good tempered, healthy – a good choice.' Mary Ann looked pleased, but James did not notice. His attention had returned inexorably to Fanny. 'I've often thought that Fanny ought to have a puppy,' he said. 'It's nice for a child to grow up with a dog; and when she's a bit older, it will take care of her.'

Fanny jumped up at once and clamoured. 'Oh yes, Papa, please! I want a puppy, I want a puppy. I want that one.'

James laughed. 'That's my contrary daughter! You can't have this one, chick, it's the one your Mama has just chosen.'

'But I want it,' Fanny cried, her lower lip jutting. He hesitated, and the glow went out of Mary Ann's eyes, and James, looking at her questioningly a second later, never knew it had been there.

'Well, of course, I meant it for Fanny,' she said. 'What would I do with a dog of my own?'

'Did you?' He was too pleased in pleasing Fanny to wonder at his wife's change of position. 'There, then, Fan, it shall be yours. Thank Mama nicely, chick. And what shall you call it, do you think?'

'Puppy,' said Fanny.

'That's not a name, that's what it is,' James laughed.

'Let her call it Puppy if she wants,' Mary Ann said indifferently, turning away. 'It's as good a name as any. Nurse, I think it is time the children went in, don't you?'

Left alone, James continued to watch the tumbling puppies, his expression thoughtful. He picked them up one by one and examined them, and determined which was the biggest and strongest, a very dark-brindled dog pup with a white mark on its breast. When he held it up before him, it yawned and licked his face, and he smiled, returned it to the litter, and went to find Edward.

Early the next morning Durban set out for Coxwold, driving the cocking-cart, with the big dog-pup confined, rather unwillingly, in the compartment under the seat.

'Lady Strathord said to me in conversation one day,' James had told him when he gave him his orders, 'that she had thought to get herself a dog or adopt a child to keep her company. Pray tell her that I can't do anything about the child, but that I can at least provide her with the dog.'

Durban was received with great pleasure by Marie, who had formed a very favourable opinion of him in the time they had shared the house.

'How is she?' Durban asking, cocking his head towards the parlour.

'Very low,' Marie said. 'It is not her way to brood – my lady is as brave as a lion, and she never complains, never. But I often find her sitting, Monsieur Durban, just sitting, with her hands in her lap.'

'It's a bad business,' Durban said, shaking his head. 'I don't know what anyone could have done different, however. Have you found another housemaid yet?'

'That is another thing,' Marie sighed. 'Not that I mind the work – I was used to work far harder, I assure you, when we lived in London, when Monsieur was alive. But it is not right that my lady should be without servants.'

'You cannot find anyone hereabouts?'

'Absolutely no. That Charlock has spoken out against my lady, and the young women may not come here – as though she were a *femme du monde* instead of next thing to an angel!'

'She must go to London, then,' Durban said wisely.

'We shall go, quite soon,' Marie nodded, 'to see

241

Monsieur de Chelmsford about selling the jewels.'

'And when she is there, she must find a housemaid in London and bring her back. What she really needs,' he added thoughtfully 'is a respectable older woman to live with her, like a chaperone, to lend her countenance.'

Marie looked cross. 'Lend her countenance? What has my lady need of anyone to do that for her!'

Durban said soothingly, 'I know that, mademoiselle, and you know it, but the simple folk of this village don't. And now, do you think your lady would see me? I have brought her a present.'

He went back to the cocking-cart and drew out the big pup by the neck. Marie's eyes grew wide.

'*Zut, alors!* Have we not trouble enough without that!'

Durban smiled. 'If she don't want it, mademoiselle, I'll take it away again. But you might ask her. She expressed to my master a wish to have a dog.'

'But yes, a little dog, a lady's dog, not that monster! However, you shall ask her, as you have come so far.'

Durban was brought into Héloïse's presence, leading the pup by the collar, and made a deferential bow. She was sitting by the fire, a shawl round her shoulders, her head bare, staring absently into the flames. Above her head, over the chimney piece, was the portrait James had painted of her during his brief residence, and Durban could not help noticing the difference between the joyful expression of the painted Héloïse, and that of the flesh-and-blood one.

'Durban! How good of you to come. How do they all go on at Morland Place? Is my aunt well?'

'Yes, my lady, she is well. Things are a little more settled now.'

'And what is this you have brought me?'

Durban released the pup's collar, and while it was dashing round Héloïse and pawing at her knees in an indiscriminate ecstasy of greeting, he gave his message. He watched her face as he spoke, and saw no immediate pleasure in the dog. She fended it from the fire and caressed it, but absently, and when she had heard the message, she winced, and gave an extraordinary smile, painful and ironic.

'If you do not wish to have the trouble of the dog, my

242

lady, I can take it away again,' he offered when he had finished. She said nothing for a while. The dog left her to course about the room, nose down, and she watched it with unseeing eyes. Then at last she seemed to come to a decision and he saw her gather herself together.

'Does it have a name, Durban?'

'No, my lady.'

'I can only think of French names, and that would not do for a Morland dog. Do you know any Morland names for dogs?'

'Well, my lady, Kithra is a traditional name in the family, and Fand, so I believe.'

'Fand – I cannot say that! No, Kithra it shall be. I shall keep the dog, gladly. Thank your master for me, if – if it can be done discreetly. Now you shall take some refreshment after your journey. Please to go into the kitchen, and ask Marie to look after you.'

Durban bowed, and left her. As he turned to close the door behind him, he saw that the dog had come back to the hearth, and was sitting in the warmth from the fire, looking up at Héloïse curiously. She was staring at the flames again, her hands folded in her lap, and her eyes were shining with tears in the flickering light.

The mild weather had kept many people in Town who would otherwise have gone into the country, and the carriage-way in Hyde Park was unusually full during the hours of promenade. Many of the gentlemen strollers wore red coats, but otherwise there was little evidence of the war which had been going on for nearly five years. Smart ladies drove or were driven at snail's pace, gentlemen were taken up for a circuit or two and put down again, carriages blocked the way by stopping alongside each other for the occupants to exchange greetings and examine each other's clothing with critical eyes. The fashionable went through the necessary process of being seen, flirtations were carried on and assignations made.

Lady Aylesbury was there most days, dashing and conspicuous. Her horses were the envy of many a sporting

243

gentleman, some of whom knew in their hearts that she handled the reins a great deal better than they. 'Lady Aylesbury's chestnuts' were as famous as Stantonbury's greys, or Mildmay's bay geldings, and everyone knew the name of her stony-faced groom, sure sign of her fame. When she drove her curricle, Parslow sat beside her, only getting down when she took up a gentleman for a turn; and when she rode her dancing golden mare, Mimosa, Parslow rode behind at a discreet distance on a horse fine enough to have been a gentleman's hack.

Of Lord Aylesbury little was seen. He was an indolent man, not much given to airings in the Park. He spent a good deal of time at Wolvercote, and when he was in Town he was usually either in bed, or at Whites or sauntering down St James's Street. When the Aylesburys entertained at home, he was in evidence, playing whist or leaning against the chimney-piece deep in conversation with some Smart or other, while his wife held court at the other end of the room. He and my lady were known to be on polite terms, but led separate lives. He lent countenance to her retinue of admirers and laughed publicly at her flirts, and thus the *ton* knew that everything was in order.

Lucy rode, walked, drove, danced, shopped, chatted and entertained frantically, and thought she was happy, dismissing her strange feelings of restlessness merely as a sign that she was not cramming enough of those activities into each day. The young officers of the 10th Dragoons, especially Wiske, Brummell, and Horatio Morland, were at the heart of her court, but she had to some extent taken over Flora's naval patronage, and such distinguished officers as were ashore were frequently to be found in her drawing-room, charming her with stories of thrilling exploits, or themselves with the unexpectedly technical discussions it was possible to have with her ladyship.

It was not in the least surprising that the up-and-coming Lieutenant Weston was almost always to be found at her elbow, and if the *ton* noticed that he was more often silent in her company those days, they cheerfully put it down as 'a flirt' and forgot about it.

Weston brought her the earliest news of her family. It

had been a good year for the navy: while the army seemed able to do nothing right, the navy could do nothing wrong, and though England was left without an ally except Portugal by the end of the year, the strength of the navy meant that the Directory's *Armée d'Angleterre*, which was gathering in northern France, was likely to remain there indefinitely.

The West India fleet had done well in the Caribbean under Rear-Admiral Hannibal Harvey. In a combined operation with the army under Sir Ralph Abercromby, Trinidad and Puerto Rico had been captured, and Captain 'Bloody Bill' Morland had been justified once again in his assertion that the West India station was the best for prize money.

In home waters, there had been another victory in October, when Admiral Duncan's fleet had beaten a Dutch fleet of fifteen of the line off Camperdown. The *Africa* had been in the engagement, and since eleven Dutch vessels had struck their colours, Captain Haworth would a richer man that winter. With the destruction of the Texel fleet, the *Africa* had been sent to reinforce Lord Bridport's blockading squadron outside Brest.

Lucy had listened to the news with mixed feelings – pride and envy, tempered by a sisterly concern for Mary's safety; but no English ship had so much as lost a mast, and Weston was soon able to assure her that the *Africa*'s losses had been light.

'There were fifteen wounded, mostly splinter wounds, and only three seriously. Seven dead, all seamen. No shots penetrated the hull. Most of the damage was on the maindeck, with shot ploughing along the deck.

Lucy nodded gravely, well able to imagine the injuries. 'I wish I had been there,' she said wistfully. Weston raised an eyebrow.

'Do you indeed? Why, Mr Proom, I rather thought you had become addicted to life on shore,' he teased gently. He often called her Mr Proom when they were alone together.

'Don't you wish to be at sea, when things like this are happening?' she asked curiously. 'If I were a man, I could not bear to be idle.'

'How unkind! You think me idle – but you must see that

245

someone has to be at the Admiralty, making decisions. And besides, if I were at sea, I couldn't be here talking to you, could I?'

Lucy felt breathless. Whenever he said anything directly flirtatious she felt a mixture of excitement and panic. Weston attracted her. She liked his company, enjoyed talking to him, and was proud to be seen with someone so handsome and personable; but there was something else, which troubled her. There was a hidden world, just under the surface of the world she was accustomed to, and sometimes the membrane between the two seemed very thin – perilously so, she thought, for whatever was that dark knowledge, it was not only exciting, it was dangerous.

She looked at him now wide-eyed, apprehensive, very different from the dashing Lady Aylesbury known to the world of fashion. Weston's smile changed minutely. 'You wouldn't really like me to go away to sea, would you, Lucy?' he asked. He was too close to her. She felt as though she could not draw her breath. 'Sure you would miss me?'

Some answer was necessary. 'I enjoy your conversation, Lieutenant Weston,' she said with a brave attempt to restore the balance. He reached across, took her hand and lifted it to his lips.

'Of course you do,' he said with a long, slow smile which made her feel as though all her bones had been removed, 'but won't you call me James when we are alone like this?'

'I – ' She gazed at him, almost mesmerized. Had it been any other name, she might have yielded then; but there were two other Jameses in her life – her husband, and her brother, whose recent actions had been the cause of much delightedly scandalous talk in the fashionable world. Sanity tapped her shoulder, and though she had not the strength to withdraw her hand, she did at least manage to say, 'I can't – I – I mustn't.'

Weston held her gaze a moment longer, and then, seemingly satisfied, restored her hand to her. 'Of course,' he said smoothly. 'Forgive me, ma'am. Shall you be at the Haymarket this evening? Captain Brummell says that the new opera is very good, and his judgement is usually sound on such matters.'

'Yes, I go with the Chelmsfords and a party. I am to dine with them first,' Lucy said, and was so grateful that the crisis had passed she added impulsively, 'I wish you might be with us, for it will be dull without you.'

His smile now was gentle. 'I shall do myself the honour of visiting you in your box, if you will permit it.' She nodded, and he continued in a cheerful, lively manner, 'But have you heard Captain Macnamara is to meet his man tomorrow?'

'No! Again? But this is the second time, is it not?' Lucy said, diverted.

'He is as proud and poisonous as a scorpion,' Weston said. 'He'll fight anyone, on any pretext, and put it all down to "the feelings of a gentleman", as he says. Well, he has chosen his equal this time – he is to meet Skeering on Primrose Hill at dawn, and if their tempers do not heat the air to a pleasant temperature I shall be surprised. I dine with Skeering at Fladong's before the opera, so I shall be able to tell you all tomorrow – if he survives!'

Lucy laughed, quite her old self again. 'You always have the best gossip, Weston! I should be lost without you.'

Chapter Fifteen

The stern cabin of the *Africa* was the most spacious room in the ship, and though when she first came on board, Mrs Haworth had not thought that was saying much, a six-months' trial of naval conditions had taught her to think it quite luxurious. It benefited from having been newly painted at the beginning of the commission, and though the Dockyard's choice of colours was limited, the grey picked out with yellow and black was quite subtly pleasing, once Mary had added her own touches.

She had discovered that the Purser had some yellow silk amongst his bales of cloth – for lining waistcoats, he said, although it did not take long for Mary to learn that the Purser had an extraordinary variety of things amongst his stores that there was no accounting for. As the ship was a kind of floating city, the Purser was all the shops of that city put together. Pursers, she was told, varied in their efficiency, honesty, and general character just as shopkeepers on shore did, but in Mr Harding they were fortunate: he was not more than ordinarily rapacious, and he placed his pride in being omniprovident.

At all events, she had fashioned some very pretty yellow curtains trimmed with black rick-rack braid for the stern cabin, and had made some cushions for the long window-seat from fine grey canvas, stuffed with oakum, trimmed with the same braid, which made the colour-scheme appear to have been chosen deliberately.

'I learnt very early in life,' she told her husband, 'that the best way to carry off an unsuccessful outfit was to be sure to look as though you *meant* to look like that.'

'I can't believe you ever wore an unsuccessful outfit, my love,' said her husband. 'I firmly believe you were born fully-clothed in the height of fashion.'

'Ah, what would the *ton* think if they could see me now?' she sighed. Life on shipboard had not been without its difficulties. Like all sailors, she missed the fresh food, especially fresh fruit and vegetables, and she had not expected to miss fresh flowers so much as she did. The sea-air made her hair frizzy, and washing in salt water left her skin feeling sticky and dirty. Washing her hair in salt-water was even worse, and she made arrangements with her husband's servant, Dipton, to keep back a little of her drinking-water day by day so that when she washed it, she could at least rinse it in fresh water, but it made little difference.

Clothes were difficult, too. The light, pretty muslins and silks she had grown accustomed to on shore would not do on ship-board, and could not have been kept clean and mended in any case. It was many weeks before she could stop feeling like a fright. Only the fact that there were no other gentlewomen with whom to compare herself comforted her. There were other females on board, but they rarely came above-decks, and the only one she had met was the carpenter's wife, who was helping in the sick-bay when she went down there during the battle of Camperdown to see if she could do anything.

It was fortunate, she reflected, that the battle had not happened until she had been ten weeks on board, and had had time to grow used to conditions. She had been very frightened, and nothing had saved her from her terror except the need to ensure that her husband had no cause to regret having brought her to sea with him. She controlled her panic, stitched an unconcerned smile on her face, and invoking the spirit of her younger sister, went below to offer her help to the surgeon.

The *Africa* was lucky in him, too, for he was a young man, well-trained, intelligent, and sober. All the same, Mary wondered afterwards how she had survived the hell of the cockpit during that battle, and even more how Lucy had survived her weeks of service and still at the end of it wanted more. Her respect for her sister increased enormously as she helped to bandage the horrible splinter-wounds.

The surgeon was not at all anxious for her help, and would not let her come near the operating table or the badly wounded. Nursing wounded men was not an occupation for gentlewomen, he insisted; but she was equally insistent that she must do something, both to prove to her husband that he had been right to bring her, and to take her mind off her own fear. Besides, she thought less nobly, how could she face Lucy's scorn if she hid in the cabin throughout the action?

Fortunately the battle, though fiercely fought – for the Dutch were proud of their naval tradition, and a very different kind of enemy at sea from the French – produced little damage to the English ships and, she was assured, a very moderate butcher's bill. Mary came through with distinction, and for the first time in her life was able to pride herself on what she had done, rather than what she was. Not that she could ever boast about it: it would rather lower her than raise her in the eyes of London Society if it were spoken of when she was next on shore; but Captain Haworth had been proud of her, and a new layer of homage had been added to his tenderness when they made love.

Mary was helping Dipton to prepare the cabin for the captain's weekly dinner-party that January day, and feeling grateful for the pallid sunshine that was coming in through the stern windows. It was still very cold, and the sea was still rough – though fortunately Mary had suffered very little from seasickness – but the sunshine was cheerful and made one think that spring was on its way.

'I do wish we had some flowers,' she said suddenly, with a sigh, as she folded napkins. 'It would make such a difference.'

'Yes, miss,' said Dipton. He and Mary had shaken down happily enough together, once he had understood that she did not mean to usurp his duties or interfere with his relationship with his captain. They were united by a love of Captain Haworth, and a conviction that he did not take enough care of himself. 'They say Captain Collingwood has a long box full of earth under the stern windows, Miss, what he grows flowers in. Daffodils and such-like.'

'What a good idea,' Mary said, struck with it. 'Daffodils would be the very thing for this cabin, wouldn't they? They'd make it look so bright – and hyacinths would smell lovely. How I wish I'd thought to bring some bulbs with me!

I must remember to do so next autumn.'

'Yes, miss. Here's the Cap'n, miss,' said Dipton. He always knew when Captain Haworth was approaching – he seemed to have developed a sixth sense for knowing exactly where in the ship his master was. It was several seconds before Mary heard, amidst the unregarded background cacophony of ship-noises, the stamp and click of the sentry outside the door coming to attention.

'Ah, my dear,' Haworth said as he came into the cabin, and both his and his wife's faces lit in a way that Dipton found very touching, as he often told the cook, his especial friend, when they were finishing off a bottle of something together down in the warmth of the galley. 'That all looks very nice.'

'I was just saying to Dipton that I wish we had some flowers for the table,' Mary said, coming forward to help him unbutton his pea-jacket, not because he needed help, but because she needed to touch him.

Haworth laughed. 'Flowers? I think we have more need of wishing for some fresh food. Still, at least we shall have something better to drink to offer our guests today, since we captured that coaster last week. Two dozen of real French claret!' he gloated. 'Do you know what people on shore back in England would give for that?'

'Perhaps you ought to keep it back,' Mary smiled. 'You could sell it for a small fortune when we next put in.'

'Ah, but a captain must keep his table, you know, my love. It would be a poor thing if the navy ever abandoned that tradition; and if you keep a table, you must offer the best you have.'

'I know – I was only funning,' Mary said.

'And who have we to dine today?' Haworth asked.

'Wilson, Doby, Cartwright, Webb, and young Morpurgo,' Mary replied, rattling off the names before Dipton could speak.

'Oh, has it got round to him again?' Haworth smiled at the name of the youngest midshipman on board, a boy of whom he was very fond. 'You must be sure to suggest a round-game after dinner, my love. The young people will enjoy it more than whist.'

251

'So will the Anchovy,' Mary said, referring to the first lieutenant, Angevin, who was always included in the dinner rota, along with the master and the officer of the forenoon watch. 'He really hates whist, you know, though he is at pains to please you by playing.'

'Darling, you really mustn't call him that,' Haworth said, leading her towards the night-cabin. 'We shall go and dress now, Dipton. I'll pass the word for you when I need you.'

'Aye aye, sir.'

'But he looks like a fish,' Mary continued the inconsequential argument.

'To be sure he does, but not like an anchovy. More like a cod.'

'Do you know what the young mids call you, my love? Haystack!'

'Because of my baldness, I suppose?'

'Well, it can't be because your skin smells deliciously like warm grass, for they can't know that, can they?'

'Foolish!' Haworth laughed, opening the communicating door for his wife.

'I shall be glad when the sea moderates and we can have some new guests at dinner from the other ships,' she said.

'Pity the poor frigate-captains of the inshore squadron,' Haworth replied, 'who never see another ship from month to month. And they have fewer officers amongst whom to ring the changes.' He closed the door behind them, threw off his pea-jacket, and opened his arms for his wife. They kissed long and tenderly, and then broke off with an identical, satisfied sigh which made them both laugh.

'You know, this is the best time of the week for me, despite the dullness of so many of our guests,' he said, sitting down on his cot and pulling off his boots. 'I love to see you sitting at the foot of my table, and being the gracious hostess, and making the young officers feel at home. I like to imagine it a proper dining-table in a large saloon in a grand house, and you entertaining in the manner your birth and beauty entitle you to.'

She stopped his lips with her fingers. 'When will you learn that I require nothing more than I have? I would not change one minute of being with you for a whole year of the

252

fashionable life.'

He kissed the fingers as they withdrew. 'I hope at least you won't mind my being a *little* more wealthy? My share of the prize money from Camperdown will be not inconsiderable, you know.'

'Not as considerable as it should be, in my view. Duncan was made a viscount, and given a pension of £3,000 a year,' Mary said, 'and he wasn't in any more danger than you.'

Haworth laughed. 'It's nothing to do with danger, my love, as you know very well. It's responsibility. If we had lost, Duncan would have taken the blame, so why shouldn't he have the benefits of victory? When I am an admiral, you won't complain if they give me a title and a pension, I hope?'

Mary came over to sit beside him. 'I'm glad you said when, and not if, though you know I couldn't love you more if you were Admiral of the Fleet and a duke into the bargain.'

Haworth's grey-blue eyes were warm with love. 'And I couldn't love you more if you were – ' he paused to think of some analogy, and Mary interrupted him with a smile.

'Oh, but I am, Captain Haworth.'

It was a moment before he caught her drift, and then his eyes became very blue. 'Oh my darling! Are you sure?'

Mary laughed. 'Of course I am – as you should be, if you had any idea of the passage of time. The child should be here in August. I hope you are pleased?'

'Pleased!' he cried, and then a frown crossed his brow. 'But not here, my love. It would be very dangerous for you to be confined here on board. Not that young Daniels isn't a very fine surgeon, but conditions on ship-board – and suppose there was another battle? No, it wouldn't do. We must see about getting you a passage for England as soon as possible. In your delicate condition you should not be here at all.'

'Now don't talk fustian, George. I am not in the least delicate, and I absolutely refuse to leave you until the last minute. What, be separated from you during the very months when I most want and need to be with you? In the summer it will be quite time enough to be getting rid of me.

253

No, no, I won't argue about it. I am as firm as – as – as Anchovy's handshake,' she finished, and in making him laugh, achieved her objective.

In January 1798, Sydney Street once again saw the smart town-chariot with the Earl of Chelmsford's arms on its side panels. This time Héloïse chose Sunday for her visit, so as to coincide with the weekly gathering of the emigrés, and she was careful to bring with her a hamper of food and a dozen bottles of champagne.

They gathered round her, glorying in her good fortune, patting her lovingly, fingering the thick pile of her velvet pelisse with wonder. Romorantin grinned to the limit of his naked gums, and did a little shuffling dance on the spot with delight. Madame Chard burst into tears when she saw three chickens and a whole roast sirloin lifted out of the hamper, and Thiviers, unpacking the champagne, let out a shout which he quickly changed into the rousing chorus of a song, which seemed however to have only one word, endlessly repeated.

They sat her in state by the fire, brought her a glass of the blessed effervescence, toasted her, France, the King, and the Vine, and then begged to hear her story. It made very good telling, too, having all the elements of drama, horror, excitement, mystery, romance, sadness, and happiness.

'My dear,' said Madame Chard, 'what a story! Secret drawers, hidden treasure, Marie-Antoinette's jewels – you live in a fairy tale!'

'So do we all, dear Chard,' said the Comte de Thiviers sadly, 'so do we all; but alas our stories do not have the happy ending. Too much of the ogre and the dungeon about ours, and not enough of the good fairy and the handsome prince! But let us rejoice at least that our dear Henriette-Louise has slain her dragon Poverty.'

Later when she was alone with Madame Chouflon, the latter said, 'Such talk! Fairy tales and handsome princes – I could have wrung Thiviers' neck.'

'Oh,' said Héloïse in a small voice. 'So you have heard all about that?'

'Well, *ma petite*, not all, I imagine, but it has been much talked of in the houses of fashion, how Monsieur Morland had run away from his wife to live with a French comtesse; and then again, how he had been persuaded to return to his wife. Those of us who serve the rich for our living must have heard so much at least.'

'There is little more to tell,' Héloïse sighed, 'apart from what I told the others, about finding the treasure. That is partly why I have come to London, to ask my cousin of Chelmsford to help me sell the jewels. I am staying with him, of course, and his wife is very kindly helping me to find housemaids. The people of my village think me a wicked woman, and won't let their daughters serve in my household; but I must have two housemaids. It is not right that Marie should continue to serve as a *bonne-à-tout-faire*, she who came to me as a lady's maid.'

'Marie does not mind what she does – you know that.'

'Yes, but I mind.' Héloïse gazed into the fire for a moment, and roused herself to say, 'I have a dog, too, did I mention? A huge dog like a wolf, with yellow eyes. They breed them at Morland Place, and, I must tell you, Flon, they are so strange, because they never bark; indeed, just like wolves! It is quite unnerving until you get used to it. I did not bring him here tonight, because in a confined space there seems to be so very much of him.'

'*Ma petite fleur*, you did not come here to tell me about housemaids and dogs,' Flon said shrewdly.

'Oh, I have told you all the story now.'

'No, not all. What is it, child?'

Héloïse looked at her, and her lip quivered, and she was forced to catch it with her teeth. Madame Chouflon held out her arms to her, and Héloïse knelt in the firelight and cried into the stiff flounces of her lap, while the old, crooked hands stroked her head.

'Oh my dear, I should have guessed,' Flon exclaimed gently. 'That's right, cry your tears out, little one, it's the best way. I expect you've been keeping up a brave face for everyone until now, haven't you?' Héloïse said something incoherent in her lap, and Flon went on soothing her until the flow of tears slowed and clotted, and she reached the hiccoughing stage, and there was some point in thrusting a handkerchief into her fingers.

When she had blown and mopped, and was sitting, dishevelled and red-eyed on the hearth-rug with the damp linen crumpled in her hand, Héloïse said, 'I'm sorry. I'm better now.'

'No need to be sorry, my child. Everyone needs to cry sometimes. But now we must be practical.'

'Yes, madame,' Héloïse said with a watery sort of smile. She felt better already. There was something about speaking French and having someone suggest being practical which made her feel as though she were back at home.

'So,' Flon said, placing her hands squarely on her knees, 'first of all, when is the child due?'

'I am not sure – you see, I have never had a baby before.'

'Stupid! When was your last flux?'

'In – in October,' said Héloïse shyly.

'Beginning or end?'

'The middle of the month.'

'Then the baby will come at the end of July,' Madame Chouflon said firmly, 'and I shall think you a simpleton if you can't work that out. Now, the next thing is, who knows of it?'

'No-one,' said Héloïse quickly. 'Except – I think perhaps Marie may have guessed, but I have not told her.'

'You have not told the father?'

'Oh no!' Héloïse said, shocked. 'How could I do that? He has returned to his wife, to try to do what is right. Do you think I would make it more difficult for him than it must be already? If he were to know, he might run away again – or if he stayed, he would suffer twice as much.'

'Don't you know that you are likely to suffer?' Madame Chouflon said.

'But it cannot help me to hurt him,' Héloïse said simply.

'I think he will be bound to find out sooner or later. Children make a great deal of noise in the world.'

'Better later than sooner. But, dear Flon, what am I to do? The people of my village disapprove of me already because I lived with someone else's husband. Now, if I have a baby as well – '

'Well, dearest, there is nothing much we can do about that, except to stare them out. And I think the circumstance of your being rich and extending your house will help.'

'James said that,' Héloïse frowned. 'I don't see why.'

'Because a rich woman in the neighbourhood benefits everyone; and in time they will get used to your circumstances. An unexplained baby is not nearly so hard to swallow as a man they know perfectly well belongs to someone else. You are quite right to think of two housemaids, but you must do more: you must give yourself all the trappings of a woman of consequence. Another footman, at least, and a cook you must have, and a respectable older woman to be your chaperone.'

Héloïse smiled up at her suddenly. 'You, Flon?'

Flon smiled back. 'I hoped you would ask me. I am certainly older, and if I am not entirely respectable, well, they will not know that! I shall come very gladly.'

'I wish you had come before, when I first asked you,' Héloïse said. 'Why didn't you?'

'That was entirely different. Before, you were asking me out of kindness; now you have need of me.'

'I think that is called the sin of pride,' Héloïse said sternly. Madame Chouflon patted her cheek.

'At my age, and in my circumstances, pride is all I can afford, *ma chère.*'

Héloïse returned to London that evening much happier than she had left it. Her future seemed secure, laid out before her in all its detail, and she realized that she was a great deal luckier than she deserved to be. She had a home, wealth, faithful servants, a friend, and a child to come, on whom to lavish her love. God is merciful, she thought, and her heart filled with gratitude, and a longing to express it. It was difficult, she reflected, living in a Protestant country: at home, she could simply have stopped the carriage in any street and gone into the church to light a candle.

The chariot was making its way along Piccadilly when a child darted out from a side street and ran heedlessly across the road, right under the hooves of the Chelmsford horses.

The carriage lurched violently as the horses plunged; a woman screamed and there were shouts, and Héloïse fumbled with the door, and jumped down without waiting for the steps.

The child was sitting at the road's edge, and there was blood on her face. Two of the bystanders were holding her, but she was struggling violently to escape. As Héloïse went towards her, a servant came running across the street through the stationary traffic crying,

'Matilda Nortiboys, you wicked girl, come here this minute!'

Héloïse's heart lurched. Accustomed as she now was to English corruptions of French words, she was easily able to translate Matilda Nortiboys back into Mathilde Nordubois. But could it be? Could it be the daughter of her old friend Lotti, the child she had promised years ago to cherish and protect? She stared at the child with wide eyes: a thin, gangling girl with a long, white freckled face and a tangle of fox-red hair. It must be she. But what was she doing here in London? The servant was still thrusting her way through the gathering crowd, as Héloïse knelt beside the child, drawing out her handkerchief to wipe the blood away, and said in French, 'Mathilde, is it you? Do you remember me? I am Héloïse, Mama's friend!' The child stopped struggling, but stared at Héloïse with no more than bewilderment.

'Don't let her go, the naughty runaway!' the servant was shouting as she struggled through.

'Don't be afraid, *chérie*,' Héloïse went on, still in French. 'I am your friend. I knew you when you were a baby, in France. Don't you remember Paris?'

'Oh Ma'am, don't trouble with that – you'll get yourself all messed.' The servant had now reached them, and took hold of the child's arm, trying to drag her to her feet. 'She's a wicked, disobedient girl, ungrateful too, when people have been so kind to her. She's always running away, the naughty sprite. You come with me, Matilda Nortiboys. It's a whipping for you this time, my girl, and don't say you haven't been warned.'

Héloïse intervened, placing her hand on the servant's arm to restrain her. 'The child is hurt, you know. Look, her head is cut. I'm afraid she must have caught it on some part of my carriage.'

'Don't you worry about that, ma'am,' said the servant. 'She's as tough as they come.' And she resumed hauling on the thin arm.

'No, please don't do that. Let me convey her – and you – in my carriage. Where have you come from?'

'Lord Burlington's school, ma'am, the girls' charity school in Boyle Street, just over yonder. It's only a step, ma'am, you mustn't trouble. This naughty girl climbed out of a window and ran away. She's forever doing it. Lucky I spotted her this time, for it was the Watch brought her back before.'

'I will take you there now, both of you. I wish to speak to your headmistress. You see, I think I know this child.'

The servant stared. 'Do you, ma'am? Why, I thought I heard you speaking Dutch to her. Mrs Webb is the matron, ma'am, and she'll be pleased to see to you, I'm sure.' Her eyes had taken in the rich attire and the coat of arms on the coach. No doubt, Héloïse reflected, such schools were always in need of wealthy patrons. She addressed a few words of explanation to the coachman and footman, and then turned to the red-haired child.

'Don't be afraid,' she said in French. 'Come with me now. I am your friend.' There was no knowing if she understood or not, for she only stared in fright and defiance. Héloïse reflected that she had been only four years old when she left France, and now perhaps understood only German. But what had happened to her since her father took her away from her uncle's house in Leipzig? Where was he, and where was her brother Karellie? The footman had put down the steps now, and she urged the child into the carriage, keeping a gentle but wary hand on her arm. That was another question – why had she run away? Did they ill-treat her? The servant mounted gingerly and sat on the very edge of the seat, the steps were put up and the door closed, and they lurched away.

In a well-furnished study in the plain but handsome school building, Héloïse was received with great deference by Mrs Webb. She seemed a respectable woman, quietly spoken, with sharp, intelligent eyes, and a conscientious frown between her brows. The child was seated in a corner, the servant keeping guard over her, and Mrs Webb told her story.

'The school is not an orphan asylum, my lady. It was founded to educate the daughters of poor people of the parish, but from time to time we take on girls in difficult circumstances, at the request of our patrons. It was Lady Winchcomb who brought this little girl here. She was the survivor of a shipwreck – a fishing boat went aground on the Goodwin Sands – and she had been taken to a sailor's home in which Lady Winchcomb also has an interest. It was obviously not a suitable place for her, and so her ladyship asked us to take her in.'

'When was this?' Héloïse asked.

'Only last autumn, ma'am.' She glanced at the child and sighed. 'The Trustees weren't too happy about it, my lady, because the child speaks no English.'

'She does not seem to understand French either,' Héloïse said. 'Have you tried speaking to her in German?'

Mrs Webb looked offended. 'No-one here speaks German, my lady.'

'And you say she keeps running away? Why is that?'

'I cannot tell you, my lady. She has never been ill-treated. How do you come to know her, may I ask?'

'I was a great friend of her mother, in Paris, from the time she was born. Her name is Mathilde Nordubois – '

'Yes, my lady, that's what we call her. Matilda Nortiboys. So it is the same child – I don't suppose there could be two with a name like that.'

'Her mother was killed in the Revolution,' Héloïse continued, ignoring the interruption. 'I escaped, bringing Mathilde and her younger brother and sister with me. But our ship, too, foundered, and we were separated. I heard later that she had been rescued and taken to her uncle in Germany, and later still that her father had taken her away from there. But you know that news is not reliable in war time. How could she have come to be on a fishing-boat? And where is her brother Karellie?'

The child gave a low cry, and started up, staring at

260

Héloïse with enormous eyes. 'Karellie!' she cried, and added something incomprehensible in German. Héloïse shook her head and smiled apologetically, and to her surprise the little girl said very slowly in awkward French, with a very odd accent, 'Where is my brother? You have news of my brother Karellie?'

Héloïse shook her head. '*Non, ma chère.* So you speak French, do you?'

'A little. I understand – not speak well.'

'Was Karellie with you in the ship?'

'Yes. But the lady took me away. I must find him.'

'Wait a little. I will ask.' She turned to Mrs Webb and reverted to English. 'I can solve your problem for you. She runs away to look for her brother. Do you know what has become of him? She says he was with her in the boat.'

Mrs Webb shook her head. 'No, my lady. I never heard of a brother. Lady Winchcomb never mentioned one. Perhaps her brother was sent to a boys' school of the same sort. There are several boys' charity schools in London.'

Héloïse leaned forward and clasped her hands before her on the desk. 'Madame, I have a request to make of you – that you let me take the child with me. I wish to adopt her and bring her up as my own.'

'Well, I don't know – '

'I promised her mother, you see, that if anything happened to her, I would take care of her children. I failed, through no fault of my own – but here is a chance to keep my promise. You must agree that she would be better off in a private home than in your school, though I'm sure you do your best for the children.'

'I'm sorry, my lady, but it is not for me to decide. It would have to be put to the Trustees – and Lady Winchcomb, of course. I don't know what they would say. I mean – I beg your pardon, my lady, but do we know who you are?'

Héloïse smiled gently. 'Of course, you must satisfy yourselves that I am a fit person to take the child, but I beg that you will put your enquiries in hand with all speed. I am staying at present with my cousin, the Earl of Chelmsford, of whom, no doubt, you have heard.'

261

Mrs Webb's face cleared. 'But of course, my lady. His lordship is one of our patrons. Indeed, his family have been patrons of the school since its beginning. I'm sure there will be no trouble about it, my lady. I shall write to the Trustees first thing in the morning.'

'Thank you. And enquire too, if you will, about her brother.' Héloïse stood up and picked up her muff. 'I shall be grateful if you will act as quickly as possible in this matter.' She turned to the child. 'Mathilde, I am going now,' she said in French, 'but I will come back, and then you shall come and live with me in a proper house, and we will find your brother, and bring him to live with us too. Do you understand me?'

'*Oui, madame.*'

'In the meantime you must stay here. I hope it will be only a few days. You must not try to run away again.' Mathilde looked doubtful. 'I promise I will come back. Do you promise you will not run away?'

'*Oui, madame,*' she said at last, with a little sigh.

It took two weeks for the Trustees of the school to meet and discuss the case, and a further week for them to acquire Lady Winchcomb's approval for the transfer of custody. Neither the Trustees nor Lady Winchcomb knew anything about Mathilde's brother, however.

'He may have been rescued by different people and taken elsewhere along the coast,' Charles said sympathetically. 'I can put enquiries in hand for you, if you wish.'

'Oh, if you please, Cousin Charles,' Héloïse said gratefully. 'It is most important to me that I fulfil my promise to Lotti, if I can.'

'If it weren't for this damned war,' Charles complained, 'we might have some hope of finding out where her father is, and what she was doing on that boat.'

'She may be able to tell me something of that, when I have a chance to talk to her at length,' Héloïse said.

'You say she did not know you?' Roberta asked.

'I'm not sure. She did not seem to remember me, but she was greatly shocked at the time. It may come back to her, in time.'

'Forgive me, my dear Héloïse, but do you really want to take on the responsibility of this child? You know nothing of her recent history. She may have a bad disposition. She may prove to be very troublesome,' Roberta said.

'Oh no, I cannot believe it. Why, she is only nine years old, and the poor thing has gone through so much! I must give her a home,' Héloïse said firmly. 'She will be no trouble.'

'I wonder,' Charles said with a wry smile.

Héloïse went back to the school several times while the enquiries were going on, to reassure Mathilde that she was not forgotten, and found out a little more of her story.

'We lived with Uncle Ernst and Aunt Anna, in a big house in Leipzig,' she said in her hesitant French. 'That was many years past. Then Papa took us away. We went to a school in Antwerp. He said he would come back, but he didn't come.'

'Before Leipzig, do you remember where you lived?' Héloïse asked. 'Do you remember Paris?' She took her head. 'Do you remember the boat that took you from France? You were with me, and Marie, and Karellic, and baby Clothilde. Do you remember Clothilde?' Again the shake of the head.

'I think I was in France once, because at the school they say we are French, but I don't remember it.' She frowned. 'I didn't like the school. They are not nice.'

'And how did you come to leave the school?'

'There was – ' She hesitated, seeking the words. 'No money. And a letter. They say, "You go to England". Then the boat, and – ' She made a gesture expressive of catastrophe. 'In England they take me to a place and another place and the school. I ask for Karellie, and no-one knows.'

'When the boat was wrecked, in England, what happened to him? Was he with you in the first place that you went to?' But Mathilde only shook her head, seeming to have no language for more detail. Héloïse thought that having been in two disastrous shipwrecks in her short life had perhaps affected her memory, making her shut out the horror and tragedy.

At the end of February the day came when Héloïse was able to take her back with her to Chelmsford House. The place, its size and the number of servants, awed the child to the brink of tears, and it was Kithra who saved the day by frisking up to her and nudging her in a friendly way, inviting her to play. Marie took advantage of the moment to put an arm round her shoulder and take her and the dog upstairs to the nursery, where Bobbie's nurses were ready and eager for an increase in their duties.

'*Viens avec moi, Mathilde, chérie. Tu te rappelles de moi?*'

'*Non, madame.*'

'*Mais si! Je suis Marie. Je t'ai connue à Paris –* '

Talking cheerfully she coaxed the child upstairs, and Charles smiled. 'It won't be long at that rate before she has learnt enough French for you to begin to teach her English.'

'Oh, but cousin, it is only to reassure her that we speak in French. When she is settled, we shall speak English, of course.'

'I know, I was only teasing you. Well, now I suppose we had better put matters in hand to make her your legal ward. You are sure you want it?'

'Why not?' said Héloïse.

'Because I believe you will soon have a child of your own to care for,' Charles said gently. Héloïse blushed scarlet, and he patted her arm. 'I did not mean to distress you, my dear. You know that I have always had your welfare at heart. I wish I could help you.'

'Oh please,' she begged, 'please don't tell Maman, or James!'

'Of course not, if you don't wish me to. But they are bound to know sooner or later, don't you think?'

'Once the baby is born, it will be easier to hide,' Héloïse said. 'James mustn't know.'

Charles shrugged. 'As you wish. But you must look upon Roberta and me in the light of parents, if you will, and come to us if you need help of any sort. I shall speak to my lawyer about the guardianship of the child tomorrow.'

'And you and I, my dear,' said Roberta, 'can have a lovely day shopping, for your little friend will need almost everything new; and there will be things to buy for the baby, too.'

Héloïse smiled, suddenly glad to be sharing the knowledge of her condition, especially with kind, practical Roberta, who was so newly a mother herself. And her desire to shew her gratitude had been answered, she realized, by the providential meeting with Lotti's child. Truly, she thought wonderingly, I am greatly blessed.

Chapter Sixteen

At the end of February, 1798, work began at last on the draining and cleaning of the moat. It was decided to do the work in sections, for the sake of the swans, who resented any interference with their environment. At first they tended to attack the workmen, and had to be persuaded to keep to the undrained section by a mixture of threats and bribes. The worst tempered of all was a solitary old penn, whose mate had died some years ago, and who lingered morosely, swearing horribly at each new generation of cygnets, and consoling herself with food.

'Poor thing, she's lonely,' Jemima said, trying to soothe the nerves of a workman who had been forced to donate his noon bread-and-cheese to this avian delinquent. 'They mate for life, you know. I know just how she feels.'

The moat had become silted up with two-and-a-half centuries' worth of mud and rubbish, which all had to be dug out and carted away.

'Extraordinary things you find at the bottom of a moat,' Edward mused over one day's haul. 'Why is everything metal? I suppose because it lasts the longest,' he answered himself. There were quantities of old coins from different periods – 'How careless people were with their money,' James remarked – and a single, very beautiful gold candlestick which no-one could explain, but nothing else of value. The mud was taken off to be spread on the fields, and the rubbish to be buried, but Jemima pounced on two cannon balls and insisted that they be cleaned up and kept.

'Mother, who wants two lumps of rusty iron?' Edward said.

'But they're historical,' she protested. 'They must have come from the time the house was held against William of Orange's men. It's always said that we were never fired on in the civil war, because the master kept changing sides just in time. Someone will be very interested in them some day.'

'And that's all. A pity,' James said, throwing down an ancient castiron hinge. 'I thought there might be a chest full of treasure.'

'Well, there isn't,' said Edward, 'so you had better be sure not to run off again, because we are paying for all this out of Mary Ann's dowry.'

He walked off to speak to the workmen. When he had gone Jemima said, 'He doesn't mean to hurt you.'

'I know, Mama. It's quite all right.'

'I wish you weren't unhappy,' she said.

'Unhappy? I don't know. It's more like having lost a limb, I think. Does a man with one arm feel unhappy, or only that he's missing something? But I'm well enough as long as I keep busy. It's only when I have time on my hands that I begin to think.'

'You have worked very hard since you came back,' Jemima said. 'I'm very proud of you.'

He gave a tight smile. 'It's accepting that it's for ever that's hard. Everything else follows easily enough.'

A servant came out from the house. 'Mr Pobgee's here, my lady. He says you sent for him.'

'Yes. Shew him into the steward's room. I'll come at once.'

'Pobgee?' James quizzed. 'Now what, Mama? Are you changing your will?'

'As a matter of fact, yes,' Jemima said. She gave him a searching look. 'It seems to me that you don't intend having any more children.' James looked away, and said nothing. 'So circumstances have changed a little since I last saw Mr Pobgee. Certain provisions must be altered.'

'Suppose – ' Jemima turned back inquiringly. 'Suppose Mary Ann were to have another child?'

She shrugged. 'I can always send for the lawyer again.'

In March an alarming report reached them that there were violent disturbances in Manchester. Cotton spinners were said to have rioted, marching on the mills, breaking windows and attempting to set fire to the buildings, in a protest over wages.

Mary Ann was naturally alarmed for the safety of her father, and angered that the actions of his own employees should endanger him. 'They are so ungrateful!' she cried. 'My father gives them employment, without which they would starve.'

'They say that their wages aren't enough to live on,' Edward read from the paper.

'The rates are fixed. Everyone pays the same,' she said indignantly. 'But some people are always discontented. The more you give them, the more they want.'

She was particularly worried that no message had come from her father to assure her of his safety, and tended to think the worst. 'He would know I would be worried. He would be sure to write, if he were all right.'

James, intrigued by this new side to his wife, who had quite lost her customary serenity, entered into the discussion with interest. 'But consider, ma'am, at a time like this he would hardly have leisure to write. And besides, the mails may have been delayed or even prevented from leaving. It may be impossible to get a message to you.'

'Then the news that he had been harmed would not reach us either!'

She was so obviously not to be comforted, that James said, 'Very well, I'll go there myself and see what's happening. It's not so very far. I can be there in a day, even at this time of year.'

She looked surprised and pleased, but Edward intervened hastily. 'No, Jamie, I think it best, if anyone's to go, that it should not be you. Remember you are not exactly in favour with your father-in-law.'

'The more reason, surely, to shew I'm concerned for his welfare.'

'He might not take it that way,' Edward said. 'Better you stay here with your wife. I'll go, and report back. I've a great curiosity to see the mills, anyway.'

James shrugged and argued no further. He had no great desire to go on a long uncomfortable journey with nothing but his father-in-law at the other end, and if Edward went, he would still get the credit of having offered, but without the pains of performance.

*

There was plenty of evidence of the rioting to be seen. Troops had been called in to control the marchers, and everywhere there were smashed windows and the smouldering remains of fires while the streets were littered with stones and bricks, and broken pieces of fencing and lengths of iron which had been used as weapons. Soldiers were in evidence on guard at various gateways and vantage points, and such civilians as were to be seen had a nervous, subdued air about them as they hurried along.

Edward had no idea where the Hobsbawn mills were, so he went straight to Hobsbawn House, where he found a trooper on guard at the gate, though the house appeared not to have been damaged. He stated his business and was admitted, and the butler let him into the house with a nervous blink to either side, and took him into the drawing-room.

'Master's with his agent, in the business room, sir. I'll tell him you're here, and he'll come to you shortly, I'm sure.'

'Is he all right?' Edward asked. 'He was not harmed by the rioters, I trust?'

'Oh no, sir, he's quite sound, only amazing vexed about it all. Well sir, if you'll excuse me –'

Edward was left alone for some time, and wandered about the drawing room, renewing his acquaintance with the exotic, elaborately decorated and oppressively luxurious furnishings. There was a faintly neglected air to the room – the mirrors were not bright, and there was a fine film of dust over everything – which revealed that Hobsbawn House lacked a mistress. In March it was not wonderful to find vases empty, but the Chinese bowl on the marble-topped commode contained brown and mummified roses which at the kindest estimate must have been there since October.

'Aye, well, Mr Morland.' Hobsbawn entered the room abruptly and Edward turned to greet him. 'And to what do I owe this pleasure?' He looked past Edward at the bowl of dead roses and frowned. 'We're at sixes and sevens, you see. I don't use this room much, since my daughter went. Don't have time to entertain, nor reason to, without her to show off; and my business friends I take to the library, where they can smoke. How is Mary Ann?'

'She's well, sir, but very worried about you. Indeed, we all were. We heard such uncomfortable reports of how things went on in Manchester, that we couldn't be easy until we had made sure that you were all right.'

'All right?' Hobsbawn frowned.

'Not harmed by the rioters,' Edward amplified. The brow cleared.

'Oh, it was my safety as exercised you, not my financial standing? You did not want to know if I was wiped out?'

'Of course not, sir,' Edward said, expressing hurt and surprise, and inwardly blessing his good sense in not allowing James to come. 'We had heard nothing from you, and your daughter felt sure that you would have written to reassure her about your safety.'

'Aye, well, I suppose I would eventually, but I have had too much to do. These damned spinners, ungrateful dogs that they are! Glass everywhere – well, by God, I wish I were a glazer in Manchester this day, for they're the only gainers by this week's work! Mind, I've not suffered the worst, I will say, for there are acquaintances of mine whose mills have been burnt down to the ground, and others who've lost near all their machines. I'm not so bad off as some – but all the same, there's thousands of pounds worth of damage done – machines smashed – walls and gates broken down. And all for what?'

Edward made a polite noise of enquiry.

'All to give them more money for the same day's work! I told them, if you don't want the work, there's others will do it! Aye, and cheaper, too! I can get women and children and train them up in a couple of weeks to do the same job. Young girls – they've nimble fingers, and they don't eat so much, and they're docile. By God, if I could get my hands on their leaders – !'

'The apprentices, sir – the children we sent you – I hope they were not involved in this unfortunate business?'

'Well, no, not directly. They didn't rise up, at all events, though one or two were hurt when the rioters smashed the windows of the 'prentice-house – it's hard against the number one mill, you see, a sort of lean-to. Cut by flying

270

glass, some of them, and some others with burns, but we've had the surgeon to 'em, and they'll be back to work as soon as the mills open again.'

They were interrupted by the butler bringing in a tray of wine and biscuits. 'Just a minute, Bowles – you'll stay the night, of course?' Hobsbawn said to Edward.

'Indeed, yes, thank you.'

'Right – then it's one more for dinner, Bowles.'

'Very good, sir.'

Hobsbawn poured two glasses of wine. 'Claret,' he said proudly. 'I don't want for French wines.'

'How do you come by them, sir?' Edward asked.

'Oh, there are ways, my boy,' Hobsbawn said, pleased with himself. 'The trade winds blow, you know, war or no war. I had several dozen come to me through America. I trade in cotton with New England; they trade in tobacco with the islands; and some of the islands are owned by the French. The great folk of Martinique like to drink their claret, same as us, and they're not averse to selling some if the profit's large enough.'

'Well, however it comes, it's a welcome change. Your health, Mr Hobsbawn.'

'And yours, Mr Morland.'

They drank and Edward put down his glass and said, 'It would very much interest me to see your mills, sir, if you would allow me? Perhaps if you are going there tomorrow, I might accompany you?'

'Aye, lad, and welcome, if it interests you, though they're a sorry sight at the moment. Thank God the rioters had no cannon, hey?'

'Indeed. My mother and father, you know, went to visit a spinning mill many years ago, in Derbyshire, and my mother was very impressed with it. She'd be glad to have my impressions of your mills.'

'In Derbyshire? Water mill, was it?'

'Yes, sir.'

Hobsbawn chuckled. 'Ah well, this is a very different go altogether, young man. Mine are steam-mills – the spinning machines are driven by steam-engines. Oh, a different go entirely, I promise you!'

271

So Edward found the next day. He also discovered why the mill-owners of Manchester did not live near their factories, as they did in Derbyshire. From the pleasant, tree-shaded, large-gardened streets around Hobsbawn House, and the handsome, broad thoroughfares and noble public buildings around the Exchange, they passed into a very different country altogether. The mills clustered along the banks of the river Irwell, ten and twelve stories high, shutting out the light. Their tall chimneys reared higher still, and from their mouths belched black smoke which hung in palls to bring a kind of unnatural twilight to the streets.

Soot was everywhere, coating every surface, and where it met with damp, turning into an indelible slime like black ink. Between the factories the houses of the workers were crammed, and as their carriage passed Edward caught a glimpse of little airless courts and mean and squalid streets of blackened brick tenements, cramped and unwholesome. Black mud was their only paving, and heaps of rubbish, offal and filth lay openly everywhere.

Mr Hobsbawn made no comment on it, nor on the condition of the river itself, which could hardly be said to be flowing, so dense was it with detritus. Its waters were greenish black, stiff with slime, and here and there great bubbles of gas broke on the surface from things rotting in its depths. Between the brick-built embankments and the water itself were narrow mud beaches on which such rubbish festered that Edward felt obliged once or twice to look away. It was clear that all the factories – mills, tanneries, dye-works, bone-mills – pumped their waste into it, along with the privies of the private houses nearby, and matters were not helped by the weirs which had been built at intervals to hold back the water for industrial purposes, against which choice selections of the debris were leaning and rotting glutinously.

When they finally stepped out of the carriage in the forecourt of the number one mill, Edward took a breath and felt for one moment of panic that he was choking. The smoky air contained a stench which seemed to be a comprehensive *resumé* of all he had seen. He gasped and coughed, and painful tears burst from his tear-ducts, and Mr Hobsbawn slapped him hard on the back and grinned.

'Catches you a bit sharp the first time, don't it? Aye, but you get used to it soon enough. It's worse than this when all the mills are working.' His face darkened. 'Had to let the engines stop, God damn it, after those bloody rioters smashed their way in! That's the worst of it! Never let the engines stop as a rule, nor the fires out. That's not the way to turn a shilling. Takes time, you see, to build up the fires and get the steam up, so once they're off and running, you leave 'em running. Day shift and night shift, one on and one off. We've gas light in the mills by night,' he added proudly, and then gave a hearty laugh. 'You know what they say, young man? The beds of Lancashire never grow cold! For when the day shift tumbles out of a morning, the night shift tumbles in! Well, it's something in winter, to have a warm bed to get into.'

Edward said nothing, and followed Hobsbawn in to the silent mill. It was eight storeys high, and the rioters had broken in and smashed the machines on three floors before they had been driven back. Debris was everywhere.

'Wanton!' Hobsbawn cried, his voice breaking tragically. 'Wanton destruction! By God, hanging's too good for the rats that did this! To think I worked my fingers to the bone all my life, to come to this!'

After a long and, to Edward, boring conversation with the watchmen, overseers and agents about repairing the damage, Hobsbawn took Edward to the number two mill, further along the bank. This was newer and bigger, fourteen storeys high, and here the rioters had been prevented from doing more than breaking windows and throwing in flaming rags, which the watchmen had been able to put out without much damage.

Hobsbawn shewed him round a floor of the factory with great pride, pointing out the salient features of the machines, and Edward experienced for the first time the deafening noise of running machines in an enclosed space. The mill-workers did not seem to notice it – indeed, it would be hard to say that they noticed anything. They were mostly children and young women – the only men he saw were overseers and engineers – and they moved in a curious manner about their work, both lethargic and mechanical, their eyes fixed and dull, seeing nothing. They worked standing up at the machines, though a good deal of the children's work seemed to involve crawling under the machines to doff the bobbins or mend the threads.

'I won't shew you namore,' Hobsbawn bellowed in his ear. 'All the floors are the same as this one. Quite a sight, ain't it? By God, there's power! There's industry!'

Edward nodded, feeling unequal to competing with the noise of the machines, and followed him out into the comparative sanity of the courtyard. It was all very different, he reflected, from what Jemima had described to him of Cromford, and it was on Cromford that she had based her decision to send the asylum children to Manchester as apprentices. It would be better, he thought, if he did not tell her all that he had seen.

'When they finish their work,' she had said, 'they come out into a beautiful green valley, and they have fine, stout, stone houses to live in.'

It was not that the workers he had seen were pale and thin and dirty – all poor people were, and they would not be mill-workers if they weren't poor; and indeed, they had a job, and a wage, in which they were better off than others who had neither. But the appalling filth and stench of their surroundings was a far cry from the green spaces of the Peak district, and Edward knew that Jemima was much too tender about her dependents to be able to accept that knowledge equably.

Lucy and Chetwyn were at a reception in Carlton House, which seemed to be being given for the purpose of cheering up the Prince of Wales, who had again been refused permission to go on active service. 'Military command is incompatible with the situation of the Prince of Wales,' the King had written to him.

Carlton House, was, as usual, overheated and full of flowers, and despite the Prince's continued penury, the entertainment was lavish and the supper sumptuous: soup, fish, veal, hare, venison, fricassee of chickens, cutlets, tarts, puddings, fruits and creams were laid out in splendid array, with the appropriate wines to drink – claret, hock, champagne, tokay, sherry and port – in plenty.

Lucy rather enjoyed these occasions, for though she did not know the Prince well enough to like him – his virtues, as Captain Brummell said, being more real than apparent – she enjoyed contact with the 'Carlton House Set'. Language was usually coarse and behaviour often gross, but she was a great favourite amongst the large-drinking, loud-swearing men, for here it was a virtue to be 'dashing', and women were not expected to be Quaker-like, retiring, and oppressively proper. Here she might talk and do as she pleased. The Carlton House set had a passion for nick-names, and Lucy's was 'Lady Curricle': it was thought a great jest that she had beaten the Prince's time to Brighton.

Lucy had George Brummell to her left at the supper-table, which was pleasant, for the Lord Cummings, on her right, was liberally doused in a heavy perfume which just failed to drown the smell of him. She mentioned the circumstance to her friend, to explain why she was leaning so far over in his direction, and he gave her his charming smile.

'It is my ambition to be the arbiter of polite society,' he said. 'Society should be a form of poetry, fastidious, elegant, witty – above all, fastidious! There are all too many who still think it effeminate to be clean. Dirt is as much an affectation as red heels or spangled waistcoats, you know. If a man have fine linen, plenty of it, and country washing, he has no need of perfumes.' He paused to wave away a dish of stewed leeks, one of the removes, which a footman was offering him.

'Do you never eat vegetables?' Lucy asked curiously. 'I don't think I have ever seen you do so.'

'Never,' he said, and then, frowning in thought, 'Wait! I think I may once have eaten a pea. I tell you as a friend: I am sure you won't repeat it.'

'How absurd you are,' Lucy laughed. 'But tell me, is it true, what my cousin Horatio tells me, that you have sold out?'

'Oh yes. What else could I do, dear Lady Aylesbury,

when the 10th Dragoons were ordered up to Manchester?'

'Yes, of course, to the riots,' Lucy agreed. 'My brother's wife's father has some mills there, which were damaged. But what of it?'

He raised an eyebrow. 'My dear ma'am, can you imagine *me* in Manchester? Quite unthinkable! As soon as I heard my troop was on warning, I went straight to the Prince – positively got him out of bed, the poor creature – and he saw it at once. "By all means, my dear fellow," he said, "sell out immediately". So you have relations there, have you? Ah, but they are not blood relations, my dear ma'am, and that is *everything*!'

'Horatio was quite upset,' Lucy said, ignoring the jibe. 'He says it will be monstrous dull without you.'

'What a fellow he is for the truth! But I shall often be dining with them. I dare say they will hardly notice the difference. Once they have come back from Manchester – for one must draw the line somewhere – I shall make a point of driving out to them wherever they are. I have just discovered the delights of travelling with four horses, by the by – the speed and convenience is wonderful. I have my valet to thank for that, of course.'

'Your valet?'

'The dear man gave me notice for expecting him to travel with only a pair. Indeed, it is true,' he said, opening his eyes wide, as Lucy laughed. 'When I first offered to take him into my service, he asked for £150 a year. "My dear fellow", said I, "give me £200, and *I* will work for *you*!" There is your cousin now, looking at us. I shall give him a nod, to shew I bear him no ill feelings. I was forced to be somewhat scathing about his driving yesterday, when he took a tandem into the Park.'

'Yes, he told me. How can you be so critical, when you are never seen handling the ribbons yourself?'

'One does not need to be able to do a thing, to know when it is well done. What an idea! Did he tell you he was selling out as well?' he asked.

'No, is he? Because of you?' Lucy asked, helping herself from a dish of mutton cutlets as it came past.

Brummell bowed. 'Thank you for your good opinion,' he

said, smiling. 'But I fear in this case it is unwarranted. The *on-dit* is that he is buying into a cavalry regiment – the Scots Greys, I believe – in order to go on active service and make his fortune. It appears that he has quite despaired of the reversion, now his nephew has reached his first birthday in perfect health.'

'It might be the best thing for him,' Lucy said thoughtfully.

'Not a doubt of it,' said Mr Brummell cheerfully. 'And it will stop him trying to drive a tandem in the Park, which will be a good thing for everybody else.'

Very early one April morning, Jemima was in the courtyard being helped up onto Hazel, who was fidgeting restlessly and making Jemima wonder for the first time in her life whether she ought to think about changing to a more staid mount. Since her father gave her her first horse, Jewel, for her thirteenth birthday, she had always ridden fiery, high-bred animals whose idea of repose was to have more than one hoof on the ground at the same time; but the troubles of the previous autumn had taxed her more than she had realized at the time, and that winter, at the age of sixty-five, she had begun to feel old.

She had just put her boot into the stirrup for the third time, when a commotion broke out in the kitchen and the noise, emerging from the open buttery door, startled Hazel and made her dance, goggling and snorting like a young dragon. Jemima stood back on the block in exasperation and said, 'What on earth is going on?' Hoskins and the two grooms attending her having no way of answering, she stepped down and bade the younger of the grooms go and find out what the matter was. It was probably, she reflected, nothing more than one of M. Barnard's outbursts of temperament, which afflicted him more frequently in the spring when the kitchen chimney sometimes would not draw; but it was an excuse not to mount Hazel for a few minutes, and to spend them standing in the blessed April sunshine.

The groom was away longer than she would have

expected, and that indication that the trouble was serious was confirmed when both Oxhey and Mrs Mappin appeared at the door looking anxious and embarrassed.

'Well, what is it?' Jemima asked.

'My lady, it is not something I would normally consider mentioning to you,' Oxhey said, casting a nervous glance at his colleague, who frowned and said, 'I told him it was nonsense, my lady, to be troubling you, especially as you're just about to go out. Depend upon it, we can deal with the matter without delaying you.'

'I beg your pardon, my lady', Oxhey said, 'but I thought, in the circumstances –'

'Well, since I already am delayed, perhaps you had better tell me what the circumstances are. Hoskins, walk Hazel around for a few minutes.' Jemima went up the steps into the great hall, and turned to Oxhey enquiringly.

'It's a boy, my lady,' he began hesitantly.

'A dirty little thief, my lady and that ungrateful girl no better than he – '

'His sister my lady,' Oxhey interrupted as if in exculpation. Jemima held up her hand.

'I cannot understand a word you say. Mappin, pray hold your peace. You may have your turn at my ear later. Oxhey, tell me from the beginning, if you please, what is going on.'

'Yes, my lady. Well, my lady – ' he paused lengthily to assemble his words, and Jemima knew better than to hurry him. 'It seems, my lady, that one of the housemaids has stolen a quantity of food and clothing, and was caught in the act of passing it on to – '

'Her accomplice!' Mrs Mappin cried triumphantly.

'Her brother,' Oxhey corrected mildly. 'It is not a matter I would normally trouble your ladyship with, but the girl – '

' – the naughty, wicked, ungrateful minx – '

' – the girl is the orphan your ladyship was so good as to take in from St Edward's, and her brother was one of those bound apprentice to Mr Hobsbawn.'

'Run away, my lady, and wants whipping for it,' Mrs Mappin interjected.

'Peace, Mappin. Why has he run away, Oxhey?' Jemima said. He looked more than ever unhappy.

'My lady, he says he has been ill-treated, and it was on that account – a matter of some delicacy, my lady, in view of – but I thought it best to consult your ladyship before – '

'You did quite right, Oxhey,' Jemima said, frowning. 'Where is the boy?'

'I shut them both in the end pantry, my lady, when the groom you sent came in,' Mrs Mappin said, 'otherwise no doubt they'd be three counties away by now.'

'Very well, I'll come,' Jemima said. 'Oxhey, you may take me there. Mrs Mappin, I need you to exercise your tact and authority in putting the servants back to work and ensuring they don't talk about this.'

'Yes, my lady,' Mrs Mappin said unwillingly, not entirely deceived by the flattery. Oxhey led Jemima away, passing through the inner court rather than the kitchen so as to avoid the eyes of the other servants. He began apologizing again as soon as they were away from the housekeeper.

'I beg your ladyship's pardon for troubling you,' he said, 'although your ladyship had made an enquiry as to the upset, but the boy being one of ours, so to speak, and his condition – well, my lady, I was quite shocked to see him, and I think – I fear – he may be telling the truth.'

One of the footmen was standing on guard outside the pantry prison, which had obviously been chosen, Jemima thought, because it had no window and contained nothing but rarely-used pans and kitchen implements. Oxhey unlocked the door, and standing aside, bade the young criminals come out. The maid Betsey came first, dishevelled, a red mark on her cheek where she had been struck, and the marks of freely-shed tears on her face. She looked frightened, but defiant and angry too. She blinked after the darkness at her gaolers, and then seeing Jemima, she flung herself on her knees before her.

'Oh my lady, my lady, I didn't mean to steal! I wouldn't do such a thing for myself, not ever, so kind as you've been to me, but it was for Timmy, my lady, my brother, and if you knew what they did to him! Oh my lady, don't send him back, I beg you! They'll kill him if you do!'

Now the boy had come out behind her, crawled out, in fact, and Jemima's eyes widened in shock at the sight of

him. She had never seen any living creature so thin. His face
was like a skull, his arms and legs were so thin that his joints
were the thickest parts of them. He was filthy, and his
clothing was in rags, and his bare feet were bruised and
bleeding from his long walk. One hand was wrapped in
filthy bandages. He looked exhausted and frightened, and as
he crawled to her feet he was evidently too weak to speak,
but looked up at her with the silent and terrified appeal of a
calf about to be slaughtered.

'Good God,' Jemima said when she could find her voice,
'what has happened to you, child? Who has done this? And
what has happened to your hand?'

Betsey began to weep again, and clutched at Jemima's
skirt, sobbing incoherently. The footman, outraged, tried to
snatch her away, but Jemima stilled him with a gesture, and
reaching down, unfastened the child's fingers herself quite
gently, saying, 'Be calm, Betsey. It's all right. No-one is
going to hurt you or your brother.'

Oxhey, much distressed, said, 'As he's 'prenticed, my
lady, we're bound to restore him under the terms of the
indenture.'

'Oh my lady, don't send him back, please don't send him
back!' Betsey wailed, and Jemima patted her hand.

'He shall not go back to the people who have permitted
this to happen to him, I promise you. Get up now, there's a
good girl, and dry your tears, and see if you can't be useful
to me and your brother.'

'Yes, m'lady,' Betsey said, much steadied by the calm
and practical tone of Jemima's voice.

'Run upstairs to Jenny as quick as you can, and bid her
send all the children into the day-nursery and keep them
there, and ask one of the maids to make up the end bed in
the night-nursery with clean sheets, and put screens around
it. Joseph, go and find Mrs Mappin and tell her I want hot
water for bathing in the night-nursery, and some warm
bread and milk. Now, Oxhey, you take one side of this poor
boy, and I'll take the other. Be careful of that hand: I expect
it is very painful.'

Stripped of his rags, the boy looked even more pitifully
thin, and there were a great number of bruises and stripes

on the grimy skin, some quite fresh, others old.

'See how he has been beaten,' Jemima said.

Boys had been beaten since the world began, and it would be a bad thing for the world if the time ever came when they weren't beaten; but this particular specimen did seem to have a surprising number of marks on his skinny torso. 'Probably he had a bad disposition, my lady,' Oxhey whispered.

Jemima did not reply, but began taking off the bandage. The boy cried out in pain when she touched his hand, and the bandage proved so stiff with filth, blood and pus that she had to resort to scissors and cut it away little by little. When the hand was revealed, it proved to be lacking two fingers. The wound was partly healed, but was oozing and swollen, and when Jemima saw the red streaks running along the forearm, she said, 'Oxhey, you had better send someone at once for Doctor Swindells.'

Jemima washed the child with her own hands, and when Oxhey came back, he helped her. It was far below his dignity as butler, but if her ladyship could do it, he reasoned, so could he. Then they dressed him in a clean nightshirt and put him to bed, and Jemima fed him the bread and milk from a spoon. At first he ate avidly, and she had to restrain him; but his famished appetite soon sickened, and he turned his head away. Jemima put the bowl aside and felt his forehead, and found it very hot. With such a wound, he would be likely to be feverish she thought.

'My lady,' Oxhey murmured discreetly in her ear, 'Mr Edward is desirous of knowing what has happened, and Mrs James has sent to ask if she can assist you in any way.'

Jemima frowned. 'Not yet, Oxhey. I want to get to the bottom of this. Please tell Mr Edward that I will speak to them all later, and pray do not let anyone – anyone at all – come into this nursery without my permission.'

The doctor came, and examined the hand, shook his head gravely, and dressed it, and drawing Jemima aside said, 'I'm afraid the wound is infected. There is little I can do at this stage beyond dressing it. One can only hope that his own body will cure him.'

'How much hope?' Jemima asked.

'Well, Lady Morland, you know that recovery depends a great deal on the state of the individual. This boy is weak and famished, and I fear may lack the strength to fight the infection.'

When Swindells had gone, Jemima returned to the boy's side, and sat staring at him unseeingly for a while. Then a movement drew her back from her thoughts, and she saw that the boy was looking at her. She smiled.

'Do you think you could eat a little more now?' she asked. He nodded, and she propped him up and fed him a few more spoonfuls, and when she laid him back on the pillows he sighed and gave her a feeble smile.

'Thank you, ma'am,' he said.

'How do you feel?'

'Comfortable,' he said after a moment. Jemima made up her mind.

'Timmy, my dear, I very much want to know what has happened to you since you went away to Manchester.' A shadow crossed his face. 'I know it must pain you to think about it, but I believe it is very important that you tell me your story. If I asked you questions, do you think you could answer them?'

'Yes, ma'am,' he said, his eyes fixed on her face. She stroked his rough hair back from his brow and said, 'You're a good boy. I'll be back in a moment.' And she went to the door and passed the word for Father Thomas to come, with pen and paper.

It took a long time. Jemima sat to one side of the bed, holding the child's skeletal hand, and occasionally breaking off to feed him a little pap or give him a sip of barley-water; while Father Thomas sat to the other side, taking down Jemima's questions and Timmy's answers. He was very weak, and Father Thomas once or twice hinted that they should leave him alone and come back another time when he had rested; but he had not seen the wounded hand. Quite soon, Jemima thought, the boy would become too feverish to know what he was being asked, and quite soon after that he would die. It was important, she believed, to

282

get his story down on paper while there was time.

So, painfully, by question and answer, it was told.

'We all lived in the Prentice House, sixty of us boys, and seventy girls. The Prentice House is built on to the side of the mill, with a door between them, so we could pass from one to the other without going outside. There was a common room below where we ate, and two chambers above for sleeping, one for the boys and one for the girls.

'The beds were in two tiers, the upper ones fixed by a square frame above the lower ones, all along the walls. We slept three in a bed. There was a door between the two chambers but it was not locked. Sometimes the older boys would go into the girls' room at night.

'We got up at five in the summer and six in the winter and went into the mill. Then we worked until eight or nine, when breakfast was brought to us. A bar would be put across the door to the house, and we would go up in turn to fetch our breakfast, which was porrage flavoured with onions. We had ten minutes to eat it, except when the mill was busy, and then we had to eat while we worked as best we could.

'Then we worked until dinner time, half past twelve, or one o'clock. Dinner was oat cake with butter or treacle spread on it, and a drink of milk. Twice a week we had an hour allowed us for dinner, while the machines were oiled. On other days we had half an hour by turns, for the machines never stopped turning.

'We worked until six or seven at night, except in busy times, and then it might be nine or ten. We got very tired, and then the overseers would beat us to keep us awake. The little ones particularly kept falling asleep. There were often accidents because they fell asleep and got caught in the machinery.

'That's how I lost my fingers. They got caught in a wheel and torn off. The surgeon was sent for at once, but I think the wound has gone bad.

'We had our supper after we had finished, in the Prentice House. Usually it was thick porrage, or potatoes, or pudding.

283

'On Sundays we only worked in the morning, cleaning the machinery. We had boiled pork and potatoes for dinner, with peas or turnips or cabbage, which made us feel very sleepy. In the afternoon we went to school and then to church, and then we were allowed to play, but mostly we just slept.

'I ran away because I couldn't bear it any more. Every day was just like the last. We never sat down all day long, and we were always hungry, and so tired at the end of the day. And then my hand wouldn't heal. I thought if I came back here, Betsey would help me. I thought if I could hide somewhere until my hand healed, I could get as far as Hull and get work on a ship.

'I knew if I stayed at the mill, I would just die one day at the machine. They never stop, day or night.'

In the drawing room, Jemima faced her sons and daughter-in-law and read to them what Father Thomas had written down. Their reactions were very different. Edward looked embarrassed and indignant, Mary Ann shocked and unhappy, while James's face was thoughtful and inscrutable.

When she had finished reading she said, 'I need not tell you how shocked I am. My dear,' she looked at Mary Ann, 'I fear I may offend you by plain speaking, but I hope you know that I do not wish to hurt you.'

Mary Ann made a vague gesture. Various loyalties were warring inside her, and her strongest desire was to run away and cry. James looked at her with sudden sympathy, and took her hand and pressed it. Edward jumped up.

'Really, Mother, I can't understand what you are making all this fuss about. Ten to one but the boy is exaggerating anyway.'

'Would he have run away if he had not been unhappy?' Jemima asked. Edward snorted.

'Unhappy? Good God, Mother, are we to enquire now about the happiness of these people?'

'These are our dependants, Ned,' Jemima said. 'We have a responsibility to them.'

'Yes, a responsibility to provide for them, which is exactly what we have done. We have taken orphans, found-lings, illegitimate children out of the gutters and off the roads, and given them useful employment whereby they can support themselves. What more can you possibly want? Do you want to bring them all up to the house and have them lie about on sophas all day eating strawberries?'

'It's true, Mother,' James said mildly. 'The poor are the poor. They are different from us. They have their work, and we have ours.'

'We don't work thirteen or fourteen hours a day in vile conditions,' Jemima said.

'Of course we don't, but our villagers do,' James said. 'Why, even their children work just as long hours, from the time they are able to stand. How often have you seen a child of four or five gleaning stones, or standing by a gate all day, to earn pennies by opening it for travellers? Ned is right. What do you want for them?'

Jemima clenched her hands. 'Of course our village children work hard, but that is quite different. They are out in the fresh air, not shut in a factory, with the noise and fumes; and they work at their own pace, and their work follows the seasons in the natural way. You heard what this boy said — every day is like the last, and the machines never stop.'

Edward sighed. 'For heaven's sake, Mother, someone has to work in the mills; and if these people cannot get farm-work, they must do factory work. You refine too much upon it, I am sure. Your poor have not your sensibilities, depend upon it.'

Jemima said deliberately, 'This boy has been starved, and beaten, and ill-treated. His hours of work and living conditions have been other than was agreed upon. It is a breach of contract.'

'And what do you propose to do about it?' Edward asked more quietly. He flicked a glance at James and Mary Ann. 'Don't forget we are bound to the Hobsbawn mills by more than apprentices.'

Jemima stared at him. 'You knew about it, didn't you? When you went to Manchester last month, you must have seen. Why didn't you tell me?'

'For this very reason,' Ned said. 'Oh, I didn't see the Prentice House, or any signs of ill-treatment. But the fact is, Mother, that you had got fixed in your mind the image of a mill in a green valley, and you were not going to like giving it up for reality. If you had never seen that damned place at Cromford, you would think this boy's story nothing out of the ordinary.'

Mary Ann stood up suddenly. 'I never saw the mills,' she said to Jemima. 'I knew nothing about them.'

'No-one blames you ...' Jemima began, but Mary Ann interrupted.

'Is there blame in the case? The poor must work. It is for us to provide them with work. And yet – they look to us also for protection. I don't know. I don't know.' She bit her lip, her expression deeply troubled.

Jemima looked at her with more sympathy than she had ever felt for her, and then said firmly to Edward, 'We shall send no more children to the mills; and as to those we have sent already, I shall make my decision in a day or two, when I have had time to reflect. For now, the discussion is at an end. I need hardly mention, I hope, that this business must be kept between us, and must go no further.' She turned towards her daughter-in-law. 'My dear, I am going to the chapel. Will you come with me? Father Thomas – '

Left alone, James and Edward looked at each other.

'She'll get over it,' James said. 'She is too tender.'

'We had better hope she does. Can you imagine what Hobsbawn will say if we accuse him of cruelty and contract-breaking? Mother's too old to cope with matters of business such as this – she should leave it to me. I'd have sent the boy back under guard, and dismissed the girl, and no-one would have known a thing about it.'

'What will you do?' James asked, regarding him thoughtfully.

'We'll have to wait and see. Once all the fuss has died down, I dare say we can continue in the old way, without Mother's knowing anything about it. What the devil can we do with all the pauper children if we don't send them to the mills?' he burst out irritably. 'Mother's living in a different age. She just doesn't realize how many of them there are, or what a drain they are on the parish. The mills are the best solution for everyone.'

'I dare say you are right,' said James.

Chapter Seventeen

While Mary Ann took a turn at sitting with Timmy, Jemima went down to breakfast. She sat down heavily in her chair at the breakfast table, too tired to want to eat, and James with silent sympathy put down the *Mercury* and poured her a cup of coffee. Edward was half way through carving a thick slice from the fragrant mutton ham in front of him and could not pause in the delicate labour until he had it safe and symmetrical upon his knife, when he offered it by a gesture to his mother. She shook her head, and Edward laid it carefully on his own plate, added two handsome pork cutlets fried in oatmeal and a couple of veal kidneys.

'Well, Mama, how's the patient?' he asked.

'His fever is higher,' Jemima replied mechanically. 'I don't think he knows where he is, now.'

James broke a piece of bun off the wig, split and buttered it, and placed it on his mother's plate, and as an afterthought lifted her hand from her lap and rested it beside the plate. She looked at him blankly for a moment, and then gave a tired smile and began to eat.

'That's probably all to the good,' Edward said. 'This ham is really delicious. Won't you let me carve you a slice?'

Jemima put down the bun. 'What do you mean, it's all to the good?'

'I mean that there's been enough talk about this business already. That deposition you took, Mama – well, it was unwise, in my view.' James coughed a mild warning, and Edward shrugged. 'Oh well, I'm sorry for the child, of course, but he's obviously going to die, and nothing will change that. It's better for him that he is delirious and does not know his pain.'

'What are you talking about?' Jemima said dangerously.

'Oh Ned, let mother have her breakfast in peace, can't you?' James interposed, but neither of them paid him any heed.

'What I mean, Mother, is that the best thing that you can do now is forget about the whole unpleasant business. Bury the boy, send the girl as far away as possible, and say no more about it to anyone.'

'You mean that you believe that we should go on sending apprentices to Manchester?' Jemima asked. James picked up the newspaper and retired from the scene, while Edward actually put down his knife and fork.

'Yes, I mean exactly that. You can have no idea, Mama, how much the foundlings cost the parish. We can place one or two as domestic or farm servants, but there simply aren't places for all of them, and there are more vagrants coming in all the time. We have to provide for them, and the mill-owners are the only employers who can absorb such numbers.'

'You can say that, knowing what you know?' Jemima said slowly. Edward ran his fingers through his hair in exasperation.

'I just don't know what you want, Mother! Frankly, I'm surprised to find you taking up such a revolutionary attitude, when you've two sons out there at sea, fighting against those very ideas!'

Jemima thrust her chair away and stood up, glaring across the table at her son. 'How dare you speak to me like that?' she said in a low, angry voice. 'You presume to tell me my duty? I think I know it a great deal better than you. These people look to us for protection and guidance. There will be no more apprentices – and Betsey shall not be sent away. Those are my final words on the subject.'

'But Mama, we must have progress!' Edward cried, and Jemima's voice rose in answer.

'Not at the cost of the old values! No, Ned! No more!' She looked from him to James, who gave a small shrug and picked up his coffee cup, declining to take sides. 'I don't understand any more,' she said wearily. 'My own children – what has happened to the world? I don't understand anything any more.' And she turned away and left the room.

Edward made a face of exasperation and went back to his plate, tackling the cutlets with a compensatory ferocity. James sipped his coffee and turned a page.

'I wish you would let Mother alone for long enough to eat her breakfast,' he said. 'Now you see she has had nothing. You could have said those things later.'

'Oh shut up, Jamie,' Edward said crossly. 'Just because you have no principles, it doesn't mean to say that everyone else must abandon theirs.'

'And what do you mean to do about yours?' James asked cynically.

'I just have to hope that Mother comes to her senses. Fortunately all the mail comes to me for franking, so I can stop any inflammatory letter going to Hobsbawn; and once she has calmed down a little I'll quietly get rid of that maid, and we may all ride out the storm in safety.'

'My wife will be pleased,' James said politely.

'It isn't funny,' Edward said crossly. 'I don't know what you find to smile about.'

'I suppose,' James said mildly, 'it is the fact that you are all so completely certain that you know what is right, whereas all I'm certain about is that I don't know anything.'

'That,' said Edward, spearing the last of the ham, 'is just shirking.'

Jemima was still keeping vigil at the bedside of the dying boy when the news came that *Pelican* had paid off at the end of her commission. William's letter preceded him only by a matter of hours, so that he and Harry arrived at Morland Place in a flurry of noise and greetings and dittybags before preparations had been made for their reception.

Jemima came downstairs at the sound of the voices, which, not having yet been adjusted for dry land, penetrated easily as far as the nursery, and found her two huge, sunbrowned, salt-bleached sons filling the great hall. Edward was out, but James and Fanny were greeting them, while Puppy revolved around the group like a top, beating their legs with his excited tail.

'Mother – there you are!' William roared as she came in from the staircase hall. 'Dog's got a tail like an anchor cable – hold him off, Jamie, there's a good fellow!'

Jemima went forward to embrace William, and found it

was like putting her arms round an outcrop of rock. He smelled of tar and salt, and his long pale pigtail, which was hanging forward over his shoulder, prickled her face. She stepped back to look up at him, and found the bronzed, firm face above her rather frightening. It was set in hard lines of authority, and the pale blue eyes seemed remote as if still fixed on distant horizons. His hair, which had been flaxen when he was a child, had been bleached colourless by years of sea-going, and the fronds around his hairline that were too short to catch back framed his face without doing anything to soften it. He had been gone from her too long. She could not find anything in him of the son she bore and remembered; he was not her William, he was Captain 'Bloody Bill' Morland, and a stranger.

'William, my dear,' she said feebly, 'how lovely to see you.'

'You're looking younger than ever, Mama. Don't know how you do it.'

She turned to Harry, and he gave her a shy smile. He had grown again, she thought. He was hard and muscular about the shoulders, but still with that softness about the jawline and the well-developed stomach which shewed he liked his food. His soft hair was cropped rather untidily, and he smelled like a human being, not a ship's timber. Jemima embraced him with more genuine warmth than she had been able to feel for his big brother.

'How long do you stay?' she asked. 'I'm afraid you have come upon us at a troubled time, but you are no less welcome for that.'

'I can't stay above a week, Mama,' William said. 'I've got my new commission – the *Venus*, 74. She's on her way back from New England on convoy duty to Liverpool, and I'm to take her over at London Pool. She should be in Liverpool next week some time, so I'll have to get back to London and chivvy the victualling yard, but I can leave this young lubber with you a few days longer.' And he gave Harry a resounding thump on the back.

After a few more words, Jemima quickly explained her duties upstairs, and left the boys in James's care, promising to see them at dinner. When she had gone, and Harry had followed the footman upstairs, William took James's arm conspiratorially. 'Want a word with you,' he said. 'So this is little Fanny, is it? Why, she's practically grown up, by God, and as pretty as a kitten! Send her away, will you, Jamie?'

Jamie smiled to himself, kissed Fanny and sent her with her nurse to play with Puppy in the garden, and then braced himself for whatever confidence William was anxious to impart. 'Well, brother, what is it?'

'It's a bit delicate,' William frowned. 'It concerns Mrs Smith.'

'Oh yes, your mistress. What of her?'

William opened his eyes. 'You mean to say you know about her?'

'Oh yes, we all do. Mary's husband mentioned her to Mary, and Harry talked about her when he was here with the chickenpox.'

'Mother too?'

'Mother too,' James said. William looked uncomfortable. 'Damn. Didn't want Mother to know about it. Was she very upset?'

'Not the least bit,' James said lightly. 'Good God, William, after my exploits, I don't think Mother has it in her to be surprised by the ordinary sort of iniquity. How is Mrs Smith, anyway? I should love to meet her. To tell the truth, I think we're all fascinated by the idea of a woman who could win your heart. She must be something very special.'

William reddened under his tan. 'Well, she is – she's the most wonderful creature in the world. I wouldn't part with her for command of a three-decker and a knighthood into the bargain! Thing is, brought her with me – anchored her at the Hare and Heather, and I've got to get back to arrange a berth for her for the week. Wouldn't do to bring her here, things the way they are. Fact is, Jamie, she's – well, she's with child.'

'Congratulations,' James said, biting his lip to prevent himself from bursting into laughter at William's expression of intense and sentimental pride, so at odds with his granite face. 'But my dear brother, if you love the lady so much, and she's going to bear your child, why don't you marry her, and make an honest woman of her?'

'Fact of the matter is,' William said unhappily, 'that she's got a husband already. Regular brute of a man – rich as Croesus, big estate on Martinique – sugar planter, you know. Drank like a fish, kept mistresses in the house. Well, Mrs Smith couldn't stand that. I took her away.'

'Do you always call her Mrs Smith?' James asked, enjoying himself. William's eyebrows made innocent arcs over his pale eyes.

'Yes – what of it?'

'Oh, nothing. Go on, do.'

'Nothing more to tell, really. She and I fell in love, and I took her away, and now she's in litter. Well, that's partly why I can only stay a week. I've got to have time before I sail to find lodgings for her, where there's a decent landlady to keep an eye on her. She don't like it above half, you know.'

'No?'

'No, she wants to come to sea with me, and have the baby on board. Says there's nothing to it. Plenty of women give birth on ships – had one in the *Pelican* back in '96 – gunner's wife – fine boy, their third, all live in the gunroom, snug as a hammock. But I said to her, that's different. Gunner's wife's a good soul, but she ain't a lady. See what I mean?'

'Of course,' James said gravely. 'There's every difference. Tell me, William, as a matter of interest, is she really black, your Mrs Smith?'

'Black? Wherever did you get that idea?' William asked in astonishment.

'I think Harry said she was a blackamoor,' James said.

'That bloody boy! Of course she ain't black! She's a Creole. To say truth, she does have a bit of foreign blood – great-grandmother was an Indian. I suppose that makes her an octoroon, but she's as white as you or me to look at. I'll take you to meet her, once I've got her settled, if you like.'

'I can't tell you how much I'd like that!' James said, and William looked gratified, and gave his brother a friendly slap which silenced him for several minutes and left him aching for half an hour.

*

Timmy died the following day. His illness had followed the expected course from the time he arrived at Morland Place: at first he had grown stronger, the effect of care and food and the absence of fear and strain; but as the infection from his wounded hand had taken hold, he had grown feverish, gradually weakening as it crept up his arm towards his heart. Jemima and Mary Ann had shared the nursing of him, with Betsey a dumb, frightened and wretched little messenger, but in the last days there had been little to do but sit beside him, comforting him, and watching his fingers slip little by little from the rim of the world.

Often delirious, his fever-bright eyes searching the shadows restlessly, his good hand twitching at the bed-clothes, he had mumbled and raved about his life at the mill, called for Betsey, cried out for someone to help him, and the watching women had had much ado to calm him. The sight of men frightened him, and he sometimes screamed when Doctor Swindells or Father Thomas came near. Jemima had found in Mary Ann a loyal and quick-thinking helper, and, knowing how inwardly torn she must be over her father's part in all this, Jemima respected her more than she could have thought possible.

Timmy finally slipped into a coma and died quietly just before dawn, with Jemima and Father Thomas by his bed. Jemima said a brief prayer, and then left her priest to watch over the body while she went to her room and penned a searing letter to Mr Hobsbawn. She sealed it, wrote the direction, and, hearing that the servants were abroad, rang for a footman to take it down to put with the rest of the post; and then composed herself to go and wake Betsey and break the news to her.

Mrs Smith received James and William in a private parlour at the King's Arms with all the dignity and propriety of a respectably married woman meeting a brother-in-law for the first time. She shook James's hand, said she was glad to make his acquaintance, hoped that they would be friends, and invited him to sit down while she rang for refreshments.

James did his best not to stare rudely. She was not above

293

middle height for a woman, and of a matronly build which, with her advanced pregnancy, made her look almost circular. She moved unexpectedly lightly when she crossed the room to the bell-pull, rolling a little on the balls of her feet like a sailor. James told himself that was only to be expected after so long at sea.

He judged her to be in her middle forties, perhaps ten years older than William, and he would have been surprised if she had ever been thought handsome. She was very dark, almost swarthy, with a sallow skin and black eyes, and thick black hair going grey in streaks at the sides. She was as plain as pudding, her expression kindly, her features undistinguished, except for a very fine set of teeth in her rather wide mouth.

She was dressed in a neat gown of light wool, grey trimmed with white, her only decoration being a very fine gold locket on a chain about her neck, and the heavy, long-fringed Cashmere shawl over her elbows. She looked, James thought, like the wife of a prosperous shop-keeper who had come up in the world.

She had a pleasant voice with a lilting accent, and spoke sensibly without exhibiting either too much reserve or too much familiarity towards her keeper's brother, a balance which James acknowledged inwardly must be hard to achieve. But then, he reflected, if William was as sociable on board his ship as most captains, she must have had plenty of practice at coping with her anomalous situation.

William evidently adored her. He seemed curiously shy with her, addressing her quite formally, as if he were a young man addressing an adult friend of his parents. Yet his pride in her was evident and he exhibited her to James as a possession of great value which would make him the envy of the world. James could quite see that he would address her always as Mrs Smith; he wondered, in fact, that William had ever been able to attain to the intimacy of making her pregnant.

On her side, she treated William kindly and affectionately, rather like a warm-hearted aunt with a favourite nephew. James had little doubt that she had initially seen in William's infatuation a providential way of escaping an unpleasant situation, and wondered how bad it must have been to make her want to exchange it for the confines of a two-decker and the horrors of ship-board food. She was a soldier of fortune, he thought, and he respected her as such, and wished her well.

As he rode home alone afterwards, having left William to enjoy a few minutes of connubial bliss, James could not help reflecting that Morland Place had reason to be grateful to the unknown Mr Smith, if that was his name. William was so besotted with his lady, that had she been free, he would have seen no reason not to marry her; and then Jemima might have felt obliged to make their children her heirs.

It was on the day of Timmy's funeral, the day before William was to leave for London, that Harry accidentally revealed Mrs Smith's presence and condition to his mother. He thought the whole thing a good joke, and was surprised that Jemima was upset.

'Lord, Mama, men have mistresses all the time, and the mistresses have brats. That's in the way of things. You mustn't take it to heart. The Cap'n's desperate fond of the old lady, and she won't want for anything. And you mustn't think there'll be a scandal, for she's as sensible as a muffler on a winter morning, and knows how to keep her colours hidden.'

Jemima did not attempt to explain her feelings to him. If Edward and James, who had lived with her for most of their lives, could not share them, she could expect little from Harry, whose understanding was not quick in any case. She did, however, seek out William, and asked him what provision he had made for the expected child.

'Don't worry, Mama,' William said awkwardly, much embarrassed. 'Mrs Smith will be quite all right. I'll find some snug lodgings for her, where the landlady's used to sailors' ways, and will keep an eye on her, and I'll make arrangements for her to draw half my pay month by month. I wouldn't let her want for anything.'

'But why don't you marry her? Surely the child makes a difference?' Jemima asked him, as James had done, and

William avoided her eyes and told her.

Jemima thought of Mary Skelwith and her child, of Héloïse and Mary Ann, of her own father and mother and Marie-Louise, of all the complications that came of doing wrong. Sins must in time be forgiven and forgotten, but an illegitimate child could not simply be cancelled out: it was an error which could not be corrected. She felt a great weariness come over her, and William looked at her stricken face and said miserably, 'I'm sorry, Mother. I wish it could be all above-board – no-one could wish it more! But it don't signify. No-one's hurt by it.'

'Do you believe that?' she asked. 'No, don't answer – I see that you do.' She left him and went to the chapel, her tread as heavy as her heart. Father Thomas was there, saying the prayers for the dead, and Jemima did not disturb him, but went into the Lady-chapel and knelt stiffly at the rail. The world has gone mad, she thought; was it the war? Did men turn from devouring each other to devouring themselves? Things had seemed so simple in her childhood. She thought of Allen going off to fight in the '45, because King James was his king, and that was that. She remembered how he had stayed in exile long after he could have come home, because she was married to another, and there was nothing to come home for. But had William or James considered themselves under that kind of constraint? Did Edward or Harry condemn them for it? Her sons seemed to have no more moral sense than wolves. Her sons – Allen's sons.

She looked up and saw that Father Thomas had come over to her, and was looking at her enquiringly. She met his eyes, wondering what to say. He's an old man, she thought suddenly; we're both old. Perhaps that's what happens to old people – the world moves on and they find they can't understand it any more.

'They say the Lady weeps when danger is coming to the house,' she said at last, 'but there are no tears today. Is that a sign? Is the absence of a sign, a sign?'

He came and knelt beside her. She thought he did not know what she was talking about.

'Everything is in James's hands,' she said. 'Is that mad-

ness? Is he the worst of them, or the best? I loved him best –
I thought he was like his father. That seems strange now.'

'Sometimes the greatest sinners can become the greatest
saints,' Father Thomas said.

'Better, you think, to do wrong, knowing it's wrong, than
to be virtuous out of ignorance? James knows God's name,
and perhaps that's better than nothing.'

'He's a thoughtful man,' Father Thomas said, and it was
painfully obvious to Jemima that he was trying to comfort
her. 'He'll come about, given time.'

She looked up at the Lady's golden face, wavering in
the candle-light, and images seemed to be streaming
through her mind at an extraordinary speed, as though she
were being shewn the portrait of everyone she had ever
known, one after the other. Faces, faces, eyes and mouths,
smiling, speaking: her father, mother, brothers; her uncles,
forever bickering, and her acquisitive cousins; Annunciata,
Marie-Louise, Allen, Henri, the brother she had never seen
– Charles and Flora, Héloïse, their children and her children. All the complex warp and weft of family and history,
of relationship, love, and duty; the shining thread spinning,
spinning, a tapestry whose pattern only God would ever see
completed.

It seemed very dark in the chapel; the candle flames were
hooded in darkness.

'My lady?' Father Thomas said, near and far away. There
were tears on her cheeks, she discovered. It was not the
Lady who was crying, after all.

'I'm tired,' she said. 'I think I'll go to my room.'

Jemima had not kept a lady's maid for many years, since she
stopped going out into society. Two of the housemaids took
care of her clothes, and took turns to draw her curtains in
the morning, though she rarely needed waking, for she was
usually astir as early as the servants. It was one of these who
came running down the backstairs the next day, eyes wide
with panic, crying out for Mrs Mappin. The housekeeper
was not down at that hour, and she hurtled into the kitchen
to find it occupied only by Monsieur Barnard and his

297

minions, and the lower-housemaids whose job it was to carry hot water up to the senior servants.

'Oh law, oh law!' she cried, 'whatever shall I do? Where's Mrs Mappin? It's the mistress – she won't wake up, and she looks ever so funny! Oh what shall I do?'

Monsieur Barnard took command of the situation, pushed the hysterical maid down into a chair, sent two under-housemaids flying upstairs for Mrs Mappin and Mr Oxhey, one kitchen boy to fetch Father Thomas and another to run out to the stables to send a groom for Doctor Swindells; and then took off his apron and climbed the backstairs and for the first time in his life made his way to the Red Room where he knew the mistress slept.

She was lying on her back, her mouth partly open, her face very pale and curiously dead-looking. She was breathing heavily, and Barnard thanked God for that, and took up her hand and felt for her pulse, and found it rapid and faint. He replaced her hand on the bedspread, and looked down at her with love.

'My dear mistress,' he said aloud, in English, 'do not go, please do not go.' And he stood quietly, keeping her company until the help he had summoned should come and take over from him.

It was a stroke, said Doctor Swindells, addressing Jemima's four sons, daughter-in-law, chaplain, butler, and house-keeper in the drawing-room. It was too early yet to say how serious it was – that must wait until she regained consciousness.

'When will that be?' Edward asked. His face had a pinched look, as though his bones were trying to escape through his skin.

'I cannot tell you. There is a possibility that she will not wake at all. Even if she does, she may not recover; or another stroke may carry her off. I'm afraid I cannot give you any very cheerful news. Everything depends on the damage that has been caused.'

'What can be done?' William asked.

'Nothing, I'm afraid. Watch and hope – and pray,' he

added for the sake of Father Thomas. 'There is nothing medicine can do in this situation.'

When he had gone upstairs again, taking Father Thomas with him, and the servants had gone, William said, 'The matter is quite clear. There is nothing anyone can do, and therefore no reason for me to delay my departure.'

'You mean to go, with Mother perhaps on her deathbed?' James exclaimed in outrage.

'My being here can't help her. I must take up my commission – we are at war, you know. If there were anything I could do, of course I would stay, but she's unconscious, and even the doctor don't know if she'll ever wake again. What use can I be here?' He looked from one to another, reading disapproval in James's and Harry's faces. Edward hardly seemed to know he had spoken, and Mary Ann was as impassive as ever. 'You had better stay, Harry,' he said.

'I should in any case,' Harry retorted, the first time in his life he had spoken other than respectfully to the brother who was also his senior officer and personal hero. 'Do you think I would run off until I knew Mother was out of danger?'

'If you don't join the *Venus* before we sail you will have to look for a berth elsewhere,' William warned him.

'To hell with that!' Harry cried angrily, and William shrugged and went away to pack.

James watched him go, and then said quietly, 'Poor Mother. She thought she had dogs on the leash, but let them loose, and they're wolves after all.'

Edward stared at him blankly, not understanding much through his shock, and then said, 'I had better get on with my work. The estate still has to be run, even though – ' He did not finish the sentence.

'Can I help you, Ned?' Harry asked. 'I'd like to have something to do, to keep me busy.'

They went out together. James looked at his wife, meeting her eyes and finding them warm and kind. 'If Mother were to die – ' he began, and then his voice failed him. Mary Ann came to him and put her arms round him, and with a little sigh he relaxed into them, leaning against her, resting his cheek on her hair. 'Oh Mary, I love her so,' he said, and felt his wife's hand gentle as it stroked his hair comfortingly.

Jemima woke at last from a confusing and horrible dream, a black tumult of faces and voices, light and dark; bitter-tasting, throbbing with distorted sounds, strangely twisted and threatening; and finally, blessedly, thinning out into a grey silence through which she drifted weightlessly, like a mote drifting in the ocean, gradually upwards towards the surface. She did not know where she was, or what had happened; she only knew that the grey silence was good after the dreams, and she was reluctant to leave it for the brighter, golden air above.

She woke, and found herself in her own bed, in the Red Room. The bed curtains were drawn back, as were the window curtains, and bright sunshine was pouring in. It was full daylight. What was she doing in bed? Had she been ill? Had she had a fall? She tried to sit up, and found that she had no body. A terrible panic washed over her for a moment: where sensation ought to be, there was nothing, no arms, legs, hands, nothing.

She rolled her head on the pillow, and saw Father Thomas sitting by the bedside. He looked worn and haggard, as though he had not slept for a long time. His head was bent over a book on his knee, but his eyelids were drooping with weariness. Then he must somehow have sensed that she was awake. He raised his head, with an effort, as though it were a great weight, and turned to her. Their eyes met, and a long clear look passed between them.

'Father Thomas,' she said, and it was clear her voice had not been used for a long time, for nothing but a whisper would come, and her lips felt numb, and would not shape the words properly. 'Am I dying, then?'

For a long time he only looked at her, and then he nodded. 'Ah,' she sighed. She saw him lean across and take her hand, but she felt nothing, and he must have realized it, for he let it go again, and with trembling fingers stroked her cheek. She tried to smile her thanks, and saw to her amazement that great tears were welling up in his eyes and rolling

300

over onto his grey and weary cheeks.

'No,' she whispered kindly, 'no, don't. I'm not unhappy.'

She still didn't know what had happened to her, and there were a great many questions she could have asked, but she found suddenly that she did not very much want to know the answers. She was very tired, and now that the horrible dreams were gone, she felt peaceful, warm and relaxed. It was like the sensation of being in a hot bath after a strenuous day's hunting.

It was all over, then. She was to pass on, through the mysterious doors, to that other place that she had spent so much of her life wondering about, and preparing for. She felt little curiosity about that, either. Here, at the very edge, she felt nothing, and wanted nothing. She thought briefly of her long life, and it seemed irrelevant, uninteresting. She watched the sunlight moving imperceptibly across the wall and thought, it's beautiful; I'm glad the sun is shining. She would be with Allen again: she had been so long away from him, and she had missed him so much. The sun shining, and going to be with Allen, and no pain or fear, only this sweet tiredness. Death was good, after all.

She turned her head to Father Thomas again, and he bent forward, wetting her face with his tears, to catch her words. 'Don't tell them, Father,' she whispered. 'Don't let them come in, until afterwards.' He nodded, unable to speak, and not knowing what else to do, stroked her head tremblingly. 'Yes,' she murmured, smiling a little, 'that feels good.' The golden light was fading, and sleep beckoned, and there was nothing left to do. She unclasped her mind, and let go.

Chapter Eighteen

The mistress was dead. The beating heart of the house was stilled, and Morland Place lay numb and helpless as though under some evil enchantment.

The machinery of the household, which had run so smoothly for so long that no-one noticed it any more, ground to a halt; beds were left unmade, floors unswept. No meals were prepared that day. Monsieur Barnard had disappeared, the kitchen fire had gone out, and the door stood open on the yard. Cautious hens stepped in to forage, and there was no-one to drive them out, or the cats that followed them.

Mrs Mappin had shut herself in her room to cry, while Oxhey remained in his pantry, frantically polishing every piece of plate the family owned, as though the exercise eased some unbearable pressure in his soul. Brach had retreated under a table in the hall, from the depths of whose shadows, like a Sibyl in a cave, she rolled her eyes and moaned at anyone who passed; and out in the yard the peacocks sat in a row along the stable roof shrieking dismally, for the poultry-maid had forgotten to feed them.

The horses had been fed and watered, a horseman's instincts, even those of the youngest lad, being stronger than the strongest grief. The youngest lad had got on quietly with filling the water buckets, until, coming into Hazel's box, he had found Mr Hoskins, his hand suspended in the act of brushing her over, weeping into the indignant mare's mane. This proved too much for the youngest lad, who gulped several times and retreated, scrambled up into the hayloft, burrowed into the heap of loose hay, and abandoned himself to sobs.

James could not bear to stay in the house. He went out to the yard, waving away Durban and the grooms, saddled Nez Carré himself, and took him out alone and rode fast until they were both tired. Coming at length to Harewood Whin he pulled up and slid from the saddle, and stood leaning against Nez Carré's shoulder waiting for the tears to come; but they would not. His throat and eyes and chest, even his jaws, ached with the need to cry, but it all seemed somehow locked inside him.

She was dead and gone, he thought. The common phrase had new meaning for him now. *She was dead* – a form of words, with so many echoes and connotations, of fear and expectation and religious belief; but *she was gone* – ah, that was different! The body of Jemima, Lady Morland, lay on the bed in the Red Room, waiting for the women to prepare it for its coffin, but it was mere untenanted clay: *she* was not there. She had gone away, and would never come back, and he would never see her again. The inmost part of him, dumb, dark and unreasoning, cried out for her like an abandoned child, and refused explanation or comfort. His intelligence stood aside and observed it in astonishment: he was thirty-one years old, and yet inside he was whimpering for his mother like a three year-old.

Hunger made itself felt at last. He did not want to go back home, to the house where his mother no longer lived; and in any case, there would be likely to be no comfort there today. Nez Carré turned his head and regarded him curiously, and then nudged him in a friendly way. James gathered the reins and swung himself back into the saddle, and turned the big horse onto the track towards the city. He would go to the club, he thought; stable Nez Carré at the Bunch of Grapes as usual, eat whatever was the ordinary in the dining room; and then climb inside a bottle of brandy and stay there for the rest of the day. Reality could have its turn with him tomorrow: for today, he was excusing himself.

It was Mary Ann who took charge, in the end. She had spent some time in the chapel, the only part of the house where there was any activity. Here the shadows had been driven up to the furthest corners of the rafters, for Father Thomas had lit every candle in every candlestick, torchère and sconce, so the very air glittered and dazzled, and the altars seemed weighted with stars, all dancing together with the movement of air. The air was heavy with incense, and the priest and his two boys dipped and rose rhythmically at their prayers, he heavily, they lightly, like one large and two small boats on the same ocean swell.

They had their own tasks to occupy them, but everyone else in the house seemed to be in a state of paralysis. In the end it was a sense of propriety as much as hunger which drove Mary Ann to take action. She went first to the kitchen. Monsieur Barnard was still nowhere to be found, so she dragged a kitchen boy from his retirement and made him relight the fire, and set the scullery maids to gathering together what cold food they could find, to fill the gap until a proper meal could be cooked. Passing into the servants' hall, she found some housemaids sitting at the table, their heads together, telling dreary stories abut strange happenings in graveyards, and corpses that sat up and spoke; and she took a grim delight in driving them out to light a fire in the drawing-room, set a kettle to boil over it, and take in the tea-things.

Having set these matters in train, she climbed the back-stairs to the top of the house and frightened Mrs Mappin to her feet by suddenly appearing at her bedside with the brisk injunction to dry her eyes, wash her face, and take up her duties.

'The women must be sent for to lay out the body – it should have been done long since – and if the cook cannot be found, you will have to prepare something for supper. I will help you, but you must rouse yourself now, and set to work.'

'Yes, ma'am,' Mrs Mappin muttered, half resentful, but half relieved to have someone take up the reins again.

Oxhey was still in his pantry, surrounded by a pirate's treasure of glittering plate. His face looked grey and exhausted, his eyes red-rimmed, and he was staring blankly into space, while his gloved hand still mechanically rubbed the cloth over and over the salver he was holding. It took time and patience for Mary Ann to gain his attention, and even longer to make him understand his orders. He is too old, she thought to herself; and then, with a rather grim pleasure, it is time for him to retire, and once I am mistress

304

of the house, I shall see he does. There will be a number of changes from now on, she thought, and had to exert self-discipline not to start thinking of them immediately.

So it was that by the time James rode reluctantly back home, a modicum of order and comfort had been restored. One of the footmen, Jacob, opened the door to him, and told him that Mr Oxhey had retired to his room, sir, quite done-up, he was, and Madam and the gentlemen was in the drawing-room taking tea. He spoke with an undertow of enormous gratification, which James had no difficulty in separating from the words as the emotions of a man who believed his chance had come at last.

In the drawing-room James found Ned and Harry sitting by the fire with the dogs. Leaky got up to greet James as he came in; Brach had changed caves from the hall table to Edward's chair, and now was sleeping busily with her head between his feet. Mary Ann was at the tea-table operating amongst the silver and porcelain, the jugs and kettles, like an alchemist preparing to turn the base metal of grief into the gold of social intercourse. It was evidently working as far as his brothers were concerned, for their eyes were fixed on her, bemused but comforted.

She looked up at James standing in the doorway, absently stroking Leaky's ears, and said, 'When did you eat? We have had supper, but I can ring for something for you.'

James shook his head. 'I had dinner at the club.'

'Some tea, then.'

'If you like.' He looked about the room, and said, 'You have been busy.'

She looked at him cautiously, detecting no praise in his voice, and yet unable to guess what else there might be. 'Someone had to take the reins,' she said.

'And what more natural than it should be you,' he said. She decided to leave the comment alone, handed him his cup, and carried two more over to the fireplace.

'Everything's in a way to be done,' Edward said. He sounded tired, but no more tired than a man who has laboured hard. James envied him the ability to take comfort from Mary Ann; would I might give her to you, he thought. They would deal splendidly together, bed uncomplicatedly,

305

and fill the empty nursery with a large brood of handsome children. How easy it would be to do what was expected of one, to win the world's approval, if it weren't for love. Edward and Chetwyn, James and Héloïse: he began to see the justice with which old-fashioned people condemned this love business as being dangerous, vulgar and unnecessary.

He sipped his tea, and watched his wife moving about the room, a tall and handsome woman, even-tempered and well-principled, with everything about her to admire and nothing to disgust. There was no reason why he should not love her and be a husband to her, except that he could never feel that she was other than separate from him. She fitted into no place inside him, and he had been raised by parents who had been two halves of one soul. They were together again now; but they had left James wanting no less than they had had.

Edward was talking about the arrangements he had made for the funeral, but feeling at last that he had less than the whole of his brother's attention he stopped and frowned and said, 'Have you been in the club all day? I suppose you are bosky.'

'On the contrary, I am horribly sober,' James said sadly. 'Have you arranged the vigil for tonight?'

'I thought Edward should take the first four hours,' Mary Ann said quickly, 'so that he can have an unbroken night's sleep. He works so hard during the day, he needs his rest.'

James met her eyes with a faint and cynical smile. 'Then since I, as you plainly imply, madam, do nothing during the day, I should take the middle watch.'

Mary Ann flushed. 'I implied nothing of the sort.'

'I thought I could do the middle watch,' Harry said, noticing nothing of the exchange. 'I'm used to sleeping in four-hour periods, so I could sleep before and after with no ill-effects.'

'Then I am to take the morning watch,' James said. 'Very well, I had better retire early, and make sure of my sleep. You seem very comfortable here – I should be no addition. I bid you all goodnight.'

He was at the foot of the stairs when he heard the drawing-room door open and shut again, and turned to find

306

his wife coming towards him. He waited for her courteously, but with that same forbidding smile which made her feel clumsy and stupid. 'Well, ma'am?'

She took a moment to assemble the words. 'James, I wish – I wish you will let me take vigil with you.'

He raised his eyebrows. 'I always thought my mother behaved towards you with nothing warmer than neglect. Surely she was nothing to you?'

But *you* are! she cried inwardly. If she could have spoken it, would it have made a difference? She didn't know; and she said, a little stiffly, 'I imagine you will not forbid me, at least.'

He bowed. 'I shall be glad of your company,' he said courteously.

'I'll leave orders for one of the housemaids to wake you,' she offered shyly.

'Thank you,' he said. A little, just a little, warmth sprang up in the hall, and they both waited to see what there might be to say. James tried to share his earlier amusement with her. 'Jacob thinks you mean to promote him to Oxhey's position. He opened the door to me with an entirely new flourish.'

But she took it amiss, and blushed with vexation. 'Oxhey was unable to perform his duties today, and someone had to take them over. I do think him too old, and that he should retire, but I shall do nothing you dislike, I assure you.'

'Now you are mistress of the house, the decisions are yours. You must do as you please about these matters,' James said. The words were courteous, even generous, but Mary Ann could not help feeling she was being baited. She made no reply, and after a moment James bowed again, and went upstairs to his solitary couch.

Jemima had made a great many friends and even more acquaintances in the course of a long life, too many to fit into the chapel at Morland Place. It was decided, therefore, to have the funeral service at St Edward's church, and the interment afterwards at the chapel for the family and servants only. The children from St Edward's School were to sit in the gallery, and were to sing an anthem during the service, and carry torches in the procession back to the house.

All the family came, except for Mary and her husband, who would not yet even have heard of Jemima's death. Charles and Roberta opened Shawes to accommodate themselves, Horatio and Lady Barbara, Horatio's two sisters and their husbands, and the Ballincreas from Northumberland. Lucy and Chetwyn, of course, stayed at Morland Place. The local inns were full of Akroyd and Pratt cousins not seen for years, and old friends and racing acquaintances from all over the country. The Ansteys, the Fussells, the Shawes, in fact the whole of York society, would be crowding into St Edward's, and even King George sent a message of sympathy, to remind the family that Jemima had been a great lady, and the wife of an important special emissary of the Crown.

Looking around him during the service, James saw that almost the only person missing was Héloïse. Even as Jemima's neice she ought to have been there, but she had been more than that. Guilt seared him, knowing that it was through his fault that she had not been able to be with them; and then loneliness and longing for her drowned out even the guilt. He moved restlessly with frustration and misery, and his wife beside him, handsome in black, which suited her, felt the movement and glanced at him in sympathy. Harslett, the vicar of St Edward's, was speaking the eulogy, and James tried to listen, to escape his unwelcome thoughts and the even more unwelcome notice of his wife.

'She was a great lady, born of a great age and a great tradition,' the nasal, fluting voice declaimed. 'In Shakespeare's words, we shall not see her like again.'

And, oh, it was true, James thought, and the enormousness of their loss engulfed him. He thought of those of them who were left, and saw that there was no-one of her stature. They were all such little people, selfish and nervous, grubbing after their own concerns, without the greatness, the long vision, the – yes, old-fashioned word though it was – the *piety* to be truly Master or Mistress of Morland Place. The world had changed, he thought sadly. She was the last of her generation. Perhaps there would be no more people like her, and the age of greatness was gone for ever.

The torchlit procession wound its way slowly back to Morland Place, the torches blowing sideways like flags, red and smokey in the breeze, villagers and tenants and labourers joining it as it passed their gates until it had swollen to a river of humanity. At the house Father Thomas was waiting to receive the coffin into the jewelled cave of the chapel, and though only the family and household were to follow it, the procession did not disperse. The torches made a ring of fire around the house, and the mourners stood like a besieging army, but a strangely silent one, pressed together for companionship, and waiting, for what they did not know.

In the chapel Father Thomas's reedy old voice wavered and failed, and kneeling with his brothers and sister, with the weeping servants all around him, James too wept at last: not for his mother, gone to live in eternal light, but for those of them left behind in darkness.

The coffin was lowered into the crypt, and at a signal from Father Thomas to one of the boys, the bell began to toll. Outside the crowd heard it, and a long sigh ran through them like a fluttering breeze. One of the torch bearers stepped forward and plunged his torch into the moat, dowsing it with a hiss, and one by one the others followed suit. The flames plunged into the black water like falling stars, leaving darkness behind; and when they were all gone, the mourners turned away in silence and went home.

Edward's letter to Mary went out with the despatches to the squadron blockading Brest, but by the time it arrived there, the *Africa* had left for other waters.

The news was that the French government, frustrated in its desire to conquer England, had turned its attentions elsewhere. In March 1798 the Directory had begun to assemble an *Armée d'Orient* in the south of France, giving the command to Buonaparte, who had done so well in Italy. The Admiralty believed that this force was to be aimed at the King of Naples, and would attack either Sicily, Sardinia, or Malta, and Admiral Lord St Vincent had quickly to gather a squadron together to send into the Mediterranean to destroy it.

Command was given to Nelson, who, recovering from the loss of his arm, had recently hoisted his flag as Rear-Admiral in the *Vanguard*, 74, and amongst the ships detached from other duties to form the squadron was the *Africa*.

'It's a compliment,' Mary said when her husband told her the news, 'and a reward, for all those years of faithful blockade duty.'

'I think you may be right. Jervis may well want to put me in the way of a little prize-money,' Haworth said.

'And he may well wish to send his most able officers on this assignment,' Mary added with an amused smile. 'So, my love, what is there to make you frown? I don't suppose there's a captain within sixty miles of us who wouldn't change places with you.'

'You know very well,' Haworth said, 'that I'm worrying about you.'

'Then don't,' Mary said. 'I am perfectly all right – indeed, I've never felt better or stronger. Don't I look well?'

She turned her glowing face to him, and he could not but smile. She carried her second child easily, and claimed that it was because she was with him that in this pregnancy she had known no single day of sickness or discomfort.

'You know it's a healthy life on board ship. Think of all the things I might have contracted if I had been on shore – smallpox, typhoid, measles – '

'That's all very well, my darling,' Haworth said, interrupting the list, 'but you know I want to see you sent safely back to England in good time for your confinement. Now we are sailing to Toulon, and who knows where we will go from there? At any rate, it is likely to be further from England, and if the talk is right, that this Buonaparte has designs on India – '

'You have so often told me that the seas are England's,' Mary said, taking his arm comfortingly, 'and wherever the squadron is, there will be ships coming and going. And we may well be back with the Brest blockade, or even back in port, in a few weeks' time,' she added hastily, to forestall his protest.

He kissed the end of her nose, and smiled. 'I know what's going on in your mind – you hope to persuade me to let you have the baby on board; but let me assure you, my darling, that there is nothing you can say to change my mind. At the first opportunity, I shall send you home to England.'

Mary merely smiled. She had her own ideas about that; but one thing she had learned during a lifetime of getting her own way was that there was no sense in fighting before the battle.

The squadron reached the Gulf of Lions on May the seventeenth, and found the French invasion fleet still in Toulon harbour. Scout ships venturing close in reported three hundred transports at anchor there – a probable army of thirty thousand – and sixteen or seventeen warships. The orders were to attack and destroy the fleet at all costs, but a severe gale blew up in the night and drove the English squadron off station, and by the time they had managed to beat back, the French had taken their chance and sailed.

What would be their first objective was a matter for guesswork, and the Mediterranean was a large place and full of vulnerable islands. It was not until a month later that definite news was heard of the French, and then it was unhelpful. The fleet, under Vice-Admiral Brueys, had sailed to Malta, where Buonaparte had taken and garrisoned Valletta with four thousand soldiers, and they had sailed again on the nineteenth of June.

'All captains' was signalled from the flagship, and Haworth with the others hurried on board the *Vanguard*, where the situation was discussed. Was Buonaparte on his way to conquer Sicily, or to take Egypt and thence India? Should the squadron sail to Malta, Sicily, or Alexandria? Mary was on the quarterdeck of the *Africa* along with the Anchovy and as many other officers as could make themselves inconspicuous when Captain Haworth came back on board, to learn the news.

'We sail for Alexandria,' he said briefly. 'Mr Angevin, will you be so good as to call all hands? Mr Wright, don't you see the flagship signalling?'

Mary, after exchanging one glance with her husband, took herself quietly out of the way of the preparations to make sail. As soon as he could absent himself, Haworth went to his cabin, and found Mary standing by the open stern windows enjoying the fresh breeze now that they had come before the wind again. She turned and smiled at him.

'Ruinous to the complexion, I know, but do not scold me – it is so delicious! So we are for Egypt?'

'Everyone agreed that was the greatest threat. If Buonaparte takes Egypt, India is in danger, and he is hard to resist on land. Better by far to stop him while he is still on the sea. But here we are, within six weeks, perhaps, of your confinement, and still I have not had a chance to send you home.'

'I am so glad of it,' Mary smiled. 'What could be more delightful than a cruise in the Mediterranean in summer? How the people at home would envy me, if they knew.'

They reached Alexandria on the twenty-eighth of June, to find no French there, and immediately set sail for Sicily, supposing that to have been Buonaparte's objective after all. But he was not in Sicily either, and it was not until a month of fruitless searching had passed that they learned that their first guess had been the correct one. Buonaparte had gone to Alexandria, but sailing more slowly than the English squadron, had not arrived until three days after them, by which time the English ships were already on their way back to Sicily.

On the twenty-fourth of July, Nelson's squadron set sail once again for Alexandria, this time to do battle with the French. Mary was now very close to her time, though still fit, healthy and active, and there had been no opportunity to set her on shore or send her safely back to England, and Haworth was beginning to think that she may have to have the baby on board after all. Mary knew it, and her smile as she went about her little tasks in the captain's cabin was a lovely thing to see.

Madame Chouflon's opinion proved to be right about Héloïse's reception in Coxwold. The news of her increased wealth, combined with James's return to his lawful wife, had already done a great deal to rehabilitate her with the inhabitants; and when she returned to her house, accompanied by an elderly lady dressed in antique style, two undoubtedly superior housemaids who looked as though they had as little desire as ability to speak French, and a completely inexplicable little red-headed girl, it all became too much for them to go on wondering about.

Her pregnancy, like her enormous dog, became merely another of her eccentricities; and then someone remembered that as Countess of Strathord she had been received at Court by King George. The aristocracy were always strange; and as she was certainly colourful, driving about, fashionably dressed, in her pretty little park phaeton, her smart French maid beside her and her huge dog running alongside, she became their particular property, and from merely staring at her, the local inhabitants took to waving and smiling as she passed, and pointing her out to visitors as Our Countess.

Héloïse had too much to do at first to worry about it, or to be unhappy. Her new household took time to settle down. The housemaids were at first inclined to feel the establishment too limited for them, and pined for the smoke and noise of London. Alice said the silence at night got on her nerves, and Nell was depressed by the absence of shops and tradesmen calling, and both were united in their determination to leave at the end of their half-year; but gradually the peace of the sunny little house seeped into their souls, and they began to love their mistress, and even, for her sake, to inject a measure of affection into their expostulations about 'that dog' and 'that child'.

Mathilde – for Héloïse could not call her by the English version of her name – had been willing to make her home with Héloïse, and had no preconceptions about the country to make her wish to return to the town, but she took a long time to settle down. No news had been heard of her brother, though Charles, on Héloïse's behalf, was still pursuing enquiries. Héloïse, believing that the truth was kinder in such circumstances, told Mathilde that it was unlikely they would ever learn anything now, and that she must not hope;

but Mathilde insisted that Karellie was still alive somewhere, and continued to grieve and worry.

Kithra became her best friend, and together they romped about the fields and got themselves into mischief. Héloïse was glad to let her play, hoping that the good air and sunshine and healthy exercise would heal her mind as they strengthened her body; but when she was racing noisily around the house driving the maids to distraction, or when a farmer came cap in hand, apologetic but firm, to claim compensation for stolen eggs or fruit or animals 'scared out of their wits by miss's antics', then Héloïse felt doubts as to the wisdom of what she had done.

But she would never admit them. This was Lotti's child, whom she had promised to care for, who had suffered terrible bereavement, and who deserved all the love Héloïse could give. When the baby was born, she told herself, she would take Mathilde in hand, give her proper lessons, teach her accomplishments, and make a lady of her.

The news of Jemima's death reached her in a roundabout way, for Kexby, the carrier, heard it talked of in York and mentioned it to Marie in conversation while driving her to Thirsk for her day off. He did not suggest by his manner that he knew of any particular interest she might have in the news, but when Marie burst into tears, he shewed no surprise. He comforted her as best he could, and when they reached Thirsk he took her straight to the Green Man and sat her down in a quiet corner with a glass of port wine by way of a stiffener.

Official news reached Héloïse later, in the form of an embarrassed letter from Edward, which so clearly longed to apologize for not asking her to the funeral that she felt no offence, only sadness. In the same batch of letters, collected by Stephen from the post-office, was a communication from Mr Pobgee of Pobgee and Micklethwaite concerning the Will of the late Lady Morland of Morland Place, and begging leave to do himself the honour of waiting on her on Tuesday forenoon.

When Mr Pobgee arrived, he found that numbers in the already crowded household had again increased, and Héloïse was engaged in trying to placate the servants and determine where the newcomer should sleep, and wishing she had not decided to put off the enlargement of the house until after the baby was born.

A few days before, not long after the funeral, Monsieur Barnard had sought audience with Edward, who received him in the steward's room with some surprise, never having spoken more than a few words to the cook in all the years of his service.

'What can I do for you, monsieur?' he asked in response to Barnard's low bow.

Barnard straightened, and looked full into Edward's eyes. 'I go.'

'Go where?' Edward asked, startled.

Barnard paused, apparently to assemble vocabulary. 'My lady dead. I no work here no more. I go,' he said.

Edward looked perplexed. 'I can understand your feelings,' he said, 'but you have been with us for a long time, and we should be very sorry to lose you. Besides, where would you go to? Have you friends? I should not wish to think of you wandering friendless in a foreign country. If you really wish for a change, perhaps I could find another place for you, through my sister in London. But you had much better stay, depend upon it. If there is anything you want, you have only to mention it. I shall be pleased to give you an increase in salary, if that will help.'

Barnard smiled through all this, and at the end of it said, 'I go. Thank you.'

Edward ran his hand through his hair distractedly. The trouble with the cook was that you never knew how much he had understood. 'I'll get madam to speak to you,' he said, and missed the slight narrowing of Barnard's eyes at the suggestion. 'In any case, you had much better not decide all at once. We are all upset at the moment. Take your time, and consider afresh when you feel more yourself.'

At this Barnard smiled, and bowed again, to indicate that the interview was at an end. Pressure of work drove the curious episode from Edward's mind until Mary Ann sought him out towards supper time with the news that the Frenchman had put his few possessions into a bag and gone.

'Gone? Where? And how?'

'On foot, towards York, according to the kitchen maids. They were too stupid to tell anyone in time to stop him.'

'Someone must go after him,' Edward said. Mary Ann raised her eyebrows.

'Go after him? What on earth for? We are better off without him, you know. He was far too autocratic. He thought he could do just as he liked, and ignore orders whenever he felt inclined.'

'But he's the best cook we have ever had. Everyone in York has envied us him,' Edward exclaimed.

'And I dare say one of them now has him, and welcome,' Mary Ann said. 'Cooks are easy enough to come by, and if we can get a young one and train him, so much the better. Or her – some houses have female cooks, you know, and they are much more biddable.'

Edward was too upset and confused to listen to this heresy. 'He is all alone in a foreign land. He doesn't speak English. We must find out that he is all right.'

'Barnard is well able to take care of himself, depend upon it,' Mary Ann said. 'And as for not speaking English, I'll wager he can speak it well enough when he wants to. We'll hear of him in a day or two, established with some family in York at twice the wage. Don't worry, Edward.'

Barnard's ability to understand English, at least, was proved by his knowing where to find Héloïse; and his determination, if it had ever been in doubt, was proved by the fact that he walked most of the way to Coxwold. When he finally came before Héloïse, he fell to his knees, clutched her hands, and kissed them in a silent ecstasy of devotion. He had with him his clothes, and a beautiful ebony crucifix which was all he had brought with him from France. For his accumulated wages for the years of his service at Morland Place he had no thought. He lived for his art, which he laid, with his life, at the feet of the person he served. Now that Jemima was dead, he had brought these things to Héloïse, her successor in his mind. Money did not enter into it.

Héloïse, with her usual practicality, took him straight to the kitchen and fed him, while Marie prepared a hot herbal bath for his feet. The English servants stood around, half resentful, half curious, while her ladyship sat at the other side of the kitchen table and carried on a conversation with the strange little man in rapid French, liberally sprinkled with exclamations and enormous shruggings.

'But you see,' said Héloïse last, 'that I have a very small household here – indeed, a very small kitchen! I do not entertain. There will be no great balls and feasts and dinner parties for you, no challenge at all. Would you not be happier staying on at Morland Place with the new mistress?'

'That one – pooh!' Barnard said. '*Elle n'est pas gentille – elle n'est qu'une gouvernante*! She wished to change my kitchen, to put in a vulgar Romford – as though I would cook on a stove! She spoke to me like a servant – make this dish, make that one. Pah! Food to her is *nécessaire – rien plus que ça*! She knows nothing of art, nothing of God. She is not *comme il faut*, that one – she is simply a *bourgeoise*.'

Héloïse felt rather sorry for Mary Ann at the end of this tirade, and smiled gently and said, 'But I, too, am only a *bourgeoise*. My mother was a café-owner's daughter, you know, and I am just like her.'

'No, my lady,' Barnard said sternly. 'It matters not who the parents are, nor the style of living. What matters is in *here*.' And he struck himself firmly on the chest with his fist. 'You are a lady, and I will work for no-one less.'

Since he was not proposing that Héloïse should hire him, it was plain, to her at least, that there could be no question of her refusing, but it was not so easy to explain that to the other servants, or to satisfy their very reasonable demands to know how the house could accommodate him; and while the arguments were still going on, Mr Pobgee arrived, and was shewn into the parlour by Alice, who could not resist telling the visitor the reason for all the excitement.

'Mr Edward Morland, at least, will be glad to know that his cook is safe and well,' Pobgee said to Héloïse when she finally joined him. 'He has been worried, especially as it seems that the man spoke no English and had no money with him.'

317

Héloïse gave a harrassed smile. 'Monsieur Barnard walked here; and he cares nothing for money. Please tell my cousin Edward that he is safe with me, if you wish – but, I beg you, tell him nothing else.' She blushed as she spoke, but did not need to be more specific, but Pobgee could not have failed to notice her advanced pregnancy, though his eyes never strayed from her face.

'You may trust me, my lady,' he said gently. 'I shall speak discreetly to Mr Edward, and arrange for Monsieur Barnard's accumulated wages to be transferred to your charge. Also, I wish you will charge me, my lady, with any business you need undertaken, of however delicate a nature. I assure you I have the liveliest interest in your welfare, and will act with the greatest discretion. The late Lady Morland, who was a friend as well as a valued client, commended your interests to my care shortly before she died.'

'You are very kind,' Héloïse said faintly, 'but there is nothing I want. Did – did Lady Morland –' She found she could not yet speak of her. Pobgee became businesslike.

'Lady Morland sent for me in February, my lady, to instruct me to make a new Will for her. In essence it was no different from her old one. Morland Place and the estate were to go to her granddaughter Frances Mary James, to be held in trust until her majority.' Héloïse nodded. 'She did, however, make certain other changes. The one which immediately concerns you is that she left certain items of her personal property to you, and charged me to bring them to you myself. This happy task I now perform.' And he placed in Héloïse's hands a small but handsome cedarwood box.

Héloïse looked at it, and then up, enquiringly, at Pobgee. He smiled. 'The box and its contents were given to Lady Morland in her childhood by the Lady Annunciata, your common ancestress. Lady Morland wanted you to have them.'

Héloïse opened the box and took out, one by one, the contents: two exquisite miniatures, painted on ivory and framed in gold, one of Martin Morland, the other of the Princess Henrietta Stuart; a lock of brown hair, tipped with gold, enclosed in a gold locket; and the fabulous diamond collar, given to Annunciata by King Charles. As she drew the diamonds out, flashing rainbow colours in the light, she glanced again at the lawyer, who, understanding her thought, said, 'Yes, the contents of the box were specified. There is no mistake. Those things belonged to Lady Morland personally, not to the estate.'

Héloïse sat with the treasures in her lap, remembering the conversation she had had with Jemima, on the day they had walked together around the lake at Shawes. Many thoughts ran through her head; and then the baby kicked restlessly, bringing her to another line of reasoning.

'You said, the provision which immediately concerns me – is there another?' she asked Pobgee. He smiled at her quickness.

'There is, my lady, but I am not at liberty to divulge it until certain circumstances appertain. When they do – if they ever do – I shall at once make it my business to make it known to you. In the meantime, I am obliged by Lady Morland's Will, as well as by her wishes, to keep a watchful eye on your welfare, and ensure that you want for nothing. She did not,' he added with a delicate hesitation, 'I suppose, know about – ?'

'About the baby? No. It – it was not in my power to tell her.'

'Indeed. A pity. Well, my lady, I hope you will not hesitate to call on me, should you need anything – anything at all – be it money or advice or simply someone to talk to.'

'You are very kind, monsieur. I shall not forget, though you see I have many friends, and want for nothing,' Héloïse said, rising.

Pobgee bowed over her hand and departed with a troubled frown. The difficulty about Wills was that they were necessarily static, while circumstances changed, which made for confusion and litigation. Good for business, you might say, Pobgee addressed an imaginary critic in his head, but in the case of the Morland family, he was enough of a friend, and sure enough of the business, to wish for everything to be straightforward. He must keep a finger on the pulse. Perhaps the Circumstances would never arise; and then he wondered whether he hoped that they would, or wouldn't.

Chapter Nineteen

A series of hot days and a strong desire to gallop had led Lucy to arrange a riding-party to Richmond Park; and a desire to be with Lucy had led Weston, who was no more enthusiastic a horseman than most sailors, to borrow a horse and join it. Half a dozen other young ladies and gentlemen completed the party, the gentlemen either officers or Bond Street sportsmen, the ladies dashing young women who admired Lady Aylesbury's style and whose collective ambition was to be known as bruising riders and hard to hounds in their own country.

Chetwyn had declined to come, observing with a faint smile that Lucy would be safe enough with her watchdog, Danby Wiske, by her side, and that he had promised Greyshott a hand or two of picquet at the club.

'I shall see you at dinner tonight,' he said.

'Very well, but be back in time to dress,' Lucy had said. 'You know we are engaged.'

'I know it; I was not sure if you did,' Chetwyn said. 'However, I think your ride may be curtailed. The weather will very likely turn dirty.'

'Oh, nonsense,' Lucy retorted. 'It's a beautiful day.'

'Don't you see that bank of cloud in the west? If I were you, I should stay close to the gates, or you may find yourselves without shelter when it turns off.'

Lucy only smiled, and twirled her gloves gaily. 'Oh, I don't regard a wetting! It can be quite exciting, galloping with the rain in your face.'

Chetwyn thought of her galloping Mimosa, an exciteable mare at the best of times, over ground made slippery by a sudden shower, in visibility obscured by dark clouds and driving rain, and bit his tongue to stop himself protesting. He knew how headstrong she had become lately, and opposition was only likely to make her more stubborn. He still did not have his heir, and a bad fall could make that impossible for ever; but more than that, he cared for Lucy, and worried about her. She was his little sister, as she had always been; but lately, for what reason he did not like to enquire too deeply, she had become more than that to him.

'I suppose it reminds you of the spray on your face while you were in the good old *Diamond*?' he heard himself say acidly, and was shocked with himself. Lucy, however, noticed nothing.

'Oh no,' she said matter-of-factly, 'I was never above decks in the *Diamond*. I thought you knew that. There weren't even any gun-ports on the orlop.' A thoughtful expression crossed her face. 'Strange to think that Mary must be a more experienced sailor than me by now! I wonder if she has had the news about Mama yet?'

'Can't your friend Weston tell you that? I thought he knew everything about the navy.'

'Well, of course, it was thanks to him that we knew the *Africa* went off with Nelson's squadron, but even he can't know where they are, until despatches come in,' Lucy said, and then tilted her head, alerted at last to her husband's tone of voice. 'What is it, Chetwyn? Don't you like Weston? I can't think why you should not.'

'I can't think why not, either. He seems to me a most agreeable young man,' Chetwyn said cynically.

'Well, everyone says his address is particularly good,' Lucy said, half pleased, half puzzled.

'And he is so very handsome,' Chetwyn added in spite of himself.

'Is he? I suppose so – I had not much noticed.'

'Had you not?' Chetwyn felt a surge of affection, and took her hand. 'That is just like you, Luce. I remember you when you used to be covered in mud and straw, trotting round after that old horse doctor. You're still the same inside, aren't you?'

The last words seemed to have a note of entreaty as well as enquiry in them. Lucy laughed nervously, and drew back her hand. 'Oh, Lord, that was years ago! I hope I have grown up since then. But I must go – it would be monstrous to keep them all waiting; and I can't wait to see what sort of a hireling they have given Weston! I told him to borrow a horse, but he would not. Proud!' she snorted in healthy derision, and was gone, leaving Chetwyn feeling ruffled, and dissatisfied with himself.

By the time the party met at the Roehampton gate, the clouds had formed a long, low bar in the western sky, but since the sky overhead was clear and cloudless and the sun was shining brightly, no-one felt inclined to postpone the treat. Weston had had a good look around, and had sniffed the wind, and frowned, but whatever his apprehensions, he kept them to himself.

'For a hireling, that's not a bad-looking horse,' Lucy told him, trying to persuade Mimosa to stand still and succeeding only in turning her in tight circles. 'A little goose-rumped, perhaps, but that's not a bad fault.'

'I may not be a polished horseman, ma'am,' Weston said in injured tones, 'but I'm no Johnny Raw. Did you think I would let them fob me off with any cow-hocked, spavined, broken-winded screw?'

'It looks as though it might be fast,' Lucy said, setting her heel covertly to Mimosa's girth. 'Shall we try?'

The mare snorted with excitement and plunged forward, and with a laughing glance at the others by way of warning, Lucy let her go, and went thundering away up the tan. Weston and Danby Wiske sprang after her as one man, and the rest of the party joined the pursuit perforce, their horses not wanting to be left behind.

At the end of the first long gallop, when everyone was flushed and laughing and thoroughly warmed up, Lucy led the way off the tan and onto a narrow path that wound through the bracken towards the wilder country in the middle of the park. There was not room for more than two horses abreast, and after a brief and silent struggle, Wiske yielded to the determination of Weston and dropped back, to let the lieutenant ride beside Lucy.

'This is a better arrangement,' Weston said. 'Now we can have a comfortable chat. Shall you be at the opera tonight?'

'Why no, I thought you knew. I am going to dinner and a ball at Chelmsford House, for Helena McNeill's engagement

– you know, Viscount Ballincrea's sister. They are cousins of a sort. The Ballincreas don't have a London house, so Charles and Roberta are giving the party for them. I thought you would have been there.'

Weston gave her an amused look. 'My dear ma'am, there are still a few houses where I am not automatically invited when you are.' She blushed at this, and looked upset, so he went on, 'The Honourable Helena McNeill – a rather handsome young woman, as I remember. Who is she to marry?'

Lucy made a face. 'That awful Greyshott! I can't think why she accepted him. He's so pale and spindle-shanked, and he looks as though he doesn't know one end of a horse from the other.'

'Hard though it is to believe, Lady Aylesbury, there are those who don't measure a man by his horsemanship, or the shape of his calves,' Weston laughed. Lucy glanced automatically at his calves, which filled his top-boots admirably, and at the bulge of his thigh-muscles under his close-cut breeches, and felt herself growing pink again.

'I know that, and I would not have thought Helena was one of them,' she said faintly. 'What can she see in him?'

'Greyshott is as rich as a nabob,' Weston said succinctly.

'Well, the Ballincreas are not exactly under the hatches,' Lucy retorted.

'The war hasn't helped people like them, whose income is all from rents. Taxes are high, and they can't raise their rents enough to make up for it, for their tenants just can't afford them. No, I think Ballincrea will be extremely glad of the match. Greyshott isn't a bad sort, and will likely come down handsome, if he gets the lovely Helena.'

'Well I think it's all fustian,' Lucy said. 'I'm sure she doesn't like him. She shouldn't be made to marry him.'

'How very romantic of you,' Weston smiled. 'I never thought to hear you advocating the love-match. What has happened to change your mind?'

Lucy met his eyes for a moment, which was a mistake. She looked away and bit her lip. 'I haven't – it isn't – ' she said in confusion. 'I don't think anyone ought to marry a man they dislike, that's all. I know nothing about love. I believe it's all – '

'Yes?' he asked sweetly.

'All gammon,' she said firmly, and sought about for a new topic. 'Did you hear that Harry has his ship at last?'

'Yes,' said Weston obligingly. 'Captain Collingwood has taken him into the *Excellent*. That will be a good thing for him. Collingwood is certain to rise high, and your brother will benefit.'

'It was too bad of William to refuse to have him.'

'Well, he had already sailed for the West Indies,' Weston pointed out fairly.

'But Harry could have gone out on a despatch ship, and joined the *Venus* there. That's what William arranged for his extraordinary Mrs Smith. She had a son, did you know? She called him Frederick. I suppose that makes him Frederick Smith. Poor Mother,' she added obscurely, with a sigh. Something rustled in the bracken just ahead, making Mimosa breenge and shake her head, and Lucy was occupied for a moment in soothing her.

'How are things at Morland Place?' Weston asked, when the crisis was over.

'Uncomfortable, I should think,' Lucy said, and then grinned. 'Not a decent meal for weeks, reading between the lines, with Monsieur Barnard walking out, and cooks not so easy to come by as some people thought.'

'Where do you suppose he went?'

'If my guess is right, that he left because he doesn't like James's wife, I shouldn't be surprised if he had not gone to Héloïse,' Lucy said shrewdly. She sighed. 'I always felt rather sorry for Mrs James, but there's no denying she has the knack of upsetting people. Poor old Oxhey, of all people, turned off after all these years! I know he's being paid a pension, but that won't make it up to him. Morland Place was his whole life. And I wouldn't mind betting there'll be others. She'll go slowly, until they're out of mourning, but after that, there'll be so many changes, it'll be like a gale blowing through the old house.'

'Well, changes aren't necessarily bad,' Weston said, to comfort her.

'You only say that because you've never had a home. When it's your *home*, where you spent your childhood, you want it to stay the same.'

'My poor Lucy, does it make you feel afraid?' Weston said, half laughing, half caressing, and the use of her name, and the tone of his voice, made her feel breathless.

'Let's trot on,' she said abruptly. 'Mimosa's getting restless.'

They were deep into the park when one of the gentlemen called out, 'I say, it's getting very dark, ain't it? Where did all those clouds come from?'

Everyone looked around, and exclaimed. The bank of clouds had drawn up fast and silently, and the outlook was now very threatening. One of the ladies suggested a little shamefacedly that they should turn for home.

'Oh, fustian!' Lucy said at once. 'How can you be such a ninny, Minerva? Well, I'm not turning back. A little rain never hurt anyone.'

'No, damn it, your ladyship,' cried a languid young Guards officer, whose duelling scars seemed at odds with his feline elegance, 'this won't be just a little rain. It looks damned bad to me – a downpour, nothing less. We should turn back.'

'But we are too far from the gate to get back before it begins,' said another. 'We ought to try for those woods.'

'Not if there's going to be lightning,' said the officer. 'What do you say, Weston? You're the man for the weather.'

'I wonder you didn't notice it when we set out, Weston,' said Danby Wiske a little reproachfully. 'Lord Aylesbury will be put out if we let her ladyship take a soakin'.'

'Oh, don't be so cow-hearted,' Lucy said, and rode on, and the others, glancing doubtfully at each other, followed.

'Here it comes!' someone cried a while later. 'Too late for talking now.'

There was a fine, cold spattering by way of warning, and then the skies opened. The party milled in confusion as the horses laid back their ears and protested at the cold rain. There was no shelter in sight but the distant trees, and after a moment Danby Wiske shouted.

'No lightnin' that I can see. Better get under the trees, before we drown.'

325

He turned his horse and led the way, and the others followed him, but Weston laid his hand on Lucy's rein and leaned towards her to say, 'I've a better plan. We're not so far from Ham Gate – over that way. We'll find shelter there.'

'We'd better tell the others,' she said, but he closed his hand over hers and shook his head. She met his eyes, and a cold fear gripped her stomach. The rain was running down her face and dripping off her nose and chin, and already her clothes felt clammy. Weston had his head turned a little to try to keep the rain out of his eyes. There were drops clinging to his eyelashes, and his hair was plastered in strands to his forehead, but he did not look cold. His eyes were bright, and he bared his teeth in a fiercely excited grin.

'There's an inn just beyond the gates. We can shelter there, and get dry,' he said, and though the cold hand still gripped her stomach, she felt the blood begin to run hot under her skin. Some instinct told her that here was grave danger, yet she had never been so excited, and excitement was what she craved to fill the emptiness in her life, to crowd out the sense of loss that she had never understood. She gave a faint nod, and Weston laughed aloud in triumph, turned his horse, and drove it into the rain, away from the rest of the party. Mimosa sprang after him, eager to be out of the rain, and Lucy let her go, closing her eyes against the teeming rain.

The inn was small, but evidently used to catering for people of quality, who might stop for refreshment on their way to or from a ride in the park. Servants came out with umbrellas and helped Lucy dismount, but she waited to see the horses were led away, with strict injunctions to rub them down well, before she would go in.

'Oh dear me, come in, ma'am, do. What a terrible downpour,' the hostess cried as Lucy dripped her way into the passage. 'I declare, you're soaked to the skin! You must get out of them wet clothes, ma'am.'

'Yes, a good idea,' Weston said, coming in behind her. 'Have you a bedchamber above with a fire lit?'

'Why, no sir, but I can get a fire lit in two twos, if your good lady would condescend to step into the coffee room for the minute. There's no-one in there now, and there the fire is lit, for I saw them clouds coming up this morning, and thought it would be wanted, one way or another. However did you come not to notice them, sir? That's right, ma'am, just you set down in here, and put your poor feet on the fender! Jem! Go up and light the fire in number one, and the parlour, and tell Betty to take up some towels, and some hot water as soon as the fire's bright. There now, sir, can I get you and your lady a little something to warm you? A nice cup of wine, with a lump of sugar, and a hot poker put in it?'

When they were alone, Lucy, having taken off her sodden hat and wrung out her gloves, looked at Weston and said, 'She thinks I'm your wife.'

'A natural assumption. No reason to disabuse her, that I can see,' he said lightly.

'And how did you come not to see the clouds?' she asked.

'Of course I saw them.'

'And ignored them.'

'As you did.'

Lucy sat down and put her feet up to the blaze. 'Chetwyn warned me about the rain before I set off. I'm afraid it only made me more determined to go. I have a bad character, you see, Weston.'

He leaned against the chimneypiece on the other side of the fire so that he could look at her. 'Hadn't you better call me James, since we're supposed to be married? The landlady might think it strange.'

She looked up at him, faintly apprehensive. 'What's going to happen?' she asked abruptly. He thought it better to take the question literally.

'Our good hostess is going to prepare a room where we can take off our wet clothes and dry ourselves. Then I imagine she will take our clothes away and dry them, by which time it will have got to dinner time, and we will be extremely hungry.'

'If we told her – she might have two rooms up above –

327

with fires,' Lucy said with difficulty. For some reason she was finding it hard to breathe.

'Oh, I think it's too late to tell her now,' Weston said smilingly. 'It takes time for a fire to burn up, you know, and I might catch my death of cold waiting for it.'

The door opened, and the landlady bustled in with a tray bearing two goblets, from which steam and an aromatic smell were rising. 'There now, ma'am, just you get this inside you, and 't'will keep out the cold. I put a bit of cinnamon to it, to warm it up. And there, sir, yours. Lord, the rain's coming down in stair-rods! Your room'll be ready very soon, ma'am, and if you'll forgive the liberty, I've looked out a couple of dressing gowns for you and your husband, to put on while your clothes dry, for if you've a dry stitch between you, it's more than I'll compound for.'

She went away again, and Lucy sipped the hot, spiced wine, and stared into the fire, and thought of nothing. She didn't want to think: it was too much of a struggle. A different instinct was working here, and if it was dangerous, it was also new and exciting, and her life was very dull. By the time the landlady came to say the fire was bright in the chamber and the hot water waiting, she was down to the dregs of her cup, and the eyes she lifted to Weston's were no longer apprehensive, but calm and curious.

'There we are, ma'am, our best bedchamber, and there's hot water, and the dressing gown, like I said. And if you put your wet clothes outside the door, the girl'll take them downstairs, and dry and press them for you. And through here, sir, there's a parlour, and a fire likewise, if you'd like to do the same. I'll leave you to it then, ma'am, sir. Just ring if you want anything.'

Weston left Lucy in the bedchamber, and went through into the parlour closing the communicating door. Lucy undressed quickly, for she was beginning to feel chilled, and standing naked by the fire, she towelled herself briskly. The wine on an otherwise empty stomach had induced a pleasantly dream-like feeling, warm and slightly drowsy. She put on the dressing gown, picked up the bundle of wet clothes distastefully and dropped them outside the door, and was drying her hair by the fire when she heard the communicating door open, and turned to see Weston standing there, watching her.

She smiled, a smile, though she did not know it, which transformed her face, and he came across and took the towel from her to rub her head.

'You must be glad you have a short crop,' he said, and, peering under the towel, 'It's as curly as a lamb's fleece from the rain. Stand up.'

She obeyed him without thinking, and he turned her to face him. From a very short distance she examined his face, the fine brows, the long-lashed brown eyes, the straight nose, the humourous mouth which for some reason made her feel rather faint. His hands came up to her shoulders, and he said, 'This is quite the most dreadful gown I have ever seen. It is a crime to cover you up with it.'

Gently, he removed it so that she was standing quite naked in the fireglow. She felt her skin tighten and her nipples start with the cold air, but there was no shame or embarrassment at being thus, for the first time, naked before a man. She watched his lips and his eyes, and thought with distant surprise, is this it? Is this being in love?

He took off his own robe, and stood naked before her, silently offering her his own body to look at, equal to equal, and she was pleased with the gesture. It seemed a friendly thing to do. She had never seen a man quite naked before. From the delicate collar-bones downward, his skin was fair and milky-white, smooth and hairless. His body was well-proportioned, like a Greek statue, broad at the shoulders, firm at the waist, tapering inwards to the tangle of light-brown hair and the strong arching penis which seemed, all of a sudden, to be the focus of his body, as though everything were curving towards that point, as though that were the centre of his being from which all his life was springing.

She looked up into his eyes, and found that she was experiencing two quite distinct sensations, a strange, weak, loosening, quivering of her body for his body, and a strong, glowing feeling in her mind for the him that was not his body, that was her friend Weston. She thought she would like to tell him about these things, and then she thought she didn't really want to speak just at the moment; and then she thought he probably knew it anyway. He stepped forward and put himself lightly against her, and kissed her, and she closed her eyes and lifted her arms round his neck, and gave herself up to the piercing sweetness of the new sensation.

Later, when they lay on the bed together, and he made love to her, and there was no difficulty or shyness as there had been with Chetwyn, she found that the two sensations were not separate after all, but had blended together in a kind of all-encompassing bliss that wiped out everything except the pleasure of being with him. Love she had thought of as a grave, cerebral thing, and what they were doing as mating, a physical act for the making of children. Now she knew differently. When poets talked of love, it must be this they meant, this extraordinary melting together of mind and body, so that to think and act were the same thing.

Later again, when they were quiet again in each other's arms, she told him what she had thought, and he looked at her gravely, and said, 'I'm glad you understand, Lucy, that *is* love, and not just – something else. What is between you and me is different from anything we will ever feel for anyone else.'

'Yes, of course,' she said, surprised that he should need to say it.

'But you see, love, other people won't understand. I only want to arm you, against the troubles to come. They won't understand, and they'll say unpleasant things.'

Dimly, she knew this to be true, but it had no power just then to hurt her. 'Don't worry,' she said. She felt strong with her love for him, and since she had no love-words, for her life had never taught her them, she said instead, 'Can we do it again, do you think?'

He laughed and rolled over to look down at her, freckle-faced, hay-haired, plainly beautiful, beautifully plain-spoken, and said, 'Yes, Mr Proom, I rather think we can. You like it, then?'

'With you – it's splendid.'

Their clothes came back, and they debated what to do. 'The rain has passed over,' Weston said, going to the window.

'We could ride back. On the other hand, we are a long way from home, and it is getting near dinner time.'

'I have an engagement tonight,' she said. 'I shall be late in any case.'

They looked at each other, holding their breath. If either one of them advocated the sensible thing, the other would agree to it. It was a perilous moment.

'I don't want to go to Chelmsford House,' Lucy said at last.

'We are going to be in the suds anyway. It's bound to get out,' Weston said. Lucy was calm.

'We knew that before we came here: it was part of the bargain. It would be simple to worry about it now. Oh Weston, don't let's go!'

He grinned. 'Are you going to call me Weston always?'

'I think so,' she said apologetically. 'Listen, it's too far to ride back. We couldn't get there before dark. It will be better if we have dinner here, and stay the night, and go back tomorrow.'

He kissed her with relief. 'Thank God! I thought you were going to be sensible! There will be a shocking brew to face tomorrow, but never mind. We'll enjoy today while it lasts.'

She looked perturbed. 'It isn't only today, is it? Aren't we going to go on?'

'That must be for you to decide. I have nothing to lose – nothing much, anyway. You are a married woman, and of rank.'

'I want to go on,' she said without hesitation, and he kissed her hand, acknowledging her courage.

'Then we will, as long as we can, and as privately as we can. Until the world catches up with us.'

'Let's have dinner,' she said practically.

The hot days of July deepened the green of the grass and the white curdle of meadowsweet in the lanes, and ripened Héloïse like an apple, and her household gathered round her protectively, waiting for the moment and making calm and sensible plans.

331

When she finally went into labour, however, all the preparations came to nothing, and the house was thrown into panic. Marie and Flon discovered that they had violently opposing views about the management of a lying-in chamber, Monsieur Barnard drove the maids into hysterics by kneeling in the kitchen and praying to the Virgin to deliver his mistress, thus convincing them that he thought she was going to die, and Mathilde expressed her excitement, anxiety, and desire for attention by racing round the house with Kithra, knocking things over and shrieking in three broken languages.

Only Stephen kept his head. He shook it sadly at the folly and improvidence of women, took off his apron, and walked down to the village to ask the apothecary to come up to the house. On his return he set the big kettle to boil on the fire, and took upstairs the beautiful elm-wood crib he had been making all summer in his spare time.

The baby, a girl, was born late in the afternoon. Marie placed her, small, long, and very dark, in Héloïse's arms, and Héloïse stared at her in astonished delight. It seemed extraordinary that she had had no idea, all these months, what the baby would look like. The reality of the baby who had kicked her lustily in the ribs and made sleeping in any position an impossibility for weeks past, and the reality of this minute scrap of humanity in her arms, were quite different.

The baby, having yelled once or twice to assure everyone that all was well, now seemed bent on making up some of the sleep she had caused Héloïse to lose. Her eyes were screwed shut in her dark and wrinkled face, her fists clenched beneath her chin, and her lips pursed as though she were savouring the quality of life so far, and finding it wanting.

'She is so small!' Héloïse exclaimed.

'She's beautiful,' Flon said sentimentally. 'Dear little black baby!' And Héloïse smiled, realizing that to Flon, the baby was beautiful because she was Héloïse's. She does not really see her, as I do, she thought. No-one does.

'I have a daughter,' she said softly to herself. Her daughter; James's daughter. She scanned the sleeping face to find some likeness, but she seemed to look only like herself. Yet she was part of them both, the living proof of their love. 'Little love-child,' she murmured. James's skin was truly fair – fair as a lily – but the baby was dark. A Stuart, not a Morland.

'My lady, Monsieur Barnard has sent you up a cordial drink,' Marie said, and knowing that it would offend him if she refused, Héloïse took it, reluctantly yielding the baby to Marie. Marie smiled down at the sleeping face. She does not really see her, either, Héloïse thought. 'To think this little mite will be a countess one day, after you,' Marie said. 'Have you decided on a name yet, my lady?'

'Just this minute,' Héloïse said. 'I shall call her Sophie-Marie. Do you like it?'

'Oh yes, my lady that's very pretty. Have you finished? I'll take the cup, then.'

'Give her back to me,' Héloïse said, but Flon intervened.

'You ought to sleep now, my dear. Let Marie put the baby down. She shall bring the cradle in here, so you can see her if you wake. Such a handsome cradle Stephen has made. I think you should send a word of thanks to him.'

Héloïse submitted again, with an inward sigh. The cradle was handsome, and Stephen would want to know that she had used it, just as Barnard would want to know that she had drunk the cordial, and Flon that she had taken her advice about sleeping. They all wanted to be part of the birth, she understood that, and as they were her people, and she loved them, she must allow them their part. But what she would have liked best of all was to be allowed to be alone with the child: birth seemed to her to be a sweet and private thing between them, and everything else, however kindly meant, was an intrusion.

Chetwyn was not at home when Lucy arrived back at Upper Grosvenor Street. The butler informed her with an impassive face that his lordship had gone to his club but would be back at noon, and Docwra, coming into the hall at the sound of Lucy's voice, hurried her away to her room to change her clothes.

'A rare state you're in, my lady! A regular little Turk you look, and however did you do your buttons this morning? What shall I lay out for you, my lady? Your habit'll have to be properly cleaned before you can wear it again.'

'It doesn't matter,' Lucy said vaguely, stepping out of her habit as Docwra stooped before her. She wandered over to the looking-glass and stared at herself. She had never been a great one for mirrors, but she thought she looked different now. The strong-boned face with the firm chin above the long neck, its set emphasised by the short and curly crop of mouse-fair hair, were tolerably familiar, but suddenly she seemed to herself older, and in a strange way beautiful. The expression of the eyes seemed deeper, as if they were viewing things far distant from the present; the lips seemed redder, their curve softer and more full. Yes, you know about kissing now, don't you? she addressed them silently, and saw them part in a smile.

Docwra moved into view behind her, and Lucy said, 'Put out the blue crêpe, and my silk shawl, will you?' It was a dress which became her, though she had hardly thought about it before. Her eyes met the reflection of her maid's, and Docwra saw the changes too, and grew pale.

'My lady – ' she began tremblingly.

'What happened yesterday?' Lucy forestalled her. 'Did his lordship go to Chelmsford House?'

'Yes, my lady. Captain Wiske came back to say you had got separated in the rain, but would be sheltering somewhere on the other side of the park. His lordship went on, and left word you was to follow later. Oh my lady, where have you been all night?'

'Never mind that,' Lucy said. 'Just get me dressed and do something with my hair, and don't chatter. I'm not in the mood for it.'

Docwra bit her lip, and got on with her task, taking pains with the curl of the hair, thinking she had better look her best to meet her husband. When she had finished, Lucy got up without a word and went downstairs, her face calm and unconcerned, and to Docwra that was the worst of all. One of her brothers had had that same sweet, almost holy look the day he had gone out to burn a rick, and had been shot in

334

the act by the armed guard he had known was there.

Lucy sat in the drawing room and waited, having told the butler to inform his lordship that she wished to see him as soon as he returned. Just after noon she heard the sounds of arrival, and a few moments later Chetwyn came in, closing the door behind him, and stood just inside it looking at her with his most inscrutable expression.

Lucy stood up and they faced each other in silence for a long moment. Then Chetwyn said, mildly interrogative, 'Well, ma'am?'

'You were quite right about the rain,' she said.

'Of course I was. Danby Wiske said you dashed off in the other direction when the downpour started. Doubtless you did the wise thing. The whole party was sadly drenched, with no better cover than trees. I should not wonder if the ladies caught their deaths of cold.'

His voice was one of the mildest social interest, but his eyes were watchful. Yesterday, Lucy would have noticed neither. Today she stepped delicately amongst the thorny words.

'Weston knew that we were not far from one of the further gates, and that there was an inn there where we could shelter,' she said.

'You expected the others to follow, but for some reason they did not,' Chetwyn offered. He is saving me from lying, she thought in surprise. She had not wanted to lie, had hoped only not to have to tell everything.

'The landlady provided a chamber where I could take off my clothes. They were soaked through,' she said. 'By the time they were dry enough to put on, it was too late to ride back before dark, so we thought we had better stay the night.'

Out loud, the words sounded as bad as they could be. Now was the time for him to ask the other questions, the ones she could not lie to, to storm and rage at her as he had every right to. She lifted her chin, standing very straight, like a soldier waiting for the first volley, but Chetwyn turned his head away and walked over to the window, and leaned there with his languid grace looking out into the sunny street.

'I made your excuses to the Chelmsfords,' he said in a

335

perfectly normal voice. 'You were lucky to miss it – it was monstrous dull, and a sad crush, despite so many people being out of Town. I left as early as I decently could.' He turned back to look at her, and with the sun behind him, she could not properly see his expression. 'They are all going into the country tomorrow. I was wondering what your plans are for the summer? Should you like to go to Brighton for a week or two? I shall have to go to Wolvercote in August of course.' She said nothing, and he added, quite kindly, 'Of course, there is no necessity for you to accompany me. You may wish to stay in Town for the summer. Some people say that it is as quiet as the countryside once all the families have gone.'

He doesn't care, Lucy thought in astonishment. He knows everything, and he doesn't care, and he's giving me permission to carry on. But if he was making it easy for her, why did it seem to her such a bitter thing? She was forced to swallow once or twice before she could say in a neutral voice, 'I don't think I want to leave Town at the moment.'

Did Chetwyn sigh? She could not tell, for the sun behind him was making his shape a blackness to her eye. Then he thrust himself upright and walked back across the room to the door. Lucy's eyes followed him, and he turned his head as his hand reached the door-knob and said, 'You look almost pretty this morning. I always liked that dress.'

She felt the blood rush to her cheeks in a mixture of consternation, anger and pain, but she said nothing, standing very straight with her hands lightly clasped before her.

'Yes, there is something different about you this morning, Luce,' Chetwyn said, and he smiled a small and horrible smile, and went away.

BOOK THREE

Falcon Jessed

But though first love's impassioned blindness
Has pass'd away in colder light,
I still have thought of you with kindness,
And shall do, till our last goodnight.
The ever-rolling, silent hours
Will bring a time we shall not know,
When our young days of gathering flowers
Will be an hundred years ago.

Thomas Love Peacock: *Love and Age*

Chapter Twenty

Dinner in the great stern cabin of the *Africa* on the afternoon of the first of August was a dreary affair, and Mrs Haworth found the effort of sustaining conversation almost too much for her. She was feeling the heat and her condition, and all the officers were out of spirits after two months of sailing around the Mediterranean looking for the French. By the very nature of it, any news they might receive was likely to come too late for action, which was a depressing thought.

One by one the topics she set afloat foundered, and eventually she too fell silent. She felt as though she were a cushion which had been stuffed overfull with oakum; and whoever had sewn up her seams had carelessly left their needle inside, for she could feel it sticking her in the back whenever she moved. The only point of triumph for her was that she had managed to stay aboard and with her husband all through her pregnancy, but just then she felt too uncomfortable and weary to savour it.

Dipton came in to remove the cloth, and Haworth made an effort to rouse himself from his thoughts. 'Well, gentlemen,' he began with a forced smile, but the sentence was not be be completed. There was a sound of excited voices from the quarter-deck which instantly froze everyone's attention. Even Dipton stopped in the act of placing the decanter and listened, and a moment later the door to the cabin was opened and young Morpurgo darted in, his eyes as round as bottle-stops, and squeaked, 'Mr. Cossey's compliments, sir, and the flagship's signalling that the enemy's in sight!'

There was commotion in the cabin, through which Morpurgo continued to shrill the rest of the news. 'The whole fleet, sir, at anchor in Aboukir Bay, in line of battle, sir!'

'I'll come,' said Haworth, springing to his feet with a lightness that would have been astonishing five minutes ago.

'So we were right in the beginning! It was Egypt! My dear,' to his wife, 'forgive me. Gentlemen, I'm afraid dinner will have to be curtailed.'

Mary nodded in a rather preoccupied way. She was very glad for them all that the French had been discovered at last, but her internal sensations were rather more immediately interesting to her. The cabin emptied as though by magic, until only Dipton was left, mechanically clearing the table. Mary began to rise, caught her breath sharply, and sat down again. Dipton met her eyes with alarm. She bit her lip and tried to smile.

'I don't know,' she answered his unspoken question. 'It may be nothing. On the other hand – ' On the other hand, it may be very bad timing indeed, she thought wryly.

'I'll call your maid, miss, and tell the Cap'n,' Dipton said.

'No – call Farleigh, by all means, but say nothing to Captain Haworth. This is not the time to be troubling him, and it may yet be nothing. I don't want him to be distracted from more important matters, Dipton.'

'Yes, miss,' he said, and gave her a nod of approval.

Once again all captains were summoned aboard the flagship, and the situation was discussed. The bay was shallow and sandy, its entrance made hazardous by shoals and breakwaters, and one end of it was guarded by an island mounting a battery. The French ships were anchored across the bay in a crescent formation with the massive treasure-ship, the 120-gun *L'Orient* at the centre. They were close in to the shore, so that they had the shallows and sandbanks behind them, and their starboard broadsides facing outward towards the enemy.

Lookouts reported that although the French had obviously seen the English ships, they appeared to be making no preparations for battle. Since the English had no charts of the bay, and it was already late in the day, the French were evidently assuming that they would not be so mad as to attempt a battle which would quickly become a night engagement.

'It would be madness to risk those shoals,' Nelson said thoughtfully, 'and the French do not expect it. Therefore it is exactly what we must do. We must cut through their lines, and attack them on their blind side, from the landward. We will take them completely by surprise.'

'They're anchored close in to the shallow water, sir,' said Berry, the Fleet Captain.

'They must have left themselves room to swing at anchor, and where there's room enough for them to swing, there's room enough for us. The risk is great, but so are the rewards. If we destroy this fleet, including the treasure-ship, we cut off their army, and their dream of taking India. Gentlemen, these are your orders.'

Mary heard the bosuns' call announcing the return of her husband to the ship, and got up from the bunk where she had been lying to sit in a chair and try to look unconcerned when he came in. She knew enough about the situation to know that it meant battle, either immediately or the following morning, and she was determined not to let worry about her distract him from his duty. She was almost sure now that she was going into labour.

He entered the cabin, his face stern with concentration, and told her the situation briskly, with the faintest tremor of excitement in his voice.

'My love, we are going to attack at once, to take them by surprise. We'll cut through their line and attack from the landward side – the admiral thinks they won't have cleared away their portside guns. You must go below now to the orlop. Ask Daniels to put you somewhere safe – and for God's sake, don't go trying to help him, not this time! I wish to God you were safe on shore somewhere, but there's no point in repining now. We must do the best we can.'

Mary forced a smile to her face. It felt like a ghastly grin, but fortunately he was too preoccupied to notice its quality.

'I shall be perfectly all right, my darling,' she said, rising with difficulty and putting her hands to his shoulders. 'I'm glad to be here, and not the least afraid, and you must put me completely out of your thoughts from this moment, and concentrate on winning a famous victory.' She kissed him, and calling to Farleigh, took herself out of his way. By the time she had gathered what she thought she needed, he was on the quarter-deck giving orders, and she was fairly sure he had forgotten her entirely.

341

The ship was in an orderly pandemonium as bulkheads were knocked away and equipment stowed, fire buckets filled and sand strewn on the decks. She and Farleigh picked their way through it all and went below into the stinking blackness of the 'tween decks. Here the hands scurried back and forth in near darkness, and bent almost double, which seemed to trouble them not a whit. On the lower deck, they stepped aside to let the gunner's party go down the companion first, heading for the powder room. The gunner and his mates were followed by the marine sentry, tramping and rattling in his uniform and boots, and by the soft rat-pattering of half a dozen powder boys and three women, all barefoot. The women glanced at Mary with sharp interest as they passed. They must all have heard of her, but it was quite likely that they had never set eyes on her before.

On the orlop they were below the waterline, which was traditionally thought to be the safest place. French gunners tended to aim high – it was their battle tactic to try to cripple a ship by destroying its masts and sails, whereas English gunners were trained to fire into the enemy's hull and sink her. It was for this reason that the sick and wounded were brought to this airless place, and clearing for action here included the grisly preparations of the after-cockpit.

Daniels was supervising the creation of an operating table out of sea-trunks and a table-top when Mary arrived. He looked up and frowned with annoyance. 'For God's sake, ma'am,' he began, but Mary forestalled him with a gesture.

'No, no, I haven't come to help. I've come to take shelter. Can you find a place for me? I think I ought to mention that – that I seem to be in labour.'

Daniel's jaw dropped, more in outrage than surprise. 'Dear God, woman, what a time to choose!' he cried, quite forgetting himself.

'I assure you, I had no choice in the matter,' she said tautly.

'But you realize that once we join battle, I shall have more wounded down here than I can cope with? I won't be able to help you. You'll have to get on with it yourself. It isn't your first, however, is it?'

342

'Madam and I will manage,' Farleigh said, deeply disapproving. 'We only need a safe place for madam to lie down in.'

He ran a distracted hand through his hair, and said, 'Everything's been knocked away, don't you understand? Wait, let me think. You, Wibley, go and rig a canvas for them between the ship's knees to the side of the lamp-room. That'll be out of the way. A hammock's no good to you,' he added, looking at Mary critically. 'It'll have to be a mattress on the deck. Wibley, drag mine out and lay it for them; and find them a lamp.' The loblolly-boy darted off to perform these tasks, and Daniels dismissed them with a wave of a hand. 'I've done my best for you. It will be no place for a woman down here, but then there is no place for a woman on a man o'war.'

Mary had a number of things to think about, all of which were more important than Daniel's rudeness, which in any case she understood and forgave. Just then the idea of a bare mattress on the deck sounded close to Heaven.

The English ships sailed in line-ahead towards the van of the French fleet. The *Culloden* went aground on the shoaling edge of the island, and remained there, a marker for the other ships, but there were no other mishaps. *Goliath* led the way and together with *Zealous* and *Theseus* cut the French line to the stern of the first ship; *Orion*, *Audacious* and the *Africa* passed between the second and third ships. It was about half past six, and the sun was setting.

The admiral had been right about the French ships being unprepared on the landward side. Within a quarter of an hour, the leading English ships had anchored themselves alongside the enemy, and were pounding them without a shot being fired in return, as the French struggled to clear away, load and run out their portside battery in the middle of that hellish bombardment.

The first French ship, *Le Guerrier*, had already been dismasted, and *Goliath* and *Orion* had shifted anchor to attack new ships further down the line, when the rear of the English line, led by the flagship, joined the attack on the

343

starboard side, so that the French were being pounded from both sides. At the end of only two hours, five French ships had surrendered, and within another hour two more had struck, and the great treasure-ship, *L'Orient*, had caught fire.

On the orlop deck of the *Africa*, the noise of the battle was continuous and maddening. The loose thunder of the gun-trucks rumbling over the decks above, the deafening boom of the broadside, the irregular and horrible thuds and crashes of enemy shot striking – all were transmitted through the fabric of the ship's timbers, drowning out the other, more familiar ship noises, the pattering of horny bare feet, the squeal of the jeers, the creak of the yards coming round as course was changed. Nearer to hand there was the confusion of screams and groans and babblings of the wounded, waiting for or enduring the attentions of the surgeon and his mates.

The motion of the ship was strange, at anchor in a shallow bay, reeling and heaving like a netted bull from the recoil of her own broadsides and the irregular strikes of the enemy; but from what Mary could tell she had not been seriously damaged. It was insufferably hot in their tiny screened-off alcove, and the lamp made it hotter still. Farleigh knelt beside her mistress and wiped the trickling sweat from her face, and as the hours extended, it all began to seem unreal, and she felt that she was trapped in an extraordinary nightmare.

Then at ten o'clock there was a massive explosion, the concussion of which stunned their ears, and actually thrust the ship sideways through the water. It was followed by an extraordinary, death-like silence. Even the wounded stopped groaning for a matter of minutes; it was as though a giant, unseen hand had been clapped down over every ship and every mouth.

'Some ship has blown up,' Farleigh whispered at last, as the sound of firing resumed. 'I wonder if it was one of ours or one of theirs?' Mary did not reply. The quality of her pains had changed: the baby was on its way out into the world. She reached for Farleigh's hand to warn her, but for once it was not there. The canvas screen had been drawn back, and a rough-looking woman, her hair escaping from her cap and her sleeves rolled up to the elbow, stood there, holding an iron cup.

'Mr Daniels sent me to see if you was all right, mum,' she said. 'I brought you a drink of water. All the wounded is gettin' one. It's savage hot down here, ain't it, mum? How're you gettin' on then? Any sign o' the babby?'

'What was that explosion?' Farleigh asked her, too glad to see another human being to rebuke her for her boldness.

'That big Frenchy, what's been on fire this hour, the treasure ship – blew up, miss,' she said with relish. 'Gor, that didn't half blow! You should 'a seen what come down on deck – my friend Tilda, what's carrying powder, says it was rainin' knives an' forks an' silver cups, an' all sorts! Stolen out o' Malta off o' them Knights, so Mr Daniels says. Well, that's all gorn to the bottom o' the bay now, Miss. That'll larn that Froggy general – he won't be conquerin' no Egypt now! We're givin' 'em a hell of a lickin', miss. Here, shall I give your missus this water?'

She made to come forward, but the smell of her preceded her into the confined space, and Farleigh said sharply, 'Stop there! There's no room for you in here. Give the water to me.'

A hand as black and shiny as anthracite with ancient dirt came forward into the lamplight, holding the cup, and then the woman said in a different voice, 'Here, miss, if I ain't far wrong, that babby's prac'ly come. You ain't been doing your job, miss, an' that's a fact. I'll give a hand, shall I?'

Mary groaned, and Farleigh in her agitation thrust at the woman with an outstretched hand. 'Go away! And drop that curtain! Do you want everyone to see? Go away, I say.'

The woman sniffed offendedly, but obeyed, and Farleigh bent over her mistress in readiness.

'It was the explosion did it,' Mary said faintly. 'Frighte- ned it out of me.' And in a very few minutes, the baby had emerged, and amongst the terrible noises of the battle sounded a new and hopeful one, the lusty yelling of a healthy baby.

'It's a girl, madam,' Farleigh said, sounding more relieved than pleased. The curtain was twitched again, and the surgeon stood there, attracted by the baby's cries, and sparing one minute from his duties.

'Everything all right, here?' he said. His eyes took in the situation, and all in one movement he squatted and reached for the child, tied the ligature, and severed the birth-cord. He looked the baby over, and examined Mary briefly. 'All in order,' he said. 'I dare say you can manage now, can't you?' He stood up. 'Congratulations,' he said tersely, and was gone.

The battle went on until three in the morning. When finally the signal to discontinue was hoisted, the English ships drew off, took the land breeze out of the bay just far enough to get clear water, and hove to. The exhausted men dropped where they stood, falling instantly asleep, their heads pillowed on their hands, on each other, even on the iron ring-bolts in the deck.

When dawn broke the results of the battle could be properly assessed. Of the French fleet, two of the line and two frigates had run for it and escaped. One ship had sunk and one had run aground, nine had been captured, and of *L'Orient* nothing remained but a few pieces of charred driftwood. Of the nine ships taken, three were so hopelessly battered that, along with the grounded ship, they would have to be burnt, but the others would be sold as prizes, to the comfort and profit of everyone in Nelson's squadron.

All the English ships were damaged, but none seriously except the *Majestic*, and the poor old *Billy Ruffian*, which, after a hopelessly mismatched engagement with *L'Orient*, was drifting out to sea hardly more than a dismasted hulk. But no English ship had been lost, and casualties, for such a battle, were light. On the *Africa* there were eighteen dead and fifty-one wounded.

'And,' said Daniels, concluding his report to the captain, who was still on the quarter-deck, directing repairs and collating reports from his officers, 'there is one new soul on board, sir.'

Haworth stared at him for a moment, so dazed with weariness that he had difficulty in understanding. Then the

346

light dawned. 'Good God! My wife – you mean – ?'

'Your good lady, sir, has presented you with a daughter, born just after the treasure-ship blew up. I've made her as comfortable as I can on the orlop, but as soon as your cabin's put to rights, I'll have her moved up there, if you agree, sir. The wounded are rather noisy.'

'Yes – yes of course. A daughter you say? Good heavens! I don't know what to say. They are well, both well? I didn't even know – '

Daniels grinned. 'Mrs Haworth is a brave woman, if you'll forgive me, sir. She was in labour before the battle began, but didn't want you to know. Congratulations, sir.'

There was no opportunity for Haworth to go below and see Mary – there was far too much to be done, from the securing of the guns to the laying out of the dead, from the telling off of prize crews to the ordering of the hands' dinner. Haworth, pale with fatigue, did not leave the quarter-deck all morning. He was dealing with the carpenter's request for a party to help plug the numerous shot-holes when Dipton came across the deck to him, bearing a tray of hot coffee and ship's bread.

'Seeing as you haven't got time to set down, sir,' Dipton said smoothly, 'I thought I'd bring you a bit o' something out here. I took some breakfast down to Mrs Haworth, sir, but she didn't want nothing to eat, sir, only some coffee. I dessay she'll take something later, when we gets her up to the cabin.'

'You've seen the baby?' Haworth said between thirsty gulps. Dipton grinned.

'That I have, sir. A right little beauty, sir, excuse me. Congratulations, sir.'

'Thank you, Dipton. You'll look after them for me, until I have a moment? And tell Mrs Haworth – give her my fondest regards.'

'Aye aye, sir,' Dipton said, and then added, 'That makes two, sir.'

'Two what?'

'Two babbies born during the battle, sir. T'other was on the *Goliath*. That was right after the explosion, too, sir. Scotch woman, from Edinburgh. One of the hands' wives.'

'How the *devil* can you know that?' Haworth asked in astonishment. The way news got around a fleet was utterly mysterious.

'Common knowledge, sir,' Dipton said, and went away.

At eleven o'clock all hands were called, and by that time the *Africa* was almost back to normal, apart from her patched sides and sails, and the row of corpses sewn into their hammocks along main deck under the bulwarks. Haworth had no chaplain on board, and so he read the service for the burial of the dead himself, and one by one they were tipped over the side from under the flag into the sunlit water.

Then he spoke a few words to the men about the victory, which had been glorious and complete. 'I don't doubt that anyone who fought at the battle of Aboukir Bay will be a hero back home,' he said. 'England will be proud of you, my lads. I know I am.'

'Three cheers for the Cap'n!' someone shouted, and they were roared out heartily. Haworth made no attempt to stop them. They were cheering as much for themselves as for him, he thought, for their victory, for the prize-money they would receive, for danger met and survived. There was cheering from every ship in the fleet. Around him, his officers grinned at each other, even the dear old Anchovy, his long face topped off with a vast white bandage wound around his brow. Down in the waist, little Morpurgo, standing with his division, threw his hat in the air in sheer high spirits.

When the noise had died down a little, Haworth held up his hand for silence. 'You will probably all have heard by now, that in the heat of the battle, my dear wife presented me with a baby daughter. I'm glad to tell you that Mr Daniels reports they are both doing well.' Another cheer. 'I want you all to know that in honour of the courage and discipline you displayed in the battle, I intend to name my daughter after this ship. So when you drink your noon grog, my lads, pray drink a toast to the health of Miss Africa Haworth!'

The cheering this time went on for fully five minutes,

348

sailors, for all their toughness, being the most sentimental creatures alive.

The news of the victory was received with enormous excitement in England, where the army had for a long time failed to produce anything to rejoice over. It was soon renamed The Battle of the Nile – few Englishmen had heard of Aboukir Bay, and to them Egypt and the Nile were more or less synonymous. The names of all the Nile captains became as familiar as those of Robin Hood and his men: they were the popular heroes of the hour.

Admiral Nelson sent his report back to England with Fleet Captain Berry in the *Leander*, but on the journey home it was captured by one of the two French ships which had escaped from Aboukir Bay. Berry and the *Leander*'s captain, Thompson, finally arrived back expecting to be court-martialled for the loss of their ship, but they discovered that nothing was too good for heroes of the Nile: they both received knighthoods instead.

Nelson had received a peerage from King George, and a dukedom from the grateful King of the Two Sicilies.

'And Captain Haworth has received a baby daughter,' Lucy said to Weston, for it was as popular a piece of news as anything that had happened in the battle. 'I wonder which of them values his reward more?'

They were lying on the bed of a room in an inn in Finchley, eating cherries. Weston had driven them out of Town in a hired curricle, to get away from the heat, and they had taken a bedchamber and private parlour under the name of Mr and Mrs Illingworth. They took reasonable precautions to avoid gossip, never staying at the same inn twice, nor choosing one where they were likely to be recognized. With London in its state of August emptiness, they had as yet escaped detection. There was no-one but the Aylesbury servants to wonder about Weston's frequent and prolonged visits to Upper Grosvenor Street, or Lucy's heavily-veiled visits to Weston's lodgings in Brook Street.

'Is it really such an important victory, though?' Lucy asked idly. They were both naked in the heat, and propped on one elbow, she had been laying out her cherry stones in a pattern across Weston's smooth white chest with the minute attention of a child.

'I think so,' he said. With his hands folded under his head he could squint down the length of his body and watch what she was doing. 'It puts a stop to the French plan to take India, and gives us virtual control of the Mediterranean. And it demonstrates that even a land campaign is not safe from the long arm of the navy. I think it may be the turning-point of the war. It may even encourage other nations to join us against the French.'

'If the war ends, we will have peace, and what will poor Weston do then, poor thing?' Lucy asked, eating another cherry and attempting to balance the stone on one of his nipples.

'Ah yes, what?' he said. 'Peace could be devastating to a friendless young officer like me. A lieutenant's half pay is not enough to live on.'

'Not in the style you like to enjoy,' Lucy said. 'But I'd hardly call you friendless. Admiral Scorton says that Lord St Vincent thinks the world of you.'

'If the war ends, I think I might try politics,' he mused. 'It seems to me a Member of Parliament leads a very pleasant life. Or the law – even more money, for even less work.'

'It's impossible to imagine peace. We've been at war so long now, it's just the way the world is.'

He raised himself on one elbow, scattering stones. 'It's the way you are!' he said. 'You are so very childlike, my love. Whatever is happening around you at the moment, you think of as a permanency. I warrant you can't remember a time before you knew me.'

'No,' she said, frowning in thought, 'I can't. How did you know?'

'I love you. I know everything about you,' he laughed, and rolled her over to kiss her.

'Ouch! Cherry stones!' she exclaimed through his kisses.

'Your own fault,' he said, pressing her back into the pillows. There was a long and satisfactory silence, after which, holding him in her arms, she said, '*Do* you love me?'

'Of course. You know I do.'

350

She sighed. 'I was married so young. I never really knew – ' She broke off thoughtfully, and then resumed, 'But perhaps if you and I had been married we should not have felt like this about each other.'

Weston smiled. 'I think you may just have discovered the secret of life. Listen, my love, would you like to get away from London for a while? I want to have a few weeks with you without interruption.'

'Can we manage it?' Lucy asked.

'Your husband will be away from London until October, won't he? I know of a cottage we could rent in a little village in Kent. Very remote – rather primitive, perhaps, but adequate for a few weeks of rural bliss. We could take your maid, if you think she can be trusted, and my man. All we have to do is to go.'

Lucy was silent for a long time, and eventually Weston freed himself from her arms to sit up and look at her.

'My love? Does the idea not appeal to you?'

'Well, why not?' she said at last, as if in conclusion to an argument. 'Yes, I think it would be delightful. But I must have Mimosa, if we are going for a long time, and Parslow to look after her. We can hire a horse for you. Parslow's devoted to me, and Docwra scolds a great deal, but she'll do anything I tell her.'

'We'll do it, then,' he said, stroking her hair lovingly. 'I shall have you all to myself at last.'

'You have me pretty much to yourself now,' she pointed out practically, and then added with a small frown, 'He doesn't care, you know. Chetwyn – he doesn't care.'

'I wouldn't go so far as to say that,' said Weston, lying down again.

After the battle, Nelson's squadron was divided, some sent to Gibraltar, some to Naples with the *Vanguard*, and three ships of the line, including the *Africa*, remaining to guard the Egyptian coast, to prevent the stranded French army from receiving supplies or reinforcements.

It was a pleasant assignment – fine weather, calm seas, fresh water and food from the shore, and no immediate

351

prospect of danger, with all the French fleets bottled up in harbours by the English blockade. The three captains had nothing worse to worry about than how to keep their crews from growing bored.

After the strain and worry of the last few months, Haworth was delighted to have the leisure to sit with his wife as she lay propped up in bed in the sleeping-cabin. The clean, mild air poured in through the open windows, the sunlight glinted off the wake, and there was the soothing sound of the water chuckling under the keel. Haworth sat with Mary's hand in his and made endless plans for Africa's future.

'I think you might have asked me before you named the poor child after your ship,' Mary teased him gently.

'Oh dear! I'm sorry, my love. I suppose I got rather carried away by rhetoric. But don't you think it a pretty name?'

'Oh, certainly, and very romantic, too. She is bound, with a name like that, to have adventures, just like one of Mrs Radcliffe's heroines. But suppose, my dearest, that she grows up fat and plain and dull?'

Haworth looked indignant. 'How can you suppose such a thing! Africa, tell your Mama what you think of that idea.' He leaned over the crib which the ship's carpenter had made, and which was drawn up close to the bed so that the doting parents could gaze at the child. Africa, apparently watching the dancing of the sunbeams on the deck planks above her, blew a few bubbles and waved her fists at the sound of her father's voice. 'I think she looks like you, darling,' Haworth said critically.

'But she has your eyes,' Mary said. 'And there's something of you about her mouth, too. I think she will be intelligent.'

'And handsome. She must have the right sort of governess, who will inform her mind, but also teach her the accomplishments and the social graces. I want her to be able to take her place in society – '

'As I did?' Mary said with amusement. 'Balls and dinners and operas and presentation at Court?'

'Of course,' he said firmly. 'And eventually a good marriage – '

'Like mine, to the best man in the world, whom she will love and admire,' Mary concluded.

'Oh no, she shan't marry a dull old sea-dog – it must be an earl at the very least for her.'

'Now I understand – you wish I had married Billy Tonbridge instead of you. Forgive me, Captain Haworth, I had not realized I was mistaken all this while.'

Haworth smiled at her lovingly. 'You know, Mary, though I should not admit it, I am so very glad you stayed with me all this summer. When you were having Hippolyta, I saw nothing of you, and I've seen very little of her. It is a great privilege and joy to me to have little Africa here, to see her every day. Sailors can so rarely spend time with their wives and children. It was shocking of me to allow you to risk yourself like this – '

Mary lifted his hand to her cheek. 'Allow me? I don't quite see how you could have prevented me.'

Haworth frowned. 'Why, darling, your cheek is burning.' He released his hand and felt her brow. 'Your forehead, too. Are you feverish?'

'It's nothing but the heat of the day, that's all,' Mary said. 'With the sunlight coming in through the stern-lights, it is hot in here. I feel perfectly all right.'

Haworth did not consider it particularly hot in the cabin, for there was a fresh breeze ruffling the yellow curtains. 'I think Daniels had better have a look at you, just in case,' he said.

'Oh no, darling, please don't fuss – ' Mary began, but the door opened at that moment, and Farleigh came in.

'I've brought you some lemonade, madam,' she said. Haworth got up to let the maid past, and having seen how thirstily Mary drank, he went quietly to the door.

'Pass the word for Mr Daniels,' he said to the sentry outside. When he returned to the bed, Farleigh was taking the empty glass away, and she met his eyes for a moment as she passed him with a frown, and a nod of approval.

The following morning Mary was definitely feverish, though she did not otherwise feel ill. Daniels shook his head. 'It may be nothing but overheating, sir.' He met Haworth's eye reluctantly. 'The other possibility – it has to be admitted – '

Haworth's mouth was dry. 'Childbed fever?'

'It's too early to say, yet, sir, Mrs Haworth gave birth in less than ideal circumstances, and there is a possibility that there is some infection. We must simply wait and see.'

'But – if it is – ?'

'There's no sense in worrying about it, sir, until we see how things develop.'

Haworth had a rare outburst of temper. 'I asked you a question, damn it!'

Daniels straightened to attention. 'Childbed fever is caused by an infection entering the body at the time of birth, sir,' he said rigidly. 'Sometimes a strong woman can fight it off, but it is more usually fatal.'

There was a silence. Haworth's face was white under his sea-tan. After a while he managed to say, 'Thank you, Mr Daniels. You may go now. Keep me informed of progress.'

He sat with Mary for most of the day, leaving her only when the ship's business required him on deck, but with calm seas and gentle breezes the interruptions were few. She was so cheerful, and seemed so well apart from the fever, that he grew cheerful too. It was nothing but overheating after all, he thought, and he had been worried for nothing.

But towards evening the fever mounted, and Mary began to feel ill. Her throat was dry, the glands in her neck swollen, and she felt as though her bones were hurting her. Daniels examined her again, palpated her abdomen, and looked grave. After a bad night, he came to report to his captain in the day-cabin.

'I'm sorry, sir, but I think there is little doubt that it is puerperal fever. The symptoms are there.' He looked at Haworth with enormous pity. The captain was seated at his desk, his eyes ringed with sleeplessness, his hands turning a paperknife with slow restlessness over and over.

'What happens now?' he asked at last.

'There is no treatment, sir. The patient's own constitution governs the course of the disease. Usually the fever comes and goes, and the patient grows weaker, until – '

'Will she live?' he asked abruptly, almost as if he hadn't

heard. Daniels hesitated a long time, wondering what to say. 'The truth, Mr Daniels,' Haworth said, meeting his eyes. 'That's an order.'

'Truly, sir, I don't know. Some women do recover. But it's – unlikely. I'm sorry, sir.'

'No, no need to be sorry. It is my own fault, for bringing her with me. Isn't that right? No, you don't need to answer. I know. If she had had the child at home, this would not have happened.'

'It happens on shore just the same, sir, even in the best houses. There's no knowing where it will strike.'

'Thank you,' he said, with a faint wry smile. 'Does she know?'

'I haven't said anything to her, sir.'

'Very well. I will tell her myself. Thank you, Daniels. You may go now.'

Haworth took a moment to compose himself, and then went back into the sleeping cabin. Farleigh had been bathing Mary's face, and withdrew to leave them alone, and he sat down beside the bed and took up the hot hand from the sheet where it was lying.

'How are you feeling now, my love?' he asked.

'A little better, I think,' Mary said. They were silent for a while. 'I was just thinking,' she went on, 'about flowers, and how much I miss them on board. The only thing I really miss, I think. One can get used to all the other privations.' Haworth nodded. 'Dipton told me once about a captain who grew daffodils in a long box of earth under the stern windows. It seemed such a good idea.'

'There's no reason why we shouldn't do the same,' Haworth said. 'If we put them in now, we could have hyacinths for Christmas, and next spring – ' Something odd seemed to have happened to his voice. He tried to clear his throat, and Mary met his eyes.

'What did Daniels say? It's childbed fever, isn't it?'

Haworth could only nod. Mary seemed to be strangely blurred. He turned his head away for a moment to look at Africa, sleeping beside them. Mary went on speaking.

'Don't be afraid, dearest. I'll get well again. I'm very strong, you know. People do get well, don't they?'

He looked at her, and as their eyes met, a great sob broke out of him. 'Oh my darling!' He slid clumsily from the chair to kneel beside her, and she put her arms round him and held him close. 'Oh Mary, my own love. I love you so much. I couldn't bear to lose you.'

'No, no,' she comforted him, stroking his head, tears of weakness breaking past the barriers. 'You won't lose me. I'm not going to die. I couldn't bear to leave you either. I'll get well, I promise. It will be all right.'

Africa woke and began to cry, but for once neither parent noticed Farleigh put her head round the door a moment later, assess the situation, and tiptoe past her master and mistress to scoop the baby out of the crib and take her away.

The *Africa* and her sister ships beat up and down the coast of Egypt in the August sunshine, and almost a holiday mood prevailed. The officers strolled on deck, leaned against the taffrail, smoked cigars and chatted; the hands skylarked on the forecastle, danced hornpipes after dinner, entered into complex negotiations over their grog-rations, and pursued their extraordinary hobbies of embroidery, painting, carving, scrimshaw work, knitting, crochet. The scrimshaw school was making a series of delicate little carved figures,which, when finished, they intended to thread together on a string to stretch across the baby's crib for her to look at and play with. The whole crew was intensely proud of 'our baby', and daily bulletins on her health and progress were demanded of the surgeon's mates.

The news that the Captain's lady was ailing could not be kept secret in a crowded ship, but all but a few believed it to be a mild indisposition, for with fine weather, fresh water, and no danger, it was hard for the men to believe that anything in the world could be wrong. In the stern cabin Haworth sat with Mary hour after hour, and they talked cheerfully together as they had always done, remembering past happinesses and planning future ones, and never spoke of her illness; but day by day he saw her grow weaker, and hope quietly died in his heart.

The day came when he found that he was doing all the talking, and Mary, her fever-bright eyes fixed on him unwaveringly, could only lie there panting shallowly, listening, but too weak to talk. His line of conversation petered out, and silence fell between them. What more was there to say, but the unsayable? It was no use to pretend any more. They read the truth in each other's eyes.

Haworth lifted her hand to his lips and kissed it, and she smiled faintly.

'Dearest George, I've been so happy with you,' she said at last in a whisper of a voice. 'It's only been too short a time.'

'Oh Mary, my heart, how can I go on without you?' he asked.

'You must, for the children.'

'I don't care about the children – it's you I want.'

'But you will, when I'm gone.' He was crying, and it tore her heart. 'I don't want to leave you,' she said weakly. 'I don't want to die.' He leaned down to kiss her and lay his cheek against hers, and his tears wet her face. There was no comfort either could offer the other.

'I love you, Mary. I love you so much.'

'I love you too.' They were silent a long while; then, 'I always knew – '

'Knew what, my darling?'

He felt her lips smiling as she whispered against his cheek. 'All those earls and dukes I refused. I always knew I'd find you one day.'

Chapter Twenty-one

Mary died on the fifteenth of August. Throughout the day she had drifted deeper and deeper into unconsciousness, and the end came quietly at sunset when the tide turned. 'She died like a sailor,' Dipton told his friend the cook as they hunched mournfully over their rum.

The whole ship's company was shocked and grieved, and many of the men cried like children at the service held the next morning. There was no question of a burial at sea – even had the Captain wished it, the men would hardly have permitted it. The body was sealed in a lead-lined coffin to await the first transport back to England. It was assumed that Farleigh and the baby would return in the same ship, but a few days later, Haworth sought out Mary's maid in the sleeping-cabin, where she was rocking the child, more for her own comfort than Africa's.

Since Mary had become too ill to breast-feed, the problem had arisen of how to feed the baby where there was no possibility of acquiring a wet-nurse. Fortunately goats were plentiful on that coast, and the watering parties that went ashore were able to obtain a supply of goat's milk until they could locate and purchase a ewe in milk to bring aboard. After one or two digestive troubles, Africa had now settled down comfortably with her ovine foster-mother.

Farleigh looked up as Haworth came in. They had liked and understood each other from the beginning, united in a love of Mary, and though she had not approved of Mary's going to sea, she had to admit that her mistress had been happy, and that it would have been hard to dissuade her, even had Haworth wanted to.

'A ship's been sighted,' he told her now. 'It's the frigate *Lively*, bound for England with despatches and taking us in on her way. She should be with us in two hours.'

'Then I had better pack,' Farleigh said, putting the baby back in her crib and getting to her feet.

'Yes,' said Haworth hesitantly. 'Farleigh – '

'Sir?' she paused.

'I wonder, would you consider staying?'

'Staying? What ever can you mean, sir? Who's to take Miss Africa home if not me?'

'I mean, would you stay and look after her?' She did not look so surprised as he had thought she would. 'I want to keep her with me, you see,' he went on. 'Do you think me foolish? But I have lost Mary, and Africa is part of her, all that's left to me. I have such joy in her, Farleigh, and if she goes back to England, who knows when I will see her again? She will grow up like Hippolyta, not knowing me, and when I see her again, I will be nothing more than a stranger to her.'

'But sir, it's impossible,' Farleigh said, without conviction. 'A baby on a war ship? It isn't likely.'

'Not impossible,' he said, smiling a little. 'Here she is, you see!'

'But the hazards, sir!'

'All life is hazardous, even on shore. At least here we are free from infectious diseases. Mary always said it was a healthy life. And the men all adore her – it puts such heart into them! She *belongs* here, Farleigh.'

'Well, sir, if you want to keep her, I can't stop you,' Farleigh said doubtfully.

'You can – by refusing to stay yourself. She needs a woman to take care of her, and it ought to be you. You were like a second mother to Mary. Won't you do the same for Mary's daughter?'

'Oh sir!' Farleigh's eyes filled with tears.

'Please, Farleigh.' He pressed home his advantage.

'Well, sir, if you wish it, I'll stay, just for a little while, and see how it goes. Lord knows, it's not for me to deprive you of your own child.'

'I knew you would! Bless you, Farleigh!' He clasped her hand.

'Just for the time being, sir. And if there's any trouble, home we both go, the very first thing.'

*

When the three weeks of rural bliss were over, and Weston had to report back to the Admiralty for duty, Lucy parted from him reluctantly but calmly, and went back to Upper Grosvenor Street. The sight of the chariot being led away from the front door towards the mews warned her that her husband had just arrived back from Brighton, and she felt a faint qualm, which she quickly shut out from her mind. Lucy in love could not be less straightforward than Lucy in any other situation. She wanted to be with Weston, and if she had no apprehension of trouble to come it was not because she deluded herself that there would be none. She simply refused to waste the time of happiness by thinking about it.

Docwra hurried nervously past her and up the stairs and a footman went out to fetch in her trunk, while Lucy stood calmly in the hall stripping off her gloves and asked the butler where her husband was.

'He has gone into the business-room, my lady, to open the letters. He has asked for refreshments to be brought to him there. Can I get your ladyship anything?'

'No, nothing. I shall go and speak to his lordship.'

Chetwyn was seated behind his desk, a pile of letters before him, an opened one in his hand. He looked up as she appeared and said expressionlessly, 'You have been away for some time, to judge by the number of unopened letters.'

'Did Hicks not tell you so?' Lucy said.

'I didn't ask him,' Chetwyn said, looking down at the letter again. 'I have no wish to share the secrets of the household with the servants. Where have you been?'

'Staying in the country. In Westerham.'

'Do we know anyone in Westerham?' he asked without looking up.

'No,' she said, and waited for him to ask with whom she had been staying, but he said nothing. Then at last he sighed and held out the letter he was holding.

'This has come from Portsmouth. From Captain Haworth on the *Africa*, somewhere off the coast of Egypt. It seems you have a new niece, and your sister is dead.'

Lucy heard the news with distant shock. 'Mary, dead?'

'Of the childbed fever,' Chetwyn said. He continued to

hold out the letter, but Lucy made no move to take it, and eventually he laid it on the desk before him. 'He has sent her body back for burial. It lies at Portsmouth, awaiting arrangements for its transportation to Morland Place. He wanted her to be buried at home. God knows,' a sudden break into emotion, 'what he must be feeling! He must blame himself bitterly. Any man would.'

'Yes,' Lucy said. Her voice sounded numb. Chetwyn looked down at the letter again.

'The most extraordinary thing, he is keeping the baby with him on the ship, and Mary's maid has agreed to stay and look after it.' Still Lucy did not speak, and he went on, 'I shall have my agent make the arrangements for carrying the body back to Yorkshire, but you had better come down to Wolvercote tomorrow with me and break the news to Hippolyta.'

She started, as though out of a reverie. 'What? Go to Wolvercote? No, no, I can't.'

'She will be very upset. She's four years old, Lucy, old enough to understand.'

'I can't leave London at the moment,' Lucy said. 'You go. You would do it better than me, anyway. I'm not good with children.'

He stared at her for a moment, his eyes hard and bright, and then the veil came down over them again. 'As you please,' he said indifferently. 'I shall go down tomorrow, and stay for about a month. Various friends will be coming and going. Join us if you wish.'

'Yes – perhaps. Later, perhaps,' she said, and went quickly away.

When Chetwyn brought the children to Morland Place for Christmas, he arrived without Lucy. It was hard weather, bright and bitter, and though it was past noon when the two coaches pulled into the yard, the roof-tiles were still rimed with last night's frost, and the steam rose from the horses like smoke into the brilliant air.

'Too cold for snow!' Edward called cheerfully, coming forward from the door to meet his friend. 'The hunting's

361

been shockingly poor – ' He stopped abruptly and cocked a brow at Chetwyn. 'No Lucy?' He glanced at the second coach, as if she might have travelled with the children, but it was little Polly, all in black, who was descending, followed by Flaminia, coming down backwards but by herself, and the nurses carrying Rosamund.

Edward gave his friend a hard embrace, and felt, with the sympathy of long-established love, how thin and brittle he was. He released him and searched his face for the trouble.

'No Lucy,' was all Chetwyn replied.

'Is she coming later?' Edward asked, having waited in vain for more.

'No, she won't be coming,' Chetwyn said, and stopped while Edward greeted his nieces and sent them running indoors. They watched them go, and then Chetwyn turned to face Edward again and said, 'She's going to Belvoir Castle, the Duke of Rutland's place. She'll be there for three or four weeks.'

'But didn't they invite you?' Edward asked, shocked.

'Oh yes, they asked me, but I didn't care to go.' He heard the hardness in his voice, and tried to cover it up. 'It's the Prince of Wales, you see – he's got up a party to celebrate Rutland's twenty-first. Rutland's brothers are officers in the 10th Dragoons, and its all that set who are going. Lucy's friends – Wiske, Brummel and so on. And others.'

Edward looked puzzled, but trusting. 'Oh well, if Danby Wiske is there, he'll look after her. I suppose she'll have taken Mimosa? If the weather's anything like it is here, they'll have poor sport, however. Well, come in, my dear fellow, and get warm. I've been making punch all morning, and I think I've got it just right.'

Edward put his arm round Chetwyn's shoulders and led him into the house, which was warm and smelled pleasantly of spiced wine and log fires and evergreens and mincemeat pies. Leaky and Brach came mincing up to him to bow and yawn and nudge him in affectionate greeting; Fanny and Puppy were driving each other almost to hysteria with their excitement at the arrivals; and Mary Ann and James alternately tried to restrain her and welcome him.

'She spends so much time alone,' Mary Ann said apologetically. 'I mean, without companions of her own age. I'm so glad you brought the children. Poor Little Polly – it is so sad to see her all in black, poor child. Take them upstairs, nurse. Is Lucy not with you, then? I suppose she will be coming later. Ottershaw, Lord Aylesbury's great-coat! The new butler, Ottershaw, you know. There have been a few changes since you were last here.'

'Yes,' said Chetwyn. 'So I see.'

'You haven't seen the half of it yet,' James said with his lazy smile. 'But come in and have a glass of punch. Now you are here, the festivities can really begin.' He ushered Chetwyn before him into the drawing-room, and murmured into his ear, 'Lucy still off the leash, then? Ned don't know the story, by the by. He reads nothing but agricultural news!'

There was another new face: standing by the fireside with his hands behind his back stood a tall young man, with an aesthetic and extremely handsome face, and his fair hair cut in a fashionable crop. Mary Ann hastened to make the introduction, with an unexpected smile and a note of pride and pleasure in her voice. 'I'd like to make Father Aislaby known to you, the new chaplain. Father Thomas felt it was time for him to retire. The duties were getting rather too much for him. Father Aislaby, the Earl of Aylesbury.'

Chetwyn nodded a greeting, and glanced at Edward ruefully. 'Break it to me gently — who else is gone?'

'Oh, it's like a change of regime, you know,' James answered for him, lightly. 'When there is a new monarch, all the principal ministers have to go: cook, butler, chaplain, and housekeeper, in this case.'

'Mrs Mappin too?' Chetwyn asked.

'She didn't want to stay on after Oxhey went,' Edward said. 'They'd been together for so long, you see. We have a Mrs Scaggs now. I must say, she seems very efficient.'

Chetwyn looked from face to face, to assess the situation. Mary Ann was proud but anxious: all this was her idea, and she wanted approval for the efficient way she had taken over the running of the house, but wasn't sure she was going to get it. Edward cared not one way or the other. The house had always been run without his help, and though he might be sorry to see old faces go, it made no more difference than that to him. And James was enjoying everyone's reactions with the faint amusement of an outsider.

They drank punch, and chatted, and exchanged news, and then Ottershaw interrupted them to tell Edward that one of the tenants had arrived asking to see him. Edward excused himself apologetically, and James took the opportunity to say to Chetwyn, 'Come and see how my latest project is getting on. My dear,' to Mary Ann, 'you'll excuse us for a few moments, won't you?'

'I was just about to ask you to excuse me,' Mary Ann said, getting to her feet. 'I have to discuss the arrangements for the Christmas services with Father Aislaby.'

'I'll shew Chetwyn his room while we're up there,' James said. 'Come along, old fellow.'

Upstairs, Chetwyn said, 'I suppose I am in my old room, in the bachelor's wing?'

'Certainly, unless you want to sleep in state. So Lucy would not come? You are being very lenient with her, Chetwyn. I hear nothing but praise for you in the club.'

'My affairs are the common gossip then, even as far north as this?' Chetwyn said bitterly.

'York ain't so far off the track, old fellow. But everyone thinks you're doing the right thing. "Chetwyn's letting her go her length", they say. With a headstrong mare like Lucy, to do anything else would be making yourself ridiculous. Even Mother couldn't govern her, you know.'

'How much is known?' Chetwyn asked quietly.

'She's seen everywhere with young Weston,' James said seriously. 'Balls, routs, ridottos. The latest *on-dit* is that they went unaccompanied three times to Astley's Amphitheatre, to see the female equestrienne.'

'Yes, that's true. Lucy was fascinated. I think she thought she had missed her career. They went to a masquerade at Putney, too. They do their best to be discreet, but as well try to carry on a love-affair in a cage at the Royal Exchange.' He looked at James awkwardly. 'It is love, you see. That's what makes it so shocking. One might laugh off a mere flirt. You say Ned doesn't know?'

'Not a thing. Nor Mary Ann, as far as I know. They don't go out much in the world.'

'Well, that's something to be thankful for.'

'Wales has invited Weston in his party to Belvoir, I take it?'

'Yes. There are one or two other Admiralty staff going – Admiral Scorton, Captain Montgomery and some others – so that it won't look too obvious – except to those that know.'

James touched Chetwyn's arm gently. 'Don't take it too hard,' he said. 'After all, it wasn't a love-match, was it? And Lucy's scandals don't last long. It will all be forgotten about five minutes after it ends.'

Chetwyn gave no sign of having heard him. They were passing the Red Room, whose door was open to shew the bed denuded of hangings, and the larger pieces of furniture covered in hollands. 'Our first Christmas without her. It's hard to believe she's gone,' he said abruptly. 'I still can't stop feeling that she will come out of a room or round a corner at any moment. As if she's somewhere near, but out of sight.'

'Perhaps she is,' James said. 'Morland Place without Mother doesn't make sense, does it? And I doubt whether she's able to feel easy about it, as things are.'

'All the changes?' Chetwyn said. 'Couldn't you have stopped them?'

James gave him his most cynical smile. 'I? What has Morland Place to do with me? Ned holds it in trust for Fanny, and Mary Ann is the lady of the house. Neither you nor I have command of our situations.' He looked around him rather bleakly. 'The ranks are thinning, Chetwyn: now Mary's gone, and Lucy's running away as hard as she can. Without Mother to care what we do, what is there to keep us together?' He paused and then answered himself. 'Only the children, I suppose. You should try taking an interest in yours, you know. Fanny gives me something to hope for. Come and see what I'm making for her.'

He led Chetwyn to his own room in the bachelor's wing, and opened the door onto a smell of wood-shavings, and a muddle of carpenter's tools and paint-pots. An old table had been set up as a work-bench, and on it, almost completed, stood a wooden baby-house.

'What do you think?' James said proudly.

'It's magnificent,' Chetwyn said, shaken out of his gloom for a moment. 'I had no idea you were so good with your hands, Jamie. Did you really make it all yourself?'

'Every inch. Fanny saw a baby-house in a shop in York when Mary Ann took her shopping one day, and she's been wanting one ever since. But I wanted her to have a better one than any other child in the land, so I started to make this. Besides, I like working with wood – it's soothing. Do you recognize it? It's a replica of Shawes, perfect in every detail – or it will be when it's finished. Look?' He opened the front of the house, which was hinged like a door. 'I've even reproduced the *trompe l'oeil* paintings I did in the great hall of the real Shawes.'

'It's exceedingly handsome,' Chetwyn conceded, 'Only rather bare, don't you think?'

James laughed. 'True! I haven't got around to making any furniture yet. Fan will have to be patient for that – or rather, she'll have to wait, for a more impatient child I never met. It will be a fine project to keep me busy for the next few years. After all, one must have something to do.'

Chetwyn looked at him with some sympathy. 'That other business – is it all over, Jamie?'

'Yes, all over,' James said quietly. 'One can struggle against the current only so long. I shall be a respectable country squire from now on, a polite husband and dutiful father, help old Ned with the horses, take my mutton at the club once a week to keep up with the news, and watch Fanny grow up and take over her inheritance. When she reaches her majority, my job will be over. I wonder what I'll do then? I'll be no more use to anyone. Perhaps I'll just go quietly into a decline.' He smiled to take the sting out of the words, but Chetwyn didn't smile back. He looked unhappy, and James tried to make a joke of it. 'Mother used to say, in the days when she still made formal visits, that it was the height of bad manners not to know when to leave.'

'Yes,' said Chetwyn. 'I remember.'

James smiled at him. 'Cheer up, old fellow. Let's go back downstairs and have another drink. We're going to have a jolly Christmas, and get three parts foxed every day, and forget all the troubles of the world. You and I are to organize the Twelfth Night play, by the way. I think we ought to give Little Polly the main part, to cheer her up, poor thing, though how we are to square it with Fanny I don't know. And the day after, we're holding a grand Epiphany feast for the tenants and villagers – roasted ox and jugglers, the usual sort of thing – so let's hope Ned is right that it's too cold for snow.'

Everyone made a great effort, and the Christmas festivities went better than Chetwyn expected. Father Aislaby, for all his aesthetic appearance, proved to have a talent for thinking up extremely silly games, fit to make even the most determinedly unhappy person break into giggles, and he shewed great tact in organizing things without appearing to do so.

The services in the chapel were extremely beautiful. At Mary Ann's instigation and with Edward's approval, the old custom of the boy's choir had been revived. Six boys of around eight years old were brought to live at Morland Place, to be educated by the chaplain and in return to sing in the chapel and serve the altar. When their voices broke, they would go back to their parents with the benefit of a sound education.

It was a scheme of mixed piety and benevolence which did something to soothe Mary Ann's conscience after the business of the mill children. Edward had most tactfully refrained from discussing it with her, but she was perfectly well aware that after Jemima's death, he had gone on sending foundlings to Manchester, and the maid Betsey had been sent away to a position Edward had found her in a household in London.

The weather continued hard and cold, and the St Stephen's day meet was not a great success, there being so little scent that the Morland pack kept hunting rabbits by sight; but there was no snow to postpone the villagers' feast on the day after Epiphany. A cook pit was dug with the greatest difficulty in the bone-hard ground, and the ox roasted, though it was so cold that the bastings froze on one side of the caracase while the other side was in the flames.

The cleaning of the moat had been finished, but its greater depth did not stop it freezing. Father Aislaby arranged skating races for the young people, four circuits to a race, with various handicaps, like having the knees tied together with a scarf, or having to balance a tankard of ale on the head. Edward organized an archery competition, and James the ever-popular wrestling matches; and there were all the usual booths, and the jugglers and fire-eaters and stilt-walkers and the pieman and the man who swallowed knives.

As the early dusk came on, torches were lit, and there was dancing under the blue-bright stars to a variety of local bands. The fire in the cook-pit burned up red and gold with the frost, and now roast pork supplemented the hot pasties, and the chestnuts and potatoes roasted in the embers. James, well wrapped up in coat and scarves and a woodman's hat with ear-lappets, passed unrecognized through the crowds, enjoying the innocent verve with which the village people enjoyed themselves. There were lamps in all the windows of the house, and by their lights a number of young people and children skated to the music of the bands.

He stopped to watch, as one young lad of twelve or so, bright as a robin in a scarlet jacket and a woollen hat, darted amongst the skaters, ducking in and out without ever once losing his own balance. He seemed intent on building up a greater and greater speed, circling the moat with his head forward and his hands behind him to compensate, and James waited, much entertained, for the inevitable crash.

When it came, it produced more amusement than wrath, for others had noted his flying passage, and eventually an enormously stout young man deliberately put himself in the way. The lad bounced off him unhurt as though he had struck a mattress, and travelled backwards for a few yards almost as fast as he had been going forwards, before landing on his seat looking very surprised.

Everyone roared with laughter, and the boy grinned good-naturedly; but a woman standing near James called out anxiously, 'John, dear, are you all right? You aren't hurt?'

James turned sharply to look at her, for he knew the

368

voice. Wrapped in a dark-blue cloak with a large, fur-edged hood and an even larger muff, she had escaped his notice. Now as she started forward the hood fell a little back, and her face was turned towards the light.

Somehow he had contrived not to set eyes on Mary Skelwith for years. She lived in York, but he rarely went into the city, except to visit his tailor or to go to the club, neither of which establishments she frequented, and he had not happened to pass her in the street. He scanned her face, and found no feeling in himself for her. Perhaps it was the way the light caught her, but she looked suddenly old to him, her face gaunt, her eyes deep set and lined. How old was she? Not above forty, he thought, but she looked ten years more. He saw nothing there of the Mary he had loved. Life must have been hard for her, despite her husband's wealth.

And that, then, was his son, the bright boy in the robin's jacket, flying amongst the slower skaters and laughing with exhilaration. Lord, but he had grown! James remembered with unabated pain the incident, so long ago, when old Skelwith had come up to the house weeping, and demanding James's punishment for what he had done. Well, he had been punished all right, not once but many times, and this was a punishment that went on for ever. Mary Skelwith had gone forward to the edge of the ice and was holding the boy's arm while she brushed the crystals off his back and admonished him for his carelessness. He was only a few feet away, but when he looked at James, his eyes passed over him with the indifference of a stranger.

I have no son, James thought. That boy is now no more mine than any of the village lads devouring pasties at the cook pit or tormenting the dancers by throwing hot chestnuts under their feet. We are strangers to each other. It was a pain that would never end; but he had grown up enough now to see the justice of it. I'm learning, Mother, he thought; if not trust and hope, at least patience and submission. Once, before Héloïse, he would have gone forward and spoken to them, stirred up God knew what troubles. Now he only pulled his scarf a little further up over his face, dug his hands into his pockets, and went away.

*

One morning in February 1799 Lucy took a hackney carriage to Brook Street, and was admitted with a faint air of affront by Weston's manservant. Weston was in the breakfast parlour, still in his dressing-gown. He was sitting in the window-seat lingering over his coffee and reading the newspaper, his lap occupied to their common benefit by his ginger cat Jeffrey.

'Her ladyship, sir,' his man said unnecessarily as Lucy rushed past him.

'Thank you, Bates. I'll ring when I need you. My love,' he said to Lucy when they were alone, 'don't you think this is a little rash? To come unveiled in broad daylight! I know Town is still thin of company, but you are not inconspicuous, you know.'

'I had to see you,' she said impetuously. He grinned at her.

'So early in the morning? And we only parted a few hours ago. I'm flattered.'

'Oh don't play the fool, Weston,' she pleaded. 'I've been out in the Park, and I met Admiral Scorton. He told me – he said – '

'What the devil was he doing up at this hour?' Weston commented, putting his newspaper aside. 'He told you about my promotion, I suppose?'

'He told me you had been made post, and would be leaving within a few days to join your ship. Oh, say it isn't true!' she cried, and flung herself down beside him. Jeffrey sprang indignantly out of the way and sat down at a safe distance pointedly to lick a paw. Weston put aside his coffee cup and stroked Lucy's ruffled hair tenderly.

'It's true,' he said. 'In many ways I wish it weren't; but it's what every officer dreams of, to be made post. Well, you've two brothers in the navy – you must know. My shore commission was almost done in any case. You knew I must go back to sea sooner or later.'

'I knew it, but I didn't want to think about it,' she said, pressing her tragic eyes with her fingers. Then she made an effort to smile. 'Well, you have your ship at last. What have they given you?'

'A sloop of war, the *Semele*, twenty-eight guns. I don't

know much about her – I seem to have served all my sea-time aboard big ships.'

'Do you know yet where you will be sailing?'

'Oh yes, it's no secret. You heard that Naples has fallen to the French? Troubridge has gone out with a squadron to blockade Naples Bay, and I'm to report to him, and act as messenger between all the Mediterranean squadrons.' He saw how hard she was trying to be interested and happy for him, and his heart lurched. 'Oh my darling, don't look like that!'

'I can't help it. I don't want you to go away,' Lucy said. 'Oh dear, what a shocking thing to say!'

He laughed. 'You absurd creature. Why shouldn't you say it?'

'Because it's weak and foolish.' She picked up his hand and rubbed her face against it like a cat. 'When do you go? How long have we got? Why didn't you tell me sooner?'

'I only knew last night. The letter was waiting for me here, after I had left you. I have to join the *Semele* on the twelfth. That means I must take the mail the day after tomorrow.'

Lucy tore herself away from him and walked about the room, her hands clenched together, her brow drawn in thought. His going back to sea was another of the things she had not allowed herself to think about. He would be gone two years, perhaps three, and who knew when she would see him again?

But she must not make a fuss. Everything that happened to them, good and bad, had been implicit from the beginning, that day in Richmond Park. It had not been accidental, she saw that now. She had seen the clouds in the west before she ever left the house, as he must have done: though on her part it had been deeply subconscious, they had used the situation, and they could have no complaint to make about anything that happened afterwards, however much it hurt.

She unclenched her hands and turned to him. He was watching her, his eyes bright and full of conflict. It did not occur to her for an instant that she was a rich woman, and could beg him not to go. The navy was his career, and even if she could have changed him, she would not have wanted to. She loved him, and her body and soul craved him as a thirsty man craves water, but her smile was calm as she said, 'Well, then, we must not waste a minute of our two days. I will spend every moment with you, until you step onto the coach.'

He stood up and put his arms round her, and felt her body press against him in an instinctive response. 'Beginning now?' he said.

'This instant,' she said.

Jeffrey watched them, his pale green eyes bright in his golden face. When he judged that they were too preoccupied to notice him, he took the opportunity to jump lightly onto the breakfast table and finish off the butter in the butter-dish.

He had gone. She had driven with him in a hired chaise to the coaching-inn to catch the mail, dry-eyed to the last, smiling as she gave him her farewell gift, a long silk muffler. 'Silk is very warm, you know, and won't absorb the damp as much as wool.' Bates was waiting for them at the inn, having gone on ahead with the luggage, and Jeffrey, cursing comprehensively in a covered basket.

'I hope he takes to the sea-faring life,' Lucy said.

'Oh, he'll love it. Cats have a wonderful time on board ships.' He climbed out of the chaise and closed the door, and Lucy let down the window and leaned through it to clasp both his hands.

'I won't wait until the mail leaves,' she said practically. 'You had better start putting your mind into naval frame.'

He lifted her hands and kissed them. It was he who was close to tears. 'You'll write to me?' She nodded. 'And I'll write to you – under cover to Docwra. I expect she has brothers all over the world. The Irish always have.' His voice failed him on the last sentence. He kissed her, brief and hard, and went quickly away, and Lucy closed the window and lay back in the corner, closing her eyes as the chaise lurched away over the cobbles.

She did not see her husband until dinner. They were dining at home for once, and without guests, which was fortunate. Docwra dressed her as though she were a rag doll, pushing her this way and that, and finally setting her in motion down the stairs when the bell rang. She entered the dining room to find Chetwyn already at the table. He stood and bowed to her; Hicks pulled out her chair and she sat; dinner began.

Chetwyn tried one or two neutral remarks, to which Lucy responded with little more than a grunt. She picked listlessly at her food, and watching her he was suddenly moved with pity. He had been about to make some remark about Weston's departure, but desisted at the last moment. Her face was all planes and angles in the candlelight, as though drawn by a new artist with a firmer hand. Her eyes were bright, a faint flush along her cheekbones, her lips slightly parted above her pointed chin. He thought suddenly that she looked beautiful, not as a woman is beautiful, but like a wild animal, when it turns for an instant to look at you before it disappears into the undergrowth.

When they had sat long enough before the untasted dishes, Lucy rose, and with a glance at Hicks, Chetwyn followed her into the drawing-room. She sat down on the edge of the sopha, and he took up his usual position leaning against the chimney-wall. Hicks furnished him with a glass of brandy, trimmed the candles, and retired. As soon as they were alone Lucy rose almost as if she were unaware of her movements and walked up and down the room.

'My dear,' Chetwyn said at last, unable to bear it any longer, 'you will wear holes in that extremely expensive carpet.' She stopped abruptly, and her hands found each other and clasped before her.

'I must speak to you, Chetwyn,' she said.

'Here I am,' he said with a languid gesture of the brandy glass. She walked a few more turns and then stopped in front of him, standing very straight, her eyes fixed on a point somewhere over his right shoulder, like a soldier about to make a report. Beneath his lazy smile, something in him became watchful.

Lucy licked her lips. 'Chetwyn – I am with child,' she said.

Whatever he had expected, it had not been that. He

stared at her in shock and growing anger as she faced him rigidly, uncontrite, unafraid, waiting for him to do what he would do. He thought that if he had taken out a pistol just then, she would have stood still and let him shoot her. She was not like a woman at all – no, nor like an animal: she was like a soldier under discipline.

'I don't understand you!' His voice was a low cry. 'You stand there and tell me – dear God alive, Lucy, it's unnatural! Any other woman would have slept with me a few times, and pretended it was mine, at least given it the semblance of propriety. But not you – oh no! That would be too easy, wouldn't it? You have to come blurting out with the truth!'

Her focus changed from the wall behind him to his face. She looked completely bewildered 'What? What are you saying? Do you mean you would have *preferred* me to lie to you?'

'I would have preferred the opportunity to salvage a little pride, yes. Does that surprise you?'

'But what pride could there be in a lie?'

His mouth turned down bitterly 'You're such a child! You live in a world of make-believe: everything must be either black or white for you. Do you think the real world deals solely in the truth? Did you never think I might prefer a little comfortable obscurity?'

She shook her head slightly, puzzled. 'It would have been dishonourable,' she said at last.

'Dishonourable? Sweet Jesu, *dishonourable*!' She flinched as his voice rose to a shout, and looked at the wall again.

'I don't understand you,' she said.

'No, that's painfully obvious,' he said angrily. After a long silence, he saw her sigh deeply, and draw herself together a little more to ask the important question.

'What will you do, Chetwyn? Will you cast me off? I suppose you will want to divorce me. I imagine it will be quite easy, in the circumstances – '

'Don't be a fool,' he said shortly. 'Divorce, in our position?' She said nothing. Her face was white and pinched, with relief or pain, he didn't know which.

'Don't you know what marriage is?' he said at last,

bitterly. 'It's an institution under law for the protection of inheritance, that's all. Since we are married, all the children of your body are deemed to be mine.' Her eyes flickered. 'Oh yes, mine. Let that be your punishment.' He set the brandy glass down on the chimney-piece carefully, and walked away. At the door, without turning, he said, 'I'll acknowledge your child, Lucy. What else can I do?'

'Thank you,' she said.

Chapter Twenty-Two

James was right that Lucy's scandal would be forgotten by Society as soon as Weston was out of sight. Adulteries might not be precisely acceptable, but there were plenty of them around to blunt the appetite. The royal dukes set the pattern, from the Prince of Wales downward; then there were such notorious cases as Lord Robert Spencer, the Duke of Marlborough's son, who took Mrs Bouverie, married woman and mother of eight, for his mistress in 1786 and had been living with her ever since; and Fox's uncle, General Fitzpatrick, who had purportedly sired a large number of his closest friends' children.

Lady Aylesbury's brief, though exceedingly public, infatuation with a naval lieutenant was not much more than a nine-days' wonder, especially as she immediately retired to the country, out of sight and mind. There may have been those who wondered about her pregnancy, but since Lord Aylesbury received congratulations just as he should, there was really nothing to talk about.

At Wolvercote, Lucy settled in for the term of her pregnancy, and since she could never bear to be doing nothing, she set about recreating the well-ordered household that had existed at the time of Flaminia's birth and which she had neglected ever since. It was not difficult. The permanent staff were willing to forgive her her defection now that she had returned, especially as she was pregnant again. The newcomers to the servants' hall quickly fell under the spell of her charm and authority, and found that any tendency to revive old gossip was quickly quashed by their seniors.

She turned her attention also towards the nursery, though she still could not feel much interest in Rosamund, who at eighteen months was a difficult, colicky baby with a singular lack of any infant charm. The other two were more promising. Hippolyta, who would be five by the time the new baby arrived, already had a great deal of Mary's porcelain beauty. The loss of her mother had not affected her deeply, for she had been very young when Mary went away, and hardly remembered her; of her father she had no recollection at all. She had a curious dignity for a child, the result, Lucy thought, of being not only the eldest in the nursery, but also the senior grandchild of the family. She was everyone's pet wherever she went, but it did not make her spoiled and difficult like her cousin Fanny, only rather solemn and oddly consequential: the infant alderman, Chetwyn had called her once.

Lucy thought that she would turn out to be intelligent, though at the moment she shewed no remarkable aptitude except for organization. It was mostly Flaminia she organized, who at three had become chubby and garrulous, and whose greatest happiness was to be Hippolyta's lieutenant, confidante, and live plaything. The days of heaving Flaminia around like a good-humoured and confiding sack were over, but she trotted after her friend wherever she went, took the supporting role in all their plays, and accepted as from the oracle everything Hippolyta said. It was 'Polly says' and 'Polly thinks', and her whims were as the laws of Medes and Persians; in return 'Minnie' was Polly's darling, bullied, petted, and protected.

Chetwyn had gone back to Town as soon as he had escorted Lucy to Wolvercote, but he came down at Easter, bringing a small party with him — to act as a buffer state, Lucy guessed. They were mostly his own friends, bachelors or pseudo-bachelors, and they came to shoot and fish all day and to play cards or billiards all evening. Of Lucy's friends he had brought only Danby Wiske, sad-eyed now and more monosyllabic than ever, and George Brummell, who assured Lucy that his leaving London even for a few days was an act of the greatest heroism.

'For you know, my dear Countess, that I have just been elected to both Brooks's and White's, and I was on the point of beginning my campaign.'

'Campaign?' Lucy said vaguely. 'I thought you had left the Dragoons.'

Brummell tapped her on the back of the hand. 'You are not paying attention! My campaign to civilize London, of course. I shall establish myself as the arbiter of graceful living, and create around me the kind of society in which I belong but which does not, alas, yet exist! And when you have rid yourself of your burden,' he gave a significant glance downwards at his own trim waistline, 'you must come back to London and help me, my dear ma'am.'

Lucy shook her head. 'I don't think I have the heart for it.'

'Nonsense! You must come – you cannot be spared,' Brummell said calmly.

'It's true, ma'am,' Wiske put in a word. 'London ain't the same without you. Damn' dull. Your wit and beauty – ' Surprised by his own eloquence he turned red and fell silent. Brummell dismissed him with an airy wave of the hand.

'Oh, those are very well,' he said, 'but what we chiefly need you for, dear ma'am, is your back.'

'My back?' Lucy said, startled into full attention. Brummell smiled angelically.

'Your back, Lady Aylesbury.' He sketched a line in the air with one hand. 'There isn't another female back in all London which even comes close. Oh, the humps and round shoulders I am forced to view, even in the best houses, positively like camels! To say nothing of the freckles and blemishes whenever the poor dears go *décolletées*. I must have yours, Countess, on which to rest my eyes for relief, when my sensibilities have been racked!'

Wiske looked disapproving, but Lucy laughed out loud for the first time in weeks. 'You really are absurd,' she said.

'That's better,' Brummell said approvingly. 'I can't bear to see you so down in the mouth – besides, it makes you look quite old!'

'I feel a thousand years old,' Lucy sighed.

'It will pass,' Brummell said comfortingly. 'Everything does.'

Since Horatio had now gone abroad with his regiment, Chetwyn had invited his wife, Lady Barbara, and her two children to stay for a few weeks, and she had accepted with alacrity, welcoming the opportunity to shut up the house in Park Lane and live at someone else's expense for a while. She calculated that as Lady Aylesbury was enceinte and had no female companion, she ought reasonably to be able to extend her visit at least until Lucy rose from childbed.

Marcus and Barbarina, four and two years old, had inherited their father's pink and white colouring and protruberant pale-blue eyes; while a stern nurse and an unbending mother had crushed out of them any tendency to exhibit individuality. Brought to the Wolvercote nursery, they stood, holding hands for comfort, just inside the door where they had been left, lacking the initiative to move any further. Dressed alike in white muslin frocks, identical pale eyes bulging, pink triangular mouths slightly open, they looked like two startled white mice. Hippolyta, having looked them over with a professional eye, received them with relish. She saw at once that they were docile and dull, and would never complain at always playing the page and never the king.

With this increase to the nursery, Lucy saw the necessity of engaging a governess. She went about it with her usual energy, and soon discovered a Miss Trotton, an elegant, well-spoken young woman with an intelligent eye and an air of quiet authority. Lady Barbara questioned her sharply, discovered that she painted in water-colours and played the harp, and put her down at once as a very genteel, well-educated girl, fit to have temporary charge of her Dear Angels.

To Jemima's daughter she must seem but poorly educated, since she had never studied Latin, Greek, Astronomy, or Philosophy, but Lucy decided she had an intelligent, liberal mind, not fettered by rigid prejudices, combined with a central core of good principles and self-discipline, and engaged her at a handsome salary.

When the house party broke up, Chetwyn sought out Lucy in her room to say goodbye. He had treated her with extreme politeness at all times, both publicly and in the rare moments when they were alone together, but there was none of the old brotherly friendliness, and she missed it. The farewell now was nothing but formal, his smile merely polite, his eye as flat as his boot-sole.

'I shall be in Town until the end of June, then Brighton for a few weeks, and then I shall go straight to Morland

Place,' he said. Lucy heard him with a lowering of spirit.

'You will not return here in August?' she asked, for that was his usual time.

'There is nothing here that the steward can't handle,' he said. 'I shan't return unless he tells me there is some serious problem that requires my personal attention. I don't imagine there will be.'

'Then I shan't see you until October?' she asked, trying to sound indifferent. The baby was due in September. Chetwyn raised an eyebrow.

'That must be as you please,' he said politely. 'You know where I will be.' He bowed and turned to go.

'Chetwyn!' she said desperately. He turned, and there was nothing in that frozen, polite face to which she could appeal. 'Oh, nothing,' she said. 'I hope you have a pleasant summer.'

Lucy's pregnancy was not difficult, and she began to feel bored, not with Wolvercote, which she was enjoying after several years spent mostly in Town, but with the lack of company. Lady Barbara she mildly disliked, and she certainly had no pleasure in the company of a woman whose sole subjects of conversation were money and her children. She was glad, therefore, when in May Charles and Roberta, going down to Shawes early on account of Charles's health, which had been poor for eighteen months past, stopped off for a visit.

It was good to see them again: Charles, urbane, kindly, interested in everything that interested her, full of pleasant small gossip about London happenings; Roberta the same good-natured, sensible, soldier's daughter she had always been. But there was a change. Charles had begun to grow old when his first wife Flora died, and now, seeing him with his travelling-wig and cane, with Roberta supporting his arm and fussing gently over him, it was like watching a dutiful daughter attending to an elderly father.

They had with them young Robert St Vincent Morland, Lord Meldon, more usually known simply as Bobbie. At a little over two, and still in petticoats, he was a precocious

380

child, bright, friendly, and biddable. He was also robustly healthy, and Lady Barbara regarded him with a hostile and jealous eye as he slipped his confident hand out of his mother's and into Miss Trotton's, and went off to join the nursery-party.

The Chelmsfords had also brought Héloïse with them. She had travelled post to London to attend to some legal business, and was taking the opportunity of travelling back to Coxwold in their company. While Charles and Roberta were seeing Bobbie settled, with Lady Barbara in close attendance, Lucy was able to have a long chat with Héloïse, whom she hadn't seen for some years.

'What were you doing in London?' Lucy asked. 'Has something been heard about Mathilde's brother?'

Héloïse shook her head. 'We still have not been able to find him. We now know that after the shipwreck he was taken to a foundling hospital for boys in Tonbridge, but he ran away almost at once, and has not been seen since. I think he must certainly be dead, for Charles's agents have made the most thorough enquiries, but Mathilde says she knows he is alive, and nothing will persuade her that he is not.'

'You left her at home in Yorkshire?' Lucy said.

Héloïse chuckled. 'Oh yes, along with all my other waifs and strays! It will be a very good thing when the improvements to my house are finished, for it is already as full as it can hold. Two months ago poor Father Jerome arrived at my door – he was our priest in London, you know, we poor *émigrés*. He was cast out of his lodging and could not find another, so he came to me, and what could I do but take him in? They are not so unkind to Catholics in my part of Yorkshire, so I hope he will be safe at Plaisir.'

'It must be a great comfort to you to have him there,' Lucy said.

'*Vraiment*, it is, and we may even make a convert out of Stephen, who is already, I think, half a Catholic from sharing a room with Monsieur Barnard, who is a very devout man, apart from making choux pastry the way no English cook ever did. But it will not end with Father Jerome, I fear. While I was in London, Cousin Charles put me in the way of helping a poor Frenchwoman who had got into trouble with the law and did not know enough English to help herself.' She sighed. 'There are a great many of my people in trouble or need, and no-one to help them. The children, in particular, one must pity.' She gave Lucy a considering look. '*Je me demande ...*' she mused.

'Yes?' Lucy asked warily.

'Well, there is no harm to ask you,' Héloïse decided briskly. 'Maman once told me that you had an ambition to start a school, and it occurs to me that you might perhaps help some of the *émigré* children in that way. Without parents or money or education, one can see they must sink into degradation, particularly the girls, who will end all as *prostitueés* if someone does not help them.'

Lucy shook her head. 'I have not thought about a school for a long time. Besides, my plan was for a select establishment for the serious education of young ladies.'

Héloïse clasped her hands. '*Eh bien*, if you will provide the school, I will provide the girls.' Lucy shook her head again. '*Mais pourquoi pas*? Don't you see poor emigrant girls who must take care of themselves will learn more eagerly than the daughters of the rich, who wish only for husbands? You could do so much good, Cousin Lucy, and they would be so grateful.'

'It's out of the question,' Lucy said firmly. 'I have enough to do with my household to run, and my own children to take care of.'

Héloïse smiled. 'Well, I do not mean to tease you. I shall say no more, and perhaps you may consider again. You have only to think what it would mean to your daughters if they were left destitute. That is what I think so often – I look at those poor girls, and I see my own little Sophie-Marie, and I think, there but for – '

'I beg your pardon?' Lucy interrupted in surprise. 'Your own little who?'

Héloïse made a face. 'Oh dear, my tongue runs away with me! But there is no harm in your knowing, after all. I am sure you will not betray us.'

Lucy stared at her. 'You have a child? Oh Héloïse! Oh, I am so sorry! I mean, of course, she must bring you great

382

joy, but at the same time – '

'Yes,' said Héloïse. 'There are many causes for joy, and many for sorrow also. But mostly for joy.'

'Then,' Lucy said slowly, 'you never told Jamie?'

'No. How could I? It would only have made things worse for him. I suppose one day he will find out the truth, but I shall not tell him. He is married to another, and that is a fact that cannot be escaped.'

Lucy gazed at her, stricken. Héloïse's words had brought her own situation to her mind, and the conflict inside her that she had hardly yet allowed herself to acknowledge. She longed to pour out the whole story, and ask her advice. Lucy had never cared much for women or women's company, but there were similarities between them which attracted her to her cousin. They had both undergone experiences early in life which had set them aside from the generality of their sex, and though Héloïse, more than Lucy, was essentially a womanly woman, they both had a strong streak of practicality and courage which made them alike.

But before she had any opportunity to unburden herself, Lady Barbara returned to the drawing-room, and Lucy retreated again behind her protective camouflage. It was just as well they were interrupted, she thought afterwards: it would be unfair to add to Héloïse's burdens, and in any case, one must always work out one's own salvation.

After two weeks, the Chelmsford party left to resume their journey, and when she had waved them out of sight, Lucy went back inside, and felt that she had never been so lonely in her life. Mother was dead, and Mary was dead; Chetwyn had abandoned her, and who could blame him; and Weston was far away. She went back into the drawing-room, and to avoid Lady Barbara, who wanted to talk about how many changes of clothes little Lord Meldon had in a day, she said she had a letter to write, and went and sat down at the writing-table.

She wished now, futilely, that she had confided in Héloïse who, she felt, was the only person who would have understood without condemning. How lightly she had dismissed James's conduct in running away to Héloïse, as just James being difficult as usual. Yet, however little he loved his wife, the decision to go must have been hard to make, and still more so the decision to come back.

What a child I've been, she thought; and then, resentfully, but it was not my fault. They had married her off when she was only fifteen, to get her out of the way. It seemed to her now a monstrous thing, to marry her to Chetwyn, whose heart had been given so long ago to Edward that there was no possibility he could ever love anyone else. They had condemned her to a life without love. Ah, how she had used to scoff at the idea of love! Romantic nonsense she had called it, until Weston.

Weston! She had not written to him, despite saying that she would, because the child made everything different. Loving Weston, even committing adultery with him, seemed forgiveable, understandable; but she was Chetwyn's wife, she was the Countess of Aylesbury, and her children would inherit the title and the estate. Marriage, children, property – they were inseparable; love was something quite other. She could not tell Weston the child was his, because that would be a betrayal in a way that loving him was not; and she could not write to him, because it would be equally impossible not to mention her pregnancy, or to tell him that the child was Chetwyn's.

Oh, but she missed him! Why was so much of life simply a matter of luck? Mama and Papa, Mary and Captain Haworth on the one side, Jamie and Héloïse, her and Weston on the other. Virtue and wickedness, happy marriage and adultery, and the difference was so small and so insurmountable. I'm only twenty-one years old, she thought: what am I going to do with the rest of my life?

Weston wrote, as he had promised. In his first letter, he said, 'I have news of your brother Harry, which you may not yet have heard: he is made acting-lieutenant, and only waits for the Commander-in-Chief to confirm the commission, which I make no doubt he will do, as he and Captain Collingwood are old friends. I took despatches to the *Excellent* only last week, and saw Lieutenant Morland proudly clutching the telescope as officer of the watch and looking completely the thing. He charged me to send you his love if I were to write, for he was much too busy. Brothers have not the same incentive to write as lovers! I await *your* letters more eagerly than I can say. I suppose they follow me around the Mediterranean, and will all arrive together, weeks of happiness all in one bag!'

In his second letter he said, 'I must tell you that I dined yesterday with your brother Haworth aboard the *Africa*. I like him exceedingly. He bears his bereavement well, and speaks of your sister with affection, as though she were waiting for him somewhere onshore. I suppose we sailors get used to being separated from our loved ones.

'His daughter is the delight of the whole ship's company. When I first saw her, she was on the fo'c'sle, sitting on the deck clutching a large camel carved out of wood, while a grizzled old tar played to her on his flute. About half a dozen other hands were standing by awaiting their turn at entertaining her!

'Haworth tells me that there is never any shortage of volunteers to look after her, and the men take the tenderest care of her. She has had a wonderful effect on discipline: they have not had a single flogging in months, for the threat of not being allowed to approach the baby is a far greater deterrent than the cat, and the men inflict their own condign punishment on any jack who dares to cuss or behave unseemly in her presence. She has more clothes and playthings than she can use, Haworth says, for the men are always making things for her.

'We are on our way to Gibraltar at this moment, where I will consign this letter to the homeward-bound bag, and hope to find something from you awaiting me. I prefer to think your letters have been delayed, than that you have not written any!'

His third letter spoke of the political situation: 'We have the Frogs on the run! The Russians and Turks have taken Corfu, and are using it as a naval base; the Russians are driving the French from Italy, and the Austrians are fighting back on the Danube. The Egyptian venture is such a failure that the illustrious General Buonaparte has abandoned his army and sailed for home, which must mean the end of his career! And our intelligence from France is that the troops are still unpaid, the country over head and ears in debt, and the Directory so discredited that it seems likely there will soon be either a renewal of the Terror under General Bernadotte, or a counter-revolution to restore the Bourbons.

'So perhaps we may have peace before my present commission ends. How shall I feel about that, I wonder? But why do you not write to me? I wish you may not be unwell. Have pity at least on my anxiety, and write to say that you are in good health.'

As soon as he arrived at Morland Place, Chetwyn was driven over to Twelvetrees by Edward in his gig, where work had begun at last on the new stables which Jemima had been wanting ever since she first married Allen.

'It's going to be a slow business,' Edward said, as they turned into the main yard. 'We have to go on using the old stables while we build the new, so we can only do it a little at a time. It would be much better if we could simply knock the whole lot down, but then where could we put the horses? Ah, there's Jamie – and Fanny, too.'

'Doesn't her mother mind her grubbing around in all this dirt?' Chetwyn asked mildly, seeing Fanny, grimed from her forehead to her boots, sitting on a pile of bricks.

'She's never said anything. I expect she's glad that James takes an interest in her. Hullo!'

'Ned – and Chetwyn! You've arrived at last,' James said, turning round from his contemplation of the plans spread out before him on a plank.

'Only just. Ned was so eager to shew me the building that I didn't even have time to change,' Chetwyn said, jumping down from the gig as a groom came up to take the horse's head. Fanny rushed over to greet him, with Puppy bouncing beside her. She had the dog attached to her by a rope tied around her waist. 'Hello, Fanny! I do believe you've grown again. How old are you now?'

'I'm four, nearly,' Fanny said proudly. 'Uncle Chetwyn, don't you think four is old enough to have a pony of my own?'

'Well, that depends a lot on the person,' Chetwyn said gravely. 'For instance, if a person hasn't managed to train their dog not to jump up at people, it might look as though they weren't very good at controlling animals, mightn't it?'

Fanny's lip jutted, but she hauled on Puppy's rope, albeit rather ineffectually.

'That dog's a damned nuisance,' Edward said. 'You see we've had to insist she keeps it tied to her, or she lets it go, and it gets under everyone's feet and frightens the horses.'

'I thought perhaps the rope was to keep Fanny tied down, not the dog,' Chetwyn said, and James grinned.

'About half and half – isn't that so, Fan? You need putting in a cavesson and lungeing for an hour every morning, according to your uncle Ned.' He smiled down affectionately at his daughter, and she wound herself round his leg and gazed up at him wheedlingly.

'I'd be *really* good if I had my own pony,' she coaxed.

James laughed. 'Put you on horseback, and we'd never know where you were,' he said, ruffling her dark curls. 'It'd take more than Puppy to weigh you down. But how are you, Chetwyn? You're looking fagged to death! Too much frowsting indoors in Brighton, and too many late nights, I'll be bound. We must get you out in the fresh air now you're here. Have you seen my plans for the new stables? It's my latest project, you see. I always had a fancy to dabble in architecture.'

He spread out the plans and the three men bent over them.

'Rather ambitious, ain't it?' Chetwyn said, poking at it with a finger. 'Like a glorified greenhouse. What's this thing? It looks like a fountain.'

'That's what it is,' James said defensively. 'You're not very appreciative. This is my masterpiece, you know. Don't you see the benefits? A circular building, with the boxes all facing into a central courtyard covered with a great glass dome, so that the weather need never bother us; and in the centre the fountain, with a large basin for filling buckets.

Every stall is the same distance away, you see. You obviously have no idea how much time is spent watering in a stable like this – probably more time than on any other single job.'

'Well, I see the point of the basin – but what are the statue and the fountain for?'

'For beauty, of course,' James said indignantly. 'What a philistine you are!'

'He's roasting you,' Edward said. 'I've already described your plan to him on the way over. It's going to be quite a sight when it's finished, don't you think?'

'And when will it be finished?' Chetwyn asked, looking around him doubtfully at the evident lack of progress.

'Oh, not for four or five years, I don't suppose,' said James.

'You sound positively cheerful about it,' Chetwyn commented, and James grinned.

'It keeps me occupied. Fanny, what's Puppy eating? Don't let him do that.'

'I'm looking forward to the races next week. What's the favourite?' Chetwyn asked. 'I hope the Gold Plate will be coming back to Morland Place for another year.'

'Of course it will – our colt Aboukir is going to come home by a street, or even two. He's so fast he'll be past the winning post before the others reach the first turn. Come and see him,' James said, rolling up the plans.

'Papa, Papa, then can Uncle Chetwyn see me ride?' pleaded Fanny.

'Yes, all right, my star,' James said, and grinned at Chetwyn. 'It is a great treat, you understand. She don't perform for everyone.'

'So you keep telling us,' Edward said cynically, 'but we've never yet discovered who it is she *won't* perform for.'

Later they all went back to Morland Place together for dinner. Ned and Chetwyn took Puppy in the gig, and James rode Nez Carré alongside, with Fanny astride the saddle in front of him, her short legs almost at right angles, and her stout boots waggling at the end of them.

'She reminds me sometimes of Lucy when she was a little girl,' James said, 'except that Mama could never keep shoes on Lucy.' Chetwyn's face revealed nothing as he concentrated on preventing Puppy from walking over the side of the gig.

'This dog seems to have absolutely no sense whatever,' he commented with a sort of scientific interest.

'Not my fault – Mary Ann picked him out,' James said cheerfully. 'But how is Lucy? Is she never going to come to Morland Place again? I thought her latest little adventure was over.'

Chetwyn shot him a hard look as Edward said, 'What adventure?'

'All her adventures are over for the time being,' Chetwyn said lightly. 'She's pregnant again. That's why she didn't come – she don't care to travel so near her time.'

'You didn't say,' Edward said in surprise. 'Why didn't you tell us before? When's the baby due?'

'In September,' Chetwyn said, and sought about for some way to change the subject, which amused James, who obviously knew all about it. 'But tell me, Ned, who is going to give the mid-week ball, if the Chelmsfords don't, on account of Charles's health?'

'We are,' Edward said, successfully diverted, 'though of course it can't be such a big affair, since we only have the long saloon to dance in. But we are going to have twenty to dinner, and thirty couples for the ball, and if they can't all dance at once, they will have to make do. We'll have supper laid out in the dining saloon, and the drawing-room for cards, and those who aren't dancing can stroll about the great hall. I dare say it will work very well.'

'People never mind a crush,' Chetwyn said, out of a wealth of London experience. 'It convinces them that they are enjoying themselves. And if you can't ask so many people as the Chelmsfords, it only makes *your* ball the more exclusive. But how will you know who to leave out?'

'Oh, Mary Ann is seeing to all that,' Edward said. 'She has made out the guest list, and sent the invitations, and she's been in conference with the cook for weeks.'

'Danvers is a very different proposition from Monsieur

Barnard,' James said with amusement. 'Try to confer with Barnard, and he would be as likely to attack you with a basting spoon, but Danvers says yes, madam and no, madam and squirms like a puppy, and says what a privilege it is to work for someone who takes so much interest in his art.'

'It makes for a quieter household,' Edward said defensively.

'Yes, but *so* dull!' James replied, and then gave in to Fanny's ceaseless demands for a canter just as far as the barbican.

Aboukir won his race, not precisely by streets, but by a good margin, which gave added zest to the celebrations, although his name had made him so popular with the public that the Morlands had not been able to get good odds anywhere.

All the same, the Gold Plate was prominently displayed in the dining-saloon when the dinner party sat down. Enthusiastic toasts were drunk, and James declared that he would try his hand at equestrian painting, and have a portrait of Aboukir on the wall by the same time next year.

An elegant dinner was spread on a table elaborately decorated, as was the new style. Mary Ann, now seated at the foot of the table as mistress of the house, admired her handiwork, and felt that the occasion was a kind of culmination. Her place was now secure: she had staff who were loyal to her, her orders were obeyed, and everything was done as *she* liked it.

The centrepiece of the table was a peacock with its tail on, and the flowers, ribbons, and other decorations were in blue, green and gold to complement it. The removes were green soups – chicken and verjuice, pigeon and pistachio, and pea soup with forcemeat balls. In the first course there was a salmon pie in the shape of the fish, with a gilded crust, a roast goose set about with golden apples, a lemon pudding, and a dish of pike with spinach; in the second chickens in egg-sauce, a tansy custard, and pistachio creams amongst the many dishes. As the china service was blue and gold, the colour of the dinner itself matched the decorations, and Mary Ann, gracious and smiling, received many compliments from the delighted and amused guests.

After dinner, the party gathered in the drawing-room while they waited for the evening guests to arrive. Then Fanny made her appearance, dressed in a new frock of white muslin sewn all over with tiny knots of pink ribbon, and a broad pink satin sash. Awed into her best behaviour, she made a good impression, holding Dakers' hand, smiling, curtseying, and allowing the gentlemen to pat her cheek or tweak her curls. Then James caught Dakers's eye, and she was hurried away before the strain of being good became too much for her and she began to demand cakes and to be allowed to stay up for the ball.

Some time later, when the ball was in full swing, Edward and Chetwyn were strolling along the edge of the long saloon arm in arm, watching the dancers.

'How red-faced they are, and how they puff and blow at their pleasures!' Chetwyn remarked languidly. 'They must all be in love, to go at it so hard. Look at that one – her feathers are drooping with the heat, but she skips like a spring lamb!'

'Just as you said, they don't seem to mind the crush,' Edward said. 'I think it's a success, don't you?'

'Do you remember,' Chetwyn said a while later, 'how your mother used to pursue us around the house to make us dance with the young women no-one else would stand up with?'

'Poor Mother,' Edward said. 'She worked so hard to get us married.'

'Well, age has released us now, my dear!'

'Yes, we need never dance again. Now Jamie's master of the house, he can stand up with all the ugly women, while you and I enjoy ourselves.'

They stopped at the corner and watched the couple at the head of the set dance down, cheeks bright, eyes sparkling, feet flying.

'Poor Mother indeed,' Chetwyn mused. 'Isn't it frightening to think, my dear, that now there's a new generation growing up, Fanny and Polly and Minnie, and Bobbie and Marcus, to start the whole thing going again? Like an infernal engine, grinding away, year after year; and all the things we've learned at such cost they will have to learn for themselves just as painfully. What's it all for, Ned? Where does it all end?'

Edward considered for a moment. 'You need some more wine,' he concluded. 'Let's go and find a bottle and take it to the steward's room, away from all this noise, and have a comfortable coze.'

'Good idea,' said Chetwyn, and flung an arm across his shoulder, and they slipped out from the brilliantly-lit saloon and down the chapel stairs to privacy.

'The indefatigables,' James said much later still to his wife as they watched the last six couples dancing down yet another set. 'I think perhaps this ought to be the last, however.'

'Yes,' said Mary Ann. 'I shall give the signal to the musicians. It's very late. Besides,' she added briskly, 'all the soup is gone, and the patties.'

James smiled at that. 'I think it has been a great success,' he said after a moment. 'I am surprised at how many dancers managed to squeeze in here. I'm sure more people came than were invited.'

Mary Ann frowned. 'Yes, I had that impression, too, but I couldn't pick out anyone who wasn't on my list, except for the party the Ansteys brought, and I knew about them, for Louisa Anstey sent me a note about it yesterday.'

'What would you have done, if you had seen anyone not on the list?' James asked, intrigued.

'Why, asked them to leave, of course,' Mary Ann said, surprised. James grinned.

'My dear ma'am, I should take off my hat to you, if I were wearing one. Ah, the end of the set. Do nod to your musicians, my dear, or we shall be up until dawn.'

'It isn't far off dawn now,' Mary Ann said, complying. 'Do you know it is past three o'clock?'

'Ah well, none of us rises as early as Mother used to,' James said. They stood at the door and bade farewell to the young people as they passed. 'I suppose you noticed Ned and Chetwyn slipping away hours ago? Mother used to have terrible trouble with them years ago, in the days when she still thought she might persuade them to marry. But it was worse when they danced than when they did not, for they could never be brought to know the name of one young lady from another, which the young ladies found extremely insulting.'

'Your mother is much on your mind tonight,' Mary Ann commented.

'Yes – I suppose, because this is the first formal occasion at which you have presided instead of her,' James said.

'I hope you think I have not disgraced you,' Mary Ann said. James looked at her appraisingly, his mouth lifted at one corner in one of his strange smiles which she never understood. 'It is difficult to plan a ball with such limited space. You know, James, if we are to entertain a great deal, it would be worth filling the moat, or covering part of it, in order to build on some larger rooms for parties and balls.' James, still smiling enigmatically, was looking around the long saloon as though he had not heard her. 'Don't you think so? James?'

'What's that? I beg your pardon, my dear – I was just imagining having Fanny's coming-out ball here. How I shall frown at all the young men, and think no-one fit to stand up with her!'

'Well, there you are, exactly,' Mary Ann said, taking his proffered arm and walking with him to the door of her room. 'A coming out ball for Fanny, with only thirty couples, and only two-thirds of them able to dance at once? It won't do, James, not for Miss Morland of Morland Place.'

'Perhaps we ought to build a new house entirely, in the modern style, like your father's,' James said ironically. 'After all, she'll be Miss Morland of Hobsbawn Mills too, won't she?'

She turned at her door to face him and looked up at him gravely. 'A new house would be entirely to the good, except that I think you would not like to abandon this old place, for all its inconveniences.'

'No,' James said gently mocking, 'you're quite right, I would not. Besides,' to salve her pride, 'we could not afford it.'

'With Papa's money we could,' she said, and then blushed surprisingly. 'I know you despise Papa's money.' James murmured a protest. 'But after all, it helps you to do things you want to do, like rebuilding the stables. Of course, Fanny being a girl, Papa won't leave her everything, because he doesn't think a female could run his mills, even with an agent in charge, but still there will be a great deal of money, and the terms of the trust would allow – '

'Who do the mills go to, Fanny being a girl?' James asked abruptly, breaking in.

'I think, to my cousin Jasper. Well, he's a second cousin, really, descended from Papa's aunt – quite a distant relative. I've never met him. I don't think even Papa knows him very well.'

James studied his wife's face, fair, lightly flushed, alabaster and rose, framed by the soft brown hair, silky as a spaniel's ears, which for several hours now had been slipping from its pins. It was almost two years since he had shared a woman's bed, and she really was very pretty.

'And this unknown Jasper is to have your father's fortune, for no better reason than that he is male?'

'I – I suppose so – not all Papa's fortune, of course – only – ' Her eyes slid away from his, and her cheeks grew hotter. James picked up one of her hands and kissed it lightly.

'It seems very unfair to me,' he said. 'Don't you think we ought to do something about it?'

Mary Ann opened her mouth automatically to ask what, but managed to close it again, the folly unspoken. She kept her eyes down, but felt him watching her, waiting, his eyes amused, his mouth curled in that inscrutable smile. She thought briefly of the five years of marriage and the slights and insults she had borne from him. He had ignored, hurt and humiliated her, and one foolish, un-Christian part of her wanted to snub him now in retaliation.

But it was a small part. Most of her mind was under her control, and was glad that he was coming at last to the right way of thinking. Her patience and forgiveness had softened him and were about to reap their reward. And then there was a large, and largely mute, part of her which simply wanted to be close to him, after the years of loneliness.

She opened the door of the west bedchamber, and pushed it wide. Dakers, sitting half asleep in a chair beside the bed, startled awake and stood up. Her eyes went past her mistress to the master, standing just outside the door, and she frowned.

'It's all right, Dakers, I don't need you any more,' Mary Ann said smoothly. 'You may go to bed now.'

Dakers was too good a servant to make any protest, but the warning look she bestowed on James as she walked past him out of the room would have melted doorknobs.

395

Chapter Twenty-three

The Earl of Aylesbury went home to Wolvercote in the autumn of 1799 with a grim face and despair in his heart. Edward knew everything. Chetwyn had hoped to keep the truth about Lucy's adultery and pregnancy from him, for Edward, the epitome of a country squire, had little interest in Society doings, rarely read a newspaper, and never listened to gossip. Chetwyn valued this extraordinary innocence, and wished to preserve it, for while Edward did not change, Chetwyn could revisit the carefree, sunlit days of his own youth in Edward's company.

But a letter came from Lucy announcing that the child was born, and begging her husband to visit her. When Edward discovered in surprise that Chetwyn did not intend to obey the summons, he had begun to ask questions which soon resulted in his learning the whole truth. Learning it, he had not sided wholeheartedly with his friend.

'I know she has behaved badly,' he said, 'but you ought to forgive her, Chet. To refuse to visit her at a time like this is too unkind. Besides, think of the scandal it will stir up. People are bound to wonder why you don't go.'

'You blame me for that, rather than her?' Chetwyn said, hurt.

'Lucy's just a child,' Edward said. 'She doesn't always think what she's doing.' Chetwyn snorted at this view of her. 'Besides, you and she didn't marry for love. It was convenient for you, because you did not want to have to woo a woman, and she has never complained, as she has every right to, of your neglect of her. If she has taken a lover, it is at least partly your fault.'

'Your view of the world is so distorted I hardly recognize the people and places,' Chetwyn said angrily. '*I* am the aggrieved party! Lucy has wronged me, yet you condemn me, while Lucy is to be excused, on what grounds I hardly understand. Pray what gives you the right to judge me? Or is it simply that your sister has first claim with you, and that I am nothing to you any more?'

From there the discussion had deteriorated into a quarrel, the remarks passed had descended to the personal, and the first breach in their long friendship had occurred. It had been patched over when Chetwyn agreed to reply to Lucy's letter and to go and visit her, but it had left him wounded where he was most vulnerable, and bitter against Lucy as the cause of it.

Hicks met him in the hall, his expression a curious mixture of relief and apprehension. 'Welcome home, my lord,' he said, 'and if I may add, congratulations, my lord.'

'On what am I to be congratulated, Hicks?' Chetwyn asked uncompromisingly. Hicks met his eye with a look which conveyed sympathy, regret, anxiety, and a fatherly warning.

'On the birth of a son, my lord,' he said.

A son! Chetwyn stared at him in dismay and dawning understanding. Had this new child been a daughter, or had Chetwyn bred a number of sons before it, it would not have been so important. Chetwyn might have let the world know, directly or indirectly, that he was not the progenitor, and the world would have shrugged. But this child, the firstborn son, would inherit the title and the estate, would become in turn the seventh Earl of Aylesbury, and there was nothing Chetwyn could do to change that. It would be worse than folly, therefore, to cast doubts upon the child's parentage: it would be a crime against his heritage.

'Her ladyship is in her own bedchamber, my lord,' Hicks said, gently reminding him of his duty. 'She instructed me to request you to step up to her as soon as you arrived, my lord, if it should be convenient.'

'Yes,' said Chetwyn. 'I'll go.'

Lucy's chamber was no less cluttered than before the birth of Flaminia and Lucy herself was sitting up in bed, wearing a robe of yellow tamboured silk, eating potted shrimps and washing them down with a quart of champagne which she was sharing with Docwra. The maid, who was sitting on the edge of the bed with a tankard in her hand, jumped up with a startled cry as Chetwyn came in, dislodg-

397

ing a heap of letters and a ginger kitten onto the floor, and trying guiltily to hide the tankard behind her.

'Oh, my lord! There, my lady, didn't I say I heard the carriage ten minutes since? Mercy on me, what a muddle! Will I get you a tankard, my lord? You'll want to be drinking a toast, I've no doubt.'

'Thank you, Docwra. I see you have been drinking toasts already. But then, my lady has something to celebrate, hasn't she?'

'Champagne is very good for women in childbed, as I've always told you, Chetwyn,' Lucy said calmly, though her eyes were watchful.

'Yes, you always have,' Chetwyn replied. He took the profferred cup from Docwra, held it to be filled, and then lifted it with an ironic smile in Lucy's direction. 'To your child, madam. You have a son at last.'

He drank. Lucy looked at Docwra and gave a small jerk of her head towards the door, and the maid curtseyed and left them alone. Chetwyn drained the tankard, set it down, and said, 'Where is the baby?'

The cot was by the bedside. He walked across to it and looked down at the tiny, sleeping scrap of humanity. It was much as all babies are, indistinguishable to Chetwyn from any other child which was not his; smaller than Flaminia had been, prettier than Rosamund. 'Is it healthy?'

'Yes,' Lucy said.

'A boy,' he said. Oh, it was a bitter thing! 'I suppose you have written to the father, to congratulate him? There will be rejoicing around the fleet, and a double rum-ration aboard the – what is the name of his ship?'

'The *Semele*,' Lucy answered him automatically.

Chetwyn bowed ironically. 'As you say. Well, you must make do with my congratulations. I'm sorry I shan't be able to rejoice as heartily as he will when he hears the news.'

Lucy's face was taut and white. 'You are quite wrong,' she said. 'You may abuse me – indeed, you have every right – and I do not expect you to understand my feelings. But I have not written to him.'

Chetwyn regarded her with hostility. 'Surely you don't expect me to believe that such fond lovers would part without a promise of correspondence?'

Lucy seemed to shrink together. 'I cannot govern what you believe. But I did not tell Weston that I was with child, and I shall not tell him that he is the father.'

There was a silence, in which Chetwyn looked puzzled, doubtful, then apprehensive. 'May I ask the reason for such forbearance? I was under the impression that you valued honesty above all other considerations. Or perhaps you pity me too much to expose me to your lover's wit?'

'I never knew,' she said in a small voice, 'that you minded. Oh Chetwyn, I'm sorry! I never meant to hurt you, indeed I didn't. But we did not marry for love, and I thought – '

'You thought I should not mind who fathered my sons? Well, perhaps it does not matter. Your friend has saved us both a great deal of trouble, for who knows but what I mightn't have gone on giving you daughters for ever? Now we need not trouble each other again. I wish you joy of your son, madam. Have you decided what to call him? Perhaps James would be the most tactful choice?'

'I didn't tell him, ' Lucy said desperately, 'because it would be disloyal. You are my husband, and the children are yours. You said so yourself. I did not think, since ours was a marriage of convenience, that it mattered where I gave my heart, but for the rest – I would not tell *anyone* that the child was not yours!'

Chetwyn thought of his quarrel with Edward, and a sense of futility washed over him. He lifted his hands in a gesture of frustration. 'For God's sake, Lucy, why did you have to tell *me*?'

The baby woke, and began to cry. Chetwyn looked at Lucy helplessly. 'I'm sorry,' she said. The baby's crying grew in strength, and almost instinctively, Chetwyn reached into the crib and lifted the white bundle, remembering anew how small and light new babies were. As soon as he picked it up, the baby stopped crying, and lay red-faced in his arms, making surprised gestures with its eyebrows. He tried to wonder how he would feel if it had been his own son he held, and found that he could not. This was Lord Calder, the future Earl of Aylesbury. He had arrived in the world, and that was that.

'You did not write to Weston?' Chetwyn said carefully.

'No,' said Lucy. The baby began to whimper, and Chetwyn rocked it a little and made crooning noises, and Lucy saw the lines at the corners of his mouth soften. 'About a name for the child,' she said diffidently. 'Have you any thoughts? Perhaps it could be something Roman, to go with Flaminia?'

'Like Marcus, perhaps?' Chetwyn enquired ironically. The baby opened its eyes, and he looked down into its face, almost smiling. 'No, I think not. Let it be something modern and fashionable. What do you say to Roland?'

Lucy's heart lifted. 'Yes, I think that sounds very well,' she said. Chetwyn laid the baby carefully back in the cradle and stood looking down at it for a moment; then he turned to Lucy, his face expressionless.

'May I ask what are your plans, madam?' he enquired politely.

'Plans?' she said, taken by surprise.

'For the immediate future. Do you intend returning to London, or will you stay at Wolvercote?'

'Docwra won't let me go anywhere for the moment,' she said, trying for a smile. 'I thought of asking some people down for the cub-hunting, and going up at the end of October.'

Chetwyn bowed. 'Then perhaps I shall see you in London. I go up first thing tomorrow morning.'

Lucy's smile froze, and her heart sank again. So there was to be no reconciliation. She returned him his bow in kind, and watched him leave without another word. She was still thinking deeply when Docwra came back into the room.

'Is everything all right, my lady?' Docwra enquired cautiously.

'His lordship is going up to London tomorrow,' Lucy said absently.

Docwra clucked in disapproval, and Lucy seemed to come to a decision. 'Well, that sets the tone for the future. He has his son, and a couple of daughters in addition. I have kept my side of the bargain. I need concern myself no longer. Docwra, fetch me my writing case. I have a letter to write – one that's long overdue.'

400

The new year came in quietly at Morland Place. There had been no guests for the Christmas season, and Shawes had not been opened up, for the Chelmsfords had stayed in London, since Charles had not felt well enough to travel so far. William was in the West Indies, where Admiral Seymour's squadron was enjoying moderate success, and Harry was off Gibraltar keeping watch for any attempt by the French to re-open communications with its lost *Armée d'Orient*.

Mary Ann had wanted to hold a grand dinner and ball to celebrate the start of the new century, until Father Aislaby had pointed out, not entirely tactfully, that she was a year in advance of the fact. It took all the combined reasoning powers of the priest and her husband to persuade her that 1800 was the last year of the old century, not the first year of the new, and even then James was never sure she had properly understood the argument.

But she was not too unhappy at spending a quiet Christmas, for she was pregnant again, and suffering intermittently from nausea. She satisfied her desire for society with the St Stephen's Day meet, and a small dinner at which Lord and Lady Anstey and Sir Arthur and Lady Fussell were the only guests. She received their congratulations on her hopes with a shy smile, and a glance at James, whose expression was inscrutable.

James had decided that Nez Carré, though as willing as ever, was getting too old to risk on the hunting field, and took out a young horse which Edward wanted to sell as a schooled hunter. He rode hard that day, and took risks which roused indignation in Edward on his youngster's behalf. He rode up to James at the first check to remonstrate with him, but seeing his brother's expression, moved away again, the reproof unspoken. He had hoped Mary Ann's condition meant that James was finally reconciled to his fate, but the grim and bleak unhappiness in his face as he waited by the covert revealed even to Edward, who was not a noticing person, that with James the outside rarely matched the inside, and that he grieved as much as ever for Héloïse.

Lucy was spending Christmas in London, but Chetwyn had gone down to Oatlands, the Surrey home of the Duke and Duchess of York. The Duchess, or 'pretty little Princess Fred' as she was known, was Prussian, and liked to keep the season in the lavish German manner, with spectacular decorations, a splendid dinner, and a table laden with gifts for her guests. In the centre of the great dining room there would be a large fir-tree in a pot, also decorated, and hung with oranges and sweetmeats and gilded gingerbread. After the distribution of presents, children from orphan asylums and charity schools would be brought in and allowed to strip the tree of its good things.

The Duchess was very fond of animals, but did not like women, so the Duke, who was very fond of her, took only gentlemen and dogs to Oatlands. Horatio, who was also home for the winter recess, met up with his commander-in-chief at Morning Service in the Chapel Royal. He spoke to him of Chetwyn's engagement with such wistful envy that the bluff, good-natured Duke felt constrained to say that he would be glad of Colonel Morland's company at Oatlands, only that he thought Lady Barbara might not take kindly to being left alone.

'Indeed, no, sir,' Horatio said hastily, 'Lady Barbara would not mind in the least. She has no taste for parties, and would much sooner spend the time quietly at Park Lane. I assure you, she would be glad to have me out of the way.'

This was no more than the truth. After her delightfully economical summer at Wolvercote, Lady Barbara had been reluctant to resume living at her own expense. Since being obliged to leave Wolvercote in the autumn, she had discovered the joys of thrift, and in the short time between her return to Park Lane and Horatio's arrival home, she had become obsessed with the making of economies.

While this mode of behaviour satisfied something in her inmost soul, its joys seemed to Horatio esoteric. His home had become austere and comfortless, and if he could find some way of indulging his taste for luxury without breaking his wife's very laudable resolve not to spend money, he would be glad of it.

The Duke of York's invitation thus made them both very

happy, and when Chetwyn offered to take Horatio to Oatlands in his chariot, their happiness was complete; for in Horatio's absence, Lady Barbara had dispensed with their own chariot and horses, assuring him on his return that there was an excellent job-stable only a step away in Hays Mews.

'Depend upon it,' she told her rather startled husband, 'it is folly to be keeping a carriage, and having a pair of horses eating their heads off day after day, whether they go out or not. I have so much to do at home that I do not venture out above twice a week, and then, you know, a hired turn-out will do just as well for my purposes; and someone else may feed the horses the rest of the time.'

It did not entirely suit Horatio's ideas of their consequence to think of going to evening parties in a hired chaise behind job-horses; but when he found himself bowling down the road towards Oatlands in the Aylesbury chariot, behind four high-fed prime goers whose keed had not cost him a penny, he saw the force of his wife's argument, and blessed Heaven for her wisdom, and his own good sense in having married her.

Lucy's Christmas in London was quiet. There was no large party at Carlton House, for the Prince of Wales was in the throes of a reconciliation with Mrs Fitzherbert. He had dismissed Lady Jersey in June, and the following month sent his brother Prince Edward to negotiate with Mrs Fitzherbert, who finally agreed to come back to him if the Pope gave permission. They had been married by the Roman Catholic rite, and though the King would not recognize the marriage, the Prince of Wales now declared that Maria Fitzherbert was his 'wife before God' and that he would acknowledge no other while he lived. A Roman Catholic priest had been sent to Rome, but until the Pope's decision was known, Mrs Fitzherbert insisted that she and the Prince must not see each other.

So with no Carlton House party, and much of her set away at Oatlands or Belvoir, Lucy spent her time quietly, riding and driving in the Park, visiting the theatre and the opera, and dining with friends. Brummell had gone to Oatlands, but Danby Wiske, dumb with bliss, resumed his place at her side. He became so accepted as her cicisbeo that those hostesses who remained in Town over the Christmas season sent out invitations to Lady Aylesbury and Major Wiske without thinking twice about it.

One day in January Lucy and Wiske made up a small party to drive out to Ascot for the races. The war had caused a shortage of food which brought hard times to the poor, and footpads and highwaymen had grown more numerous and more bold of late, but even so Lucy was astonished as she drove across the heath when two brutish-looking men jumped out from the bushes at the side of the road. One brandished a pistol and yelled at her to stop, while the other made a jump for the leaders' heads.

Lucy was too angry to be afraid, for her horses were very much startled. The leaders threw up their heads and went back on their haunches, and the nearside wheeler, driven forward by the impetus of the carriage-pole, tried to turn sideways and began to kick.

'Let them go!' she yelled. 'If he gets his leg over the trace he'll break it.'

'You stop still, my lady, an' give us yer jools an' yer reddicool,' growled the man with the pistol. 'An' you, Capting, less 'ave yer bowse, quick as yer like, an' no-one won't get 'urt. Ah, would ye!'

This last was addressed to Parslow, who had got down from his seat behind and was attempting to come up along the side of the curricle to get to his horses. The frightened wheeler was jerking from side to side in panic, trying to get free, and Parslow was too anxious for its safety to worry about his own.

'Stay where you are!' the footpad shouted, turning his pistol on the groom.

'No!' Lucy screamed. As Parslow jumped for the wheeler's head, a shot rang out, dull in the damp air, and he span round and fell to the ground, clutching his arm. The leaders reared up in alarm, knocking the second villain away. Danby Wiske saw his chance, leapt from the curricle, and seized him from behind with an arm round his neck. Wiske was not a big man, but he was regular in his exercise and well-fed, more than a match for the footpad, who struggled weakly, tugging ineffectually at the restraining arm.

Wiske's body was thus shielded by that of the second man, and the first man hesitated, unable to shoot. Then Wiske began tugging at his sword, trying to get it from its sheath without letting go of his prisoner, and he saw that the game was up and took to his heels, hoping for easier pickings another time. His confederate wriggled in terror in Danby Wiske's grip.

'Let me go, Capting, let me go! I ain't done nothing! I never meant no 'arm!'

'No harm? Here's a man shot!' Wiske said sternly.

'T' warn't me, Capting! I never carried no pop! T'warn't me as done it!'

'For God's sake, Danby, let him go and see to Parslow,' Lucy cried. She was standing up in the curricle, the better to hold her horses, who were still nervous and fretful. Wiske saw that he would have to let the man go, for they had got a long way ahead of the rest of the party, and help would be some time coming.

'I never meant nobody no 'arm, Capting,' the footpad cried. 'I juss done it fer the money, fer summink to eat. Wass a man to do when e's starving?'

'Rub off, then,' Wiske said abruptly, releasing the man's neck, and he bolted like a rabbit and disappeared into the bushes.

'You'd better hold the horses while I see to Parslow,' Lucy said. For a moment he was about to protest, before he realized that Lucy certainly had more experience of treating wounds than he, however little he liked the idea of a woman doing such things. He went to the leaders' head, while Lucy hitched the reins round the rail and jumped down.

Parslow was trying to sit up, his hand pressed to his shoulder, and Lucy helped him, and supporting him from behind began to ease his coat off.

'It's nothing, my lady, a flesh wound only,' Parslow said faintly.

'Hush, save your breath for groaning,' Lucy said. 'It's a good job you wear your coat loose, or this would hurt you a great deal more than it does. Ah, that's it!' Under the scorched coat the shirt was rent and bloody, and Lucy tore the rent wider with strong fingers and looked at the ugly, purpling gouge in the fleshy part of her groom's shoulder. Gently she felt around it and articulated the joint. 'As you say, a flesh wound only. You are extremely lucky. At that range he ought to have broken your shoulder at the very least, if he had not put the shot directly into your lungs and killed you. What the devil did you do it for, you fool?' she demanded crossly.

'Why, my lady,' Parslow began feebly, 'I could not allow –'

'Fudge! Do you think I care more for a few trumpery jewels than for you? How could I replace you if you were killed? Hold still, now, while I bind you up. I shall have to tear a strip off your shirt, but it's ruined already. I wonder what became of the ball? It must have just injured you in passing. Perhaps we'll find it embedded in the weather-board.'

She chattered lightly to distract him while she bound the shoulder as tightly as she could, and then took over the horses while Wiske helped the groom up into the curricle and got up on the other side of him.

'We'll stop at the first inn we see so that I can clean and bind it properly – and get a tot of brandy for each of us, by the by!' Lucy said, sending the team on. She glanced at her friend curiously. 'You were very brave, Danby, jumping down like that. Foolhardy, when the man with the pistol still had another shot, but brave all the same. I never really thought of you as a man of action before, but I see now how wrong I was. The way you seized that man was splendid!'

Wiske blushed rosily. 'Nothing to it,' he murmured deprecatingly. 'Saw m' chance – weed of a fellow – like wrestlin' with cow-parsley! Thing is,' he added thoughtfully, 'times must be desperate hard if they're willing to try it on a road like this – open, lots of traffic.'

'It's nothing to do with hard times. A man must have a very bad disposition if he's willing to risk the gallows for highway robbery instead of working honestly for his bread.' Lucy countered.

'May not be able to find work,' Wiske said apologetically.

'Then let him take the shilling! We are at war, you know, and the army's not particular. I'm surprised at you Danby, talking such radical nonsense. What will come of us if we start excusing criminals?'

'Lord, ma'am, I didn't mean – only that – never knew anyone so thin! Said he was starving – believed him! Here's an inn, however,' he said with relief at the prospect of escape from philosophy's tangled web. 'Let me jump down, and I'll rouse 'em out directly.'

A week later Lucy heard that Lord Chelmsford was laid up with an influenza. She offered to help nurse him, and sent Docwra round with a draught, but Roberta refused all help gently but firmly. As soon as he was allowed visitors, Lucy drove to Chelmsford House to see how he went on.

'It's very good of you to come,' Roberta said as she conducted Lucy upstairs. 'Charles will be so glad to see you. You are his first visitor. Horatio and Lady Barbara enquired every day, but they say they will not come in case they take the infection home to the children.'

'Well, I'm not afraid of infection,' Lucy said. 'I'm as strong as a horse, and besides, my children are still down at Wolvercote. But you are looking very pulled, Roberta. I wish you may not have knocked yourself up with nursing him.'

'Oh no,' Roberta said in her gentle voice. 'Charles was no trouble at all. I wish he had been more, for there was little he would let me do for him. I'm a little tired and worried, that's all. But you will cheer him up,' she added, and opened the door of his chamber. Charles was propped up on a small mountain of pillows, and though he looked drawn, and his breathing was laborious, he presented no other immediate signs of illness. A welcoming smile spread across his face as Lucy entered.

'My dear little cousin, what a delicious sight you are! Is that a new gown? That deep cream colour suits you, and the sleeves are very cunning. Are they your own thought?'

'How are you, Charles?' Lucy asked with a grin. 'You needn't try to entertain me, you know. I'm very sure you aren't the least bit interested in my gown.'

'Oh, but you're wrong,' Charles replied. 'I've found a new interest in fashion ever since I learnt that Lady Barbara is selling off her old gowns to a shop in Kensington. I believe they make them over and sell them to the wives of well-to-do trades people.'

'You are joking me,' Lucy said, staring.

'No, I assure you, it's true,' Roberta smiled. 'She says there is no point in having a wardrobe full of clothes she never wears, and that they were far too expensive to give away.'

'I've told Roberta she ought to go down to Kensington for her next new gown,' Charles said. 'Such an example of thrift ought to be followed by all you gentlewomen. It would be a graceful compliment to Lady Barbara, to appear in her company in one of her made-over gowns.'

'Illness has not made you less wicked,' Lucy observed. 'But how came you to be so foolish as to catch an influenza, Charles?'

'It was not an influenza, just a feverish cold,' Charles said quickly. 'But my wife likes to worry, so I let her have her head.' He and Roberta smiled at each other.

'He was sitting too long in debate,' Roberta said sternly, 'and then insisted on walking home – '

'I wanted a breath of fresh air,' Charles protested.

' – despite the fact that it was cold and drizzling. He got thoroughly chilled, and then went back the next day for another long sitting.'

'I can hardly tell my colleagues, some of whom are much older than me, that I am not fit to sit two days in succession,' Charles objected pleasantly. 'Besides, the Irish question is as pressing as it is complicated, and dear to Pitt's heart.'

'I should think it would be, after the rebellion in '98, and the threat of French invasion,' Lucy said. 'As long as we are at war with France, Ireland is like a knife at our backs.'

'Exactly so,' Charles said, 'just as Scotland used to be, with its French connections, before the Union. Well, we solved that once for all by uniting the two countries, and Pitt believes that we must do the same with Ireland. We are looking to have a union by next year, but of course there is a great deal of opposition.'

'I should think there may,' Lucy said with a smile.

Charles grinned. 'You don't know the half of it, my dear. For Pitt, the union is just another step in the road to Catholic emancipation, and the present Irish Parliament will not like to have its ranks diluted or its privileges removed. It's as corrupt a body as ever breathed, but that is the nature of humanity, it seems. Which of us would not do the same, if we were given the power?'

'You would not, to begin with,' Roberta said firmly.

'He'll never get such a scheme past the King,' Lucy said. 'It's well known the King hates Catholics.'

'Oh, it isn't that so much,' Charles said, 'but he promised in his Coronation Oath to defend the Protestant church, and he takes it very literally. However, he's an old man, and unwell. If Pitt takes things slowly, he may find it all comes out his way in the end.'

'If it's to be taken slowly,' Roberta said sternly, 'there was no need for you to risk your health by sitting all day when you had a chill.'

Charles laughed, and pressed his wife's hand. 'You are delightfully single-minded, my dear. But if you want to worry, worry about Lucy. What's this we hear, cousin, about your being attacked by highwaymen?'

'Oh, they were nothing but a couple of footpads,' Lucy said airily, 'and Major Wiske drove them off with no trouble.'

'But Parslow was shot, was he not?'

'A shot was fired, and creased Parslow's shoulder, but it was only a scrape, and it's healing well, with no sign of mortification. He'll have nothing but a handsome scar to shew for it. I was very proud of Danby, however. I bought him a gold snuff-box to thank him, and had it engraved with the date and "For Valour". It made him laugh a good deal, but he loves to use it and have people ask about it. If you see him, don't forget to enquire.'

'Oh Lucy,' Charles said, laughing, 'you do one such a lot of good.'

*

The season was cold and damp, and Charles did not mend as he should. A week later Lucy found him lying back on his pillows, and breathing with such difficulty that he could only speak slowly, with frequent pauses. Roberta was clearly worried about him, though she said little, except that he had a troublesome cough for which the doctor had sent some soothing syrup.

'If only it were cold and dry,' she said to Lucy, 'it would not be so very bad; but the damp air oppresses him, and even the best of fires does not seem to help much.'

Lucy visited every day after that, when engagements permitted, and though he did not get worse, he did not improve either. Then came the day when she called at Chelmsford House on her way back from a drive in the park, and Hawkins greeted her with an air of suppressed excitement. With a glance towards the porter's room he said, 'His lordship has a visitor already, my lady, who arrived unexpectedly a few minutes ago.'

Lucy paused in the act of taking off her gloves. 'Oh, then I had better not disturb him, Hawkins. Perhaps you will tell her ladyship that I called?'

'I am quite sure her ladyship will wish you to step up, my lady,' Hawkins said, 'the gentleman being of your acquaintance. It is Captain Weston, my lady.'

Lucy's heart seemed to jump into her throat, and she knew she was staring like an idiot, but for the moment she could not govern herself. Hawkins gave her what was almost a friendly nod. 'I understand that Captain Weston called at Upper Grosvenor Street before coming here, my lady. May I shew you up to his lordship's room?'

Lucy found her voice at last. 'Thank you, Hawkins, but don't trouble to announce me. I know my way by now.'

She mounted the stairs slowly to give herself time to think, and paused before the huge mirror on the wall at the turn of the stairs to examine her appearance. Her face looked pale and her eyes wide, and she adjusted her expression carefully. She was wearing a pelisse of grey grosgrain deeply trimmed with muscovy sable, and a ridiculous hat decorated with a veritable salad of fruit – plums, cherries, grapes and apricots – and with a half-veil of fine black net, which she knew became her. She presented a smart, fashionable, and expensive appearance, and yet she suddenly felt as shy and awkward as a schoolgirl at the thought of seeing him again.

She continued up the stairs to Charles's room, scratched at the door, and opened it. Roberta was sitting beside the bed holding Charles's hand. Weston was standing on the other side, and all three faces turned towards her as she entered, but Lucy saw only his. His colour was a shock to her – she had forgotten how brown he must be after a year in the Mediterranean – and she noticed that the front part of his hair was bleached by the sun, and that the back part had grown so long he had tied it in a queue with a bit of ribbon. As if he had heard her thoughts, he bowed his greetings to her and said, 'Yes, Lady Aylesbury, I need to send for the hairdresser before I am fit for company! But I knew Lady Chelmsford would forgive me, and I hope you will too.'

'Weston,' Lucy said foolishly, 'how came you here?'

'Why, I walked up from Whitehall, ma'am,' he said with a teasing smile.

'You know very well what I mean,' Lucy said unguardedly.

'My ship lies in London Pool. We brought in despatches, and when I had made my number at the Admiralty. I called at Upper Grosvenor Street, but your servants told me you were gone to the Park, and would probably call here afterwards. So I took the liberty of coming to pay my respects to Lady Chelmsford – '

'And hoped to take two birds with one shot,' Roberta finished for him.

Lucy recovered her composure sufficiently to greet Roberta and ask Charles how he was. He was not looking well, his face grey and pinched, his lips with a bluish tinge, and his breathing audibly no better. But he returned her a cheerful answer, and said, 'It's good to have Weston back, even though it will be but a short visit.'

Lucy turned an enquiring look on the captain.

'No more than a week,' he said, meeting her eyes. 'I hope not less, but I have no security of that.'

In that case, she wanted to cry, we must waste no time; but she forced her eyes away from his glowing brown ones,

411

and said, 'You find poor Charles in bad case. If only he could have a cruise in the Mediterranean like you, I believe he would get better. He needs sunshine, you see, and there is nothing else we can give him that does him any good – though I did prevent the burning of pastilles Sir Arthur Bury recommended,' Lucy added, with a stern look at Roberta. 'The folly of it – to be taking up the air with burning rubbish, when Charles can hardly breathe!'

'But tell us about the war, Weston,' Charles intervened tactfully. 'What news do you bring?' Talking made him cough, and Roberta proffered a cup of watered wine, but he waved it away, and nodded to Weston to continue.

'Well, what can I tell you?' he said. 'We still have the upper hand at sea, though things have not all gone our way of late. Admirals Nelson and Keith cannot agree about anything, and quarrel continually, and Nelson is making a great cake of himself over Lady Hamilton – wife of Sir William Hamilton, you know, the ambassador to the Court of Naples. She flatters him in the grossest of terms, and he takes her advice about everything. It is quite absurd.'

'But is peace any nearer?' Roberta asked.

Weston shook his head. 'I'm afraid it may be a little further off. That fellow Buonaparte – he has taken supreme power in Paris, set himself up as first consul and moved into the Tuileries, for all the world as though he were king.'

'I thought there were three consuls,' Lucy objected. Weston bowed.

'That is true. The *coup d'état* last December replaced the Directory with a three-man consulate, Buonaparte, Cambacérès, and Lebrun. The wits call them "he, she and it". Buonaparte may be a soldier, but Cambacérès is a devoted gourmet with strange sexual tastes, and Lebrun is a book-keeper and dedicated to figures. Neither has any desire to argue with Buonaparte, and in any case, they are intended only as makeweights. Their powers are defined purely as advisory: only the first consul can promulgate laws, and now that he has had the constitution endorsed by plebiscite, it is virtually a dictatorship.'

'Until he loses a few more battles, and his supporters turn on him,' Charles said.

'He who lives by the sword shall die by the sword,' Roberta nodded. 'He took power by force of arms, and he can be removed in the same way.'

'Well, yes,' Weston said cautiously. 'However, I don't think it does to underestimate the man. We all thought he was finished when he abandoned his army in Egypt, but somehow he has turned it to his advantage. God knows what he is going to do next, but one thing is sure – whatever his move, it will be a bold one.'

'As long as we keep control of the seas, we are safe,' Lucy said, rather tactlessly, considering Roberta came of a long line of soldiers. But Roberta turned it graciously into a compliment towards her other guest, and said smilingly, 'As long as we have able captains like Mr Weston, I am sure we need fear nothing.'

Weston laughed and said, 'Now I know it is time to take my leave! Indeed, I am sure I have tired the invalid long enough. I will call again before I sail, Lady Chelmsford, if you will allow me?'

'Please do,' Roberta said.

'I had better go too,' Lucy said. 'Charles is looking fagged to death with our noise. I'll call again tomorrow, Roberta. Captain Weston, I have my curricle outside. May I convey you somewhere?'

Alone at last in the morning room at Upper Grosvenor Street, Lucy and Weston faced each other. It was not as she had imagined the first meeting. She had thought that she would fling herself at once into his arms, but there was a curious shyness to be overcome first.

'Why did you take so long to write to me?' Weston asked at last.

'I told you in my letter – I was very busy.'

'Your letter told me nothing. It was an example of its kind – two pages, crossed, telling me all and revealing nothing! What was it, Lucy? Did you have any doubts? I guessed that that was the case. And yet now I see you face to face, you do not seem to want to send me away.'

'I don't,' she said bluntly. 'Yes, I had doubts. They are

413

resolved now. Chetwyn and I –' She hesitated.

'You need tell me nothing about that. It is not my business,' he said gently.

'Oh, there is nothing to tell. We go our own ways, and see little of each other.'

'You sound as if you minded. Poor Lucy,' said Weston. 'I wonder if your doubts are as firmly resolved as you think?'

She met his eyes squarely. 'Do you love me?' she asked abruptly.

'You mean, do I love you *still*? Oh yes – more than ever. A year at sea,' he added with a grin, 'concentrates a man's mind wonderfully!'

Lucy was satisfied; but there remained this strange shyness, and she couldn't find the right words to carry her over the breach. 'Did Jeffrey enjoy life aboard the *Semele*?' she asked at last, diffidently.

Weston gave her an amused look. 'What do you care about Jeffrey? Come here.'

'Why?' she said defensively, but took a step forward all the same.

'Because,' he said, meeting her half way and taking her in his arms, 'I want to kiss you, fool.'

When she removed her lips from his at last, she sighed and rested her chin on his shoulder and remarked obscurely, 'Yes, I was a fool. So we have a week,' she went on, 'before you go back to sea.'

'More or less.'

'Then we must not waste a minute of it, I once said of Mary that it was a foolish trick to fall in love with a sailor, and I'm still of the same opinion.'

'Are you in love with me, Lucy?' Weston asked. 'You have not said so.'

'I don't know. I feel –'

'Yes? What do you feel?'

'A great gladness that you are here. A great dread of your going away again.'

'It will do very nicely to begin with,' he smiled, releasing her from his arms and taking her hand. 'And now, do you think we might retire to your chamber? A year is a very long time, and you did say something about not wasting a minute.'

Chapter Twenty-four

Lucy certainly had every intention of visiting Chelmsford House every day, but somehow there never seemed to be an opportunity. Weston was obliged to call at the Admiralty the following day, so Lucy drove him there, and waited until he was finished to drive him home again. By then it was time for dinner, Weston being accustomed to ship-board hours, and the rest of the day just disappeared in mysterious fashion.

On the day after that he had to go to his ship, and Lucy went with him, as eager to inspect the pride of his heart as he could be to shew it to her. They took oars from Westminster Steps to London Pool, and Lucy was astonished at how rapidly they crossed the width of London. 'It would have taken so much longer by road,' she marvelled. 'London traffic is beyond anything.'

The shore-boat took them right up to the *Semele*, riding the making tide at anchor. She was Spanish-built, a prize of the American war, and though carrying only twenty-eight guns, and officially a sloop, she was not flush-decked, as was usually the case, but had a raised fo'c'sle and quarter-deck, like a frigate.

At the moment she presented the aspect of a kicked ants' nest, for she had the victualling-yard hoy hooked on to her starboard side, swaying up barrels of salt pork and beef and sacks of peas and biscuit, the navy-yard hoy hooked on to port, replenishing her bo'sun's stores, and working parties scurrying about the decks under the sharp encouragement of their petty officers.

Despite all this tremendous activity, the officer of the watch spotted the shore-boat at once, with the familiar form of his captain in the stern. A bellowed order brought the sideboys running and the principal officers to the quarter-deck as the shore-boatman turned his craft skilfully down-river of the ship and ran up under her flank with the make.

'She's riding light, of course, without her stores,' Weston said apologetically to Lucy. 'It will be quite a climb for you. Perhaps I had better have them lower a chair.'

'Nonsense,' Lucy said stoutly, though regarding the side of the ship with some misgiving. 'I'm not made of glass.'

'Well, you're not Mr Proom now, you know,' Weston grinned. 'And you're wearing a skirt. Consider my reputation, if not your own.'

Lucy was received with flattering attention aboard the *Semele*, the officers, down to the youngest mid, staring at her with a mixture of admiration and disbelief, and, in the case of the first lieutenant, a keen interest which suggested he had heard about Lucy's naval adventure.

Politenesses over, however, they were soon clamouring for the captain's professional attention, and it became clear that Weston's duties would be too numerous for him to be able to go ashore again. It seemed the obvious thing, therefore, for Lucy to remain on board too, and share the captain's quarters with him and Jeffrey, so that she could be with him until the last moment.

A message was sent for Docwra to come to the ship with a bag of necessities for herself and her mistress. Four days passed rapidly and, for Lucy, blissfully: to be with Weston, and to be in a ship again, was a double ration of happiness. Then the wind veered the necessary point for the *Semele* to be able to make the Channel, and at first light on the fifth day, Lucy and Docwra found themselves seated in a shore-boat watching the graceful little ship glide away down the river.

The dark surface of the water was wreathed in coils of milky mist, barely disturbed by the ship's wake, for the airs were light and she moved as though asleep, her topsails ghostly in the grey murk, the ensign hanging limp above her tall stern. Then a single gleam of sunlight broke through, turning her stern-lights suddenly to square gold coins, and catching the gilded scroll-work and the arched lettering of her name below them.

It was a moment of magical beauty. Even the grizzled, one-legged boatman, leaning on his oars, watched in wrapt silence until the lovely vessel disappeared into the mist; and then as Docwra drew a sigh of pure pleasure, he nodded sympathetically and said, 'Aye, it don't matter 'ow often you see it, it still brings a lump to yer throat. I musta seen 'undreds of ships set sail in my time, but I dunno 'ow it is – ' and overcome with emotion, he sniffed and cleared his throat, and then turned away to spit eloquently over the side. 'Thassa lovely sight,' he concluded. 'There ain't one better. Where to, ladies?'

When they arrived home, Lucy went to her room to bathe and change. Docwra kept a sympathetic silence while she dressed her and did her hair, and Lucy's absent expression suggested that her inner eye was still fixed on that tiny day-cabin with the long, velvet-squabbed seat below the sternlights, the chart-deck and chair, the small oval dining-table, the square of rich crimson carpet, the handsome silver lamp swinging from its chain, whose chasing matched that of the silver rose-bowl on the desk.

The cabin furnishings had to be few and simple, but the touches of luxury were entirely in keeping with Weston's character. Even Jeffery had a deep mahogany box lined with sheepskin in which to recline, which was usually placed on the long bench where he could catch the sunshine through the stern-lights. Like master, like cat, she thought, and a smile touched her lips at the thought of the two sensualists, who used each other shamelessly. Her parting gifts for the voyage, sent on board last night, reflected her view of them: six dozen of good claret and six of port, and a cold roast chicken for Weston and Jeffrey to share for today's dinner.

Well, she thought, suddenly brisk, another year might bring them back again; and whatever Weston said, there was no knowing how close they might be to peace. The war had been going on for seven years, and everyone was sick of it: the French must long for it to end as much as the English.

'I must have breakfast, Docwra,' she said, standing up and shaking out her skirts. 'I am unaccountably hungry all of a sudden.'

She was half way through a second handsome plate of ham and eggs when Chetwyn arrived from Wolvercote, where he had gone when the Oatlands party broke up.

'You are very late with breakfast, ma'am,' he said politely.

'Yes, and amazingly hungry,' she agreed pleasantly. 'Will you join me? Have you eaten?'

'Before I left,' he said, 'but I will take a cup of coffee with you.'

'How are the children?' Lucy asked when the servant had brought another cup and left them alone again.

'Well, I suppose,' he said vaguely. 'Miss Trotton brought Polly and Minnie to curtsey to me once a day. I didn't see Rosamund. She was covered with spots, apparently, but I understand the illness was not serious. Chicken-pox, or something of the sort.' He sipped his coffee again. Lucy noticed he did not mention Roland at all, and, deciding that the omission was deliberate, forbore to ask.

She ate, and he drank, in silence for a while, and then he said, 'Weston has been here, I suppose?'

Lucy looked up. 'How can you know?'

'The shipping page in the *Morning Post* is remarkably detailed. As his ship was reported come in to the Pool, I assumed you would have seen him.'

'He sailed again this morning,' she said diffidently.

'Ah!' he said, and drained his cup, and set it down in its saucer precisely and soundlessly. 'I have something to propose to you,' he went on, and then, with a faint, wry smile, 'No, perhaps propose is not the right word, I have something to tell you.'

Lucy looked at him apprehensively. 'I don't think – ' she began, but he held up his hand.

'I'm not going to quarrel with you, Lucy. Please hear me out. You know that when we married, it was principally, on my part at least, in order to provide me with an heir. Well, now we have achieved that, by what means it is profitless to discuss, there is no need for us to live together any more. Unless, that is, your son should die before me, but we need not consider that possibility until it happens.'

His eyes looked through her, his smile was the coldest thing Lucy had ever seen that lived.

'Do you like this house?'

'Do I – yes, I like it well enough,' Lucy said, startled by the apparent change of subject.

'Good. Then you may keep it. I have found myself some

comfortable rooms in Ryder Street for when I am in Town, handy for my clubs and St James's Palace, and a short walk across the park from Westminster. Wolvercote, I dare say, is large enough for us both, if we happen to be there at the same time. You may do as you please with the children, leave them at Wolvercote or have them here as you choose. I shan't interfere.'

He stood up, and Lucy's bewildered eyes followed him up and around the table. 'I shall make an arrangement with my bank concerning your personal allowance. I imagine it will be sufficient, but if it is not, you must speak to my agent, and he will attend to it. The household bills for this house and Wolvercote, and the servants' wages, he will also attend to, so you need not concern yourself with them.'

'But – but Chetwyn, are we never to see each other at all?' Lucy asked at last.

He raised an eyebrow. 'I should think it inevitable that we must bump into each other from time to time, in a city the size of London, but it will not be intentional on my part. You look surprised: I wonder why? I am merely making formal what is already fact.'

He walked to the door, turning as he reached it only to say, 'I shall give Hawkins my direction, of course, in case you should need to consult me.' His eyes met hers for a second and moved away again. 'I'm sure this is the most comfortable arrangement for both of us. Your servant, ma'am.' He bowed, and was gone.

The servant who came to clear the breakfast-things found my lady standing by the window staring out into the street. He coughed discreetly, but she was so deep in thought that she did not hear him, so he took the opportunity to clear as quietly as he could. He had just got to the door with the tray when it opened from the other side and Hicks came in with a letter on a salver.

Lucy turned, frowning. 'Ah yes, Hicks, I was just going to ring for you,' she said vaguely.

'I beg your pardon, my lady,' Hicks said smoothly, sending the servant out with a small jerk of the head, 'but a letter has just come by hand from Chelmsford House. I thought you would want to see it at once.'

Lucy took it and broke the seal, and Hicks went over to brush up a little fallen ash in the grate. From long practice, he was able to straighten up and turn to his mistress just as she finished reading and folded the page again.

'Not bad news, I hope, my lady?' he enquired delicately.

'The Earl of Chelmsford has taken a turn for the worse. I shall go immediately to Chelmsford House, Hicks. Have Parslow bring my curricle round with a pair put-to, and send Docwra up to me in my chamber. Who brought the letter?'

'The porter's boy, my lady, but he did not wait.'

'No matter. I'll be there as soon as a message.'

'Sir Arthur says it is the lung-fever,' Roberta said quietly. Her calm was impressive, even to Lucy, who took her own in the face of sickness for granted. There was no wringing of hands or weeping or vapouring. Roberta was pale, and her eyes were shadowed, and about her mouth there were grim lines, but she was well in control of herself.

'I'm afraid that for once, Sir Arthur seems to be right,' Lucy said, looking down at Charles's unnaturally flushed face against the pillow. The symptoms were all there – high fever, shallow, rapid pulse, difficult breathing, shivering fits; Charles had complained of severe pain in the side of the chest and a metallic taste in the mouth, but now his fever had mounted so high that he was in no case to complain of anything. Lucy doubted if he were aware of their presence by his bed.

Roberta touched his forehead with the tip of her fingers. 'He's so hot,' she said, then and looked up at Lucy with despair in her eyes. 'There's no hope, is there?'

Lucy hesitated, her natural impulse to honesty warring for once with sympathy. 'There's always hope,' she said at last, briskly. 'What did Sir Arthur prescribe?'

Roberta looked guilty. 'Burning pastilles for the breathing,' she said, and went on hastily, 'and iodine to break up the sputum, and oil of camphor to reduce the internal swelling. Hot poultices to the chest and feet – oh, and

420

laudanum for the pain.'

Lucy nodded, and felt Charles's pulse again, frowning. 'I'll get Docwra to make him a pneumonia-jacket,' she said. 'There isn't much we can do until the crisis comes, but it's essential to keep the heart going at this stage. Sir Arthur shouldn't have given laudanum, you know. No use at all in these cases: he should have stimulants. Oil of foxglove, that's the thing. We'll send a boy to the apothecary's straight away.'

Roberta looked down at her husband's flushed, unconscious face. 'Whatever you think best,' she said, and then her lip trembled, and she caught it between her teeth and drew a shaky breath. Lucy put a tentative hand on her arm, little used to offering physical comfort to human beings, but Roberta seemed to take strength from it. 'Will you stay here with me?' she asked in a steadier voice. 'I feel so much safer with you here.'

'Of course I will,' Lucy said. 'I won't leave you. Docwra and I will stay until he's well again.'

Charles's fever did not go down. In the afternoon, Sir Arthur called again, shook his head, and decreed that he should be bled. He took two ounces of blood from his left foot, trickled a little brandy into Charles's mouth, pronounced himself satisfied for the moment, and promised to call again later that day.

'We can only wait for the crisis, dear Lady Chelmsford. But his lordship has led a regular life, and there is every hope of a happy outcome,' he said magnificently. He took out his snuff-box, applied a pinch to his right nostril, put the box away again, dusted his nose and hands with his handkerchief, bowed profoundly to Roberta, and took himself off.

Lucy had hidden herself, at Roberta's request, in the dressing-room while Sir Arthur was there, for Roberta was afraid that he would refuse to treat Charles if Lucy argued with him, which she was very likely to. Now she came out and resumed her vigil at the bedside. Bleeding seemed to have produced some relief, but the effect was only tempor-

421

ary. Soon the fever was mounting again, and higher than before.

'He's burning up like a piece of paper,' Roberta said, and Lucy met Docwra's eye across the bed and read the message in them.

'I think perhaps you should send for the priest,' she said gently.

Three hours later Charles's breathing stopped. The silence in the room was dreadful. Roberta stared for a moment blankly at his face, and then lifted the hand she held to her lips, and kissed it, and laid it against her cheek, before replacing it gently on the counterpane.

Lucy went through the motions of feeling for his pulse. She felt hollow inside, and aching, for though it was several hours since she had expected him to recover, still the fact of his death was a different matter, something for which she could not have prepared herself. Kind Charles, everybody's friend, always there, always understanding, always ready to help; what would life be like without him to depend on?

'It was the damp air that did the damage, you know?' said Roberta. Her face was white and exhausted, and she spoke with an unnatural calm. 'He used to say he had a southern constitution. Being born in Italy, he ought to have lived in a hot climate.'

'Was he?' Lucy asked in surprise.

'Oh yes. His father served in the court of James III in Rome until he came into the title; then he came back to England. Charles was only a child, but he always loved Italy. He went there on his Grand Tour. When Bobbie's older, and the war is over, he shall go to Italy too. It's what Charles wanted.'

She was talking almost at random, her shadowed eyes blank in her white, strained face. Lucy got up and went around the bed to her, and urged her to her feet.

'Come,' she said, 'you must rest now. You're worn out.'

'Yes,' Roberta said automatically. 'He didn't want to live, you know. Well, now he's with Flora, and I'm happy for him. He always loved her best. After she died, he was never the same.'

'Oh, no, you mustn't say that. He loved you. Anyone

could see that,' Lucy said firmly.

'Yes, he loved me, in his way. We had a happy life together. But he was only marking time, until he could be with her again.'

'Come, you need to rest. Let me take you to your room. I'll make you up a draught, and then you'll sleep,' Lucy said, putting an arm around her.

Roberta resisted. 'He shouldn't be left alone.'

'Docwra will sit with him. She knows what's necessary.'

Roberta allowed Lucy to draw her out of the room and along the corridor to her own chamber. 'Will you stay with me, Lucy? Until I'm asleep? I feel better with you near me.'

'Yes, of course I'll stay,' Lucy said. 'I'll still be here when you wake up, I won't leave you.'

'Will you do something else for me?' she asked a while later, when Lucy was helping her take off her gown. 'Will you have Bobbie to stay with your children at Wolvercote? He likes Miss Trotton. He'd be safe there.'

'Of course. Parslow can take him and his nurse down tomorrow, if you like. It's probably better for him to be out of the way for the next few days.'

'Yes,' Roberta said, turning to face Lucy, 'and I don't want Lady Barbara to offer to have him.'

Lucy hesitated over a reply, not knowing quite what Roberta meant. 'Well, I suppose she is rather strict with her children, but –'

'It isn't that,' Roberta blurted out. 'Don't you realize that Bobbie is all that stands between Horatio and the title? Oh, I wish Charles could have waited, at least until Bobbie was older. My poor little boy! What's to become of us now?'

Lucy stared at her, shocked. 'You surely don't mean that you think – ? Oh no, really, it's too much! I confess I don't like Lady Barbara, but you can't think she would harm your son?'

'She and Horatio both, they want the title for Marcus. They always have. They'd stop at nothing to get it.'

'But you're talking about murder! This is the eighteenth century, things like that don't happen any more – not in England, anyway. You're upset, you don't know what

423

you're saying. When you've rested, you'll see things in a different light.'

But Roberta clutched her arm so hard that it hurt. 'Promise me you'll send Bobbie to Wolvercote! Promise me you won't let them take him away!'

'Yes, of course, I promise,' Lucy soothed her. 'Now lie down and rest, and I'll bring you up a draught. And as soon as everything has been done here, you and I will go down to Wolvercote, and join the children for a few weeks. We'll ride and walk, and Danby has promised to teach me how to shoot, in case we meet any more footpads. We'll have a lovely time, away from prying eyes, and you'll feel well and strong again.'

There was so much to be done. Charles's agent, Athersuch, took over much of the burden, and with the secretary dealt with such things as notices for the newspapers, writing to relatives, answering formal letters of condolence, and arranging the funeral; but there were still domestic matters to arrange, and Roberta was quite prostrated and unable to deal with anything. She did not cry, only lay motionless in bed as if she had been flattened against the pillows, hardly speaking, eating obediently when Docwra or her own maid fed her with a spoon, but making no voluntary movement at all.

So Lucy took command, ordered the blinds drawn, the liveried servants into their mourning, the others into weepers; had the door knocker wreathed in black crape; received the callers on Roberta's behalf and gave them burnt wine and biscuits.

True to her promise, she sent little Robert St Vincent, now seventh Earl of Chelmsford at the age of three and too bewildered to cry, off to Wolvercote on the morning after Charles's death, in the Chelmsford chariot. He clung tightly to Nursey's hand, and looked from face to face with round eyes, and was little consoled to know he was going to stay with his cousins, for he was too young properly to remember them. However, he knew and liked Parslow, and was gratified at all the consequence of having not only Parslow and

424

Nursey to attend him inside the chariot, but a footman and two postillions outside, *and* two outriders.

The latter were Docwra's thought. Lucy had not been inclined to accord so much consequence to such a little boy, but Docwra had said, 'You can't be too careful, m'lady, not with someone else's child. You know how many ugly customers there are hangin' about the post-roads these days, and how'd you ever face Lady Chelmsford if anything was to happen to his little lordship?'

Lucy concurred, though not entirely convinced, and even let Parslow take the two enormous horse-pistols which he was wont to carry when he accompanied his mistress on a long journey. She was a little shaken when, only an hour after the chariot departed, Lady Barbara arrived in heavy mourning to pay her condolences, and offered to take Bobbie back to Park Lane with her.

'For I'm sure you won't want the trouble of a child with everything else you have to do. He won't be any bother to me, I assure you! It cannot signify to nurse whether she has two children or three to take care of, and dear Marcus and dearest Barbarina will like above all things to have the little earl to stay.'

'Most grateful to you, ma'am, but the matter's already arranged,' Lucy said, blinking. 'The child is gone to Wolvercote this hour past.' An expression of fury crossed Lady Barbara's face fleetingly. 'Roberta wished it so,' Lucy added hastily.

'Well, then, I'm sure it's for the best,' Lady Barbara said with an effort.

'I shall tell Roberta of your kind offer, however,' Lucy said blandly. 'I am sure she will know just how to value it.'

The funeral was carried out with all the melancholy splendour of black-draped carriages, plumed horses, muffled drums, and a torchlit procession of servants and dependants. The standard over the pediment of Chelmsford House hung at half-mast, and the coffin itself was draped in a heavy cloth with a bullion fringe, embroidered with the Chelmsford arms, which had originally been made for the funeral of Annunciata's son Charles, the second earl.

It was extremely well attended, for Charles had made friends everywhere, amongst peers and ministers, in naval circles largely through Flora, and latterly in army circles too. The Prince of Wales, and the Dukes of York and Clarence attended, representing the King; there was a large contingent from the world of fashion, and one as large from amongst the merchants, bankers, and other gentlemen of enterprise from the City.

The Chelmsford estate comprised no land other than the demesne of Shawes and Chelmsford House itself, but partly owing to the undertakings of Charles's father, who had married the daughter of a rich banker, it had fingers in a great many financial pies, including shipping, banking, and maritime insurance. The seventh earl was starting life a very wealthy young man, and Roberta's widow's portion was extremely generous.

Lucy had time to think about Charles a great deal during the weeks following his death, and though she had no doubt that he had loved Roberta sincerely, she could not help coming to conclusion that he had married her after Flora's death largely to get an heir, and thus keep Horatio out of the succession. It seemed a little hard on Horatio, who had for so many years quite reasonably expected to come into the title eventually. Because of his expectations he had developed expensive tastes, while Roberta had been brought up to thrift and had tastes both modest and simple. While she was glad for Roberta's sake that she had been raised from her unmerited poverty, she did discover in herself an unwilling sympathy for Horatio.

Weston's guess about Buonaparte proved correct: his next move was a bold one. He led an army over the Alps in May, through the St Bernard pass, and coming down on northern Italy like a wolf on the fold, took the Austrians completely by surprise. By the second of June he had occupied Milan, and on the fourteenth he defeated the Austrian army in the battle of Marengo. On the following day the Austrian army of occupation signed an armistice. Whatever credit Buonaparte may have lost in Egypt, he regained in the Italian campaign.

It was a hot summer in England, and the harvests were early and abundant, and as day followed perfect day of sunshine and blue sky, it was hard to believe in the war at all. Mary Ann sat in the rose-garden under the tangled arbour of scented white roses like many a mistress of Morland Place before her, and embroidered baby-shirts and grew larger. James sometimes read her bits of war news out of the newspaper, but it meant little to her. Her world was bounded by the muffling walls of fertility, which distant alarms could not hope to penetrate.

Edward rejoiced in a large crop of spring lambs, and with the grass coming through early, they grew big and strong. In view of the hot weather he decided to start shearing a fortnight early, and hoped thereby to get the shearers before the time of their greatest demand; but everyone else had the same idea, so he got no benefit from it.

Fanny's ceaseless demands for a pony of her own had finally persuaded James. He decided on a Fell pony for her, for they were reliable and gentle-tempered, narrow enough for a very little girl, but strong enough to continue to carry her as she grew older. He found one at last, already schooled, and brought it back to Morland Place, and though Mary Ann thought it looked rather common, with its large head and heavily-feathered legs, it found favour at once with Fanny on account of its immensely long mane and tail.

She named her new pet, rather inappropriately, Tempest; and Tempest soon won Mary Ann's approval by his unshakeable good sense and temper. He did not object to anything Fanny might do, only turning to look at her with grave interest when she swung on his tail or ducked between his legs, and even when Puppy bounced around him and bit his heels, he simply moved aside and snorted a little.

Edward was growing more and more exasperated with Puppy, and when the dog crowned his bad behaviour by developing a taste for chasing sheep, Ned rounded on James in fury and told him that if he didn't take Puppy in hand and train him properly, he, Edward, would have no compunction in shooting him.

'An untrained dog's no use to anyone – you know that'
he said angrily. 'I know he's Fanny's dog, but he's your
responsibility, Jamie, which you've ignored from the beginning. Well, I tell you now, he's to be kept on a lead at all
times, until you prove to me that he's safe to be let off. And
if I see him chasing sheep again – or horses, or cattle for that
matter – I'll shoot him anyway, and that will be that.'

So James had two tasks in hand, teaching Fanny to
handle her horse, and trying to impress some sense into
Puppy's flighty brain. Fanny liked her riding lessons –
especially as James was teaching her initially to ride across,
which annoyed her mother considerably – but was bored
with Puppy's training, which was left more and more to
James to conduct alone. But she went almost everywhere
with her father, either riding Tempest on a leading-rein, or
sitting in front of James's saddle, and she grew as brown as a
gypsy, much to Mary Ann's disgust.

James would not take her complaints seriously. 'Oh, she's
only a child. You can worry about her complexion when
she's fourteen. Lucy was as brown as a nut when she was
Fanny's age, and she grew up to marry an earl! You mustn't
fret: it's bad for the new baby.'

His days were spent teaching Fanny, supervising the
building works at the new stables, schooling the horses
which were to be sold as hacks or hunters, breaking in the
young carriage horses, and helping Edward at times of
universal effort, like lambing, shearing or harvest. Twice a
week he dined at the Maccabbees, to meet old friends, read
the papers, and gather the gossip, and about once a month
he would stay late, drinking brandy, and have to be brought
home by Durban. He always felt dreadful the following day,
and Edward sometimes told him he was a fool and asked
him why he did it. James would only shrug and say that he
was a wire-walker, and that it was necessary for balance.

By mid-June they were coming to the end of shearing,
and most of the Morland flocks were back out in the fields,
looking strangely knobbed and gawky without their uniform
fleeces. In the barn the clip mounted up in tightly-packed
bundles to the rafters, but still the smell and the sound of
sheep were everywhere, and the taste of sheep-yolk

428

permeated everything, to the despair of Danvers, the cook.

James was helping one day to move the hurdles of the temporary paddock where the unshorn sheep waited their turn, making the paddock smaller, so that the reducing numbers would be easier to handle. Out of the corner of his eye he was watching Fanny, who had just helped to bring up the baskets of food and jugs of ale for the shearers' midday meal, and was now doing her best to save them the trouble of eating it. He moved a post and held it steady for his companion to knock in, when a hallooing caught his attention.

It was Birkin, the groom, bareback on one of the message-cobs, riding up from the direction of the house and waving his free arm excitedly. James guessed at once what it must mean – Mary Ann had gone into labour. He moved incautiously, and received the blow of the mallet intended for the post on his thumb. The next few minutes were all confusion, with apologies, explanations, requests and commands taking the air together, liberally laced with oaths from James, who had instinctively put his injured thumb in his mouth, and was now sincerely wishing he had not. At the end of that time James had taken over the cob from Birkin, vaulted astride, scooped Fanny up before him, and was cantering down towards the house.

'What's the matter, Papa?' Fanny asked jerkily as the cob lumbered homewards with a great deal more enthusiasm than he had made the outward journey.

'You Mama's time has come,' James said briefly.

'You mean the new baby's coming?' Fanny pouted. She was not at all sure she wanted the new brother or sister she had been promised. 'Why can't I stay with the shearers? It's nearly dinner time.'

'They're too busy to look after you,' James said. 'The next thing you know you'd have gone too close and got your fingers snipped off.'

Fanny's sense of injury was increased when she discovered that she was not to have any part in the excitement, but — crowning indignity — was to be packed off to the schoolroom with Father Aislaby and the chapel boys.

'But I don't want to!' she howled. "I want to stay here. I

want to see the baby come.'

'Father Aislaby will begin teaching you to read,' James offered coaxingly. 'Wouldn't you like to learn to read?'

Fanny only howled louder. 'I want to see Mama,' she cried. 'Polly says Mamas die when they have new babies. I don't want Mama to die.'

'She won't die,' James said, distracted.

'Polly's did,' Fanny said triumphantly. Father Aislaby gave James an admonitory look and took Fanny's hand, and led her firmly towards the stairs.

'Come along, my child,' he said. 'Your father will come and tell you all about it afterwards. There's no use making a fuss.' Fanny's experience of life so far had taught her that, on the contrary, it was well worth making a fuss, and she made it, all the way up the stairs, until they turned out of sight of James, and the priest was able to administer a sharp slap and shake and some good advice about not being naughty, which so surprised Fanny that she actually stopped for a good few minutes.

The silence lasted until they reached the day nursery, where Fanny, regarding the priest with narrowed eyes, demanded to have Puppy with her, to be allowed to play with her baby-house, not to learn to read, and to have strawberry tarts and junket for dinner. Aislaby was a pragmatist, with no love of Fanny and six energetic young boys waiting for him in the schoolroom: he made counter demands of complete silence from Fanny while he was next door, and the treaty was concluded amicably, with the reservation only that the strawberry-tart end of the business was not within his province, and that she must wheedle the nursery maid for them.

The ringing of the house-bell late in the afternoon took Father Aislaby from the schoolroom to the great bed-chamber, bringing relief to the chapel-boys, who were knee-deep in Virgil and sinking fast. At six o'clock, when the household gathered in the chapel for vespers, they were also able to give thanks for the safe delivery of the mistress, and witness the baptism of the new soul, who was given the name Henry, and also Anthony, since it was just past St Anthony's day..

The new baby's father was so deeply moved by conflicting emotions that he escaped after the service into the solitude of the Italian garden, and walked, deep in thought, amongst the dusky shadows of the tall hedges; undisturbed until one of the maids, escaping Durban's vigilance, came to tell him that Miss Fanny was carrying on fit to choke.

He was recalled forcibly to his duty. He had promised to go and tell Fanny all about it, and he had forgotten. The maid, trotting anxiously at his heels as he headed for the house, told him that the news had been brought to the nursery by a servant, and that Miss Fanny had clapped her hands over her ears and screamed, because she wanted to hear it from her father.

'We didn't know where you were, sir,' she said breathlessly, 'and Miss Fanny, poor little soul, cried as though her heart was broke, and said her Mama was dead, and she wouldn't believe anyone to the contrary, sir, and she called for you again and again, and we're in that much of a moither you wouldn't think!'

James would, and hurried to the nursery, leaving the maid well behind. Fanny had passed through wailing to screaming rage, in which she flung her toys with wild abandon at anyone who came near her, finally making herself sick, and losing the benefit of the hard-won strawberry tarts. When James arrived, she had got her second wind and was well into her stride, sobbing with a regular mechanical whoop. She was a sorry sight, her muslin dress torn, her curls disordered and ribbonless, her face white and wet and her eyes swollen, and the nursery staff fussing round her and vainly coaxing her with all manner of sweetmeats and playthings.

When she saw James she flung herself at his legs. He picked her up and held her against his shoulder where she hiccoughed dismally that everyone had forgotten her and that her mother was dead and that he had not come as he promised.

'Now, chick, now, it's not true. Your Mama is perfectly all right, and you have a new brother, and I didn't forget you, only I was too busy to come before. Everything's all

431

right. Do stop crying, Fanny. There's nothing to cry for. Papa's here.'

'They took P-P-Puppy away,' she sobbed, though less forcefully.

'Only to feed him,' James soothed.

'I thought you'd never come,' she said, pressing her wet face against his neck. 'And I broke my b-best b-b-baby!' she remembered. In the height of her throwing fit, she had wrenched open her treasured baby-house and flung its contents to the winds, including the cunning little wooden baby James had made with jointed arms and legs, and for which Mary Ann had made a beautiful silk gown with real lace on it and petticoats and a muslin tucker and cap. Fanny had been fascinated by it, and now it lay sadly mangled, for when she had flung it against the wall, an arm had broken off, and then Puppy, thinking it a game, had chewed it, to the serious detriment of the clothing.

'Never mind, my pigeon, we can make it all right again. Don't cry. Papa will mend her, and Mama will make some new clothes for her, and she'll be as good as new. Now, my darling, why don't you let Sarah wash your face and brush your hair, and put on a clean frock, and then I'll come up and have supper with you. How would you like that?'

Fanny nodded dumbly, her face still pressed against him.

'And afterwards I'll read you a story,' he added, setting her down gently and nodding to the nursery-maid. Fanny allowed herself to be led away, but stopped after a few paces to look at her father doubtfully.

'Papa, you won't love the new baby more than me, will you?'

James smiled painfully, 'No, chicken, I won't. I promise.'

Mathilde, perched on a stool, wriggled, and Héloïse, kneeling at her feet, felt the hem of the dress which she was attempting to pin up twitched out of her hands for the fourth time.

'Oh, Mathilde!' she cried despairingly. Mathilde looked down in surprise.

'Did I move?' she asked innocently.

'You wriggled,' Héloïse affirmed, searching on the floor for the pin she had dropped.

'I didn't know. I'm sorry,' Mathilde said humbly. Héloïse smiled up at her.

'It's partly my fault. I'm so slow. I'll never make a dressmaker,' she said thoughtlessly. Madam Chouflon, sitting by, her swollen fingers twitching in her lap with the desire to take over the bungled business, groaned.

'Oh, my useless hands!' she said. 'I should be doing that, and all I can do is sit here and watch.'

'You are not just watching,' Héloïse said. 'Do you think I could do this without your instructions?'

Flon was not to be comforted. 'I'm nothing but a burden to you.'

'Nonsense,' Héloïse said, but a fraction wearily. Plain sewing she had learned as a child, and practised all her life, but dressmaking was another matter, especially working with soft muslins like this fine jaconet. It was Mathilde's first grown-up dress, and when an attack of her old trouble disabled Madame Chouflon, Héloïse did not want to disappoint her ward, and offered to complete the work under Flon's direction. But she worked inexpertly, and it made Flon feel useless.

'I don't know what I would do without you,' she went on, but Flon shook her head, making her long earrings rattle.

'A burden,' she said. 'We all are, one way and another. There's Barnard, cooking as though for a Court banquet, in spite of all you say to him, and weeping when you order only one course. Three-colour soup and Florence oranges ! Goose stuffed with capons and Paradise tart!'

'He has just learned to make the lemon curd which I like,' Héloïse offered in defence of her cook.

'Aye, but twenty pounds at a time,' Flon retorted, 'and it doesn't keep. He won't learn that he is not cook to a great household any more. And then there's Father Jerome, wanting to say Mass three times a day, and for you to build a chapel onto the house instead of a new drawing-room.'

'But he is of the greatest help to me,' Héloïse said. 'He teaches Mathilde, and he has got her to speak grammatical French, which was more than I ever managed. Perhaps you

433

had better get down now, my love,' she smiled up at her ward apologetically. 'I'll finish the hem later. I'm sure you need a rest, after standing still for so long.'

'He ought to teach her grammatical English, that would be more to the point,' Flon went on relentlessly. 'But you don't need a chaplain any more than you need a cook like Barnard – or a tame dressmaker, especially one who can't hold a needle for three months out of four. We're just burdens, child, and you know it, for all that you like to pretend we pay our way.'

Héloïse, still kneeling, moved over and put her arms round her old friend. 'Well, call yourself a burden if you like! What do you think I would do without you all? Live alone with my great wealth? Spend my days counting my money? Don't you think I am paid fourfold in love for any little trouble I might go to?'

Flon patted the dark curly head fondly. 'I know you are a great deal too good for us, and next thing to an angel, as Marie says. God will reward you in Heaven, dearest child.'

Kithra, lying on his side in a patch of sunlight from the window, lifted his head suddenly, whined, and beat his tail against the carpet.

'That must be Marie returning,' Héloïse said, though she could not yet hear the sound of Kexby's mare or the rattling of his cart. 'Mathilde, my love, run upstairs and put on your frock. I expect Marie will want some tea,' she said to Madame. 'Would you ask Alice, dear Flon, while I go and get Sophie up from her nap? I think it's cool enough now for us to take it in the garden, under the mulberry tree.'

Sophie-Marie still slept in Héloïse's own room, though she had long outgrown the elm-wood crib, and had a low truckle, which Stephen had also made for her. Héloïse went in quietly and found her asleep, lying on her side with her cheek nestled in her hand. The muslin curtains had been drawn across the open window, and a little breeze had got up at last, and was blowing them softly above Sophie's head.

She would be two years old next month. Héloïse, gazing down at her sleeping daughter, thought that every passing month made her only more beautiful. She seemed the image of James, to Héloïse's partial eyes: she had his features, his fine, silky, dark brown hair, with the hint of fox when the sun shone on it, and when she smiled, it was James's smile, and fit to melt one's heart. Her eyes were his in shape, though in colour they were as black as midnight, and her skin was not lily-fair like James's, but Stuart-dark.

Héloïse loved her with a passion which was humble, grateful, and astonished. Sophie-Marie was a gift from God, His sign of forgiveness, His blessing on Héloïse. She could not view it any other way, for the child was too lovely simply to be the sum of her parents, and her sweet and loving nature could surely only come from the kindly and all-forgiving Father.

Héloïse bent over the bed and kissed the rose-velvet cheek, savouring the innocent smell of her skin and hair, and Sophie-Marie woke and smiled.

'Time to get up, my darling,' Héloïse said. 'Marie is back from Thirsk, and we shall go into the garden and have some tea.'

When she came downstairs, with the baby, still a little sleepy, on her hip, she found Flon and Marie waiting for her in the drawing room. Marie still had on her bonnet, and they both looked anxious.

'Ah, here's my little sweetheart,' Flon said, too quickly, holding out her arms for Sophie. 'Come to Flon, my darling! let me take her out into the garden, my dear. Marie wants to speak to you.'

She took Sophie and hurried away. Héloïse went forward to untie Marie's bonnet-strings. 'What is it, Marie? Don't you wish for some tea? Have you asked Kexby to stay? Did you have an agreeable day?'

Marie, made nervous by the attention, tried to push Héloïse's hands away, and only succeeded in creating a knot. Kithra, sensing the atmosphere, came up and whined and thrust his muzzle up at them. Héloïse desisted and regarded her maid with her head slightly tilted.

'Well, then, what is it? You look upset, Marie. Has someone spoken unkindly to you?'

'Oh, madame, I have heard some news. I did not know whether to tell you, but Flon says I should, for you would hear it sooner or later. Only now I don't know how.'

Héloïse stood very still. 'If it is so very bad,' she said carefully, 'you had certainly better tell me at once.'

Marie clasped her hands together, her face creased with sympathy. 'It is not bad news, madame, at least, not really, only I'm afraid you will not like it.' She gathered her courage, and said baldly, 'They have got a son, madame, at Morland Place. A son named Henry.'

She watched as the news sank slowly in. Héloïse said nothing for a long time. She stared at Marie as though she hoped to be told it was a mistake, or a jest. Then she said, 'A son named Henry. I think they must be very happy.'

'Oh, madame – '

'Please, Marie, please don't,' Héloïse said gently. 'Your strings are all in a tangle. You had better go and ask Alice to undo it for you. Yes, please go,' she forestalled a protest. 'I wish to be alone.'

Some time later Father Jerome went to look for her, and found her in her bedchamber, sitting on the bed, staring at nothing. Kithra was sitting at her feet, his head laid helpfully in her lap, and she was stroking his ears absently.

'My child,' said the priest, and Héloïse looked up. He sat beside her on the bed and said gently, 'Whatever your trouble, it will be eased by sharing it with God.'

'Oh Father,' she said, 'I don't know. I think I must be very wicked. It is a great and good thing to have a child, and one ought to rejoice for them.' Her voice sank to a whisper. 'But it *hurts*, Father, it hurts so much.'

He captured one of her hands and stroked it. 'I know,' he said.

'It's foolish,' she went on. 'Why should this make any difference? I told him to go back, I wanted him to, because it was the right thing. And yet – and yet, I suppose I always thought that he would go on loving me, and that it would be a marriage only in name. Oh, that was wicked, wasn't it?'

'Yes, my child, that was wicked.'

'Then I am punished,' she said, her mouth turned down in pain. She looked down at Kithra, gazing anxiously into her face, and her eyes filled with tears. She tried to swallow them back. 'Oh Father, what can I do? I love him so, and he loves me, and yet we cannot be together. How can such love be a wrong thing? We might so easily have been married. Why are we punished for what was never our fault? I don't understand,' she burst out passionately. 'I don't understand any of it!'

Father Jerome stroked her hand gently. 'God has His reasons for everything. It would be a poor thing, would it not, if God were not wiser than men?'

She bowed her head. 'But what am I to do?' she asked again.

'Trust Him. It is not for us to understand all things, only to trust and obey. Our Father loves us, child. He sees even the sparrow fall – do you think He would let you out of His sight? He has His plan for you as for everyone.'

She said nothing, and after a moment the priest stood up and went away, hoping his words would work on her good sense. Héloïse smoothed Kithra's head and said, 'Yes, you love me, I know.' He beat his tail in agreement. 'Am I ungrateful? I am surrounded by love.' Kithra shuffled a fraction of an inch closer to her. 'Oh, but it isn't the same!' She looked across his head at the window and the bright day beyond, remembered James here with her in this very room; and then thought of Sophie-Marie sleeping below the blowing curtains. A boy. He and his wife had a boy. She had gone full circle. The tears held back were making her throat ache. 'Henry,' she said. 'I wish I did not know his name.'

Chapter Twenty-five

Contrary to her expectations, Lucy enjoyed her quiet spell at Wolvercote with Roberta and the children. The hunting was virtually over by the time they went down, but the weather was perfect for riding, fresh and sunny and not too hot, and Lucy exercised her restless spirit by arranging and competing in a number of private cross-country races, riding Mimosa, and a big, strong, ground-eater of a colt called Minstrel, which Chetwyn had bought as a second hunter from 'Cheerful Charlie' Rutland, but couldn't get on with.

Roberta's maid, Sands, was much scandalized that Lucy rode cross-saddle in these races, and complained so frequently to her mistress that a bad example was being set to the children, that Roberta felt obliged at last to mention the matter as delicately as possible to Lucy.

'Oh, stuff,' Lucy said firmly. 'It's not as if I'm doing it in public – I make a point of keeping the races to our own land. These things are only a matter of foolish convention, anyway.'

'I don't think it's quite – decent,' Roberta said hesitantly, 'for a female to sit *astride* a horse.'

'Now don't be fusty, Roberta,' Lucy said. 'I wouldn't do it in London, in the Park, because it would be too tiresome to have the old hens clucking at me all the time, but here on my own land, I shall do as I please.'

Apart from Roberta the company at Wolvercote was exclusively male, and the young men who ran tame about the house and stables thought her ladyship a trump card, a great goer, and absolutely up to the rig. Roberta let the subject drop, and told Sands to hold her tongue. The matter resolved itself when the continuing hot weather made the ground too hard for races, and the steeplechasing petered out into innocent picnics and sight-seeing rides.

At the beginning of June a letter came from Captain

Haworth, dated from Portsmouth, with the news that the *Africa* had been recommissioned under him, with his whole crew, for a further two years, and had been ordered to sail immediately her stores were completed to join the blockade of Brest under Lord Bridport.

'He may see something of Harry, then,' Lucy said as she read the letter to Roberta. When the *Excellent* had paid off, Cuthbert Collingwood had got his flag at last, hoisting it in the old *Triumph*. Of his kindness, he had taken Harry with him, and they too were now with the Brest squadron. 'Your blockade captains are amazingly sociable, always in and out of each others' ships.'

Haworth's letter concluded with the hope that, now he was in home waters, he might have more opportunities for shore leave. Until then, he sent Hippolyta his love, and a guinea under the seal for ribbons.

'Now that Hippolyta is nearly six,' Lucy decided, 'it's time she learned to ride. I shall teach her myself, rather than leave it to a groom. Mary was taught by a groom, and she was never more than an indifferent rider,' she explained to Roberta. 'I mean to see Polly has a better start. I owe it to Captain Haworth.'

'Is he a good rider, then?' Roberta asked, looking up from her tambour-work.

'Why, no – I don't know. I don't suppose so – sailors hardly ever are, are they?' Lucy said.

'Then, I don't quite understand,' said Roberta. 'Why do you owe it to him?'

Lucy found herself puzzled. 'Because I like him,' she said at last, a little lamely.

'Oh,' said Roberta, and looked down at her work again. 'It does seem hard that he should have been sent off to sea again without any time on shore.'

'I expect he liked it of all things,' Lucy said practically. 'He'd have but just got his crew used to his ways.'

'But he hadn't even time to come to see Hippolyta. I don't suppose she would recognize him now.'

'I wonder about his other child. I do think he must be forced to send her home, at least at the end of summer. It was one thing to have her with him in the Mediterranean

439

but when the autumn gales hit the Channel, and then when winter comes – '

Roberta shook her head. 'I don't know how he can think of it. And Mary's maid is still with him, taking care of the child, isn't she?'

'Yes, dear old Farleigh,' Lucy chuckled. 'She must be as tough as ship's beef after all! But I suspect she would endure anything for the sake of the baby. She adored Mary, you know, for all her crusty ways.'

Roberta stitched in silence for a while, and then said tentatively, 'I wonder, if you are really going to teach Hippolyta to ride, would you consider teaching Bobbie, too? I know he's only three, but he's very sensible, and boys ought to learn sooner than girls, don't you think?'

'Of course I will,' Lucy said at once. 'It's a capital idea. Perhaps I'll start a regular school – Lady Aylesbury's Academy of Equitation! He and Polly will help each other on – it's always better to learn in company. And you're quite right that Bobbie ought to begin as soon as possible. Perhaps I'll put Minnie up, too?' she added, and then had a mental image of plump, bolster-shaped Flaminia on a pony. 'On second thoughts, perhaps not. I don't think Minnie is destined to be a horsewoman.'

So with running the house, riding, walking with Roberta, teaching the children to ride, and taking lessons in shooting from the faithful Danby Wiske, Lucy found the days passed pleasantly; and lest she should miss London Society, she gave Major Wiske a standing order to invite people to Wolvercote every weekend, or, if there was anything happening in Town that he thought would amuse her, to procure her an invitation and escort her to it.

Of Chetwyn she saw little. From courtesy she always sent her card to his lodgings when she came up to Grosvenor Street; she saw him once standing with a friend outside Asprey's in Bond Street, and he raised his hat to her as she bowled past in her curricle; and once they were in adjacent boxes at the Haymarket theatre, and he strolled round during the entr'acte to ask her how she did. At Easter he came down to Wolvercote with a party of his own for the shooting, and for four days his guests and hers met at dinner, before he took his off to Cheveley.

She found, however, that she did not miss him. The idea of their separating had upset her a great deal more than the fact; she had not liked to have it spelled out, but once she got used to it, she found she hardly ever thought of him at all. How he liked it, it never crossed her mind to wonder.

In June the Pope gave his decision on Mrs Fitzherbert's marriage to the Prince of Wales: he was her lawful husband in the eyes of the Church, and she might therefore live with him without sin. In his gratitude, the Prince declared that Roman Catholicism was the only religion for a gentleman; he and his Maria once more became inseparable, and on the seventeenth Mrs Fitzherbert gave a public breakfast at her house in Tilney Street, by way of announcing formally that they were reconciled.

Obedient to the promptings of curiosity, and to Wiske's affirmation that 'Everyone would be there', Lucy accepted her invitation. It was a grand occasion, with four hundred guests, for whose better accommodation three huge marquees had been erected in the garden. Mrs Fitzherbert, still an attractive woman, was looking almost bridal in her triumph, as the Prince stood beside her to receive the guests.

'Ah, Lady Curricle, good of you to come,' the Prince greeted Lucy smilingly, bending his tall bulk over her hand. He was looking splendid in a white morning-coat with gold frogs and a muscovy sable collar, across which his blue ribbon and star shewed up beautifully; a lilac and white striped Marseilles quilted waistcoat; finest doeskin pantaloons, tasselled boots of blinding brilliance; a new, elegantly oiled nut-brown peruke; and hanging from his sleeve a muslin handkerchief embroidered all over with gold spots and well-scented with rose-water.

'Highness,' said Lucy, curtseying low.

The perfectly manicured, perfumed and bejewelled hand raised her. 'Wiske brought you, I see. Well, you'll find plenty of friends here today, eh, Maria? All friends, you know. They tell us so themselves, so it must be true, what?'

He was in the best of moods, merry, affable, full of little

jokes and pleasantries. His charm was considerable where he felt himself loved and respected, and that day he seemed to have no doubts. His behaviour towards his beloved Maria was almost boyish, and the effect of her influence was clearly seen in that though he drank heavily throughout the long entertainment – which involved two changes of costume, beginning at two in the afternoon, continuing through dinner at seven, and lasting until five the following morning – he was never nearer to being drunk than a slight unsteadiness.

Lucy joined the throng and was claimed at once by old Admiral Scorton, who had with him Captain Macnamara, a friend of William's – they had been lieutenants together – who was famed equally for his pet Newfoundland dog, and his passion for duelling. They begged leave to introduce another sea captain, an extremely handsome young man named Thomas Manby, who bowed and mentioned diffidently that he was acquainted with James Weston.

'Manby's just back from Naples,' Macnamara said. 'Says Nelson's got himself into the deuce of a scramble over Hamilton's wife.'

'Damned lot of fustian,' Admiral Scorton grumbled. 'Let a man have his batter puddin', I say. What's it got to do with it? Is he a good sailor or ain't he, that's all I want to know.'

'I don't know that Admiral Keith would agree with you, sir,' Macnamara smiled. 'According to Manby here, he says he's tired of having the fleet commanded by a woman. Nelson does whatever Emma Hamilton commands.'

'I know Keith,' Scorton said. 'A good man, but stuffy, He don't understand. When a man ain't in the petticoat line, which Nelson never has been, he falls hard if he falls at all. But Nelson's a damned fine sailor, and he'd never do anything amiss in the naval way, just because a woman told him to.'

'But Lady Hamilton, sir, admires Admiral Nelson exceedingly, and does not hesitate to tell him so,' said Captain Manby. 'What man could resist such flattery? He says he is not happy anywhere but by her side, and has idled in Naples month after month in order to be so.'

'Pah! She's a silly woman – and not out of the top

drawer, neither. I don't know why Hamilton ever took her on. But why shouldn't she admire him? Hero of the Nile, and all that sort of thing.'

'Well, the hero's on his way home now,' Macnamara said with a grin, travelled overland, if you like, with Lady Hamilton *and* Sir William! And in spite of the Nile, I wonder whether St Vincent will be able to save his Protégé's bacon this time. Keith has made no secret of his opinion.'

'Johnny Jervis won't be swayed by a lot of idle gossip,' Admiral Scorton said firmly.

'They say Nelson's sworn to have Lady Hamilton presented at Court,' Macnamara went on teasingly. 'I wonder how he will introduce her to Lady Nelson? Is the *ménage à trois* to become *à quatre*?'

Admiral Scorton was beginning to grow red in the face, and Manby took pity on him and said with a bow, 'But I am sure we are boring Lady Aylesbury. We must find a topic more suitable for her ears.'

'I assure you,' Lucy said, 'nothing to do with His Majesty's navy bores me. But tell me,' she went on casually, 'have you happened to meet with Captain Weston recently? I believe he was in Naples a few weeks ago.'

'I did have the pleasure of dining with him last month,' Manby said with a faint smile. 'I am delighted to be able to inform your ladyship that he was in excellent health, and in as good spirit as could be expected in the circumstances.'

'Eh? What circumstances?' Admiral Scorton asked inopportunely.

Lucy frowned, and Macnamara said with a grin, 'Not all sailors, sir, are lucky enough to be able to have their loved ones with them.'

Admiral Scorton looked from one face to another, and then enlightenment cleared his brow. 'As you say, as you say,' he said hastily, and crooked an arm towards Lucy. 'What say we go and look for a glass of champagne, m'dear? It's damned hot in here. Can't think how the Prince can wear fur in this weather – and a flannel waistcoat, if I know him, under that fancy Marseilles confection he's sportin'.' Lucy, with a glance at the two young captains, slipped her hand demurely under the Admiral's, and let him lead her away. When they were clear of them, the Admiral squeezed her hand against his coat and said, 'Don't you mind it, m'dear, if those two tease you a little.'

'Tease me, sir?' Lucy murmured innocently.

'Aye, aye, you know very well what I mean. Thing is, no-one minds a man takin' a shine to a lady, provided he don't make a fool of himself. Wouldn't admit it in front of Macnamara or young whatsisname, but Nelson's doin' himself no good, lettin' that woman drag him about the Courts of Europe, presentin' him like a bear in a cage, puffin' him off to all and sundry. Writes songs in his praise, if you please, and sings 'em herself – with encores! Pah! Couldn't stand to see it m'self, though he's as fine a sailor as I've ever met, or hope to. But this other business of yours – different thing altogether!'

'I can't think what business you mean, Admiral,' Lucy said.

'Aye, you may laugh at me, you naughty puss,' he chuckled, 'but I mean what I say; and you may always count on one friend at least while I live. And if I were twenty years younger, I'd give young Weston a run for his money, too!'

Lucy was touched, and comforted too. There was no denying she had sometimes worried that their liaison might harm Weston's career, and it was good to have an official opinion on the matter, especially from someone like Scorton, who had influence with Their Lordships.

Weston continued a reliable correspondent. His letters, read and re-read until they grew quite dog-eared, combined amusing stories of day-to-day life aboard the *Semele* with news of the world at large and the progress of the war.

Through him she learnt that the French General Buona-parte had returned to Paris after the victory at Marengo, only to face plots to replace him, one of them hatched by his own brother, Joseph. The Austrian Court had repudiated the armistice signed after Marengo, saying that it had in any case only applied to the army in Italy, not to Austria as a whole.

'So it looks as though Buonaparte will be kept busy in Paris for the next few months at least, which is good news for all of us. There is every chance that one of his rivals will assassinate him, as long as he stays in the capital!'

In September Weston was on the spot when the French garrison in Malta finally surrendered to the British.

'So we have driven the Frogs another step backwards, but in doing so have angered the Russians, for their Tsar Paul is hereditary Grand Master of the order of St John, and feels that Malta ought to be in the hands of the Knights and none other. Needless to say, we do not agree with him. He is, in any case, as mad as a hatter, and has conceived the wildest admiration for the Corsican general.'

His letters always ended with love, telling her how much he missed her, how he thought about her in all his spare moments, how often he wished for peace, so that he could be with her, how he looked forward to receiving her letters, and treasured them when they did come.

Lucy sometimes wondered how much comfort they could bring him. Though she thought about him constantly, and longed for him fiercely, she did not have it in her to write such things. Her vocabulary included no words of love, and her letters to him were cheerful and busy and matter-of-fact, ending almost curtly with a trust that he was well and a diffident hope that she would see him soon.

No matter how she bit the end of her pen or ruined the nib by digging it into the desk-top, she could never write the sort of things that he said to her, and the fear haunted her that she disappointed him, that he might not know how much she cared for him. Her love was dumb, and she had not yet come to realize that he understood that, and was well able to read between the lines and supply her feelings for himself.

In October Lucy arrived in Town for the Little Season, accompanied by Roberta, who was now in half-mourning, and on whom she thought a little urban noise and variety might work favourably. The young Earl remained at Wolvercote with the other children, and Roberta stayed at

Upper Grosvenor Street, rather than open up Chelmsford House.

'It's too big for me, anyway,' Roberta said. 'I will have to think seriously about where Bobbie and I are going to live. The thought of either Shawes or Chelmsford House is very daunting. One poor widow and one small boy would be entirely dwarfed by those mansions.'

'I'd hardly call you poor,' Lucy said.

'There are other ways of being poor than having no money,' Roberta said sadly. 'I've tried both, and I'd much prefer to be without money.'

'Yes, I know,' Lucy said. 'Still, Bobbie is the Earl of Chelmsford. You must live in some style, or you'll bring Horatio and Lady Barbara down on you. And as soon as you breech him, you'll have to find him a suitable governor. Miss Trotton and Nursey won't do for a young man in trousers.'

'How to know who is suitable? My ideas will certainly not match with Lady Barbara's, and if I take her recommendation, I shall never know a moment's security.'

Lucy looked at her curiously. 'You don't really think she would harm him, do you?' she asked. 'I thought that was only a wild fantasy.'

Roberta looked grave. 'I don't know,' she said. 'It's a terrible thing to think, but greed is the strongest of all human passions – greed and jealousy.' She fell silent, deep in thought.

'I wonder you don't ask your Papa's advice,' Lucy said idly. 'He seemed to me a most sensible man, the one time I met him.'

Roberta looked up, and a slow smile transfigured her face. 'Why, of course! Lucy, you are so clever. Why didn't I think of it? Papa will know what to do. I wonder – perhaps he may agree to come and live with us permanently? I don't suppose at his age he will want to go on active service again. We could live very comfortably together, and I should feel so much happier with a man about the house.'

A week later Chetwyn fell ill. He had been walking home

446

alone, drunk, from one of his clubs, when he had stumbled and fallen while crossing St James's Square. It was very late, and the square was quiet, and no-one had happened to pass by, and he had lain half-conscious for several hours, during which time it came on to rain, until he was thoroughly soaked and chilled.

His man, Thorn, had eventually begun to worry about him. He sent an enquiry round to the club, and on learning that his lordship had left some time ago, set out to trace his master's probable route, and found him shivering and groaning under the bushes in the centre of the square. He got him home and to bed, but a fever had rapidly developed, and Thorn, worried by its severity, sent word round to Upper Grosvenor Street.

Lucy went at once to Ryder Street, and after one glance at her husband proclaimed that she would nurse him herself, and not leave him until he was well again.

'Oh, but my lady, you can't think of it!' Thorn cried, shocked. 'Not here, not in Ryder Street. These are bachelor apartments! It – it wouldn't be fitting!'

'Don't talk such nonsense,' Lucy said tersely. 'I am his wife.'

'But my lady, there isn't anywhere for you to sleep, or for your maid. There's only this room, as you see it, and the drawing-room, and the dressing-room where I sleep.'

Lucy considered. She was indifferent to comfort as a rule, but there was no denying that the rooms were very small, and if the illness were to be protracted, they would be very inconvenient. She came to a decision.

'Parslow, do you think you could lift his lordship, if Thorn were to help you, and carry him down to the chaise?'

'Yes, my lady,' said the excellent Parslow imperturbably. 'If I may suggest, my lady, you might go down ahead of us with blankets, and have the carriage door open, and the footman inside to help us lift his lordship in.'

'Of course. Well, Thorn, what are you waiting for? Pack your master's bag immediately.'

'Pack, my lady?' said the man in bewilderment. His mind did not work as swiftly as Parslow's.

'Yes, pack. We are taking his lordship home to Upper

Grosvenor Street, where I can nurse him properly. It's a short journey, and the greater comfort at the end of it will be worth the trouble of moving him.'

'Yes, my lady,' said Thorn. 'Pack, you said, my lady?'

'Not his clothes, simpleton! His night-things, his brushes, his razors! Parslow, you had better go with him and see to it. The man's got windmills in his head.'

They disappeared into the dressing-room, and Lucy went over to the bed to feel Chetwyn's pulse, and to wipe the sweat from his face, where it had gathered in his eye-sockets like tears. The touch of her hand brought him to consciousness, and he opened his eyes and looked at her, evidently puzzled.

'Lucy?' he whispered at last.

'Yes, it's me,' she said.

'Where am I?'

'In your lodgings. You had a fall, and hurt your head, and now you've got a fever, so I'm taking you home to look after you properly. Let me lift your head, while you take a sip of water.'

He drank gratefully, and she put him gently back on the pillows. He looked up at her, his eyes clouded with fever. 'You're a good girl,' he said, closing them. 'Mother'll look after me.'

'What's that?' Lucy asked, startled, before she realized that the fever had confused him. He had used to call Jemima Mother. Probably when she said 'home', he had thought she meant Morland Place.

'Tired,' he said. 'So tired.' She laid her fingers on his forehead, and he smiled and moved a little towards her hand. 'Nice,' he mumbled. 'Don't leave me, Luce.'

Chetwyn's general health had been undermined by drinking, and for the second time in a year Lucy found herself nursing a case of the lung-fever. The similarity of the symptoms unnerved Roberta so much that she burst into tears, and Lucy suggested that she go back to Wolvercote.

'Docwra and I will manage between us, don't worry,' she said, but Roberta wouldn't hear of it.

'I couldn't leave you at a moment like this,' she said, drying her eyes and blowing her nose vigorously. 'Besides, I'm sure you will need me, to take over while you sleep. I shall be all right now. I'm sorry I was so weak and foolish – it won't happen again.'

Lucy did not call in a doctor, not even the eminent Sir Arthur, who had presided over so many notable deaths. 'He didn't make such a hand of treating Charles,' she pointed out tactlessly to Roberta when she suggested sending for him. 'Lung-fever cases need careful nursing, and peace and quiet.'

Outside the windows a glorious golden autumn was stretching out that lovely summer. Hicks had straw spread in the street to muffle the noise of the traffic, and the two footmen stood guard to beg passers by to keep their voices down, for Lucy was insistent that the windows of the sick-room should be kept open. 'He needs fresh air,' she said. Docwra had been converted over the last four years to the principle Lucy had inherited from her father, though Roberta still hankered after the closed windows and hot fires of traditional nursing.

Docwra made a pneumonia-jacket of double flannel, filled with duck-down; Lucy propped Chetwyn as high as possible on pillows, and administered her own specific, champagne well-laced with brandy, along with small doses of foxglove-oil to stimulate the heart. But despite all this Chetwyn's condition declined. He sank into semi-consciousness, his pulse grew faint and rapid, and his breathing laboured as his fever grew higher and higher.

On the seventh day, late in the evening, Docwra left Lucy alone with the patient for half an hour, and returned with the priest from the nearest church. Lucy met her eyes across the bed, and then stepped back without a word to let the priest perform his task. When he had gone, Lucy said to the other two. 'You had better rest. I'll watch him. Yes, go on. There's nothing for you to do here. I'll call for you if I need you.'

Left alone, she sat beside the bed and watched her husband's face. The flesh had been stripped away by the consuming fever, the lines smoothed out, and he looked oddly boyish, with the flush across the cheekbones and the ears suddenly prominent. He was Chetwyn, her brother's friend, whom she had known all her life, and loved as a brother. They should not have married, she thought, for other things had got in the way of that pure and natural feeling, and made it impossible for them to be either man and wife, or brother and sister.

She realized suddenly, that she knew nothing of how he felt about things. Did he mind about her and Weston? And if so, in what way? Why had he moved to Ryder Street? Was he unhappy, or merely indifferent? She pushed his hair back from his forehead – conker-coloured hair, cut in a fashionable crop – and found that there were threads of silver in the crown, and suddenly she was crying. She didn't want him to die. She leaned over him, and her tears dropped on his cheek, and he was so hot she half expected them to sizzle. He was forty-three, too young to die; but then, Charles had been very little older.

The candles burned low, and guttered; the church bell struck quarters indefatigably; the household slept heavily and uneasily. Lucy sat beside the bed, alone with her thoughts and memories, until the darkness outside was suddenly shot through with the thrilling silver of the first birdsong. Dawn was coming, she thought gladly. She left the bedside and went to the window to look at the sky.

She smelled the dawn before she saw it, smelled it through the London perfume of horse-manure and wood-smoke like the cold clarity of a high hill-stream. The sky was suffused with a silvery greyness, shading to aquamarine in the west, primrose in the east, and as the birdsong reached a crescendo the sun rose, still hidden from her by the houses, but revealing its presence in the suddenly gilded edges of the small clouds above the rooftops.

Behind her, in the shadowed bedroom, there was silence. Lucy stiffened, listening for the sound she had grown so accustomed to she had ceased to notice it – the harsh, rapid labouring of Chetwyn's breathing – but the silence was absolute. A stillness came over her. It was all over then. He was dead. She tried to feel, tried to move, but she could do nothing, only stand at the window in the cool dawn air and watch the transparent colours of morning deepen into day.

Some time later – she did not know how long – she heard the door of the bedchamber open.

'My lady?' said Docwra's voice tentatively. She sounded as though she had only just woken up. Lucy heard her draw a small, quick breath, heard the rustling of her clothes as she hurried to the bed, and then another drawn breath, longer, like a sigh.

And then her voice, lilting with gladness, making Lucy turn from the window at last. 'Our Blessed Lady be praised! The fever's broken! The crisis is over, my lady. He's going to get well!'

The convalescence was long, marked with the lassitude characteristic of the illness. He was very weak, and had no appetite, but not all his fretfulness and indifference could wear the patience of the three women. They had brought him through the sickness which had killed Charles, and would have run up and down stairs twice as often, and have spent all day in the kitchen if need be, concocting trifles to tempt his weary appetite.

By the end of November he was up and about again, though going no farther than the garden on warm days, and spending a good deal of time on the sopha. Lucy brought Chetwyn tidbits of news to tempt his curiosity. All London was buzzing with the scandal of Lord Nelson and the Hamiltons. They had landed at Yarmouth on the 6th of November, and had been greeted rapturously by the crowds, who made nothing of the sailor-hero's private peccadillos, and unhitched the horses from his carriage to draw it themselves through the streets to the first tavern, whose landlord begged permission to rename his house *The Nelson Arms*.

This adulation continued all the way to London, where Lady Nelson had came up from Norfolk to join her husband, and to meet for the first time her notorious rival. The Hamiltons had a house in Grosvenor Square, and Lucy's servants buzzed every day with fresh details of the meetings between the two families. Lord Nelson and Lady

Hamilton evidently laboured under the delusion that they were invisible, a delusion which Sir William seemed only too glad to foster, but Society was quick to shew its disapproval. Lady Hamilton was received nowhere, and when Sir William went to Court, he had to go alone, for the Royal Family had made it very plain they would not admit her to their presence.

December brought other, graver news. On the third, the Austrians suffered a crushing defeat at Hohenlinden on the Danube at the hands of the French general Moreau, and at once began to negotiate peace with the French. On the sixteenth the Russian Tsar Paul revived the old Armed Neutrality with Denmark, Sweden and Prussia against England, and seized all the English vessels in Russian waters. England once more stood alone, and the closure of the Baltic to English ships meant that the supply of pitch, hemp and timber vital to ship-building was cut off, particularly the supply of tall trees for replacement masts, always problematical since the loss of the American colonies.

December also brought the *Triumph* into port, and Harry to Upper Grosvenor Street.

'There doesn't seem any point in going home to Morland Place, now Mother's not there,' he said to Lucy. 'Shall you mind if I stay here? Apart from anything else, Admiral Collingwood says he'll present me at court. He really is a trump card, you know, Luce: absolutely top of the trees! He's the kindest man in the world. The jacks all love him – we hadn't the cat out once this last voyage! And what a sailor – !'

'Perhaps we ought to have this paragon to dinner. What do you say, Lucy?' Chetwyn suggested, amused. 'Someone ought to play host to our sailor heroes when they are ashore.'

'Of course,' said Lucy, pleased. 'We've known Admiral Collingwood for ever, Harry – he was a great favourite of Flora's and we used to meet him at her dinners.'

'We won't ask Admiral Nelson, however,' Chetwyn said, keeping a straight face, 'for it would be difficult to know which of his wives to invite with him.'

Harry blushed at this, for like most young sailors, he

452

worshipped the Hero of the Nile, and found it hard to reconcile his private weakness with his professional prowess. Lucy took pity on him and said evenly, 'We'll ask Admiral Scorton, though, for he has influence at the Admiralty, which might be of use to you, Harry.'

'It's very good of you, Lucy – and you, sir. I hope it won't be too much for you, however. You're looking horrid pulled after your illness. Are you quite well again?'

'Well enough to withstand a naval dinner,' Chetwyn said gravely, and added with a glance at Lucy, 'I had excellent nursing, you know. I have almost come to feel there are compensations to being ill.'

Admiral Collingwood presented Harry at the first available levee, and a few days later, Lucy and Chetwyn met up with him at a Court reception, the first public function they attended together in more than a year. Cuthbert Collingwood was fifty, a tall, slender, extremely handsome man, white-haired now and brown-faced, as were so many sailors, but with a charm and magnetism which made him as likeable to men as he was attractive to women. His eyes were remarkably beautiful beneath fine brows, his nose straight, his chin firm, his lips both sensitive and sensual. He was intelligent, an individual thinker, kindly, humane, and a fine sailor.

He had been at sea since he was eleven, with the exception of six years on half-pay during the gap between the American war and the outbreak of the French war, but he had never lost the traces of a lilting Northumberland accent. He and Hannibal Harvey were old friends, and he was also godfather to Lord Tonbridge who had been one of Mary Haworth's most constant suitors.

The first thing Lucy asked him was for news of Captain Haworth.

'I made sure he would send his little daughter home at the end of the summer, for winter in the Channel is not what I would expose a child to,' she said.

'And Lady Aylesbury is not notoriously a fussy parent,' Chetwyn added drily.

Collingwood smiled at the sally. 'I have no idea that he means to part with the child in the near future,' he said. 'All

I can tell you is that she seems to thrive. I see him tolerably often when we are on station. We all try to dine together as often as possible, to relieve the monotony of blockade, you know, and Miss Africa is a great favourite with everyone. Of course, we've had an exceptionally tranquil autumn. If we had had storms Haworth might have changed his mind about keeping her on board, or her nurse might have changed it for him.'

'Pray tell him when you return that I will be glad to have the child if he wants to send her ashore,' Lucy said.

'Of course, you have care of his other daughter,' Collingwood remembered.

'My wife collects children,' Chetwyn put in. 'She has young Bobbie Chelmsford too. If you know of any other youngsters in need of succour, do send them along!'

Just then, Admiral Nelson arrived, and an incident occurred which, though distressing, was ultimately of use to the Morland interest. A muted buzz followed Nelson's progress towards the King, and all eyes were on him as he made his bow, for it was well-known that the King shared the rest of the Royal Family's view about his affair with Emma Hamilton.

Nelson straightened up. The King, his bulging eyes hostile, said, 'You are well, I trust, my lord?' and before Nelson could answer, the King had turned pointedly away to enter into conversation with the person standing nearest to him on the other side, which by chance happened to be Harry.

Lucy saw Harry's naturally bright cheeks redden further, and he bent his brown-locked head deferentially to the King and answered what was evidently a professional enquiry. The buzz of comment rose at Nelson's discomfiture, and Collingwood excused himself with a bow to Lucy, and hastened away to his friend's rescue. Half an hour later when he joined Lucy and Chetwyn again, the King was still apparently in rapt conversation with Harry.

'What on earth can they be finding to talk about?' Lucy wondered, and Collingwood smiled rather wickedly.

'Well they can't be discussing his naval successes!' Then he looked across at Nelson, now talking to St Vincent, and frowned. 'Poor fellow, he has done himself great harm with his indiscretion! But it's like him, you know – he can never feel anything by halves. He is all passion, all heart. It cuts him up terribly.'

'Hmm,' said Chetwyn coolly. 'He might shew a little more heart towards Lady Nelson, don't you think?'

There was an awkward pause. Lucy was embarrassed that Collingwood's friend had been criticized so openly by Chetwyn; but Collingwood was upset to realize that he had forgotten about Lady Aylesbury's affair with Captain Weston, and that Lord Aylesbury was more likely to feel sympathy with Lady Nelson than with her husband. He had spoken tactlessly, stirring up old trouble, and he hastened to make amends.

'At all events, His Majesty has certainly singled out your brother for attention, whatever the reason,' he said to Lucy. 'We must see if we can't turn the circumstance to some good. St Vincent thinks there will be an expedition to the Baltic in the new year, so there are bound to be promotions, and vacancies in the captains' list. It might present the opportunity to get our young friend made post.'

Lucy's face lit with a smile, and she seized Collingwood's hand impulsively. 'Oh, how kind you are! Harry will be so grateful – we all will! You are so very good to interest yourself in our family. I don't forget how you helped poor Jack.'

'He was the most likeable of young men,' Collingwood said, 'and a fine sailor. He was a great loss to the service. Ah, here comes the *succés fou* of the evening!' he added as Harry rejoined them, his cheeks burning and his eyes bright from his experience. 'Lady Aylesbury, may I do myself the honour of calling on you in a day or two? I should like to pay my respects to Lady Chelmsford, and I may perhaps have some news for you by then.'

Lucy caught her first glimpse of Lady Hamilton that same evening, as she and Chetwyn and Harry were driving home in the chariot to Upper Grosvenor Street. As they went through Grosvenor Square, they saw a carriage drawn up in front of the Hamilton's house, saw old Sir William descend and then turn back to offer his hand to his lady.

'Is that her?' Lucy said in astonishment. 'Good God, she is enormous! How can Lord Nelson be so fond of her? And not even handsome,' she added, as they passed the house and the light from the flambeau fell across Lady Hamilton's face.

Docwra had a thing or two to say about it as she undressed Lucy for bed an hour later. 'She's generally held to be handsome, my lady, though there's differences of opinion about *how* handsome,' she said when Lucy repeated her opinion to her. 'But she's not lookin' at her best at the moment. She'll be a mite puffed up in the face.'

'More than a mite,' Lucy said. 'She's monstrous fat! All swathed in layers and layers of muslin, she looked like an enormous ham.'

Docwra pursed her lips. 'Fat she may be, my lady, but it's what you'd call a temporary condition, and I wouldn't wonder if she didn't be losing some of that figure before very long.'

'What?' Lucy said, startled. 'You don't mean – ?'

'I do an' all,' Docwra nodded. 'Cook had it off one of the housemaids, but sure I don't need gossiping servants to tell me that she's increasing and like to come off at any moment!'

'Dear me,' said Lucy. 'How very awkward.'

456

Chapter Twenty-six

A week later Cuthbert Collingwood brought the good news round to Upper Grosvenor Street. It was doubly worth waiting for: Harry had been made post into *Semele*, and to make room for him, Captain Weston was promoted to command of a frigate, the *Thames*, 32.

'The commissions in both cases are effective immediately,' Collingwood told Lucy, 'though it will be several weeks before the news reaches the *Semele* and Weston can bring her in. The *Thames* probably won't arrive before February – she's on her way back from the West Indies.'

'You are so very kind,' Lucy said, taking his hand. 'You have made the occasion to do me two good services. I can't thank you enough.'

'Believe me, there was very little to do. Your brother recommended himself to His Majesty with his modest good sense, and Captain Weston's reputation is already high with Their Lordships.'

'Nevertheless, I know what trouble you must have been to for things to have moved so quickly.'

'I am always glad to do my country the service of helping her to reward good sailors,' he smiled, bowing over her hand.

'And the *Thames*, of all ships,' Lucy marvelled as the thought struck her. 'She was my brother William's very first command! He had her for a summer cruise, the year before the war began.'

'Yes, in the April of '92, I remember,' Collingwood said.

'Do you?' Lucy asked, surprised.

He gave a wry smile. 'Very well indeed. Your brother was much luckier than I. I had six years on the beach. In those days, one scanned the papers for the details of every ship in commission – there were few enough of them to remember!'

'I seem to recall William spoke very well of the *Thames*,' Lucy mused.

'Yes, she's a nice ship, though she's had a chequered career. She was in French hands for three years, you know. They took her after a single-ship action with the *Uranie* in '93. Poor Cotes had her then – he was terribly cut up. She and *Uranie* fought each other for four hours, until the French broke off the engagement. The *Thames* had lost two of her three masts and her rudder, and had no way of manoeuvring to re-engage, so she made sail in the only direction she could hold, straight before the wind. Her opponent was too badly damaged to follow, but no sooner was she hull-down of the *Uranie* than she ran straight into another French squadron of three frigates and a brig.'

'Oh, what bad luck!'

'Yes, indeed it was. She had no choice but to strike. The French renamed her *Tamise*, and she carried the tricolour for three years, until Byam Martin won her back off the Scillies in '96, in a single-ship action with the *Santa Margarita*.'

'How nice for Weston to have a frigate with a history,' Lucy said.

'Oh, all our ships have a tale to tell,' Collingwood smiled. 'And one always has an affection for one's first command. Mine was the old *Hinchinbroke* – I took her over from Nelson, when he transferred to the *Janus*. I dare say Weston will be quite sorry to leave the *Semele*.'

Harry was out when Collingwood called, so it fell to Lucy to tell him the good news on his return, and to hand him the Admiralty letters that had been left for him. Harry expressed himself delighted, but Lucy felt there was something missing from his excitement, and when pressed, he finally admitted his trouble.

'I can't help knowing that he's doing all this not for me, but in memory of Jack. That was why he took me into the *Excellent* in the first place, to sort of make it up to cousin Charles. I just wish I could be promoted on my own merits, that's all.'

'Oh, don't be such a buffle-head,' Lucy said. 'In the first

458

place, he wouldn't have helped you at all if you weren't a good sailor – surely you must know that much about him? And in the second place, everyone, however good they are, needs interest. Even your precious Admiral Nelson got on at the beginning through interest, because his uncle was Comptroller of the navy. So don't stand there talking fustian, but go straight away and write him a proper letter of thanks, because he has put himself out a great deal to do this for you, and whatever he says, it can't be agreeable to ask favours.'

The *Semele* wasn't expected until the middle of January, and Harry, whose spirits soon rose to the proper level for a man who had achieved post rank at the age of only twenty-three, with all its concomitant glory, and the knowledge that he now had only to live long enough to become an admiral one day, said that he might as well go to Yorkshire for the Christmas season.

'But why don't you come with me?' he said to Lucy and Chetwyn at the dinner table, 'and bring the children, too? We could make a real occasion of it. After all, who knows when we'll all be together again?'

Chetwyn and Lucy exchanged cautious glances. 'What do you think, Ma'am?' Chetwyn said diffidently. 'I expect the children would like it of all things.'

'Perhaps I will,' Lucy said, studying the pattern on her plate. 'I haven't yet seen what Mary Ann has made of the old place.'

'You haven't yet seen the new baby,' Harry pointed out. 'My namesake.'

'Not so new any more,' Chetwyn said. 'But wait – we are not fair to the absent. We must not forget Roberta.' She was dining out that evening. 'Will she want to come?'

'She's already told me she's taking the boy to stay with her father and some of his relatives in Gloucestershire,' said Lucy.

'Good, then it's all settled,' Harry said, reaching for the roast duck. 'Can I carve you some more of this, Luce? I say, wouldn't Mama be pleased to have another son a captain? I once told her I'd settle down with a nice girl and raise some grandchildren for her once I'd got my ship. Perhaps I'd better look around in York over Christmas.'

'But now Mother's dead, there's no need for the grand-children. You needn't marry if you don't want to,' Lucy pointed out.

Harry's knife paused with the arresting thought. 'Very true! I hadn't thought of that.' The knife took up its carving again. 'But I think I might as well do it as not, after all. I expect I might like it prodigiously, once I got used to it.' Chetwyn snorted into his wine, and Lucy choked a little over her pickled peas, and Harry looked at them with a smirk of puzzled amusement. 'Now what are you two laughing at? Is it something I said?'

Everyone was pleased with the decision. Edward was glad to see Chetwyn again, especially as he and Lucy seemed to be on better terms – not loving, nor even close, but at least comfortable. James was always glad of a distraction from the monochromatic unhappiness of his life, and he had always got on best with Lucy of all his brothers and sisters.

'We should have better hunting this year,' he promised her. 'The ground's soft, and there's plenty of scent, and Ned and I have found out half a dozen earths.'

'Yes, I thought there would be good sport, so I sent Parslow on ahead with Minstrel. We passed him just this side of Doncaster, so he should be here by tomorrow night,' said Lucy.

Chetwyn shuddered. 'If she's taking Minstrel out, I shall stay at home by the fire. I'd as lief not actually see her break her neck. You can tell me about it afterwards, Jamie.'

James grinned. 'Oh, Minstrel's the colt you bought from Rutland, is it? John Anstey told me about it. Can you really manage it, Luce?'

'Don't be silly,' Lucy replied shortly.

'Well, I'll join you by the fire, sir,' Harry said. 'I can't see the fun in dashing about on a horse through fathoms of mud when you might have your feet in a fender and your hand around a tankard. And a horse is about as comfortable as the fore t'gallant masthead after a sprat supper.'

'You'd get on well with George Brummell,' Lucy said drily.

Edward had been regarding his friend closely, and put a solicitous hand on his arm and said, 'Are you really well again, Chet? You're looking worn to the socket.'

Chetwyn returned the pressure briefly, 'I'm well enough,' he said. 'It's just the years catching up with me.'

Edward, his brow creased with concern, felt the first cold breath of a very human fear. Chetwyn was five years his senior, and the time marched for all of them. He had thought his mother immortal, until she had gone away and left him. 'I won't hunt either,' he said. 'We'll coze together, like old times, and roast chestnuts, and tell stories. We'll get you well and strong again. Morland Place will cure you.'

Fanny was delighted with the advent of so many cousins over whom to queen it, and as first lady of the nursery, with a pony and a dog of her own, she felt she had every right to superiority. Hippolyta, however, was a very difficult person to impress. She was a year older than Fanny, and of an imperturbable disposition, and the fact that she, too, had been learning to ride proved the deciding factor.

To Fanny's surprise, the pleasure of displaying her prowess on Tempest to a silently admiring audience, paled before the prospect of actually going out for a ride with her cousin Polly. Aunt Lucy and Papa arranged it all. Papa found a suitable mount for Polly, and Aunt Lucy instructed the formidable Parslow to be their guide and guard, with a Morland Place groom to help him.

Fanny's chagrin when she discovered that Hippolyta was allowed to handle her own mount, while Tempest must stay on the leading-rein, almost put an end to the outing. But Papa promised that if she behaved herself very well, she might be let off next time, and Polly herself pointed out that she was a year older, and that her mount was old and steady and only called Robin, so Fanny allowed her ruffled feelings to be soothed, and even agreed without fuss to leave Puppy behind.

'Hippolyta has a good influence on Fanny,' Edward remarked as the little girls set off demurely through the barbican.

'Early days yet,' Lucy replied. 'Let's see if they come back in one piece. Fanny might corrupt Polly, for all we know.'

It was not a comment to please Mary Ann, who forgave it, however, in view of Lucy's gratifying interest in the changes she had made about the house. At Lucy's request, she took her on a tour of the principal sites. The kitchen was their first port of call, where she had had a Rumford installed, and introduced various improvements of which she was intensely proud. Danvers, the new cook, spoke of the advantages of a stove over an open fire, and Mrs Scaggs, the new housekeeper, praised Madam's arrangement of the pantries as most felicitous, but Lucy watched their eyes and felt that they would have said anything to turn Madam up sweet.

'Oh, the swan window's still there,' she exclaimed with pleasure as her roving eye found a familiar landmark.

'Oh yes, we couldn't break with tradition, you know, however inconvenient it is,' Mary Ann said quickly. Lucy learned afterwards from James that Mary Ann had got as far as having a man in to block it up, before Edward heard about it and intervened.

The chapel was their next stop. It had been newly decorated, with a great deal of gold-leaf, and a new chandelier, whose central globe of bright ormolu sprouted graceful swan-necked stems, each bearing a crystal lustre as well as the candle-rose. There were new gold and crystal vases on the high altar, and in the Lady-chapel the wooden statue once more wore its blue robes and its crown of pearls. It all looked very beautiful, and Lucy said so, glad to be able to praise something sincerely.

She could say nothing pleasant about the drawing-room, which seemed crowded with over-elaborate furniture and ornaments. She was amused to note that the pianoforte again occupied the corner where Mary's harpsichord used to stand. She asked what had happened to the harpsichord, and Mary Ann told her briefly that it had been sent as a gift to the girls' school in York.

But the changes Lucy most disliked were to the red room, where she slept, since Mary Ann still used the blue room, and Lucy had never cared for the great bed chamber.

'It hadn't been redecorated for eighty years or more,' Mary Ann said. 'It looks very different now don't you think?'

'Very different,' Lucy agreed. The old four-poster, Eleanor's bed as it was known, had been stripped out of its hangings and tester of red damask. A new canopy had been made, of pleated yellow silk drawn up to a pinnacle crowned with a gold knob. There was a fringed frieze, gold knobs atop the posts themselves, and the bed curtains were of the same dark-yellow silk, while the counterpane was of quilted satin. The walls were covered in a modern yellow and green wall-paper, and there were mustard-coloured moreen curtains at the window. Modern furniture had replaced the old dark oak, and there were two large mirrors.

'It was Mother's room,' was all Lucy said.

'Only after your father died,' Mary Ann said, a little puzzled. 'Before that she slept in the great bed chamber.'

Useless to tell Mary Ann what she had told Weston, that she wanted her childhood home to stay always the same. Useless and selfish – it was not her home now. It was borne upon her forcibly that her mother's death had changed everything. She was no-one's child any longer, and it seemed to her suddenly a lonely thing, to be grown-up.

On the thirteenth of January, an express arrived for Harry, to say that the *Semele* had been sighted off Portland. Harry's indolence fell from him like a discarded cloak.

'I must pack my bag at once,' he said. 'Ned, do you think one of the men could be sent out to hire a po'chaise? If I sleep on the road, I could be at Portsmouth almost as soon as she is.'

'Of course,' said Ned obligingly. 'What men of action you sailors are!' Everything was action and bustle, but it had not escaped Chetwyn's eye that Lucy turned very pale when Harry read out his letter, nor that she took the opportunity to slip out of the room when Ottershaw answered the bell. He found her, as he expected, with Docwra in her room, packing. She straightened up guiltily as he appeared in the

463

doorway, and then, with a glance at Docwra, she came out into the passage and closed the door.

'You're leaving, then?' he said, Lucy bit her lip, searching for a reply. 'Harry will be glad, I imagine, to share the cost of the chaise,' he went on mildly.

'Chetwyn – ' she began helplessly.

'I suppose,' he interrupted her, 'it's no use asking you not to go?'

She looked down at her hands, and up again, and shook her cropped head.

'No use,' she said. He regarded her a moment longer, and then nodded, and turned away.

'I see,' he said, 'I may perhaps see you in London.'

'Why don't you stay here?' Lucy said anxiously. 'It's early for London. There'll be no-one there. You'll be much more comfortable here than at Grosvenor Street.'

'Thank you for your concern, but I shan't be going back to Grosvenor Street,' he said. 'When I leave here, I shall go to my lodgings.' He met her eyes with a hard look. 'I should not like to be in your way. That, I imagine, would embarrass both of us equally.'

Lucy reached out a hand to him. 'Oh Chetwyn, please – can't we be friends? I thought that things were better since your illness.'

'Ah yes, how wise of you to remind me of what I owe you,' he said, looking away.

'Oh, don't,' she said exasperated, letting her hand drop again. 'You know I didn't mean that.'

'No,' he admitted. 'That was ungenerous of me. I'm sorry. But in answer to your question, no, I don't think we can be friends.'

Lucy felt tears prickling her eyes, of frustration, or of pity for his pain, she didn't know which. She swallowed them back determinedly, and said in a steady voice, 'But at least – not enemies?'

He didn't answer for a long time, and then she thought he sighed before lifting his eyes for a moment to hers. 'Not enemies. I think we can manage that.'

*

On Lucy's offering to pay all the expenses of the journey, Harry was quite willing to allow her and her maid to take up two thirds of the room in the chaise. Parslow was left to take Minstrel back to Wolvercote, forming an escort for Miss Trotton and the children at the same time.

'I don't know where I will be going from Portsmouth, so you had better go on to Grosvenor Street and wait for me there. I'll send for you if I want you,' Lucy said.

Brother and sister were equally anxious to make all possible haste, and did their part by hiring four horses and sleeping in the chaise. Encouraged by Harry's exhortations to 'put 'em along' and Lucy's judicious distribution of coin, the postboys entered into the spirit of the thing, and the journey was made most expeditiously. On reaching Portsmouth they drove straight to the dockyard, where Harry's enquiries established that the *Semele* was already in, and lying at Spithead.

'We had better find an inn and bespeak rooms,' Lucy said. Harry stared.

'What for? I want to take a shore-boat out to my ship. I don't need a room. Once I've read myself in, I'll be sleeping on board.'

'But we need rooms,' Lucy said firmly. 'You need to change into your uniform, and we all need dinner. It's after four o'clock.'

'Aye, and it'll be dark any moment,' said Harry agitatedly. 'I'll come with you while you bespeak a room, and change my clothes, but I can't wait for dinner. I'll get mine on board.'

Lucy agreed to the compromise, and told the post-boys to drive to the Golden Lion. It was thrilling to be in Portsmouth again, almost eight years since the day she had arrived here by the stage, dressed in boy's clothing and looking for adventure. She craned eagerly out of the window as they drove along the Hard, past the Keppel's Head, where she had first met Weston. How little she had guessed then what would come of it all! The horses turned, slipping a little on the cobbles, into the High Street and up towards the smart new square behind the Garrison Chapel where the Golden Lion was situated. It was beginning to drizzle, and everything was dull and grey, but nothing could dampen the joy in two of the three hearts that beat inside the hired chaise.

My Lady Aylesbury, with the dignity of four horses and a stern-faced maid, had no difficulty in acquiring the best bed chamber, with a private sitting room, and an adjoining dressing-room for her maid.

'And how long will you be staying, my lady?' asked the landlord.

'I don't know. A few days, perhaps. My brother has come to take command of his ship, and I shall probably stay until he sails.'

The landlord regarded Harry with an experienced eye. 'Your first command, sir? My felicitations, sir. May you confound the French and take a hundred prizes,' he offered with more courtesy than conviction.

Harry had no fault to find with the sentiment. 'You may depend upon it!' he said with an irrepressible grin.

He used Lucy's dressing-room in which to put on his uniform and shave himself in the hot water sent up, and emerged to find Lucy had changed into a very sober round gown of grey twilled stuff, and was putting on a small bonnet with long, broad ribbons, calculated to resist the wind.

'I'm coming with you,' she said firmly. Out of the corner of his eye, Harry saw Docwra looking disapproving, and took courage to protest.

'But I thought you wanted your dinner? Besides, a shore-boat will be very uncomfortable. It's choppy today, and the wind is very sharp.'

'My dear brother, I know all about small boats and sea breezes, and I assure you I wouldn't miss seeing you taking up your first command for the world.'

Harry shifted uncomfortably. 'Aye, but look here, Luce, what will they think if I turn up with a woman in tow? They'll think I'm tied to your apron strings. It will look damned odd.'

'Nonsense,' Lucy said serenely. 'I promise you the officers of the *Semele* will know perfectly well why I am there. Worry about that if you want to worry about anything. Now come along. I've had a chaise and pair waiting these ten minutes, while you preened yourself before the mirror. Docwra, have your dinner! I will send word if I am to be late.'

It was almost dark by the time they reached the ship. She hung a darker grey bulk between the colourless masses of the sea and the sky, snubbing herself restlessly against her anchor on the choppy swell. She was already shewing her riding lights, and as they rounded the stern, someone lit the lamps in the captain's cabin, and suddenly her stern windows were a row of yellow jewels dancing in the grey half-light.

The lookout hailed them. 'Boat, there!'

'Aye aye!' the oarsman hailed back; and then there was a muffled cry and a flurry of activity which told Lucy that someone had recognized her. By the time she reached the quarter-deck, Weston and his officers were assembled to greet them. Hats were touched, hands were shaken, introductions made, but Lucy saw only Weston's face, and his eyes devouring her, and the astonished delight of his smile. Her hand tingled from the pressure of his, and from the light brush of his lips against it, which was all that, with respect for naval discipline, he could allow himself by way of touching her.

'I had not thought to see you so soon,' Weston said, looking at Harry but really addressing Lucy.

'I hoped you wouldn't mind, sir,' Harry said. 'I didn't want to waste a minute in taking over my command. After all – '

'I understand perfectly,' Weston grinned. 'I felt the same way. Come to my cabin, and I'll tell you all about her, while Bates packs my dunnage.'

Harry blushed. 'I don't want you to think I'm trying to hurry you away,' he stammered.

'Don't give it a thought, my dear fellow,' Weston said, leading the way. 'I assure you I am perfectly happy to hand her over to you at once and go ashore.' He met Lucy's eyes again, and an irresistible smile came to the lips of both.

'Have you dined?' he asked her softly. She shook her head, her eyes glowing with delight simply at being near him again. 'Then we shall dine on shore, if it pleases you, my lady.'

In the day-cabin that Lucy remembered so well, she sat on the long window-seat and renewed acquaintance with the ecstatic Jeffrey while Bates received his orders.

'Put my immediate necessities in a cloak-bag,' Weston told him, 'and I'll take that with me. You can pack everything else in my trunk and follow on with it. I'll make arrangements with Mr Morland about my furniture.' He turned to Harry with a smile. 'I dare say you have not had time yet to think about cabin furniture? I shall be happy to allow you to use mine for a day or two, until you have had time to go ashore and buy your own. Now then, these are the watch bills and the station bills – '

Lucy listened with half her attention as Weston gave Harry useful information about the way the ship handled, and about the qualities and foibles of the officers and men, and admired his patience, when she knew perfectly well that all he wanted to do was to get to some private place with her so that they could touch each other. At the end of an hour Weston was ready to leave, Jeffrey was forced, spitting furiously, into his basket, and Bates took him and the cloak-bag to the boat while Weston ordered all hands, his last act as captain of the *Semele*.

When the hands had assembled in the waist, Harry, standing at the rail, read himself in in a voice that barely trembled with excitement. Then the hands were dismissed, the officers not on duty touched their hats and retired, and Lucy embraced the newest captain in the King's Navy and whispered, 'You did that *beautifully*, Hal! One would think you'd done it a hundred times!'

Weston grinned and shook hands, and said, 'If there's anything you want to ask me, don't hesitate to send word.' He glanced at Lucy. 'I dare say you'll know where to find me.'

'And do let us know when you are coming ashore, Harry,' Lucy said. 'Perhaps you will dine with us in a day or two, when you are settled in?'

'Your dunnage is in the boat, sir,' mentioned a midshipman at Weston's elbow.

'Thank you, Mr Wells. Well, goodbye, then, for the present, Captain.'

'Goodbye, sir. Thank you,' said Harry.

A few moments later Lucy and Weston were in the stern-sheets of the shore-boat, with Jeffrey howling mutedly in his basket between their feet, the big warm bulk of the *Semele* growing smaller behind them, and the cold black eternity of the sea opening around them. Lucy shivered a little, and Weston's warm hand crept under her cloak and captured her.

'There are the lights of the shore, look,' he said, knowing, as he so often seemed to, what was in her mind. She fixed her eyes on them, and spoke in a normal voice.

'I'd never seen that done before. It's a solemn thing, isn't it?'

'Reading in a new captain? Most solemn. Harry will never forget it. And for me – from captain to passenger in a matter of minutes! Satan took longer than that to tumble from Heaven.'

Lucy looked at him cautiously. 'But you will have your new ship as soon as she comes in,' she said. Weston pressed her hand and grinned.

'Long may she be delayed! I am in the best of positions, my lady, don't you know that? I have shore leave, but without the misery of doubt as to whether I will get another commission. I can be with you all day and every day until the *Thames* makes harbour, and I don't even have to get special permission to sleep out of my ship!'

Lucy thought of the rooms she had taken at the Golden Lion, of the private sitting-room where they could have their dinner alone together, with Jeffrey stretched out luxuriously before the first fire he would have seen in two years. She thought of the big bed and the night to come, and the bliss of being able to wrap herself unreservedly in Weston's arms; and all the other days and nights to come, at least two weeks of them, perhaps four or even six, when they could be together and do exactly as they pleased, until duty and the *Thames* called him away again. She was so happy she felt as though she might burst.

'Well, that's all right then,' she replied.

After only a brief discussion, Weston and Lucy decided to remain at the Golden Lion. It didn't matter much to either of them where they stayed, as long as they were together. Their rooms there were comfortable, and the landlord, in view of Lucy's liberality with her purse, raised no objection to the addition of Weston and Bates to her entourage.

Their time together was longer even than they had expected, for contrary winds delayed the *Thames* in the Channel, and she did not reach Spithead until the middle of February. After a long commission and a difficult voyage home, she was in need of extensive refitting, and had to go immediately up to the dockyard where she spent a week in dry dock. When she was returned to her moorings, Weston had too much to do to sleep ashore, but it was another two weeks before she was ready to go to sea, and Lucy took up residence in the captain's quarters, which she found a little more commodious than on board the *Semele*.

A great many things happened during those weeks they spent together. Prime Minister Pitt, pushed to the wall over the Catholic Relief Bill, felt obliged to stand by his principles and resign, and the King chose Henry Addington to replace him. Addington had been the Speaker of the House of Commons since the beginning of the war, and though a quiet man of modest abilities, he was known to be honest, reliable, and a staunch churchman, which the harrassed King, at that moment, was likely to value most of all.

Only a week later,the King, perhaps because of the strain he had been under, fell ill, and began to shew symptoms alarmingly reminiscent of those he had displayed back in '88.

On the naval front, the *London Gazette* had announced that Lord Nelson had been promoted to Vice-Admiral of the Blue, and was to return in the *San Josef* to the Mediterranean as second in command to Sir Hyde Parker. The Austrians had signed the treaty of Luneville, making peace

470

with the French, and a strong presence in the Mediterranean was more than necessary.

'On the other hand,' Weston said to Lucy as they breakfasted together – a source of unfailing delight to Lucy, who could not conceive how poets had failed to remark that ham and eggs and requited love were perfect foils for each other – 'I shall be astonished if Their Lordships do not put together a squadron to go to the Baltic. If we can't persuade the Armed Neutrality to disband itself, we shall be properly in the suds.'

His guess proved correct, for at the beginning of February the news filtered back that Sir Hyde Parker was to take his squadron into the Baltic instead of the Mediterranean, with Nelson still his second in command, but in the *St George* instead of the *San Josef.*

'So if the *Thames* comes in before they sail, I suppose I shall be attached to them,' Weston said. 'The Baltic at this time of year would not be my choice. Let's hope the winds blow contrary for the *Thames* for a good few weeks yet.'

'But if they have their orders, won't they sail at once?' Lucy asked.

'Oh no, there will be plenty to do before they weigh anchor,' said Weston, and added with a grin, 'besides, Parker has a new young wife, and he won't be in any hurry to leave her behind.'

Lucy was intrigued by the rumour which Docwra brought to her that Lady Hamilton's figure had undergone a sudden and marked reduction. 'Twins, they say, my lady, though I set no store by that. There's some people as'd say anything! Herself was up and about again in no time, as she'd need to be, if she was to pretend there was nothing amiss; and they say Lord Nelson's as thrilled as a lark.'

By the end of February, the King's condition had deteriorated so far that there was some fear that he would die. It was confirmed that his illness was the same flying gout which had caused his bout of madness back in '88. He was confined in the care of the Willises, who had been his gaolers on the previous occasion, and there was much speculation as to whether a Regency would be necessary.

On the ninth of March Weston reported his ship ready

for sea, and was ordered to take her up to Yarmouth Roads to join the Baltic squadron. Lucy sailed with Weston and they arrived to find preparations for sea going ahead at a leisurely pace, and a grand farewell ball arranged by Admiral Parker for the thirteenth.

Weston, like the Admiral, was perfectly happy with that plan, but it soon appeared that Vice-Admiral Nelson was not. He wrote a letter of complaint about the delay to Troubridge, who passed it on to St Vincent. St Vincent sent orders to Parker that he should sail the moment the wind served. The ball was cancelled, and on the twelfth of March Lucy found herself ashore again, watching the fleet sail out into the grey choppy waters of the Channel. She watched until even she could not believe there was anything more to see on the murk of the horizon, and then turned away to the comfort of Docwra's sympathy, who handed her a clean handkerchief and chose to pretend that her mistress's streaming eyes were caused by the sharp wind.

There being nothing further to stay for, Lucy and Docwra at once set off by post-chaise for London and the comforts of Grosvenor Street. The journey was made hideous by the bitter complaints of Jeffrey at yet another incarceration in the hated basket. Weston had asked Lucy to take care of him until his return, for he didn't think the freezing cold, damp and fogs of the Baltic in March would suit the constitution of such a hedonistic cat.

Lucy found London in a state of ferment over the possibility of a Regency. Fortunately for her curiosity, George Brummell called as soon as the knocker was back on the door.

'Come and ride with me, my dear ma'am, and I will tell you all the latest gossip,' he offered. 'You are the only woman in Town it is not a punishment to ride beside, and I must have a turn about the Park, for I have a most delightful new horse, whose colour matches mine perfectly. You had better change your gown at once, before Wiske gets wind that you are returned, and comes to interrupt us. But you must wear your blue velvet habit with the Hussar frogging, and that delicious little black hat of yours, with the half-veil.'

Lucy laughed. 'Do you remember my wardrobe so exactly? How you must wish I were more like my sister Mary. You and she could have talked about clothes for ever.'

'She was one of the three most beautiful women in England,' he sighed, 'and probably *the* best dressed. Her death was a great tragedy.'

Lucy was a little piqued. 'You needn't sound as though you wish I had gone instead of her.'

He put his head on one side and smiled. 'Come, ma'am, pouting don't become you! Your oddities endear you far more to me than beauty and elegance, I assure you. I'm a faithful old body, as you shall find, besides being an oddity myself, so I know how to value such things.'

She changed into her habit, and they went downstairs where Parslow and Brummell's groom were holding the horses. Lucy admired Brummell's chestnut, whose red-gold coat was indeed a very similar shade to his hair, and he bowed and said, 'Yes, and your yellow horse makes a very nice contrast, so I am satisfied.'

'You absurd creature!' Lucy laughed, and was lifted into Mimosa's saddle by Parslow, whose rigidity of mouth told her that he enjoyed Mr Brummell's absurdities too. Mimosa curvetted around as the cold saddle touched her back, but Lucy mastered her in a moment, for she was eight years old, and her playfulness was by now more habitual than convinced. The grooms fell in behind, and the cavalcade made its way into the Park.

'Well, now,' said Brummell, 'first of all I must tell you that there have never been such comings and goings at Carlton House! It's astonishing how many friends the Prince has who have quite suddenly taken it into their heads to assure him of their unswerving loyalty and undying affection. It's touching, you know – quite brings tears to the Prince's eyes.'

'Then a Regency is likely?' Lucy asked, Brummell shrugged.

'Likely. Possible. Who can tell? Pitt and Addington mentioned the word to His Royal Highness, and then added the words "limited powers", which quite took the thrill out

473

of it. But even Clarence and Kent have been seen lounging about looking casual just where the Prince is expected to pass, and starting with surprise when he appears, and feeling they might as well take the opportunity to mention their willingness to undertake responsibility.'

'And the Duke of York?' Lucy asked innocently, knowing Brummell's partiality for him.

'To his eternal credit, York remains aloof. He don't favour the Catholic Relief Bill any more than the King, and he's not one to go a-mongering.'

'But how grave is the King's condition?' Lucy asked.

'We'd all like to know the answer to that one. The Willises keep him a prisoner, and the Prince has only been allowed to see him once, though they say he's recovered enough to be able to feed himself. But there's no doubt he has been, and still is, very ill, and the Prince has already approached various people privately about forming a government: Devonshire, Buckingham, Norfolk, Aylesbury —'

'What?' said Lucy, startled.

Brummell smiled. 'Does that surprise you? The Prince has always liked your husband.'

'But Chetwyn has no political ambitions,' Lucy said.

'A man must have something to fill his days,' Brummell said obliquely. 'Besides, a man lacking ambition makes an easier bed-fellow than someone always fidgeting for advancement. His Highness, for instance, gets on much more comfortably with Addington than ever he did with Pitt.' He glanced at her thoughtful face with amusement. 'But however,' he went on, 'it may all come to nothing. Now, ma'am, what else is there to tell you? Lady Hamilton's curious indisposition? But no, I am persuaded you must have all the naval news before me. Ah, yes, of course, I have it! Your fair cousin, the lovely Lady Greyshott, has been the cause of a duel — her first of many, I imagine!'

'No, really?'

'Oh yes, at Chalk Farm last week, a meeting between Colonel Lord Bolito and Sir Henry Graves. Shots were exchanged, and Bolito's arm was broken — the left arm, not that it makes any difference in his case, for he's equally clumsy with either. Where *his* ball went, only the gods can tell, for he is the very worst shot in the army, which makes it all the more strange that he should have offered to meet Graves at all.'

'But what was it about? And if it was an affair of honour, why was not Lord Greyshott involved?'

'My dear Lady Aylesbury, you *have* been away a long time!' said Brummell, with relish at the prospect of a long story. 'I had better tell you all about it from the beginning.'

Chapter Twenty-seven

Roberta's father, Colonel Taske, agreed to take up residence with her and to give her the benefit of his advice in bringing up his grandson.

'But we have decided not to live in Chelmsford House, at least until Bobbie is older,' she told Lucy. 'It's far too big for us. Athersuch is going to find us a suitable tenant, and we'll let it, and take a small Town house.'

'And Shawes?' Lucy asked.

'We're keeping that on. Papa thinks it important for a boy to have a taste of the country life. He's going to help me to find a tutor, too, so that I can take Bobbie out of petticoats and cut his hair.' Her mouth turned down. 'I must say, I don't like the idea of that at all. He won't be my little boy any more.'

Lucy had nothing to say to that. Her own baby Roland seemed to her to be of no possible interest to anyone *until* he went into trousers, but then she had never cared much for babies. The young of animals seemed to her much more attractive, and more interesting.

'Is Athersuch going to pick your Town house for you?' she asked.

'Well, no,' Roberta said. 'I rather hoped you might help me to choose one.'

Lucy was glad of the commission, to give her an interest and keep her mind occupied. From amongst the houses Athersuch found them, Lucy advised Roberta to choose a very pretty modern house in Brook Street, not far from where Weston had had his lodgings. The redoubtable Hawkins gave his approval to the choice, personally selected a loyal corps from amongst the Chelmsford House servants, and soon proved he could be just as terrifying in his new surroundings as in the noble spaces of his old domain.

'After all, my lady,' he said to Roberta, 'the change of abode is only temporary, and it would be most unwise to

476

permit a lowering of standards. His lordship should be served in this house in the manner in which he will expect to be served when he returns home again.'

Roberta also asked Lucy to be present when she interviewed the cleric her father recommended to the post of tutor. He was the son of a friend of Colonel Taske's, of an old and respectable family, and just down from Oxford. He was a short and stocky young man, very fair, good-looking, with excellent teeth and an engaging smile. Lucy could see that Roberta was very favourably taken with him.

'I like him,' Lucy said when Firth had left. 'I like the way his ears stick out. It makes him look trustworthy.'

'Oh Lucy, how can you be so absurd?' Roberta said. 'I wish you will be serious.'

'I am perfectly serious. Haven't you noticed that horses with big ears are always good tempered? It's a very good sign.'

'Mr Firth is not a horse.'

'The principle's the same. I like his eyes, too.'

'He has very nice eyes,' Roberta said, giving herself away.

'Yes, large, and very clear, and hazel,' Lucy grinned. 'There is something about hazel eyes, don't you think? I should engage him at once!'

Roberta looked shocked, and a little offended. 'I meant, that I thought his eyes honest,' she said stiffly.

'Now don't starch up,' Lucy said 'I was only teasing you. He seems a very decent, respectable young man, sensible, and kind too, and I'm sure he will suit Bobbie admirably. Of course, Horatio and Lady Barbara will want someone much more fashionable and smart, but – '

'They may mind their own busines,' Roberta said firmly, and Lucy saw that young Mr Firth had found a friend for life. Well and good, she thought. Long experience with animals had given her very reliable instincts about people. Kindness, good sense, and loyalty would be the hallmarks of Mr Firth's actions.

*

News from the Baltic was not long in coming. On the first of April the English ships inflicted a thorough defeat on the hostile Danish fleet at Copenhagen. While the news of the victory was good, Lucy knew for the first time the agony of waiting for the casualty lists, and when Hicks finally brought up the newspaper containing them, she could not bring herself to read it, and it was Docwra who finally scanned the columns and assured her mistress that Captain Weston's name was not there.

The fleet pressed on northwards to attack Sweden and Russia. At the end of April the news came that the mad Tsar Paul had been murdered in his bed by some of his own officers, and that his successor, Alexander, had ordered his ships to refrain from hostilities, and was willing to negotiate an end to the Armed Neutrality.

The Baltic threat was thus virtually at an end, and in May the Regency crisis ended too, when the King's recovery was sufficient for him to be able to go to his beloved Weymouth for a convalescence.

In June, the French began to move troops to the north of France, and to assemble a fleet of small craft in the harbour at Boulogne. With the capitulation of Austria in December and of Portugal in June, England was now France's only enemy, and the implications were clear. Another invasion was being threatened.

In July the Baltic fleet, no longer needed in northern waters, was recalled and a new squadron formed from its numbers, with Admiral Nelson in command, to defend the coast of England, and if possible to destroy the invasion fleet in Boulogne. Lord St Vincent was adamant that England's sea power was too great for an invasion to succeed, and soon his words to the Cabinet were being quoted joyfully in every street and tavern: 'I do not say the French cannot come, I only say they cannot come by sea.'

Cartoons appeared in the newspapers of a French army crossing the Channel by a variety of ingenious contrivances, such as air balloons, tunnels under the sea and giant catapults. But everyone was weary of war, and while England was invincible at sea, France was invincible on land. At the end of August, the news that Addington had sent envoys to

France to negotiate an armistice was greeted everywhere with relief.

The armistice was signed on the first of October, 1801. Marie brought the news to Héloïse as she sat at her desk in her study, working on her history of the revolution. She had not been getting on very fast that day. The long windows were open onto the garden, and the sweet autumn air was stirring memories in her. Under the desk, at her feet, Kithra slept, head on paws, snoring a little, and in a patch of sunlight on the carpet sat Sophie, dressing and undressing the wooden baby Stephen had made for her, and croodling to it like a pigeon.

From the walled garden came the distant sound of voices, echoing flat and high in the warm air, where Flon, Barnard and the maids were picking apples. Within the house there was the halting sound of Mathilde's lesson with Father Jerome on the cabinet piano, a new acquisition. A domestic peace was over everything. Héloïse looked out into the garden where the autumn colours lay warm under the hesitant, gauzy sunlight, smelled the ripening sweetness of the air, and wondered why beauty was so sad. She was surrounded with love; child, dog, ward, friend and servants all poured it out on her every day, and yet she felt lonely and full of pain. The love hurt her as much as the beauty.

She sighed deeply, and Kithra groaned in his sleep in answer, and Sophie looked up at her and smiled the smile that happy children reserve for their parents; and Héloïse laughed, and rebuked herself for feeling anything but profound gratitude for her lot. She picked up her pen again determinedly, and had just dipped it into the ink, when Marie came running into the house calling out for her.

'In here, Marie,' she called back. Marie appeared in the doorway, her face red and her eyes brilliant with some excitement. She looked unusually ruffled, as though she had been running. She had been down to the village for one or two things, but the basket on her arm was still empty.

'Oh madame! Oh madame!' she cried breathlessly.

'Be calm, Marie. Catch your breath, and tell me what has

happened,' Héloïse said gently. Behind Marie she saw Father Jerome and Mathilde appear in the passage, attracted by the commotion.

'It is news, madame,' Marie babbled. 'In the village, I heard it in the village. They are all talking about it. Everyone is so happy, and there is free ale at the Fauconburg Arms for everyone. The armistice, madame, they have signed it! It is peace, madame! We can go home!'

Héloïse could not speak. Kithra had got up and was circling Marie, wagging his tail, and Sophie was tugging her mother's arm to be lifted up. Héloïse picked her up absently. Father Jerome and Marie were chattering excitedly in French and Mathilde was asking questions in English. Home! The peace did indeed mean they could go home, and Héloïse could not begin to think what she felt about that. What sort of France would it be, after eight years of war, and numerous changes of government? So many had died under the blade, or before the firing squad, so many others had fled; whole families wiped out, houses pillaged, destroyed. Would she recognize it? Would it welcome her?

Yet it was home – that very English word, which embodied a longing all hearts knew, and which in French could be felt only wordlessly. Her own country, her own people – Paris, her own city! And somewhere in Paris, she hoped still alive, was her friend Marie-France, and the son she had borne to Héloïse's father. Héloïse herself had helped to bring Marie-France's son into the world, and though she had not seen him since, she often thought about him. He was, after all, her brother.

She looked from one excited face to another, and knew she must say something. 'Tell the others,' she said with an effort. 'Tell Flon and Barnard.' Mathilde dashed away on the errand; Father Jerome kissed Marie, who shrieked with laughter, and then took Sophie from Héloïse's arms and hugged her and jigged around the room with her, with Kithra circling her like a mad thing, his yellow wolf-eyes shining with his own secret delight.

Father Jerome took Héloïse's hands and pressed them, and she saw his lips moving, but she didn't seem to be able to understand what he was saying. She became aware that her face was aching, and realized that it was because a most ridiculous smile was stretching her mouth as wide as it would go, which was odd, because at the same time there were definitely tears on her cheeks.

At Morland Place, they gave an Armistice Party for the leading families of the neighbourhood. It was Sir Arthur Fussell who first mentioned the new craze for visiting Paris.

'Lord, yes, goin' over by scores,' he said. 'Visit the Tuileries, see the little Corsican at home, take a look at the place where the French King was made a head shorter.'

'Please, my dear,' Lady Fussell protested.

'It's true,' said Lady Anstey. 'John says there are hand-bills all over London, advertising the services of couriers, and places on ships making the crossing. It's quite the fashionable thing to do.'

'Well, why not?' Lord Anstey replied to a quizzical look from James. 'After eight years of war, people are eager for a little diversion. There's a whole generation grown up who have never set foot outside these shores.'

'And another generation – of soldiers and sailors – who've done nothing but,' Edward put in.

'I suppose you will be expecting to have your brothers home?' said Lady Fussell, turning the subject gracefully.

The seed, however, lodged itself in Mary Ann's brain, and flowered into a strange fascination with the idea, which she brought up with her husband at breakfast the next day.

'Why on earth should you want to go to Paris?' James asked in astonishment.

'Why shouldn't I want to?' she retorted, nettled. 'Doesn't everyone want to travel?'

James remembered his father's diatribes on that point, and said, 'No, not everyone. What is it you want to see in Paris?'

'What everyone sees,' she said. 'Don't pretend not to understand. It's all very well for you,' she added as James gave a sideways smile and went back to his toast, 'you've always gone wherever you wanted to. But I've never been anywhere but home – I mean, Manchester – and here. And

481

since we married, I've never been further than five miles from Morland Place. I should dearly love to take a journey to Paris,' she went on cajolingly. 'To go on a boat across the Channel! I've never even *seen* the sea. Oh James, do say we can go!'

'My dear ma'am, there's nothing I can do to stop you,' James said, buttering another slice. 'If you want to take tea in the Tuileries with the Corsican and Madame Josephine, by all means do!'

'Don't be odious,' Mary Ann said. 'You know perfectly well I can't go without you.'

'Ah, now we come to the nub of it.'

'Oh please, James, you'd like it of all things, I'm persuaded! A vacation would do us both so much good, and improve our minds, too. Edward wouldn't mind. There's nothing very much to do at the moment, and he could well spare you.'

'Do you know what a Channel crossing would be like at this time of year?' James said.

'But everyone says the weather is very settled at the moment! It's September when there are gales.'

'My dear, once the peace is concluded, you'll have the rest of your life to visit Paris if you want to. There's no hurry. Why not wait until next year, or the year after, and go in the summer, when the weather's good?'

But Mary Ann was firm in wanting to go immediately. For one thing, she was restless, and longing for change. For another, if one was going to do the fashionable thing, one must do it *before* everyone else, not after them. And for a third, she had a wonderful new set of Russian sables her father had given her, which she wanted to wear, and which deserved a wider audience than the Fussells and the Ansteys.

The following day Birkin brought her further ammunition which she did not hesitate to put to use.

'There's a man staying at the Hare and Heather,' she told James, 'a very respectable man called Climthorpe, who's arranging passages on a boat, the *Magpie*. It's to be a very select party – only a few people from the very best families. He arranges the passage from Dover to Boulogne, and the journey post from Boulogne to Paris, and there's a courier to accompany the party all the way, who speaks French, and another who goes ahead and arranges the accommodation at the best inns. So you see,' she finished eagerly, 'you wouldn't be put to any trouble at all, James. It would all be done for you. All you would have to do would be to step into a carriage at one end of the journey, and step out of another in Paris.'

'I've never heard of Climthorpe,' James protested feebly, but his resistance was weakening. For one thing, there was no good reason he could give for denying his wife this pleasure except his own indolence, and for another, he was beginning to experience faint stirrings of curiosity himself. Edward, appealed to by Mary Ann, gave his opinion mildly on her side, that James could be spared, and there was no reason why they shouldn't go if they wished. Further enquiry established that Climthorpe was perfectly respectable, the accredited agent of a merchant who owned three well-founded privateers. James gave in, and Climthorpe was sent for.

He spoke well, assuring them that their journey would be attended by every luxury, and that they would share the crossing in the *Magpie* or one of her sister ships with a small number of the very best people. 'Only such people, I assure you, dear Mrs Morland, as you would be happy to receive into your own house. The journey from Boulogne to Paris will be accomplished in two days, spending the night in a very respectable posting-house, the Lion d'Or at Amiens. Would you desire our courier to arrange accommodation in Paris for you? Very good, ma'am. And how many of you will be travelling? Yourself and your husband, and your maid and man. Just so. Now, as to the length of your stay – '

Fanny's rage was ungovernable when she discovered that she was not to be included in the treat, and not all her father's promises of presents brought back from Paris would mollify her. Edward looked forward gloomily to days of sulks and tantrums, but cheered considerably when Father Aislaby hinted at the improvement that might be wrought in Fanny once her father and mother were out of reach of appeal. He hastened to assure James that there was not the least need in the world for him to hurry back.

The *Magpie* was certainly a handsome vessel, and shewed signs of having been recently refitted, presumably to suit her for her new business, and repainted. She was gay with flags when the chaise carrying James and Mary Ann drew up beside her gangplank, and there appeared to be a large number of smartly-dressed sailors moving about her deck, whose grey jackets piped with red, red waistcoats, and grey trousers made a favourable impression on Mary Ann.

She was in a mood to be pleased with everything, for the excitement of travelling and the new things she had seen had raised her spirits almost to euphoria. Her first sight of the sea, though it was uniformly grey and restlessly heaving under a blank grey twilight sky, thrilled her inexpressibly. 'It's so big,' was all she could manage to say, but her eyes shone so delightedly that James for the first time felt glad that he had granted her this indulgence.

The captain greeted them and shewed them to their well-appointed cabins, where Mary Ann admired everything, from the plush curtains over the portholes to the raised frame on the beds to stop them rolling out.

'We shall sail when the tide turns, just after midnight,' he told them, 'and provided the wind doesn't back any further, we should reach Boulogne at first light. There will be no need for you to leave your beds then unless you wish to see the approach. Once we have anchored, we shall leave you to sleep until a more respectable hour,' he added with a smile, 'and breakfast will be provided at an inn in the harbour.'

Mary Ann expressed disappointment that the crossing was to take place while they were asleep. As it was her first time in a boat, James privately doubted that she would sleep very much, but forbore to say so, and only promised her that the return crossing would be made in daylight.

An excellent dinner, provided by the Ship Inn, was served to them in the larger of their two cabins.

'For all Climthorpe's assurances about sharing the journey with only the best families,' James said, 'I can't see that it would have mattered who they were, if we are never going to meet them. Here we are dining alone, and we'll sleep through the crossing. I suppose we may see them at breakfast in Boulogne – '

'How wonderful that sounds – breakfast in Boulogne!' Mary Ann interposed rapturously.

'And dinner in Amiens,' James added for her benefit. She smiled across the table at him.

'Thank you for bringing me,' she said shyly. 'I know you didn't want to come at first, but, oh, I am so glad you agreed, and I'm sure you will like it in the end.'

'I am liking it already,' James assured her. Animation had brightened her eyes and cheeks, and she looked rather pretty. 'Do you know what tomorrow is?'

'Tell me,' she said.

'It is the anniversary of the day we were married,' he said. 'Seven years ago. Didn't you know that?'

'Yes, I knew, but I didn't think you did,' she said. She hesitated and then said, 'Do you remember having dinner at the George in Huddersfield that night?' She looked down at her plate. 'We had duck then, too. With chestnuts.'

He didn't remember the meal, but he remembered the occasion, and the night that followed. It had been a long, weary road since then, for him at least; and none of it her fault.

'Are you sorry that you married me?' he asked her abruptly.

'No,' she said very quietly. Her head was bent even further over her plate, so that he could only see the crown of her head and the soft nest of her mouse-brown hair. 'But I think you have been.'

'I never meant to make you unhappy,' he said at last. 'It was just – '

'Yes,' she said. 'I understand.' She looked up at last. 'I'm not unhappy now,' she offered tentatively. He examined her cream-and-rose face, neat featured, her calm, light-brown eyes, and realized that he had grown rather fond of her, of late. If he had never known more, it would have seemed enough to him. He might have made her happy, and in doing so, been contented himself. Perhaps even now it was

485

not too late to make the effort, for her sake. He knew she wanted to love him, would do so if he let her.

One of the ship's servants came in to clear – Durban and Dakers would be having their own dinner elsewhere at the moment – and James asked him idly who were the other passengers on the *Magpie*.

'Well, sir, there's Sir Phillip Goodman and his party: Lady Goodman, Miss Goodman, and Mr Bernard Goodman,' he began.

'Yes, of course, I know Sir Phillip,' James said. 'Who else?'

'There's Mr and Mrs Norton Le Clay, and Lord and Lady Husthwaite and their two daughters, and yourselves, sir, that's all aboard, and one more party that's expected shortly, sir, the French lady.'

'French lady?' Mary Ann said.

'Yes, ma'am, Lady Strathord. Very strange it must seem to her, ma'am, to be going back after all these years. The Cap'n was saying – '

'Thank you, that will do,' James said, stemming this disastrous flood of information.

'Yes, sir. Will there be anything else?'

'Nothing, thank you,' James said firmly, aware out of the corner of his eye of the rigidity of Mary Ann's posture.

'Very good, sir.' The servant bowed and retired, and James turned to face his wife.

'I want to go home,' she said tautly. 'Will you be so good as to ring for Dakers?'

'No, I will not,' he said. 'Do you want a scandal? If you leave now you will set everyone talking.'

'I don't care,' she said. 'I won't stay on this boat a moment longer. How could you suppose that I would? Did you think I had no pride at all?'

'Don't be a fool,' he adjured her tersely. 'I didn't know she was going to be here. It's the most infernal bad luck, that's all.'

'I don't believe you,' she said, low and tense, a spot of bright colour flaming in each cheek. 'You arranged it all. You don't care how you humiliate me – '

'Oh, for God's sake! If I wanted to see her, I could do it

486

at home, easily and privately. Why should I go to all this trouble to meet her in conditions of the greatest difficulty and discomfort? Use what little sense God gave you!'

'You don't need to add insult to injury,' she said stiffly.

'What injury?' he said desperately, running his hand backwards through his hair. 'Didn't I leave her to come back to you? What more do you want?'

'I want to go home.'

'Well, you can't. You asked to come on this journey, and here you stay. I'm not going to have you make fools of us both. Look,' he said more gently, 'we've already said that we didn't see how we should have any contact with the rest of the party. Once she knows we are here, she'll do her best to avoid us too. There's no reason why we should meet at all.'

She said nothing, only stared at him, miserable and resentful, and he saw that he had done nothing to convince her. Exasperated, he bowed and said coldly, 'I think we had better retire for the night. I'll send Dakers to you, and hope you see things in a clearer light in the morning.'

The night was calm, a slow swell lifting the *Magpie* soporifically, a light breeze rolling the clouds slowly across the moonwashed sky. The mast creaked as the bows lifted and again as they sank, the ensign at the stern flapped languidly, and a halliard somewhere rattled fitfully: peaceful, calming sounds. James leaned against the taffrail and stared down at the gap between the ship and the dockside, now widening, now narrowing, and the water, slapped by the one against the other, jumping upwards like a live thing, smelling of weed and rotting wood. Two sailors standing aft by the binnacle conversed in low voices; from a cabin nearby came a rattling of crockery and sudden burst of laughter; and someone somewhere was smoking a cigar.

A two-horse hack chaise came into view along the harbour-side, the postboy in his drab coat going slowly, keeping an anxious eye for his charges' hooves on the moonlit cobbles, while trying to read off the names of the ships tied up alongside. One of the sailors came forward to the entry port and hailed him, and he pulled up opposite the gangplank, and three hands went scurrying down, one to open the carriage door and fold down the steps, the other two to deal with the luggage.

A woman in a grey cloak and a straw hat tied with a scarf stepped down, a cloak bag in her hand. Hidden in the shadows of the deck-housing, James found his palms damp, and wiped them slowly and carefully on his handkerchief. Now a second woman in an all-enveloping, hooded cloak appeared, putting her gloved hand in that of the sailor and stepping lightly down onto the cobbles, and lifting her head to look at the ship.

It gave James the strangest feeling, the feeling he imagined he would have if he were suddenly able to see himself from a distance, every movement completely familiar, yet strange. He did not need to see her face to recognize her. He knew the curve of her wrist, the flex of her ankle, the exact way she lifted her head when she was excited, the way she stood, the way she moved. These things were etched deeper than memory, in some dark and dumb part of him which ached with longing for her, and knew no words for what it could never forget.

The luggage was being lifted down, words were exchanged, and now they were coming up the gangplank, Marie first, nervously, feeling her way, gripping the hand-rope tightly as though she expected a tempest to rise up at any instant and whisk her way; her mistress coming after her, her fingers barely touching the rope, her feet finding their way without help over the slatted duckboards.

And then she stopped, so abruptly that the sailor behind her with the trunk on his shoulder walked into her and staggered for his balance. James saw a glimmer of white as her face lifted, and turned towards him. He was only a dark shape in the darkness, he had made no sound or movement, but her eyes found him out, came straight to him as though he had called her.

They met at the head of the gangplank.

'James,' she said – how his name on her lips shook him! 'But what is this? What are you doing here?'

'Going to Paris. Mary Ann wants to drink tea in the

488

Tuileries,' he said. His eyes devoured her upturned face, his body ached with the effort of not touching her. 'But you – are you well? Is all well with you?'

'It was a man called Climthorpe,' she said. 'Stephen brought back a handbill from the inn in the village. He said that the passage would be for a few select people only.' She laughed nervously. 'But how he has selected us! James, what are we to do?'

'Do? Nothing. There's nothing to do. For the sake of peace we must try not to meet. Mary Ann knows you are here, and I do not trust her to meet you without an uncomfortable scene.'

'It will not be difficult,' she said. 'At Boulogne I will leave the boat quickly and depart before you are up. Where will you stop on the road?'

'At Amiens, the Lion D'or.'

'Then I will be sure to stay somewhere else.'

'Alone?'

'France is my country,' she said. 'I will be safe enough, as far as Paris. Stephen did not wish to come, and I would not press him. I brought only Marie this time.'

'This time?' He looked at her searchingly. 'Marmoset, why *are* you going to Paris?'

'To see how things have changed. To see whether we should go back to live there, permanently.'

'No,' he said, and at her nervous start, lowered his voice, but spoke no less urgently. 'No, please, you must not! If you go to live in France, I shall never see you again.'

'But my James,' she said in a breaking voice, 'I can never see you again in any case.'

'We don't know that,' he said quickly, taking her hand – ah, the touch of her! 'We don't know what may happen.'

Her eyes widened in her upturned face. 'No, James, no, you mustn't say so. If you think that, it is like wishing – like wishing for her to die.' She took her hand away from him. 'If you think that, I must certainly go.'

They faced each other, a few inches apart on the gently lifting deck. James examined her face, noted the tiny lines around her eyes which had not been there before, found her only the more dear. 'I love you,' he said, low and desperate.

'I don't forget. I try to do my duty, but the days are so long, and so lonely. I need to know that you are somewhere near.' He took both her hands, and she let him. 'Sometimes, when I wake in the morning, I don't know how I am to get through the day. I think of you, and – '

'I know,' she said. 'For me too. If it weren't for – ' She stopped.

'For what?'

'For Marie and Flon, I could not go on.'

He stared at her. 'That is not what you were going to say.' He searched her face, and the knowledge came to him like a physical thing, through her hand in his. 'A child,' he whispered. 'There was a child.'

She nodded once, painfully.

'Why didn't you tell me?'

'I thought it would make it harder for you,' she said.

'Boy or girl?'

'A girl. Sophie-Marie.'

He closed his eyes for a moment. 'Yes, it does make it harder. But it wasn't for you to choose that. You should have told me. We are one soul, you and I, one life. You must not have pains that I don't share.'

Her mouth turned down. 'Must I not? But what of your son? The pain of *that* is all mine.'

He pressed her hand, his expression gentle. 'You think so?' he said.

'Madame!' Marie's voice, low and warning: someone was coming. James released Héloïse's hand and they moved a little apart, and Mary Ann appeared from around the deck housing.

'You should have told me you were taking the air on deck, James,' she said. 'I would have joined you.' Her eyes passed on, burning and hostile, to rest on Héloïse's tired white face. 'But I see you have company after all. Madame.' She executed a slight and frigid curtsey, and Héloïse returned it.

James looked a weary warning at her. 'You remember my cousin, of course.'

'Of course,' Mary Ann said in an icy voice. 'What a coincidence that we should all meet here. Shall we have the pleasure of your company all the way to Paris, madame?'

'I regret,' Héloïse said, very French in her distress. 'I leave the boat very early. We shall not meet, I think. And now I must go to my cabin. Madame – cousin James.' She curtseyed again and went quickly away, Marie falling in anxiously beside her, a hand under her arm to support her.

James watched her go, and then turned to remonstrate with his wife; but she met his gaze burningly, hurt and anger in her eyes and a retort on her lips, and his intention sank under the weary weight of inevitability. 'You had better return to your cabin, ma'am,' he said quite gently. 'The night air is not good for you.'

Often and often, Héloïse felt she should not have come. The ways in which Paris was unchanged only emphasized distressingly the ways in which it was different, and made her a stranger in her own city.

The Parisians themselves, after a decade of upheaval, bloodshed, misery and war were rejoicing at the prospect of peace and stability, and were ready to enjoy themselves with all the frivolity for which they had formerly been famous. The theatres, the opera, the restaurants, the smart strolls and the shopping streets were thronged, and at private parties every night the native French and visiting English met and wondered at each other.

But Héloïse wandered the streets like a restless ghost, and everything hurt with a surprisingly fresh pain. She went to the Rue St Anne and stood before the gates of her own house, on which a new, well-polished brass plate announced that it belonged to the Ministry of Justice, Department of Civil Proceedings. There was much coming and going, but between each arrival or departure the gate was closed with a clang by a gatekeeper with an uncompromising aspect. It was evident that no-one without official business was admitted.

Héloïse could only gaze wistfully through the bars at the house where she had grown up, and lived most of her life. She imagined its interior as it had been, the little white attic room of her childhood, the green saloon where Tante

Ismène had held her meetings, the bedroom and dressing room Papa had fitted out and decorated for her on her marriage, the handsome dining room where she and Olivier had entertained the up-and-coming young men of the Convention.

'It would have been foolish,' she said to Marie, 'to imagine it would stay the same; and yet – '

'Yes, madame,' Marie said wistfully. The gatekeeper had begun to look suspiciously at them, and so they moved on.

The house in the Rue de St Rustique was closed up, the shutters and the gate crossed with locked iron bars, and judging from the condition of the exterior and the tangle of creeper growing over the wall, it had been unoccupied for years. Héloïse wondered what had happened to Duncan, whether he had remained in Paris after Papa's execution, whether he, too, had fallen a victim of the Terror. She thought that if he had come to England, he would have sought her out, so she guessed that, alive or dead, he was in France still.

Her enquiries could establish no trace of Marie-France and the child. Héloïse had no idea even whether they were alive, and if alive what name they used, or what part of Paris they might live in. Nevertheless, she walked the grimier *faubourgs* with the uncomplaining Marie at her heels and asked endless questions and parted with many a coin; and every ten-year-old urchin who ran past her was followed with a wistful and enquiring eye. The more she searched, the more she appreciated what a hopeless task it was.

She saw James and his wife only once, when she was coming out of the Palais Royal gardens, as they were stepping out of a carriage outside the Comédie Française. Mary Ann was looking magnificent in sables, with a vivid glitter of diamonds and sapphires at her throat, and James, in evening garb and a silk cloak, held her elbow with automatic courtesy as he ushered her across the pavement to the foyer. Héloïse stopped still, too far away and too hidden amongst the crowd to be seen, but before he entered the theatre in his wife's wake, James turned and looked around him with a faintly puzzled air, as though he thought he had heard his name called.

It was that evening, when they returned to their room at the posting-house, that Héloïse said to Marie, 'I am accomplishing nothing here. I think we should go back.'

Marie's face lit with relief. 'Oh yes, madame.'

'You really wish to go?' Héloïse asked with a quizzical smile. 'I would not insist, if you wished to stay in Paris. After all, it is your *home*.' She used the English word.

Marie shook her head. 'No, madame. *Home* is where you are, and the children. They will be so excited to have you back.' She hesitated. 'We don't belong here anymore.'

'No,' Héloïse agreed sadly. 'We don't belong anywhere now.'

Chapter Twenty-eight

The Treaty of Amiens which ended the war was signed in March 1802. It concluded a peace of which everyone was glad, and no-one was proud, for under its terms, England resigned all its conquests except Trinidad and Ceylon, while France kept only Belgium. Everything was therefore much as it had been before the war began, a suitable conclusion to a conflict which had ended in the deadlock of French invincibility by land and English by sea.

At the same time, Buonaparte signed a concordat with the Pope in which he agreed to restore the Sabbath and Holy Orders, and to allow the Holy Father to consecrate the bishops, provided he appointed them.

'It's a clever move on the Corsican's part,' Father Jerome said thoughtfully. 'It recognizes Catholicism as the religion of the majority, without restoring to the Church its old power, and allows the juring and non-juring priests to be reconciled. All in all, it will tend to unite men and content them with his rule.'

'Do you think he is so calculating?' Héloïse asked. 'Has he really done it for those reasons, or is that merely what has happened?'

Jerome said, 'I am perfectly sure that it was intended. It would be a foolish move to underestimate this man: everything he has done has been marked by an intelligence, restless but acute, energetic but practical. I believe we will see him rule France for a long time. After all, a benevolent despotism is the most stable form of government.' He met Héloïse's eyes with an apologetic smile. 'The concordat means that I can go home.'

'Yes,' said Héloïse. 'And will you?'

'I think I must. A new state is being born, and every birth needs a priest on hand. But what will you do? Will you come too?'

She frowned. 'I don't know. I don't know if I could.'

'There has been a general amnesty,' he reminded her, 'and Buonaparte is actively encouraging *émigrés* to return. There are so many new institutions and official positions to be filled.'

'I didn't mean that,' Héloïse said with a faint smile. 'I meant that I don't know if I can leave England.'

Jerome regarded her for a long moment. There was no need for him to remind her of the danger in which she stood. He was aware both of her strength and her weakness: it was not the sins of the body he feared for her, but the sins of the mind and heart. They, of course, might be committed anywhere, but he thought that in France they would be easier to resist. In the end he said merely, 'It would be better for you to go.'

'Perhaps,' said Héloïse. 'At all events, I must give the others the opportunity. If anyone wishes to go, I shall see that it is made possible.'

She asked them that same day. Flon sighed and said she wished more than anything to go back to France, but that she was too old to uproot herself. Marie said that she had not stayed with Héloïse through danger and hardship only to leave her in prosperity, and Barnard merely shrugged and said, 'I cook for you. You live here, I cook here.'

Héloïse was grateful for so much loyalty, but as she said afterwards to Father Jerome, it was a worry, too. 'For what it comes down to is that they would all go if I went, and that they stay here because I do.'

'You must have known that before you asked,' Jerome said.

'I suppose so,' Héloïse sighed, 'but it means that I can't decide whether to stay or to go on my own account alone. I must consider what they really want, and act accordingly.'

'All love is a responsibility,' Jerome said. 'My advice to you is to take your time and think about it carefully. After all, now that there is peace, there is no hurry for you to decide. France will always be there.'

Roberta and Lucy met at the door of Harding and Howell's in Pall Mall as Roberta was being bowed out by two senior assistants. They greeted each other with pleasure.

'I didn't know you were in Town,' Lucy said.

'We only arrived yesterday,' Roberta said, 'and I haven't a thing fit to be seen in. I have just been choosing some materials to have sent round to my mantuamaker. Were you about to go in? I rather thought your Madame Genoux was too autocratic to allow you to choose your own materials.'

'She is. I came out of the merest idleness, having nothing better to do. But now I have met you, we can go home and have a comfortable chat.'

'Come to Brook Street, then,' said Roberta, 'and see Bobbie. He has grown so much over the past few months, you'll hardly know him.'

'I shall be delighted to. Here's my curricle, you see. You're not afraid to be driven by me? Docwra, you can walk back to Brook Street with Sands.'

Roberta settled herself in the curricle beside Lucy, who glanced over her shoulder to see that Parslow was up, and sent her horses forward.

'How was your business in the draper's?' she asked politely. 'Did you find some pretty materials? There's an apple-green silk I've seen that would suit you to perfection. Light greens are so difficult. Madame Genoux tried to get me to wear it, but I told her that only a true golden blonde would look well in it. I sometimes think she has no sense at all. She certainly has no idea of what colours suit me. I have a battle with her every time.'

Roberta regarded her with an indulgent smile. 'Then why do you go to her?'

'Oh, well, she is a very good dressmaker. Her seams are always neat and strong, and she sets a sleeve so that I can lift my arm. Besides, I'm too lazy to change. As long as I'm firm with her, the results are well enough.'

'You always appear killingly smart to me,' Roberta said. Lucy glanced sideways at her as she turned her pair into Berkeley Street.

'And you,' she replied, 'are looking more than usually pretty, I believe. Has something pleasant happened, to put you in such good looks?'

Roberta blushed. 'No, nothing, of course. How can you

be so absurd? I believe I am glad to be in London, that's all.'

At the house in Brook Street, Lucy was received very kindly by Roberta's father, who had been promoted to General on his retirement, and was keeping himself occupied by advising the Minister for War on the best way to dismantle the army and bring the troops home. Lucy had been in the drawing-room only long enough to exchange civilities with him, when the door opened, and young Bobbie came running in, followed more sedately by Mr Firth. The boy had certainly grown, and was promising all his mother's golden beauty.

'I knew it was you, Mama,' he cried, running to embrace her, 'but Mr Firth said it couldn't be, because you had gone out on foot, not in a carriage.'

'Now, Bobbie, remember your manners,' General Taske said. 'Don't you see we have a visitor?'

'Sorry, Grandpapa,' the boy said, and turning to Lucy, executed a short scrape and a rather jerky bow, and said gruffly, 'How d'e do, ma'am? Your most obedient.'

Roberta burst into laughter, and Mr Firth said with a rueful smile, 'I beg you will not believe, ma'am, that this is the sum of my teaching!'

'Was that not right?' Bobbie said, turning an innocent face up to his preceptor. 'It's how Great-uncle Bertrand does it. But Uncle Horace does it like this!' And he laid a hand on the hilt of an imaginary sword, smirked, and doubled himself willowily.

'You are an abominable child,' Roberta said. 'Mr Firth is supposed to be your pattern.'

'Yes, Mama. I can do it like Mr Firth as well, if you wish,' said Bobbie, and was restrained from the demonstration by his tutor's firm hand on his shoulder.

'He has such a talent for mimicry,' Roberta explained to Lucy. 'He has us in whoops of laughter, though I sometimes wonder whether it is quite a proper talent for an earl.'

'Was it your carriage we heard, ma'am?' the boy now asked Lucy eagerly. 'It sounded like a curricle to me – you can't see down into the street from our window. Is it still outside? Is Parslow walking the horses? Might I go and see them?'

497

'Yes, Parslow is there, but you had best ask your Mama,' Lucy said, and watched with interest as Firth looked at Roberta, and various messages passed between them with a facility which suggested a well-established sympathy. As a result, Firth took the boy outside, and a few minutes later General Taske excused himself, to walk off to his club.

'Is there any news yet of Captain Weston?' Roberta asked when they were alone.

'My last news was from Gibraltar,' Lucy said. 'The *Thames* was going from there to Malta with the garrison's pay, and then coming home, so I expect to hear at any moment that he is arrived.'

'And then what? Is the *Thames* to pay off?' Roberta asked.

'I don't know. Only a very few ships are being kept in commission, and I haven't been able to discover whether the *Thames* is to be one of them.'

'And what of Harry? He is still with the Revenue Service, I suppose?'

'Yes, and commands his cutter as if it were a seventy-four, so I'm told,' Lucy laughed. 'He sank a boatload of owlers last month off the Sussex coast, because they did not heave-to when he hailed them. The reverberations are still shaking Whitehall. Nobody seems to know whether to prosecute them for smuggling or compensate them for the loss of their boat.'

'I wish Harry may not find himself in trouble,' Roberta said. 'By what one hears, he was lucky to get the commission when the *Semele* paid off.'

'He's a good sailor,' Lucy said, 'and Admiral Harvey spoke up for him. There's so much smuggling since the war ended, it seems likely that the Revenue Service will be expanded still further. I imagine Harry is secure in his position.'

'It seems hard that the younger captains should be favoured over the older ones,' Roberta said. 'Harry and Captain Weston both employed, while William and Captain Haworth are on the beach.'

'It's understandable,' Lucy said with a shrug. 'The big warships were the first to be laid up after the armistice, and

498

the fighting captains are less adaptable to peace-time duties. But I don't think Captain Haworth wanted another ship – not immediately, anyway. He was happy enough to stay on shore, and set up his house, and have time to spend with his children. He has his half pay, and his prize-money invested in the Funds – enough to live on.'

'I often think about little Africa,' Roberta mused. 'It must have been very strange for her, to be on shore for the first time in her life.'

'I think it would have frightened a less bold-spirited child into fits,' Lucy said, 'suddenly to find all that space around her, and solid green grass instead of rolling blue sea. You know they spent some weeks at Wolvercote when the *Africa* paid off? We had the deuce of a job keeping track of that child!'

'Yes, I imagine you would, in a large house like that.'

'The devil of it was that in the ship, she was free to wander where she would. She couldn't get lost, of course, and wherever she went, she had six hundred besotted sailors to see she came to no harm. So of course she couldn't understand our wanting to confine her – and added to that, she's as agile as a monkey, and completely fearless. The very first day she wandered off, and we found her on the leads, if you please, proposing to climb the chimney to see what was inside!'

Roberta shuddered. 'Imagine if she had slipped!'

'Yes, but she never does, you know. She climbs as easily as she walks – in fact I don't think she distinguishes at all between forward and upward progress. She won't wear shoes, either, so she clings on to things with her feet – exactly like a monkey, in fact. Poor old Farleigh is torn between adoration, and despair that she will ever make a lady of her.'

'She must have been glad to have Hippolyta back: she's such a ladylike child.'

Lucy frowned. 'Yes, she was, but of course Polly didn't remember her, or her Papa. I'm not at all sure it was the right thing to do, for Haworth to take her away when he set up his house in Southsea. Of course, she's his daughter, and he has the perfect right to, but she and Minnie are so fond of each other, and they've been together ever since Minnie was born.'

'Did she seem upset when Captain Haworth took her away?' Roberta asked.

'Well, no, not really, but then Polly's such an obedient, well-behaved child, she never makes a fuss about anything. Flaminia cried for hours. I think Haworth should have left Polly at Wolvercote, but now he's settled down on shore, I can see that he'd want his children with him.'

'Well, there's nothing more you can do about it,' Roberta said comfortingly, 'and children soon adapt. They'll have forgotten all about each other in a few weeks.'

'I suppose so,' Lucy said. 'How were things at Morland Place? Did you visit much when you were at Shawes?'

'Oh yes,' said Roberta. 'There was a great deal of visiting and entertaining. Mrs James Morland seems a very enthusiastic hostess.'

'I suppose she's bent on making her mark in the district,' Lucy said. 'Now that the men are back from the war, and the shortages are over, there'll be a plenty of chances for her to shine. Are she and James on terms?'

Roberta blushed at being asked so very direct and personal a question. 'To say true,' she said hesitantly, 'I didn't see very much of your brother James. He was often out when I called, and away a good deal, when there were dinners and balls being held.'

'So they are not upon terms,' Lucy said grimly. 'I believe their trip to Paris was not a great success – Edward said that they both looked extremely fagged when they came back, and I know what *that* means. How does Mrs James get on with Mrs Smith? I was never more surprised in my life than when William took her home to Morland Place, except when Edward allowed her and her child to stay! Mother would turn in her grave. I'll warrant Mrs James didn't like it above half, having William's mistress under her roof.'

Roberta picked a careful way through the social hazards of the conversation. 'Edward likes Mrs Smith very much. She's a very respectable-seeming woman, quietly spoken, well-mannered, and she doesn't put herself forward. Edward seems to enjoy her company, and often sits with her in the evening.'

'By which you mean that Mrs James loathes her,' Lucy grinned, 'and Edward's put his foot down and insisted she stays.'

'I believe William is undertaking enquiries to find Mr Smith,' Roberta said, 'to discover whether there is any possibility of his divorcing her, so that they can be married.'

'Well, he's fair and far off there, for she's a Catholic, so it don't signify if Mr Smith divorces her ten times over, she still can't marry William. Of course, he may be dead by now. That would answer.'

'Yes, I believe that he was considerably older than her,' Roberta said.

Lucy looked thoughtful for a moment. 'I must say, I think it the outside of enough for William and Edward to foist Mrs Smith on Mrs James, however agreeable she may be. James, of course, would do nothing to help. I expect he just stands aside and stirs everyone up for the fun of it.' She saw from Roberta's expression that she had guessed correctly. 'And then there's the child. Mrs James won't like Fanny and Henry sharing the nursery with a bastard.'

Roberta made no comment. It was too thorny a subject for discussion, and she greatly wished to get away from it.

'Well, I'm glad to be out of it, at all events,' Lucy concluded her own thoughts. 'Morland Place must be extremely uncomfortable, for everyone but Edward.'

They were interrupted at that moment by the return of Bobbie and Mr Firth, and Lucy was interested to see how gladly Roberta's eyes lifted to the tutor's, and how openly he returned her smile. It was easy to account, she thought, for Roberta's increased prettiness and her new interest in clothes. And why not, Lucy's mind jumped on agilely. Roberta's portion was generous, and had no conditions attached to it, and Charles had trusted her sufficiently to make her sole guardian of the young Earl, so she had no trustees to appease or offend. She had been two years a widow, and was not above four-and-twenty, too young to wear weeds all her life. It would be a very good thing, Lucy thought, if she and Mr Firth were to come to an understanding.

But for the moment, the seventh earl was claiming her attention. 'Oh ma'am,' he said rapturously, 'your horses are first-rate! Prime blood and bone! Parslow took us around the square, and he let me take 'em for a bit, on the straight, and he says I've got light hands, and would make a driver if I was taught!' It was evident that Parslow's praise was the highest he could attain to.

'I can guess what comes next,' Roberta smiled, 'and the answer is, not until you are older.'

'But Mama – !'

'Your mama's quite right,' Lucy said, feeling she should extricate them from the tangle her groom had got them into. 'Parslow didn't mean that you should learn now, Bobbie. You aren't strong enough yet to hold a horse in harness, but when you are, if your mama permits, I will teach you myself.'

'Thank you, ma'am,' Bobbie said doubtfully, 'but if you don't mind very much, I should prefer to have Parslow teach me.'

'Bobbie!' Roberta exclaimed. 'And after Lady Aylesbury taught you to ride, you ungrateful child.'

'Holed and sunk,' Lucy grinned ruefully. 'I hope the *Thames* comes in soon, or I shall have no self-esteem left.'

Lucy was right in thinking that Mary Ann would object to having Mrs Smith and her child to live at Morland Place. She objected seriously and strenuously, tackling first her husband, and then Edward on the subject, with a notable lack of success. James merely smiled cynically, and said that it was nothing to do with him.

'I am merely in lodgings here, as you know very well. I have no say in the running of the house or the estate. You'll have to speak to Edward about it.'

'But don't you care that Henry and Fanny are to be exposed to the evil influence of *that woman*? To say nothing of being brought up with – with – '

'A bastard?' James supplied the word helpfully. 'Well, I don't see much harm in Mrs Smith, or in young master Smith. They seem very quiet, well-behaved folk. In any case, I'm not Fanny's trustee. Your Papa didn't think me a fit person, you know, so my opinion must be worthless.'

Mary Ann glared at him, but she knew there was no purpose in pursuing the discussion further. James was in what she considered one of his worst moods, flippant, caustic, and care-for-nothing, and the gleam of amusement in his eye at her discomfiture made her want to hit him. Ever since that ill-fated visit to Paris, the little kindness that had been painstakingly built up between them had vanished, and he had treated her instead with a rigidly correct politeness which frustrated her, because she knew he meant it for an insult. He absented himself from home more frequently, and was more often drunk, besides going away for several days every month on the sort of trips she had hoped he had given up for ever.

Occasionally she had seen glimpses of the torment underneath which provoked this behaviour, and if he had borne his grief in some other way, she might even have found it in her to pity him, and be kind. But he did not want her kindness, of course.

She wished she had not seen them together. The image of her husband and Héloïse as she had seen them, standing close together on the deck of the *Magpie*, and the way they had looked at each other, was branded on her memory. No, he did not want her kindness. He hated her, because she kept him from the woman he loved.

All the same, she was his wife, and mistress of Morland Place, and she was not prepared to accept her brother-in-law's whore under her roof. She went to Edward to demand her removal.

Edward listened to her with a frown, and then said, 'Well, I know it isn't the usual thing, but William would marry her if he could, you know. It isn't as if he was bringing lightskirts here. As for harming Fanny, why, Mrs Smith behaves with the greatest propriety. You couldn't want a higher stickler, as far as manners are concerned.'

'That isn't the point,' Mary Ann began, and Edward interrupted her.

'Isn't it? Then I don't quite see what is. William's my brother, and this is his home, and Mrs Smith's his wife, in

503

everything but a small point of law, which neither of them can help. And Frederick's a perfectly well-behaved child, and William's as strict as can be with him, and makes sure he never strays out of line, so I don't really see what you've got to object to.'

'The small point of law, as you call it, is what I object to. Whatever you say, they are not married to each other, and that makes Mrs Smith – makes her an undesirable companion,' she concluded a little feebly, seeing Edward's frown deepen.

'I find her a very pleasant companion,' he said firmly. 'And as far as I'm concerned, William and his wife and child – for so I regard them – are welcome to stay here as long as they like.'

He indicated politely that the argument was terminated, but Mary Ann was not willing to let things rest there. The next day she ordered the horses put-to in her vis-à-vis, and drove into York to visit the offices of Messrs Pobgee and Micklethwaite in Davygate. Mr Pobgee received her kindly, but could offer no help.

'Morland Place is Captain William Morland's home while he chooses so to regard it,' he told her. 'Under the terms of Lady Morland's Will, any of her children has the right to reside at Morland Place while unmarried.'

'But that's a direct inducement to immorality,' Mary Ann said angrily.

'I assure you, ma'am, it was not meant thus,' Pobgee said. 'It's a curious clause, but then the circumstances were not usual. In leaving the estate to the offspring of her third son, she had no wish to render the elder two homeless.'

'But what about this Mrs Smith?' Mary Ann asked. 'Surely she has no rights under the terms of the Will?'

'Naturally not,' Pobgee said. 'That is a matter which you must take up with Mr Edward Morland. As sole Trustee, such decisions are his. He is quite within his rights to invite Mrs Smith to remain at Morland Place.'

'Until Fanny reaches her majority,' Mary Ann said grimly. Pobgee bowed. 'So what you are saying is that as long as Edward agrees, William may live at Morland Place with fifty women if he wishes?'

504

'I think it highly unlikely that he would want to do any such thing,' Pobgee said with a faint smile. 'But in essence, that is correct.'

Since she could not send Mrs Smith and her brat away from Morland Place, Mary Ann decided that the best thing she could do was to remove herself and her son, at least temporarily. Her father had for a long time been pressing her to come and stay, and to bring his grandson, so as to acquaint the neighbourhood with the heir to Hobsbawn Mills. That evening, Mary Ann announced her decision to accept the invitation.

It aroused only the mildest of interest. Edward nodded over his beef and said, 'Quite right, the lad ought to see his grandpapa. How long will you stay?'

'I am not sure,' Mary Ann said. 'For a month, at least. Perhaps more.'

'And will you take Fanny, too?' William asked, more out of politeness than because he really wanted to know.

'I think not,' Mary Ann said with dignity, avoiding James's eye. Fanny was so much her father's child, that it would have been difficult to detach her, even had she wanted, and she didn't really want to. She didn't much like Fanny, especially now she had a son. It seemed wrong to her that Fanny should inherit Morland Place over little Henry's head.

'I hope you will have an enjoyable stay,' James said with belated cordiality as Mary Ann set off on her journey, accompanied by Dakers, Birkin, and baby Henry in the care of Jenny, the senior nursery-maid. 'Give my respects to your father.'

'Thank you,' Mary Ann said stiffly.

'Bring me back a present,' said Fanny, holding her father's hand and fidgeting, wishing her mother would hurry up and go, so that she and Papa could go out riding.

The two carriages jerked into motion, and as they drew away from Morland Place, Mary Ann looked back with a sense of escape and relief. It would be delightful to be at home again, at Hobsbawn House. She would take charge of the household for Papa, in whose eyes she could do no wrong, and make him comfortable again, and bask in his

505

approval. She would help him to entertain, and would visit the leading ladies of the neighbourhood and display her pretty son and her expensive, fashionable clothes. How delightful it would be, she thought, as the carriage turned a bend and the house disappeared from view, if she never had to return!

The *Thames* came in to Plymouth at the end of April, and a week later sailed up to Portsmouth to be paid off and laid up. Captain Weston was given two months' leave, after which he would go onto half pay. The navy was shrinking daily, though a few ships would be kept in commission for messenger and diplomatic duties, to transport army pay to the overseas garrisons, and to support the Revenue Service in its losing battle against the smugglers.

'I don't intend to seek an appointment immediately,' he said to Lucy. 'After three years at sea, I mean to have the whole of the summer to myself. What would you like to do? Do you want to go to London? I suppose the Season's in full swing at the moment. Or would you like to go to Brighton, or into the country? I'll do anything you like. I'm in a very pliant mood, you see. Peace must have gone to my head.'

'Are you really glad about the peace?' asked Lucy curiously. 'I thought perhaps you wouldn't be.'

'Oh, the war was enjoyable in some ways, but it's good to feel that we have time before us to be together, that I won't suddenly be called away. It's good to be able to make plans, for a change. Now, what would you like to do?'

'There is something I've been thinking about for a long time,' Lucy said cautiously. Weston grinned.

'Out with it! It's something outrageous, by your expression.'

'I want to dress as a boy again. I enjoyed the freedom so much, when I ran away to join the *Diamond*. You can have no idea, Weston, what it's like to put on breeches after a lifetime in petticoats.'

'Well, I must have done it once, but I was only four years old at the time, and can't remember,' he laughed. 'By God, I remember you in breeches, though! It was how I first set eyes on you, and a most captivating youth you made, too. I wouldn't mind the chance to meet Mr Proom again – but, my love, you are older now, and I think you will be hard put to it to convince anyone that you are a boy.'

'Oh, I don't wish to go into society,' Lucy said hastily. 'I've no wish to masquerade – just to enjoy the freedom. I thought perhaps we could go away somewhere really quiet and remote, where no-one knows us. I could be your nephew perhaps, or your younger brother, and if we kept our distance from everyone, I should pass well enough.'

'Where no-one knows us? Not Westerham, then,' he mused. 'Wait – I have it – Great Wakering!'

'I've never heard of it,' Lucy said, wrinkling her nose.

'It's a village in the Essex marshes, close to the sea. It has a church, one or two houses, a few cottages, and the rest is farmland. It also happens to be where my family comes from.'

'I didn't know you had any family.'

'I haven't now. There's no-one left there to recognize me. But it's as quiet and remote as you could wish. We can go riding, and there's good shooting on the marshes, and – yes, I'll teach you to fish, and to handle a small boat! I couldn't do that if you were in skirts. I must say, this notion of yours looks better and better. I'm only afraid that if I see you in breeches, I shall never want you to wear dresses again.'

It was a glorious summer. Weston and his 'nephew' rented a cottage outside the village on the edge of one of the numerous reedy inlets which joined the marshland to the sea, and there they lived in great harmony out of sight of the world, served by their faithful and only mutely critical servants. Lucy, bare-headed and bare-legged in breeches and a shirt, won praise from Weston in her handling of the small sailing-boat they hired. They spent many hours in it, tooling about the inlets and on fine days taking it out to sea. They fished from it, ate many a picnic meal in it, swam from it when they found a private enough stretch of the coastline, and once or twice, returning home late on moonlight nights, even made love in it.

507

When they weren't boating, they went walking or riding, or took guns out after duck, snipe, pigeon or rabbit, taking great delight in eating the result of their labours. Lucy had a good eye, and with practice soon became a fair shot. Her skin grew very brown, which she knew would be a nuisance when she returned to Town, and her hair was bleached pale by the sunshine.

'You look more like a boy every day,' Weston told her. 'I think you might even pass for a freckle-faced lad before an uncritical eye.'

Lucy was quite happy not to put it to the test. She wanted no contact with the outside world, needing nothing more than to be with Weston every hour of the day, and freed at last from the restraints society had placed upon her from her birth. A deep and satisfying companionship built up between them, which she felt owed its particular strength and rich complexity to their being on equal terms, and sharing their pursuits. It could not have happened, she firmly believed, had she worn a dress these last weeks.

He took her, one day, to look at the village. 'The old house used to stand here,' he told her as they halted their horses before a row of four farm-labourers' cottages. 'My grandfather, Sir Edwin Rivers – my mother's father – was Member of Parliament for the constituency, and owned half the land hereabouts. The other half was owned by Burchett, the squire, who lived in that long red house we passed earlier. When Sir Edwin died, he left everything to my uncle Edgar, who I'm afraid was a shocking loose screw, and gambled it all away. Burchett bought the land piece by piece as uncle Edgar was forced to sell to pay his debts, until there was only the house left. Then one night it burnt down – it was an old timber-framed house, largely Tudor, and it burnt like a torch, taking uncle Edgar with it.'

'How terrible!' Lucy said. 'Did he have a wife and children?'

'No, he never had time to marry, between hands of cards. At any rate, there was nothing left for my mother to inherit. She had to sell the land the house was built on to settle his outstanding debts. Squire Burchett bought it, of course, and built these cottages for his employees; and that's that. A sad and cautionary tale, don't you think?'

'So if your uncle Edgar hadn't been a gamester, you'd have been lord of the manor?'

'Would you have loved me more?' Weston enquired with interest.

'Don't be silly,' Lucy said.

'Come and look at the church, and see the tombs of my forefathers,' he said. They hitched the horses to the gate, and wandered about the churchyard, examining the gravestones of all the Rivers and Westons of former ages, and then looked inside the church, and signed their names in the visitors' book which stood on a lectern just inside the door. Weston signed it 'Captain Jas Weston, grandson of Sir Edwin Rivers MP', and Lucy signed underneath 'L. Morland, nephew of the above', and the date, '13th August, 1802'.

'One day, when we're old and sere, we can come back and look at this book, and remember the summer we spent here in our green days,' Weston said, closing the book with satisfaction.

Lucy shivered. 'It's cold in here after the sunshine,' she said. 'Let's go now.'

October came, and they went back to Town, the servants with some relief, Lucy and Weston with the greatest reluctance. To savour the very last of their freedom, they decided to travel by boat from Southend, the nearest town to Great Wakering, from where a regular service would take them right to the Westminster steps.

Lucy dressed again in woman's clothes, and felt very strange and confined in them. The day was sunny, but cool, which made it easier for her to wear gloves to hide her brown, calloused hands, and a veil over her face, to conceal her sunburn. The boat was crowded and both of them felt uneasy suddenly to be in contact with so many people. They were very quiet, and pressed close together like nervous horses smelling thunder.

The man beside Weston, a decent-looking citizen, probably a well-to-do tradesman by his clothes, glanced at them curiously from time to time, wondering perhaps about their air of preoccupation, and eventually offered Weston his newspaper with a civil bow and deprecatory cough.

'Would you care to take a glance, sir, at the *Post*? Bad business, this, about Swisserland, don't you think, sir? That Buonaparte's a restless cove.'

'I beg your pardon, sir,' Weston replied. 'I have been away, and have not heard any news for a long time.'

'Ah,' said the citizen, encouraged, 'I thought perhaps – you being a little weathered, if you'll pardon my noticing. You haven't heard about the French invading Swisserland, then?'

'No, sir, I've heard nothing all summer,' Weston said. On the side away from the helpful man, Lucy's hand crept anxiously into his, and he held it firmly, as much for his comfort as hers.

'That Buonaparte – invaded Swisserland, conquered it, made himself king there – not that they call it king, being foreigners – Mediator of the Republic, or some such. And last month it was Italy – the Cisalpine Republic – and the month before it was Elba. And he's never withdrawn his troops from Holland, which it was stipulated in the Treaty he was supposed to. Ah, he's a restless cove, all right, and what next, I ask you? Means to make himself Emperor, that's what I've heard.'

'Emperor?' Weston said, sounding dazed. How could so much have happened in so short a time? 'Surely not?'

'Well, it's a wonder, when the Frogs was so anxious to get rid of their king, but he made himself Consul for life back in August, and not a vote was cast against it, and what's that but a king under a different name, I ask you? And the talk is that he means to declare himself Emperor of the French before very long, and the way he's been going on, I wouldn't be at all surprised.'

Weston took the newspaper and read the article pointed out to him, and looked up in amazement to meet the citizen's satisfied gaze.

'If you ask me, sir, and I'm not a book-learned man, but I've my wits about me, as anyone who knows me would tell you, and there's not a few folk at London Wall, which is where I live, sir, as ask my advice about a great number of things – if you ask me, sir, we're going to have to fight him again, sooner or later. Ah, that's what it'll come to, all right, and this time, we'll have to lick him good and proper.'

When they arrived at Westminster, they took a hack to Upper Grosvenor Street, and pausing only to change his clothes, Weston went straight off to Fladong's. He returned in time for dinner, which he and Lucy ate at home alone together, though the desk in the business-room had been covered in invitations, several of them for that evening.

'Fladong's was full of officers,' Weston said. 'Lots of them had come up from the country for much the same reason as I went there. It's all true, as the cit told us. The Peace has been nothing to the French but a breathing space, a chance to consolidate their gains and prepare their next move. Buonaparte's got troops in Belguim and Holland, he's taken over Switzerland and northern Italy, and he's threatening Egypt. He's bought back Louisiana from the Spanish, and sent an expedition to Haiti. He's retaken the French coastal bases in India and South Australia. And he's operating an embargo on our goods in all the ports he controls.'

Lucy listened in silence, the food untouched on her plate. 'Does nobody oppose him?' she asked in a small voice.

'He is the most popular man in France,' Weston said grimly. 'He's brought order to a state sinking into anarchy, and won battles all over the world. They are calling him the new Charlemagne.' He picked up his glass, and put it down again untouched. 'It's clear that we will have to fight him. With his troops swarming all over the Low Countries, we cannot be safe, even if it were possible to allow him to conquer where he liked in Europe and America. No, we'll have to fight. It's just a question of when.'

'You'll go back to sea,' Lucy said. It was not a question. He looked at her tenderly.

'England will need every fighting captain she has. Everything that floats will be put into commission. The fleet will be built up to its former levels, and – '

511

'You needn't sound so glad!' Lucy cried out. 'You needn't sound as though you were longing to go.'

He got up and went round the table, despite the presence of the servants, and put his arm round her, and kissed her averted cheek. 'I don't want to leave you, not for a moment, not ever,' he said. 'But you know that I will have to. And,' he added, because they were honest with each other, 'that part of me wants to.'

He felt her sigh, and lean against him for a moment, and then she straightened up and pushed him gently away. He released her and went back to his place.

'Of course, you're quite right,' she said, picking up her fork again. 'We can't allow that little brigand to call himself Emperor. And I imagine there were plenty of smiling faces at Fladong's, at the thought of going to sea again. I wish I could come with you – you'll have the best of it, you know. It's harder to be the one left behind with nothing to do.'

'Yes, I know,' he said. She looked up at him, but her eyes were far too bright, and she looked hastily down at her plate again.

'Perhaps they'll give you a seventy-four this time,' she said.